Tactics of Mistake

The men of the Dorsai were the finest fighting soldiers in the universe, mercenary troops without equal. Their talents were devastatingly employed on Kultis, where a bloody little war raged between the Western Alliance and Eastern Coalition. But not even the Dorsai could anticipate the dramatic effect of Cletus Grahame's brilliant mind and the galaxy-shaking theory he called The Tactics of Mistake.

Time Storm

Marc Despard was one of the handful to survive the Time Storm – or keep a remnant of sanity. Mist walls moving endlessly across the surface of the Earth created a devastated, shifting patchwork of temporal anarchy, wrenching both inanimate and living things between the past and the future. But Despard saw strange, dazzling patterns in his head that he knew were instruments that might enable him to beat the Time Storm. And if he could do that . . . he could do anything.

The Dragon and the George

Jim Eckert leads a peaceful, happy campus life – until his girlfriend Angie disappears while taking part in a laboratory experiment on astral projection. In an attempt to find out what's happened, he (unwisely) submits himself to the equipment. Next thing he knows he's in the Middle Ages, and Angie has been nabbed by a dragon and taken to the Loathly Tower. But it could be worse – because Jim now appears to be a dragon, too!

Also by Gordon R. Dickson

The Childe Cycle

Dorsai! (1959, abridged as The
  Genetic General, 1960)
Necromancer (1962, aka No Room
  For Man)
Soldier, Ask Not (1967)
Tactics of Mistake (1970)
The Spirit of Dorsai (1989)
Lost Dorsai (1980)
The Final Encyclopedia (1984)
The Chantry Guild (1988)
Young Bleys (1991)
Other (1994)

The Dragon Knight

The Dragon and the George (1976)
The Dragon Knight (1990)
The Dragon on the Border (1992)
The Dragon at War (1992)
The Dragon, the Earl and the Troll
  (1994)
The Dragon and the Djinn (1996)
The Dragon and the Gnarly King
  (1997)
The Dragon in Lyonesse (1998)
The Dragon and the Fair Maid of
  Kent (2001)

Underseas

Secret Under the Sea (1960)
Secret Under Antarctica (1963)
Secret Under the Caribbean (1964)

Dilbia

Spacial Delivery (1961)
Spacepaw (1969)

Novels

Alien From Arcturus (1956, aka
  Arcturus Landing, 1979)
Mankind on the Run (1956, aka On
  The Run)
Time to Teleport (1960)
Delusion World (1961)
Naked to the Stars (1961)
The Alien Way (1965)
Mission to Universe (1965)
Space Winners (1965)
Planet Run (with Keith Laumer, 1967)
The Space Swimmers (1967)
None But Man (1969)
Wolfling (1969)
The Hour of the Horde (1970)
The Outposter (1971)
Sleepwalker's World (1971)
The Pritcher Mass (1972)
Alien Art (1973)
The Far Call (1973)
The R-Master (1973, rewritten as The
  Last Master, 1984)
Gremlins, Go Home! (1974)
Lifeboat (1975 with Harry Harrison,
  aka Lifeship)
Time Storm (1977)
Home From the Shore (1978)
Pro (1978)
Masters of Everon (1979)
Jamie the Red (with Roland Green,
  1984)
The Forever Man (1986)
Way of the Pilgrim (1987)
The Earth Lords (1989)
Wolf and Iron (1990)
The Magnificent Wilf (1995)
The Right to Arm Bears (2000)

Gordon R. Dickson

SF GATEWAY OMNIBUS

TACTICS OF MISTAKE
TIME STORM
THE DRAGON AND THE GEORGE

GOLLANCZ
LONDON

First published in Great Britain in 2013 by Gollancz
An imprint of the Orion Publishing Group
Orion House, 5 Upper St Martin's Lane, London WC2H 9EA
An Hachette UK Company

A CIP catalogue record for this book
is available from the British Library

ISBN 978 0 575 12989 4

1 3 5 7 9 10 8 6 4 2

Typeset by Input Data Services Ltd, Bridgwater, Somerset

Printed and bound by CPI Group (UK) Ltd, Croydon, CR0 4YY

The Orion Publishing Group's policy is to use papers
that are natural, renewable and recyclable products and
made from wood grown in sustainable forests. The logging
and manufacturing processes are expected to conform to
the environmental regulations of the country of origin.

www.orionbooks.co.uk
www.gollancz.co.uk

CONTENTS

ENTER THE SF GATEWAY . . .

Towards the end of 2011, in conjunction with the celebration of fifty years of coherent, continuous science fiction and fantasy publishing, Gollancz launched the SF Gateway.

Over a decade after launching the landmark SF Masterworks series, we realised that the realities of commercial publishing are such that even the Masterworks could only ever scratch the surface of an author's career. Vast troves of classic SF & Fantasy were almost certainly destined never again to see print. Until very recently, this meant that anyone interested in reading any of those books would have been confined to scouring second-hand bookshops. The advent of digital publishing changed that paradigm for ever.

Embracing the future even as we honour the past, Gollancz launched the SF Gateway with a view to utilising the technology that now exists to make available, for the first time, the entire backlists of an incredibly wide range of classic and modern SF and fantasy authors. Our plan, at its simplest, was – and still is! – to use this technology to build on the success of the SF and Fantasy Masterworks series and to go even further.

The SF Gateway was designed to be the new home of classic Science Fiction & Fantasy – the most comprehensive electronic library of classic SFF titles ever assembled. The programme has been extremely well received and we've been very happy with the results. So happy, in fact, that we've decided to complete the circle and return a selection of our titles to print, in these omnibus editions.

We hope you enjoy this selection. And we hope that you'll want to explore more of the classic SF and fantasy we have available. These are wonderful books you're holding in your hand, but you'll find much, much more . . . through the SF Gateway.

www.sfgateway.com

INTRODUCTION
from The Encyclopedia of Science Fiction

Gordon R. Dickson (1923–2001) was a Canadian-born writer, resident in the USA since age 13 and who became a US citizen many decades before his death. He was educated (along with Poul Anderson) at the University of Minnesota, taking his BA in English in 1948, and remained in Minnesota. Through the Minneapolis Fantasy Society, which he re-established after World War Two, he became friends with Anderson, with whom he later collaborated on the Hoka series – *Earthman's Burden* (1957), *Star Prince Charlie* (1975) and *Hoka!* (1982) – and with Clifford D Simak. Along with these writers, Dickson early demonstrated a sympathy for hinterland settings peopled by solid farming or small-town stock whose ideologies, when expressed, violate any simple, conservative-liberal polarity, even though urban readers and critics some-times responded to them as right-wing. As late as the Ruined Earth tale *Wolf and Iron* (1990) – which embodies a Survivalist plot considerably deepened by the author's detailed and compassionate attachment to the kind of hero who understands and loves the physical world – he was still mining this fertile soil.

Dickson began publishing SF in Spring 1950 with "Trespass", written with Anderson, and he remained a prolific and consistent short-story author. Dickson's first novel, *Alien from Arcturus* (1956), established from an early date the tone of underlying seriousness which, especially in later works, transformed genre models into vehicles for significant explorations into the human condition. In this way, he was able to transform a certain diffidence about the expression of emotional intensities into "safer" (but at the same time innovative) explorations into how *Homo sapiens* might engage with an expanding universe full of challenges, including other species; he had a particular ability to describe the kind of relations that might obtain between human and dependent Alien (or, as in *Wolf and Iron*, Terran mammal). The aliens in *Alien from Arcturus* are decidedly attractive, with shining black noses, and much resemble those who appear in *Space Winners* (1965), a Young Adult tale, and *The Alien Way* (1965), about an Earthman's telepathic rapport with the representative of a species that may invade the home planet. But the strong narrative skills Dickson applied in the sophisticating of comparatively rudimentary Space-Opera models, along with an idiomatic capacity to meet the challenge of writing novel-length fiction (a skill Poul Anderson only slowly gained), has ensured the survival of these seemingly unambitious works. Some later singletons – like *Sleepwalker's World* (1971), a dystopian vision of Overpopulation, and *The R-Master* (1973), in which a society is ambiguously guided by a saviour whose origins lie more in Pulp-magazine ideas than in philosophy – failed to maintain the elation of the earlier books; but by this point Dickson had already embarked on the project that would define the remaining decades of his active career.

The Childe Cycle was planned to begin with novels set in historical times, but these tales seem not to have been drafted; the existing volumes, which are SF, make up the sustained and internally coherent Dorsai sub-series, which (as Dickson may have discovered) successfully stands alone. The Childe Cycle as a whole was intended to present an evolutionary blueprint, in highly dramatized fictional terms, a prospectus for humanity's ultimate expansion through the Galaxy as an inherently ethical species; the Dorsai books self-sustainedly represent the climax of that long tale. "In order to make this type of story work effectively," Dickson said:

> *'I developed by the late 1950s a new fictional pattern that I have called the "consciously thematic story". This was specifically designed to create an unconscious involvement of the reader with the philosophical thematic argument that the story action renders and demonstrates. Because this new type of story has represented a pattern hitherto unknown to readers and writers, my work has historically been criticized in terms that do not apply to it – primarily as if it were drama alone.'*

It may be that Dickson discovered that some of the "philosophical thematic argument" – presumably lost to us through the absence of the earlier volumes – may have been difficult to couch so as to gain readers' "unconscious participation"; and it may be he felt that the full integrity of his argument remained, therefore, undemonstrated. Lacking the full projected series, we cannot properly guess what might have been. But the vast torso that remains is both internally satisfying, nor does it affect the reader as incomplete; and probably introduces as much naked philosophy as the author would have ever felt comfortable espousing in works of fiction.

In rough order of internal chronology, the Childe Cycle comprises *Necromancer* (1962); *Tactics of Mistake* (1971); *Soldier, Ask Not* (1967), the short form of which won a Hugo for 1964; and *The Genetic General* (later republished as *Dorsai!* 1976; *The Spirit of Dorsai* (1979) and *Lost Dorsai* (1980); and a final grouping of texts, all set about 100 years further into the future: the overlong *Young Bleys* (1991), *Other* (1994) and *Antagonist* (2007) with David W Wixon, all focused on the Antihero Bleys – who has a disruptive effect on the flow of history, rather like the Mule in Isaac Asimov's Foundation trilogy – then *The Final Encyclopedia* (1984), whose great length is entirely justified, and *The Chantry Guild* (1988), the last volume – Dickson claimed as early as 1983 – being hived off from a projected final volume to be called *Childe*.

As the sequence develops, human space is divided into four spheres plus Old Earth herself, with her vast genetic pool: Dorsai, whose inhabitants are bred as professional soldiers, stories featuring them closely resembling Military SF at its most cerebral; the Exotic worlds, whose inhabitants are bred to creative (sometimes sybaritic) mind-arts; those worlds (like Newton) which emphasize physical science; and the God-haunted Friendly worlds, whose folk are bred for faith. The task of mankind's genetic elite is somehow to merge these variant strains, and the philosophical burden of the sequence tends to be conveyed through plots whose origins lie somewhere between the Superman tales of earlier genre sf and the philosophical epics of Olaf Stapledon. It may indeed be fair to suggest that Dickson was the only American SF writer to take Stapledon on board, and in the process to humanize the British philosopher's sweeping but impersonal vision.

The Genetic General, which in its restored form as *Dorsai!* remains the most arousing title of the entire series, features Donal Graeme, the central incarnation of a triune evolutionary superman whose earlier life is told in *Necromancer*, and who is reborn as Hal Mayne to climax the series – and the genetic selection it promulgates – through its final (but apparently never written) volumes, though the enormous Slingshot Ending effect that now ends the series is certainly rousing enough, and may in fact represent an outcome so inherently successful that Dickson realized he need not continue an argument already visualized so vividly. The terms Dickson uses to describe his superman's capacities – Graeme, for instance, being capable of a potent sort of cognitive intuition – are perhaps best appreciated within the massive, ongoing rhythm of the series; for it is as a novelist, not as a philosopher, that Dickson (as he himself seems to have understood) reveals his strength.

Very little of Dickson's fiction, though some of it seems hasty compared to his magnum opus, fails to pose questions and arguments about humankind's fundamental nature. From 1960 much of his work specifically reflected his preoccupation with the concept that humankind is inevitably driven to higher evolutionary states, a notion often expressed in relatively traditional genre sf tales – like *None But Man* (1969) or *Hour of the Horde* (1970) – that contrast humankind's indomitable spirit with that of Aliens whose lack of comparable *élan* makes them into straw horses for *Homo sapiens* to defeat. More serious presentations of material – from *The Far Call* (1978), an ambitious novel involving Politics on Mars, to the fine *Time Storm* (1977) – clearly manifest a revisionary attitude toward the SF he imbibed when young, but whose triumphalist agenda he subjected to increasingly strict scrutiny. Though his continued use of modified genre conventions to provide solutions to serious arguments undoubtedly retarded full recognition of his talent and seriousness, the later volumes of the Childe Cycle series have increasingly encouraged the serious attention his work merits.

Dickson won the Nebula for Best Novelette with "Call Him Lord" (1966). He was President of the Science Fiction Writers of America 1969-1971. In 1981, he won Hugos not only for the novella "Lost Dorsai" (1980) but also for a novelette, "The Cloak and the Staff" (1980). He was inducted into the Science Fiction Hall of Fame in 2000.

Of the three novels selected here *Tactics of Mistake* needs the most explanation, and the least. It is part of Dickson's long Childe series, set in the early years when the Dorsai warrior clan needed organizing, which it gets here. What needs no explanation is the sheer exuberance of the story, with battles and revelations galore; and a superhero aborning. *Time Storm* is something else, a tale which starts in confusion, and triumphs. Reality has been fractured (by whom or what?), the Earth has been diced into various time zones, and the protagonist attempts to find his wife in this churning chaos; and he does. The conception is grand, impressively laid down, and the quest of the hero through realities galore never ceases to grasp hold of the reader. In *The Dragon and the George* – expanded from "St Dragon and the George" (September 1957 *Magazine of Fantasy and Science* Fiction) – Dickson unlaces his stays. No more do we deal with the nature of history or of reality, though we're glad we had the chance. We are in a version of medieval England where dragons roam, and a young researcher discovers that, in the process of tracing his lost loved one, he has turned into a dragon. To redeem himself, he must learn to be a whole man. Throughout his career, Dickson focused on growth: the growth of individuals; the growth of the species. He taught us lessons in becoming whole. In these three tales, those lessons are conveyed through stories that convey what may be his most telling gift: that they make us want to be there, again and again.

For a more detailed version of the above, see Gordon R. Dickson's author entry in *The Encyclopedia of Science Fiction*: http://sf-encyclope dia.com/entry/dickson_gordon_r

Some terms above are capitalised when they would not normally be so rendered; this indicates that the terms represent discrete entries in *The Encyclopedia of Science Fiction*.

TACTICS OF MISTAKE

Trouble rather the tiger in his lair than the sage amongst his books. For to you Kingdoms and their armies are things mighty and enduring, but to him they are but toys of the moment, to be overturned by the flickering of a finger ...

LESSONS: *Anonymous*

1

The young lieutenant-colonel was drunk, apparently, and determined to rush upon disaster.

He came limping into the spaceship's dining lounge the first night out from Denver on the flight to Kultis, a row of bright service ribbons on the jacket of his green dress uniform, and looked about. He was a tall, lean officer, youthful to hold the rank he wore in the Expeditionary Forces of Earth's Western Alliance; and at first glance his open-featured face looked cheerful to the point of harmlessness.

He gazed around the room for a few seconds, while the steward tried unsuccessfully to steer him off to a booth nearby, set for a single diner. Then, ignoring the steward, he turned and headed directly for the table of Dow deCastries.

The white-faced, waspish little man called Pater Ten, who was always at deCastries' elbow, slipped away from his chair as the officer approached, and went toward the steward, still staring blank-faced with dismay after the lieutenant-colonel. As Pater Ten approached, the steward frowned and bent forward to talk. The two of them spoke for a moment in low voices, glancing back at the lieutenant-colonel, and then went quickly out of the lounge together.

The lieutenant-colonel reached the table, pulled up an empty float seat from the adjoining table without waiting for an invitation and seated himself across from the tawny-haired, beautiful young girl at deCastries' left.

'Privilege of first night out, they tell me,' he said pleasantly to all of them at the table. 'We sit where we like at dinner and meet our fellow passengers. How do you do?'

For a second no one spoke. DeCastries only smiled, the thin edge of a smile that barely curved the lips in his handsome face, framed by the touches of gray in the black hair at his temples. For five years, now, Secretary of Outworlds Affairs for Earth's Coalition of Eastern Nations, he was known for success with women; and his dark eyes had concentrated on the tawny-haired girl ever since he had invited her – with her mercenary soldier father and the Exotic Outbond who made up the third in their party – to join his table, earlier. There was no obvious threat in that smile of his; but reflexively at the sight of it, the girl frowned slightly and put a hand on the arm of her father, who had leaned forward to speak.

'Colonel …' The mercenary wore the pocket patch of an officer from the Dorsai World, under contract to the Bakhallan Exotics, and he was a full colonel. His darkly tanned face with its stiffly waxed mustache might have looked ridiculous if it had not been as expressionlessly hard as the butt-plate of a cone rifle. He broke off, feeling the hand on his sleeve, and turned to look at his daughter; but her attention was all on the interloper.

'Colonel,' she said to him in her turn – and her young voice sounded annoyed and concerned at once, after the flat, clipped tones of her father, 'don't you think you ought to lie down for a while?'

'No,' said the lieutenant-colonel, looking at her. She caught her breath, finding herself seized, suddenly, like a bird in the hand of a giant, by the strange and powerful attention of his gray eyes – entirely at odds with the harmless appearance he had given on entering the room. Those eyes held her momentarily helpless, so that without warning she was conscious of being at the exact focus of his vision, naked under the spotlight of his judgment. '… I don't,' she heard him say.

She sat back, shrugging her tanned shoulders above her green dinner gown, and managed to pull her gaze from its direct link with his. Out of the corner of her eye she saw him look about the table, from the blue-robed Exotic at its far end, back past her father and herself to the dark, faintly smiling deCastries.

'I know you, of course, Mr. Secretary,' he went on to deCastries. 'In fact, I picked this particular flight to Kultis just so I could meet you. I'm Cletus Grahame – head of the Tactics Department at the Western Alliance Military Academy until last month. Then I put in for transfer to Kultis – to Bakhalla, on Kultis.'

He looked over at the Exotic. 'The purser tells me you're Mondar, Outbond from Kultis to the Enclave in St. Louis,' he said. 'Bakhalla's your home town, then.'

'The capital of Bakhalla Colony,' said the Exotic, 'not just a town, nowadays, Colonel. You know, I'm sure we're all pleased to meet you, Cletus. But do you think it's good judgment for an officer in the armed forces of the Alliance to try to mix with Coalition people?'

'Why not – on shipboard?' said Cletus Grahame, smiling unconcern-
edly at him. 'You're mixing with the secretary, and it's the Coalition
who's supplying Neuland with arms and material. Besides, as I say, it's
the first night out.'

Mondar shook his head. 'Bakhalla and the Coalition aren't at war,'
he said. 'The fact the Coalition's given some aid to Neuland Colony is
beside the point.'

'The Alliance and the Coalition aren't at war,' said Cletus, 'and the
fact that they're backing different sides in the brush war between you
and Neuland's beside the point.'

'It's hardly beside the point—' began Mondar. But then he was
interrupted.

There was a sudden hush in the buzz of conversation about the lounge.
While they had been talking, the steward and Pater Ten had returned,
behind an impressively large, uniformed man wearing the stripes of a
spaceliner's first officer, who now reached the table and dropped a big
hand heavily on Cletus' shoulder.

'Colonel,' said the shipman, loudly, 'this is a Swiss ship of neutral
registry. We carry Alliance and Coalition people, both, but we don't
like political incidents on shipboard. This table belongs to the Coalition
Secretary of Outworlds Affairs Dow deCastries. Your place is back
there across the room ...'

But from the first word, Cletus paid him no attention. Instead, he
looked back to the girl – at her alone – and smiled and raised his eyebrows as if leaving it up to her. He made no move to rise from the table.

The girl glared back at him but still he did not move. For a long second
her glare held; then it wavered and broke. She turned to deCastries.

'Dow ...' she said, interrupting the ship's officer, who had begun to
repeat his words.

DeCastries' thin smile widened slightly. He too, raised his eyebrows,
but with a different expression than Cletus. He let her gaze appealingly
at him for a long second before he turned to the shipman.

'It's all right,' he said, his deep, musical voice stilling the voice of the
other, instantly. 'The colonel's just making use of his first-night privi-
leges to sit where he wants.'

The shipman's face reddened. His hand dropped slowly from Cletus'
shoulder. Suddenly his size made him seem no longer large and impressive, but clumsy and conspicuous.

'Yes, Mr. Secretary,' he said stiffly, 'I see. Sorry to have bothered you
all ...'

He darted a glance of pure hatred at Pater Ten, which affected the little man no more than the shadow of a rain cloud affects the glowing radiance of a white-hot iron ingot; and, carefully avoiding the eyes of the other passengers, he turned and walked from the lounge. The steward had already evaporated, at deCastries' first words. Pater Ten slid into the seat he had vacated earlier, scowling at Cletus.

'About the Exotic Enclave at St. Louis,' Cletus said to Mondar – he did not seem to be disturbed by what had just happened – 'they've been very good about lending me library materials for research.'

'Oh?' Mondar's face was politely interested. 'You're a writer, Colonel?'

'A scholar,' said Cletus. His gray eyes fastened now on the Exotic. 'I'm writing volume four right now, of a twenty-volume work I started three years ago – on tactics and strategical considerations. But never mind that now. May I meet the rest of the people here?'

Mondar nodded. 'I'm Mondar, as you say.'

'Colonel Eachan Khan,' he said turning to the Dorsai at his right, 'may I introduce Lieutenant-Colonel Cletus Grahame of the Alliance forces?'

'Honored, Colonel,' said Eachan Khan, in a clipped, old-fashioned British accent.

'Honored to meet you, sir,' said Cletus.

'And Colonel Khan's daughter, Melissa Khan,' went on Mondar.

'Hello,' Cletus smiled again at her.

'How do you do?' she said, coldly.

'Our host, Secretary Dow deCastries, you've already recognized,' Mondar said. 'Mr. Secretary – Colonel Cletus Grahame.'

'I'm afraid it's a little late to invite you to dinner, Colonel,' said deCastries deeply. 'The rest of us have eaten.' He beckoned the steward. 'We can offer you some wine.'

'And, finally, the gentleman on the secretary's right,' said Mondar. 'Mr. Pater Ten. Mr. Ten's got an eidetic memory, Colonel. You'll find he's got an encyclopedic fund of knowledge on just about everything.'

'Pleased to meet you, Mr. Ten,' said Cletus. 'Maybe I ought to arrange to borrow you, instead of library materials, for my next research.'

'Don't bother!' said Pater Ten, unexpectedly. He had a creaky, high-pitched, but surprisingly carrying, voice. 'I looked at your first three volumes – wild theories, backed up by warmed-over military history. They must've been going to kick you out of the Academy if you hadn't requested a transfer first. Anyway, you're out. Now, who'll read you? You'll never finish a fourth book.'

'I told you,' said Mondar in the conversational pause that followed this small verbal explosion. Cletus was gazing at the small man with a faint smile not unlike that of deCastries earlier. 'Mr. Ten has an encyclopedic fund of knowledge.'

'I see what you mean,' said Cletus. 'But knowledge and conclusions are two different things. That's why I'll be finishing all sixteen of the other volumes in spite of Mr. Ten's doubts. In fact that's why I'm headed for Kultis, now, to make sure I get them written.'

'That's right – haul victory out of defeat there,' creaked Pater Ten. 'Win the war at Bakhalla in six weeks and become an Alliance hero.'

'Yes, not such a bad idea,' said Cletus, as the lounge steward deftly slid a clean wineglass in front of him and filled it from the bottle of canary-yellow liquid on the table. 'Only it isn't either the Alliance or the Coalition that's going to win in the long run.'

'That's a strong statement, Colonel,' said deCastries. 'Also, a little close to treason, isn't it? That part about the Alliance, spoken by an Alliance officer?'

'You think so?' Cletus said, and smiled. 'Is someone here thinking of reporting me?'

'Possibly.' There was abruptly a note of something chilling in deCastries' deep voice. 'Meanwhile, it's interesting to hear you talk. What makes you think it won't be either the Alliance or the Coalition that'll end up having the strongest voice among the colonies on Kultis?'

'The laws of historical development,' said Cletus, 'are working to that end.'

'Laws,' said Melissa Khan, angrily. The tension she had been feeling beneath the calm talk had become too much to bear. 'Why does everybody think' – she glanced a moment, almost bitterly at her father – 'that there's some impractical set of principles or theories or codes that everybody ought to live by? It's practical people who make things happen! You have to be practical, nowadays, or you might as well be dead.'

'Melissa,' said deCastries, smiling at her, 'honors the practical man. I'm afraid I have to agree with her. Practical experience works.'

'As opposed to theories, Colonel,' flung in Pater Ten, gibingly, 'as opposed to bookish theories. Wait'll you get out among practical field officers in the Neuland-Bakhalla jungle in a practical fire-fight, and discover what war's really like! Wait'll you hear your first energy weapon sending its sizzle overhead, and you'll find out—'

'He's wearing the Alliance Medal of Honor, Mr. Ten'

The sudden, flat, clipped tones of Eachan Khan chopped across the small man's tirade like an ax. In the new silence Eachan pointed a steady, brown forefinger at the red, white and gold bar at the far right of the row of ribbons decorating Cletus' jacket.

9

2

The silence continued a moment at the table.

'Colonel,' said Eachan, 'what's the trouble with your leg?'

Cletus grinned wryly. 'It's part prosthetic about the knee, now,' he said. 'Perfectly comfortable, but you can notice it when I walk.' He looked back at Pater Ten. 'Actually, Mr. Ten's pretty close to being right about my practical military experience. I only had three months of active duty after being commissioned, during the last Alliance-Coalition brush war on Earth seven years ago.'

'But you ended up those three months with the Medal of Honor,' said Melissa. The expression with which she had watched him before had now changed completely. She swung about to Pater Ten. 'I suppose that's one of the few things you don't know anything about, though?'

Pater Ten stared hatingly back at her.

'Do you, Pater?' murmured deCastries.

'There was a Lieutenant Grahame decorated seven years ago by the Alliance,' spat out Pater Ten. 'His division had made an attack drop and landing on a Pacific island held by our garrisons. The division was routed and cut up, but Lieutenant Grahame managed to put together a guerrilla force that was successful in bottling our people up in their strong fortified areas until Alliance reinforcements came a month later. He ran into a traveling mine the day before he would have been relieved. They stuck him in their Academy because he couldn't qualify physically for field duty after that.'

There was another, but shorter, moment of silence at the table.

'So,' said deCastries, in an oddly thoughtful tone, turning in his fingers the half-filled wineglass on the tablecloth before him, 'it seems the scholar was a hero, Colonel.'

'No, Lord no,' said Cletus. 'The lieutenant was a rash soldier, that's all. If I'd understood things then as well as I do now, I'd never have run into that mine.'

'But here you are – headed back to where the fighting is!' said Melissa.

'That's true,' said Cletus, 'but as I said, I'm a wiser man now. I don't want any more medals.'

'What *do* you want, Cletus?' asked Mondar, from the end of the table. The Outbond had been watching Cletus with an un-Exotic-like intensity for some few minutes now.

'He wants to write sixteen more volumes,' sneered Pater Ten.

'As a matter of fact, Mr. Ten's right,' said Cletus quietly to Mondar. 'What I really want to do is finish my work on tactics. Only I've found out first I'm going to have to create the conditions they'll apply to.'

'Win the war on Neuland in sixty days!' said Pater Ten. 'Just as I said.'

'Less time than that, I think,' said Cletus, and he gazed calmly about at the sudden changes of expression on the faces of all but Mondar and Pater Ten.

'You must believe in yourself as a military expert, Colonel,' said deCastries. Like Mondar's, his gaze upon Cletus had grown interested.

'But I'm not an expert,' said Cletus. 'I'm a scholar. There's a difference. An expert's a man who knows a great deal about his subject. A scholar's someone who knows all there is that's available to be known about it.'

'It's still only theories,' said Melissa. She looked at him puzzledly.

'Yes,' he said to her, 'but the effective theorist's got an advantage over the practician.'

She shook her head, but said nothing – sinking back against the cushion of her seat, gazing at him with her lower lip caught between her teeth.

'I'm afraid I'd have to agree with Melissa again,' said deCastries. For a moment his gaze was hooded, as if he looked inward rather than outward at them all. 'I've seen too many men with nothing but theory get trampled on when they ventured out into the real world.'

'Men are real,' said Cletus. 'So are weapons ... But strategies? Political consequences? They're no more real than theories. And a sound theorist, used to dealing with unreal things, is a better manipulator of them than the man used to dealing only with the real tools that are actually only end products ... Do you know anything about fencing?'

DeCastries shook his head.

'I do,' said Eachan.

'Then maybe you'll recognize the tactic in fencing I use as an example for something I call the *tactics of mistake*. It's in the volume I'm writing now.' Cletus turned to him. 'The fencing tactic is to launch a series of attacks, each inviting ripostes, so that there's a pattern of engages and disengages of your blade with your opponent's. Your purpose, however, isn't to strike home with any of these preliminary attacks, but to carry your opponent's blade a little more out of line with each disengage so gradually he doesn't notice you're doing it. Then, following the final engage, when his blade has been drawn completely out of line, you thrust home against an essentially unguarded man.'

'Take a damn good fencer,' said Eachan, flatly.

'There's that, of course,' said Cletus.

'Yes,' said deCastries, slowly, and waited for Cletus to look back at him. 'Also, it seems a tactic pretty well restricted to the fencing floor, where everything's done according to set rules.'

'Oh, but it can be applied to almost any situation,' said Cletus. There were coffee cups, as yet unfilled, spaced about the table. He reached out and captured three of these and lined them up, upside down between himself and deCastries. Then he reached into a bowl of sugar cubes standing on the table and brought his fist back to drop a cube onto the tablecloth by the central cup.

He covered the sugar cube with the central cup and moved all the cups about, interchanging their positions rapidly. Then he stopped.

'You've heard of the old shell game,' he said to deCastries. 'Which one of those cups would you say the sugar cube's under?'

DeCastries looked at the cups but made no attempt to reach out to them. 'None of them,' he said.

'Just for purposes of illustration – will you pick one, anyway?' asked Cletus.

DeCastries smiled. 'Why not?' he said.

He reached out and lifted the middle cup. His smile vanished for a second and then returned again. In plain view sat a sugar cube, white against white on the tablecloth.

'At least,' said deCastries, 'you're an honest shell-game operator.'

Cletus took up the middle cup, which deCastries had set down, and covered the sugar cube. Once again he rapidly switched around the positions of the overturned cups.

'Try it again?' he asked deCastries.

'If you want.' This time deCastries chose to lift the cup at the right end of the row as it faced him. Another sugar cube was exposed.

'Once more?' said Cletus. Again he covered the cube and mixed the cups. DeCastries picked up the cup now in the center and put it down with some force when he saw the sugar cube he had exposed.

'What's this?' he said. His smile was definitely gone now. 'What's the point of all this?'

'It seems you can't lose, Mr. Secretary, when I control the game,' said Cletus.

DeCastries looked penetratingly at him for a second, then covered the cube and sat back, glancing at Pater Ten.

'You move the cups this time, Pater,' he said.

Smiling maliciously at Cletus, Pater Ten rose and switched the cups about – but so slowly that everyone at the table easily kept track of the cup deCastries had last handled. That particular cup ended up once more in the middle. DeCastries looked at Cletus and reached for the cup to the right of the one that plainly contained the cube. His hand hesitated, hovered over it for a moment, and then drew back. His smile returned.

'Of course,' he said, looking at Cletus, 'I don't know how you do it, but I do know that if I lift that cup there'll be a sugar cube under it.' His hand moved to the cup at the opposite end of the line. 'And if I choose this one, it'll probably be there?'

Cletus said nothing. He only smiled back.

DeCastries nodded. The customary easiness of his manner had returned to him. 'In fact,' he said, 'the only cup I can be sure doesn't have a sugar cube under it is the one that we all know must have a cube – the one in the middle. Am I right?'

Cletus still only smiled.

'I am right,' said deCastries. He extended his hand out over the central cup for a second, watching Cletus' eyes, then withdrew the hand. 'And that was what you were after, in this demonstration with the cups and sugar cubes, wasn't it, Colonel? Your aim was to make me figure out the situation just the way I have – but also to make me so unsure of myself after being wrong three times in a row, that I'd still have to turn the center cup over to prove to myself it really was empty. Your real purpose was to strike at my confidence in my own judgment according to these *tactics of mistake* of yours, wasn't it?'

He reached out and snapped the central cup with his fingernail so that it rang with a sound like that of a small, flat-toned bell.

'But I'm not going to turn it over,' he went on, looking at Cletus. 'You see, having reasoned it out, I've gone one step further and worked out your purpose in trying to make me do it. You wanted to impress me. Well, I am impressed – but only a little. And in token of just how little, suppose we leave the cup sitting there, unturned? What do you say?'

'I say your reasoning's excellent, Mr. Secretary,' Cletus reached out and gathered in the other two cups upside down, covering the mouth of each briefly with his hand before turning them right-side-up to expose their empty, open mouths to the lounge ceiling. 'What else can I say?'

'Thank you, Colonel,' said deCastries, softly. He had leaned back in his chair and his eyes had narrowed down to slits. He reached out now with his right hand to take the stem of his wineglass and rotate it once more between thumb and forefinger with precise quarter turns, as if screwing it delicately down into the white tablecloth. 'Now, you said something earlier about taking this flight to Kultis only because you knew I'd be on it. Don't tell me you went to all that trouble just to show me your tactical shell game?'

'Only partly,' said Cletus. The tension in the atmosphere around the table had suddenly increased, although the voices of both Cletus and deCastries remained pleasant and relaxed. 'I wanted to meet you, Mr. Secretary, because I'm going to need you to arrange things so I can finish my work on tactics.'

'Oh?' said deCastries, 'And just how did you expect me to help?'

'Opportunities ought to present themselves to both of us, Mr. Secretary' – Cletus pushed back his chair and stood up – 'now that you've met me and know what I'm after. With that much done it's probably time for me to apologize for intruding on your dinner party and leave—'

'Just a moment, Colonel ...' purred deCastries.

A small sound of breaking glass interrupted them. Melissa's wineglass lay spilled and shattered against a saucer before her, and she was pushing herself unsteadily to her feet, one hand holding her forehead.

3

'No, no – it's all right!' she said to her father. 'I'm just a little dizzy, suddenly, that's all. I'll go lie down ... No, Dad, you stay here. Colonel Grahame, you can help me to my cabin, can't you – as long as you are leaving anyway?'

'Of course,' said Cletus.

He came quickly around the table and she took hold of his arm. She was tall, and she leaned the not inconsiderable weight of her healthy young body heavily against him. Almost irritably, she waved her father and deCastries back into their seats.

'Really!' she said. Her voice sharpened. 'I'm all right. I just want to lie down for a bit. Will you please not make a fuss about it? Colonel ...'

'Right here,' said Cletus. They moved off together slowly, she still leaning against him as they crossed the lounge and went out into the corridor turning left.

She continued to lean on him until they had made a turn in the corridor that hid them from the lounge entrance, then she stopped abruptly, straightened up and pulled away, turning to face him.

'I'm all right,' she said. 'I just had to do something to get you out of there. You aren't drunk at all!'

'No,' said Cletus, good-humoredly. 'And not a very good actor either, evidently.'

'You couldn't have fooled me, if you were! I can feel ...' She half-raised her hand, fingers spread out as if to touch him on the chest; and then dropped the hand abruptly as he looked curiously at it. 'I can see right through people like you. Never mind that. It would have been bad enough if you *were* drunk. Trying to play games with a man like Dow deCastries!'

'I wasn't exactly playing games,' said Cletus, soberly.

'Oh, don't tell me!' she said. 'Don't you think I know what kind of idiots professional soldiers can make of themselves when they try to deal with people outside their own special military world? But a Medal of Honor means something to me, even if most civilians don't know what it is!' Her eyes had slipped into line with his again. She almost wrenched her gaze away. 'And that's why I helped get you away from him just now. The only reason! ... And I'm not going to do it again!'

'I see,' said Cletus.

'So you get back to your cabin now, and stay there! Stay away from Dow deCastries from now on. From Dad and me, too ... Are you listening?'

'Of course,' said Cletus. 'But I'll see you the rest of the way to your cabin, at least.'

'No thanks. I can get there by myself.'

'What if someone sees you doing just that and the word gets back to the Secretary that your dizziness cleared up this quickly, once you were out of the lounge?'

She glared at him, turned and stalked off down the corridor. Cletus caught up with her in two long strides and fell into step.

'About professional soldiers,' he said, mildly. 'One isn't just like another ...'

She stopped and faced him abruptly, forcing him to stop also. 'I suppose,' she said, grimly, 'you think my father never was anything but a mercenary.'

'Of course not,' Cletus said. 'A lieutenant-general in the Royal Army of Afghanistan, wasn't he, up until ten years or so ago?'

She stared at him. 'How did you know?' Her tone was accusing.

'Military history – even recent military history – is part of my field,' he said. 'The University Revolution at Kabul twelve years ago, which ended up by taking over the government at Kabul, is part of it. The Afghanistani Army wouldn't have had more than one General Eachan Khan. He must have emigrated from Earth not more than a couple of years after the takeover.'

'He didn't have to leave!' she said. 'They still wanted him in the Army, even after Afghanistan gave up its independence to become a sector area of the Coalition. But there were other things ...' She broke off.

'Other things?' asked Cletus.

'You wouldn't understand!' She turned and began walking once more down the corridor. But, after a few steps, the words came from her as if she could not keep them in. 'My mother had died ... and ... *Salaam Badshahi Daulat Afghanistan* – when they began enforcing the death penalty for anyone singing the old Afghanistani anthem, he resigned. So he emigrated – to Dorsai.'

'It's a new world full of soldiers there, I understand,' said Cletus. 'It shouldn't have been too—'

'They found him work as a captain – a *captain* in a mercenary battalion!' she flashed at him. 'And since then, in ten years, he's managed to work his way just back up to colonel – and there he'll stay. Because the Dorsai mercenaries can't find employment for anything larger than a short regiment – and after his expenses are paid we don't have enough left over from what he makes to visit Earth, let alone live there again, unless the Exotics or someone pay our way there on official business.'

Cletus nodded. 'I see,' he said. 'But it's a mistake for you to try to mend things through deCastries. He's not capable of being influenced the way you hope.'

'Mend things . . .' She turned her head and stared at him, meeting his eyes this time in unthinking shock, her face suddenly pale.

'Of course,' said Cletus. 'I'd been wondering what you were doing at his table. You'd have been underage at the time your father emigrated to Dorsai, so you must have dual Coalition – Dorsai citizenship. You have the right to go back and live on Earth any time you want to take up your Coalition citizenship. But your father can't be repatriated except by special political dispensation, which is almost impossible to get. Either you or he must think you can get deCastries to help you with that—'

'Dad's got nothing to do with it!' Her voice was fierce. 'What kind of a man do you think he is?'

He looked at her. 'No. You're right of course,' he said. 'It must have been your idea. He's not the type. I grew up in a military family back on Earth, and he reminds me of some of the generals I'm related to. In fact, if I hadn't wanted to be a painter—'

'A painter?' She blinked at the sudden change of topic.

'Yes,' said Cletus, smiling a little wryly. 'I was just starting to make a living at it when my draft number came up, and I decided to go into the Alliance Military Academy after all, the way my family had wanted me to from the beginning. Then I got wounded, of course, and discovered I liked the theory of military art. So painting got left behind.'

While he was talking she had come to a halt automatically before one of the stateroom doors lining the long, narrow corridor. But she made no attempt to open it. Instead she stood, staring at him.

'Why did you ever leave teaching at the Academy, then?' she asked.

'Someone,' he said, humorously, 'has to make the worlds safe for scholars like myself.'

'By making a personal enemy out of Dow deCastries?' she said, incredulously. 'Didn't it teach you anything when he saw through your game with the teacups and the sugar cubes?'

'But he didn't,' said Cletus. 'Oh, I ought to admit he did a very good job of covering up the fact he hadn't.'

'*He* covered up?'

'Certainly,' Cletus answered. 'He lifted the first cup out of over-confidence, feeling sure he could handle whatever came of my shell game. When he turned up the first cube he thought I had blundered, not he. With the second cube, he revised his ideas, but was still over-confident enough to try again. When he turned up the third cube he finally woke to the fact that the game was completely under my control. So he had to find an excuse for stopping it and refusing to choose a fourth time.'

She shook her head. 'This is all the wrong way around,' she said, unbelievingly. 'You're twisting what happened to make it look the way you want it.'

'No,' said Cletus, 'DeCastries was the one who twisted it, with his actually very clever explanation of why he wouldn't lift a cup a fourth time. The only trouble was, it was a false explanation. He knew he'd find a sugar cube under any cup he lifted.'

'How could he?'

'Because I had cubes under all three cups, of course,' said Cletus. 'When I lifted one cube from the bowl, I palmed two others. By the time he got around to the fourth choice, deCastries had probably fig-ured that out. The fact that the game turned out to be the avoiding of finding a cube, instead of trying to find one, misled him at first. But pointing it out by then would have been too late to keep him from look-ing foolish at having played the game three times already. People like deCastries can't afford to look foolish.'

'But why did you do it?' Melissa almost cried. 'Why do you want to make an enemy like that?'

'I need to get him involved with me,' said Cletus, 'so I can make use of him. Unless I can make him annoyed enough to thrust, I can't parry. And only by successfully continuing to parry every attempt he makes can I finally get his whole attention ... Now you see,' he went on, a little more gently, 'why you ought to be worrying about your own involve-ment with Dow deCastries instead of mine. I can handle him. On the other hand, you—'

'*You* ...' Suddenly blazing with anger, she turned and jerked open the door. 'You absolute – go mix yourself up with Dow. Get yourself chewed up to mincemeat. I hope you do. But stay away from me . . . And from Dad! Do you hear me?'

He looked at her, and a slight shadow of something like pain passed through him. 'Of course,' he said, stepping back. If that's what you want.'

She went in, slamming the door behind her. He stood for a second, looking at its blank surface. For a moment with her there, the self-imposed barrier of isolation he had set up around himself many years ago, when he found others did not understand him, had almost melted. But it was back now.

He drew a short, deep breath that was almost a sigh. Turning, he went off down the corridor in the direction of his own stateroom.

4

For the next four days Cletus punctually avoided Melissa and her father – and was ignored in turn by deCastries and Pater Ten. Mondar, on the other hand, grew to be almost a close acquaintance, a circumstance Cletus found not only pleasant, but interesting.

The fifth day out from Earth, the spaceliner went into parking orbit around Kultis. Like its sister planet Mara, Kultis was a green, warm world with transient icecaps and only two major continental masses, north and south, as it had been true with Earth during the Gondwanaland period of the home planet's geological past. The shuttleboats from the chief cities of the various Kultan colonies began to come up to take off passengers.

On a hunch, Cletus tried to phone down to Alliance Headquarters in Bakhalla for reporting and billeting information. But the space-to-surface circuits were all tied up by the party for Neuland, in the forward evacuation lounge. Which meant, Cletus discovered with a little quiet inquiry, Pater Ten speaking for Dow deCastries. This, of course, was blatant favoritism on the part of a vessel of supposedly neutral registry. Cletus' hunch flowered into suspicion. One of those calls could well be concerned with him.

Glancing around as he turned from the phone, Cletus caught sight of the blue robe of Mondar, who was standing by the closed hatch of the midship lounge, only a few steps from Melissa and Eachan Khan. Cletus limped briskly over to the Exotic.

'Phones tied up,' Cletus said. 'Thought I'd ask Alliance Forces HQ for instructions. Tell me, is there much activity in close to Bakhalla by Neuland guerrillas these days?'

'Right up to our front doors,' answered Mondar. He looked at Cletus shrewdly. 'What's the matter? Just now remembering how you impressed Dow at dinner, that first day on board here?'

'That?' Cletus lifted an eyebrow. 'You mean deCastries goes to the trouble of making special guerrilla targets out of every light colonel he meets?'

'Not every one, of course,' said Mondar, and smiled. 'But in any case there's no cause for alarm. You'll be riding into Bakhalla with Melissa, Eachan and myself in a command car.'

'That's reassuring,' said Cletus. But his thoughts were already half-way elsewhere. Clearly, whatever effect he had achieved with Dow deCastries had been at least partly transparent to Mondar. Which was all right, he thought. The trail he had laid out toward his announced goal was baited along its length for just the sort of subtle mind that could envision purposes at work invisible to less perceptive men. It was that sort of mind deCastries possessed, and Mondar's was complex and deep enough in its own way to prove a useful control subject.

A gong rang through the lounge, cutting through the sounds of conversation.

'*Shuttleboat for Bakhalla, now docking,*' droned the first officer's voice from a wall speaker. '*Now docking, midships lounge hatch, the shuttleboat for Bakhalla. All passengers for Bakhalla should be ready to board ...*'

Cletus found himself swept forward as the hatch opened, revealing the bright metal connecting tunnel to the shuttleboat. He and Mondar were separated by the crowd.

The shuttleboat was little more than a cramped, uncomfortable, space- and atmosphere-going bus. It roared, dropped, plunged, jerked and finally skidded them all to a halt on a circle of scarred brown concrete surrounded by broad-leaved jungle – a green backdrop laced with what seemed to be threads of scarlet and bright yellow.

Shuffling out of the shuttleboat door into the bright sunlight, Cletus stepped a little aside from the throng to get his bearings. Other than a small terminal building some fifty yards off, there was no obvious sign of man except the shuttleboat and the concrete pad. The jungle growth towered over a hundred feet high in its surrounding circle. An ordinary, rather pleasant tropical day, Cletus thought. He looked about for Mondar – and was abruptly jolted by a something like a soundless, emotional thunderclap.

Even as it jarred him, he recognized it from its reputation. It was 'reorientation shock' – the abrupt impact of a whole spectrum of differences from the familiar experienced all at once. His absentmindedness as he had stepped out into this almost Earth-like scene had heightened its effect upon him.

Now, as the shock passed, he recognized all at once that the sky was not blue so much as bluish-green. The sun was larger and a deeper golden yellow than the sun of Earth. The red and yellow threads in the foliage were not produced by flowers or vines, but by actual veins of color running through the leaves. And the air was heavily humid, filled with odors that intermingled to produce a scent something like that of a mixture of grated nutmeg and crushed grass stems. Also, it was vibrant with a low-level but steady chorus of insect or animal cries ranging from the sounds like the high tones of a toy tin flute to the mellow booming of an empty wooden barrel being thumped – but all with a creakiness foreign to the voices of Earth.

Altogether the total impact of light, color, odor and sound, even now that the first shock was passed, caught Cletus up in a momentary immobility, out of which he recovered to find Mondar's hand on his elbow.

'Here comes the command car,' Mondar was saying, leading him forward. The vehicle he mentioned was just emerging from behind the terminal building with the wide shape of a passenger float-bus behind it. 'Unless you'd rather ride the bus with the luggage, the wives and the ordinary civilians?'

'Thanks, no. I'll join you,' said Cletus.

'This way, then,' said Mondar.

Cletus went with him as the two vehicles came up and halted. The command car was a military, plasma-powered, air-cushion transport, with half-treads it could lower for unusually rough cross-country going. Overall, it was like an armored version of the sports cars used for big game hunting. Eachan Khan and Melissa were already inside, occupying one of the facing pair of passenger seats. Up front on the open seat sat a round-faced young Army Spec 9 at the controls, with a dally gun beside him.

Cletus glanced at the clumsy hand weapon with interest as he climbed aboard the car over the right-side treads. It was the first dally gun he had seen in use in the field – although he had handled and even fired one back at the Academy. It was a crossbreed – no, it was an out-and-out mongrel of a weapon – designed originally as a riot-control gun and all but useless in the field, where a speck of dirt could paralyze some necessary part of its complex mechanism inside the first half hour of combat.

Its name was a derivative from its original, unofficial designation of "dial-a-gun", which name proved that even ordnance men were capable of humor. With proper adjustment it could deliver anything from a single .29 caliber pellet slug to an eight-ounce, seeker-type canister shell. It was just the sort of impractical weapon that set Cletus' tactical imagination perking over possible unorthodox employments of it in unexpected situations.

But he and Mondar were in the car now. With a hiss from its compressor, the command car's heavy body rose ten inches from the concrete and glided off on its supporting cushion of air. An opening in the jungle wall loomed before them; and a moment later they were sliding down a narrow winding road of bonded earth, with two deep, weed-choked ditches on each side unsuccessfully striving to hold back the wall of jungle that towered up on either side to arch thinly together, at last, over their heads.

'I'm surprised you don't burn back or spray-kill a cleared area on each side of the road,' said Cletus to Mondar.

'On the important military routes, we do,' said the Exotic. 'But we're short-handed these days and the local flora grows back fast. We're trying to variform an Earth grain or grass to drive out the native forms, and plant it alongside our roads – but we're short-handed in the laboratories, too.'

'Difficult – the services and supply situation,' jerked out Eachan Khan, touching the right tip of his waxed gray mustache protectively as the command car came unexpectedly upon a giant creeper that had broken through the bonded earth of the roadway from below, and was forced to put down its treads to climb across.

'What do you think of the dally gun?' Cletus asked the Dorsai mercenary, his own words jolted from his lips by the lurching of the command car.

'Wrong sort of direction for small arms to go ...' The creeper left behind, the car rose smoothly onto its supporting air cushion again. 'Nagle sticks – dally guns – ultrasonics to set off, jam or destroy the components in your enemy's weapons – it's all getting too complicated. And the more complicated, the more difficult the supply situation, the tougher to keep your striking forces really mobile.'

'What's your idea, then?' Cletus asked. 'Back to crossbows, knives and short swords?'

'Why not?' said Eachan Khan, surprisingly, his flat, clipped voice colored with a new note of enthusiasm. 'Man with a crossbow in the proper position at the proper time's worth a corps of heavy artillery half an hour late and ten miles down the road from where it should be. What's that business about "... *for want of a nail a horseshoe was lost ...*"?'

'"*For want of a horseshoe a horse was lost. For want of a horse a rider was lost ...*"' Cletus quoted it through to the end; and the two men looked at each other with a strange, wordless but mutual, respect.

'You must have some training problems,' said Cletus, thoughtfully. 'On Dorsai, I mean. You must be getting men with all sorts of backgrounds, and you'd want to turn out a soldier trained for use in as many different military situations as possible.'

'We concentrate on basics,' said Eachan. 'Aside from that, it's our program to develop small, mobile, quick-striking units, and then get employers to use them as trained.' He nodded at Mondar. 'Only real success in use so far's been with the Exotics, here. Most employers want to fit our professionals into their classical tables of organization. Works, but it's not an efficient use of the men, or the units. That's one reason we've had some arguments with the regular military. Your commanding officer here, General Traynor—' Eachan broke off. 'Well, not for me to say.'

He dropped the subject abruptly, sat up and peered out through the open window spaces in the metal sides of the command car at the jungle. Then he turned and called up to the driver on the outside seat.

'Any sign of anything odd out here?' he asked. 'Don't like the feel of it, right along in here.'

'No sir, Colonel!' called the driver back down. 'Quiet as Sunday din—'

A thunderclap of sound burst suddenly all around them. The command car lurched in the same moment and Cletus felt it going over, as the air around them filled with flying earth. He had just a glimpse of the driver, still holding the dally gun but now all but headless, pitching into the right-hand ditch. And then the car went all the way over on its side and there was a blurred moment in which nothing made sense.

Things cleared again, suddenly. The command car was lying on its right side, with only its armored base and its left and rear window spaces exposing them to the outside. Mondar was already tugging the magnesium shutter across the rear window and Eachan Khan was pulling the left window-space shutter closed overhead. They were left in a dim metal box with only a few narrow, sunlit apertures toward the front and around the armored section behind the driver's seat.

'You armed, Colonel?' asked Eachan Khan, producing a flat, little, dart-thrower sidearm from under his tunic and beginning to screw a long sniper's barrel onto it. Solid pellets from sporting guns – theoretically civilian weapons, but deadly enough at jungle ranges – were already beginning to whang and yowl off the armor plating of the car surrounding them.

'No,' said Cletus, grimly. The air was already close in the car and the smell of crushed grass and nutmeg was overwhelming.

'Pity,' said Eachan Khan. He finished screwing on the sniper barrel, poked its muzzle through one of the aperture cracks and squinted into the daylight. He fired – and a big, blond-bearded man in a camouflage suit came crashing out of the jungle wall on the far side of the road, to lie still.

'The bus will hear the firing as it comes up behind us,' said Mondar out of the dimness behind Cletus. 'They'll stop and phone ahead for help. A relief squad can get here by air in about fifteen minutes after Bakhalla hears about us.'

'Yes,' said Eachan Khan, calmly, and fired again. Another body, invisible this time, could be heard crashing down out of a tree to the ground below. 'They might get here in time. Odd these guerrillas didn't let us pass and wait for the bus in the first place. Bigger package, less protection, and more prizes inside ... I'd keep my head down, Colonel.'

This last sentence was directed at Cletus, who was heaving and wrenching in a fury at the shutter on the down side of the car. Half-propped off the road surface as the car was by the bulge of that same surface under it, opening the shutter gradually produced a space facing on the ditch into which the dead driver had pitched – a space large enough for Cletus to crawl out.

The jungle-hidden riflemen became aware of what he was up to, and a fusillade of shots rang against the armored underside of the car – though, because of the narrow angle it made with the ground, none came through the opening Cletus had produced. Melissa, suddenly recognizing what was in his mind, caught at his arm as he started through the opening.

'No,' she said. 'It's no use! You can't help the driver. He was killed when the mine went off—'

'The hell ... with that ...' panted Cletus, for a fire-fight did not encourage the best in manners. 'The dally gun went with him when he fell.'

Wrenching himself free of her grasp, he wriggled out from under the armored car, jumped to his feet and made a dash for the ditch where the body of the driver lay unseen. An explosion of shots from the surrounding jungle rang out, and he stumbled as he reached the ditch edge, tripped, spun about and plunged out of sight. Melissa gasped, for there was the sound of thrashing from the ditch, and then an arm was flung up into sight to quiver for a second and then hang there in plain view, reaching up like a last and desperate beckoning for help.

In response, a single shot sounded from the jungle and a slug blew away half the hand and wrist. Blood spattered from it, but the hand was not withdrawn; and almost immediately the bleeding dwindled, with none of the steady spurt and flow that would have signaled a still-pumping, living heart behind it.

Melissa shuddered, staring at the arm, and a shivering breath came from her. Glancing about for a minute, her father put his free hand for a moment on her shoulder.

'Easy, girl,' he said. He squeezed her shoulder for a second and then was forced back to his loophole as a new burst of shots rang against the body of the car. 'They'll rush us – any minute now,' he muttered.

Sitting cross-legged in the dimness like a figure meditating and remote, Mondar reached out and took one of the staring girl's hands in his own. Her gaze did not move from the arm in the ditch, but her own grip tightened, tightened, on Mondar's hand with a strength that was unbelievable. She did not make a sound, but her gaze never moved and her face was as white and still as a mask.

The shots from the jungle stopped suddenly. Mondar turned to look at Eachan.

The Dorsai looked back over his own shoulder and their eyes met.

'Any second now,' said Eachan, in businesslike tones. 'You're a fool if you let them take you alive, Outbond.'

'When there is no more point in living, I can always die,' answered Mondar, serenely. 'No man commands this body but myself.'

Eachan fired again.

'The bus,' said Mondar, calmly, 'ought to have gotten close enough to hear the firing and phoned, by this time.'

'No doubt,' said the Dorsai. 'But help'd have to be on top of us right now to do any good. Any second, as I said, they'll give up sniping at us and make a rush. And one pistol won't hold off a dozen or more ... Here they come now!'

Through the aperture, over the soldier's shoulder strap, Mondar could see the two waves of camouflaged-overalled figures that erupted suddenly from both sides of the jungle trail and came pouring down upon the car. The little handgun in Eachan's hand was speaking steadily, and, magically – for its voice was almost lost in the general din and uproar – figures in the front of the rush were going down.

But there was only a matter of fifteen meters or so for the attackers to cover; and then the jungle and the little patch of sunlight Mondar could see were blotted out by camouflaged overalls.

The gun in Eachan's hand clicked empty – and in that second, just as the shape of the first guerrilla darkened the opening through which

Cletus had gotten out, the wild yammer of a dally gun roared from behind the attackers, and they melted like sand figures under the blow of a heavy surf.

The dally gun yammered on for a second longer, and then stopped. Stillness flowed in over the scene like water back into a hole made in a mountain lake by a falling stone. Eachan pushed past the frozen figures of Mondar and Melissa and crawled out from the car. Numbly, they followed him.

Limping on his artificial left knee joint, Cletus was climbing out of the ditch, dragging the shape of the dally gun behind him. He got to his feet on the roadway just as Eachan came up to him.

'Very well done,' said the Dorsai, with a rare note of warmth back in his usually stiff voice. 'Thank you, Colonel.'

'Not at all, Colonel,' said Cletus, a little shakily. Now that the excitement was over, his one knee that was still flesh and blood was trembling with reaction, invisibly but perceptibly under his uniform trouser leg.

'Very well done, indeed,' said Mondar, as quietly as ever, joining them. Melissa had halted and was staring down into the ditch where the dead driver lay. It was his arm that had been up-flung, obviously with intention, by Cletus, as he lay thrashing about like a deeply wounded man, unseen in the ditch. Melissa shivered and turned away to face the rest of them.

She stared at Cletus out of her white face, in which a strange mixture of emotions were now intermingled. Mondar spoke:

'Here come our relief forces,' commented the Exotic, gazing skyward. A couple of battle aircars, with a squad of infantry aboard each, were dropping down to the roadway. A hiss of a braking airjet sounded behind them and they turned to see the bus slide into view around a turn in the road. 'As well as our signal section,' he added, smiling a little.

5

The command car, its compressor damaged by guerrilla fire, was left behind. One of the battle aircars carried its four surviving passengers the rest of the way into the port city of Bakhalla. The aircar dropped the four of them off at the transport section of Alliance Headquarters in Bakhalla. Eachan Khan and Melissa said goodbye and left by autocab for their own residence in the city. Mondar opened the door of another autocab and motioned Cletus inside.

'You'll need to go to Alliance HQ for your assignment and billeting, and that's on my way. I'll drop you off.'

Cletus got in; Mondar reached to punch out a destination on the control board of the autocab. The cab rose on its air cushion and slid smoothly off between the rows of white-painted military buildings.

'Thanks,' said Cletus.

'Not at all,' said Mondar. 'You saved all our lives back in the jungle just now. I want to do more than just thank you. I take it you might like to talk to Dow deCastries again?'

Cletus looked at the Outbond curiously. All his life he had enjoyed watching people of strong aims at work to achieve them; and in the five days since he had met Mondar he had become aware of a purposefulness in the Exotic that might well be as dedicated as his own.

'I thought deCastries went down to Capital Neuland.'

'He did,' said Mondar, as the autocab made a right turn into a somewhat broader boulevard and began to approach a large building of white concrete with the Alliance flag flying on top of it. 'But Neuland's only twenty-five minutes from here by air. The Coalition hasn't any direct diplomatic relations with our Exotic government here on Kultis, and neither our people nor Dow want to pass up a chance to talk. After all, it's really the Coalition we're fighting – Neuland couldn't last six weeks without them. So I'm giving an unofficial little party at my home this evening – with a buffet supper and general conversation. Eachan and Melissa will be there. I'd appreciate having you, too.'

'Be happy to come,' said Cletus. 'May I bring my aide?'

'Aide?'

'A second lieutenant named Arvid Johnson, if I'm lucky enough to find him still unassigned,' Cletus said. 'One of my former students at the Academy. He came to visit me when he was home from here on leave a couple of months ago. It was what he told me that got me interested in Bakhalla.'

'Was it? Well, bring him by all means.' The autocab slid to a halt before the walkway leading up to the entrance of the large white building. Mondar pressed a button and the autocab door next to Cletus swung open. 'Bring anyone you think might enjoy it. About eight o'clock.'

'We'll be there,' said Cletus. He turned and let the walkway carry him up into the Headquarters building.

'Colonel Cletus Grahame?' echoed the narrow-faced, young second lieutenant at the cluttered desk behind the glass door of the billeting and assignments office, when Cletus confronted him. 'You're to report to General Traynor immediately – *immediately* when you arrive.'

He had a high tenor voice and he grinned unpleasantly as he spoke. Cletus smiled agreeably, asked directions to the general's office and left.

The glass door he finally found marked *Brigadier General John Houston Traynor* led him first into an outer office where a square-set, half-bald colonel in his early fifties stood, evidently just completing the giving of some directions to an overweight, thirtyish captain behind the room's single desk. Finishing, the colonel turned around and eyed Cletus.

'You're Grahame?' he asked abruptly.

'That's right, Colonel,' said Cletus pleasantly, 'and you …?'

'Dupleine,' said the other, ungraciously. 'I'm chief of staff to General Traynor. You're not going into the Officers' Pool, then?'

'I'm on special assignment from Geneva, Colonel,' said Cletus.

Dupleine grunted, whirled around and went out the door Cletus had just entered. Cletus looked back at the fat captain behind the desk.

'Sir,' said the captain. His voice held the hint of a note of sympathy. His face was not unkind, and even intelligent, in spite of the heavy dewlap of the double chin supporting it from beneath. 'If you'll just sit down a moment, I'll tell General Traynor you're here.'

Cletus sat down and the captain leaned forward to speak into the intercom grille of his desk. The reply he received was inaudible to Cletus, but the captain looked up and nodded.

'You can go right in, Colonel,' he said, nodding to another door behind his desk.

Cletus rose and obeyed … As he stepped through the door into the farther office, he found himself directly facing a much larger desk, behind which sat a bull-like man in his mid-forties with a heavy-boned face decorated by a startling pair of thick, black eyebrows. 'Bat' Traynor, the general had been nicknamed, Cletus recalled, because of those brows. Bat Traynor stared now, the brows pulled ominously together as Cletus walked forward toward his desk.

'Colonel Cletus Grahame reporting, sir,' Cletus said, laying his travel orders on the desk. Bat shoved them aside with one big-knuckled hand.

'All right, Colonel,' he said. His voice was a rough-edged bass. He pointed to a chair facing him at the left side of his desk. 'Sit down.'

Cletus limped gratefully around to the chair and dropped into it. He was beginning to feel the fact that he had strained one or more of the few remaining ligaments in his bad knee during the episode in the ditch outside of town. He looked up to see Bat still staring point-blank at him.

'I've got your dossier here, Colonel,' Bat said after a moment. He flipped open the gray plastic folder that lay on the desk before him and looked down at it. 'You come from an Academy family, it says here. Your uncle was General Chief of Staff at Geneva Alliance HQ just before he retired eight years ago. That right?'

'Yes, sir,' said Cletus.

'And you' – Bat flipped papers with a thick forefinger, scowling a little down at them – 'got that bad knee in the Three-Month War on Java seven years ago? … Medal of Honor, too?'

'Yes,' said Cletus.

'Since then' – Bat flipped the folder shut and raised his eyes to stare unwaveringly once more across it at Cletus' face – 'you've been on the Academy staff. Except for three months of active duty, in short, you've done nothing in the Army but pound tactics into the heads of cadets.'

'I've also,' said Cletus, carefully, 'been writing a comprehensive "Theory of Tactics and Strategical Considerations."'

'Yes,' said Bat, grimly. 'That's in there, too. Three months in the field and you're going to write twenty volumes.'

'Sir?' said Cletus.

Bat threw himself back heavily in his chair.

'All right,' he said. 'You're supposed to be here on special assignment to act as my tactical adviser.' The black eyebrows drew together in a scowl and rippled like battle flags in the wind. 'I don't suppose I've got you because you heard some rumor they were going to clean out all the dead wood at the Academy and you pulled strings to be sent to some nice soft job where there's nothing for you to do?'

'No, sir,' said Cletus, quietly. 'I may have pulled a string or two to get sent here. But, with the General's permission, it wasn't because I thought this a soft job. I've got to do a great deal out here.'

'I hope not, Colonel. I hope not,' said Bat. 'It just happens I put in a request for a dozen jungle-breaker tanks three months ago ... You're what I got instead. Now, I don't give a damn what the Academy wants to do with its Tactics Department. The kids just have to come out here into the field and relearn it all over again under practical conditions, anyway. But I needed those tanks. I still need them.'

'Possibly,' said Cletus, 'I can come up with some means to help the General get along without them.'

'I don't think so,' said Bat, grimly. 'What I think is that you're going to hang around here for a couple of months or so and turn out not to be particularly useful. Then I'm going to mention that fact to Alliance HQ back on Earth and ask for my jungle-breakers again. I'll get them, and you'll be transferred back to Earth – if with no commendations, at least without any black marks on your record ... That's if everything goes smoothly, Colonel. And' – Bat reached across to a corner of his desk and pulled a single sheet of paper toward him – 'speaking of the way things go, I've got a report here that you got drunk your first night out, on the ship headed here, and made a fool of yourself in front of the Outworld's Secretary for the Coalition, who was aboard.'

'That's fast reporting,' said Cletus, 'considering that, when our party for Bakhalla left the ship, the phones aboard were all still tied up by Coalition people. I take it this report to the General comes from one of them?'

'It's none of your business who made the report!' rumbled Bat. 'As a matter of fact, it comes from the captain of the spaceship.'

Cletus laughed.

'What's the joke, Colonel?' Bat's voice rose.

'The idea, sir,' said Cletus, 'of a civilian ship commander reporting on the fitness of an Alliance officer.'

'You won't find it all that funny if I have the information entered in your record, Colonel,' said Bat. He stared at Cletus, at first grimly, and then a trifle disconcertedly, when Cletus did not seem greatly sobered by this threat. 'But, never mind the Coalition or any civilian shipmaster. I'm your commanding officer, and *I'm* asking for an explanation of your drunkenness.'

'There isn't any explanation ...' began Cletus.

'Oh?' said Bat.

'No explanation, I was going to say,' continued Cletus, 'because no explanation's necessary. I've never been drunk in my life. I'm afraid the ship's captain was wrongly advised – or drew the wrong conclusion.'

'Just made a mistake, eh?' said Bat, ironically.

'As it happens,' said Cletus, 'I think I've got a witness who'll testify I wasn't drunk. He was at the table. Mondar, the former Outbond from here to St. Louis Enclave.'

Bat's mouth, opened to retort before Cletus was half done, closed instead. The general sat silent for several seconds. Then his eyebrows quivered and the frown line between his eyes smoothed somewhat.

'Then why this report?' he asked in a more neutral voice.

'The ship's people, from what I saw,' said Cletus, 'seemed partial to the Coalition people aboard.'

'Well, then, damn it!' exploded Bat, 'if you saw them jumping to the wrong conclusion, why didn't you set them straight?'

'As a matter of elementary strategy,' said Cletus, 'I thought it wouldn't do any harm to let the Coalition people pick up as low an opinion of me as possible – of me, and my usefulness to you, as a tactical expert.'

Bat looked balefully at him. 'Their opinion couldn't be any lower than mine, anyway,' he said. 'You're no use to me, Colonel. This is a dirty, little, hole-in-the-wall war, with no room for strategical mysteries. This Exotic colony's got brains, money, technical developments and a seacoast. The Neulanders've got no seacoast, no industry and too much population for their back-country farms to support – because of this multiple-wife religious cult of theirs. But that same excess population's just fine for supplying guerrillas. So, the Neulanders want what the Exotics've got and the Coalition's trying to help them get it. We're here to see they don't. That's the whole situation. What the Neuland guerrillas try to do, and what we do to stop them from doing it, is just plain obvious. I need a book-strategy and tactics expert like I need a hundred-piece symphony orchestra. And I'm sure deCastries and the other Coalition people on that ship knew it as well as I do.'

'Maybe I won't be quite as useless as the General thinks,' said Cletus, unperturbed. 'Of course, I'll have to survey and study the situation, starting by setting up a plan for trapping those guerrillas that'll be infiltrating through Etter's Pass, up country, in the next few days.'

Bat's eyebrows shot up into flag position again. 'New guerrillas? Who told you anything about Etter's Pass?' he snapped. 'What kind of a rabbit is this you're trying to pull out of your hat?'

'No rabbit,' said Cletus, 'not even a professional judgment, I'm afraid.

Just common sense. With Dow deCastries here, the Neulanders have to try to put on some sort of spectacular during his visit ... Have you got a map handy?'

Bat jabbed a button on the surface of his desk, and the wall of the room to Cletus' left lit up suddenly with the projection of a large map showing the long, narrow coastline country of the Exotic colony, and the interior range of mountains that divided it from the Neuland colony inland. Cletus stepped over to the projection, looked it over and reached up to tap with his left forefinger at a point in the middle of the mountain range running down the left side of the map.

'Here's Etter's Pass,' he said to Bat. 'A good, broad cut through the mountains, leading from Neuland down to Bakhalla – but, according to reports, not much used by the Neulanders, simply because there's nothing much worth raiding on the Exotic side for over a hundred miles in any direction. On the other hand, it's a fairly easy pass to get through. There's nothing but the small town of Two Rivers down below it, here. Of course, from a practical standpoint, the Neulanders are better off sending their guerrillas into the country through passes closer to the larger population centers. But if they aren't after profit so much as spectacle, it'd pay them to infiltrate a fairly good-sized force through here in the next few days, so that a week from now they can hit one of the smaller coastal towns in force – maybe even capture and hold it for a few days.'

Cletus turned, limped back to his chair and sat down. Bat was frowning at the map.

'At any rate,' Cletus said, 'it shouldn't be too difficult to set up a net to sweep most of them in, as they try to pass Two Rivers. In fact, I could do it myself. If you'd let me have a battalion of jump troops—'

'Battalion! *Jump troops!*' Bat started suddenly out of his near-trance and turned a glare on Cletus. 'What do you think this is? A classroom, where you can dream up whatever force you need for a job? There's no jump troops on Kultis. And as for giving you a battalion of any kind of troops – even if your guess has something going for it ...' Bat snorted.

'The guerrillas are coming, all right. I'd bet my reputation on it,' said Cletus, undisturbed. 'In fact, you might say I've already bet it, come to think of it. I remember talking to some of my fellow staff members at the Academy, and a friend or two down in Washington, and forecasting that infiltration, just as soon as Dow deCastries reached Neuland.'

'You forecast ...' Bat's tone became thoughtful – almost cunning – suddenly. He sat behind his desk, pondering Cletus with knitted brows. Then his dark eyes sharpened. 'So you bet your reputation on this, did you, Colonel? But spare troops are something I haven't got, and in any case, you're here as a technical adviser … Tell you what. I'll pull a company off Rest and Retraining and send them out with a field officer in charge. He'll be junior to you, of course, but you can go along if you want to. Officially, as an observer only, but I'll tell the officer commanding that he's to keep your advice in mind … Good enough?'

The last two words were barked sharply at Cletus, in a put-up-or-shut-up tone of voice.

'Certainly,' said Cletus. 'If the General wishes.'

'All right!' Bat beamed suddenly, showing his teeth in a hearty, wolfish grin. 'You can go on and see about your quarters, then, Colonel. But stay on call.'

Cletus rose to his feet. 'Thank you, sir,' he said, and took his leave.

'Not at all, Colonel. Not at all,' he heard Bat's voice saying, with almost a chuckle in it, as Cletus closed the door of the office behind him.

Cletus left the Headquarters building and went to see about establishing himself. Once set up in the Bachelor Officers' Quarters, he strolled over to the Officers' Pool HQ with a copy of his orders and checked to see if that Second Lieutenant Arvid Johnson, of whom he had spoken to Mondar, was still unattached. Informed that he was, Cletus filed a request for the lieutenant to be assigned to him as a research staff member and requested that he get in touch with him at the BOQ immediately.

He returned to the BOQ. Less than fifteen minutes later, the signal outside his room buzzed to announce a visitor. Cletus rose from his chair and opened the door.

'Arvid!' he said, letting the visitor in and closing the door behind him. Arvid Johnson stepped inside, turned and smiled happily down at Cletus as they shook hands. Cletus was tall, but Arvid was a tower, from the soles of his black dress boots to the tips of his short-cropped, whitish-blond hair.

'You came after all, sir,' Arvid said, smiling. 'I know you said you'd come, but I couldn't believe you'd really leave the Academy for this.'

'This is where things are going on,' said Cletus.

'Sir?' Arvid looked incredulous. 'Away out here on Kultis?'

'It's not the locality so much,' said Cletus, 'as the people in it that makes things happen. Right now we've got a man among us named Dow deCastries and the first thing I want for you is to go with me to a party for him tonight.'

34

'Dow deCastries?' Arvid said, and shook his head. 'I don't think I know—'

'Secretary to the Outworlds for the Coalition,' said Cletus. 'He came in on the same ship from Earth as I did ... A gamesman.'

Arvid nodded. 'Oh, one of the Coalition bosses,' he said. 'No wonder you say things might start to happen around here ... What did you mean by gamesman, sir? You mean he likes sports?'

'Not in the usual sense,' said Cletus. He quoted, '"*Whose game was empires and whose stakes were thrones. Whose table, earth – whose dice were human bones ...*"'

'Shakespeare?' asked Arvid, curiously.

'Byron,' said Cletus, 'in his "The Age of Bronze", referring to Napoleon.'

'Sir,' said Arvid, 'you don't really mean this deCastries is another Napoleon?'

'No more,' answered Cletus, 'than Napoleon was an earlier deCastries. But they've got points in common.'

Arvid waited for a moment longer, but Cletus said nothing more. The big young man nodded again.

'Yes, sir,' he said. 'What time are we supposed to go to this party, Colonel?'

6

Thunder, deeper toned than Earth's, muttered beyond the ridge of hills inland from Bakhalla like a grumbling of giants, as Cletus and Arvid arrived at the residence of Mondar. But above the city the sky was clear. Out over the rooftops of the buildings leading down the harbor, the yellow sun of Kultis was filling the sky and sea alike with pinkish gold.

Mondar's home, surrounded by trees and flowering shrubs, both native and Earth variform, sat alone on a small hill in the eastern suburbs of the city. The building itself was made up of an assortment of basic building units put together originally with an eye more toward utility than appearance. However, utility no longer controlled any but the basic forms of the house. In everything else an artistic and gentle influence had been at work.

The hard white blocks of the building units, now tinted by the sunset, did not end abruptly at the green lawn, but were extended into arbors, patios and half-rooms walled with vine-covered trellises. Once Cletus and Arvid had left their car and passed into the first of these outer structures of the house, it became hard for them to tell at any time whether they were completely indoors or not.

Mondar met them in a large, airy half-room with solid walls on three sides only, and an openwork of vines on the fourth. He led them deeper into the house, to a long, wide, low-ceilinged room deeply carpeted and scattered with comfortably overstuffed chairs and couches. A number of people were already there, including Melissa and Eachan Khan.

'DeCastries?' Cletus asked Mondar.

'He's here,' said Mondar. 'He and Pater Ten are just finishing their talk with some of my fellow Exotics.' As he spoke he was leading the two of them toward the small bar in one corner of the room. 'Punch for whatever you'd like to drink. I've got to see some people right now – but I'd like to talk to you later, Cletus. Is that all right? I'll look you up just as soon as I'm free.'

'By all means,' said Cletus. He turned toward the bar as Mondar went off. Arvid was already picking up the glass of beer for which he had punched.

'Sir?' asked Arvid. 'Can I get you ...'

'Nothing right now, thanks,' said Cletus. He was glancing around again and his eye lit upon Eachan Khan, standing alone with a glass in his hand next to a wide window screen. 'Stay around here, will you, Arvid? So I can find you easily when I want you?'

'Yes, sir,' said Arvid.

Cletus went toward Eachan Khan. The older man glanced around with a stony face, as though to discourage conversation, as he came up. Then, seeing who it was, Eachan's face relaxed – insofar as it could ever be said to be relaxed.

'Evening,' Eachan said. 'I understand you've met your commanding officer.'

'News travels fast,' said Cletus.

'We're a military post, after all,' said Eachan. His gaze went past Cletus for a moment, and then returned. 'Also, I hear you suggested something about a new infiltration of Neulander guerrillas through Etter's Pass?'

'That's right,' said Cletus. 'You don't think it's likely?'

'Very likely – now you've pointed it out,' said Eachan. 'By the way – I got hold of those three volumes on tactics you've already published. The Exotic library here had copies. I've only had time to glance through them, so far' – his eyes suddenly locked with Cletus' – 'but it looks like sound stuff. Very sound ... I'm still not sure I follow your tactics of mistake, though. As deCastries said, combat's no fencing match.'

'No,' said Cletus, 'but the principle's applicable, all the same. For example, suppose a simple tactical trap you lay for an enemy consists of enticing his forces to strike at what seems to be a weak section of your line. But when they do, your line pulls back and draws them into a pocket, where you surround them and pinch them off with hidden, superior forces of your own.'

'Nothing new about that,' said Eachan.

'No,' Cletus said, 'but apply the tactics of mistake to essentially the same situation. Only this time, in a succession of contacts with the enemy, you entice him into picking up a series of what seem to be small, easy victories. Meanwhile, however, you're getting him to engage a larger amount of his available forces with each contact. Then, when he finally commits the greatest part of his strength for what he conceives as one more easy win – you convert that contact into a trap and he discovers that you've gradually drawn him into a field position where he's outflanked and completely at your mercy.'

'Tricky,' Eachan frowned. 'Too tricky, perhaps ...'

'Not necessarily,' said Cletus. 'Imperial China and Russia both used a crude version of this, drawing invaders deeper into their territories, until the invader suddenly realized he was too far from his supply and support bases and completely surrounded by the native enemy ... Napoleon and the retreat from Moscow.'

'Still—' Eachan broke off suddenly. His gaze had gone past Cletus; and Cletus, turning, saw that Dow deCastries was now in the room. The tall, dark and elegant Secretary to the Outworlds for the Coalition was now standing in conversation with Melissa, by the opposite wall.

Glancing from the two figures back to Eachan, Cletus saw that the older man's face had become as cold and still as the first sheet of ice on the surface of a deep pond on a windless winter day.

'You've known deCastries awhile now?' Cletus asked. 'You and Melissa?'

'The women all like him,' Eachan's voice was grim. His gaze was still on Melissa and Dow.

'Yes,' said Cletus. 'By the way—' He broke off, and waited. With reluctance, Eachan removed his gaze from the pair across the room and looked back at him.

'I was going to say,' said Cletus, 'that General Traynor came up with something strange when I was talking to him. He said he didn't have any jump troops here in Bakhalla. That surprised me. I did some reading up on you Dorsais before I came out here, and I thought a jump course was part of the training you gave your mercenaries?'

'We do,' replied Eachan, dryly. 'But General Traynor's like a lot of your Alliance and Coalition commanders. He doesn't think our training's good enough to qualify the men for jump-troop work – or a lot of other combat field duties.'

'Hmm,' said Cletus. 'Jealousy? Or do you suppose they look on you mercenaries as competitors of a sort?'

'I don't say that,' said Eachan, frostily. 'You draw your own conclusions, of course.' His eyes showed a desire once more to wander back across the room to Melissa and Dow.

'Oh, and something else I was going to ask you,' said Cletus. 'The assignment sheets for Bakhalla that I looked at back on Earth listed some Navy officers, on detached duty as marine engineers – something about river-and-harbors work. But I haven't seen any Navy people around.'

'Commander Wefer Linet,' said Eachan, promptly, 'wearing civvies, down at the end of the couch across the room there. Come along. I'll introduce you.'

Cletus followed Eachan at a long slant across the room, which brought them to a couch and several chairs where half a dozen men sat talking. Here, they were less than a quarter of the distance they had been before from Dow and Melissa – but still too distant to catch the conversation going on between the two.

'Commander,' said Eachan, as they reached the couch, and a short, square-faced man in his middle thirties got up promptly from the end of the couch, a drink still in his hand. 'I'd like you to meet Colonel Cletus Grahame, just out from Earth, to be attached to General Traynor's staff – tactical expert.'

'Happy to meet you, Colonel,' said Wefer Linet, shaking Cletus' hand with a hard, friendly grip. 'Dream something up for us to do besides dredging river mouths and canals and my men'll love you.'

'I'll do that,' said Cletus, smiling. 'It's a promise.'

'Good!' said Wefer energetically.

'You've got those large, underwater bulldozers, haven't you?' asked Cletus. 'I read about them in the Alliance Forces Journal, seven months back, I think.'

'The Mark V, yes,' Linet's face lit up. 'Six of them here. Care for a ride in one someday? They're beautiful pieces of machinery. Bat Traynor wanted to take them out of the water and use them knocking down jungles for him. Do it better than anything you Army people have, of course. But they're not designed for land work. I couldn't tell the general no, myself, but I insisted on direct orders from Earth and kept my fingers crossed. Luckily, they turned him down back there.'

'I'll take you up on that ride,' said Cletus. Eachan was once more watching Melissa and Dow with a stony concentration. Cletus glanced about the room and discovered Mondar, standing talking to a pair of women who looked like the wives of diplomatic personnel.

As if Cletus' gaze had an actual physical touch to it, the Exotic turned toward him just then, smiled and nodded. Cletus nodded back and turned once more to Wefer, who had launched into an explanation of how his Mark V's worked, at depths down to a thousand feet or in the teeth of thirty-knot currents and tides.

'It looks as if I may be tied up for the next few days, out of the city,' Cletus said. 'But after that, if for some reason I shouldn't leave town ...'

'Give me a ring, anytime,' Wefer said. 'We're working on the main harbor here at Bakhalla right now. I can have you off the docks and down inside my command unit in ten minutes, if you'll just phone me half an hour or so ahead of time to make arrangements ... Hello, Outbond. The Colonel here's going to take a ride with me one of these days in a Mark V.'

Mondar had come up while Wefer had been speaking.

'Good,' said the Exotic, smiling. 'He'll find that interesting.' His gaze shifted to Cletus. 'But I believe you wanted to talk to Dow deCastries, Cletus? His business with my people's over for the evening. You can see him, right across the room there, with Melissa.'

'Yes ... I see,' said Cletus. He looked around at Wefer and Eachan. 'I was just going over there. If you gentlemen will excuse me?'

He left Wefer with a promise to phone him at the earliest opportunity. As he turned away, he saw Mondar touch Eachan lightly on the arm and draw him off to one side in conversation.

Cletus limped over to where Dow and Melissa were still standing together. As Cletus came up they both turned to look at him, Melissa with a sudden, slight frown line between her darkened eyebrows. But Dow smiled genially.

'Well, Colonel,' he said. 'I hear all of you had a close call coming in from the spaceport earlier today.'

'Only the sort of thing to be expected here on Bakhalla, I suppose,' said Cletus.

They both laughed easily, and the slight frown line between Melissa's eyes faded.

'Excuse me,' she said to Dow. 'Dad's got something to say to me, I guess. He's beckoning me over. I'll be right back.'

She left. The gazes of the two men met and locked.

'So,' said Dow, 'you came off with flying honors – defeating a guerrilla band single-handed.'

'Not exactly. There was Eachan and his pistol.' Cletus watched the other man. 'Melissa might have been killed, though.'

'So she might,' said Dow, 'and that would have been a pity.'

'I think so,' said Cletus. 'She deserves better than that.'

'People usually get what they deserve,' said deCastries. 'Even Melissa. But I didn't think scholars concerned themselves with individuals?'

'With everything,' said Cletus.

I see,' said deCastries. 'Certainly with sleight-of-hand. You know, I found a sugar cube under that middle cup after all? I mentioned it to Melissa and she said you'd told her you'd had cubes under all three cups.'

'I'm afraid so,' Cletus said.

They looked at each other.

'It's a good trick,' said deCastries. 'But not one that'd work a second time.'

'No,' said Cletus. 'It always has to be different, a second time.'

DeCastries smiled, an animal smile.

'You don't sound much like a man in an ivory tower, Colonel,' he said. 'I can't help thinking you like theory less, and action more, than you admit. Tell me' – his eyes hooded themselves amusedly under his straight brows – 'if it comes down to a simple choice, aren't you tempted to practice rather than preach?'

'No doubt about it,' said Cletus. 'But one drawback to being a scholar is you're likely to be an idealist, too. And in the long run, when these new worlds are free to work out their own destinies without Earth's influence, one man's theories could have a longer and more useful effect than one man's practice.'

'You mentioned that, back aboard ship,' deCastries said. 'You talked about Alliance and Coalition influence being removed from worlds like Kultis. Do you still feel as safe talking like that here, with your Alliance superiors all around the place?'

'Safe enough,' said Cletus. 'None of them would believe it – any more than you do.'

'Yes. I'm afraid I don't.' DeCastries picked up a wineglass from the small table beside which he was standing and held it briefly up to the light, twisting it slowly between thumb and forefinger. He lowered the glass and looked back at Cletus. 'But I'd be interested in hearing how you think it's going to happen.'

'I'm planning to help the change along a little,' said Cletus.

'Are you?' said deCastries. 'But you don't seem to have anything to speak of in the way of funds, armies or political influence to help with. Now, for example, I've got those things, myself, which puts me in a much stronger position. If I thought a major change could be accomplished – to my benefit, of course – I'd be interested in altering the shape of things to come.'

'Well,' said Cletus, 'we can both try.'

'Fair enough.' DeCastries held the wineglass, looking over it at Cletus. 'But you haven't told me how you'd do it. I told you what my tools are – money, armed troops, political power. What have you got? Only theories?'

'Theories are enough, sometimes,' said Cletus.

DeCastries slowly shook his head. He put the wineglass back down on the small table and lightly dusted against one another fingertips of the hand that had held the glass, as if to get rid of some stickiness.

'Colonel,' he said, quietly, 'you're either some new kind of agent the Alliance is trying to fasten on me – in which case I'll find out about you as soon as I can get word back from Earth – or you're a sort of interesting madman. In which case, events will take care of you in not much more time than it takes to establish the fact you're an agent.'

He watched Cletus for a second. Cletus met his eye expressionlessly.

'I'm sorry to say,' deCastries went on, 'you're beginning to sound more and more like a madman. It's too bad. If you'd been an agent, I was going to offer you a better job than the one you have with the Alliance. But I don't want to hire a madman – he'd be too unpredictable. I'm sorry.'

'But,' said Cletus, 'if I turned out to be a successful madman ...?'

'Then, of course, it'd be different. But that's too much to hope for. So all I can say is, I'm sorry. I'd hoped you wouldn't disappoint me.'

'I seem to have a habit of disappointing people,' said Cletus.

'As when you first decided to paint instead of going on to the Academy and then gave up painting for a military life, after all?' murmured deCastries. 'I've been a little disappointing to people in my life that way. I've got a large number of uncles and cousins about the Coalition world – all very successful managers, business chiefs, just as my father was. But I picked politics—' He broke off, as Melissa rejoined them.

'It wasn't anything ... Oh, Cletus,' she said, 'Mondar said if you wanted to find him he'd be in his study. It's a separate building, out behind the house.'

'Which way do I go?' asked Cletus.

She pointed through an arched entrance in a farther wall of the room. 'Just go straight through there and turn left,' she said. 'The corridor you'll be in leads to a door that opens on the garden. His study building's just beyond it.'

'Thank you,' said Cletus.

He found the corridor, as Melissa had said, and followed it out into the garden, a small, terraced area with paths running to a line of trees, the tops of which tossed sharply in a hot, wet wind against a sky full of moonlight and torn cloud ends. There was no sign of any building.

At that moment, however, just as Cletus hesitated, he caught sight of light glimmering through the trees ahead of him. He went out across the garden and through the trees. Past their narrow belt he came into the open before a low-roofed, garage-like structure so comfortably fitted in among the vegetation surrounding it that it gave the impression of being comfortably half-sunk in the earth. Low, heavily curtained windows let out the small amount of light he had seen just now. There was a door before him; and as he approached, it slid noiselessly open. He stepped inside and it closed behind him. He stopped, instinctively.

He had walked into a softly but clearly lit room, more library than study in appearance, although it had something of both about it. Its air tasted strangely thin and dry and clean like air on some high mountain peak. Bookshelves inset in all four of the walls held a surprisingly large collection of old-fashioned, printed volumes. A study console and a library retrieval system each occupied a corner of the room. But Mondar, the only other person in the room besides Cletus, was seated apart from these devices on a sort of wide-surfaced and armless chair, his legs up and crossed before him, so that he sat like a Buddha in the lotus position.

There was nothing except this to mark the moment and place as anything out of the ordinary – but as Cletus stepped through the door, a deep, instinctive warning shouted loudly at him, checking him just inside the threshold. He sensed an impalpable living tension that held the very air of the room – a feeling as of a massive, invisible force in delicate, temporary balance. For a second his mind recoiled.

Then it cleared. For one fleeting but timeless moment he saw that which was in the room – and that which was not.

What his eyes registered were like two versions of the same scene, superimposed on each other, but at the same time distinct and separate. One was the ordinary room, with Mondar seated on his chair, and all things ordinary.

The other was the same room, but filled with a difference. Here, Mondar did not sit on his chair but floated, in lotus position, a few inches above its seat cushion. Stretching out before and behind him was a succession of duplicating images, semitransparent, but each clearly identifiable – and while those closest to him, before and behind him, were duplicates of himself, those farther from him wore different faces – faces still Exotic, but of different men, different Outbonds. Before and behind him, these stretched away until they were lost to sight.

Cletus, too, he became aware, had his images in line with him. He could see those before and he was somehow conscious of those behind him. Before him was a Cletus with two good knees, but beyond this and two more Cletuses were different men, bigger men. But a common thread ran through them, tying the pulses of their lives to his, and continuing back through him to a man with no left arm, on and on, through the lives of all those others behind him until it ended, at last, with a powerful old man in half-armor sitting on a white horse with a baton in hand.

Nor was this all. The room was full of forces and currents of living pressures coming from vast distances to this focal point, like threads of golden light they wove back and forth, tying each other together, connecting some of Cletus' images with Mondar's, and even Cletus, himself, with Mondar, himself. They two, their forerunners and their followers, hung webbed in a tapestry of this interconnecting pattern of light during that single moment in which Cletus' vision registered the double scene.

Then, abruptly, Mondar turned his gaze on Cletus, and both tapestry and images were gone. Only the normal room remained.

But Mondar's eyes glowed at Cletus like twin sapphires illuminated from within by a light identical in color and texture to the threads that had seemed to fill the air of the room between both men.

'Yes,' said Mondar. 'I knew ... almost from the moment I first saw you in the spaceship dining lounge. I knew you had potential. If it'd only been part of our philosophy to proselytize or recruit in the ordinary way, I'd have tried to recruit you from that minute on. Did you talk to Dow?'

Cletus considered the unlined face, the blue eyes, of the other, and slowly nodded.

'With your help,' he said. 'Was it actually necessary to get Melissa away, too? DeCastries and I could have talked over her head.'

'I wanted him to have every advantage,' Mondar said, his eyes glowing. 'I wanted no doubt left in your mind that he'd been able to bid as high for you as he wanted to go ... He did offer you a job with him, didn't he?'

'He told me,' said Cletus, 'that he couldn't – to an interesting madman. From which I gathered he was extremely eager to hire one.'

'Of course he is,' said Mondar. 'But he wants you only for what you can do for him. He's not interested in what you could make of yourself ... Cletus, do you know how we Exotics came about?'

'Yes,' said Cletus. 'I looked you up before I put in my request for transfer to here. The Association for the Investigation and Development of Exotic Sciences – my sources say you developed out of a black-magic cult of the early twenty-first century called the Chantry Guild.'

'That's right.' Mondar said. 'The Chantry Guild was the brainchild of a man named Walter Blunt. He was a brilliant man, Cletus, but like most of the people of his time, he was reacting against the fact that his environment had suddenly been enlarged from the surface of one world to the surfaces of any number of worlds spread out through light-years of interstellar space. You probably know the history of that period as well as I do – how that first, instinctive, racial fear of space beyond the solar system built up and erupted in a series of bloody social eruptions. It spawned any number of societies and cults for people attempting to adjust psychologically to feelings of vulnerability and insignificance, deep down on the unconscious level. Blunt was a fighter, an anarchist. His answer was revolution—'

'Revolution?' asked Cletus.

'Yes. Literally – revolution.' Mondar answered. 'Blunt wanted to destroy part of actual, objective physical reality as well – by using primitive psychic leverage. He called what he wanted to do "creative destruction". He called on people to *"Destruct!"* But he couldn't quite push even the intense neurotics of his time all the way over the emotional brink. And then he was deposed as head of the Guild by a young mining engineer who'd lost an arm in a mine accident—'

'Lost an arm?' said Cletus sharply. 'Which arm?'

'The left – yes, I think it was the left that was gone,' said Mondar. 'Why?'

'Nothing,' said Cletus. 'Go on.'

'His name was Paul Formain—'

'Fort-Mayne?' Cletus interrupted a second time.

'No *t*.' answered Mondar, 'F-o-r-m-a-i-n.' He spelled it out, looking curiously at Cletus. 'Something about this interests you particularly, Cletus?'

'Only the coincidences,' said Cletus. 'You said he had only one arm, so the right arm he had left would have been overmuscled from compensation development. And his name sounds almost like *fort-mayne*, which are the words used by the Norman French to describe their policy to the conquered English after they took over England in the eleventh century. *Fort-mayne* – literally, "strong-hand". It described a policy of using whatever force was necessary to keep the native English under control. And you say he took over the Chantry Guild, deposing this Blunt?'

'Yes.' Mondar frowned. 'I see the coincidences, Cletus, but I don't see why they're important.'

'Maybe they aren't,' said Cletus. 'Go on. Formain took over the Chantry Guild and started your Exotic Association?'

'He almost had to wreck the Chantry Guild to do it,' said Mondar. 'But he did. He changed its aim from revolution to evolution. The evolution of man, Cletus.'

'Evolution.' Cletus repeated the word thoughtfully. 'So, you don't think the human race is through evolving? What comes next, then?'

'We don't know, of course,' said Mondar, folding his hands in his lap. 'Can an ape imagine a man? But we're convinced the seeds of further evolution are alive in man, still – even if they aren't already germinating. We Exotics are dedicated to searching for those seeds, and protecting them once we've found them, so that they can flourish and grow until evolved man is part of our community.'

'Sorry,' Cletus shook his head. 'I'd make a poor Exotic, Mondar. I've got my own job to do.'

'But this is part of your job – and your job is part of it!' Mondar leaned forward, and his hands slid apart. 'There's no compulsion on our members. Each one searches and works for the future the way he thinks best. All we ask is that when the skills *of* anyone are needed by the community, he makes them available to it. In return the community offers him its skills to improve *him,* physically and mentally, so he can be that much more effective in his own work. You know what you can do now, Cletus. Think what you might be able to do if you could make use of all we can teach you!'

Cletus shook his head again.

'If you turn us down,' said Mondar, 'it signals a danger to you, Cletus. It signals an unconscious desire on your part to go the deCastries way – to let yourself be caught up by the excitement of directly manipulating people and situations instead of dealing with what's much more valuable, but less emotionally stimulating – the struggle with ideas to find principles that'll lift people eventually above and beyond manipulation.'

Cletus laughed, a little grimly. 'Tell me,' he said, 'isn't it true that you Exotics won't carry or use weapons yourself, even in self-defense? And that's why you hire mercenaries like the Dorsais, or make agreements with political groups like the Alliance to defend yourselves?'

'Yes – but not for the reason most people think, Cletus,' said Mondar, swiftly. 'We haven't any moral objection to fighting. It's just that the emotions involved interfere with clear thinking, so people like myself prefer not to touch weapons. But there's no compulsion on our people on this. If you want to write your work on military tactics, or even keep and carry guns—'

'I don't think you follow me,' said Cletus. 'Eachan Khan told me something. You remember when you were in the command car after it overturned, earlier today, and he suggested you not let yourself be taken alive by the Neulander guerrillas – for obvious reasons? You answered that you could always die. "No man" you said, "commands this body but myself."'

'And you think suicide is a form of violence—'

'No,' said Cletus. 'I'm trying to explain to you why I'd never make an Exotic. In your calmness in the face of possible torture and the need to kill yourself, you were showing a particular form of ruthlessness. It was ruthlessness toward yourself – but that's only the back side of the coin. You Exotics are essentially ruthless toward all men, because you're philosophers, and, by and large, philosophers are ruthless people.'

'Cletus!' Mondar shook his head. 'Do you realize what you're saying?'

'Of course,' said Cletus, quietly. 'And you realize it as well as I do. The immediate teaching of philosophers may be gentle, but the theory behind their teaching is without compunction – and that's why so much bloodshed and misery has always attended the paths of their followers, who claim to live by those teachings. More blood's been spilled by the militant adherents of prophets of change than by any other group of people down through the history of man.'

'No Exotic spills blood,' said Mondar, softly.

'Not directly, no,' said Cletus. 'But to achieve the future you dream of means the obliteration of the present as we know it now. You may say your aim's changed from revolution to evolution but your goal is still the destruction of what we have now to make room for something different. You work to destroy what presently is – and that takes a ruthlessness that's not my way – that I don't agree with.'

He stopped speaking. Mondar met his eyes for a long moment.

'Cletus,' said Mondar at last, 'can you be that sure of yourself?'

'Yes,' said Cletus. 'I'm afraid I can.' He turned toward the door. As he reached the door and put his hand on its button, he turned back.

'Thanks all the same, Mondar,' he said. 'You and your Exotics may end up going my way. But I won't go yours. Good night.'

He opened the door.

'Cletus,' said Mondar, behind him, 'if you refuse us now, you do it at your own risk. There are larger forces at work in what you want to do than I think you understand.'

Cletus shook his head. 'Good night,' he said again, and went out.

Back in the room where he had left Arvid, he found the young lieutenant and told him they were leaving. As they reached the parking area together and Cletus opened the door of their aircar, the sky split open above them in a wild explosion of lightning and thunder, with raindrops coming down like hailstones.

They bolted for the interior of the car. The rain was icy and the few seconds of being exposed to it had left their jackets soaked and clinging to their shoulders. Arvid put power on the vehicle and lifted it out of the lot.

'All hell's broke loose tonight,' he murmured, as they swung back across the city. Then, startled, he looked at Cletus, sitting beside him.

'Now, why did I say that?' he asked. Cletus did not answer and after a second Arvid answered himself.

'All the same,' he said, half to himself, 'it has.'

7

Cletus woke to the sensation that his left knee was being slowly crushed in a heavy vice. The dull, unyielding pain of it had roused him from his sleep, and for a moment he was its captive – the sensation of pain filling the whole universe of his consciousness.

Then, practically, he took action to control the crippling sensation. Rolling over on his back, he stared up at the white ceiling seven feet above him. One by one, starting with his thigh muscles, he commanded the large muscles of his arms and legs to lose their tensions and relax. He moved on to the neck and face muscles, the belly muscles, and finally into a feeling of relaxation pervading him completely.

His body was heavy and limp now. His eyes were drooping, half-closed. He lay, indifferent to the faint noises that filtered to him from other parts of the BOQ. He drifted, sliding gently away, like a man lax upon the surface of some warm ocean.

The state of relaxation he had induced had already muffled the dull-jawed, relentless grip of the pain upon his knee. Slowly, so as not to reawaken an alertness that would allow tension to form in him once more, he propped the pillow behind and pulled himself up in the bed. Half-sitting, he folded the covers back from his left leg and looked at it.

The knee was puffed and swollen to stiffness. There was no darkness or bruise-shade of discoloration about it, but it was swollen to the point of immobility. He fastened his gaze steadily on the swollen knee, and set about the larger job of bringing it back down to normal size and movement.

Still drifting, still in that more primitive state of mind known as regression, he connected the pain response in his knee with the pain message in his mind, and began to convert the message to a mental equivalent of that same physical relaxation and peace which held his body. Drifting with it, he felt the pain message lose its color. It faded, like an instruction written in evaporating ink, until it was finally invisible.

He felt what he had earlier recognized as pain, still present in his knee. It was a sensation only, however, neither pain nor pressure, but co-equal with both. Now that he had identified this former pain as a separate sensation-entity, he began to concentrate upon the actual physical feeling of pressure within the blood and limb, the vessels now swollen to the point of immobilizing his leg.

He formed a mental image of the vessels as they were. Then, slowly, he began to visualize them as relaxing, shrinking, returning their fluid contents to those pipe systems of the leg to which they were severally connected.

For perhaps as much as ten minutes there was no visible response from the knee area. Then, gradually, he began to be aware of a yielding of the pressure and a sensation of faint warmth within the knee itself. Within another five minutes it was possible to see that the swelling was actually going down. Ten minutes later, he had a knee that was still swollen, but which he could bend at a good sixty-degree angle. It was good enough. He swung good leg and bad out of bed together, got up and began to dress.

He was just buckling on a weapons belt over his jungle suit, when there was a knock at his door. Cletus glanced over at the clock beside his bed. It showed eight minutes before 5 A.M.

'Come on in,' he said.

Arvid stepped into the room.

'You're up early, Arv,' Cletus said, snapping the weapons belt shut and reaching for his sidearm on top of the chest of drawers beside him. He slid the weapon into its holster, hanging from the belt. 'Did you get the things I wanted?'

'Yes, sir,' said Arvid, 'the loudspeaker horn and the singleton mines are tucked away out of sight in duffle packs. I couldn't get the rifle into a pack, but it's with the packs, clipped onto the electric horse you asked for.'

'And the horse, itself?'

'I've got it in the back of a courier car, outside ...' Arvid hesitated. 'I asked to go with you, sir, but the orders just called for you and the field officer in charge of the company. I want to tell you about him. They've given you a first lieutenant named Bill Athyer.'

'And this Bill Athyer is no good, is that it?' asked Cletus, cheerfully, picking up his communications helmet and leading the way out of the room.

'How did you know?' Arvid stared down at Cletus, following him as they went out down the long center aisle of the BOQ.

Cletus smiled back at him, limping along, but delayed his answer until they had stepped out the front door into the misty, predawn darkness where the courier car waited for Cletus. They got in, Arvid behind the controls. As the big young lieutenant sent the vehicle sliding off on its air cushion, Cletus went on:

'I rather thought the general'd be giving me someone like that. Don't worry about it, Arv. You're going to have your hands full enough today, as it is. I want you to find office space for me and line me up a staff – a warrant officer, if you can get one for office manager, a couple of clerical tech fives and a file clerk tech two with a research specialty. Can you get right to work on that?'

'Yes, sir,' answered Arvid. 'But I didn't know we had authority for something like that—'

'We don't, yet,' said Cletus. 'But I'll get it for you. You just find the premises and the people, so we know where to lay hands on them as soon as we have authorization.'

'Yes, sir,' said Arvid.

Having arrived at the transport area, Cletus found his company, under the command of First Lieutenant William Athyer, standing at ease in ranks, equipped, armed and apparently ready to take off. Cletus assumed that the men had had breakfast – not being the field officer in command of them, it was not up to him to see that they had; and asking Athyer about it would be impolitic, not to say insulting. Cletus descended a little stiffly from the courier car and watched as Arvid unloaded the electric horse, with its equipment.

'Colonel Grahame?' a voice said behind him. 'I'm Lieutenant Athyer, in command of this company. We're ready to take off . . .'

Cletus turned. Athyer was a short, dark, fairly slim man, in his mid-thirties, with a beak-like nose. A vaguely sour expression sat on his features, as if habit had made it permanent there. His speech was abrupt, even aggressive, but the words at the end of each speech tended to thin out into a whine.

'Now that you're finally here, sir,' he added.

The extra, unnecessary statement verged on impertinence. But Cletus ignored it, looking past Athyer's shoulder at the men behind the lieutenant. Their tanned skin and the mixture of old and new equipment and clothing about them suggested experience. But they were more silent than they should be; and Cletus had little doubt about the reason for this. To be put back under weapons and flown off into combat in the middle of Rest and Retraining was not likely to make soldiers happy. He looked back at Athyer.

'I imagine we'll start loading right away, then. Won't we, Lieutenant?'

he said pleasantly. 'Let me know where you want me.'

'We're taking two atmosphere support ships for transport,' growled Athyer. 'I've got my top sergeant in the second. You'd better ride with me in the first, Colonel—'

He broke off to stare at the electric horse, as its overhead vanes whined into movement. Arvid had just switched its satchel turbine on, and the single-person vehicle had lifted into the air so that it could be moved easily under its own power to the support ship. Evidently, Athyer had not connected the horse with Cletus until this moment. In truth, it was an unlikely little contraption for such an outing – designed for spaceport inspection work, mainly, and looking like a wheel-less bicycle frame suspended fore and aft from metal rods leading down from a side-by-side pair of counter-rotating ducted vanes driven by a nuclear-pack, satchel turbine just below them. Cletus' cone rifle and duffle bags were hung before its saddle on the crossbar.

It was not pretty, but that was no reason for Athyer to scowl at it as he was doing.

'What's this?' he demanded.

'It's for me, Lieutenant,' said Cletus, cheerfully. 'My left knee's half-prosthetic, you know. I didn't want to hold you and your men up if it came to moving someplace along the ground in a hurry.'

'Oh? Well ...' Athyer went on scowling. But the fact that the sentence he had begun trailed off was evidence enough that his imagination was failing him in its search for a valid excuse to forbid taking the electric horse. Cletus was, after all, a lieutenant-colonel. Athyer turned, snapping at Arvid. 'Get it on board, then! Quick, Lieutenant!'

He turned away to the business of getting the company of perhaps eighty men into the two atmosphere support ships waiting on the transport area pad some fifty feet distant.

The boarding of the ships went smoothly and easily. Within twenty minutes they were skimming northward over the tops of the jungle trees toward Etter's Pass – and the sky beyond the distant mountain range was beginning to grow pale with the dawn.

'What're your plans, Lieutenant?' began Cletus, as he and Athyer sat facing each other in the small, forward passengers' compartment of the ship.

'I'll get the map,' said Athyer, ducking away resentfully from Cletus' gaze. He dug into the metal command case on the floor between his boots and came up with a terrain map of the Exotic side of the mountains around Etter's Pass. He spread the map out on the combined knees of himself and Cletus.

'I'll set up a picket line like this,' Athyer said, his finger tracing an arc through the jungle on the mountain slopes below the pass, 'about three hundred yards down. Also, place a couple of reserve groups high up, behind the picket line on either side of the pass mouth. When the Neulanders get through the pass and far enough down the trail to hit the lower curve of the picket line, the reserve groups can move in behind them and we'll have them surrounded ... That is, if any guerrillas do come through the pass.'

Cletus ignored the concluding statement of the lieutenant's explanation. 'What if the guerrillas don't come straight down the trail?' Cletus asked. 'What if they turn either right or left directly into the jungle the minute that they're on this side of the mountains?'

Athyer stared at Cletus at first blankly, and then resentfully, like a student who has been asked an exam question he considers unfair.

'My support groups can fall back ahead of them,' he said at last, ungraciously, 'alerting the rest of the picket line as they go. The other men can still close in behind them. Anyway we've got them enclosed.'

'What's visibility in the jungle around there, Lieutenant?' asked Cletus.

'Fifteen – twenty meters,' Athyer answered.

'Then the rest of your picket line is going to have some trouble keeping position and moving upslope at an angle to enclose guerrillas who're probably already beginning to split up into groups of two and three and spread out for their trek to the coast. Don't you think?'

'We'll just have to do the best we can,' said Athyer, sullenly.

'But there're other possibilities,' said Cletus. He pointed to the map. 'The guerrillas have the Whey River to their right as they come out of the pass, and the Blue River to their left, and both those rivers meet down at Two Rivers Town, below. Which means that any way the Neulanders turn, they've got to cross water. Look at the map. There're only three good crossing spots above the town on the Blue River, and only two on the Whey – unless they'd want to go right through the town itself, which they wouldn't. So, any or all of those five crossings could be used.'

Cletus paused, waiting for the junior officer to pick up on the unspoken suggestion. But Athyer was obviously one of those men who need their opportunities spelled out for them.

'The point is, Lieutenant,' Cletus said, 'why try to catch these guerrillas in the jungle up around the pass, where they've got all sorts of opportunities to slip past you, when you could simply be waiting for them at these crossings, and catch them between you and the river?'

Athyer frowned reluctantly, but then lent over the map to search out the five indicated crossing points that Cletus had mentioned.

'The two Whey River crossings,' Cletus went on, 'are closest to the pass. Also they're on the most direct route to the coast. Any guerrillas taking the passes on the Blue River are going to have to circle wide to get safely around the town below. The Neulanders know you know this. So I think it's a fairly safe bet that they'll count on your trying to stop them – if they count on anyone trying to stop them at all – at those two passes. So they'll probably merely feint in that direction and make their real crossing at these three other fords over on the Blue River.'

Athyer stared at Cletus' finger as it moved around from point to point on the map in time with his words. The lieutenant's face tensed.

'No, no, Colonel,' he said, when Cletus had finished. 'You don't know these Neulanders the way I do. In the first place, why should they expect us to be waiting for them, anyway? In the second place, they're just not that smart. They'll come through the pass, break up into twos and threes going through the jungle and join up again at one, maybe two, of the Whey River crossings.'

'I wouldn't think so—' Cletus was beginning. But this time, Athyer literally cut him short.

'Take my word for it, Colonel!' he said. 'It's those two points on the Whey River they'll be crossing at.'

He rubbed his hands together. 'And that's where I'll snap them up!' he went on. 'I'll take the lower crossing with half the men, and my top sergeant can take the upper crossing with most of the rest. Put a few men behind them to cut off their retreat, and I'll bag myself a nice catch of guerrillas.'

'You're the field officer in command,' said Cletus, 'so I don't want to argue with you. Still, General Traynor did say that I was to offer you my advice, and I'd think you'd want to play safe, over on the Blue. If it was up to me ...'

Cletus let his voice trail off. The lieutenant's hands, with the map already half-folded, slowed and ceased their movement. Cletus, looking at the other's lowered head, could almost see the gears turning over inside it. By this time Athyer had left all doubts behind about his own military judgment. Still, situations involving generals and colonels were always touchy for a lieutenant to be involved in, no matter who seemed to be holding all the high cards.

'I couldn't spare more than a squad, under a corporal,' muttered Athyer to the map, at last. He hesitated, plainly thinking. Then he lifted his head and there was a craftiness in his eyes. 'It's your suggestion,

Colonel. Maybe if you'd like to take the responsibility for diverting part of my force over to the Blues …?'

'Why, I'd be perfectly willing to, of course,' said Cletus. 'But as you pointed out, I'm not a field officer, and I can't very well take command of troops under combat conditions …'

Athyer grinned. 'Oh, that!' he said. 'We don't stick right with every line in the book out here, Colonel. I'll simply give orders to the corporal in charge of the squad that he's to do what you say.'

'What I say? You mean – *exactly* what I say?' asked Cletus.

'Exactly,' said Athyer. 'There's an authority for that sort of thing in emergencies, you know. As commanding officer of an isolated unit I can make emergency use of any and all military personnel in whatever manner I feel is necessary. I'll tell the corporal I've temporarily allowed you status as a field officer, and of course your rank applies.'

'But if the guerrillas do come through the Blue River crossings,' said Cletus. 'I'll have only a squad.'

'They won't, Colonel,' said Athyer, finishing his folding of the map with a flourish. 'They won't. But if a few stray Neulanders *should* show up – why, use your best judgment. An expert on tactics like yourself, sir, ought to be able to handle any little situation like that, that's liable to turn up.'

Leaving the barely concealed sneer to linger in the air behind him, he rose and went back with the map into the rear passenger compartment where the soldiers of half his command were riding.

The support ship in which they were traveling set Cletus down with his squad at the uppermost of the three crossing points on the Blue River, and took off into the dawn shadows, which still obscured this western slope of the mountain range dividing Bakhalla from Neuland. Athyer had sorted out a weedy, nineteen-year-old corporal named Ed Jarnki and six men to be the force Cletus would command. The moment they were deshipped, the seven dropped automatically to earth, propping their backs comfortably against nearby tree trunks and rocks that protruded from the unbroken, green ferny carpet of the jungle floor. They were in a little clearing surrounded by tall trees that verged on a four-foot bank over the near edge of the river; and they gazed with some curiosity at Cletus as he turned about to face them.

He said nothing. He only gazed back. After a second, Jarnki, the corporal, scrambled to his feet. One after the other the rest of the men rose also, until they all stood facing Cletus, in a ragged line, half at attention.

Cletus smiled. He seemed a different man entirely, now, from the officer the seven had glimpsed earlier as they were boarding and descending from the support ship. The good humor had not gone from his face. But in addition, now, there was something powerful, something steady and intense, about the way he looked at them, so that a sort of human electricity flowed from him to them and set all their nerves on edge, in spite of themselves.

'That's better,' said Cletus. Even his voice had changed. 'All right, you're the men who're going to win the day for everyone, up here at Etter's Pass. And if you follow orders properly, you'll do it without so much as skinning your knuckles or working up a sweat.'

8

They stared at him.

'Sir?' said Jarnki, after a moment.

'Yes, Corporal?' said Cletus.

'Sir ... I don't understand what you mean.' Jarnki got it out, after a second's struggle.

'I mean you're going to capture a lot of Neulanders,' said Cletus, 'and without getting yourselves hurt in the process.' He waited while Jarnki opened his mouth a second time, and then slowly closed it again.

'Well? That answer your question, Corporal?'

'Yes sir.'

Jarnki subsided. But his eyes, and the eyes of the rest of the men, rested on Cletus with a suspicion amounting to fear.

'Then we'll get busy,' said Cletus.

He proceeded to post the men – one across the shallow ford of the river, which here swung in a lazy curve past the clearing, two men down below the bank on each side of the clearing, and the four remaining in tree-top positions strung out away from the river and upslope of the direction from which any guerrillas crossing the ford would come.

The last man he posted was Jarnki.

'Don't worry, Corporal,' he said, hovering on the electric horse in midair a few feet from where Jarnki swayed in the treetop, clutching his cone rifle. 'You'll find the Neulanders won't keep you waiting long. When you see them, give them a few cones from here, and then get down on the ground where you won't get hit. You've been shot at before, haven't you?'

Jarnki nodded. His face was a little pale, and his position in a crotch of the smooth-barked, variform Earth oak he perched in was somewhat too cramped to be comfortable.

'Yes, sir,' he said. His tone left a great deal more unsaid.

'But it was under sensible conditions, with the rest of the men in your platoon or company all around you, wasn't it?' said Cletus. 'Don't let the difference shake you, Corporal. It won't matter once the firing starts. I'm going to check the two lower crossings. I'll be back before long.'

He swung the electric horse away from the tree and headed downriver ... The vehicle he rode was almost silent in its operation, producing nothing much more than the kind of hum a room exhaust fan makes. Under conditions of normal quiet it could be heard for perhaps fifteen meters. But this upland Kultan jungle was busy with the sounds of birds and animals. Among these was a cry like the sound of an ax striking wood, which sounded at intervals; and another sound that resembled heavy snoring, which would go on for several seconds, only to break off, pause, and then begin again. But most of the woodlife noises were simply screams of different pitches and volumes and musical character.

Altogether these made an unpredictable pattern of sound, among which the low hum of the electric horse could easily be lost to ears not specifically listening for it – such as the ears of a guerrilla from Neuland who was probably both unfamiliar with the noise and not expecting it in any case.

Cletus flew downriver and checked both the lower crossings, finding them empty of all human movement. He turned from the lowest crossing to move through midair into the jungle from the river, upslope, in the direction of the pass. Luck so far, he thought, since they had the longest distance to cover if several crossings were being used. Undoubtedly a rendezvous point and time would have been set up for all groups on the far side of the river.

He drifted forward just under treetop level, some forty to sixty meters above the ground, at a speed of not more than six kilometers per hour. Below him, the upland jungle flora showed less of the yellow veining than there had been in the greenery near the shuttleboat landing pad; but the threads of scarlet ran everywhere, even through the outsize leaves of the variform Earth trees – oak, maple and ash – with which Kultis had been seeded twenty years back.

The Earth flora had taken more strongly in these higher altitudes. But there was still a majority of the native plants and trees, from fernlike clumps reaching ten meters into the air, to a sprawling tree-type with purple fruits that were perfectly edible but exhaled a faint but sickening scent through their furry skins as they ripened.

Cletus was about eight hundred meters away from the river crossing before he spotted his first sign of movement, a waving of fern tops below him. He checked his forward movement and drifted downward.

A second later the foreshortened figure of a man in a brown- and green-splashed jungle suit moved into sight from under the fern.

The infiltrator was unequipped except for the pack on his back, a soft camouflage-cloth cap on his head and the pellet-gun sporting firearm he carried by its strap over his right shoulder. This was to be expected where the guerrillas were concerned. The convention that had grown up on the newer worlds in fifty years of inter-colony disputes was that, unless a man carried military weaponry or equipment, he was subject only to civil law – and civil law had to prove damage to property, life or limb before any action could be taken against an armed man, even from another colony. A guerrilla caught with nothing but a sporting gun was usually only deported or interned. One with any kind of military equipment, however – even as little as a military-issue nail file – could be taken by the military courts, which usually adjudged him a saboteur and condemned him to prison or death. If this man below him was typical of the infiltrators in his group, then Jarnki and his men with their cone rifles would have a massive advantage in weapons to make up for their scarcity of numbers, which was a relief.

Cletus continued to watch the man for several minutes. He was making his way through the jungle with no real regard for silence or cover. As soon as Cletus had a line of march estimated for this individual, he turned off to one side to locate the other members of the same guerrilla force.

The rapidly rising sun, burning through the sparse leaves at treetop level, heated the back of Cletus' neck. He was sweating from his armpits, all across his chest and back under his jungle suit, and his knee was threatening to revive its ache once more. He took a moment out to force his muscles to relax and push the knee discomfort from him. There was not time for that – not yet. He went back to searching the jungle for more guerrillas.

Almost immediately he found the second man, moving along parallel to and perhaps thirty meters from the infiltrator Cletus had spotted first. Cletus continued looking, and within the next twenty minutes he ranged out to both ends of the skirmish line that was pushing through the jungle below him and counted twenty men moving abreast over a front perhaps three hundred meters in width. If the Neulanders had split their forces equally between the three crossings, which would be only elementary military precaution, that would mean an infiltration force of sixty men. Sixty men, assuming they lost something like 20 per cent of their group's strength in getting through the jungle from here to the coast, would leave about forty-eight men available for whatever assault the Neulanders planned to celebrate deCastries' visit.

Forty-eight men could do a lot in the way of taking over and hold-ing the small coastal fishing village. But a good deal more could be done with double that number. Perhaps there was a second skirmish line behind the first.

Cletus turned the electric horse in midair and drifted it back under the treetops behind the man he had just spotted advancing. Sure enough, about eighty meters back, he discovered a second skirmish line – this time with fifteen men in it, including at least a couple who looked like officers, in that they carried more in the way of communica-tion and other equipment and wore sidearms rather than rifles. Cletus turned the electric horse about, slid quietly through the air just below the tree-tops and back toward the outside lower end of the approaching skirmish line. He located it, and saw that – as he had expected – the guerrillas were already beginning to close up so as to come into the crossing point together. Having estimated the line along which their lower edge would be drawing in, he went ahead on the electric horse, stopping to plant singleton personnel mines against the trunks of trees not more than four inches thick at intervals of about twenty meters. He planted the last of these right at the water's edge, about twenty meters below the crossing. Then he swooped back to make contact with the end of the second skirmish line.

He found the end of the line just coming level with the first mine he had planted, the end man some ten meters away from it in the jungle. Cletus swooped out and around to come up behind the center of the line. Careful not to approach any closer than twenty meters, he halted the electric horse, unlimbered his rifle and sprayed a long burst up and down the line through about a sixty-degree angle.

The sound of a cone rifle firing was not the sort of noise that went unnoticed. The tiny, self-propelled cones, leaving the muzzle of the rifle at relatively low velocity but accelerating as they went, whistled pierc-ingly through the air until their passage was concluded by the dull, abrupt thud of the impact explosion that ended their career. A man not in body armor, as these guerrillas were not, could be torn in half by one of those explosions – so that it was no wonder that, for a second after the sound of his firing had ceased, there was utter silence in the jungle. Even the birds and beasts were still. Then, somewhat laggardly, but bravely enough, from immediately in front of Cletus and all up and down the invisible skirmish line of the infiltrators, pellet guns began to snap back, like a chorus of sprung mousetraps.

The firing was blind. The pellets, zipping through the leaves of the trees about Cletus like so many hailstones, went wide. But there was an uncomfortable amount of them. Cletus had already flung the electric horse about and was putting distance between himself and those who were shooting. Fifty meters back, he turned once more around the downriver end of the line and reached for the remote trigger that set off the first of his singleton personnel mines.

Up ahead of him to his left, there was a single loud explosion. A tree – the tree to which the land mine had been stuck – leaned like a sick giant among its fellows, and slowly at first, then faster, came toppling down among the underbrush.

By now, the jungle was alive with sound. The guerrillas were apparently firing in every direction, because the wildlife were screaming at the tops of their lungs. Cletus moved in at an angle to the end of the line, fired another long burst from his weapon and quickly moved up level with his second mine.

The heavy vegetation of the jungle hid the actions of the individual guerrillas. But they were shouting to each other now; and this, as well as the wildlife sounds, gave Cletus a rough idea of what was going on. Clearly, they were doing the instinctive, if not exactly the militarily wise, thing. They were beginning to draw together for mutual support. Cletus gave them five minutes in which to get well clumped, so that what had been two spread-out skirmish lines was now a single group of thirty-five individuals within a circle of jungle no more than fifty meters in diameter.

Then he swung around to the rear of this once more, set off his second singleton mine ahead of them and once more commenced firing into them from behind.

This time he evoked a veritable cricket chorus of answering pellet-gun fire – what sounded like all thirty-five weapons snapping at him at once, in every direction. The nearby Kultan wildlife burst out in a cacophony of protest; and the toppling of a tree cut down by a third singleton mine added its crash to the general uproar just as the firing began to slack off. By this time, Cletus was once more around behind his line of remaining unfired mines, downriver from the guerrillas ... He waited.

After a few minutes commands were shouted and the guerrilla firing ceased. Cletus did not have to see into the center of the hundred-meter wide area to know that the officers among the infiltrators were talking over the situation they had encountered. The question in their minds would be whether the explosions and cone-rifle firing they had heard had been evoked from some small patrol that just happened to be in this area, or whether they had – against all normal expectations and reason – run head-on into a large enemy force set here directly to bar their route to the coast. Cletus let them talk it over.

The obvious move by a group such as these guerrillas in a situation such as this was to sit tight and send out scouts. The infiltrators were by this time less than eight hundred meters from the river's edge clearing of the crossing point and scouts would easily discover that the point was actually undefended, which would not be good. Cletus set off a couple more of his mines and commenced firing upon the downriver side of the guerrilla area. Immediately the guerrillas answered.

But then this fire, too, began to dwindle and become more sporadic, until there was only a single gun snapping from moment to moment. When it, at last, fell silent, Cletus took the electric horse up and swung wide, away from the river into a position about five hundred meters upriver. Here he hovered, and waited.

Sure enough, within a very few minutes, he was able to make out movement in the jungle. Men were coming toward him, cautiously, and once more spread out in a skirmish line. The Neulander guerrillas, having encountered renewed evidence of what they thought was at least a sizable force at the lowest crossing, had chosen discretion over valor. They were withdrawing to the next higher crossing, where either their passage would not be barred or they would have the comfort of joining forces with that other group of their force which had been sent to cross at the middle ford.

Cletus swung wide once more, circled in, away from the river, and headed upstream toward the second crossing. As he approached this general area, he slowed the electric horse, to minimize the noise of its ducted fans, and crept along, high up, just under treetop level.

Shortly, he made contact with a second group of the guerrilla force, also in two skirmish lines, but a good nine hundred meters yet from the middle of the three river crossings. He paused long enough to plant another row of singleton personnel mines on trees in a line just downriver from the crossing, then slipped upriver again.

When he reached the area inland of the ford, highest up on the Blue River, where Jarnki and the others waited, he found that the third group of guerrillas, approaching this highest crossing, were not on schedule with the two other groups below. This upper group was already almost upon the crossing – less than 150 meters from it.

There was no time here for a careful reconnaissance before acting. Cletus swept across thirty meters in front of their first skirmish line, firing one long whistling burst from his cone rifle when he judged he was opposite the line's center.

Safely beyond the farther end of it, he waited until the snapping of answering fire from the guerrillas had died down, and then slipped back across their front once more, this time pausing to plant four singleton mines in their path. Once he was back beyond the downriver end of their lines, he set off a couple of these mines and began firing again.

The results were gratifying. The guerrillas opened up all along their front. Not only that, but, fortunately, the men he had left at the crossing, spooked by the guerrilla firing, began instinctively returning it with their cone rifles. The result, as far as the ear could tell, was a very good impression of two fair-sized groups in a fire-fight.

There was only one thing wrong with these additional sound effects Cletus was getting from his own men. One of the heavily whistling guns belonged to Jarnki; and evidently, from the sounds of it, the corporal was on the ground within fifteen meters of the front guerrilla lines – up where the exchange of shots could well prove lethal to him.

Cletus was tempted to swear, but stifled the urge. He pulsed a sharp message over his throat mike communicator to Jarnki to fall back. There was no response, and Jarnki's weapon went on speaking. This time Cletus did swear. Dropping his electric horse to just above the ground, he threaded the vehicle through the jungle cover up to right behind the corporal's position, led to it easily by the sound of Jarnki's firing.

The young soldier was lying in the prone position, legs spread out, his rifle barrel resting upon a rotting tree trunk, firing steadily. His face was as pale as the face of a man who has already lost half the blood in his body, but there was not a mark on him. Cletus had to dismount from the horse and shake the narrow shoulder above the whistling rifle before Jarnki would wake to the fact that anyone was beside him.

When he did become conscious of Cletus' presence, the convulsive reaction sent him scrambling to get to his feet like a startled cat. Cletus held him down against the ground with one hand and jerked the thumb of the other toward the crossing behind them.

'Fall back!' whispered Cletus harshly.

Jarnki stared, nodded, turned about and began to scramble on hands and legs toward the crossing. Cletus remounted the electric horse. Swinging wide again, he approached the guerrillas from their opposite side to ascertain their reaction to these unexpected sounds of opposition.

He was forced, in the end, to dismount from the electric horse and wriggle forward on his stomach after all, for perhaps ten meters, to get close enough to understand some of what was being said. Happily, what he heard was what he had hoped to hear. This group, like the group farthest downriver, had decided to stop and talk over these sounds of an unexpected opposition.

Painfully, Cletus wriggled back to the electric horse, mounted it and flew a wide curve once more back to the crossing itself. He reached it just as Jarnki, by this time back on his feet, also reached it. Jarnki had recovered some of his color, but he looked at Cletus apprehensively, as if expecting a tongue-lashing. Instead, Cletus grinned at him.

'You're a brave man, Corporal,' Cletus said. 'You just have to remember that we like to keep our brave men alive, if possible. They're more useful that way.'

Jarnki blinked. He grinned uncertainly.

Cletus turned back to the electric horse and took one of his boxes of singleton mines. He handed it to Jarnki.

'Plant these between fifty and eighty meters out.' Cletus said. 'Just be sure you don't take any chances on getting shot while you're doing it. Then hang back in front of those Neulanders as they advance, and keep them busy, both with the mines and with your weapon. Your job is to slow those Neulanders down until I can get back up here to help you. At a guess, that's going to be anywhere from another forty-five minutes to an hour and a half. Do you think you can do it?'

'We'll do it,' said Jarnki.

'I'll leave it to you, then,' said Cletus.

He mounted the electric horse, swung out over the river and headed down to make contact with the group of guerrillas moving toward the middle ford.

They were doing just that when he found them. The Neulanders were by this time fairly close to the middle crossing, and right in among his mines. There was no time like the present – Cletus set them off, and compounded the situation by cruising the Neulander rear and firing a number of bursts at random into them.

They returned his fire immediately; but, shortly after that, their return shooting became sporadic and ceased. The silence that followed lengthened and lengthened. When there had been no shots for five minutes, Cletus circled downriver with the electric horse and came up behind where the middle-crossing group had been when it was firing back at him.

They were not there, and, following cautiously just under treetop level, he soon caught up with them. They were headed upriver, and their numbers seemed to have doubled. Clearly, the group from the lower crossing had joined up with them and with common consent both groups were now headed for the highest crossing and a reunion with the group scheduled to cross there.

It was as he had expected. These infiltrators were saboteurs rather than soldiers. They would have been strictly ordered to avoid military action along the way to their destination if it was at all possible to avoid it. He followed them carefully until they were almost in contact with the group of their fellows pinned down at the highest crossing, and then swung out over the river to reconnoiter the situation at that crossing.

He came in from above and cautiously explored the situation of the upper guerrilla group. They were strung out in a ragged semicircle, the ends of which did not quite reach the riverbanks some sixty meters above and thirty meters below the crossing. They were laying down fire but making no real effort to fight their way across the river – as he listened, the sound of their firing dwindled and there was a good deal of shouting back and forth as the two groups from downriver joined them.

Hovering above ground level, Cletus produced a snooper mike from the equipment bar of the horse and slipped its earphone to his right ear. He swung the snooper barrel, scanning the undergrowth, but the only conversations he could pick up were by ordinary members of the guerrilla force, none by officers discussing the action they would take next. This was unfortunate. If he had been up to crawling fifty meters or so to make a personal reconnaissance – but he was not, and there was no point considering it. Reconnaissance on the electric horse would by now be too risky. There remained the business of putting himself in the shoes of the guerrilla force commander and trying to second-guess the man's thoughts. Cletus half-closed his eyes, relaxing in the same fashion as he had relaxed that morning in order to conquer the pain of his knee. Eyelids drooping, slumping bonelessly in the saddle of the horse, he let his mind go free.

For a long moment there was nothing but a random sequence of thoughts flowing across the surface of his consciousness. Then his imagination steadied down, and a concept began to form. He felt as though he was no longer sitting on the seat of the electric horse, but standing on the soft, spongy surface of the jungle floor, his camouflaged suit glued to his body by sweat as he squinted up at the sun, which was already past its zenith, moving into afternoon. An irritation of combined frustration and apprehension filled his mind. He looked back down at the circle of guerrilla under-officers gathered about him and realized that he had to make an immediate decision. Two-thirds of his force had already failed to get across the Blue River at the time and places they were supposed to cross. Now, already behind schedule, he was faced with the last opportunity for a crossing – but also with the opposition of enemy forces, in what strength he did not know.

Clearly, at least one thing was true. The infiltration of this group he commanded had turned out to be not the secret from the Exotics that it had been expected it would be. To that extent, his mission was already a failure. If the Exotics had a force here to oppose him, what kind of opposition could he expect on the way to the coast?

Clearly, the mission now stood little or no chance of success. Sensibly, it should be abandoned. But could he turn back through the paths now without some excuse to give his superiors so that he would not be accused of abandoning the mission for insufficient reason?

Clearly, he could not. He would have to make an attempt to fight his way across the river, and just hope that the Exotic forces would oppose him hard enough so that he would have an excuse to retreat ...

Cletus returned to himself, opened his eyes and straightened up in the saddle once more. Lifting the electric horse up just under treetop level once more, he tossed three singleton mines at different angles toward the guerrilla position, and then set them off in quick succession.

Immediately, also, he opened up with both his rifle and sidearm, holding the rifle tucked against his side and firing it with his right hand while firing his sidearm with the left.

From the crossing, and from the two other sides of the guerrilla position, came the sound of the gunfire of his soldiers upon the Neulanders.

Within seconds the guerrilla force was laying down answering fire. The racket was the worst to disturb the jungle so far this day. Cletus waited until it began to die down slightly, so that he could be heard. Then he took the loudspeaker horn from the crossbar of the electric horse. He lifted the horn to his lips and turned it on. His amplified voice thundered through the jungle:

'CEASE FIRING! CEASE FIRING! ALL ALLIANCE FORCES CEASE FIRING!'

The cone rifles of the men under Cletus' command fell silent about the guerrilla area. Gradually, the answering voice of the guerrilla weapons also dwindled and silence filled the jungle again. Cletus spoke once more through the loudspeaker horn:

'ATTENTION NEULANDERS! ATTENTION NEULANDERS! YOU ARE COMPLETELY SURROUNDED BY THE ALLIANCE EXPEDITIONARY FORCE TO BAKHALLA.

FURTHER RESISTANCE CAN ONLY END IN YOUR BEING WIPED OUT. THOSE WHO WISH TO SURRENDER WILL BE GIVEN HONORABLE TREATMENT IN ACCORDANCE WITH THE ESTABLISHED RULES GOVERNING THE CARE OF PRISONERS OF WAR. THIS IS THE COMMANDER OF THE ALLIANCE FORCE SPEAKING. MY MEN WILL HOLD THEIR FIRE FOR THREE MINUTES, DURING WHICH TIME YOU WILL BE GIVEN A CHANCE TO SURRENDER. THOSE WISHING TO SURRENDER MUST DIVEST THEMSELVES OF ALL WEAPONS AND WALK INTO THE CLEARING AT THE CROSSING IN PLAIN SIGHT WITH THEIR HANDS CLASPED ON TOP OF THEIR HEAD. I REPEAT, THOSE WISHING TO SURRENDER MUST DIVEST THEMSELVES OF ALL WEAPONS AND WALK INTO PLAIN SIGHT IN THE CLEARING AT THE CROSSING, WITH THEIR HANDS CLASPED ON TOP OF THEIR HEAD. YOU HAVE THREE MINUTES TO SURRENDER IN THIS FASHION STARTING FROM WHEN I SAY NOW.'

Cletus paused for a moment, then added:

'ANY MEMBERS OF THE INVADING FORCE WHO HAVE NOT SURRENDERED BY THE TIME THREE MINUTES IS UP WILL BE CONSIDERED AS INTENDING TO CONTINUE RESISTANCE, AND MEMBERS OF THE ALLIANCE FORCE ARE INSTRUCTED TO OPEN FIRE UPON SUCH INDIVIDUALS ON SIGHT. THE THREE MINUTES IN WHICH TO SURRENDER WILL BEGIN, NOW!'

He clicked off the loudspeaker horn, replaced it on the horse and quickly swung toward the river, out and around to where he had a view of the clearing without being visible himself. For a long moment nothing happened. Then there was a rustle of leaves, and a man in a Neulander camouflage suit, his hands clasped over his head and some jungle grass still stuck in his bushy beard, stepped into the clearing. Even from where Cletus watched, the whites of the guerrilla's eyes were visible and he looked about him apprehensively. He came forward hesitantly until he was roughly in the center of the clearing, then stopped, looking about him, his hands still clasped on top of his head.

A moment later another guerrilla appeared in the clearing; and suddenly they were coming from every direction.

Cletus sat watching and counting for a couple of minutes. By the end of the time, forty-three men had entered the clearing to surrender.

Cletus nodded, thoughtfully. Forty-three men out of a total of three groups of thirty guerrillas – or ninety – all told. It was as he had expected.

He glanced down along the riverbank to the place, less than ten meters from him, where Jarnki crouched with the two other men who had been left here to defend this crossing and were now covering the growing mass of prisoners.

'Ed,' Cletus transmit-pulsed at the young corporal. 'Ed, look to your right.'

Jarnki looked sharply to his right, and jerked a little in startlement at seeing Cletus so close. Cletus beckoned to him. Cautiously, still crouching low to keep under the ridge of the riverbank, Jarnki ran up to where Cletus hovered on the electric horse a few feet off the ground.

As Jarnki came up, Cletus set the vehicle down on the ground and, safely screened from the clearing by the jungle bushes before him, stepped stiffly off the horse and stretched himself gratefully.

'Sir?' said Jarnki, inquiringly.

'I want you to hear this,' said Cletus. He turned to the horse again and set its communications unit for the channel number of Lieutenant Athyer, over on the Whey River.

'Lieutenant,' he pulse-messaged, 'this is Colonel Grahame.'

There was a short pause, and then the reply came, crackling not only in the earphones plug in Cletus' ear but over the small speaker built into the electric horse, which Cletus had just turned on.

'Colonel?' said Athyer. 'What is it?'

'It seems the Neulander guerrillas attempted to infiltrate across the Blue River crossing here, after all,' Cletus said. 'We were lucky and managed to capture about half of them—'

'Guerrillas? Captured? Half …' Athyer's voice faltered in the earphones and over the speaker.

'But that isn't why I messaged,' Cletus went on. 'The other half got away from us. They'll be headed back toward the pass, to escape back into Neuland. But you're closer to the pass than they are. If you get there with even half your men, you ought to be able to round up the rest of them without any trouble.'

'Trouble? Look … I … how do I know the situation's the way you say it is? I …'

'Lieutenant,' said Cletus, and for the first time he put a slight emphasis on the word, 'I just told you. We've captured half their force, here at the upper crossing on the Blue.'

'Well … yes … Colonel. I understand that. But—'

Cletus cut him short. 'Then get going, Lieutenant,' he said. 'If you don't move fast, you may miss them.'

'Yes, sir. Of course. I'll message you again, shortly, Colonel ... Maybe you'd better hold your prisoners there until they can be picked up by support ships ... Uh, some of them might get away if you try to move them through the jungle with only your six men.' Athyer's voice was strengthening as he got control of himself. But there was a bitter note in it. Clearly, the implications of the capture of a large group of enemy infiltrators by a desk-bound theoretician, when Athyer himself was the sole field officer in command of the capturing force, was beginning to register on him. There was little hope that General Traynor would overlook this kind of a failure on his part.

His voice was grim as he went on.

'Do you need a medic?' he asked. 'I can spare you one of the two I've got here and send him right over by one of the support ships, now that secrecy's out and the Neulanders know we're here.'

'Thanks, Lieutenant. Yes, we could use a medic,' said Cletus. 'Good luck with the rest of them.'

'Thanks,' said Athyer, coldly. 'Out, sir.'

'Out,' replied Cletus.

He cut transmission, stepped away from the electric horse and lowered himself stiffly to the ground into a sitting position, with his back to a nearby boulder.

'Sir?' said Jarnki. 'What do we need a medic for? None of the men got hurt. You don't mean you, sir ...?'

'Me,' said Cletus.

He extended his left leg, reached down and took his combat knife from his boot sheath. With its blade he ripped open his left pants leg, from above the knee to the top of his boot. The knee he revealed was extremely swollen and not pretty to look at. He reached for the first-aid kit at his belt and took out a spray hypo. He put the blunt nose of the spray against his wrist and pulled the trigger. The cool shock of the spray being driven through his skin directly into his bloodstream was like the touch of a finger of peace.

'Christ, sir,' said Jarnki, white-faced, staring at the knee.

Cletus leaned back gratefully against the boulder, and let the soft waves of the narcotic begin to fold him into unconsciousness.

'I agree with you,' he said. Then darkness claimed him.

9

Lying on his back in the hospital bed, Cletus gazed thoughtfully at the stiff, sunlit form of his left leg, upheld in traction above the surface of the bed.

'So,' the duty medical officer, a brisk, round-faced fortyish major had said with a fiendish chuckle when Cletus had been brought in, 'you're the type who hates to take time out to give your body a chance to heal, are you, Colonel?' The next thing Cletus had known he was in the bed with his leg balanced immovably in a float cast anchored to the ceiling.

'But it's been three days now,' Cletus remarked to Arvid, who had just arrived, bringing, as per orders, a local almanac, 'and he promised that the third day he'd turn me loose. Take another look out in the corridor and see if he's been in any of the other rooms along here.'

Arvid obeyed. He returned in a minute or two, shaking his head.

'No luck,' he said. 'But General Traynor's on his way over, sir. The nurse on the desk said his office just phoned to see if you were still here.'

'Oh?' said Cletus. 'That is right. He'd be coming, of course.' He reached out and pressed the button that tilted the bed to lift him up into a sitting position. 'Tell you what, Arv. Take a look up and down the other rooms for me and see if you can scrounge me some spacepost covers.'

'Spacepost covers,' replied Arvid, calmly unquestioningly. 'Right, I'll be back in a minute.'

He went out. It took him more like three minutes than one; but when he returned he had five of the flimsy yellow envelopes in which mail sent by spaceship was ordinarily carried. The Earth Terminal postmark was square and black on the back of each. Cletus stacked them loosely together and laid them in a face-down pile on the table surface of his bedside console. Arvid watched him.

'Did you find what you wanted in the almanac, sir?' he asked.

'Yes,' said Cletus. Seeing Arvid still gazing at him curiously, he added, 'There's a new moon tonight.'

'Oh,' said Arvid.

'Yes. Now, when the general comes, Arv,' Cletus said, 'stay out in the corridor and keep your eyes open. I don't want that doctor slipping past me just because a general's talking to me, and leaving me hung up here for another day. What time was that appointment of mine with the officer from the Security Echelon?'

'Eleven hundred hours,' said Arvid.

'And it's nine-thirty, already,' said Cletus, looking at his watch. 'Arv, if you'll step into the bathroom there, its window should give you a view of the drive in front of the hospital. If the general's coming by ground car, you ought to be able to see him pulling up about now. Take a look for me, will you?'

Arvid obediently disappeared into the small bath cubicle attached to Cletus' hospital room.

'No sign, sir,' his voice came back.

'Keep watching,' Cletus said.

Cletus relaxed against the upright slope of the bed behind him, half-closing his eyes. He had been expecting the general – in fact, Bat would be merely the last in a long line of visitors that had included Mondar, Eachan Khan, Melissa, Wefer Linet – and even Ed Jarnki. The gangling young non-commissioned officer had come in to show Cletus the new sergeant's stripes on his sleeve and give Cletus the credit for the fact they were there.

'Lieutenant Athyer's report tried to take all the credit for himself.' Jarnki said. 'We heard about it from the company clerk. But the rest of the squad and me – we spread the real story around. Maybe over at the Officers' Club they don't know how it was, but they do back in the barracks.'

'Thank you,' said Cletus.

'Hell ...' said Jarnki, and paused, apparently at somewhat of a loss to further express his feelings. He changed the subject. 'You wouldn't be able to use me yourself, would you, Colonel? I haven't been to clerks' school, but I mean – you couldn't use a driver or anything?'

Cletus smiled. 'I'd like to have you, Ed,' he said, 'but I don't think they'd give you up. After all, you're a line soldier.'

'I guess not, then,' said Jarnki, disappointed. He went off, but not before he extracted from Cletus a promise to take him on if he should ever become available.

Jarnki had been wrong, however, in believing that Athyer's report would be accepted at face value among the commissioned ranks. Clearly, the lieutenant was known to his fellow officers for the kind of

71

field commander he was – just as it had been fairly obvious that Bat had not by chance chosen an officer like him to test Cletus' prophecy of guerrilla infiltration. As Arvid had reported to him, after that night at Mondar's party, the word was that Bat Traynor was out to get Cletus. In itself this information had originally meant merely that Cletus would be a good person for his fellow officers to avoid. But now, since he had pulled his chestnut out of the fire up on the Blue River without burning his fingers there was plainly a good deal of covert sympathy for him among all but Bat's closest supporters. Eachan Khan had dryly hinted as much. Wefer Linet, from his safe perch inside the Navy chain of command, had blandly alluded to it. Bat could hardly be unaware of this reaction among the officers and men he commanded. Moreover, he was a conscientious commanding officer in the formal sense. If anything, it was surprising that he had not come to pay a visit to Cletus at the hospital before this.

Cletus relaxed, pushing back the tension in his body that threatened to possess it in impatience at being anchored here on the bed when so many things were yet to be done. What would be, would be ...

The sound of the door opening brought his eyes open as well. He raised his head and looked to his right and saw Bat Traynor entering the hospital room. There had been no warning from Arvid, still in the bathroom. Fleetingly, Cletus permitted himself the hope that the young lieutenant would have the sense to stay out of sight now that his chance to discreetly leave the hospital room was barred.

Bat strode up to the edge of the bed and stared down at Cletus, his expressive eyebrows drawing together in a faint scowl.

'Well, Colonel,' he said, as he pulled a nearby chair close to the bed and sat down so that he stared into Cletus' face. He smiled, in hard, genial fashion. 'Still got you tied up, I see.'

'I'm supposed to be turned loose today,' Cletus answered. 'Thank you for dropping by, sir.'

'I usually drop by to see one of my officers who's in the hospital,' said Bat. 'Nothing special in your case – though you did do a good job with those six men up on the Blue River, Colonel.'

'The guerrillas weren't very eager to make a fight of it, sir,' said Cletus. 'And then I was lucky enough to have them do just what I'd guessed they'd do. The General knows how unusual it is when everything works out in the field just the way it's planned.'

'I do. Believe me, I do,' answered Bat. Under the heavy brows, his eyes were hard but wary upon Cletus. 'But that doesn't alter the fact you were right in your guess about where they'd come through and what they'd do once they were through.'

'Yes, I'm happy about that,' said Cletus. He smiled. 'As I told the General, I pretty much bet my reputation on it to my friends back on Earth just before I left.'

He glanced, as if unthinkingly, at the loose pile of facedown spaceship covers. Bat's eyes, following the direction of Cletus' gaze, narrowed slightly at sight of the yellow envelopes.

'You've been getting congratulations, have you?' Bat asked.

'There've been a few pats on the back,' Cletus said. He did not add that these had been only from such local people as Eachan, Mondar and newly made Sergeant Ed Jarnki. 'Of course, the operation wasn't a total success. I heard the rest of the guerrillas managed to get back through the pass before Lieutenant Athyer could contain them.'

Bat's eyebrows jerked together into a solid angry line of black. 'Don't push me, Colonel,' he rumbled. 'Athyer's report said he got word from you too late to take his men up into position to bar the pass.'

'Was that it, sir?' said Cletus. 'I'd guess it was my fault, then. After all, Athyer's an experienced field officer and I'm just a desk-jockey theoretician. I'm sure everybody realizes it was just luck that the contact my squad had with the enemy was successful and the contact the lieutenant and the rest of his company had wasn't.'

For a moment their eyes locked.

'Of course,' said Bat, grimly. 'And if they don't understand it, I do. And that's what's important – isn't it, Colonel?'

'Yes, sir,' said Cletus.

Bat sat back in his chair, and his brows relaxed. 'Anyway,' he said, 'I didn't come here just to congratulate you. A suggestion by you came through to my office that you set up a staff to make regular weekly forecasts of enemy activity. There was also your request for personnel and office space to facilitate your making such forecasts ... Understand, Colonel, as far as I'm concerned, I still need you like I need a fifty-man string ensemble. But your success with the guerrillas has got us some good publicity back at Alliance HQ, and I don't see how you can do any harm to the rest of the war effort here on Kultis by setting up this forecast staff. So, I'm going to approve it.' He paused, then shot the words at Cletus. 'That make you happy?'

'Yes, sir,' said Cletus. 'Thank you, General.'

'Don't bother,' said Bat, grimly. 'As for Athyer – he had his chance, and he fell on his face. He'll be coming up for a Board of Inquiry into his fitness as an Alliance officer. Now – anything else you want?'

'No,' said Cletus.

Bat stood up abruptly. 'Good,' he said. 'I don't like having my arm twisted. I prefer handing out favors before they're asked. Also, I still need those tanks, and you're still going back to Earth at the first opportunity, Colonel. Tuck that fact into your prognostications and don't forget it!'

He turned on his heel and went toward the door.

'General,' said Cletus. 'There is a favor you could do me ...'

Bat checked and swung about. His face darkened. 'After all?' His voice was hard. 'What is it, Colonel?'

'The Exotics have quite a library here in Bakhalla,' said Cletus. 'With a good deal of military text and information in it.'

'What about it?'

'If the General will pardon me,' said Cletus, slowly, 'Lieutenant Athyer's main problems are too much imagination coupled with not enough confidence in himself. If he could get away and season himself for a while – say, as Information Officer for the Expeditionary Forces, to that Exotic library – he might turn out highly useful, after all.'

Bat stared at Cletus. 'Now why,' said Bat softly, 'would you want something like that for Athyer instead of a Board of Inquiry?'

'I don't like to see a valuable man wasted,' said Cletus.

Bat grunted. He turned on his heel and went out without a further word. Looking a little sheepish, Arvid emerged from the bathroom.

'I'm sorry, sir,' he said to Cletus. 'The General must've come by air and landed on the roof.'

'Think nothing of it, Arv,' said Cletus, happily. 'Just get out in that corridor and find me that doctor. I've got to get out of here.'

Twenty minutes later, Arvid having finally located and produced the medical officer, Cletus was finally out of his cast and on his way to the office space Arvid had located for him. It was one of a set of three office suites, each consisting of three rooms and a bath, originally erected by the Exotics for housing VIP guests. The other two suites were empty, so that, in essence, they had the building to themselves – a point Cletus had stipulated earlier when he had sent Arvid out to search. When they reached the office, Cletus found it furnished only with some camp chairs and a temporary field desk. A lean major in his early forties, with a white scar across his chin, was examining these in disparaging fashion.

'Major Wilson?' asked Cletus, as the officer turned to face them. 'I'm Colonel Grahame.'

They shook hands.

74

'Security sent me over,' Wilson said. 'You said you were expecting some special problem here, Colonel?'

'I'm hoping for one,' replied Cletus. 'We're going to be handling a good deal of material here, from the classified category on up. I'm going to be making weekly forecasts of enemy activity for General Traynor. Sooner or later the Neulanders are bound to hear of this and take an interest in this office. I'd like to set it up as a trap for anyone they send to investigate.'

'Trap, sir?' echoed Wilson, puzzled.

'That's right,' said Cletus, cheerfully. 'I want to make it possible for them to get in, but, once in, impossible for them to get back out.'

He turned to indicate the walls around them.

'For example,' he said, pointing, 'heavy steel mesh on the inside of the windows, but anchored so that it can't be pried loose or cut through with ordinary tools. An obvious lock on the outer door that can be easily picked – but a hidden lock that fastens the door securely once the open lock has been picked and the door opened and shut once. Metal framing and center panel for the door frame and door itself, so that they can't break out once the hidden lock has closed the door ... Possibly a wiring system to electrify the doors, windows and ventilator system just to discourage any attempt to break loose.'

Wilson nodded slowly, but doubtfully. 'That's going to add up to a good bit in the way of work-time and materials,' he said. 'I suppose you have authorization for this, Colonel ...?'

'It'll be forthcoming,' said Cletus. 'But the thing is for your division to get to work on this right away. The general was just talking to me less than an hour ago in the hospital about getting this office set up.'

'The general – oh!' said Wilson, becoming brisk. 'Of course, sir.'

'Good, then,' said Cletus. 'That's settled.'

After discussion of a few details, and after Wilson had taken a few measurements, the security officer left. Cletus set Arvid to getting Eachan Khan on the field telephone, which, with the table and chairs, was the office's only equipment. The Dorsai colonel was finally located out in the training area set aside for his mercenary troops.

'Mind if I come out?' asked Cletus.

'Not at all.' In the small vision screen of the field phone, Eachan's face looked faintly curious. 'You're welcome anytime, Colonel. Come along.'

'Right,' said Cletus. 'I'll be there in half an hour.'

He broke the connection. Leaving Arvid to see about getting the office supplied with furniture and staff, Cletus went out and took the staff car in which Arvid had driven him here to the training area of the Dorsai troops.

He found Eachan Khan standing at the edge of a field with a ten-meter metal tower in its center, from which what looked like a company of the tanned Dorsai professionals were practising jump-belt landings. The line of those waiting their turn stretched out behind the tower, from the top of which mercenaries were going off, one by one, the shoulder jets of the jump belts roaring briefly and kicking up a cloud of whitish-brown dust as each one fell earthward. For men not trained exclusively as jump troops, Cletus noted with satisfaction as he limped up to the watching Eachan Khan, there were a great many more soft, upright landings than might have been expected.

'There you are,' said Eachan, without turning his head, as Cletus came up behind him. The Dorsai colonel was standing with his legs slightly spread, his hands clasped behind him as he watched. 'What do you think of our level of jump training, now you see it?'

'I'm impressed,' answered Cletus. 'What do you know about guerrilla traffic on the Bakhalla River?'

'Fair amount. Bound to be, of course, with the river running right through the city into the harbor here.' Eachan Khan stared at him curiously. 'Not so much infiltrators as sabotage materials, I understand, though. Why?'

'There's a new moon tonight,' explained Cletus.

'Eh?' Eachan stared at him.

'And according to the local tide tables,' said Cletus, 'we're having an unusually high tide – all the tributaries and canals will be running deeper than usual as much as twenty miles inland. A good time for the Neulanders to smuggle in either large amounts of supplies or unusually heavy equipment.'

'Hm ...' Eachan fondled the right tip of his mustache. 'Still ... if you don't mind a word of advice?'

'Go right ahead,' said Cletus.

'I don't think there'd be anything you could do about it,' said Eachan. 'River security is maintained by a half-dozen Army amphibs with half a dozen soldiers and light weapons on each one. That's not enough to do any good at all, and everybody knows it. But your General Traynor opts for dryfoot war equipment. About six months back he got five armored personnel carriers by swearing to your Alliance HQ that his river defenses were perfectly adequate and that, instead of sending him a couple of patrol boats, they could give him the personnel carriers instead. So if you go pointing out probable trouble on the river, you're not going to be making Traynor very happy. My advice would be to let any Neulander activity there go by on your blind side.'

'Maybe you're right,' said Cletus. 'How about lunch?'

They left the training ground and drove in to the Officers' Club for lunch, where Melissa joined them in response to a telephone call from her father, at Cletus' suggestion. She was somewhat reserved, and did not often meet Cletus' eye. She had come with her father for one brief visit to Cletus in the hospital, during which she stood back and let Eachan do most of the talking. She seemed inclined to let him do most of the talking now, although she glanced at Cletus from time to time when his attention was on her father. Cletus, however, ignored her reactions and kept up a steady, cheerful flow of conversation.

'Wefer Linet's been after me,' Cletus said to her when they were having coffee and dessert, 'to take one of his underwater tours in one of the Mark V submarine dozers. How about joining us this evening, and we can come back into Bakhalla afterward for a late supper?'

Melissa hesitated, but Eachan broke in, almost hastily. 'Good idea, girl,' he said, almost gruffly. 'Why don't you do that? Do you good to get out for a change.'

The tone of Eachan's voice made his words sound like a command. But the naked voice of appeal could be heard beneath the brusqueness of the words. Melissa surrendered.

'Thank you,' she said, raising her eyes to meet those of Cletus, 'that sounds like fun.'

10

Stars were beginning to fill the Bakhallan sky as Cletus and Melissa reached the gates to the Navy Yard and were met by an ensign attached to Wefer Linet's staff. The ensign conducted them inside to the ramp where the massive, black, two-story-tall shape of a Mark V squatted on its treads just above the golden-tinged waters of the Bakhallan harbor. Cletus had phoned Wefer immediately on parting from Eachan and Melissa to set up the evening's excursion.

Wefer had been enthusiastic. Navy regulations, he gleefully informed Cletus, absolutely forbade his allowing a civilian such as Melissa aboard a duty Navy vehicle like the Mark V. But, personally, he did not give a damn. For the record, he had caught only the words 'Dorsai' and 'Khan' when Cletus had phoned him earlier – and to whom, of course, could those words apply but to a mercenary colonel of his acquaintance, who was certainly no civilian? So he would be waiting for Colonel Grahame and Colonel Khan aboard the Mark V at 7 P.M.

Awaiting them he was. Moreover, he seemed to have shared the joke of his little deception of Navy regulations with his under-officers and crew. The ensign meeting Cletus and Melissa at the Navy Yard gate had gravely addressed Melissa as 'Colonel'; and they were hardly aboard the Mark V before three of the seamen, grinning broadly, had found occasion to do the same.

This small and ridiculous joke, however, turned out to be just the straw needed to break the back of Melissa's stiffness and reserve. On the fourth occasion of being addressed as 'Colonel.' she laughed out loud – and began from then on to take an honest interest in the outing.

'Any place in particular you'd like to see?' asked Wefer, as the Mark V put itself into motion and rumbled slowly down its ramp into the bay.

'Up the river,' said Cletus.

'Make it so, Ensign.'

'Aye, sir,' said the ensign who had met them at the gate. 'Balance all tanks fore and aft, there!'

He was standing at the con, a little to the left of Wefer, Cletus and Melissa, who were placed before the large, curved shape of the hemispherical screen, which looked through the muddy water ahead and about them as though it were clear as glass, to pick up the shapes of ships' undersides and other solid objects below water level in the harbor.

There was a faint hissing and rumbling noise all around them. The vibration and sound of the heavy treads on the ramp suddenly ceased, and the water line shown on the hemispherical screen moved up above the horizon mark as the huge vehicle balanced out its ballast, replacing water with compressed air where necessary, and vice versa, so that the submarine dozer – its hundreds of tons of land weight now brought into near balance with an equal volume of water – floated as lightly as a leaf in air down to the muddy bottom of the harbor, sixty feet below.

'All forward, right thirty degrees horizontal,' ordered the ensign; and they began their underwater tour up-river from Bakhalla.

'You'll notice,' said Wefer in the fond tone of a father pointing out the talents of his first newborn, 'our treads aren't touching the bottom here. There's nearly ten feet of loose silt and muck underneath us before we hit anything solid enough for the Mark V to walk on. Of course, we could settle down into it and do just that, if we wanted to. But why bother? We're as much at home and a lot more mobile staying up in the water itself and simply swimming with the treads ... Now look here ...'

He pointed to the screen, where, some two hundred yards ahead of them, the bottom dipped abruptly below their level of sight for a space of perhaps fifty yards before it rose again.

'That's the main channel – the main current line to the sea,' Wefer said. 'We clean that out daily – not because there're any ships here with draft enough to need a hundred and ten feet of water under them, but because that trench provides a channel for the current that helps keep the harbor from silting up. Half of our work's understanding and using existing patterns of water movement. By keeping that channel deep, we cut our normal silt-removing work in half. Not that we need to. It's just the Navy way to do it as efficiently as possible.'

'You mean you've got enough Mark V's and crews to keep the harbor clear even if the channel wasn't there?' Cletus asked.

Wefer snorted good-humoredly. 'Got enough ...' he echoed. 'You don't know what these Mark V's can do. Why I could keep the harbor clean, even without the current channel, with this one machine alone! ... Let me show you around here.'

He took Cletus and Melissa on a tour of the Mark V's interior, from the driver's escape chamber down between the massive treads to the arms turret at the top of the vehicle, which could be uncovered to allow the Mark V to fire either its two heavy energy rifles or the underwater laser with which it was provided.

'You see why Traynor wanted these Mark V's for use in the jungles,' concluded Wefer, as they ended their tour back in the control room before the hemispherical screen. 'It hasn't got the fire power of the Army's jungle-breaker tanks, but in every other respect, except land speed, it's so far superior that there's no comparison—'

'Sir,' interrupted the ensign behind him, 'deep-draft surface vessel coming down the channel. We're going to have to get down and walk.'

'Right. Make it so, Ensign,' answered Wefer. He turned to the screen and pointed at the V-shaped object cutting the line of the river surface some two hundred yards ahead of them. 'See that, Cletus? … Melissa? It's a boat drawing nine or ten feet of water. The channel here's less than fifty feet deep and we're going to have to get right down on the bottom to make sure that boat goes over with a good couple of fathoms of clearance.'

He squinted at the V shape growing on the screen. Suddenly, he laughed. 'Thought so!' he said. 'That's one of your river patrol boats, Cletus. Want to have a look at its topside?'

'You mean, with a sensor float?' asked Cletus, quietly.

Wefer's jaw dropped. 'How'd you know about that?' he demanded, staring.

'There was an article about it in the *Navy-Marine Journal* a little less than two years ago,' answered Cletus. 'It struck me as the sort of device a sensible navy would put aboard a vehicle like this.'

Wefer still stared at him, almost accusingly. 'Is that so?' he said. 'What else about the Mark V do you know that I don't know you know?'

'I know that with a bit of luck you might be able to capture a boatload of Neulander saboteurs and supplies bound for Bakhalla tonight, if you want to try for it. Have you got a map of the river?'

'A map?' Wefer lit up. He leaned forward and punched buttons below the hemispherical screen. The image on it vanished, to be replaced by a map showing the main river channel with its tributaries from the harbor mouth at Bakhalla to some thirty miles upstream. A barely moving red dot in the shape of a Mark V seen from above was crawling up the main channel in representation of the vehicle enclosing them. 'What guerrillas? Where?'

'About six kilometers upstream from here,' Cletus answered. He reached out to point with his forefinger to a spot ahead of the small, red, moving shape of the Mark V, where a tributary almost as large as the main river joined it at that spot. Up beyond the point of joining, the tributary spread itself out into a number of small streams and then marshland.

'There's an unusually high tide tonight, as you know,' Cletus said. 'So from this point on down there will be at least an extra eight feet of water in the main channel. Enough extra depth so that any small upriver motor launch could make it down into Bakhalla harbor towing a good load of supplies, and even personnel, behind it, safely underwater in a drogue pod. It's just a guess on my part, of course, but it hardly seems to me that the guerrillas would let a chance like this slip by without making an effort to get men and supplies to their people in the city.'

Wefer stared at the map and slapped his leg in delight. 'You're right!' he exploded. 'Ensign, we're headed for that confluence Colonel Grahame just pointed out. Button up for noise, and get the weapon turret uncovered topside.'

'Aye, sir,' answered the ensign.

They reached the juncture point between the tributary point and the mainstream, which Cletus had pointed out. The Mark V crept out of the channel into the relatively shallow water near the riverbank opposite the mouth of the tributary and stopped there, its turrets less than five feet below the river surface. The sensor float was released from the upper hull of the vehicle and popped to the surface – a small, buoyant square of material with the thin metal whisker of a sensor rod rising one meter from it into the air, the two connected by a fine wire to the communications equipment of the Mark V. The sensor rod had to view the scene around it by available light only; but its resolving power was remarkable. The image of the scene it sent down to the hemispherical screen in the command room of the Mark V below was very nearly as clear as if broad daylight, rather than a fingernail paring of a moon, was illuminating the conjunction of the two streams.

'Not a hull in sight,' muttered Wefer, rotating the view in the hemispherical screen to take in the full 180 degrees scanned by the sensor rod. 'I suppose we'll just have to sit here and wait for them.'

'You could be taking a few precautions, meanwhile.' suggested Cletus.

Wefer glanced aside at him. 'What precautions?'

'Against their getting away downstream if by some chance they manage to slip by you,' said Cletus. 'Is there anything to stop you now from moving enough material into the channel downriver so that, if they do come by, they'll run aground just below us?'

Wefer stared at him in astonishment, which slowly changed to delight. 'Of course!' he exploded. 'Ensign! Take her downstream!'

The Mark V moved roughly a hundred yards downstream; and, extending its massive dozer blade crosswise in front of it, began to shovel sand and silt from beneath the water near the river's edges into the main channel. Fifteen minutes work filled the channel for some fifty yards to a level even with the rest of the river bottom. Wefer was inclined to stop at that point, but Cletus suggested he further refine it into a barrier consisting of a wide, sloping ramp rising gradually to within half a dozen feet of the surface. Then, also at Cletus' suggestion, the Mark V returned, not merely upstream, but up into the tributary some fifty yards behind the point where it met with the waters of the main river.

Here the water was so shallow that the Mark V sat with its turret out in the air. But a few moments work with the dozer blade sufficed to dig a shallow depression so that they could lie in wait completely underwater.

Then the wait began. It was three hours – nearly midnight – before the sensor rod on its float, invisible against the shadow of the foliage lining the tributary's bank, picked up the image of a motor launch sliding down the main channel of the tributary, its motor turning at a speed barely sufficient to keep the drogue pod, towed behind it, underwater.

They waited, holding their breaths, until ship and drogue had passed. Then Wefer jumped for the command phone, from which he had, some hours since, displaced the ensign.

'Wait,' said Cletus.

Wefer hesitated, staring at Cletus. 'Wait?' he said. 'What for?'

'You know that launch isn't going to be able to get past the barrier you built downstream,' answered Cletus. 'So why not sit here a little longer and see if another boat comes along?'

Wefer hesitated. Then he stepped back from the command phone. 'You really think another one might come along?' he asked, thoughtfully.

'I wouldn't be surprised,' said Cletus, cheerfully.

The answer was hardly out of his mouth before the sensor picked up another approaching motor launch with pod in tow. By the time this was well past and out into the main river, still another launch had appeared. As Wefer stood staring with incredulous delight into the hemispherical screen, twenty boats towing pods passed within thirty yards of the submerged Mark V.

When a couple of minutes had gone by following the passage of the twenty boats and pods, Cletus suggested that probably it was time they were checking up on what had happened downstream. Wefer put the Mark V in motion. It surged up out of its shallow hole and plunged under the surface again down into the main channel of the tributary.

They reached the central channel of the main river, and turned downstream. Their infrared searchlights underwater, as well as the sensor rod being towed on its float above them, gave them a picture of wild confusion just ahead of them. Of the twenty launches that had passed them, fully half were firmly aground in the sloping ramp of river bottom that the Mark V had built. The rest, still afloat but with their drogue pods bobbing helplessly on the surface behind them, were valiantly trying to tow the stranded vessels free.

Wefer commanded the Mark V to a halt. He stared into the screen with mingled elation and dismay.

'Now what?' he muttered to Cletus. 'If I charge on down there, the ones that aren't stuck are just going to turn around and beat it upriver and get away. Of course I've got the weapons in the turret. But still, a lot of them are going to get past me.'

'As a suggestion,' said Cletus, 'how's this Mark V of yours at making a wave?'

Wefer stared at him. 'A wave?' he said – and then repeated, joyously. 'A *wave!*'

He barked orders into the command phone. The Mark V backed up a hundred yards along the channel of the main river and stopped. The two wings of its dozer blade, which had been folded back against its body to reduce drag while traveling, folded forward again and extended themselves to right and left until the blades' full area of twenty yards of width and ten feet of height were exposed. Delicately, Wefer tilted the front of the Mark V upward until the top half of the blade poked through the surface of the river and the treads were swimming freely in the water. Then he threw the engines into full speed, forward.

The Mark V rushed down the river in a roar of water, checked itself and sank itself to the bottom of the channel just fifty yards short of the still-floating launches. For a moment a wall of water hid the scene ahead; and then this passed, speeding like an ever-diminishing ripple farther downstream.

Left behind was a scene of wreckage and confusion.

Those launches that had already been aground had had their decks swept by the wave that the Mark V had created. In some cases they had been flipped on their sides by the wave or even turned completely upside down. But the greatest effect was to be seen upon those launches that had still had water under their keels and had been trying to tow the grounded ones loose.

Without exception these free-floating boats had been driven aground as well. In many cases they had been literally hammered into the soft soil of the piled-up river bed. One launch was standing on its nose, its prow driven half a dozen feet into the sand and silt below.

'I think they're ready for you now.' Cletus said to Wefer.

If anything more was needed to complete the demoralization of the guerrillas aboard the launches it was the sight of the black shape of the Mark V roaring up into view out of the river depths, the two heavy energy rifles in its turret sweeping ominously back and forth. Almost without exception those who had managed to cling to their battered crafts dived overboard at the sight and began to swim frantically for the banks of the river.

'Turret—' began Wefer excitedly. But Cletus put his hand over the phone.

'Let them go,' Cletus said. 'The important men'll still be sealed inside the pods. Let's see about collecting them before they get too worried by all that's happened and start breaking out.'

The advice was good. The Neulanders inside the pods had reached the limits of their endurance with the tossing about they had taken in the wave generated by the Mark V. Already more than one of the pods bobbing helplessly on the surface of the water, still tethered to their grounded launches, was beginning to split along the top, as those within activated their emergency exits. Wefer wheeled the Mark V into the midst of the wreckage and sent his ensign with three seamen out the Mark V's top hatch with hand weapons to cover the Neulanders as they emerged. They were ordered to swim to the Mark V, where they were searched, put in wrist restraints and herded down the hatch to be locked up in the Mark V's forward hold. Cletus and Melissa stayed discreetly out of sight.

Its forward hold crammed with prisoners, and the cargo pods filled with supplies in tow, the Mark V returned to its base at the Bakhalla Navy Yard. After disposing of their prisoners and their spoils, Cletus, Melissa and Wefer at last got into the city for that late – now early morning – supper they had planned. It was after four in the morning when Cletus took a tired but happy Melissa back to her father's residence. However, as they approached their destination, Melissa sobered and fell silent; and when they pulled up in front of the door of the house that the Exotics had put at the disposal of Melissa and Eachan, she did not offer to get out of the car right away.

'You know,' she said, turning to Cletus, 'you're pretty remarkable, after all. First those guerrillas on our way into Bakhalla, then the ones you captured up at Etter's Pass. And now, tonight.'

'Thanks,' he said, 'but all I did was anticipate the optimum moves for deCastries to make, and arrange to be on the scene when they were made.'

'Why do you keep talking about Dow as if he was having some sort of personal duel with you?'

'He is,' said Cletus.

'The Outworlds Secretary for the Coalition – against some unknown lieutenant-colonel in an Alliance Expeditionary Force? Does that make sense?'

'Why not?' Cletus said. 'He has a great deal more to lose than an unknown lieutenant-colonel in an Alliance Expeditionary Force.'

'But you're just imagining it all. You have to be!'

'No,' said Cletus. 'Remember I pushed him into an error of judgment with the sugar cubes in the dining lounge of the ship? The Outworlds Secretary for the Coalition can't afford to be made a fool of by an unknown Alliance lieutenant-colonel – as you describe me. It's true nobody but you knows – and only because I told you – that he did make a mistake, then—'

'Was that why you told me what you'd done?' Melissa interrupted quickly. 'Just so I'd tell Dow?'

'Partly,' said Cletus. She drew in her breath sharply in the darkness. 'But only incidentally. Because it really didn't matter whether you told him or not. He knew I knew. And it simply wasn't good policy to let someone like me walk around thinking that I could beat him, at anything.'

'Oh!' Melissa's voice trembled on the verge of anger. 'You're making all this up. There's no proof, not a shred of proof for any of it.'

'There is, though,' said Cletus. 'You remember the guerrillas on the way into Bakhalla attacked the command car, in which I was riding, instead of – as your father pointed out – the bus, which would have been a much more natural target for them. And this after Pater Ten had been burning up the ship-to-planet phone lines to Neuland before we left the ship.'

'That's coincidence – stretched coincidence, at that,' she retorted.

'No,' said Cletus, quietly. 'No more than the infiltration through Etter's Pass, which, while it was also made to provide a coup for the Neulanders, would have had the effect of discrediting me as a tactical expert before I had a chance to get my feet on the ground here and learn about the local military situation.'

'I don't believe it,' Melissa said vehemently. 'It has to be all in your head!'

'If that's so, then deCastries shares the delusion,' answered Cletus. 'When I slipped out of the first trap, he was impressed enough to offer me a job with him – a job, however, which obviously would have put me in a subordinate position with regard to him ... That happened at Mondar's party, when you stepped over to talk to Eachan, and deCastries and I had a few moments together.'

She stared at him through the night shadow of the car, as if trying to search out the expression on his face in the little light that reached them from the lamp beside the doorway of the house and the dawn-pale sky above the aircar.

'You turned him down?' she said, after a long moment.

'I just have. Tonight,' said Cletus, 'after the guerrillas on landing and Etter's Pass, he couldn't delude himself that I wouldn't expect that the next obvious move for the Neulanders would be to take advantage of the high tide on the river to run in supplies and saboteurs to Bakhalla. If I'd let that infiltration take place without saying or doing anything, he'd have known that I'd become, to all intents and purposes, his hired man.'

Again, she stared at him. 'But you—' she broke off. 'What can you expect to get out of all this, this ... chain of things happening?'

'Just what I told you on the ship,' said Cletus. 'To trap deCastries into a personal fencing match with me, so that I can gradually lead him into larger and larger conflicts – until he commits himself completely in a final encounter where I can use his cumulative errors of judgment to destroy him.'

Slowly, in the shadow, she shook her head. 'You must be insane,' she said.

'Or perhaps a little more sane than most,' he answered. 'Who knows?'

'But ...' She hesitated, as though she was searching for an argument that would get through to him. 'Anyway, no matter what's happened here. Dow's going to be leaving now. Then what about all these plans of yours about him? Now he can just go back to Earth and forget you – and he will.'

'Not until I've caught him in an error of judgment too public for him to walk away from or hide,' said Cletus. 'And that's what I have to do next.'

'One more – what if I tell him you're going to do that?' she demanded. 'Just suppose the whole wild thing's true, and I go to Capital Neuland tomorrow and tell him what you're planning? Won't that ruin everything for you?'

'Not necessarily,' said Cletus. 'Anyway, I don't think you'll do that.'

'Why not?' she challenged. 'I told you on the ship, that first night, that I wanted help from Dow for Dad and myself. Why shouldn't I tell him anything that might make him more likely to help me?'

'Because you're more your father's daughter than you think,' said Cletus. 'Besides, your telling him would be a waste of effort. I'm not going to let you throw yourself away on deCastries for something that'd be the wrong thing for Eachan and you anyway.'

She stared at him, saying nothing, for one breathless minute. Then she exploded.

'*You* aren't going to let me!' she blazed. '*You're* going to order my life and my father's, are you? Where'd you get that kind of conceit, to think you could know what's best for people and what isn't best for them – let alone thinking you could get what you think best for them, or take it away from them if they want it? Who made you ... king of everything ...?'

She had been fumbling furiously with the latch of the door on her side of the aircar as the words tumbled out of her. Now her fingers found it, the door swung open and she jumped out, turning to slam the door behind her.

'Go back to your BOQ – or wherever you're supposed to go!' she cried at him through the open window. 'I knew there was no point going out with you tonight, but Dad asked me. I should have known better. *Good night!*'

She turned and ran up the steps into the house. The door slammed behind her. Cletus was left to silence and the empty, growing light of the pale dawn sky, unreachable overhead.

11

'Well, Colonel,' said Bat, grimly, 'what am I supposed to do with you?'

'The General could put me to use,' said Cletus.

'Put you to use!' They were standing facing each other in Bat's private office. Bat turned in exasperation, took two quick steps away, wheeled and stepped back to glare up at Cletus once more. 'First you make a grandstand play up by Etter's Pass, and it pays off so that you collect about five times as many prisoners as you had men to collect them with. Now you go out for a midnight picnic with the Navy and come back loaded with guerrillas and supplies bound for Bakhalla. Not only that, but you take a civilian along with you on this Navy spree!'

'Civilian, sir?' said Cletus.

'Oh yes, I know the official story!' Bat interrupted him, harshly. 'And as long as it's a Navy matter, I'm letting it ride. But I *know* who you had with you out there, Colonel! Just as I know that wooden-headed young character, Linet, couldn't have dreamed up the idea of capturing those motor launches full of guerrillas. It was your show, Colonel, just like it was your show up at Etter's Pass! ... And I repeat, what am I going to do with you?'

'In all seriousness, General,' said Cletus, in a tone of voice that matched his words, 'I mean what I say. I think you ought to put me to use.'

'How?' Bat shot at him.

'As what I'm equipped to be – a tactician,' said Cletus. He met the glare from under the general's expressive brows without yielding, and his voice remained calm and reasonable. 'The present moment's one in which I could be particularly useful, considering the circumstances.'

'What circumstances?' Bat demanded.

'Why, the circumstances that've more or less combined to trap the Military Secretary of the Coalition here on Kultis,' Cletus replied. 'I imagine there's little doubt, in the ordinary way of things, that Dow deCastries would be planning on leaving this planet in the next day or two.'

'Oh, he would, would he?' said Bat. 'And what makes you so sure that you know what a Coalition high executive like deCastries would be doing – under any circumstances?'

'The situation's easily open to deduction,' answered Cletus. 'The Neulander guerrillas aren't in any different situation than our Alliance forces here when it comes to the matter of getting supplies out from Earth. Both they and we could use a great many things that the supply depots back on Earth are slow to send us. You want tanks, sir. It's a safe bet the Neulander guerrillas have wants of their own, which the Coalition isn't eager to satisfy.'

'And how do you make that out?' Bat snapped.

'I read it as a conclusion from the obvious fact that the Coalition's fighting a cheaper war here on Kultis than we are,' said Cletus, reasonably. 'It's typical of Alliance-Coalition confrontations for the past century. We tend to supply our allies actual fighting forces and the equipment to support them. The Coalition tends merely to arm and advise the opposition forces. This fits well with their ultimate aim, which isn't so much to win all these minor conflicts they oppose us in but to bleed dry the Alliance nations back on Earth, so that eventually the Coalition can take over, back there where they believe all the important real estate is.'

Cletus stopped speaking. Bat stared at him. After a second, the general shook his head like a man coming out of a daze.

'I ought to have my head examined,' Bat said. 'Why do I stand here and listen to this?'

'Because you're a good general officer, sir,' said Cletus, 'and because you can't help noticing I'm making sense.'

'Part of the time you're making sense ...' muttered Bat, his eyes abstracted. Then his gaze sharpened and he fastened it once more on Cletus' face. 'All right, the Neulanders want equipment from the Coalition that the Coalition doesn't want to give them. You say that's why deCastries came out here?'

'Of course,' said Cletus. 'You know yourself the Coalition does this often. They refuse material help to one of their puppet allies, but then, to take the sting out of the refusal, they send a highly placed dignitary out to visit the puppets. This visit creates a great deal of stir, both in the puppet country and elsewhere. It gives the puppets the impression that their welfare is very close to the Coalition's heart – and it costs nearly nothing. Only, in this one instance, the situation's backfired somewhat.'

'Backfired?' said Bat.

'The two new guerrilla thrusts that were supposed to celebrate deCastries' visit – that business up at Etter's Pass, and now last night's unsuccessful attempt to infiltrate a good number of men and supplies into the city of Bakhalla – have blown up in the Neulanders' faces,' Cletus said. 'Of course, officially, Dow's got nothing to do with either of those two missions. Naturally we know that he undoubtedly did know about them, and maybe even had a hand in planning them. But as I say, officially, there's no connection between him and them, and theoretically he could leave the planet as scheduled without looking backward once. Only I don't think he's likely to do that now.'

'Why not?'

'Because, General,' said Cletus, 'his purpose in coming here was to give the Neulanders a morale boost – a shot in the arm. Instead, his visits have coincided with a couple of bad, if small, defeats for them. If he leaves now, his trip is going to be wasted. A man like deCastries is bound to put off leaving until he can leave on a note of success. That gives us a situation we can turn to our own advantage.'

'Oh? Turn to our advantage, is it?' said Bat. 'More of your fun and games, Colonel?'

'Sir,' answered Cletus, 'I might remind the General that I was right about the infiltration attempt through Etter's Pass, and I was right in my guess last night that the guerrillas would try to move men and supplies down the river and into the city—'

'All right! Never mind that!' snapped Bat. 'If I wasn't taking those things into consideration I wouldn't be listening to you now. Go ahead. Tell me what you were going to tell me.'

'I'd prefer to show you,' answered Cletus. 'If you wouldn't mind flying up to Etter's Pass—'

'Etter's Pass? Again?' said Bat. 'Why? Tell me what map you want, and show me here.'

'It's a short trip by air sir,' said Cletus, calmly. 'The explanation's going to make a lot more sense if we have the actual terrain below us.'

Bat grunted. He turned about, stalked to his desk and punched open his phone circuit.

'Send over Recon One to the roof here,' he said. 'We'll be right up.'

Five minutes later, Cletus and Bat were en route by air toward the Etter's Pass area. The general's recon craft was a small but fast passenger vehicle, with antigrav vanes below its midsection and a plasma-thrust engine in the rear. Arvid, who had been waiting for Cletus in the general's outer office, was seated up front in the co-pilot's seat, with the pilot and the vessel's own crewman. Twenty feet behind them, in the open cabin space, Bat and Cletus conversed in the privacy provided by their distance and lowered voices. The recon craft approached the Etter's Pass area and, at Cletus' request, dropped down from its cruising altitude of eighty thousand feet to a mere six hundred. It began slowly to circle the area encompassing Etter's Pass, the village of Two Rivers and the two river valleys that came together just below the town.

Bat stared sourly at the pass and the town below it, nestled in the bottom of the V that was the conjunction of the two river valleys.

'All right, Colonel,' he said, 'I've taken an hour out of my day to make this trip. What you've got to tell me had better be worth it.'

'I think it is,' answered Cletus. He pointed at Etter's Pass and swung his fingertip from it down to the town below. 'If you'll look closely there, sir, you'll see Two Rivers is an ideal jump-off spot for launching an attack through the pass by our forces, as the first step in an invasion of Neuland.'

Bat's head jerked around. He stared at Cletus. 'Invade Neuland ...' He lowered his voice hastily, for the heads of all three men up front had turned abruptly at the sound of his first words. 'Have you gone completely out of your skull, Grahame? Or do you think I have, that I'd even consider such a thing? Invading Neuland's a decision that's not even for the General Staff back on Earth to make. It'd be the political boys in Geneva who'd have to decide that!'

'Of course,' said Cletus, unruffled. 'But the fact is, an invasion launched from Two Rivers could very easily be successful. If the General will just let me explain—'

'No!' snarled Bat, keeping his voice low. 'I told you I don't even want to hear about it. If you got me all the way up here just to suggest that—'

'Not to suggest it as an actuality, sir,' said Cletus. 'Only to point out the benefits of the appearance of it. It's not necessary actually to invade Neuland. It's only necessary to cause the Neulanders, and deCastries, to realize such an invasion could be successful, if launched. Once they realize the possibility, they'll be under extreme pressure to take some counteraction to prevent it. Then, if after they've taken such action, we move to show that invasion was never our intention, Dow deCastries will have been involved in a local blunder from which it'll be impossible for him to detach his responsibility. The Coalition's only way of saving face for him and itself will be to cast all blame on the Neulanders and penalize them as evidence that the blame-casting isn't just rhetoric. The only form that penalizing can take is a lessening of Coalition help to Neuland ... Naturally, any reduction in Coalition aid to the

Neulanders puts the Alliance contribution to the Exotics in that much stronger position.'

Cletus stopped talking. Bat sat for a long second, gazing at him with an unusual expression – something almost like awe – below the heavy, expressive eyebrows.

'By God!' Bat said, at last, 'you don't think in simple terms, do you, Grahame?'

'The complexity's more apparent than real,' answered Cletus. 'Everyone's more or less the prisoner of his current situation. Manipulate the situation and the individual often hasn't much choice but to let himself be manipulated as well.'

Bat shook his head, slowly. 'All right,' he said, drawing a deep breath, 'just how do you plan to signal this fake invasion attempt?'

'In the orthodox manner,' answered Cletus. 'By maneuvering of a couple of battalions of troops in this area below the pass—'

'Hold on. Whoa—' broke in Bat. 'I told you once before I didn't have spare battalions of troops lying around waiting to be played with. Besides, if I order troops up here on anything like maneuvers, how am I going to claim later that there never was any intention to provoke Neuland in this area?'

'I realize you haven't any regular troops to spare, General,' said Cletus. 'The answer, of course, is not to use regular troops. Nor should you order them up here. However, the Dorsai regiment under Colonel Khan is engaged in jump-belt training right now. You could agree to a suggestion which Colonel Khan might make to the Exotics – and which the Exotics will certainly check out with you – that he bring his Dorsais up here for a week of live training jumps in this ideal terrain, which combines river valleys, jungle and hill country.'

Bat opened his mouth as if to retort – then closed it sharply. His brows drew together in a thoughtful frown.

'Hmm,' he said. 'The Dorsais ...'

'The Dorsais,' Cletus reminded him, 'don't operate out of your budget. They're financed separately by the Exotics.'

Bat nodded, slowly.

'A full two battalions of men in this area,' went on Cletus, 'are too many for deCastries and the Neulanders to ignore. The fact that they're Dorsais rather than your own troops makes it seem all the more likely you're trying to pretend innocence, when in fact you've got some thrust into Neulander territory in mind. Add one more small factor, and you'll make suspicion of such a thrust a certainty, to deCastries at least. He knows I've been concerned with the two recent incidents when the Neulanders were frustrated. Appoint me your deputy general commander of this Dorsai unit, with authority to move them wherever I want, and nobody on the other side of the mountains will have any doubt left that the jump training's only a cover for an attack on Neuland territory.'

Bat jerked his head up and stared at Cletus suspiciously. Cletus returned his gaze with the calm innocence of a man whose conscience has nothing to hide.

'But you *won't* be moving those Dorsais anywhere, except between Bakhalla and this area, will you, Colonel?' he demanded softly.

'I give you my word, sir,' said Cletus. 'They'll go nowhere else.'

For a long moment Bat continued to stare, hard, at Cletus. But then, once again, slowly he nodded.

They returned to Bat's office in Bakhalla. As Cletus was leaving, headed for his staff car in the parking lot, a flyer settled into one of the marked spaces and Mondar got out, followed by the small, waspish shape of Pater Ten.

'There he is,' said Pater Ten in a brittle voice, as he spotted Cletus. 'Why don't you go ahead into the Headquarters building, Outbond? I'll stop a minute with Colonel Grahame. Dow wanted me to extend his congratulations on Grahame's success last week – and last night.'

Mondar hesitated briefly, then smiled. 'As you like,' he said, turned and went on toward the Headquarters building.

Pater Ten walked over to face Cletus.

'Congratulate me?' asked Cletus.

'The Military Secretary,' said Pater Ten, almost viciously, 'is a very fair-minded man—'

In mid-sentence he broke off. For a second some inner change seemed to wipe his face clean of expression, and then it shaped itself again into a different kind of expression – an expression like that of an excellent stage mimic who has decided to impersonate the character and mannerisms of Dow deCastries. Except that Pater Ten's eyes were fixed and remote, like a man under hypnosis.

When he spoke, it was in an eerie echo of Dow's ordinary speech:

'Evidently,' said those silkily urbane tones, 'you're still trying to raise the ante, Grahame. Take my advice. Be warned. It's an occupation that's fraught with danger.'

As abruptly as it had come, the unnatural resemblance to Dow smoothed itself from the little man's features and his gaze became normal again. He looked sharply up at Cletus.

'Very fair-minded,' Pater said. 'You underestimate him. I promise you, you've underestimated him—' The little man broke off, abruptly. 'What're you looking at me like that for?' he snapped, acidly. 'You don't believe me, is that it?'

Cletus shook his head, sadly. 'I believe you,' he said. 'It's just that I see I did underestimate him. It seems he's not just a dealer in other people's minds. He buys souls as well.'

He turned and walked off to his car, leaving Pater Ten staring after him uncomprehendingly but with the automatic rage on his face with which the violent little man viewed nearly all things in the universe.

12

They met in Eachan Khan's office a week later – Cletus, Eachan and the four other top officers among the Dorsais. There was Eachan's second-in-command, Lieutenant-Colonel Marcus Dodds, a tall, quiet, narrow-boned man. There were also a major with a shaved head and expressionless features in a hard, round, blue-black face, with the single name of Swahili, a Major David Ap Morgan, who was thin and slightly buck-toothed and as fair-skinned as Swahili was dark; and, last, there was Captain Este Chotai, short, heavy-fleshed and handsome, with narrow eyes in a slightly mongoloid face. They sat around the long conference table in Eachan's wide office, with Eachan at the head of the table and Cletus seated at his right.

'And so, gentlemen,' said Eachan Khan, winding up his explanation of Cletus' presence in their midst, 'we have a new commanding officer from the Alliance Forces. I'll let Colonel Grahame speak for himself from this point on.'

Eachan got up from his chair at the head of the table and stepped aside. Cletus rose, and Eachan took Cletus' former place at the table. Cletus moved over behind the chair Eachan had occupied, but he did not sit down immediately.

Instead, he turned about to look at the large map of Etter's Pass – Two Rivers area projected on the wall behind him. He looked at it and something deep, powerful and unyielding moved without warning through him. He drew in a slow deep breath and the silence of the room behind him seemed to ring suddenly in his ears. The features of the map before him seemed to leap out at him as if he saw, not the projected representation, but the actual features of jungle, hill and river that they represented.

He turned about and faced the Dorsai officers. Under his gaze they stiffened and their eyes narrowed as though something massive and unknown had stepped suddenly among them. Even Eachan stared at Cletus as though he had never seen him before.

'You're all professional soldiers,' said Cletus. His voice was completely flat, without inflection or emphasis, but it rang in the room with a finality that left no room for doubt or argument in its listeners. 'Your future depends on what you'll be doing in the next two weeks. Therefore I'm going to tell you what no one else on this planet yet knows, and I'm going to trust you to keep that information locked inside you.'

He paused. They sat staring at him like men in a trance.

'You're going to fight a battle. My aim isn't going to be to kill the enemy in this battle, but to force him to surrender in large numbers, so if all goes according to plan you ought to win with little or no casualties ... I don't guarantee that. I only say that it ought to be that way. But, in any case, you'll have fought a battle.'

He paused for a second, looking into their faces one by one. Then he went on.

'Behind me here,' he said, 'you see the upland area into which you're going to move at the end of this week for further jump-training and jungle practice. This practice isn't just to fill time. The better shape your men are in at the end of the training period, and the better they know the area, the better chance they'll have to survive in the fight, later. Colonel Khan will give you your specific orders. That's all I'll tell you now. As I say, I don't want you to tell anyone, not even the men you command, that any sort of real action's in prospect. If you're the kind of officers I think you are, and they're the kind of men I think they are, they'll absorb the feeling that something is going to happen without your having to tell them ... That's all.'

He sat down abruptly and turned to Eachan.

'Take over, Colonel,' he said to Eachan.

Eachan, unmoving, continued to gaze at him for just a fraction of a second longer before he rose, cleared his throat and began to describe the patterns of movement of the various units from Bakhalla into the Two Rivers area. Four days later support ships of the type that had flown Cletus with Lieutenant Athyer and his troops up to Etter's Pass began ferrying the mercenary soldiers to Two Rivers. Cletus went up on one of the early flights and toured the area with Eachan Khan. Cletus' first concern was for the town or village – it was really more village than town – of Two Rivers itself.

The settlement was actually a tight little V-shaped clump of condominiums and individual homes surrounding a warehouse and business section and filling the triangular end-point of flatland where the valleys of the Blue and Whey rivers came together. This patch of flatland extended itself, with a few scattered streets and buildings, up the valley of each river for perhaps a quarter of a mile before the river-banks became too high and steep for much building to be practical. The town was a community supported essentially by the wild-farming of a majority of its inhabitants, wild-farming being the planting, in the surrounding jungle area, of native or mutated trees and plants bearing a cash crop without first dividing up or clearing the land. A wild-farmer owned no territory. What he owned was a number of trees or plants that he tended and from which he harvested the crops on a regular basis. Around Two Rivers a sort of native wild cherry and mutated rubber plants introduced by the Exotics four years ago were the staple wild-farm crops.

The local people took the invasion by the Dorsais in good spirits. The mercenaries were much quieter and better-mannered in their off-duty hours than were regular troops. Besides, they would be spending money in the town. The locals, in general, paid little attention to Cletus, as, with Eachan Kahn, he marked out positions for strong points with dug-in weapons on the near banks of the two rivers just above the town and down within the open land of the community itself. When Cletus had finished, he had laid out two V-shaped lines of strong points, one inside the other, covering the upriver approaches to the town and the river junction itself.

'Now,' said Cletus to Eachan, when this was done, 'let's go take a look up beyond the pass.'

They took one of the support ships that had just discharged its cargo of Dorsai soldiers and was about to return to Bakhalla for another load. With it they flew up and over the area of Etter's Pass and made a shallow sweep over the some ten miles of mountainous territory beyond it to where the ground sloped away into the farther jungle that was Neuland territory.

'I expect the Neulanders will be coming around to see what we're doing,' he said to Eachan, 'as soon as their people in Bakhalla tell them the Dorsais have moved up here for training. I want this side of the mountains kept under observation by men who won't be spotted. I assume you've got people like that?'

'Of course!' said Eachan. 'I'll have a watch on up here all twenty-six hours of the day. How soon do you want it to start?'

'Right away,' answered Cletus.

'I'll have men started out in half an hour,' Eachan answered. 'Anything else?'

'Yes,' Cletus said. 'I want those defensive strong points, in and above the town, dug in, with an earth wall inside and sandbags outside so that it's at least six feet thick at the base and seven feet above the level of the ground outside.'

Eachan frowned slightly. But his reply was laconic. 'Yes, Colonel,' he said.

'That's it, then,' said Cletus. 'I'm headed back to Bakhalla. I'll have the ship drop you back down at Two Rivers first. Are you planning on coming back to town later?'

'This evening,' he answered, 'as soon as I've got all the men moved in here and set up. I'm planning on commuting. Here, days – Bakhalla, nights.'

'I'll see you back at the city then,' said Cletus. He turned to the pilots of the support ship. 'Take us back to Two Rivers.'

He dropped off Eachan and went back to Bakhalla. There he found his work waiting for him – in two stacks, for, in accepting a role as Bat's deputy commanding officer of the Dorsais, he had in essence taken on another full job. The Dorsais operated with a small to nonexistent Headquarters staff, as they did in all areas requiring non-combatant personnel. In the field, each Dorsai was his own cook, launderer and bottle washer, and each officer was responsible for all paper work involving his command. Away from the field, in barracks so to speak, men were hired from the regular fighting units, at a small addition to their ordinary wages, to work as clerks, cooks, vehicle drivers and the rest, but in the field there was none of this.

Those Dorsais, therefore, who ordinarily would have lightened Cletus' paper workload concerning the mercenary soldiers were now in battle gear up at Two Rivers. It was this fact that also required Eachan to commute back to Bakhalla every night to take care of his own paper work.

Cletus, of course, had the use of the staff Arvid had collected to help in making his forecasts of enemy activity. But members of the staff, including Arvid himself, were fully occupied with their regular jobs, at least during normal working hours. Cletus had set them to functioning as a research service. They were collecting information on both Neuland and the Exotic colony, plus all the physical facts about Kultis – weather, climate, flora and fauna – that pertained to the two opposed peoples. This information was condensed and fed to Cletus as soon as it was available; at least half his working day was taken up in absorbing and digesting it.

So it was that the first five days after the Dorsais had been moved up to Two Rivers, Cletus spent at his office between the hours of seven in the morning and midnight with very few breaks in between. About seven o'clock of the fifth evening, after the rest of the staff had already left for the day, Wefer Linet showed up unexpectedly.

'Let's go catch some more Neulander guerrillas,' Wefer suggested.

Cletus laughed, leaned back in his chair and stretched wearily. 'I don't know where there are any, right now,' Cletus said.

'Let's go have dinner then and talk about it,' said Wefer craftily. 'Maybe between the two of us we can figure out how to find some.'

Cletus laughed again, started to shake his head, and then let himself be persuaded. After the dinner, however, he insisted on returning to his desk. Wefer came back with him, and only reluctantly took his leave when Cletus insisted that the work yet undone required his immediate attention.

'But don't forget,' Wefer said on his way out, 'you'll call me if anything comes up. I've got five Mark V's, and four of them are yours on half an hour's notice. It's not just me, it's my men. Everyone who was with us there on the river has been spreading the story around until I haven't got anyone in my command who wouldn't want to go with you if another chance comes up ... You'll find something for us to do?'

'It's a promise,' said Cletus. 'I'll turn up something for you shortly.'

Wefer at last allowed himself to be ushered out. Cletus went back to his desk. By eleven o'clock he had finished the extensive and detailed orders he had been drafting to cover the actions and contingencies of the next two days. He made up a package of the orders, which were to be passed on to Eachan Khan for application to the Dorsai troops, and, going out, drove himself in a staff aircar to the Headquarters building in the Dorsai area.

He parked in front of it. There were two other cars waiting there; the one window of Eachan's office that faced him was alight. The rest of the building – a temporary structure of native wood painted a military light green that looked almost white in the pale light of the now-waxing new moon overhead – was dark, as were all the surrounding office and barracks buildings. It was like being in a ghost town where only one man lived.

Cletus got out of the car and went up the steps into the front hall of the building. Passing through the swinging gate, which barred visitors from the clerks normally at work in the outer office, he went down the corridor beyond the outer office to where the half-open door of Eachan's private office was marked by an escaping swathe of yellow light that lay across the corridor floor. Coming quietly up on that patch of light, Cletus checked, suddenly, at the sound of voices within the room.

The voices were those of Eachan and Melissa – and their conversation was no public one.

Cletus might have coughed, then, or made some other noise to warn that he had come upon them. But at that moment he heard his own name mentioned – and instantly guessed at least half of the conversation that had gone before. He neither turned and retreated nor made a sound. Instead he stood, listening.

'I thought you liked young Grahame,' Eachan had just finished saying.

'Of course I like him!' Melissa's voice was tortured. 'That's got nothing to do with it. Can't you understand, Dad?'

'No.' Eachan's voice was stark.

Cletus took one long step forward, so that he could just see around the corner of the half-open door into the lighted room. The illumination there came from a single lamp, floating a foot and a half above the surface of Eachan's desk. On opposite sides of the desk, Eachan and Melissa stood facing each other. Their heads were above the level of the lamp, and their faces were hidden in shadow, while the lower parts of their bodies were clearly illuminated.

'No, of course you can't!' said Melissa. 'Because you won't try! You can't tell me you like this better – this hand-to-mouth mercenary soldiering – than our home in Jalalabad! And with Dow's help you can go back. You'll be a general officer again, with your old rank back. That's *home*, Dad! Home on Earth, for both of us!'

'Not any more,' said Eachan deeply. 'I'm a soldier, Melly. Don't you understand? A *soldier*! Not just a uniform with a man walking around inside it – and that's all I'd be if I went back to Jalalabad. As a Dorsai, at least I'm still a soldier!' His voice became ragged, suddenly. 'I know it's not fair to you—'

'I'm not doing it for me!' said Melissa. 'Do you think I care? I was just a girl when we left Earth – it wouldn't be the same place at all for me, if we went back. But Mother told me to take care of you. And I am, even if you haven't got the sense to take care of yourself.'

'Melly ...' Eachan's voice was no longer ragged, but it was deep with pain. 'You're so sure of yourself ...'

'Yes, I am!' she said. 'One of us has to be. I phoned him, Dad. Yesterday.'

'Phoned deCastries?'

'Yes,' Melissa said. 'I called him in Capital Neuland. I said we'd come anytime he sent for us from Earth. *We'd* come, I said, Dad. But I warn you, if you won't go, I'll go alone.'

There was a moment's silence in the darkness hiding the upper part of Eachan's stiff figure.

'There's nothing there for you, girl,' he said, hoarsely. 'You said so yourself.'

'But I'll go!' she said. 'Because that's the only way to get you to go back, to say I'll go alone if I have to – and mean it. Right now, I promise you, Dad …'

Cletus did not wait to hear the end of that promise. He turned abruptly and walked silently back to the front door of the building. He opened and closed the door, banging the heel of his hand against it noisily. He walked in, kicked open the gate in the fence about the outer office area and walked soundingly down the hall toward the light of the partly opened door.

When he entered the office room, the overhead lights had been turned on. In their bright glare, Melissa and Eachan still stood a little apart from each other, with the desk in between.

'Hello, Melissa!' Cletus said. 'Good to see you. I was just bringing in some orders for Eachan. Why don't you wait a few minutes and we can all go have a cup of coffee or something?'

'No, I …' Melissa stumbled a little in her speech. Under the overhead lights her face looked pale and drawn. 'I've got a headache. I think I'll go right home to bed.' She turned to her father. 'I'll see you later, Dad?'

'I'll be home before long,' Eachan answered.

She turned and went out. Both men watched her go.

When the echo of her footsteps had been brought to an end by the sound of the outer door of the office building closing, Cletus turned back to face Eachan and threw the package of papers he was carrying onto Eachan's desk.

'What's the latest word from the scouts watching the Neulander side of the mountains?' Cletus asked, watching the older man's face and dropping into a chair on his side of the desk. Eachan sat down more slowly in his own chair.

'The Neulanders've evidently stopped moving men into the area,' Eachan said. 'But the scouts estimate they've got thirty-six hundred men there now – nearly double the number of our Dorsai troops. And they're regular Neulander soldiery, not guerrillas, with some light tanks and mobile artillery. My guess is that's better than 60 per cent of their fully equipped, regular armed forces.'

'Good,' said Cletus. 'Pull all but a couple of companies back into Bakhalla.'

Eachan's gaze jerked up from the packet of orders to stare at Cletus' face. 'Pull back?' he echoed. 'What was the point in going up there, then?'

'The point in going up there,' said Cletus, 'was to cause Neuland to do exactly what they've done – assemble troops on their side of the mountain border. Now we pull back most of our men, so that it looks as though we've lost our nerve. Either that, or never intended to be a threat after all.'

'And was that what we intended?' Eachan looked narrowly at Cletus.

Cletus laughed cheerfully. 'Our intent, just as I say,' he answered, 'was to make them assemble a large force on their side of the pass through the mountains. Now we can pack up and go home – but can they? No doubt you've heard the army rumor – and by this time the Neulanders will have heard it too – that General Traynor and myself were over-heard discussing an invasion of Neuland, and that we made a special trip up to Etter's Pass to survey it with that in mind.'

'You mean,' said Eachan, 'that deCastries and the Neulanders will be sure that we really meant to invade them?'

'I mean just the opposite,' said Cletus. 'There's a great deal of truth to the fact that a liar is always going to suspect you of lying and a thief'll always suspect your honesty. DeCastries is a subtle man, and the weakness of subtle men is to suspect any straightforward action of being a screen for some kind of trick. He'll be sure to have concluded the rumor was leaked specifically for the purpose of causing him – and Neuland – to move a lot of troops into position on a false invasion scare, which would evaporate then and leave them looking foolish. Consequently, being the man he is, he'll have resolved to play along with our game and take advantage of us at the very moment we plan to be chuckling over his embarrassment.'

Eachan frowned. 'I don't believe I follow you,' he said.

Cletus nodded at the package of papers. 'It's all in the orders, there,' he said. 'You'll start withdrawing men from the Two Rivers area early tomorrow, a shipload at half hour intervals. As each shipload gets back here and gets sorted out, turn them loose on three-day passes.'

Eachan stared at him, grimly. 'And that's it?' Eachan said, at last.

'That's it – until I give you further orders,' said Cletus, getting to his feet. He turned about and headed toward the door.

'Good night,' said Eachan behind him. As Cletus went out the door and turned left to go off down the corridor, he caught a glimpse of Eachan, still standing behind the desk, looking after him.

Cletus went back to his quarters and to bed. The next morning he allowed himself the unusual luxury of sleeping late. It was 10 A.M. by the time he drifted into the Officers' Club for a late breakfast and just short of noon when he finally arrived at his office. Arvid and the staff Arvid had accumulated there were all diligently at work. Cletus smiled at them like an indulgent father and called them all together.

'I'm flying up to Two Rivers this afternoon,' he said, 'to supervise the windup of the Dorsai exercises up there. So there's not much point in your feeding me with a lot of information material that'll go stale between now and Monday morning anyway. I've been working you all above and beyond the call of duty. So take the rest of the day off – all of you, that is, except Arvid' – he smiled at the big young officer – 'and I'll see you again at the beginning of next week.'

The staff evaporated like a scattering of raindrops on hot pavement after a tropical shower. Once they were gone, Cletus went carefully around the office, making sure all its security systems were in working order and ready to be put in operation. Then he came back, sat down opposite Arvid's desk and reached over to pick up Arvid's phone. He dialed the number of the Navy base.

'This is Colonel Cletus Grahame,' he told the duty petty officer at the far end. 'Would you try to locate Commander Linet for me, and have him call me back? I'm at my office.'

He put the phone back on Arvid's desk and waited. Arvid was watching him with curiosity. Cletus got up and walked over to his own desk. He picked up his own phone there and brought it back to exchange it for the phone in front of Arvid. Arvid's phone he took back to his own desk.

He punched out the first two digits of the five-digit number that would connect him with Bat Traynor's office. Then, with the phone activated, but the call uncompleted, he pushed the phone from him and looked over at Arvid.

'Arv,' he said, 'some time in the next few hours Eachan Khan's going to be calling me. If anyone but Colonel Eachan calls, I've just stepped out and you don't know when I'll be back. But if Colonel Eachan calls, tell him that I'm on the phone to General Traynor at the moment – and I will be. Ask him if you can take a message, or say I'll call him back in a few minutes.'

Arvid frowned in slight puzzlement – but the frown evaporated almost immediately into his usual agreeable expression.

'Yes, sir,' he said ... 'And now?' he asked, after Cletus had made the call.

'Now, we wait.'

Wait, they did – for nearly two hours, during which perhaps a dozen unimportant phone calls came in and were neatly fielded by Arvid. Then the phone Cletus had moved from his desk to that of the lieutenant buzzed abruptly and Arvid lifted the receiver.

'Colonel Grahame's office, Lieutenant Johnson speaking—' Arvid broke off, glancing over at Cletus. 'Colonel Khan? Yes, sir ...'

Cletus had already picked up Arvid's phone and was completing the punching of the proper sequence of numbers for contact with Bat's office. In the background he heard Arvid saying that he could take a message. Bat's office answered.

'This is Colonel Grahame,' Cletus said into the phone. 'I'd like to talk to General Traynor right away – in fact, immediately. It's red emergency.'

He waited. There was a fractional delay at the other end of the line. Arvid, meanwhile, had hung up. There was silence in the office. Cletus could see out of the corner of his eye how Arvid was standing, watching him.

'Grahame?' Bat's voice exploded suddenly against Cletus' ear. 'What's all this?'

'Sir,' said Cletus, 'I discovered something, and I think I ought to talk to you about it right away – privately. I can't tell you over the phone. It's got to do with the Coalition and it involves not only us, here on Kultis, but the whole Alliance. I'm at my office. I've given my staff the rest of the day off. Could you make some excuse to leave your office and come over here so that we could talk privately?'

'Talk? What is all this—' Bat broke off. Cletus heard the other's voice, suddenly withdrawn from the mouthpiece of the phone, speaking distantly to someone else. 'Joe, go get me that file on ... the plans for the new military district south of town.'

There were a few more seconds of pause, and then Bat's voice came back close to the phone but muted and cold in tone.

'*Now* you can tell me,' he said.

'I'm sorry, sir,' said Cletus.

'Sorry? You mean you don't even trust the phone circuits to my office?'

'I didn't say that, sir,' answered Cletus evenly. 'I only suggested that you make some excuse to get out of your office and meet me privately over here at mine.'

His voice was almost wooden in its lack of expression. There was a long pause at the other end of the phone circuit. Then Cletus heard Bat's indrawn breath hiss sharply.

'All right, Grahame,' said Bat, 'but this better be as serious as you're making it sound.'

'Sir,' said Cletus seriously, 'without exaggeration, it concerns not only the highest Coalition personnel presently on the planet, but members of our own Alliance command here in Bakhalla as well.'

'See you in fifteen minutes,' said Bat. The phone circuit clicked in Cletus' ear, and then went dead.

Cletus put the phone down and turned to look at Arvid, who was staring at him.

'Eachan's message?' Cletus prompted gently. With a start, Arvid came out of his trance.

'Sir, the Neulanders are attacking Two Rivers!' he burst out. 'Colonel Khan says they're coming in both by air and through the pass – and there's less than three companies of Dorsais left in Two Rivers, not counting a few scouts still out in the jungle who'll have been captured or bypassed by the Neulander troops by this time.'

Cletus picked up the phone and punched for Lieutenant-Colonel Marcus Dodds at the landing field by the Dorsai military area.

'Colonel Dodds – sir?' said the lean, quiet face of Eachan's second-in-command, appearing in the small phone screen.

'Have you heard about the Neulander attack at Two Rivers?' Cletus asked.

'Yes, sir,' Dodds answered. 'Colonel Khan just messaged us to stop all release of men. We're starting to get them turned around now.'

'Good,' said Cletus. 'I'll join you shortly.'

He broke the circuit, put the phone down and crossed the room to an arms cabinet. Unlocking it, he took out a pistol belt and sidearm. He turned and tossed these to Arvid. Arvid put out one hand automatically and caught them.

'Sir?' he said, puzzled, 'the Neulanders aren't attacking in the city, here, are they?'

Cletus laughed, reclosing and locking the arms cabinet. 'No, Arv,' he said, turning back to the tall lieutenant, 'but the Neulanders have started to move up at Two Rivers, and Dow deCastries is the kind of man to want to take out insurance, even when he has a sure thing. I'd look a little strange wearing a sidearm, but you can wear it for me.'

He turned back to his desk phone and punched for the Navy base.

'This is Colonel Grahame,' he said. 'A little while ago I put in an important call for Commander Linet ...'

'Yes, sir,' said the voice of the ensign who had answered the phone.

'The commander's been trying to get you sir, but your circuits were busy just now. Just a minute, sir ...'

Wefer's voice broke in on the line. 'Cletus! What's up?'

'You offered me the use of four of your Mark V's,' Cletus said. 'I need only three of them. But they have to move upriver between here and the town of Two Rivers, at the confluence of the Blue and the Whey. That's nearly two hundred and thirty miles of river travel. Do you think they could make it between now and, say, an hour before dawn tomorrow?'

'Two hundred and thirty miles? Between now and an hour to dawn? Nothing to it!' shouted Wefer over the phone circuit. 'What's up?'

'The Neulanders have moved regular troops across the border at Etter's Pass,' said Cletus, in a level voice. 'They'll be attacking Two Rivers shortly after sunup tomorrow. I'll give you the details of what I want you for later. But can you move your Mark V's to within a mile downstream of where the two rivers come together and hold them there without being seen?'

'You know I can!' said Wefer. 'But you'll be in touch?'

'I'll be contacting you before dawn tomorrow,' said Cletus.

'Right! We're on our way!' The phone clicked dead at Wefer's end.

'Go ahead, Arv,' said Cletus. 'Wait for me outside at the car. I'll be along in a minute.'

Arv stared. 'We're leaving?' he said. 'But, sir, isn't the general due ...'

His voice ran down into silence as Cletus stood patiently waiting. 'Yes, sir,' he said.

He went out.

Cletus put the phone in his hand back down on the desk by which he was standing. He glanced at his watch. Some eight minutes had gone by since he had spoken to Bat, and Bat had said he would be here in fifteen minutes. Cletus made a last tour of the office to make sure all the security devices were in order. Then he let himself out the front door, pulling the door to, but leaving it slightly unlatched, with the trap spring activated. The next person to walk through that door would find it closing automatically behind him, locking him into an area from which escape was not easily possible.

Cletus turned and went out to his staff car, where Arvid waited. They drove off toward the BOQ.

13

As Cletus' command car tilted on its air cushion and slid around the corner into the short street leading toward the BOQ, Cletus saw the parking lot before the BOQ half-filled with parked cars, clustered before the main entrance of the building in two rows with a narrow aisle in between.

Both ends of the parking lots were empty; the building itself, with those other buildings of the officers' compound beyond it, seemed to slumber emptily under the afternoon sun. The BOQ's occupants for the most part would now be either at work, having a late lunch, or asleep within. As the staff car slid on its air cushion toward the entrance to the parking lot Cletus raised his eyes and caught the glint of sunlight on something metallic just below the ridge of the roof over the BOQ's main entrance.

Cletus looked at the empty-windowed double row of cars sitting flat on the cement of the parking lot, with their air cushions turned off. His lips thinned. At that moment, as they turned into the aisle between the two rows of cars, there were sizzling sounds like the noise of enormous slices of bacon frying above them, followed by several licking dragons' breaths of superheated air, as energy weapons sliced into the metal sides and roof of his command car like the flames of acetylene torches into thin tinfoil. Arvid fell heavily against Cletus, his uniform jacket black and smoking on the upper right side, and the staff car careered out of control, to its right, into two empty parking spaces between cars, where it wedged itself, still on its air cushion between the grounded vehicles.

A bleak fury exploded inside Cletus. He turned, jerked the sidearm from its holster at Arvid's side, ducked down and punched open the door on his side of the staff car. He dived through it into the space between his car and the grounded one on the right. He rolled back under his own floating car and crawled rapidly to the back end of the grounded car on his left. Lying flat, he peered around its end. There was a man on his feet, energy rifle in hand, coming toward him between the two rows of parked vehicles at a run. Cletus snapped a shot from the sidearm and the man went tumbling, head over heels. Cletus ducked around the car to his right and into the next space between it and the car farther on.

The charge weapons now were silent. From memory of the sound and damage to the command car, Cletus guessed no more than three gunmen were involved. That left two to deal with. Glancing out, Cletus could see the man he had shot sprawled, lying still on the pavement, his energy weapon rolled out of his grasp, its transparent, rifle-like barrel reflecting the sunlight. Cletus backed up, opened the near door of the car on his right and crawled in. Lying flat on its floorboards, he raised it on its air cushion and set it backing out in reverse.

As it reached the center space between the two rows of parked cars, he dived out the opposite door, just as two beams cut into the other side and the roof of the car behind him. He snatched up the fallen charge weapon and, carrying it, scuttled behind the screen of the still-moving car until it slammed into the opposite row of cars. Then he ducked into the closest available space there, turned about and looked back around the nearest car end.

The other two gunmen were visible, standing out in the open now, back to back, by the car Cletus had last sent smashing into the ones opposite. One was facing Cletus' direction, the other in the opposite direction, both with their charge weapons up and scanning the spaces between the vehicles for any sign of movement.

Cletus pulled back, cradled the charge weapon in his left elbow and lobbed his sidearm in a high arc over the heads of the two standing men to fall with a clatter by Cletus' own cut-up command car.

Both of the gunmen spun about to face in the direction of the noise. Cletus, standing up and stepping out from between his two parked cars, cut them down with the energy weapon he still held in his hands.

Breathing heavily, Cletus leaned for a second against the back of the car by which he had emerged. Then, throwing aside the energy weapon, he limped hastily back toward the staff car in which Arvid still lay.

The lieutenant was conscious when Cletus arrived. He had taken a bad burn through the upper part of his chest and shoulder on the right side, but energy weapon wounds were self-cauterizing; the wound was ugly, but there was no bleeding. Cletus eased him down onto the grass and went into the BOQ to call for medical aid from an astounded military hospital unit.

'Guerrillas!' Cletus said briefly, in answer to their questions. 'There're three of them – all dead. But my aide's wounded. Get over here as soon as you can.'

He cut the connection and went back out to see how Arvid was doing.

'How …' whispered Arvid, when Cletus bent over him.

'I told you deCastries would like insurance,' said Cletus. 'Lie still now, and don't talk.'

The ambulance unit from the military hospital swooped down then, its shadow falling across them like the shadow of some hawk from the skies just before it landed softly on the grass beside them. White-uniformed medics personnel tumbled out, and Cletus got to his feet.

'This is Lieutenant Johnson, my aide,' said Cletus. 'Take good care of him. The three guerrillas out in the parking lot are all dead. I'll write up a full report on this later – but right now I've got to get going. You can handle things?'

'Yes, sir,' said the medic in charge. He was a senior, with the gold and black bars of a warrant officer on his collar. 'We'll take care of him.'

'Good,' said Cletus.

Without stopping to say anything further to Arvid, he turned and went up into the BOQ and down the hall to his own quarters. Swiftly, he changed into combat overalls and the straps for battle gear. When he came out, Arvid had already been taken away to the hospital and the three dead gunmen had been brought up and laid on the grass. Their clothes were the ordinary sort of civilian outfits normally seen on the streets of Bakhalla but the lower part of the faces of each was pale in contrast to the tan of their foreheads, showing where heavy Neulander beards had been shaved off recently.

Cletus tried his command car, found it operable, and slid off in the direction of the Dorsai area.

When he arrived there, he found most of the returned Dorsai troops already marshaled by units on the exercise ground – armed, equipped and ready to be enshipped back to Two Rivers. Cletus went directly to the temporary Headquarters unit set up at one side of the field and found Lieutenant-Colonel Marcus Dodds there.

'You haven't sent any shiploads back up yet, have you?' Cletus demanded the moment Dodds saw him.

'No, Colonel,' answered the tall, lean man. 'But we should probably be thinking about moving men back up soon. If we try to have troops jump into Two Rivers after dark, three out of four of them are going to land in the rivers. And by daylight tomorrow, those Neulander troops will probably be in position in both river valleys above the town. They'd have a field day picking off our jump troops if we send men in then.'

'Don't worry about it,' Cletus said brusquely. 'We aren't going to jump into the town in any case.'

Marc Dodds' eyebrows raised in his narrow, brown face. 'You're not going to support—'

'We'll support. But not that way,' said Cletus. 'How many of the men that were sent back and turned loose on pass are still out?'

'Not more than half a company, probably, all told. They've been hearing about this and coming back on their own,' said Marc. 'No Dorsai's going to let other Dorsais be surrounded and cut up when he can help—'

He was interrupted by the phone ringing on the field desk before him. He picked it up and listened for a moment without comment.

'Just a minute,' he said, and lowered the phone, pushing in on the muffle button. 'It's for you. Colonel Ivor Dupleine – General Traynor's chief of staff.'

Cletus reached out his hand and Marc passed the phone into it.

'This is Colonel Grahame,' Cletus said into the mouthpiece. Dupleine's choleric face, tiny in the phone screen by Cletus' thumb, glared up at him.

'Grahame!' Dupleine's voice barked in his ear. 'This is Colonel Dupleine. The Neulanders've moved troops over the border at Etter's Pass and seem to be setting up around Two Rivers. Have you still got any Dorsai troops up there?'

'A couple of companies in the town itself,' said Cletus.

'Only a couple? That's not so bad then!' said Dupleine. 'All right, listen now. Apparently those Dorsais over there with you are getting all stirred up. You're not to make any attempt against those Neulander troops without direct orders. *That's* a direct order – from General Traynor himself. You understand? You just sit tight there until you hear from me or the general.'

'No,' said Cletus.

For a moment there was a dead silence at the other end of the circuit. Dupleine's face stared out at Cletus from the phone screen.

'What? What did you say?' snapped Dupleine, at last.

'I ought to remind you, Colonel,' said Cletus, quietly, 'that the general put me in complete command of these Dorsais with responsibility only to him.'

'You ... but I'm giving you the general's orders, Grahame! Didn't you hear me?' Dupleine's voice choked on the last word.

'I've got no proof of that, Colonel,' said Cletus, in the same unvarying tone of voice. 'I'll take my orders from the general, himself. If you'll have the general tell me what you've just told me, I'll be happy to obey.'

'You're insane!' For a long moment, he once more stared at Cletus. When he spoke again, his voice was lower, more controlled, and dangerous. 'I think you know what refusing to obey an order like that means, Colonel. I'm going to sign off here and give you five minutes to think it over. If I haven't heard from you within five minutes, I'll have to go to the general with your answer just the way you gave it. Think about it.'

The little screen in the phone went dark, and the click of the disconnected circuit sounded in the earphone. Cletus put the phone back on the desk.

'Where's your map projector?' he asked Marc.

'Right over here,' he answered, leading the way across the room to a horizontal table-screen, with the black shape of a projector bolted beneath it. A map of the Etter's Pass area showed on the screen. As they both reached the edge of the table-screen, Cletus put his finger on the marked position of Two Rivers town where the streams of the Whey and the Blue came together.

'By dawn tomorrow,' he said to Marc, 'whoever's commanding those Neulanders will want to be in a position to start his attack on our troops in the town. That means' – Cletus' finger traced horseshoe-shaped curves, their open ends facing downstream, about the valleys of both the Whey and the Blue rivers just above the town – 'our men from here should be able to go in as jump troops – since they're fresh from training for it – just up-river of both those positions with comparative safety – since the Neulander forces should all be looking downriver. Now, I understand that the Neulanders don't have any real artillery, any more than we do. Is that right?'

'That's right, sir,' Marc said. 'Kultis is one of the worlds where we've had an unspoken agreement with the Coalition not to supply our allies, or our troops stationed with those allies, with anything more than portable weapons. So far as we know, they've kept to their part of the bargain as far as Neuland's concerned. Actually, they haven't needed anything more than hand weapons, just as we haven't, since up till now all their fighting's been done with native guerrillas. We can expect their troops to have light body armor, energy weapons, rocket and fire bomb launchers ...'

Together they plotted the probable future positions of the Neulander troops, particularly those carrying the launchers and other special weapons. While they worked, a ceaseless stream of orders came in and out of the field HQ, frequently interrupting their talk.

The sun had set several hours before one of the junior officers tapped Cletus deferentially on the elbow and offered him the phone.

'Colonel Dupleine again, sir,' the officer said.

Cletus took the phone and looked at the image of Dupleine. The face of the Alliance colonel looked haggard.

'Well, Colonel?' asked Cletus.

'Grahame—' began Dupleine, hoarsely, and then broke off. 'Is anyone there with you?'

'Colonel Dodds of the Dorsais,' answered Cletus.

'Could I … talk to you privately?' said Dupleine, his eyes searching around the periphery of the screen as though to discover Marc, who was standing back to one side out of line of sight from the phone. Marc raised his eyebrows and started to turn away. Cletus reached out a hand to stop him.

'Just a minute,' he said. He turned and spoke directly into the phone. 'I've asked Colonel Dodds to stay. I'm afraid I'd prefer having a witness to whatever you say to me, Colonel.'

Dupleine's lips sagged. 'All right,' he said. 'The word's probably spreading already. Grahame … General Traynor can't be located.'

Cletus waited a second before answering. 'Yes?' he said.

'Don't you understand?' Dupleine's voice started to rise. He stopped, visibly fought with himself and got his tones down to a reasonable level again. 'Here the Neulanders have moved not just guerrillas, but regular troops, into the country. They're attacking Two Rivers – and now the general's dis … not available. This is an emergency, Grahame! You have to see the point in canceling any orders to move the Dorsai troops you have there, and coming over to talk with me, here!'

'I'm afraid I don't,' answered Cletus. 'It's Friday evening. General Traynor may simply have gone somewhere for the weekend and forgotten to mention he'd be gone. My responsibility's to his original orders, and those leave me no alternative but to go ahead with the Dorsais in any way I think best.'

'You can't believe he'd do a thing like that—' Dupleine interrupted himself, fury breaking through the self-control he had struggled to maintain up until this point. 'You nearly got gunned down by guerrillas yourself, today, according to the reports on my desk! Didn't it mean anything to you that they were carrying energy weapons instead of sport rifles? You know the Neulander guerrillas always carry civilian-level weapons and tools so they can't be shot as saboteurs if they're captured! Doesn't the fact that three men with energy weapons tried to cut you down mean anything to you?'

'Only that whoever's giving the orders on the Neuland side,' said Cletus, 'would like to have me removed as command of the Dorsai troops. Clearly, if they don't want me commanding, the best thing I can do for our side is to command.'

Dupleine glared at him wearily from the phone screen. 'I warn you, Grahame!' he said. 'If anything's happened to Traynor, or if we don't find him in the next few hours, I'll take emergency command of the Alliance Forces here myself. And the first thing I'm going to do is to revoke Bat's order to you and put you under arrest!'

The tiny screen in the phone went dark, the voice connection went dead. A little wearily, Cletus put the phone down on the table-screen and rubbed his eyes. He turned to Marcus Dodds.

'All right, Marc,' he said. 'We won't delay any longer. Let's start moving our men back up to Two Rivers.'

14

Cletus went in with the first wave of six transport craft, which circled eight miles upstream from Two Rivers and dropped their jump troops on both sides of the two river valleys. A reconnaissance aircraft, swinging low over the jungle in the darkness following moon-set, two hours before, had picked up the heat images of two large bodies of Neulander troops waiting for dawn in both the river valleys, five miles above the town. Another, smaller, reserve force was camped just below the mouth of Etter's Pass – but its numbers were slight enough so that the Dorsais could disregard any counterattack from that direction. Cletus watched the flares of the jets from the jump belts of the descending men, and then ordered the pilot of his transport ship to fly low above the river, heading downstream from the town.

A quarter mile below the town, the river curved to the right, and it was just around this curve that the response came from the M5's. The transport ship came down and hovered above the water, and the turret of one of the huge submarine dozers rose blackly from the dark waters.

Cletus went down an elevator sling to the turret, and the hatch in it opened. Wefer stepped out. Together they stood on the slight slope of the wet metal casing below the tower.

'Here we are, then,' Wefer said. 'Three of us, just like the doctor ordered,' Under his black hair, his friendly, pugnacious face was excited in the dim light. 'What do you want us to do?'

'The Neulander troops – and their regular troops,' said Cletus, 'are concentrated in the two river valleys a few miles above the town. They'll be pushing down those valleys and into the town along the flatland below the river bluffs. But I don't think they'll be trying to come at the town from this downriver side. So you ought to be able to work without being seen.'

'Sure, sure,' said Wefer, sniffing the chilly dawn air like a hunting dog. 'But what do you want us to do?'

'Can you plough up the bottom of the river just below the town, to raise the water level in and above the town?'

'In this little trickle of a river?' answered Wefer. 'No trouble at all. We'll simply raise an underwater ridge at some point where the river bluffs on either side come straight down to the water's edge. The water has to rise to get over it. How high a dam? How much do you want to raise the water level?'

'I want the water six feet deep, a mile above the town,' Cletus said.

For the first time, Wefer frowned. 'Six feet? A full fathom? You'll flood the town itself. That flat spot between the rivers that the town's built on can't be more than six or eight feet above water level on both sides. You'll have another four to six feet of running water in the streets. Do you want that?'

'That's exactly what I want,' said Cletus.

'Well ... of course there's plenty of solid buildings there in the warehouse district for people to climb into,' said Wefer. 'I just don't want to get the Navy billed for flood damage—'

'It won't be,' said Cletus. 'I'm still under General Traynor's direct orders as commander here. I'll take the responsibility.'

Wefer peered at Cletus in the growing light, shook his head and whistled admiringly. 'We'll get right at it then,' he said. 'You ought to have your fathom of water up above the city there in about four hours.'

'Good,' said Cletus. He stepped into the elevator sling and waved to the transport ship to pull him back in. 'Good luck.'

'Good luck to you and your Dorsais!' Wefer replied. 'You'll need it more than we do. We're just going to be doing our daily jobs.'

Once back inside the transport, Cletus ordered it to swing back up to within line of sight of Two Rivers itself. The sky was lightening rapidly now, and the individual buildings in Two Rivers were easily picked out. Cletus had a coherent light beam trained on the curved reception mirror on the roof of the warehouse building that the Dorsais had taken over as their Two River HQ during the week of jump practice. He sent a call down the light beam and got an immediate answer from Eachan.

'Colonel?' Eachan's voice was distant, clipped and unruffled. 'Been expecting to hear from you. I haven't had any reports from my scouts out in the jungle for better than three hours now. They're all either captured or lying low. But I gather the Neulanders are clustered in both river valleys above town. I've got all strong points here manned and ready.'

'Fine, Colonel,' said Cletus. 'I just wanted to tell you to expect to get your feet wet. You might also warn the civilians in town to gather in the higher buildings of the warehouse district above the second floor.'

'Oh? Thunderstorm coming?'

'We're not that lucky, I'm afraid,' said Cletus. A good heavy rainstorm would have been all to the advantage of the well-trained Dorsai, both the jump troops and those in fixed positions in the city. 'The weather forecast is for hot and clear. But the river's going to rise. I'm told you'll have four to six feet of water in the streets there.'

'I see. I'll take care of it – with the troops and civilians too—' Eachan broke off. 'Are we getting reinforcements here in the town?'

'I'm afraid I can't spare you any,' Cletus said. 'But with luck, it'll be over one way or the other before the Neulanders are really on top of you. Do the best you can with the men you have.'

'Understood,' said Eachan. 'That's all from this end then, Colonel.'

'That's all from my end for the moment, too, Colonel,' replied Cletus. 'Good luck.'

He broke the light-beam contact and ordered the transport ship back to Bakhalla for a new load of jump troops. Now that it was open daylight over Two Rivers and there was no more secrecy to be gained by operating at low altitudes in the shadows below the peaks above the town, Cletus accompanied the next wave of jump troops riding in a courier craft, which he set to circling above the reach of hand-weapon fire from the ground.

The second wave of Dorsai troops to go down on their jump belts were harassed, but ineffectively so, by angled fire from the Neulander troops downriver.

'Good enough,' commented Marc Dodds, who had accompanied Cletus in the courier ship, leaving Major David Ap Morgan to take charge of getting off the last two remaining waves and accompanying the last as its commanding officer. 'They'll have aircraft hitting our next wave, though. I don't know why they haven't had Neulander ships in the air over here before now.'

'Another instance of the too imaginative mind,' said Cletus. Marc glanced at him inquiringly, and Cletus went on to explain. 'I was telling Eachan last night that too much subtlety would lead to mistakes. The Neulanders know that the Alliance has supplied the Exotics with many more and better air-combat craft than the Coalition supplied them. So automatically they've drawn the wrong conclusion. They think our lack of air cover is only apparent – bait to tray them into putting their own ships up so our superior air power can knock them down. Also, they know that only the Dorsais were jump-training, and they'll be suspecting that the Dorsais are the only ones who're being sent against them for that reason. They know they outnumber us two or three to one on the ground, which would tend to make them complacent.'

The third wave came in and jumped to the jungle below. True to Cletus' assessment of the situation, there was no appearance of Neuland aircraft to oppose the jump. Nor was there with the fourth and final wave. With all four waves of Dorsai jump troops now down on the ground, the pattern of Cletus' battle plan began to make itself felt. He had set his Dorsais down in the jungle on the top of the bluffs on either side of both rivers upstream from the concentration of Neulander troops. Now, spread out in skirmish lines, the Dorsais began to open up on the rear of the Neulander troops. The Neulanders fought back, but withdrew steadily, as their force began to move down into the river valleys toward the town. They showed no tendency to turn and fight and no panic at being caught by small-arms fire from their rear. Up in their circling aircraft, Cletus and Marc kept in touch with their units on the ground by line-of-sight light-beam voice transmission.

'We aren't even slowing them down,' said Marc, his mouth a straight line as he observed the scene below in the multiple reconnaissance screens set up before them.

'They'll be slowed up later,' replied Cletus.

He was very busy plotting the movements of the running battle below on the reconnaissance screen, even as he issued a steady stream of orders to individual small units of the Dorsai troops.

Marc fell silent and turned back to examining the situation on the reconnaissance screens as it was developing under the impetus of Cletus' orders. Before him the two main elements of the Neulander forces were like large fat caterpillars crawling down the inner edge of the valley troughs of the two rivers, converging as the rivers converged toward the single point that was the town of Two Rivers. Behind, and inland from the rivers, the Dorsai troops, like thin lines of tiny ants, assailed these two caterpillars from the rear and the inland sides. Not that all this was visible to the naked eye below the thick screen of jungle cover. But the instruments and Cletus' plotting on the chart revealed it clearly. Under attack the caterpillars humped their rearward ends closer toward their front, bunching up under the attacks of the ants, but otherwise were undisturbed in their progress.

Meanwhile, Cletus was extending his pursuing Dorsai troops forward along the inland side of each enemy force until the farthest extended units were almost level with the foremost troops of the enemy units they harassed. Occasionally they dented the Neulanders lines they faced. But in case of trouble the Neulanders merely withdrew over the edge of the steeply sloping bluff and fought the Dorsai back over, what was in effect, a natural parapet. Not merely that, but more and more their forward-moving units were dropping below the edge of the bluff with a skirmish line along its edge to protect their march – so that fully 80 per cent of the enemy force was beyond the reach of the Dorsai weapons in any case.

Cletus broke off abruptly from his work on the screens and turned to Marc.

'They're less than two miles from the upper edge of the town,' he said. 'I want you to take over here and keep those Neulander forces contained all along their lines. Make them get down below the bluff and stay there, but don't expose men any more than you have to. Contain them, but hold your troops back until you get word from me.'

'Where're you going, sir?' Marc asked, frowning.

'Down,' said Cletus, tersely. He reached for one of the extra jump belts with which the aircraft was supplied and began strapping it on. 'Put half a company of men on each river over on their jump belts and send them down the opposite side. They're to fire back across the river into any exposed elements of the enemy as they go, but they are not to stop to do it. They're to keep traveling fast until they rendezvous with me down here.'

He turned and tapped with his fingernail on the bend in the river below the town beyond which Wefer and his three Mark V's were at work. 'How soon do you estimate they can meet me down there?' he asked.

'With luck, an hour,' answered Marc. 'What're you planning to do, sir – if you don't mind my asking?'

'I'm going to try to make it look as though we've got reinforcements into that town,' Cletus said. He turned and called up to the pilot in the front of the reconnaissance ship. 'Cease circling. Take me down to just beyond the bend in the main river there – point H29 and R7 on the grid.'

The aircraft wheeled away from its post above the battle and began to circle down toward the river bend. Cletus moved over to the emergency escape hatch and put his hand on the eject button. Marc followed him.

'Sir,' he said, 'if you haven't used a jump belt in a long time—'

'I know,' Cletus interrupted him cheerfully, 'it's a trick to keep your feet down and your head up, particularly when you're coming in for a landing. Don't worry—' He turned his head to shout to the pilot up front. 'That patch of jungle just inside the bend of the river. Call "*Jump*" for me.'

'Yes, sir,' the pilot called back. There was a moment's pause and then he shouted, *'Jump.'*

'Jump,' echoed Cletus.

He punched the eject button. The emergency door flipped open before him and the section of decking beneath his feet flipped him abruptly clear of the aircraft. He found himself falling toward the tops of the jungle treetops, six hundred feet below.

He clutched the hand control in the center of the belt at his waist, and the twin jets angling out from his shoulder tank flared thunderously, checking him in midair with a wrench that left him feeling as though his back had been broken. For a moment, before he could catch his breath, he actually began to rise. Then he throttled back to a slow fall and began the struggle to keep himself in vertical position with his feet under him.

He was not so much falling as sliding down at a steep angle into the jungle below. He made an effort to slow the rate of his fall, but the sensitive, tricky reactions of the jump belt sent him immediately into a climb again. Hastily, he returned the throttle to its first, instinctive fall-setting.

He was very near the tops of the taller trees now, and it would be necessary to pick his way between them so as not to be brained by a branch in passing or land in one of the deadly, dagger-like thorn bushes. Careful not to twist the throttle grip in the process, he shifted the control handle slightly this way and that to determine the safe limits of a change of direction. His first attempt very nearly sent his feet swinging into the air, but he checked the swing and after a moment got himself back into a line of upright descent. There was a patch of relatively clear jungle down to his right. Gingerly he inched the control handle over and was relieved as his airy slide altered toward the patch. Then, abruptly, he was among and below the treetops.

The ground was rushing at him. The tall, jagged stump of a lightning-blasted tree, which he had not seen earlier because it was partly covered with creepers blending in with the green of the ground cover, seemed to leap upward at him like a spear.

Desperately he jammed the handle over. The jets bucked. He went into a spin, slammed at an angle into the tree stump and smashed against the ground. A wave of blackness took him under.

15

When he came to – and it may have been only seconds later – he was lying twisted on the ground with his bad knee bent under him. His head was ringing, but, otherwise, he did not feel bad.

Shakily he sat up and, using both hands, gently began to straighten out his bum leg. Then there was pain, mounting and threatening unconsciousness.

He fought the unconsciousness off. Slowly it receded. He leaned back, panting against the tree trunk, to catch his breath and use his autocontrol techniques. Gradually the pain in his knee faded, and his breathing calmed. His heartbeat slowed. He concentrated on relaxing the whole structure of his body and isolating the damaged knee. After a little while, the familiar floating sensation of detachment came to him. He leaned forward and gently straightened the knee, pulled up the pants leg covering it and examined it.

It was beginning to swell, but beyond that his exploring fingers could not tell him what serious damage had been done it this time. He could sense the pain like a distant pressure off behind the wall of his detachment. Taking hold of the tree trunk and resting all his weight on his other foot, he slowly pulled himself to his feet.

Once on his feet he gingerly tried putting a little of his weight on that leg. It supported him, but there was a weakness about it that was ominous.

For a moment he considered using the jump belt to lift himself into the air once more, over the treetops and down to the river. But after a second, he dismissed the idea. He could not risk another hard landing on that knee, and coming down in the river with as much current as there was now was also impractical. He might have to swim, and swimming might put the knee completely beyond use.

He unbuckled the jump belt and let it fall. Relieved of its weight, he hopped on his good foot to a nearby sapling about two inches in diameter. Drawing his sidearm, he shot the sapling's trunk through some six feet above the ground, and again at ground level. Stripping off a few twigs from the length of wood this provided left him with a rough staff on which he could lean. With the help of the staff he began hobbling toward the river's edge. He finally reached the bank of the gray, flowing water. He took the body phone from his belt, set it for transmission limited to a hundred yards and called Wefer on the Navy wavelength.

Wefer answered, and a few minutes later one of the Mark V's poked its massive, bladed snout out of the water ten yards in front of him.

'What now?' asked Wefer, after Cletus had been assisted aboard and down into the control room of the Mark V. Cletus leaned back in the chair they had given him and stretched out his bad leg carefully.

'I'm having a company of men, half on each side of the river, meet us here in about' – he broke off to look at his watch – 'thirty minutes or so from now. I want one of your Mark V's to take them, a platoon at a time, underwater up to the downriver end of the town. Can you spare one of your machines? How's the water level coming, by the way?'

'Coming fine,' answered Wefer. 'Those platoons of yours are going to find it knee-deep in the lower end of town by the time they get there. Give us another hour, and with only two machines I'll have the river as deep as you want it. So there's no problem about detaching one of the Mark V's for ferry purposes.'

'Fine,' said Cletus.

He rode into the town with the last Mark V load of the ferried Dorsais. As Wefer had predicted, the water was knee-deep in the streets near the downriver end of the town. Eachan Khan met him as he limped into the command room of the Dorsai HQ in Two Rivers.

'Sit down, Colonel,' said Eachan, guiding Cletus into a chair facing the large plotting screen. 'What's happening to the river? We've had to herd all the civilians into the tallest buildings.'

'I've got Wefer Linet and some of those submarine dozers of his working downstream to raise the river level,' answered Cletus. 'I'll give you the details later. Right now, how are things with you here?'

'Nothing but some long-range sniping from the forward Neulander scouts, so far,' said Eachan, coolly. 'Those sandbagged strong points of yours were a fine idea. The men will be dry and comfortable inside them while the Neulanders will be slogging through ankle-deep water to get to them.'

'We may have to get out in the water and do a little slogging ourselves,' said Cletus. 'I've brought you nearly two hundred extra men. With these added to what you've got, do you think you could mount an attack?'

Eachan's face had never inclined to any large changes of expression, but the stare he gave Cletus now was as close to visible emotion as Cletus had seen him go.

'Attack?' he echoed. 'Two and a half – three companies – at most, against six or eight battalions?'

Cletus shook his head. 'I said mount an attack. Not carry one through,' he replied. 'All I want to do is sting those two Neulander fronts enough so that they'll pause to bring up more men before starting to go forward against us again. Do you think we can do that much?'

'Hmm.' Eachan fingered his mustache. 'Something like that … yes, quite possible, I'd think.'

'Good,' said Cletus. 'How can you get me through, preferably with picture as well as voice, to Marc Dodds?'

'We're on open channel,' Eachan answered. He stepped across the room and returned with a field phone.

'This is Colonel Khan,' he said into it. 'Colonel Grahame wishes to speak with Colonel Dodds.'

He passed the phone to Cletus. As Cletus' hands closed about it, the vision screen in the phone's stem lit up with the image of Marc's face, the plotting screen of the aircraft behind him.

'Sir?' Marc gazed at Cletus. 'You're in Bakhalla?'

'That's right,' Cletus answered. 'And so's that company of men I had you send to meet me at the bend of the main river. Give me a view of the board behind you there, will you?'

Marc moved aside, and the plotting screen behind him seemed to expand to fill the full screen of the phone. Details were too small to pick out, but Cletus could see that the two main bodies of Neuland troops were just beginning to join together on the sandy plain that began where the river bluffs on adjacent banks of the converging Blue and Whey rivers finally joined and ended in a sloping V-pointed bluff above the town. Behind the forward scouts, the advancing main line of the Neulanders was less than half a mile from the forward Dorsai strongpoints defending the town. Those strongpoints and the defending Dorsais would be firing into the enemy at long range, even now.

'I've got men along the tops of the bluffs all the way above the Neulanders on both rivers,' said the voice of Marc, 'and I've got at least two energy-rifle companies down on the flats at the foot of the bluffs behind their rear guards, keeping up fire into them.'

'Pull those rifle companies back,' Cletus said. 'There's no point in risking a man we don't have to risk. And I want you to have your men on top of the bluffs stay there, but slacken off on their firing. Do it gradually, cut it down bit by bit until you're just shooting into them often enough to remind them that we're there.'

'Pull back?' echoed Marc. His face came back into the screen, frowning. 'And slacken fire? But what about the rest of you down in the town there?'

'We're going to attack,' said Cletus.

Marc stared out of the screen without answering. His thoughts were as visible as though they were printed in the air before him. He, with better than three thousand men, was being told to back off from harassing the rear of an enemy force of more than six thousand – so as not to risk casualties. Meanwhile, Cletus, with less than six hundred men, was planning to attack the enemy head on.

'Trust me, Colonel,' said Cletus softly into the phone. 'Didn't I tell you all a week ago that I planned to get through this battle with as few men killed as possible?'

'Yes, sir ...' said Marc, grudgingly, and obviously still bewildered.

'Then do as I tell you,' said Cletus. 'Don't worry, the game's not over yet. Have your men slacken fire as I say, but tell them to stay alert. They'll have plenty of chance to use their weapons a little later on.'

He cut the connection and handed the phone back to Eachan.

'All right,' he said. 'Now let's see about mounting that attack.'

Thirty minutes later, Cletus was riding with Eachan in a battle car that was sliding along on its air cushion ten inches above the water flooding the town, water that was now ankle-deep, even here at the upper edge of the town. He could see, moving ahead of him, spaced out in twenty-yard intervals and making good use of the houses, trees and other cover they passed, the closest half dozen of his Dorsai troopers in the first line of attack. Immediately in front of him, in the center of the control panel of the battle car, he could see a small replica plotting screen being fed with information by a remote circuit from the main plotting screen under Eachan's control at Dorsai HQ in the town behind him. It showed the Neulanders forming up at the base of the vertical wall of stone and earth where adjacent river bluffs came together. Their line stretched right across the some six hundred yards of sandy soil making up the neck of the land that connected the foot of the bluffs with the broader area of slightly higher ground on which the town of Two Rivers was built.

Only the apparent width of the neck of land showed on the plotting screen, however. Its actual width was lost now in an unbroken sheet of running water stretching from the bluffs on what had been the far side of the Whey River to the opposite bluffs on what had been the far side of the Blue. Under that gray, flowing sheet of liquid it was impossible to tell, except for the few small trees and bushes that dotted the neck of land, where the water was ankle-deep and where it was deep enough for one of Wefer's Mark V's to pass by on the bottom, unnoticed. Cletus had warned the attacking men to stay well toward the center of the enemy line, to avoid blundering into deeper water that would sweep them downstream.

The attackers paused behind the cover of the last row of houses and dressed their line. The enemy was only a few hundred yards away.

'All right,' said Cletus into his battle phone. 'Move out!'

The first wave of attackers rose from their places of concealment and charged forward at a run, zigzagging as they went. Behind them their companions, as well as the strongpoints with a field of fire across the former neck of land, opened up on the enemy with missile weapons.

The Neuland troops still standing on the dry footing of the slightly higher ground at the foot of the bluffs stared at the wild apparition of rifle-armed soldiers racing toward them, in great clouds of spray, with apparent suicidal intent. Before they could react, the first wave was down behind whatever cover was available, and the second wave was on its way.

It was not until the third wave had moved out that the Neulanders began to react. But by this time the fire from the attackers – as well as the slightly heavier automatic fire from the strongpoints – was beginning to cut up their forward lines. For a moment, disbelief wavered on the edge of panic. The Neuland troops had been under the impression that there was no one but a token force to oppose them in Two Rivers – and that it would be a matter of routing out small pockets of resistance, no more. Instead, they were being attacked by what was clearly a much greater number of Dorsais than they had been led to believe were in the town. The front Neuland line wavered and began to back up slightly, pressing in on the troops behind them, who were now crowding forward to find out what was going on.

The confusion was enough to increase the temporary panic. The Neuland troops, who had never fought a pitched battle before, for all their Coalition-supplied modern weapons, lost their heads and began to do what any seasoned soldier would instinctively have avoided doing. Here and there they began to open up at the charging figures with energy weapons.

At the first touch of the fierce beams from the weapons, the shallow water exploded into clouds of steam – and in seconds the oncoming Dorsais were as effectively hidden as though the Neulanders had obligingly laid down a smoke screen for their benefit.

At that the panic in the first few ranks of the Neulanders broke completely into a rout. Their forward men turned and began trying to fight their way through the ranks behind them.

'Back!' Cletus ordered his charging Dorsais by battle phone. For, in spite of the temporary safety of the steam-fog that enveloped them, their mere handful of numbers was by now dangerously close to the mass soldiery of the Neulanders' force, as his plotting screen reported, even though vision was now obscured. 'Get back! All the way back. We've done what we set out to do!'

Still under safety of the steam-fog, the Dorsais turned and retreated. Before they were back to the cover of the houses, the steam blew clear. But the Neulander front was still in chaos, and only a few stray shots chased the attackers back into safety.

Cletus brought them back to Dorsai HQ and climbed stiffly out of the battle car, whose air cushion hovered it above more than seven feet of water now lapping at the top of the steps leading to the main entrance of the building. He made a long step from the car to the threshold of the entrance and limped wearily inside toward the command room.

He was numb with exhaustion and he stumbled as he went. One of the younger officers in the building stepped over to take his arm, but Cletus waved him off. He limped shakily into the command room, and Eachan turned from the plotting screen to face him.

'Well done, sir,' said Eachan slowly and softly. 'Brilliantly done.'

'Yes,' replied Cletus thickly, too tired to make modest noises. On the screen before him the Neulanders were slowly getting themselves back into order. They were now a solid clump around and about the foot of the bluff. 'It's all over.'

'Not yet,' said Eachan. 'We can hold them off awhile yet.'

'Hold them off?' The room seemed to waver and threaten to rotate dizzily about Cletus' burning eyes. 'You won't have to hold them off. I mean it's all over. We've won.'

'Won?'

As if through a gathering mist, Cletus saw Eachan staring at him strangely. A little clumsily, Cletus made it to the nearest chair and sat down.

'Tell Marc not to let them up to the top of the bluffs unless they surrender,' he heard himself saying, as from a long way off. 'You'll see.'

He closed his eyes, and seemed to drop like a stone into the darkness. Eachan's voice reached down after him.

'... Medic, here!' Eachan was snapping. 'Damn it, hurry up!'

So it was that Cletus missed the last act of the battle at Two Rivers. From the moment of the Neulanders' momentary panic at being attacked by the Dorsais under Cletus' direction, trouble began to beset the six thousand soldiers from Neuland. It took them better than half an hour to restore order and make themselves ready to move forward upon the town again. But all that time the river level, raised by the work of Wefer's Mark V's, had been rising. Now it was up over the knees of the Neulanders themselves, and fear began to lay its cold hand upon them.

Ahead of them were certainly more Dorsai troops than they had been led to expect. Enough, at least, so that the Dorsais had not hesitated to mount an attack upon them. To go forward might cause them to be caught in a trap. Besides, to go forward was to go into steadily deepening water. Even the officers were uncertain – and caution suggested itself as the better part of valor. The word was given to withdraw.

In orderly manner, the two halves of the Neuland invading force split up and began to pull back along the river flats down which they had come. But, as they backed up, in each case, the width of the flat narrowed and soon the men farthest away from the bluff found themselves stumbling off into deeper water and the current pulling them away.

As more and more Neuland troopers were swept out into the main river current, struggling and splashing and calling for help, a new panic began to rise in the ranks of those still standing in shallow water. They began to crowd and jostle to get close to the bluff. Soon their organization began to dissolve. Within minutes, soldiers were breaking away from the ranks and beginning to climb directly up the bluffs toward the safety of high ground overhead.

But it was at this moment that Marc, following Cletus' earlier written orders, gave the command to his Dorsais lined up along the top of the bluff to fire down into these refugees from the rising waters ... And it was all over but the shouting.

They did not even have to call on the Neulanders to surrender. The panic-stricken colonists in uniform from over the mountains beyond Etter's Pass threw away weapons and began climbing the slope with their hands in the air, at first only a few, then mobs. By the time the sun was touching the western horizon, more than six thousand soldiers – as it was later to turn out, better than 70 per cent of Neuland's army – sat huddled together as prisoners under the guns of their Dorsai guards.

But Cletus, still unconscious, knew none of this. Back in a room of the Dorsai HQ in Two Rivers, a prosthetic physician flown up from

Bakhalla was straightening up from his examination of Cletus' swollen left knee, his face grave.

'How is it, Doctor?' asked Eachan Khan, sharply. 'It's going to mend all right, isn't it?'

The physician shook his head and looked at Eachan soberly. 'No, it isn't,' the physician said. 'He's going to lose the leg from just above the knee.'

16

'Prosthetic knee and ankle joints – in fact, prosthetic lower limbs,' said the physician, patiently, 'are really excellent. Inside of a couple of months after you've adapted to the prosthetic unit, you'll find yourself almost as mobile as you were before with that limp. Of course, no one likes to face the thought of an amputation, but—'

'It's not the thought of an amputation that worries me,' interrupted Cletus. 'I've got things to do that require two flesh and blood legs. I want a surgical replacement.'

'I know,' answered the doctor. 'But you remember we ran tests on you and you've got an absolute level of rejection. All the evidence is that it's a case of psychological, not physiological, rejection. If that's the case, all the immune-suppressant drugs on the list can't help you. We can graft the leg on but your body's sure to reject it.'

'You're sure it's a case of psychological rejection?' said Cletus.

'Your medical history shows you have a uniformly successful resistance to hypnosis, even under ordinary drugs,' the doctor answered. 'We find that kind of resistance almost always in people who exhibit psychological rejection of grafted organs, and whenever it's found we always – without exception – have psychological rejection. But just to put it to the test, I've brought along one of the new synthetic parahypnotic drugs. It leaves you conscious up to safe levels of dosage, but it absolutely anesthetizes volition. If you can resist hypnosis with that in you, then the resistance is below the levels even psychiatry can reach. It's probably a genetic matter. Do you want to try it?'

'Go ahead,' said Cletus.

The doctor fastened the band of a hypnospray around Cletus' forearm, with the metered barrel of the drug poised above a large artery. The level of the liquid in the barrel of the spray was visible. Resting his thumb and little finger on Cletus' arm on either side of the band, the doctor placed the top of his forefinger on the spray button.

'I'll keep asking you your name,' he said. 'Try not to tell me what it is. As you continue to refuse, I'll keep stepping up the dosage level. Ready?'

'Ready,' said Cletus.

'What's your name?' asked the doctor. Cletus felt the cool breath of the hypnospray against the skin of his forearm.

Cletus shook his head.

'Tell me your name?' repeated the doctor.

Cletus shook his head. The cool feeling of the spray continued. Slightly to his surprise, Cletus felt no light-headedness or any other indication that the drug was working on him.

'Tell me your name.'

'No.'

'Tell me your name ...'

The questioning continued and Cletus continued to refuse. Abruptly, without warning, the room seemed filled with a white mist. His head whirled, and that was the last he remembered.

He drifted back into a weariness, to find the doctor standing over his bed. The hypnospray was unstrapped from his arm.

'No,' said the doctor, and sighed. 'You resisted right up to the point of unconsciousness. There's simply no point in trying a transplant.'

Cletus gazed at him almost coldly. 'In that case,' he said, 'will you tell Mondar the Exotic Outbond that I'd like to talk to him?'

The doctor opened his mouth as if to say something, closed it again, nodded and left.

A nurse came to the door. 'General Traynor is here to see you, Colonel,' she said. 'Do you feel up to seeing him?'

'Certainly,' said Cletus. He pressed the button on the side of the bed that raised the head section, lifting him up into a sitting position. Bat came in the door and stood beside the bed looking down at him; his face was like a stone mask.

'Sit down, sir,' Cletus said.

'I'm not going to be here that long,' said Bat.

He turned about to close the door of the room. Then he turned back to glare down at Cletus.

'I've just got two things to tell you,' he said. 'When I finally smashed the door open on the arms locker in your office and got a gun to shoot the hinges off the door, it was Sunday afternoon, so I made sure I got secretly out of town and phoned Colonel Dupleine quietly, before I made any fuss. You'll be glad to hear, then, there isn't going to be any fuss. Officially, I had a slight accident Friday afternoon a little ways out-side of Bakhalla. My car went off the road. I was knocked unconscious and pinned in it. I wasn't able to get out until Sunday. Also, officially, what you did up at Two Rivers in capturing those Neulanders was done at my orders.'

'Thank you, sir,' said Cletus.

'Don't butter me up!' snarled Bat softly. 'You knew I was too bright to go around raising hell about your putting me out of the way until I'd found out what the score was. You knew I was going to do what I did. So let's not play games. You locked me up and nobody's ever going to know about it. But you captured two-thirds of the Neuland armed forces and *I'm* the one who's going to get most of the credit back in Geneva. That's the way things stand, and that's one of the two things I came to tell you.'

Cletus nodded.

'The other thing's this,' Bat said. 'What you pulled off up there at Two Rivers was one hell of a piece of fine generalship. I can admire it. But I don't have to admire you. I don't like the way you work, Grahame, and I don't need you – and the Alliance doesn't need you. The second thing I came to tell you is this – I want your resignation. I want it on my desk inside of forty-eight hours. You can go back home and write books as a civilian.'

Cletus looked at him quietly. 'I've already submitted my resignation from the Alliance Military Service,' he said. 'I'm also giving up my citizenship as an Earth citizen. I've already made application for citizenship on Dorsai, and it's been accepted.'

Bat's eyebrows rose. For once his hard, competent face looked almost foolish. 'You're skipping out on the Alliance?' he asked. 'Completely?'

'I'm emigrating, that's all,' said Cletus. He smiled a little at Bat. 'Don't worry, General. I've no more interest in making public the fact that you were locked in my office over part of the weekend than you have. We'll assume a Neulander spy got into the office, found himself trapped and managed to break his way out.'

Their eyes met. After a second, Bat shook his head. 'Anyway,' he said. 'We won't be seeing each other again.'

He turned and left. Cletus lay gazing at the ceiling until he fell asleep.

Mondar did not show up until the following afternoon; he apologized for not coming sooner.

'The message saying that you wanted to see me was sent through the regular mail,' he said, sitting down in a chair at Cletus' bedside. 'Evidently your good physician didn't see any urgency in your asking for me.'

'No,' said Cletus, 'it's outside his area of knowledge.'

'I think he assumed I'd have to tell you that I – or we Exotics, that is – couldn't help you either,' said Mondar, slowly. 'I'm afraid he may have been right. I called the hospital after I got your message and talked to someone I know on the staff here. I was told you've got a problem of almost certain psychological rejection of any organ graft.'

'That's right,' said Cletus.

'He said you thought that perhaps I – or perhaps some other Exotic, working with you, could succeed in overcoming such a psychological reaction long enough for a healthy leg to be grafted on you.'

'It's not possible?' Cletus watched the Exotic closely as he spoke.

Mondar looked down and smoothed the blue robe covering his crossed knees. Then he looked back up at Cletus.

'It's not impossible,' he said. 'It'd be possible in the case, say, of someone like myself, who's trained in the areas of mental and physical self-control since he was a boy. I can ignore pain, or even consciously will my heart to stop beating, if I wish. I could also, if necessary, suppress my immune reactions – even if they included the kind of psychological rejection that afflicts you ... Cletus, you've got a tremendous amount of native talent, but you haven't had my years of training. Even with my assistance you wouldn't be able to control the rejection mechanism in your body.'

'You're not the only one who can ignore pain,' said Cletus. 'I can do that too, you know.'

'Can you?' Mondar looked interested. 'Of course, come to think of it. Both after your first time up at Etter's Pass, and this time at Two Rivers when you damaged the knee again, you did a good deal of moving around on it when ordinarily such movement should have been unendurable.'

His eyes narrowed a little, thoughtfully. 'Tell me – do you deny the pain – I mean do you refuse to admit the pain is there? Or do you *ignore* it – that is you remain conscious that the sensation is there but you don't allow the sensation to affect you?'

'I ignore it,' answered Cletus. 'I start out by relaxing to the point where I feel a little bit as though I'm floating. Just that much relaxation takes a lot of the sting out of the pain. Then I move in on what's left and more or less take the color out of it. What I'm left with is a little like a feeling of pressure. I can tell if it increases or decreases, or if it goes away entirely, but I'm not bothered by it in any way.'

Mondar nodded slowly. 'Very good. In fact, unusually good for self-trained,' he said. 'Tell me, can you control your dreams?'

'To a certain extent,' said Cletus. 'I can set up a mental problem before falling asleep, and work it out while I'm asleep – sometimes in the shape of a dream. I can also work out problems the same way while I'm awake by throwing a certain section of my mind out of gear, so to speak, and letting the rest of my body and mind run on automatic pilot.'

Mondar gazed at him. Then he shook his head. But it was an admiring shake.

'You amaze me, Cletus,' the Exotic said. 'Would you try something for me? Look at that wall just to your left there, and tell me what you see.'

Cletus turned his head away from Mondar and gazed at the flat, vertical expanse of white-painted wall. There was a small prickling sensation at the side of his neck just behind and below his right ear – followed by a sudden explosion of pain from the site of the prick, like the pain from the venom of a bee sting following the initial puncture. Cletus breathed out calmly; as the breath left his lungs, a crimson violence of the pain was washed clean and unimportant. He turned back to Mondar.

'I didn't see anything,' he said, 'of course.'

'Of course. It was only a trick to get you to turn your head away,' said Mondar, putting what looked like a miniature mechanical pencil back in his robes. 'The amazing thing is, I wasn't able to measure any skin flinch, and that's a physiological reaction. Clearly your body hasn't much doubt about your ability to handle pain quickly.'

He hesitated. 'All right, Cletus,' he said. 'I'll work with you. But it's only fair to warn you that I still don't see any real chance of success. How soon do you want the transplant done?'

'I don't want it done,' said Cletus. 'I think you're probably quite right about the impossibility of suppressing my rejection mechanism. So we'll do something else. As long as it's a long shot anyway, let's try for a miracle cure.'

'Miracle ...' Mondar echoed the word slowly.

'Why not?' said Cletus cheerfully. 'Miracle cures have been reported down through the ages. Suppose I undergo a purely symbolic operation. There's both flesh and bone missing from my left knee where the prosthetic unit was surgically implanted after I was first wounded years ago. I want that surgical implant taken out and some small, purely token portions of the flesh and bone from equivalent areas of my right knee transplanted into the area where the original flesh and bone is missing in the left. Then we cover both knees up with a cast' – his eyes met Mondar's – 'and you and I concentrate hard while healing takes place.'

Mondar sat for a second. Then he stood up.

'Anything is eventually possible,' he murmured. 'I've already said I'd help you. But this is something that's going to require some thought, and some consultation with my fellow Exotics. I'll come back to see you in a day or two.'

The next morning Cletus had a visit from both Eachan Khan and Melissa. Eachan came in first, alone. He sat stiffly in the chair beside Cletus' bed. Cletus, propped up in a sitting position gazed at the older man keenly.

'Understand they're going to try to do something to fix that knee of yours,' Eachan said.

'I twisted some arms,' answered Cletus, smiling.

'Yes. Well, good luck,' Eachan looked away, out the window of the room for a moment, and then back at Cletus. 'Thought I'd bring you the good wishes of our men and officers,' he said. 'You promised them a victory almost without a casualty – and then you delivered it.'

'I promised a battle,' Cletus corrected, gently. 'And I was hoping we wouldn't have much in the way of casualties. Besides, they deserve a good deal of credit themselves for the way they executed their battle orders.'

'Nonsense!' said Eachan brusquely. He cleared his throat. 'They all know you're emigrating to Dorsai. All very happy about it. Incidentally, seems you started a small rash of emigrations. That young lieutenant of yours is coming over as soon as his shoulder heals up.'

'You accepted him, didn't you?' Cletus asked.

'Oh, of course,' Eachan said. 'The Dorsai'll accept any military man with a good record. He'll have to pass through our officers' school, of course, if he wants to keep his commission with us, though. Marc Dodds told him there was no guarantee he'd make it.'

'He will,' said Cletus. 'Incidentally, I'd like your opinion on something – now that I'm a Dorsai myself. If I supply the funds for subsistence, training facilities and equipment, do you suppose you could get together a regiment-sized body of officers and men who would be willing to invest six months in a complete retraining program – if I could guarantee them that at the end of that time they'd be able to find employment at half again their present pay?'

Eachan stared. 'Six months is a long time for a professional soldier to live on subsistence,' he said, after a moment. 'But after Two Rivers, I think it just might be done. It's not just the hope of better pay, much as that means to a lot of these people who've got families back on Dorsai. It's the better chance of staying alive to get back to the families that you might be able to give them. Want me to see about it?'

'I'd appreciate it,' said Cletus.

'All right,' said Eachan. 'But where's the money to come from for all this?'

Cletus smiled. 'I've got some people in mind,' he said. 'I'll let you know about that later. You can tell the officers and the men you contact that it's all conditional on my having the funds, of course.'

'Of course.' Eachan fingered his mustache. 'Melly's outside.'

'Is she?' asked Cletus.

'Yes. I asked her to wait while I had a word with you on some private matters first, before she came in ...' Eachan hesitated. Cletus waited.

Eachan's back was as stiffly upright as a surveyor's rod. His jaw was clamped and the skin of his face was like stamped metal.

'Why don't you marry her?' he said, gruffly.

'Eachan ...' Cletus checked himself and paused. 'What makes you think Melissa would want to marry me, anyway?'

'She likes you,' said Eachan. 'You like her. You'd make a good team. She's mostly heart and you're nearly all head. I know you both better than you know each other.'

Cletus shook his head slowly, for once finding no words ready to his tongue.

'Oh, I know she acts as if she knows all the answers when she doesn't, and acts like she wants to run my life, and yours, and everybody else's for them,' went on Eachan. 'But she can't help it. She does feel for people, you know – I mean, feel for what they're actually like, at core. Like her mother in that. And she's young. She feels something's so about some-one and can't see why they don't do exactly what she thinks they ought to do, being who they really are. But she'll learn.'

Cletus shook his head again. 'And me?' he said. 'What makes you think I'd learn?'

'Try it. Find out,' retorted Eachan.

'And what if I made a mess of it?' Cletus looked up at him with more than a touch of grimness.

'Then at least you'll have saved her from deCastries,' said Eachan, bluntly. 'She'll go to him to make me follow her – to Earth. I will, too, to pick up the pieces. Because that's all that'll be left of her afterward – pieces. With some women it wouldn't matter, but I know my Melly. Do you want deCastries to have her?'

'No,' said Cletus, suddenly quiet. 'And he won't. I can promise you that, anyway.'

'Maybe,' said Eachan, getting to his feet. He swung about on his heel. 'I'll send her in now,' he said, and went out.

A moment or two later, Melissa appeared in the doorway. She smiled wholeheartedly at Cletus and came in to seat herself in the same chair Eachan had just vacated.

'They're going to fix your knee,' she said. 'I'm glad.'

He watched her smile. And for a second there was an actual physical sensation in his chest, as though his heart had actually moved at the sight of her. For a second what Eachan had said trembled in his ears, and the guarded distance that life and people had taught him to keep about him threatened to dissolve.

'So am I,' he heard himself saying.

'I was talking to Arvid today ...' Her voice ran down. He saw her blue eyes locked with his, as if hypnotized and he became aware that he had captured her with his own relentless stare.

'Melissa,' he said slowly, 'what would you say if I asked you to marry me?'

'Please ...' It was barely a whisper. He shifted his gaze, releasing her; she turned her head away.

'You know I've got Dad to think about, Cletus,' she said, in a low voice.

'Yes,' he said. 'Of course.'

She looked back, suddenly, flashing her smile at him, and put a hand on one of his hands, where it lay on the sheet.

'But I wanted to talk to you about all sorts of other things,' she said. 'You really are a remarkable man, you know.'

'I am, am I?' he said, and summoned up a smile.

'You know you are,' she said. 'You've done everything just the way you said you would. You've won the war for Bakhalla, and done it all in just a few weeks with no one's help but the Dorsai troops. And now you're going to be a Dorsai yourself. There's nothing to stop you from writing your book now. It's all over.'

Pain touched his inner self – and the guarded distance closed back around him. He was once more alone among people who did not understand.

'I'm afraid not,' he said. 'It's not over. Only the first act's finished. Actually, now it really begins.'

She stared at him. 'Begins?' she echoed. 'But Dow's going back to Earth tonight. He won't be coming out here again.'

'I'm afraid he will,' said Cletus.

'He will? Why should he?'

'Because he's an ambitious man,' said Cletus, 'and because I'm going to show him how to further that ambition.'

'Ambition!' Her voice rang with disbelief. 'He's already one of the five Prime Secretaries of the Coalition Supreme Council. It's only a year or two, inevitably, until he'll get a seat on the Council itself. What else could he want? Look at what he's got already!'

'You don't quench ambition by feeding it any more than you quench a fire the same way,' said Cletus. 'To an ambitious man, what he already has is nothing. It's what he doesn't have that counts.'

'But what doesn't he have?' She was genuinely perplexed.

'Everything,' said Cletus. 'A united Earth, under him, controlling all the Outworlds, again under him.'

She stared at him. 'The Alliance and the Coalition combine?' she said. 'But that's impossible. No one knows that better than Dow.'

'I'm planning to prove to him it is possible,' said Cletus.

A little flush of anger colored her cheeks. 'You're planning—' She broke off. 'You must think I'm some kind of a fool, to sit and listen to this!'

'No,' he said, a little sadly, 'no more than anyone else. I'd just hoped that for once you'd take me on faith.'

'Take you on faith!' Suddenly, almost to her own surprise, she was blindingly furious. 'I was right when I first met you and I said you're just like Dad. Everybody thinks he's all leather and guns and nothing else, and the truth of the matter is, those things don't matter to him at all. Nearly everybody thinks you're all cold metal and calculation and no nerves. Well, let me tell you something – you don't fool everybody. You don't fool Dad, and you don't fool Arvid. Most of all, you don't fool me! It's people you care about, just like it's tradition Dad cares about – the tradition of honor and courage and truth and all those things nobody thinks we have any more. That's what they took away from him, back on Earth, and that's what I'm going to get back for him, when I get him back there, if I have to do it by main force – because he's just like you. He has to be made to take care of himself and get what he really wants.'

'Did you ever stop to think,' said Cletus, quietly, when she finished, 'that perhaps he's found tradition all over again on Dorsai?'

'Tradition? Dorsai?' Scorn put a jagged edge on her voice. 'A world full of a collection of ex-soldiers gambling their lives in other people's little wars for hardly more pay than a tool programmer gets! You can find tradition in that?'

'Tradition to come,' said Cletus. 'I think Eachan sees into the future further than you do, Melissa.'

'What do I care about the future?' She was on her feet now, looking down at him where he lay in the bed. 'I want him happy. He can take care of anyone but himself. *I* have to take care of him. When I was a little girl and my mother died she asked me – *me* – to be sure to take care of him. And I will.'

She whirled about and went toward the door. 'And he's all I'm going to take care of,' she cried, stopping and turning again at the door. 'If you think I'm going to take care of you, too, you've got another think coming! So go ahead, gamble yourself twice over on some high principle or another, when you could be settling down and doing some real good, writing and working, person to person, the way you're built to do!'

She went out. The door was too well engineered to slam behind her, but that was all that saved it from slamming.

Cletus lay back against his pillows and gazed at the empty, white and unresponsive wall opposite. The hospital room felt emptier than it had ever felt before.

He had still one more visitor, however, before the day was out. This was Dow deCastries, preceded into Cletus' hospital room by Wefer Linet.

'Look whom I've got with me, Cletus!' said Wefer, cheerfully. 'I ran into the Secretary here at the Officers' Club, where he was having lunch with some of the Exotics, and he told me to bring you his congratulations for abstract military excellence – as opposed to anything affecting the Neulander-Bakhalla situation. I asked him why he didn't come along and give you the congratulations himself. And here he is!'

He stepped aside and back, letting Dow come forward. Behind the taller man's back Wefer winked broadly at Cletus. 'Got to run an errand here in the hospital,' said Wefer. 'Back in a minute.'

He ducked out of the room, closing the door behind him. Dow looked at Cletus.

'Did you have to use Wefer as an excuse?' Cletus asked.

'He was convenient,' Dow shrugged, dismissing the matter. 'My congratulations, of course.'

'Of course,' said Cletus. 'Thank you. Sit down, why don't you?'

'I prefer standing,' said Dow. 'They tell me you're going off to bury yourself on Dorsai now. You'll be getting down to the writing of your books then?'

'Not just yet,' said Cletus.

Dow raised his eyebrows. 'There's something else for you to do?'

'There're half a dozen worlds and a few billion people to be freed first,' said Cletus.

'Free them?' Dow smiled. 'From the Coalition?'

'From Earth.'

Dow shook his head. His smile became ironic. 'I wish you luck,' he said. 'All this, in order to write a few volumes?'

Cletus said nothing. He sat upright in his bed, as if waiting. Dow's smile went away.

'You're quite right,' Dow said, in a different tone, though Cletus still had not spoken. 'Time is growing short, and I'm headed back to Earth this afternoon. Perhaps I'll see you there – say in six months?'

'I'm afraid not,' said Cletus. 'But I expect I'll see you out here – among the new worlds. Say, inside two years?'

Dow's black eyes grew cold. 'You badly misunderstand me, Cletus,' he said. 'I was never built to be a follower.'

'Neither was I,' said Cletus.

'Yes,' said Dow, slowly, 'I see. We probably will meet after all then' – his smile returned, suddenly and thinly – 'at Philippi.'

'There never was any other place we could meet,' said Cletus.

'I believe you're right. Fair enough,' said Dow. He stepped backward and opened the door. 'I'll wish you a good recovery with that leg of yours.'

'And you a safe trip to Earth,' said Cletus.

Dow turned and went out. Several minutes later the door opened again and Wefer's head appeared in the opening.

'DeCastries gone?' Wefer asked. 'He didn't take long at all then.'

'We said what we had to say,' answered Cletus. 'There wasn't much point in his staying, once we'd done that.'

17

Three days later, Mondar made his reappearance at Cletus' bedside.

'Well, Cletus,' he said, sitting down in the chair by the bed, 'I've spent most of my time since I saw you last going into your situation with other members of our group who've had more experience with certain aspects of what you suggested than I have. All together we worked out a pattern of behavior that looks as if it might give the greatest possible encouragement to the miracle you're after. The main question seemed to be whether it would be better for you to be intimately acquainted with the physiology of your knees, and the process of tissue growth and regrowth, or whether it would be better for you to have as little knowledge of it as possible.'

'What was the decision?' Cletus asked.

'We decided it would be best if you knew as little as possible,' Mondar said. 'The point is, the stimulus for what's going to be essentially an abnormal body reaction has to come from a very primitive level of the organism – you being the organism.'

'You don't want me visualizing what's going on then?'

'Just the opposite,' answered Mondar. 'You should remove your concern with the regrowth process as completely as possible from any symbolic area. Your determination to achieve regrowth must be channeled downward into the instinctive level. To achieve that channeling you're going to need practice, and so we worked up a set of exercises that I'm going to teach you to do over the next two weeks. I'll come here and work with you daily until you can do the exercises by yourself. Then I'll observe until I think you've got complete control in the necessary areas. Then we'll recommend the symbolic operation, in which the genetic pattern of your right knee will be transferred in the form of a few cells of tissue of flesh and bone to the area of the left knee, where we want regrowth to take place.'

'Good,' said Cletus. 'When do you want to start the exercises?'

'Right now, if you like,' answered Mondar. 'We start out by getting off the topic of your knees entirely and into some completely different area. Any suggestions for a topic?'

'The best one in the universe,' Cletus answered. 'I was intending to talk to you about it anyway. I'd like to borrow two million IMU's.'

Mondar gazed at him for a second, then smiled. 'I'm afraid I don't have that much with me,' he said. 'After all, out here away from Earth two million International Monetary Units are rather more scarce than they are back on Earth. Are you very urgent about your need for them?'

'Urgent and absolutely serious,' replied Cletus. 'I'd like you to talk to your fellow Exotics here in Bakhalla – and anywhere else, if necessary. I'm not wrong, am I, in thinking your organization could lend me that kind of money if you thought it was worthwhile?'

'Not wrong, no,' said Mondar, slowly. 'But you have to admit it's a rather unusual request from an essentially property-less ex-colonel in the Alliance forces who's now an emigrant to Dorsai. What do you plan doing with a sum of money like that?'

'Build an entirely new type of military unit,' Cletus answered. 'New in organization, training, hardware and tactical abilities.'

'Using,' said Mondar, 'the Dorsai mercenaries, of course?'

'That's right,' answered Cletus. 'I'm going to produce a fighting force at least five times as effective as any comparable military unit presently in existence. Such a force will be able to underbid not only the Alliance, but the Coalition, when it comes to supplying military force to an off-Earth colony such as yours. I can raise the pay of the men and officers in it and still market an effective force for less than even the Dorsai mercenaries were charging in the past – simply because we'll need fewer men to do the same job.'

'And you're suggesting,' Mondar said, thoughtfully, 'that such a mercenary force would soon pay back a two million loan?'

'I don't think there's any doubt of it,' said Cletus.

'Possibly not,' said Mondar, 'provided these new mercenaries of yours will do what you say they'll do. But how could anyone know that in advance? I'm afraid, Cletus, that our organization would need some kind of security before lending out such a very large amount of money.'

'Security,' said Cletus, 'is often unnecessary where the borrower's reputation is good.'

'Don't tell me you've borrowed two million IMU's on occasions before this?' Mondar raised his eyebrows quizzically.

'I was speaking of a military, not a financial, reputation,' Cletus said calmly. 'Your Exotics have just had the best possible proof of the military reputation in question. A small group of Dorsai mercenaries, single-handedly, have succeeded in doing what a very large and much better equipped Alliance force wasn't able to do – essentially destroy Neuland as a military power and win the local war for your colony. The conclusion to be drawn from that is that this colony of yours doesn't need the Alliance forces. It can protect itself perfectly adequately with its Dorsai mercenaries, alone. Am I right?'

'You certainly present a good argument,' said Mondar.

'The security for the loan, therefore,' said Cletus, 'is the best sort of security in the world. It's the literal security of this colony, guaranteed by the Dorsai mercenaries until the loan is paid back.'

'But what if … ah …' Mondar said, delicately, 'you Dorsais should default on your bargain? I don't mean to insult you, of course, but in matters like this all possibilities are going to have to be considered. If I don't bring up the question, someone else will. What if, after we'd lent you the money and you'd retrained your troops, you refused either to pay or to continue guaranteeing the security of this colony?'

'In that case,' said Cletus, spreading his hands on the sheet of the bed, 'who else would hire us? Successful mercenaries, like traders in any other goods, build their business on the basis of satisfied customers. If we took your money and then welshed on our agreement, what other colony would be willing to take a chance on us?'

Mondar nodded. 'A very good point,' he said. He sat for a moment, his gaze abstracted, as if he communed with himself in some secret corner of his brain. Then his eyes came back to Cletus.

'Very well,' he said. 'I'll convey your request for a loan to my fellow Exotics. That's as much as I can do, you realize. It'll take some little time for the matter to be considered, and I can't promise you any great hopes of success. As I said, it's a very large amount of IMU's you're asking to borrow, and there is, after all, no great reason why we should lend it.'

'Oh, I think there is,' said Cletus easily. 'If my estimate of you Exotics is correct, one of your eventual aims is to be completely independent of outside obligations – so that you can be free to work out your vision of the future without interference. The Alliance's military aid has been helpful to you, but it's also kept you under the Alliance's thumb. If you can buy security from mercenary soldiers without obligation, you'll have achieved a freedom that I think you all want very badly. A two million unit loan on good security is a small risk to take for the chance of gaining that freedom.'

He looked significantly at Mondar, Mondar shook his head slightly; there was a touch of admiration in his face.

'Cletus, Cletus,' said Mondar, 'what a waste it is, your not being an Exotic!' He sighed, and sat back in the chair. 'Well, I'll pass your request for a loan along. And now, I think it's time we got started with your exercises. Sit back and try to achieve that state of a floating sensation that you described to me. As you probably know, it's called a state of regression. I'm also putting myself now into such a state. Now, if you're ready, join me in concentration on that isolated pinpoint of life, that single sperm cell that was the first core and beginning of your consciousness. To that early and primitive consciousness, now, you must try to return.'

Three weeks later, healing well and with both legs stiffened by a walking cast about each knee, Cletus was swinging along on wrist-crutches with Arvid in the Bakhalla in-town terminal. They were headed toward the airbus that would lift them to that same shuttleboat landing pad on which Cletus had first set down on Kultis a couple of months before – the airbus being made necessary by new construction on the road to the pad, now that guerrilla activity had been halted.

As they passed the main lounge of the terminal, an Alliance officer stepped out in front of them. He was First Lieutenant Bill Athyer, and he was drunk – not drunk enough to stumble in his speech or his walk, but drunk enough to bar their way with an ugly light in his eye. Cletus halted. Arvid took half a step forward, opening his mouth, but Cletus stilled the young man with a hand on one massive arm.

'Leaving for Dorsai, are you, Colonel?' said Athyer, ignoring Arvid. 'Now that everything's nice and prettied up here, you're on your way?'

Cletus leaned on the crutches. Even bent over in this position, he had to look down to meet Athyer's bloodshot eyes.

'Thought so.' Athyer laughed. 'Well, sir, I didn't want to let you get away, sir, without thanking you. I might have gone up before a review board, if it hadn't been for you, sir. Thank you, sir.'

'That's all right, Lieutenant,' said Cletus.

'Yes, isn't it? Quite all right,' said Athyer. 'And I'm safely tucked away in a library instead of facing a reprimand and maybe losing one turn at an advance in grade. No danger of my getting out in the field where I might foul up again – or, who knows, might even make up for not being quite as smart as you up at Etter's Pass, sir.'

'Lieutenant . . .' Arvid began in a dangerous rumble.

'No,' said Cletus, still leaning on the crutches, 'let him talk.'

'Thank you, Colonel. Thank you, sir . . . Damn you, Colonel' – Athyer's voice broke suddenly, raw-throated – 'did your precious reputation mean so much to you that you had to bury me alive? At least you could've let me take my lumps fair and square, without any show-off kindness from you! Don't you know I'll never get another chance in the field now? Don't you know you've marked me for good? What am I supposed to do now, stuck in a library for the rest of my army life with nothing but books?'

'Try reading them!' Cletus made no attempt to hold his voice down. It carried clearly to the crowd that by now was listening, and the scorn in it was, for once in his life, cruel and unsparing. 'That way, you just might learn something about the handling of troops in combat ... Come along Arv.'

He swung his crutches out to one side and went around Athyer. Arvid followed. Behind them, as the crowd closed in about them once more, they heard Athyer's hoarse, pursuing shout:

'I'll read, all right!' it rang behind them. 'And I'll keep reading until I've got the goods on you – *Colonel!*'

18

Six months later, Cletus was not only successfully healed, but ready to begin upon the work he had anticipated, in emigrating to Dorsai.

Entering the last two miles of his fifteen-mile daily run, he leaned into the beginning of the long slope up the hill that would bring him back to the shore of Lake Athan across from the home of Eachan Khan on the outskirts of the town of Foralie, on that world known as Dorsai. His stride shortened, his breathing deepened, but aside from these changes there was no difference. He did not slacken speed.

It had been nearly five months now since the casts had been taken off his legs to reveal a perfectly healthy, regrown left knee. The local medical fraternity had been eager to keep him available for tests and study of the essential miracle that had occurred, but Cletus had other things to do. Within a week, tottering along on legs that had just begun to relearn how to walk, he took ship with Melissa and Eachan Khan for Dorsai. He had been here since, his engagement to Melissa an accepted fact, as a guest in Eachan's household, and the time from his arrival until now had been spent in unrelenting physical self-training.

The methods of that training were simple, and except in one respect, orthodox. Basically, he spent his days in walking, running, swimming and climbing. It was the climbing that provided the one unorthodox element to this routine, for Cletus had caused to be built, and continually added to since its construction, a sort of adult-sized jungle gym, a maze of steel pipes interconnected at different heights and angles that was now some thirty feet high, twenty feet wide and more than fifty feet long.

Cletus' day began now, six months after his departure from the hospital on Kultis, with a vertical climb, hands only and without pause, from the ground to the top of a rope suspended from a tree limb eighty feet above ground. Having reached the limb, he then moved a dozen feet farther out along its length, climbed down a shorter rope only fifty feet in length and set it swinging until the arc of his airborne travels

144

brought him close enough to the top bar of the jungle gym for him to catch hold. The next thirty minutes or so were spent in clambering through the jungle gym by routes that had grown increasingly complex and torturous as the gym had been extended and Cletus' physical condition had improved.

At the far end of the jungle gym, his morning's run – which, as has been said, was now fifteen miles – began. It was a run that began across country of a fairly level surface, but later led him among a variety of the steep hills and slopes that this mountainous territory provided. Here the altitude was eighty-four hundred feet above sea level, and the effect upon Cletus' red blood cell count and coronary artery size had been remarkable.

It ended with this long, steady uphill slope two miles in length. Just beyond the upper end of the slope, the ground dipped down again for about fifty yards among pine-like trees, and Cletus came to the edge of Lake Athan.

He did not even break stride as he approached the bank, but went off it in a shallow dive directly into the waters of the lake. He surfaced and began swimming the half-mile distance across the lake to the shore above which the long, low-roofed, rather rustic shape of Eachan's house could be seen, small among trees.

The water of this mountain lake was cold, but Cletus was not chilled by it. His body, heated by the run, found it pleasantly cool. He swam, as he had done all the rest of his exercise, dressed in running shoes, socks, shorts and shirt; he was by now so accustomed to the weight of these water-heavy shoes and clothes upon him that he did not notice them.

He swam powerfully, arms digging deep, his head rolling rhythmically toward his right shoulder to take deep breaths of the upland air. His feet churned a steady wake behind him. Almost before he had settled to the soothing rhythm of his swimming, he drove into the shallow water at the lake's other side and got to his feet.

He glanced at his wristwatch and trotted leisurely up the slope to the ground-floor sliding window that led directly into his bedroom. Ten minutes later, showered and changed, he joined Eachan and Melissa in the sunny dining room of the long house for lunch.

'How did you do?' asked Melissa. She smiled at him with a sudden, spontaneous warmth, and a warm current of shared feeling sprang into existence between them. Six months of close association had destroyed all obvious barriers separating them. Cletus was too likable and Melissa too outgoing for them not to be drawn together under such close conditions. They had reached the stage now where what they did not say to each other was almost more important than their words.

'Under six minutes average on the fifteen-mile run,' he answered. 'A little over ten minutes crossing the lake.' He looked over at Eachan. 'I think it's time to set up that demonstration I planned. We can use the running track in the stadium at Foralie.'

'I'll attend to it,' said Eachan.

Three days later the demonstration took place. Present in the Foralie stadium under a warm August sun were the eighty-odd ranking Dorsai officers whom Eachan had invited. They sat down front in one section of the stand before a large screen fed by a battery of physiological monitoring equipment tuned to various transmitters on and within Cletus' body.

Cletus was in his usual running outfit. Neither the jungle gym nor a pool for swimming was in evidence, since this was to be a simple demonstration of endurance. As soon as the visiting officers were all seated, Eachan stood by to monitor the reports of various instruments onto the screen so that all could see them, and Cletus started running.

The various mercenary officers present had all been made acquainted with Cletus' history, particularly the events on Kultis, and the near miraculous regrowth of his wounded knee. They watched with interest while Cletus set a pace of nearly ten miles an hour around the half-mile track. After the first mile, he dropped back to a little better than eight miles an hour; his pulse, which had peaked at 170, dropped to about 140 and hung there.

He was running quite easily and breathing steadily as he approached the four-mile mark. But then, although his speed did not decrease, his pulse began to climb once more, slowly, until by the end of the six miles it was almost up to 180. Here it peaked again, and from that point on he began slowly to lose speed. By the time he had completed the eighth mile he was down below seven miles an hour, and by the time he finished the ninth he was barely moving at six miles an hour.

Clearly, he was approaching the exhaustion point. He pushed himself twice more around the track. Coming up toward the end of the tenth mile, he was barely jogging. Clearly, he had run himself out; but this kind of performance by anyone, let alone a man who had been a prosthetic cripple half a standard year before, was enough to waken a hum of amazement and admiration from the watchers.

Some of them stood up in their seats, ready to step down into the field and congratulate Cletus as he trotted toward the conclusion of the tenth mile, which seemed obviously intended to be the end of the race.

'Just a minute, please, gentlemen,' Eachan Khan said, 'If you'll hold your seats a little longer ...'

He turned and nodded to Cletus, who was now passing the ten-mile mark directly in front of the viewers. Cletus nodded and kept on going.

Then, to the utter astonishment of the watchers, a remarkable thing happened. As Cletus continued around the track, his step became firmer and his breathing eased. He did not immediately pick up speed, but his pulse rate, as shown on the viewing screen, became slowly to fall.

At first it went down by ragged steps, dropping a few beats, holding firm, then dropping a few more. But as he continued, it began to drop more steadily. By the time he was back around in front of the watching officers, his pulse rate was again 150.

And his speed began to pick up. It did not pick up much; he gained back to just under six miles an hour. But he held steady at that pace, continuing to circle the track.

He ran six more laps of the track – three miles – and at the end of the third mile his speed and pulse rate were still constant.

At the end of that additional third mile he stopped running, walked a lap without any sign of unusual distress, and ended up in front of the watching group, breathing normally and hardly perspiring, with his pulse in the low seventies.

'That's it, gentlemen,' he said, addressing them all. 'Now I'm going to have to take a few moments to clean up, and the rest of you may adjourn to Eachan's house, where we'll be able to talk in more comfort and privacy. I'll join you there in about twenty minutes, and I'll leave you now to consider what you've just seen without any further explanation, except that what you've just seen me do, did, in fact, exact a penalty upon my bodily reserves greater than that ordinarily demanded by exertion. However, as you see, it was possible and practical, at that price.'

He turned away toward the dressing room at the near end of the stadium. The spectators moved outside to an airbus rented by Eachan, and were flown out to Eachan's house, where the window wall along one side of the long living room had been opened up so that the living room and the patio outside became one large gathering space. Food and drink had been provided, and there, a little later, Cletus joined them.

'As you know,' he said, standing facing them as they sat in a rough semicircle in chairs about him, 'all of you here were officers we invited because I hoped you might be interested in joining me in forming an entirely new military unit, a military unit I intend to command, and which would pay its officers and men only subsistence during a training period of some months, but which would thereafter pay them at least double the rate they had been receiving as mercenaries up until this time. It goes without saying that I want the cream of the crop, and that I expect that cream of the crop to invest not merely their time but their wholehearted enthusiasm in this new type of organization I have in mind.'

He paused. 'That was one of the reasons for the demonstration you've just seen,' he said. 'What you saw, in the crudest terms, was a demonstration in which I was at least half again as physically effective as my bodily energy level and conditioning would allow me to be. In short, I've just given you an example of how a man can make himself into a man and a half.'

He paused again, and this time he raked his eyes over every face in the audience before he continued.

'I am going to expect,' he said, slowly and emphatically, 'every enlisted man and officer in this military unit I'm forming to be able to multiply himself to at least that extent by the time he's finished training. This is a first prerequisite, gentlemen, to anyone wishing to join me in this venture.'

He smiled, unexpectedly. 'And now, relax and enjoy yourselves. Stroll around the place, look at my homemade training equipment, and ask as many questions as you like of Eachan, Melissa Khan or myself. We'll have another meeting out here in a few days time for those of you who have decided to join us. That's all.'

He stepped away from the center of their attention and made his way to the buffet tables where the food and drink had been set up. The gathering broke up into small groups and the hum of voices arose. By late afternoon most of the visitors had left, some twenty-six of them having pledged their services to Cletus before leaving. A somewhat larger number had promised to think it over and get in touch with him within the next two days. There remained a small group of those who had already pledged themselves to Cletus before the demonstration, and these met in the once more enclosed living room after dinner for a private conference.

Present were Arvid, now recovered from his shoulder wound, Major Swahili and Major David Ap Morgan, whose family was also a Foralie neighbor. Eachan's other officers were still back in Bakhalla commanding the force of Dorsais that remained there in Exotic pay to guard the colony, now that the Alliance had withdrawn its troops under Bat Traynor. Bat's misgivings about leaving had not been shared by

Alliance HQ back on Earth, which had been overjoyed to free nearly half a division of men to reinforce its hard-pressed military commitments on half a dozen other new worlds. In addition to Arvid, Ap Morgan, Swahili, and Eachan himself, were two old friends of Eachan's – a Colonel Lederle Dark and a Brigadier General Tosca Aras. Dark was a thin, bald man who seemed to be all bone and long muscle under a somewhat dandified exterior. Tosca Aras was a small, neat, clean-shaven man with washed-out blue eyes and a gaze as steady as an aimed field rifle in its gun mount.

'By the end of the week,' Cletus said to them all, 'anyone who hasn't made up his mind to join us won't be worth having. From those I talked to today, I estimate we'll get perhaps fifty good officers, perhaps ten of which we'll lose in training. So there's no point in wasting time. We can start setting up a table of organization and a training schedule. We'll train the officers, and they can train their men afterward.'

'Who's to be in charge of the extra energy training?' asked Lederle Dark.

'I'll have to be, to begin with,' Cletus answered him. 'Right now there's nobody else. And all of you will have to join the other officers in my classes on that. The rest of it you can all handle by yourselves – it's simply a matter of running them through the physical and practicing standard field problems, but from the viewpoint of the new organizational setup.'

'Sir,' said Arvid, 'excuse me, but I still don't seem to really understand why we need to shake up the whole table of organization – unless you want it different just so the men in this outfit will feel that much more different.'

'No – though the feeling of difference isn't going to do us any harm,' Cletus said. 'I should have gone into this with all of you before now. The plain fact of the matter is that a military body structured into squads, platoons, companies, battalions and so on is designed to fight the type of war that used to be common but which we aren't going to be encountering out here on the new worlds. Our fighting units are going to bear more resemblance to a group of athletes in a team sport than they are to the old type of fighting unit. The tactics they're going to be using – my tactics – aren't designed for structured armies in solid confrontation with each other. Instead, they're designed to be useful to what seems to be a loose group of almost independently acting units, the efforts of which are coordinated not so much by a hierarchy of command as by the fact that, like good members of a team, they're familiar with each other and can anticipate what their teammates will do in response to their own actions and the general situation.'

Cletus paused and looked around him. 'Are there any of the rest of you who don't understand that?' he asked.

Eachan cleared his throat. 'We all understand what you say, Cletus,' he said. 'But what the words are going to mean when they're turned into battle units is something we've got to see before it'll make much sense. Here you cut the squad to six men – and that's divided into two teams of three men each. You make four squads to a group, with a senior or junior groupman in charge, and two groups make up a force. It's plain enough, but how's anyone going to know how it'll work until they see it in practice?'

'They aren't. You aren't – of course,' answered Cletus. 'But what you can do now is absorb the theory of it, and the reasoning behind the theory. Shall I go over it again?'

There was a moment of silence.

'Probably better,' said Eachan.

'All right then,' said Cletus. 'As I think I've told you all, the basic principle is that, from the individual right up to the largest organizations within the total Dorsai military command, each unit should be capable of reacting like a single member of a team made up of other members equal in size and importance to himself. That is, any one of the three soldiers in any given half squad should be able to operate in perfect unison with the other two members of his team with no more communication than a few code words or signals that would cue the others to standard actions or responses to any given situation. Similarly, the two teams in any squad should be able to work as partners with no more than a few code words or signals. Likewise, the four squads should be able to operate as a team in the group with each squad knowing its role in any one of a hundred or more group actions identifiable by code word or signal. Just as the two groups must be able to react together almost instinctively as a single command, the commandant of which should likewise be trained to react in pattern with the commandants of the commands with which he is associated.'

Cletus stopped talking. Once more there was the small silence.

'You say you'll supply the patterns?' Tosca Aras said. 'I mean you'll work out all these team actions that are triggered by code words and signals and so forth?'

'I already have them worked out,' said Cletus.

'You have?' Aras' voice teetered on the edge of incredulity. 'There must be thousands of them.'

Cletus shook his head. 'Something over twenty-three thousand, to be exact,' he said. 'But I think you may be missing the point. The actions of a team are included within the actions of the squad, just as the actions of the squad are included within the actions of the group. In short, it's like a language with twenty-three thousand words. There are innumerable combinations, but there's also a logical structure. Once you master the structure, then the choice of words within the sentence is severely restricted. In fact, there's only one ideal choice.'

'Then why have such a complicated setup anyway?' asked David Ap Morgan.

Cletus turned to look at the young major. 'The value of the system,' he said, 'doesn't come so much from the fact that there are a large number of combinations of tactical actions ranging from the team on up through the command, but from the fact that any large choice of action implies a certain spectrum of choices of action for the lesser elements of the command, so that the individual soldier, on hearing the general code word for the command to which he belongs, knows immediately within what limits the actions of all the groups, all the squads and his own team must be.'

He paused. 'In short,' he said, 'no one, right up through the battle operator or the commander of the total military unit, simply follows orders. Instead, they all – right down to the individual line soldier – react as a team member in a common effort. The result is that breaks in the chain of command, misunderstood or incorrect orders, and all the other things that go to mess up a battle plan by mischance, are bypassed. Not only that, but from the lowest ranks on up each subordinate is ready to step into the position of his superior with 90 per cent of the necessary knowledge that his superior had at the moment the superior was put out of action.'

Arvid gave a low whistle of admiration. The other officers in the room all looked at him. With the exception of Cletus, he was the only one among them who had never been a practicing Dorsai field officer. Arvid looked embarrassed.

'A revolutionary concept,' said Tosca Aras. 'More than revolutionary if it works out in practice.'

'It's going to have to work,' said Cletus. 'My whole scheme of strategy and tactics is based upon troops that can operate along those lines.'

'Well, we'll see,' Aras picked up the thick manual Cletus had issued to each of them just after dinner and which had been lying since then in his lap. He stood up. 'An old dog learning new tricks is an understatement in my case. If the rest of you gentlemen don't mind, I'll be getting to my homework.'

He said good night and went out, starting a general exodus. Eachan stayed behind, and Arvid – Arvid, to apologize for that whistle.

'You see, sir,' he said earnestly to Cletus, 'it suddenly came clear to me, all of a sudden. I hadn't seen it before. But now I see how it all ties together.'

'Good,' said Cletus. 'That's half the learning process done for you right there.'

Arvid followed the others out of the living room. Eachan alone was left. Cletus looked at him.

'Do *you* see how it all hangs together?' Cletus asked him.

'Think so,' said Eachan. 'But remember, I've been living with you for the last half year – and I know most of the patterns in that manual of yours already.'

He reached for the decanter behind the glasses ranked on the small table beside his chair and thoughtfully poured himself a small amount of whiskey.

'Shouldn't expect too much too soon,' he said, sipping at it. 'Any military man's bound to be a bit conservative. In the nature of us. But they'll come through, Cletus. It's beginning to be more than just a name with us here, this business of being Dorsais.'

He turned out to be correct. By the time the officers' training program got under way a week later, all of those who had sat in the living room with Cletus that night knew their manuals by heart – if not yet quite by instinct. Cletus divided the officers to be trained among the six of them, in groups of roughly ten each, and training began.

Cletus took the class that he had labeled simply "Relaxation," the course that would train these officers to tap that extra source of energy he had demonstrated to them all at the Foralie stadium after running himself to the normal exhaustion point. His first class consisted of the six from the living room. Eachan was among them, although he already had more than a faint grasp of the technique involved. Cletus had been privately tutoring both him and Melissa in it for the past couple of months, and both had become noticeably capable with it. However, it was Eachan's suggestion – and Cletus found it a good one – that his inclusion in the class would be an example to the others that someone besides Cletus could achieve unusual physiological results.

Cletus began his class just before lunch, after they had completed the full day's physical training schedule, consisting of jungle gym, run and swim. They were physically unwound by the exercise, and more than a little empty because of the long hours since breakfast. In short, they were in a condition of maximum receptivity.

Cletus lined them up behind a long steel bar supported between two posts at about shoulder height off the ground.

'All right,' he said to them. 'Now I want you all to stand on your right legs. You can reach out and touch the bar in front of you with your fingertips to help keep your balance, but take your left feet off the ground and keep them off until I tell you can put them down again.'

They complied. Their pose was a little on the ridiculous side, and there were a few smiles at first, but these faded as the legs on which they stood began to tire. About the time when bearing all their weight upon the muscle of one leg was beginning to become actively painful, Cletus ordered them to switch legs and kept them standing with all their weight on their left legs until the muscles of calf and thigh began to tremble under their full body weight. Then he switched them back to the right leg and then again to the left, shortening the intervals each time at the leg muscles became exhausted more quickly. Very shortly they stood before him on legs as uncertain as those of men who had been bedridden for a period of weeks.

'All right, now,' Cletus said then, cheerfully, 'I want you all up in a handstand, the palms of your hands on the ground, your arms fully extended. You can balance yourselves this time by letting your legs rest against the bar.'

They obeyed. Once they were all up, Cletus gave them a further order.

'Now,' he said, 'one hand off the ground. Do your handstand on one arm only.'

When they were upside down, he went through the same process he had when they had been right side up. Only it took their arms a fraction of the time it had taken their legs to tire. Very shortly he released them from their exercise, and they all tumbled to the ground, virtually incapacitated in all their limbs.

'On your backs,' ordered Cletus. 'Legs straight out, arms at your sides – but you don't have to lie at attention. Just straighten out on your back comfortably. Eyes on the sky.'

They obeyed.

'Now,' said Cletus, pacing slowly up and down before them, 'I want you just to lie there and relax while I talk to you. Watch the sky ...' It was one of those high, bright blue skies with a few clouds drifting lazily across it. 'Concentrate on the feeling in your arms and legs, now that they've been relieved from the load of supporting your bodies against the force of gravity. Be conscious of the fact that now it's the ground supporting you – and them – and be grateful for it. Feel how heavy and limp your arms and legs are, now that they've given up the work of bearing weight, and are themselves being borne by the surface of the ground. Tell yourself – not out loud – in your own words how limp and heavy they are. Keep telling yourself that and watching the sky. Feel how heavy and relaxed your body is, with its weight being supported by the ground beneath your back. Feel the relaxation in your neck, in the muscles of your jaw, in your face, even in your scalp. Tell yourself how relaxed and heavy all these parts of you are and keep watching the sky. I'll be going on talking, but pay no attention to me. Just give all our attention to what you're telling yourself and what you're feeling and how the sky looks …'

He continued to pace up and down talking. After a while, the arm- and leg-weary men, soothed by their relaxed position and the slow movement of the clouds, lulled by the steady, pleasant, monotonous sound of his voice, ceased in fact to pay any attention to the sense of his words. He was merely talking. To Arvid, at one end of the line, Cletus' voice seemed to have gone off and become as remote as everything else about him. Lying on his back, Arvid saw nothing but sky. It was as if the planet beneath him did not exist, except as a soft grassy pressure at his back, bearing him up. The clouds moved slowly in the endless blue, and he seemed to drift along with them.

A nudge at his feet brought him suddenly and sharply back to consciousness. Cletus was smiling down at him.

'All right,' Cletus said, in the same steady low tone, 'on your feet and step over there.'

Arvid obeyed, getting heavily upright once more, and moving off, as Cletus had indicated, about a dozen feet. The rest were still on the ground, with Cletus talking to them. Then he saw Cletus, who was still pacing, pause at the feet of David Ap Morgan and nudge the sole of David's right foot with his toe.

'All right, David,' Cletus said, without breaking the pace or tone of his talking, 'up you get and join Arvid over there.'

David's eyes, which had been closed, jerked open. He got to his feet and went over to stand by Arvid. As the two of them watched, one by one other members of the class went to sleep and were quietly wakened and weeded out until no one but Eachan still lay on the grass, his eyes wide open.

Cletus abruptly ended his talking with a chuckle. 'All right, Eachan,' he said. 'There's no point in my trying to put you to sleep. You get up and join the others.'

Eachan rose. On their feet and all together once more, the class looked at Cletus.

'The idea,' said Cletus, with a smile, 'is *not* to fall asleep. But we won't worry about that for a while yet. How many of you remember feeling any kind of a floating sensation before you did drop off?'

Arvid and three others raised their hands. Eachan was one of them.

'Well, that's it for today,' Cletus said. 'Tomorrow we'll try it without the muscle-tiring exercises first. But I want you all to go back to your quarters and try doing this again, by yourself, at least three times before tomorrow morning. If you like, you can try putting yourself to sleep tonight with it. We'll gather together here again tomorrow, at this same place at the same time.'

In the next few sessions Cletus worked with the class until all of them could achieve the floating sensation without drifting off into sleep. With this accomplished, he led them by easy stages into autocontrol of pain and deep bodily sensations. When they had become fairly adept at this, he began to move them gradually from a relaxed and motionless position into movement – first getting them to achieve the floating sensation while standing upright, then when walking slowly and rhythmically forward, and finally under any kind of activity up to the most violent. This achieved, there remained for them only the ability to make use of the trance state in various types of autocontrol under all conditions of activity, and he turned them loose to become teachers, in their turn to the other officers in training – who would, again, pass on the training to the enlisted men under their command.

By this time nearly three months had gone by, and the officers in training had advanced to the point where they could begin to pass on at least the physical end of their training to the troops that would be under their orders. Recruitment was started for Dorsais to fill the enlisted ranks – and for some few extra Dorsai officers to replace those who had dropped out of the training program.

Just at this time Cletus received a thick envelope of clippings sent him by a news-clipping service on Earth he had contacted before leaving Bakhalla. He opened the envelope, alone in Eachan's study, and spread the clippings out in order of their dates to examine them.

The story they told was simple enough. The Coalition, sparked by a few key speeches by Dow deCastries himself, was attempting to raise a storm of protest against mercenary troops on the new worlds in general, and the Dorsais in particular.

Cletus replaced the clippings in their envelope and filed them in the cabinet holding his own correspondence. He went out on the terrace to find Melissa there reading.

It was high summer in these Dorsai mountains, and the sun was in late afternoon position above the farther peaks. He paused for a moment, watching her as she sat unsuspecting that he watched. In the clear sunlight, her face was untroubled, and somehow more mature-looking than he remembered it back at Bakhalla.

He went out onto the terrace and she looked up from her reading spool at the sound of his feet. He caught her gaze with his own, and her eyes widened a little at the seriousness with which he stood looking down at her. After a minute he spoke.

'Will you marry me, Melissa?' he said.

The blueness of her eyes was as deep as the universe itself. Once again, as it had in the hospital in Bakhalla, her gaze seemed to evaporate the barrier of protective loneliness that his experience with life and people had led him to build about him. She looked up at him for a long moment before answering.

'If you really want me, Cletus,' she said.

'I do,' he replied.

And he did not lie. But, as the protective barrier flowed once more into position about his inner self, even as he continued to match her gaze with his, a cold interior part of his mind reminded him of the necessity that there would be now to lie, hereafter.

19

The wedding was set for a day two weeks away. Meanwhile, Cletus, seeing the formation of the force he had begun to raise on Dorsai now beginning to operate under its own momentum, took time out for a trip back to Kultis and Bakhalla for a conversation with Mondar, and a further trip to Newton seeking employment for the newly trained Dorsais of his command.

On Bakhalla, he and Mondar had an excellent dinner at Mondar's residence. Over the dinner table Cletus brought the Exotic up to date. Mondar listened with interest, which increased visibly when Cletus got into the matter of the special training in autocontrol he had initiated for the officers and men who would be under his command. After the dinner was over, they strolled out onto one of the many terraces of Mondar's home to continue their talk under the night sky.

'And there,' said Cletus, as they stood in the warm night breeze, looking upward. He pointed at a yellowish star low on the horizon. 'That'll be your sister world, Mara. I understand you Exotics have quite a colony there, too.'

'Oh, yes,' answered Mondar thoughtfully, gazing at the star.

'A pity,' said Cletus, turning to him, 'that they aren't as free there from Alliance and Coalition influence as you've been here on Kultis since the Neulanders were taken care of.'

Mondar withdrew his eyes from the star, turned himself to face Cletus and smiled. 'You're suggesting we Exotics hire your new battle unit to drive out the Alliance and Coalition forces?' he said, humor in his voice. 'Cletus, we've strained our financial resources for you already. Besides, it's counter to our general philosophy to contemplate deliberate conquest of other peoples or territories. You shouldn't suggest it to us.'

'I don't,' said Cletus. 'I only suggest you contemplate the building of a core-tap power station at the Maran North Pole.'

Mondar gazed through the darkness at Cletus for a moment without speaking. 'A core-tap power station?' he echoed at last, slowly. 'Cletus, what new subtlety are you working at now?'

'Hardly a subtlety,' replied Cletus. 'It's more a matter of taking a square look at the facts on Mara, economic and otherwise. The Alliance and the Coalition are both still stretched to their economic limits to maintain their influence with various colonies on all the new worlds. They may have lost ground here. But they're both strong on Mara, on Freiland and New Earth under Sirius, on Newton and Cassida, and even to a certain extent on the younger old worlds of the solar system – Mars and Venus. In fact, you might say they're both overextended. Sooner or later they're bound to crack – and the one that's liable to crack first, because it's invested more of its wealth and manpower in influencing new world colonies than the Coalition has, is the Alliance. Now, if either the Alliance or the Coalition goes under, the one that's left is going to take over all the influence that the other formerly had. Instead of two large octopi, with their tentacles into everything on the new worlds, they'll be one extra-large octopus. You don't want that.'

'No,' murmured Mondar.

'Then it's plainly in your interests to see that, on some place like Mara, neither the Alliance nor the Coalition gets the upper hand,' said Cletus. 'After we took care of Neuland, and you invited the Alliance forces out, the personnel the Alliance had here were taken away and spread out generally – plugged in any place the Alliance seemed in danger of springing a leak in confrontation with the Coalition. The Coalition, on the other hand, took its people in Neuland – of which, granted, there weren't as many as there were of Alliance people, but it was a fair number – and simply shifted them over to Mara. The result is that the Coalition is headed toward getting the upper hand over the Alliance on Mara.'

'So you're suggesting we hire some of these newly trained Dorsais of yours to do on Mara what you did here?' Mondar smiled at him, a little quizzically. 'Didn't I just say that philosophically we Exotics consider it inadvisable to improve our position by conquest – or any violent means, for that matter. Empires built by force of arms are built on sand, Cletus.'

'In that case,' said Cletus, 'the sand under the Roman Empire must have been most solidly packed. However, I'm not suggesting any such thing. I'm merely suggesting that you build the power plant. Your Exotic colony of Mara occupies the subtropical belt across the one large continent there. With a core-tap power station at the North Pole, you not only extend your influence into the essentially unclaimed sub-arctic regions there, you'll be able to sell power to all the small, independent, temperate-zoned colonies lying between Mara and the station. Your conquest on that planet, if any, will be by purely peaceful and economic means.'

'Those small colonies you refer to,' said Mondar, his head a little on one side, watching Cletus out of the corners of his blue eyes, 'are all under Coalition influence.'

'All the better,' said Cletus. 'The Coalition can't afford very well to drill them a competing core-tap power plant.'

'And how are we going to afford it?' Mondar asked. He shook his head. 'Cletus, Cletus, I think you must believe that our Exotic peoples are made of money.'

'Not at all,' Cletus said. 'There's no need for you to put yourself to any more immediate expense than that for the basic labor force required to set up the plant. It ought to be possible for you to set up an agreement for a lease-purchase on the equipment itself, and the specially trained people required to set up the plant.'

'Where?' asked Mondar. 'With the Alliance? Or the Coalition?'

'Neither,' said Cletus, promptly. 'You seem to forget there's one other colonial group out here on the new worlds that's proved itself prosperous.'

'You mean the scientific colonies on Newton?' said Mondar. 'They're at the extreme end of the philosophical spectrum from us. They favor a tight society having as little contact with outsiders as possible. We prize individualism above anything else, and our whole purpose of existence is the concern with the total human race. I'm afraid there's a natural antipathy between the Newtonians and us.' Mondar sighed slightly. 'I agree we should find a way around such emotional barriers between us and other human beings. Nonetheless, the barrier's there – and in any case, the Newtonians aren't any better off financially than we are. Why should they extend us credit, equipment and the services of highly trained people – as if they were the Alliance itself?'

'Because eventually such a power station can pay back their investment with an excellent profit – by the time the lease expires and you purchase their interest in it back from them,' said Cletus.

'No doubt,' said Mondar. 'But the investment's still too large and too long-ranged for people in their position. A man of modest income doesn't suddenly speculate on distant and risky ventures. He leaves that to richer men, who can afford the possible loss – unless he's a fool. And those Newtonians, whatever else they are, aren't fools. They wouldn't even listen.'

'They might,' said Cletus, 'if the proposition was put to them in the proper manner. I was thinking I might say a word to them myself about it – if you want to authorize me to do that, that is. I'm on my way there now, to see if they might not want to hire some of our newly trained Dorsai troops.'

Mondar gazed at him for a second; the Exotic's eyes narrowed. 'I'm utterly convinced, myself,' he said, 'that there's no chance in the universe of your persuading them to anything like this. However, we'd stand to gain a great deal by it, and I don't see how we could possibly lose anything by your trying. If you like, I'll speak to my fellow Exotics – both about the project and about your approaching the Newtonians for equipment and experts to put it in.'

'Fine. Do that,' said Cletus. He turned back toward the house. 'I imagine I should start folding up, then. I want to inspect the Dorsai troops in the regiment you've got here now, and set up some kind of rotation system so that we can move them back by segments to Dorsai for the new training. I want to be on my way to Newton by the end of the week.'

'I should have our answer for you by that time,' said Mondar, following him in. He glanced curiously at Cletus as they moved into the house side by side. 'I must say I don't see what you stand to gain by it, however.'

'I don't, directly,' Cletus answered. 'Nor do the Dorsais – *we* Dorsais, I have to get used to saying. But didn't you say something to me once about how anything that moved mankind as a whole onward and upward also moved you and your people toward their long-term goal?'

'You're interested in our long-term goal now?' Mondar asked.

'No. In my own,' said Cletus. 'But in this case it amounts to the same thing, here and there.'

He spent the next five days in Bakhalla briefing the Dorsai officers on his training program back on Dorsai. He invited those who wished to return and take it, along with those of their enlisted men who wished the same thing, and he left them with a sample plan for rotation of troops to that end – a plan in which his own trained men on Dorsai would fill in for those of the Bakhallan troops that wished to take the training, collecting the pay of those they replaced for the training period.

The response from the Dorsais in Bakhalla was enthusiastic. Most of the men there had known Cletus at the time of the victory over Neuland. Therefore, Cletus was able to extend the value of the loan he had made from the Exotics, since he did not have to find jobs immediately for those Dorsais he had already trained, but could use them several times over as replacements for other men wishing to take the training. Meanwhile, he was continually building up the number of Dorsais who had been trained to his own purposes.

At the end of the week, he took ship for Newton, bearing credentials from the Exotics to discuss the matter of a core-tap power station on Mara with the Newtonian Governing Board as an ancillary topic to his own search for employment for his Dorsais.

Correspondence with the board had obtained for him an appointment with the chairman of the board within a day of his arrival in Baille, largest city and de facto capital of the Advanced Associated Communities – as the combined colonies of technical and scientific emigrants to Newton had chosen to call themselves. The chairman was a slim, nearly bald, youthful-faced man in his fifties by the name of Artur Walco. He met with Cletus in a large, clean, if somewhat sterile, office in a tall building as modern as any on Earth.

'I'm not sure what we have to talk about, Colonel,' Walco said when they were both seated on opposite sides of a completely clean desk showing nothing but a panel of controls in its center. 'The AAC is enjoying good relationships currently with all the more backward colonies of this world.'

It was a conversational opening gambit as standard as king's pawn to king's pawn four in chess. Cletus smiled.

'My information was wrong, then?' he said, pushing his chair back from the desk and beginning to stand up. 'Forgive me. I—'

'No, no. Sit down. Please sit down!' said Walco, hastily. 'After you've come all the way here, the least I can do is listen to what you wanted to tell me.'

'But if there's no need your hearing ...' Cletus was insisting, when Walco once more cut him short with a wave of his hand.

'I insist. Sit down, Colonel. Tell me about it,' he said. 'As I say, there's no need for your mercenaries here at the moment. But any open-minded man knows that nothing's impossible in the long run. Besides, your correspondence intrigued us. You claim you've made your mercenaries more efficient. To tell you the truth, I don't understand how individual efficiency can make much difference in a military unit under modern conditions of warfare. What if your single soldier *is* more efficient?' He's still just so much cannon fodder, isn't he?'

'Not always,' said Cletus. 'Sometimes he's a man behind the cannon. To mercenaries, particularly, that difference is critical, and therefore an increase in efficiency becomes critical too.'

'Oh? How so?' Walco raised his still-black, narrow eyebrows.

'Because mercenaries aren't in business to get themselves killed,' said Cletus. 'They're in business to win military objectives *without* getting themselves killed. The fewer casualties, the greater profit – both to the mercenary soldier and to his employer.'

'How, to his employer?' Walco's eyes were sharp.

'An employer of mercenaries,' Cletus answered, 'is in the position of any businessman faced with a job that needs to be done. If the cost of having it done equals or exceeds the possible profit to be made from it, the businessman is better off leaving the job undone. On the other hand, if the cost of having it done is less than the benefit or profit to be gained, then having the work accomplished is a practical decision. The point I'm making is that, with more efficient mercenary troops, military actions which were not profitable to those wishing them accomplished now become practical. Suppose, for example, there was a disputed piece of territory with some such valuable natural resource as stibnite mines—'

'Like the Broza Colony stibnite mines the Brozans stole from us,' shot out Walco.

Cletus nodded. 'It's the sort of situation I was about to mention,' he said. 'Here we have a case of some very valuable mines out in the middle of swamp and forest stretching for hundreds of miles in every direction without a decent city to be found, worked and held onto by a backward colony of hunters, trappers and farmers. A colony, though, that is in possession of the mines by military forces supplied by the Coalition – that same Coalition which takes its cut of the high prices you pay the Brozans for the antimony extracted from the stibnite.'

Cletus stopped speaking and looked meaningfully at Walco. Walco's face had darkened.

'Those mines were discovered by us and developed by us on land we'd bought from Broza Colony,' he said. 'The Coalition didn't even bother to hide the fact that they'd instigated the Brozans' expropriation of them. It was piracy, literal piracy.' Walco's jaw muscles tightened. His eyes met Cletus' across the desk top. 'You picked an interesting example,' he said. 'As a matter of theoretical interest, suppose we do go into the matter of expense, and the savings to be gained by the efficiency of your Dorsais in this one instance.'

A week later, Cletus was on his way back to Dorsai with a contract for the three months' hire of two thousand men and officers. He stopped at Bakhalla on Kultis on the way back to inform the Exotics that their loan was already promising to pay off.

'Congratulations,' said Mondar. 'Walco has a reputation of being one of the hardest men on any world to deal with. Did you have much trouble persuading him?'

'There was no persuading involved,' answered Cletus. 'I studied the situation on Newton for a point of grievance before I first wrote him. The stibnite mines, which are essentially Newton's only native source of antimony, seemed ideal. So, in my correspondence after that I dwelt upon all those aspects and advantages of our troops under this new training, which would apply to just such a situation – but without even mentioning the Brozan stibnite mines by name. Of course, he could hardly help apply the information I gave him to that situation. I think he was determined to hire us to recover the mines even before he met me. If I hadn't brought up the subject, he would have.'

Mondar shook his head with a slow smile of admiration. 'Did you take advantage of his good humor to ask him to consider the Maran core-tap plan?'

'Yes,' said Cletus. 'You'll have to send a representative to sign the actual papers, but I think you'll find he'll be falling over himself in his eagerness to sign the agreement.'

The smile vanished from Mondar's face. 'You mean he's seriously interested?' Mondar demanded. 'He's interested in a situation in which they'd put up that kind of equipment and professional services simply in return for a long-term financial gain?'

'He's not merely interested,' said Cletus. 'You'll find he's pretty well determined not to let the chance get away, no matter what. You should be able to write your own terms.'

'I can't believe it!' Mondar stared at him. 'How in the name of eternity did you get him into such a favorable mood?'

'There wasn't any real problem,' said Cletus. 'As you say, the man's a hard bargainer – but only when he's bargaining from a position of strength. I began, after our talk about the Dorsais was done, by just dropping the hint that I was on my way to Earth, where I had family connections who'd help me in getting Alliance funds to help you set up the Maran core-tap. He was interested, of course – I think, at first, more in the prospect in getting some such sort of Alliance aid for Newton. But then I happened to dwell on some of the financial benefits the Alliance would receive in the long run in return for their help, and that seemed to start him thinking.'

'Yes,' murmured Mondar, 'the Newtonian appetite for credit is real enough.'

'Exactly,' Cletus said. 'Once he showed that appetite, I knew I had him hooked. I kept drawing him on until he, himself, suggested his Advanced Associated Communities might possibly be interested in putting up a small share themselves – perhaps supply 20 per cent of the equipment, or an equivalent amount of the trained personnel, in return for no more than a five-year mortgage on property here on Bakhalla.'

'He did?' Mondar's face became thoughtful. 'It's a steep price, of course, but considering our chances of actually getting Alliance money are practically nonexistent—'

'Just what I told him,' interrupted Cletus. 'The price was so steep as to be ridiculous. In fact, I laughed in his face.'

'You did?' Mondar's gaze sharpened. 'Cletus, that wasn't wise. An offer like that from a chairman of the board on Newton—'

'Is hardly realistic, as I frankly told him,' said Cletus. 'I wasn't likely to put myself in the position of carrying an offer from them to you that was penurious to the point of insult. After all, as I told him, I had an obligation to my Dorsais to maintain good relationships with the governments of *all* independent new worlds colonies – and on second thought, I'd even begun to feel a little doubtful that I ought to have mentioned the matter to him in any case. After all, I'd only been given authority to speak to my relatives and contacts back on Earth.'

'And he stood for that?' Mondar stared at Cletus.

'He not only stood for it,' said Cletus, 'he didn't waste any time in apologizing and amending his offer to a more realistic level. However, as I told him, by this time I was beginning to feel a little bit unsure about the whole business where he was concerned. But he kept on raising his offer until he was willing to supply the entire amount of necessary equipment, plus as many trained people as necessary to drill the core-tap and get it into operation as a power source. I finally agreed – reluctantly – to bring that offer back to you before going on to Earth.'

'Cletus!' Mondar's eyes were alight. 'You did it!'

'Not really,' said Cletus. 'There was still that matter of the Newtonians requiring Bakhalla property as security in addition to a mortgage on the core-tap itself. I was due to leave the next day, so early that morning, before I left, I sent him a message saying I'd thought it over during the night and, since there was absolutely no doubt that the Alliance would be happy to finance the project with a mortgage merely on the basis of the core-tap mortgage alone, I'd decided to disregard his offer after all and go directly on to Earth.'

Mondar breathed out slowly. 'With that much of an offer from him already in your hands,' he said – and from anyone but an Exotic the tone of the words would have been bitter – 'you had to gamble on a bluff like that!'

'There wasn't any gamble involved,' said Cletus. 'By this time the man had talked himself into buying a piece of the project at any cost. I believe I could even have gotten more from him if I hadn't already implied the limits of what the Alliance would do. So, it's just a matter of your sending someone to sign the papers.'

'You can count on that. We won't waste time,' answered Mondar. He shook his head. 'We'll owe you a favor for this, Cletus. I suppose you know that.'

'The thought would be a strange one to overlook,' said Cletus, soberly. 'But I'm hoping Exotics and Dorsais have stronger grounds for mutual assistance in the long run than just a pattern of reciprocal favors.'

He returned to Dorsai, eight days later, ship's-time, to find the three thousand men, about whom he had messaged from Newton, already mobilized and ready to embark. Of these, only some five hundred were new-trained Dorsais. The other twenty-five hundred were good solid mercenary troops from the planet, but as yet lacking in Cletus' specialized training. However, that fact did not matter; since the untrained twenty-five hundred would be essentially, according to Cletus' plans, along only for the ride.

Meanwhile, before he left with them for Newton in three days' time, there was his marriage to Melissa to accomplish. The negotiations at Bakhalla and on Newton had delayed him. As a result, he arrived – having messaged ahead that he would be there in time for the ceremony if he had to hijack an atmosphere ship to make it – less than forty-five minutes short of the appointed hour – all this, only to find the first news to greet him was that perhaps all his hurry had been needless.

'She says she's changed her mind, that's all,' Eachan Khan said to Cletus, low-voiced, in the privacy of the shadowed dining room. Over Eachan's stiff shoulders Cletus could see, some thirty feet away, the chaplain of his regiment of new-trained Dorsais, along with the other guests, eating and drinking in light-hearted ignorance of the sudden, drastic change in plans. The gathering was made up of old, fast friends of Eachan and new, but equally fast, friends and officers of Cletus. Among the mercenaries, loyalties were apt to be hard-won, but once won, unshakable. Those who were friends of Cletus outnumbered those of Eachan by more than two to one. Cletus had set up the invitation list that way.

'She says there's something wrong,' said Eachan, helplessly, 'and she has to see you. I don't understand her. I used to understand her, before deCastries—' He broke off. His shoulders sagged under the jacket of his dress uniform. 'But not any more.'

'Where is she?' asked Cletus.

'In the garden. The end of the garden, down beyond the bushes in the summer house,' said Eachan.

Cletus turned and went out one of the French doors of the dining room toward the garden. Once he was out of sight of Eachan, he circled around to the parking area and the rented car he had flown out here from Foralie.

Opening the car, he got out his luggage case and opened it. Inside were his weapon belt and sidearm. He strapped the belt around his waist, discarding the weather flap that normally protected the polished butt of the sidearm. Then he turned back toward the garden.

He found her where Eachan had said. She was standing in the summer house with her back to him, her hands on the white railing before her, looking through a screen of bushes at the far ridge of the surrounding mountains. At the sound of his boots on the wooden floor of the summer house, she turned to face him.

'Cletus!' she said. Her face was quite normal in color and expression, although her lips were somewhat firm. 'Dad told you?'

'Yes,' he answered, stopping in front of her. 'You should be inside getting ready. As it is we're going to have to go ahead just the way we are.'

Her eyes widened slightly. A look of uncertainty crept into them. 'Go ahead?' she echoed. 'Cletus, haven't you been up to the house? I thought you said you'd already talked to Dad.'

'I have,' he said.

'Then ...' She stared at him. 'Cletus, didn't you understand what he said? I told him – it's wrong. It's just wrong. I don't know what's wrong about it, but something is. I'm not going to marry you!'

Cletus looked at her. And, as she gazed back at him, Melissa's face changed. There crept into her face that expression that Cletus had seen her wear only once before. It was the look he had seen on her face after he had emerged alive from the ditch in which he had played dead in order to destroy with the dally gun the Neulander guerrillas who had attacked their armored car on its way into Bakhalla.

'You don't ... you can't think,' she began, barely above a whisper. But then her voice firmed. 'You can *force* me to marry you?'

'We'll hold the ceremony,' he said.

She shook her head, disbelievingly. 'No Dorsai chaplain would marry me against my will!'

'My regimental chaplain will – if I order it,' Cletus said.

'Marry the daughter of Eachan Khan?' she blazed, suddenly. 'And I suppose my father's simply going to stand still and watch this happen?'

'I hope so – sincerely,' answered Cletus, with such a slow and meaningful emphasis on the words that color leaped into her face for a second and then drained away to leave her as pale as a woman in shock.

'You ...' Her voice faltered and stopped. Child of a mercenary officer, she could not have failed to notice that, among those present for the wedding, those bound to Cletus by emotional or other ties outnumbered those bound to her father by two to one. But her eyes on him were still incredulous. They searched his face for some indication that what she saw there was somehow not the true Cletus.

'But you're not like that. You wouldn't ...' Her voice failed again. 'Dad's your friend!'

'And you're going to be my wife,' Cletus answered.

Her eyes fell for the first time to the sidearm in the uncapped holster at his waist.

'Oh, God!' She put a slim hand to each side of her face. 'And I thought Dow was cruel – I won't answer. When the chaplain asks me if I'll take you for my husband, I'll say no!'

'For Eachan's sake,' said Cletus, 'I hope not.'

Her hands fell from her face. She stood like a sleepwalker with her arms at her sides.

Cletus stepped up to her, took her arm and led her, unresisting, out of the summer house up through the garden, through a hedge and back in through the French doors to the dining room. Eachan was still there, and he turned to face them quickly as they came in, putting down the glass he held and stepping quickly forward to meet them.

'Here you are!' he said. His gaze sharpened suddenly on his daughter. 'Melly! What's the matter?'

'Nothing,' Cletus answered. 'There's no problem, after all. We're going to get married.'

Eachan's gaze switched sharply to Cletus. 'You are?' His eyes locked with Cletus' for a second, then went back to Melissa. 'Is this right, Melly? Is everything all right?'

'Everything's fine,' said Cletus. 'You'd better tell the chaplain we're ready now.'

Eachan did not move. His eyes raked downward and stared deliberately at the weapon in its holster on Cletus' hip. He looked back up at Cletus, and then at Melissa.

'I'm waiting to hear from you, Melly,' Eachan said slowly. His eyes were as gray as weathered granite. 'You haven't told me yet that everything's all right.'

'It's all right,' she said between stiff, colorless lips. 'It was your idea I marry Cletus in the first place, wasn't it, Dad?'

'Yes,' said Eachan. There was no noticeable change in his expression, but all at once a change seemed to pass over him, sweeping away all emotion and leaving him quiet, settled and purposeful. He took a step forward, so that he stood now almost between them, looking directly up into Cletus' face from a few inches away. 'But perhaps I was making a mistake.'

His right hand dropped, seemingly in a casual way, to cover Cletus' hand where it held Melissa's wrist. His fingers curled lightly about Cletus' thumb in a grip that could be used to break the thumb if Cletus did not release his hold.

Cletus dropped his other hand lightly upon the belt of the weapon at his side.

'Let go,' he said softly to Eachan.

The same deadly quietness held them both. For a second there was no movement in the room, and then Melissa gasped.

'No!' She forced herself between them, facing her father, her back toward Cletus, his hand still holding her wrist, now behind her back. 'Dad! What's the matter with you? I'd think you'd be happy we've decided to get married after all!'

Behind her, Cletus let go of her wrist and she brought the formerly imprisoned arm around before her. Her shoulders lifted sharply with the depth of her breathing. For a moment Eachan stared at her blankly, and then a little touch of puzzlement and dismay crept into his eyes.

'Melly, I thought ...' His voice stumbled and fell silent.

'Thought?' cried Melissa, sharply. 'What, Dad?'

He stared at her, distractedly. 'I don't know!' he exploded, all at once. 'I don't understand you, girl! I don't understand you at all.'

He turned away and stamped back to the table where he had put his drink down. He picked it up and swallowed heavily from it.

Melissa went to him and for a second put her arm around his shoulders, laying her head against the side of his head. Then she turned back to Cletus and placed a cold hand on his wrist. She looked at him with eyes that were strangely deep and free of anger or resentment.

'Come along, then, Cletus,' she said, quietly. 'We'd better be getting started.'

It was some hours later before they were able to be alone together. The wedding guests had seen them to the door of the master bedroom in newly built Grahame House, and it was only when the door was shut in their faces that they finally left the building, the echo of their laughter and cheerful voices fading behind them.

Wearily, Melissa dropped into a sitting position on the edge of the large bed. She looked up at Cletus, who was still standing.

'Now, will you tell me what's wrong?' she asked.

He looked at her. The moment he had foreseen when he had asked her to marry him was upon him now. He summoned up courage to face it.

'It'll be a marriage in name only,' he said. 'In a couple of years you can get an annulment.'

'Then why marry me at all?' she said, her voice still empty of blame or rancor.

'DeCastries will be back out among the new worlds within another twelve months,' he said. 'Before he came, he'd be asking you to come to Earth. With your marriage to me, you lost your Earth citizenship. You're a Dorsai, now. You can't go – until you've had the marriage annulled and reapplied for Earth citizenship. And you can't annul the marriage right away without letting Eachan know I forced you to marry me – with the results you know, the same results you agreed to marry me to avoid, right now.'

'I would never let you two kill each other,' she said. Her voice was strange.

'No,' he said. 'So you'll wait two years. After that, you'll be free.'

'But why?' she said. 'Why did you do it?'

'Eachan would have followed you to Earth,' said Cletus. 'That's what Dow counted on. That's what I couldn't allow. I need Eachan Khan for what I've got to do.'

He had been looking at her as he talked, but now his eyes had moved away from her. He was looking out the high, curtained window at one end of the bedroom, at the mountain peaks, now just beginning to be clouded with the afternoon rains that would in a few months turn to the first of autumn snows.

She did not speak for a long time. 'Then,' she said, at last, 'you never did love me?'

He opened his mouth to answer, for the moment was upon him. But at the last minute, in spite of his determination, the words changed on his lips.

'Did I ever say I did?' he answered, and, turning, went out of the room before she could say more.

Behind him, as he closed the door, there was only silence.

20

The next morning Cletus got busy readying the expeditionary contingent of new-trained and not yet new-trained Dorsais he would be taking with him to Newton. Several days later, as he sat in his private office at the Foralie training grounds, Arvid stepped in to say that there was a new emigrant to Dorsai, an officer-recruit, who wanted to speak to him.

'You remember him, I think, sir,' said Arvid, looking at Cletus a little grimly. 'Lieutenant William Athyer – formerly of the Alliance Expeditionary Force on Bakhalla.'

'Athyer?' said Cletus. He pushed aside the papers on the float desk in front of him. 'Send him in, Arv.'

Arvid stepped back out of the office. A few seconds later, Bill Athyer, whom Cletus had last seen drunkenly barring his way in the in-town spaceship terminal of Bakhalla, hesitantly appeared in the doorway. He was dressed in the brown uniform of a Dorsai recruit, with a probationary officer's insignia where his first lieutenant's silver bars had been worn.

'Come in,' said Cletus, 'and shut the door behind you.' Athyer obeyed and advanced into the room. 'It's good of you to see me, sir,' he said, slowly. 'I don't suppose you ever expected me to show up like this ...'

'Not at all,' said Cletus. 'I've been expecting you. Sit down.'

He indicated the chair in front of his desk. Athyer took it almost gingerly. 'I don't know how to apologize ...' he began.

'Then don't,' said Cletus. 'I take it life has changed for you?'

'Changed!' Athyer's face lit up. 'Sir, you remember at the Bakhalla Terminal ...? I went back from there with my mind made up. I was going to go through everything you'd ever written – everything – with a fine-toothed comb, until I found something wrong, something false, I could use against you. You said not to apologize, but ...'

'And I meant it,' said Cletus. 'Go on with whatever else you were going to tell me.'

170

'Well, I ... suddenly began to understand it, that's all,' said Athyer. 'Suddenly it began to make sense to me, and I couldn't believe it! I left your books and started digging into everything else I could find in that Exotic library in Bakhalla on military art. And it was just what I'd always read, no more, no less. It was *your* writing that was different ... Sir, you don't know the difference!'

Cletus smiled.

'Of course, of course you do!' Athyer interrupted himself. 'I don't mean that. What I mean is, for example, I always had trouble with math. I wasn't an Alliance Academy man, you know. I came in on one of the reserve officer programs and I could sort of slide through on math. And that's what I did until one day when I ran into solid geometry. All at once the figures and the shapes came together – it was beautiful. Well, that was how it was with your writing, sir. All of a sudden, the art and the mechanics of military strategy came together. All the dreams I'd had as a kid of doing great things – and all at once I was reading how they could be done. Not just military things – all sorts and kinds of things.'

'You saw that in what I'd written, did you?' asked Cletus.

'Saw it!' Athyer reached up a hand and closed its fingers slowly on empty air. 'I saw it as if it were *there,* three-dimensional, laid out in front of me. Sir, nobody knows what you've done in those volumes you've written. Nobody appreciates – and it's not only what your work offers now, it's what it offers in the future!'

'Good,' said Cletus. 'Glad to hear you think so. And now what can I do for you?'

'I think you know, sir, don't you?' Athyer said. 'It's because of what you've written that I came here, to Dorsai. But I don't want to be just one of your command. I want to be close, where I can go on learning from you. Oh, I know you won't have any room for me on your personal staff right away, but if you could keep me in mind ...'

'I think room can be made for you,' said Cletus. 'As I say, I've been more or less expecting you. Go see Commandant Arvid Johnson and tell him I said to take you on as his assistant. We'll waive the full training requirement and you can go along with the group we're taking to employment on Newton.'

'Sir ...' Words failed Athyer.

'That's all, then,' said Cletus, raking back in front of him the papers he had pushed aside earlier. 'You'll find Arvid in the office outside.'

He returned to his work. Two weeks later the Dorsai contingent for

Newton landed there, ready for employment – and newly commissioned Force Leader Bill Athyer was among them.

'I hope,' said Arthur Walco several days after that, as he stood with Cletus watching the contingent at evening parade, 'your confidence in yourself hasn't been exaggerated, Marshal.'

There was almost the hint of a sneer in his voice, as the chairman of the board of the Advanced Associated Communities on Newton used the title Cletus had adopted for himself as part of his general overhaul of unit and officer names among the new-trained Dorsai. They were standing together at the edge of the parade ground, with the red sun in the gray sky of Newton sinking to the horizon behind the flagstaff, its flag already half-lowered, as Major Swahili brought the regiment to the point of dismissal. Cletus turned to look at the thin, balding Newtonian.

'Exaggeration of confidence,' he said, 'is a fault in people who don't know their business.'

'And you do?' snapped Walco.

'Yes,' answered Cletus.

Walco laughed sourly, hunching his thin shoulders in their black jacket against the northern wind coming off the edge of the forest that grew right to the limits of the Newtonian town of Debroy, the same forest that rolled northward, unbroken for more than two hundred miles, to the stibnite mines and the Brozan town of Watershed.

'Two thousand men may be enough to take those mines,' he said, 'but your contract with us calls for you to hold the mines for three days or until we get Newtonian forces in to relieve you. And within twenty-four hours after you move into Watershed, the Brozans can have ten thousand regular troops on top of you. How you're going to handle odds of five to one, I don't know.'

'Of course not,' said Cletus. The flag was all the way down now and Major Swahili had turned the parade over to his adjutant to dismiss the men. 'It's not your business to know. It's only your business to write a contract with me providing that we get our pay only after control of the mines has been delivered to your troops. And that you've done. Our failure won't cause your Advanced Associated Communities any financial loss.'

'Perhaps not,' said Walco, viciously, 'but my reputation's at stake.'

'So's mine,' replied Cletus cheerfully.

Walco snorted and went off. Cletus watched him go for a second, then turned and made his way to the Headquarters building of the temporary camp that had been set up for the Dorsais here on the edge of

Debroy under the shadow of the forest. There, in the map room, he found Swahili and Arvid waiting for him.

'Look at this,' he said, beckoning them both over to the main map table, which showed in relief the broad band of forest, with Debroy at one end of the table and the stibnite mines around Watershed at the other. The other two men joined him at the Debroy end of the table. 'Walco and his people expect us to fiddle around for a week or two, getting set here before we do anything. Whatever Brozan spies are keeping tab on the situation will accordingly pick up the same idea. But we aren't going to waste time. Major ...'

He looked at Swahili, whose scarred, black face was bent with interest above the table top. Swahili lifted his eyes to meet Cletus'.

'We'll start climatization training of the troops inside the edge of the forest here, tomorrow at first light,' Cletus said. 'The training will take place no more than five miles deep in the forest, well below the Newtonian-Brozan frontier' – he pointed to a red line running through the forested area some twenty miles above Debroy. 'The men will train by forces and groups, and they aren't going to do well. They aren't going to do well at all. It'll be necessary to keep them out overnight and keep them at it until your officers are satisfied. Then they can be released, group by group, as their officers think they're ready, and allowed to return to the camp here. I don't want the last group out of the forest until two and a half days from tomorrow morning. You leave the necessary orders with your officer to see to that.'

'I won't be there?' asked Swahili.

'You'll be with me,' answered Cletus. He glanced at the tall young captain to his right. 'So will Arvid and two hundred of our best men. We'll have split off from the rest the minute we're in the woods, dispersed into two- and three-man teams and headed north to rendezvous five miles south of Watershed, four days from now.'

'Four days?' echoed Swahili. 'That's better than fifty miles a day on foot through unfamiliar territory.'

'Exactly!' said Cletus. 'That's why no one – Newtonians or Brozans – will suspect we'd try to do anything like that. But you and I know, don't we, Major, that our best men can make it?'

His eyes met the eyes in Swahili's dark, unchanging face.

'Yes,' said Swahili.

'Good,' said Cletus, stepping back from the table. 'We'll eat now, and work out the details this evening. I want you, Major, to travel along with Arv, here. I'll take Force Leader Athyer along with me and travel with him.'

'Athyer?' queried Swahili.

'That's right,' replied Cletus, dryly. 'Wasn't it you who told me he was coming along?'

'Yes,' answered Swahili. It was true, oddly enough. Swahili seemed to have taken an interest in the newly recruited, untrained Athyer. It was an interest apparently more of curiosity than sentiment – for if ever two men were at opposite poles, it was the major and the force leader. Swahili was far and away the superior of all the new-trained Dorsais, men and officers alike, having surpassed everyone in the training, with the exception of Cletus in the matter of autocontrol. Clearly, however, Swahili was not one to let interest affect judgment. He looked with a touch of grim amusement at Cletus.

'And, of course, since he'll be with you, sir ...' he said.

'All the way,' said Cletus levelly. 'I take it you've no objection to having Arv with you?'

'No, sir,' Swahili's eyes glanced at the tall young commandant with something very close – as close as he ever came – to approval.

'Good,' said Cletus. 'You can take off, then. I'll meet you both here in an hour, after we've eaten.'

'Yes.'

Swahili went out. Cletus turned toward the door, and found Arvid still there, standing almost in his way. Cletus stopped.

'Something the matter, Arv?' Cletus asked.

'Sir ...' began Arvid, and he did not seem to be able to continue.

Cletus made no attempt to assist the conversation. He merely stood, waiting.

'Sir,' said Arvid again, 'I'm still your aide, aren't I?'

'You are,' said Cletus.

'Then' – Arvid's face was stiff and a little pale – 'can I ask why Athyer should be with you in an action like this, instead of me?'

Cletus looked at him coldly. Arvid held himself stiffly, and his right shoulder was still a little hunched under his uniform coat, drawn forward by the tightening of the scar tissue of the burn he had taken back at the BOQ in Bakhalla, protecting Cletus from the Neuland gunmen.

'No, Commandant,' said Cletus, slowly. 'You can't ask me why I decide what I do – now or ever.'

They stood facing each other.

'Is that clear?' Cletus said, after a moment.

Arvid stood even more stiffly. His eyes seemed to have lost Cletus, and his gaze traveled past him now to some spot on the farther wall.

'Yes, sir,' he said.

'Then you'd probably better be getting to the evening meal, hadn't you?' said Cletus.

'Yes, sir.'

Arvid turned and went out. After a second, Cletus sighed and also left for his own quarters and a solitary meal served there by his orderly.

At nine the following morning, he was standing with Force Leader Athyer five miles inside the forest fringe, when Swahili came up to him and handed him the matchbox-sized metal case of a peep-map. Cletus tucked it into a jacket pocket of his gray-green field uniform.

'It's orientated?' he asked Swahili. The major nodded.

'With the camp as base point,' Swahili answered. 'The rest of the men tagged for the expedition have already left – in two- and three-man teams, just as you said. The captain and I are ready to go.'

'Good,' said Cletus. 'We'll get started, too, Bill and I. See you at the rendezvous point, five miles below Watershed, in approximately ninety-one hours.'

'We'll be there, sir.' With a single, slightly humorous glance at Athyer, Swahili turned and left.

Cletus turned the peep-map over in the palm of his hand, exposing the needle of the orientation compass under its transparent cover. He pressed the button in the side of the case and the needle swung clockwise some forty degrees until it pointed almost due north into the forest. Cletus lined himself up with a tree trunk as far off as he could see through the dimness of the forest in that direction. Then he put the peephole at one end of the instrument to his eye and gazed through it. Within he saw the image of what appeared to be a ten- by twelve-foot relief map of the territory between his present position and Watershed. A red line marked the route that had been programmed into the map. Reaching for another button on the case, he cranked the view in close to study the detail of the first half-dozen miles. It was all straight forest, with no bog land to be crossed or avoided.

'Come on,' he said over his shoulder to Athyer. Putting the peep-map into his pocket, he started off at a jog trot.

Athyer followed him. For the first couple of hours they trotted along side by side without speaking, enclosed in the dimness and silence of the northern Newtonian forest. There were no flying creatures, neither birds nor insects, in this forest, only the amphibious and fish-like life of its lakes, swamps and bogs. Under the thick cover of the needle-like leaves that grew only on the topmost branches of the trees, the ground was bare except for the leafless tree trunks and lower branches but covered with a thick coat of blackened, dead needles fallen from the trees in past seasons. Only here and there, startling and unexpectedly, there would be a thick clump of large, flesh-colored leaves as much as four feet in length, sprouting directly from the needle bed to signal the presence of a spring or some other damp area of the jungle floor beneath.

After the first two hours, they fell into an alternate rhythm of five minutes at a jog trot, followed by five minutes at a rapid walk. Once each hour they stopped for five minutes to rest, dropping at full length upon the soft, thick, needle carpet without bothering even to remove the light survival packs they wore strapped to their shoulders.

For the first half hour or so, the going had been effortful. But after that they warmed to the physical movement, their heartbeats slowed, their breathing calmed – and it seemed almost as if they could go on forever like this. Cletus ran or walked, with the larger share of his mind abstract, far away in concentration on other problems. Even the matter of periodically checking their progress with the directional compass on the peep-map was an almost automatic action for him, performed by reflex.

He was roused from this at last by the fading of the already dim light of the forest about them. Newton's sun, hidden between its double screen of the treetops' foliage and the high, almost constant cloud layer that gave the sky its usual gray, metallic look, was beginning to set.

'Time for a meal break,' said Cletus. He headed for a flat spot at the base of a large tree trunk and dropped into a sitting position, cross-legged with his back to the trunk, stripping off his shoulder pack as he did so. Athyer joined him on the ground. 'How're you doing?'

'Fine, sir,' grunted Athyer.

In fact, the other man was looking as good as he claimed to feel, and this Cletus was glad to see. There was only a faint sheen of perspiration on Athyer's face, and his breathing was deep and unhurried.

They broke out a thermo meal pack apiece and punctured the seal to start warming the food inside. By the time it was hot enough to eat, the darkness around them had closed in absolutely. It was as black as the inside of some sealed underground room.

'Half an hour until the moons start to rise,' Cletus said into the darkness in the direction in which he had last looked to see the seated Athyer. 'Try to get some sleep, if you can.'

Cletus lay back on the needles, and made his limbs and body go limp. In a few seconds, he felt the familiar drifting sensation. Then it seemed that there were perhaps thirty seconds of inattention, and he opened his eyes to find a new, pale light filtering down through the leaf cover of the forest.

It was still only a fraction as bright as the filtered daylight had been, but already it was bright enough so that they could see to travel, and that brightness would perhaps double, since at least four of Newton's five moons should be in the night sky.

'Let's move,' said Cletus. A couple of minutes later, he and Athyer, packs on back, were once more jog trotting upon their route.

The peep-map, when Cletus consulted it by its own inter-illumination, now showed a black line paralleling the red line of their indicated route for a distance of a little over thirty-one miles from their starting point. In the next nine hours of nighttime traveling, interrupted only by hourly rests and a short meal break around midnight, they accomplished another twenty-six miles before the setting of most of the moons dimmed the light once more below the level of illumination at which it was safe to travel. They ate a final, light meal and dropped off into five hours of deep slumber on the thick needle bed of the forest floor.

When Cletus' wrist alarm woke them, the chronometer showed that over two hours of daylight had already elapsed. They arose, ate and moved on as soon as possible.

For the first four hours they made good progress – if anything, they were traveling even a little faster than they had the day before. But around noon they entered into an area of bog and swamp thick with plants of the big, flesh-colored leaf, and something new called parasite vines, great ropes of vegetation hanging from the low limbs of the trees or stretching out across the ground for miles and sometimes as thick as an oil drum.

They were slowed and forced to detour. By the time night fell, they had made only an additional twenty miles. They were barely one-third of the distance to the rendezvous point below Watershed, nearly one-third of their time had gone, and from now on fatigue would slow them progressively. Cletus had hoped to cover nearly half the distance by this time.

However, the peep-map informed him that another twenty miles would bring them out of this boggy area and into more open country again. They had their brief supper during the half hour of darkness, and then pushed on during the night. They reached the edge of the bog area just before the moonlight failed them; they fell, like dead men, on the needle carpet underfoot and into slumber.

The next day the going was easier, but exhaustion was beginning to slow their pace. Cletus traveled like a man in a dream, or in a high fever, hardly conscious of the efforts and wearinesses of his body except as things perceived dimly, at a distance. But Athyer was running close to the end of his strength. His face was gray and gaunt, so that the harsh beak of his nose now seemed to dominate all the other features in it, like the battering-ram prow of some ancient wooden vessel. He managed to keep the pace as they trotted, but when they slowed to a walk, his foot would occasionally go down loosely and he would stumble. That night Cletus let them both sleep for six hours after the evening meal.

They made less than sixteen miles in the hours of moonlight that remained to them, before stopping to sleep again for another six hours.

They awoke with the illusion of being rested and restored to full strength. However, two hours of travel during the following daylight found them not much better than they had been twenty-four hours before, although they were traveling more slowly and more steadily now, portioning out their strength as a miser portions out the money for necessary expenses. Once again, Cletus was back in his state of detachment; his bodily suffering seemed remote and unimportant. The feeling clung to his mind that he could go on like this forever, if necessary, without ever stopping for food or rest.

By now, in fact, food was one of the least of their wants. They paused for the midday meal break and forced themselves to swallow some of the rations they carried, but without appetite or sense of taste. The ingested food lay heavily in their stomachs, and when darkness came neither of them could eat. They dug down to the base of one of the flesh-colored leafed plants to uncover the spring that was bubbling there, and drank deeply before dropping off into what was now an almost automatic slumber. After a couple of hours of sleep, they arose and went on under the moonlight.

Dawn of the fourth day found them only half a dozen miles from the rendezvous point. But when they tried to get to their feet with their packs on, their knees buckled and gave under them like loose hinges. Cletus continued to struggle, however, and, after several tries, found himself at last on his feet and staying there. He looked around and saw Athyer, still on the ground, unmoving.

'No use,' croaked Athyer. 'You go on.'

'No,' said Cletus. He stood, legs stiff and braced, a little apart. He swayed slightly, looking down at Athyer.

'You've got to go on,' said Athyer, after a moment. It was the way they had gotten in the habit of talking to each other during the last day or so – with long pauses between one man's words and the other's reply.

'Why did you come to Dorsai?' asked Cletus, after one of these pauses.

Athyer stared at him. 'You,' said Athyer. 'You did what I always wanted to do. You were what I always wanted to be. I knew I'd never make it the way you have. But I thought I could learn to come close.'

'Then learn,' said Cletus, swaying. 'Walk.'

'I can't,' said Athyer.

'No such thing as can't – for you,' said Cletus. 'Walk.' Cletus continued to stand there. Athyer lay where he was for a few minutes. Then his legs began to twitch. He struggled up into a sitting position and tried to get his legs under him, but they would not go. He stopped, panting.

'You're what you've always wanted to be,' said Cletus slowly, swaying above him. 'Never mind your body. Get Athyer to his feet. The body will come along naturally.'

He waited. Athyer stirred again. With a convulsive effort he got to his knees, wavered in a half-kneeling position, and then with a sudden surge lifted to his feet, stumbled forward for three steps and caught hold of a tree trunk to keep from going down again. He looked over his shoulder at Cletus, panting but triumphant.

'When you're ready to go,' said Cletus.

Five minutes later, though Athyer still stumbled like a drunken man, they were moving forward. Four hours later they made it to the rendezvous point, to find Swahili and Arvid, together with perhaps a fifth of the rest of the men due to arrive at this point, already there. Cletus and Athyer collapsed without even bothering to take off their back packs, and they were asleep before they touched the needle-carpet ground.

21

Cletus awoke about mid-afternoon. He felt still and a little lightheaded, but rested and extremely hungry. Athyer was still sleeping heavily, like a man under deep anesthesia.

Cletus ate and joined Swahili and Arvid.

'How many of the men are in?' he asked Swahili.

'There's twenty-six who haven't shown up yet,' answered Swahili. 'We got most of the rest in during the next hour after you got here.'

Cletus nodded. 'Good,' he said. 'Then they should be slept up enough to operate by twilight. We'll get busy right now with the ones that are already rested. The first thing we need is a vehicle.'

So it happened that a Brozan truck driver sliding on his airjets down the single fused earth highway leading into the small mining town of Watershed unexpectedly found his way barred by half a dozen armed men in gray-blue uniforms, each with a small blue and white flag of the Advanced Associated Communities stapled over the left breast pocket. One of these, a tall officer wearing a circle of stars on each shoulder tab, stepped up on the foot-rest entrance to his cab and opened the door.

'Out,' said Cletus, 'we need this truck of yours.'

Two hours later, just before sunset, that same truck drove into Watershed from a highway that had been strangely unproductive of traffic during the last 120 minutes. There were two men in the cab without caps on and they drove the truck directly to the headquarters of the small police detachment that had the duty of keeping law and order in the mining town.

The truck pulled into the parking compound behind the police headquarters, and a few moments later there was the sound of some disturbance within the headquarters itself. This, however, quietened, and a few moments later the fire siren above the police headquarters burst to life with a whooping like that of some mad, gigantic creature. It continued to whoop as the townspeople poured out of their houses and other buildings to find the town surrounded and the streets patrolled by armed soldiers with blue and white flags stapled over the left breast pockets of their uniform jackets. By the time the sun was down, Watershed had awakened to the fact that it was a captured community.

'You must be crazy! You'll never get away with it!' stormed the manager of the stibnite mines when, with the mayor of the town and the head of the local police contingent, he was brought into Cletus' presence at police headquarters. 'The Brozan Army's headquartered at Broza City – and that's only two hours from here, even by road. They'll find out you're here in a few hours, and then—'

'They already know,' Cletus interrupted him, dryly. 'One of the first things I did was use your police communications here to announce the fact that we've taken over Watershed and the mines.'

The mine manager stared at him. 'You *must* be crazy!' he said at last. 'Do you think your five hundred men can stand up to a couple of divisions?'

'We may not have to,' said Cletus. 'In any case, it's no concern of yours. All I want you and these other two gentlemen to do is to reassure the local people that they're in no danger as long as they keep off the streets and make no effort to leave the town.'

There was a note in his voice that did not invite further argument. With a few additional half-hearted attempts at protest, the three officials of Watershed agreed to make a joint community call over the local phone system with the reassurance and warning he had asked them to deliver – following which, he had them placed under guard in the police headquarters.

It was in fact less than two hours before the first elements of the Brozan Army began to arrive. These were flying transports loaded with troops who quickly ringed the village at a distance of about two hundred yards inside the edge of the forest surrounding the town. Through the rest of the night, other troops, heavy weapons and armored vehicles could be heard arriving. By dawn, Swahili and Cletus concurred in an estimate that close to a division of Brozan soldiery, bristling with everything from belt knives to energy weapons, enclosed Watershed and its two hundred occupying Dorsai troops.

Swahili was in good humor as he handed the field glasses back to Cletus, after making his own survey of the surrounding forest area. They were standing together on top of the communications tower, which was the tallest structure in the town.

'They won't want to use those heavy weapons indiscriminately, with all these local people on hand,' said Swahili. 'That means they're going to have to come in on foot – probably all around the perimeter at once. I'd guess they'll attack inside the hour.'

'I don't think so,' answered Cletus. 'I think they'll send someone in to talk, first.'

He turned out to be correct. The surrounding Brozan troops did nothing for the first three hours of the morning. Then, toward noon, as the cloud-veiled sun over Newton was heating the northern landscape, a command car flying a white flag slowly emerged from the shadows of the forest and entered the town from the highway. It was met at the perimeter of Watershed by soldiers instructed in preparation for this meeting, and it was escorted by them to the police headquarters. There, a small, spare general in his early sixties, flanked by a round man perhaps ten years younger and wearing a colonel's insignia, dismounted and entered the headquarters building. Cletus received them in the office of the commander of the police detachment.

'I'm here to offer you surrender terms—' The general broke off, staring at Cletus' shoulder tabs. 'I don't recognize your rank?'

'Marshal,' Cletus answered. 'We've shaken up our table of organization and our titles on Dorsai, recently. Marshal Cletus Grahame.'

'Oh? General James Van Dassel. And this is Colonel Morton Offer. As I was saying, we're here to offer you terms of surrender—'

'If it was a matter of sending surrender terms, you'd hardly have needed to come yourself, would you, General?' Cletus broke in. 'I think you know very well that there's no question of our surrendering.'

'No?' Van Dassel's eyebrows rose politely. 'Maybe I should tell you we've got more than a full division, with a full complement of heavy weapons, surrounding you right now.'

'I'm aware of that fact,' said Cletus. 'Just as you're completely aware of the fact that we have something over five thousand civilians here inside our lines.'

'Yes, and we're holding you strictly accountable for them,' said Van Dassel. 'I have to warn you that, if any harm comes to them, the liberal surrender terms we're about to offer you—'

'Don't try my patience, General,' interrupted Cletus. 'We hold those civilians as hostages against any inimical action by your forces. So let's not waste any more time on this nonsense about our surrendering. I've been expecting you here so that I could inform you of the immediate steps to be taken by the Advanced Associated Communities with regard to Watershed and the mines. As you undoubtedly know, these mines were developed on land purchased from Broza by the Advanced Associated Communities, and Broza's expropriation has since been ruled illegal by the international court here on Newton … although Broza has seen fit until now to refuse to obey that court's order returning the mines to the Advanced Associated Communities. Our expeditionary force has already notified the Advanced Associated Communities that the mines are once more under their proper ownership, and I've been informed that the first contingents of regular AAC troops will begin to arrive here by 1800 hours, to relieve my command and begin to function as a permanent occupying force …' Cletus paused.

'I'm certainly not going to permit any such occupying forces to move in here,' said Van Dassel, almost mildly.

'Then I'd suggest you check with your political authorities before you make any move to prevent them,' said Cletus. 'I repeat, we hold the townspeople here hostage for the good behavior of your troops.'

'Nor am I willing to be blackmailed,' said Van Dassel. 'I'll expect notification of your willingness to surrender before the next two hours are up.'

'And I, as I say,' answered Cletus, 'will hold you responsible for any hostile action by your command during our relief by the regular troops from the Advanced Associated Communities.'

On that mutual statement, they parted politely. Van Dassel and his colonel returned to the Brozan troops encircling the village. Cletus called in Swahili and Arvid to have lunch with him.

'But what if he decides to hit us before the relieving troops get here?' asked Swahili.

'He won't,' said Cletus. 'His situation's bad enough as it is. The Brozan politicians are going to be asking him how he allowed us to take over Watershed and the mines here in the first place. He might survive that question, as far as his career is concerned – but only if there're no Brozan lives lost. He knows I understand that as well as he does, so Van Dassel won't take chances.'

In fact, Van Dassel did not make any move. His division surrounding Watershed sat quietly while his deadline for surrender passed, and the relieving forces from the Advanced Associated Communities began to be airlifted in. During the following night, he quietly withdrew his forces. By the following sunrise, as the newly landed, AAC soldiery began to clear an area of the forest outside the town and construct a semi-permanent camp for themselves, there was not a Brozan soldier to be found within two hundred miles.

'Very well done indeed!' said Walco, enthusiastically, when he arrived at Watershed with the last of his own troops and was ushered in to the office Cletus had taken over in the police headquarters building. 'You and your Dorsais have done a marvelous job. You can move out any time now.'

'As soon as we're paid,' said Cletus.

Walco smiled, thinly. 'I thought you might be eager to get your pay,' he said. 'So I brought it along with me.'

He lifted a narrow briefcase onto the desk between them, took out a release form, which he passed to Cletus, and then began to remove gold certificates, which he stacked on the desk in front of Cletus.

Cletus ignored the form and watched coolly as the pile of certificates grew. When Walco stopped at last, and looked up at him with another broad smile, Cletus did not smile back. He shook his head.

'That's less than half of what our agreement called for,' Cletus said.

Walco preserved his smile. 'True,' Walco said. 'But in the original agreement we envisioned hiring you for a three-month term. As it happens, you've been lucky enough to achieve your objective in less than a week and with only a quarter of your expeditionary force. We figured full combat pay for the whole week, however, for the five hundred men you used, and in addition we're paying you garrison scale not only for the rest of your men for that week but for your whole force for the rest of this month as well – as a sort of bonus.'

Cletus looked at him. Walco's smile faded.

'I'm sure you remember as well as I do,' said Cletus coldly, 'that the agreement was for two thousand men for three months, full combat pay for everybody during that period – and no pay at all if we weren't able to deliver the stibnite mines to you. How many men I used to make that recovery, and how long I took, was my concern. I expect full combat pay for three months for my entire command, immediately.'

'That's out of the question, of course,' said Walco, a little shortly.

'I don't think so,' said Cletus. 'Maybe I should remind you that I told General Van Dassel, the Brozan commander who had us encircled here, that I was holding the civilian population of Watershed hostage for his good behavior. Perhaps I should remind you that I and the men I brought here with me are still holding these people hostage – this time for *your* good behavior.'

Walco's face became strangely set. 'You wouldn't harm civilians!' he said, after a moment.

'General Van Dassel believes I would,' replied Cletus. 'Now I, personally, give you my word as a Dorsai – and that's a word that's going to become something better than a signed contract, in time ... that no single civilian will be hurt. But have you got the courage to believe me? If I'm lying, and your takeover of the mines includes a blood bath of the resident townspeople, your chances of coming to some eventual agreement with Broza about these mines will go up in smoke. Instead of being able to negotiate on the basis of having a bird in the hand, you'll have to face a colony interested only in vengeance – vengeance for an action for which all civilized communities will indict you.'

Walco stood, staring at him. 'I don't have any more certificates with me,' he said at last, hoarsely.

'We'll wait,' answered Cletus. 'You should be able to fly back and get them and return here by noon at the latest.'

Shoulders slumped, Walco went. As he mounted the steps of the aircraft that had brought him to Watershed, however, he stopped and turned for a parting shot at Cletus.

'You think you're going to cut a swath through the new worlds,' he said, viciously, 'and maybe you will for a while. But one of these days everything you've built is going to come tumbling down around your ears.'

'We'll see,' said Cletus.

He watched the door shut behind Walco and the aircraft lift away into the sky of Newton. Then he turned to Arvid, who was standing beside him.

'By the way, Arv,' he said, 'Bill Athyer wants to have the chance to study my methods of tactics and strategy at close hand, so he'll be taking over as my aide as soon as we're back on Dorsai. We'll find a command for you, out in the field somewhere. It's about time you were brushing up on your combat experience anyway.'

Without waiting for Arvid's response, he turned his back on the younger man and walked off, his mind already on other problems.

22

'Your prices,' said James Arm-of-the-Lord, Eldest of the First Militant Church, on both the neighboring worlds of Harmony and Association – those two worlds called the Friendlies, 'are outrageous.'

James Arm-of-the-Lord was a small, frail, middle-aged man with sparse gray hair – looking even smaller and more frail than he might otherwise in the tight black jumper and trousers that were the common dress of those belonging to the fanatical sects that had colonized, and later divided and multiplied, on the surfaces of Harmony and Association. At first sight, he seemed a harmless little man, but a glance from his dark eyes or even a few words spoken aloud by him were enough to destroy that illusion. Plainly he was one of those rare people who burn with an inner fire – but the inner fire that never failed in James Arm-of-the-Lord was a brand of woe and a torch of terror to the Unrighteous. Nor was it lessened by the fact that the ranks of the Unrighteous, in James' estimation, included all those whose opinions in any way differed from his own. He sat now in his office at Government Center on Harmony, gazing across the desk's bare, unpolished surface at Cletus, who sat opposite.

'I know we're priced beyond your means,' said Cletus. 'I didn't come by to suggest that you hire some of our Dorsais. I was going to suggest that possibly we might want to hire some of your young men.'

'Hire out our church members to spend their blood and lives in the sinful wars of the Churchless and the Unbelievers?' said James. 'Unthinkable?'

'None of your colonies on Harmony or Association have anything to speak of in the way of technology,' said Cletus. 'Your Militant Church may contain the largest population of any of the churches on these two worlds, but you're still starving for real credit – of the kind you can use in interworld trading to set up the production machinery your people need. You could earn that credit from us, as I say, by hiring out some of your young men to us.'

James eyes glittered like the eyes of a coiled snake in reflective light. 'How much?' he snapped.

'The standard wages for conventional mercenary soldiers,' replied Cletus.

'Why, that's barely a third of what you asked for each of your Dorsais!' James' voice rose. 'You'd sell to us at one price, and buy from us at another?'

'It's a matter of selling and buying two different products,' answered Cletus, unmoved. 'The Dorsais are worth what I ask for them because of their training and because by now they've established a reputation for earning their money. Your men have no such training, and no reputation. They're worth only what I'm willing to pay for them. On the other hand, not a great deal would be demanded of them. They'd be used mainly as diversionary forces like our jump troops in our recent capture of Margaretha, on Freiland.'

The taking over of Margaretha on Freiland had been the latest of a series of successful engagements fought by the new-trained Dorsai mercenaries under Cletus' command. Over a year had gone by since the capture of the stibnite mines on Newton, and in that time they had conducted campaigns leading to clear-cut and almost bloodless victories on the worlds of Newton's sister planet of Cassida, St. Marie, a smaller world under the Procyon sun with Mara and Kultis, and most recently on Freiland, which with New Earth, were the inhabited planets under the star of Sirius.

Margaretha was a large, ocean-girt island some three hundred miles off the northeastern shore of the main continental mass of Freiland. It had been invaded and captured by the nearest colony adjoining it on the mainland mass. The island's government in exile had raised the funds to hire the Dorsais to recapture their homeland from the invaders.

Cletus had feinted with an apparent jump-belt troop drop of untrained Dorsais over Margaretha's main city. But meanwhile he had sent several thousand trained troops into the island by having them swim ashore at night at innumerable points around the coastline of the island. These infiltrators had taken charge of and coordinated the hundreds of spontaneous uprisings that had been triggered off among the island's population by word of the jump-troop drop.

Faced with uprisings from within and evident attack from without, the mainland troops that had seized the island chose discretion as the better part of valor, and abandoned the island for their home colony. They reached home only to discover how few had been the troops that had actually driven them out, and turned swiftly about to return to Margaretha.

When they reached the island this second time, however, they found watch fires burning on all the beaches, and the population aroused, armed and this time ready to die between the tide marks rather than let a single mainlander invade ashore.

As with Cletus' other military successes, it had been a victory achieved through a careful blending of imagination and psychology with what was now beginning to be regarded, on the other colony worlds, as the almost superhuman abilities of the trained Dorsai soldiers. Clearly, for all his apparent unwillingness to listen to Cletus' offer, James was not unaware of the hard facts and advantages of the proposition. It was typical of elders such as James that they were either pro or con, but never admitted to indecision.

Cletus took his leave, accordingly, having planted the seed of an idea in a Friendly mind, and being content to bide his time and let it grow.

He took a spaceship to New Earth, that sister planet of Freiland, where his command of Dorsais and a new military campaign were waiting for him. Marcus Dodds, Eachan's old second-in-command, met him at the Dorsai camp just outside of Adonyer, the main city of Breatha Colony, their employers on New Earth. In spite of the two new stars on each of his shoulder tabs, marking him as a field commander with a full division of mercenaries under him, Marcus' face was solemn with concern.

'Spainville's formed an alliance with four of the five other city-states of the interior plains,' he told Cletus, as soon as they were alone in Marcus' office. 'They call it the Central Combine, and they've mustered a combined army of better than twenty thousand regular troops. Not only that, they're ready and waiting for us. We aren't going to be able to use surprise the way we have in other campaigns, and this short division you've given me here has less than five thousand men.'

'True enough,' said Cletus, thoughtfully. 'What do you suggest I do about it?'

'Break the contract with Breatha,' said Marcus, strongly. 'We can't possibly go up against this Central Combine now without more men. And how many other new-trained Dorsais are there? Certainly not more than a couple of hundred. We've got no choice but to break the contract. You can cite the fact that the situation has changed since we were hired. Breatha may squawk, but responsible people in other colonies wanting to hire us will understand. If we don't have the troops, we don't have the troops – that's all there is to it.'

'No,' said Cletus. He got up from his seat beside Marcus' desk and walked across the room to a map showing that flat plains area of the continental interior, which Breatha shared with its rivals, five other colonies, each of which was essentially farming communities centered around one large city – hence their common name of city-states. 'I don't want to start breaking contracts, no matter how well justified we are.'

He studied the map for a minute. Breatha, with a narrow corridor running to the coast, was surrounded by the city-states of the interior on four of its five sides. Originally it had been the manufacturing center that supplied the city-states with most of their factory-made equipment and bought farm produce from the city-states in return. But then Spainville, the largest of the five city-states, had ventured into manufacturing on its own, sparking off a similar action in the other city-states – one of which, called Armoy, had chosen to construct a deep-space spaceport in competition with the one existing in Breatha Colony.

Now, with economic ambition burning bright in the former agricultural colonies of the central plain, Spainville, which bordered on Breatha's corridor to the sea, had chosen to lay claim upon that corridor and threaten to take it over by armed force if Breatha did not yield it peacefully. Hence, the presence of the Dorsais on the Breatha payroll.

'On the other hand,' said Cletus, turning back to Marcus, 'if they believe we'd been reinforced, that might be almost as good as our actually getting the necessary extra troops in here.'

'How're you going to make them think that?' demanded Marcus.

'It may take some thought,' Cletus smiled. 'At any rate, I'll make a quick trip back to Dorsai now, as though I was going after extra men, and see if I can't work out a plan on the way.'

Having announced his intentions, Cletus wasted no time. By late that evening, after a wild trip halfway around the circumference of New Earth in an atmosphere ship, he was on board a deep-space vessel that had Dorsai as its next port of call. Three days later he was back in Foralie. Melissa met him at the doorway of Grahame House with a warmth that was surprising. Since the marriage, she had slowly been softening toward him, and since the birth of their son, three months ago, that process had accelerated, even while it seemed that all those others who had once been close to Cletus were becoming more and more estranged from him.

Typical of these was Eachan, whose greeting to Cletus was almost as detached and wary as that which might be accorded a stranger. At the first opportunity, he got Cletus away from Melissa and the child to speak bluntly to his son-in-law.

'Have you seen these?' he asked, spreading an assortment of news clippings out on the desk before Cletus. They were standing in Cletus' office-study, in the west wing of Grahame House. 'They're all from Earth news services – Alliance and Coalition alike.'

Cletus glanced over the clippings. Unanimously, they were concerned with the Dorsais and himself. Not only that, but their vituperative tone was so alike that they could have been the product of a single voice.

'You see?' Eachan challenged, as Cletus finally looked up from the clippings. 'It was the Coalition news service that started calling you a pirate after the Bakhalla business. But now the Alliance has taken it up too. These city-states you're hired to go against on New Earth are backed by Alliance as well as Coalition aid and investment. If you don't look out you'll have the Alliance as well as the Coalition laying for you. Look' – his brown right forefinger stabbed at one of the clippings – 'read what Dow deCastries said in a speech in Delhi – *"If nothing else, the peoples of the Coalition and the Alliance both can join in condemning the brutal and bloody activities of the ex-Alliance renegade Grahame..."'*

Cletus laughed.

'You think this is funny?' said Eachan, grimly.

'Only in its predictability,' answered Cletus, 'and in the obviousness of Dow's intentions.'

'You mean you've been expecting this – expecting deCastries to make speeches like that?' demanded Eachan.

'Yes,' answered Cletus. He dismissed the subject. 'Never mind that. I'm back here to go through the motions of transporting an imaginary extra division of troops to Breatha Colony. I'll need at least two deep-space transports. Maybe we can arrange to lease some empty cargo spaceships for a diversionary trip—'

'You'd better listen to something else first,' Eachan interrupted him. 'Did you know you're losing Swahili?'

Cletus raised his eyebrows. 'No,' he murmured. 'But it's not surprising.'

Eachan opened a drawer of Cletus' library desk and took out a resignation form, which he dropped on the table on top of the news clippings. Cletus looked down at it. Sure enough, it was made out and signed by Swahili, now a one-star general field commander. Promotions had come thick and fast among those men who had been with Cletus from the beginning. Only Arvid, now in the field, was still a commandant – the equivalent of his old grade of captain – and Eachan, who had refused the one promotion offered him. By contrast, the once

190

ineffective Bill Athyer was now a rank above Arvid as commandant senior grade, less than two ranks away from field commander, with command of a regiment.

'I suppose I'd better talk to him,' said Cletus.

'Not that it'll do you any good,' replied Eachan.

Cletus invited Swahili up from his post at the main new-training center, now on the far side of Foralie. The next day they met briefly in that same office-study where Eachan had confronted Cletus with the news clippings shortly after his arrival home.

'Of course, I'm sorry to lose you,' said Cletus, as the two faced each other. Swahili, a single star gleaming gold on each of his shoulder tabs, bulked larger than ever in his blue dress uniform. 'But I imagine you've completely made up your mind.'

'Yes,' said Swahili. 'You understand, don't you?'

'I think so,' said Cletus.

'I think you do,' echoed Swahili softly, 'even if it is just the opposite of the way you like to do things. You've taken all the life out of war – you know that, don't you?'

'It's the way I like it,' said Cletus.

Swahili's eyes flashed a little in the soft light of the peaceful library-office. 'It's not the way I like it,' he said. 'What I like is what nearly everyone else hates – hates or is scared sick of. And it's *that* you've taken out of the business for everybody who serves under you.'

'You mean the combat, itself,' said Cletus.

'That's right,' said Swahili, softly. 'I don't like being hurt and all those weeks in the hospital any more than the next man. I don't want to die. But I put up with all the rest of it – all the training, all the hurry-up-and-waiting, all the marking time between engagements – I put up with all that, just for the few hours when everything turns real.'

'You're a killer. Or don't you admit that to yourself?' asked Cletus.

'No,' said Swahili. 'I'm a special fighter, that's all. I like to fight. Just the killing itself wouldn't do anything for me. I told you I didn't want to get hurt, or killed, any more than the next man. I feel just as hollow inside when the energy weapons start burning the air over my head. At the same time, I wouldn't miss it for anything. It's a dirty, damn universe, and every once in a while I get a chance to hit back at it. That's all. If I knew in the morning when I started out that I was going to be killed that day, I'd still go – because I couldn't die happier than to go down hitting back.'

He stopped talking, abruptly. For a moment he simply looked at Cletus in the silence of the room.

'And it's *that* you've taken out of mercenary work,' he said. 'So I'm going someplace else where they still have it.'

Cletus held out his hand. 'Good luck,' he said.

They shook hands.

'Luck to you,' said Swahili. 'You'll need it. In the end the man with gloves on always loses to the bare-knuckle fighter.'

'You'll have your chance to test that belief, at least,' said Cletus.

23

A week later Cletus returned to New Earth with two leased cargo vessels, the crew and officers of which had agreed to being held in a locked room during the embarking and disembarking of the troops they were supposed to carry. They could testify afterward only to hearing the sounds of boots entering the ship for two and a half hours, on Dorsai, and to some four hours of similar sounds as they hung in orbit above New Earth, while landing craft shuttled from their ships to some unannounced spot on the planet below. Agents for the Central Combine of city-states, however, observed these landing craft making their sit-downs in a wooded area just inside Breatha Colony's border with Spainville. On attempting to investigate further, the agents found themselves stopped and warned back by a cordon of armed Dorsais, but their estimate of the troops landed, taken from the number of trips from the spaceship in orbit, was at least five thousand men.

General Lu May, commander of the city-states combined forces, grunted when this information was brought to him.

'That's the sort of thing this Grahame likes to pull,' said Lu May. The general was in his mid-seventies, and had been retired from active soldiering until the new ambitions and war-like fervor of the city-states had summoned him back to take over-all command of their new army. 'He'd like to shake us up with the idea that we've got to watch two separate invading commands. But I'll lay you odds he pulls them together at the first opportunity, as soon as he thinks he's got us out in the open where he can pull all sorts of fancy maneuvers. But we aren't going to fall for it. We'll stay dug in here in Spainville, and make him come to us.'

He chuckled. He was fat as well as old, and the thought of being able to frustrate this unorthodox young upstart while remaining comfortably seated in his own home in Spainville tickled him. He ordered heavy energy weapons dug in all around the perimeter of the city and all approaches heavily mined. It would take more than the light-weaponed and light-armored Dorsai mercenaries to break through defenses such as these, even if they were equal in number to the men he had under arms inside the city.

Meanwhile, Cletus' forces were already in motion. A motley horde of civilian trucks and other heavy-duty, air-cushioned sliders had earlier converged on the area where the shuttleboats had landed from the spaceships. These now moved out like a transport and supply convoy, with an armed Dorsai driving each of them. This force crossed the border into Armoy, and swung inland toward Armoy City and its new spaceport, thereby raising flutters of alarm within the community's citizens.

'Sit tight!' grunted Lu May to the frantic messages that reached him from Armoy City for an expeditionary force to defend them against the oncoming Dorsais. He did not send the force, but instead followed his own advice, sitting tight and watching Cletus' other command, which was also in movement now, across the Spainville border, heading apparently through Spainville toward one of the other adjoining city-states. Still Lu May made no move, and sure enough, once it had passed the city of Spainville, Cletus' first command of Dorsais swung about and came up on the city's rear. At the same time, the command that had been threatening Armoy City swung away and cut in to come up before the city of Spainville, so that within a few days the city was ringed by the Dorsai troops.

Lu May chortled and slapped his fat knees. Curiously enough, in Cletus' headquarters outside the city, there was hardly less satisfaction to be found in the person of Chancellor Ad Reyes, representative of the government of Breatha Colony, who was accompanying Cletus, ostensibly as an 'observer.'

'Excellent, Marshal. Excellent!' Reyes, who was a thin, eager, scholarly-looking man with a high forehead, dressed in the long, black, official gown of his chancellor-hood, rubbed his thin hands with pleasure. 'You've managed to trap their army here. And there're no other forces who can come to their rescue. Excellently done!'

'You should thank General Lu May for that, instead of me,' Cletus answered dryly. 'He has a good deal less to fear from us, sitting back behind his mine fields and his perimeter defenses, than he does in the open field, where the Dorsais are a great deal more mobile than his troops. He has more men and he's in an entrenched position.'

'But you don't have to try to take the place by assault!' protested Reyes. 'You can live off the country or supply yourself from Breatha as you want. Lu May's cut off from outside supplies. It's just a matter of starving him out!'

'That may not be easy,' said Cletus, 'unless he's been strangely forgetful, while preparing for everything else, to stock enough provisions for the city and his troops so that they can hold out longer than we can afford to sit here besieging them.'

Reyes frowned. Plainly, it seemed to him that this Dorsai marshal was taking an entirely too gloomy a view of the situation.

'Do you object to besieging the city?' Reyes demanded. 'If so, I should probably mention that the Breatha government considered this the optimum – indeed the only – course you could pursue, if you were lucky enough to trap Lu May in a fixed position.'

'I don't object – for now,' Cletus answered, quietly. 'But that's because there're military reasons for it, far removed from the opinions of your government. I might remind you, Chancellor, that one of my stipulations in accepting employment with Breatha Colony, as it is with every government with whom I sign a contract, is that I, alone, be in charge of the conduct of the campaign.'

He turned and sat down behind the desk in the office of the field structure in which they had been talking. 'And now, if you'll excuse me, I've got work to do.'

Reyes hesitated, then turned on his heel and walked out.

Cletus continued the siege for three weeks, throwing up breastworks and digging his own trenches behind them to encircle the city, as if he had every intention of staying indefinitely. Meanwhile, outside of an occasional exchange of small-arms fire, there was little open conflict between the city defenders and its Dorsai attackers.

Meanwhile, overhead, a similar unspoken truce existed. Dorsai aircraft patrolled the atmosphere above and about the city to prevent city-state vessels from entering or leaving it. But beyond this, there was no aerial conflict. As in most inter-colony armed conflicts on the new worlds, air warfare was being avoided by the sort of tacit agreement that had interdicted the use of poison gas during World War II in the twentieth century on Earth. The object of armed struggle between opposed technology-poor communities, such as the young colonies, was not so much to destroy the enemy's productive capacity as to take it away from him. One did not obliterate by bombing that which one had started a war to obtain. And if the factories and other hardware of civilization were valuable, the men who had the skills to operate them were almost as valuable.

Therefore, bombing and even the indiscriminate use of heavy

weapons in the vicinity of built-up areas was avoided, and – atmosphere craft being almost as expensive as spacecraft – any use of the skies other than for reconnaissance or the transporting of troops was likewise avoided.

At the end of three weeks, however, Cletus apparently lost patience with this stalemate and issued orders, orders that brought Chancellor Ad Reyes literally running to Cletus' headquarters office, the black gown tucked up to allow free movement to the chancellor's legs.

'You're pulling out half your forces and sending them to take Armoy City and its spaceport!' Reyes accused him, bursting into Cletus' office.

Cletus looked up from the desk at which he was working. 'You've heard of that, have you?' Cletus asked.

'Heard of it!' Reyes strode up to the edge of the desk and leaned over it almost as though he would have liked to have thrust his face nose-to-nose with Cletus'. 'I've *seen* them! All those civilian trucks you requisitioned to transport your secondary command are headed off toward Armoy! Don't tell me that isn't where they're headed!'

'That's where they're headed,' said Cletus agreeably. 'The rest of us will be following them in twenty-four hours. There's plainly no point in continuing this siege any longer. I'm going to raise it, move on Armoy City and take that spaceport of theirs.'

'Raise the siege? ... What kind of trick is this? If you'd been paid by the city-states to betray us, you couldn't have picked a better—' He broke off abruptly, shrinking a little at the sudden sound of his own words in his ears. Cletus was on his feet behind the desk.

'I hope I don't hear you correctly, Chancellor,' Cletus' voice and eyes had changed. 'Are you accusing Dorsais of dishonoring a contract with your government?'

'No ... that is, I didn't mean ...' Reyes stammered.

'I'd advise you to be careful of what you do mean,' said Cletus. 'The Dorsais don't break contracts, and we don't tolerate talk that we do. And now, for the last time, let me remind you that I – I, alone – am in command of this campaign. Perhaps you should get back to your own quarters, now.'

'Yes, I ...' Reyes fled.

Just before dawn the following morning, the rest of the Dorsais besieging Spainville mounted their military vehicles and pulled out with all armor and weapons. Only their aircraft remained above Spainville to discourage pursuit by air reconnaissance.

Dawn rose on the empty trenches and breastworks that the mercenaries had thrown up, it was nearly noon before their silence and appearance of abandonment could tempt patrols out from Spainville to investigate. When, however, the former Dorsai positions had been investigated and found to be abandoned, the patrols took note of the direction of the signs of departure visible in the pasture earth and summer grass south of the city, and passed the word hastily to General Lu May.

Lu May, roused with this news from his slumbers after a late evening, swore in a way that had gone out of fashion forty years ago.

'We've got him!' the old man exploded, rolling out of bed and beginning hastily to struggle into his clothes. 'He couldn't stand the waiting – now he's cut his own throat!'

'Sir?' protested the colonel who had brought him the news. 'Cut his own throat? I don't understand—'

'That's because you kids know nothing about war the way it's really fought!' trumpeted Lu May, getting into his trousers. 'Grahame's headed for Armoy City, idiot!'

'Yes, sir,' said the colonel. 'But I still don't see—'

'He's faced the fact that there was no hope of his taking the city here!' snapped Lu May. 'So he's pulled out and decided to take Armoy City, instead. That way he can claim that he did the best he could, and at least got Breatha Colony the spaceport that was giving them competition! With the spaceport, he'll tell them, they can make a deal to protect their corridor to the sea! Don't you see? Grahame's finally faced the fact that it was a bad contract he signed. He wants to get out of it on any terms – but he can't get out unless he has at least something to offer Breatha. Armoy City and that spaceport will be it!'

'Yes, sir,' said the colonel, earnestly. 'I see all that. But what I don't understand is why you say he cut his own throat. After all, if he's able to give Breatha Colony the spaceport and Armoy City to bargain with—'

Idiot! Double idiot!' roared Lu May. 'He has to take Armoy City first, doesn't he, fool?'

'Yes, sir—'

'Then he's going to have to occupy Armoy City with his forces, isn't he?'

Dressed at last, Lu May waddled hastily toward the door. Over his shoulder, he continued, 'If we move fast after him, we'll catch him inside Armoy City, and we can surround him! He's got no supplies to last in a city like that very long – and if we need to, we even have the men and weapons to take the city by storm! Either way we can wrap his Dorsais up and have him as a prisoner to do what we want with!'

Lu May wasted no time in getting his army in pursuit of Cletus and

197

the Dorsais. But for all his hurry, he did not fail to move out in good marching order, or without the heavy energy weapons he had dug in around the perimeter of the city, and which he now took with him, even though having them with him would necessarily slow his movement. Ponderous, but deadly, he slid along over the plain track Cletus' two departing commands had left behind through the standing grass and grain.

The direction of the track aimed directly at Armoy City, perhaps three days' travel away for Cletus' lightly equipped Dorsais. Lu May would be lucky to do it in four with his command, but the extra day should bring the Spainville general on the scene at Armoy City, as he calculated, just in good time to take advantage of that moment in which Cletus' troops were letting down, after having made their conquest of Armoy City and the spaceport an accomplished fact.

All the same, it was wise ... thought Lu May – to give himself a little time margin if at all possible. If he should find himself ahead of schedule, he could always dawdle a bit in coming up to the city at the far end of his pursuit. Therefore, he issued orders after the evening meal for his command to continue after dark, under the moonless but star-bright New Earth sky. He pushed them on through the darkness until men began falling asleep at the controls of their vehicles, or on their feet. Finally, reluctantly, he called a halt for the night about three hours after midnight.

His army had just managed to get deeply into exhausted slumber, when a series of sharp, blasting explosions jerked them back to wakefulness, and they sat up to see the heavy energy weapons they had been hauling burning with sparkling red-white flames as their energy storage units melted under their own fierce heat like butter in a furnace. In the same moment, dark-clad Dorsais were suddenly among Lu May's troops stripping them of their body weapon and herding them into groups under the watchful eyes and guns of other mercenaries standing guard.

General Lu May, himself, started out of deep slumber, and sat up in his field bed to find Cletus standing over him, an uncapped holster showing the sidearm at Cletus' side. Lu May stared in befuddlement.

'But you're ... up ahead of me ...' he stammered, after a moment.

'I've got a detachment of empty civilian trucks up ahead of you,' answered Cletus. 'Trucks that never had any men in them except the drivers. What men I had are here with me now – and your command is taken prisoner, General. You'll make things simpler by giving me your surrender, right now.'

Lu May fumbled out of bed. Suddenly he was very old, and chilly, and helpless, standing there in his pajamas. Almost humbly, he went through the motions of surrender.

Cletus went back to the field unit that had already been set up as his temporary headquarters. Waiting inside for him was Chancellor Ad Reyes.

'You can inform your government that the effective military forces of the combined city-states are now our prisoner, Chancellor ...' he began, and broke off as Arvid entered, bearing a yellow message slip.

'Signal from Colonel Khan on Dorsai,' said Arvid, 'forwarded on by our base camp at Adonyer, back in Breatha Colony.'

Cletus took the message sheet and unfolded it. He read:

Attack made through Etter's Pass from Neuland into Bakhalla territory beaten off. Alliance and Coalition forces combined in a joint 'Peace Force' for the new worlds. Dow deCastries has supreme command of this force.

Cletus folded the message and put it in a pocket of his battle tunic. He turned to Reyes.

'You've got twenty-four hours,' he said, 'to get Breatha troops here to take charge of these prisoners we've just captured. I and my troops must return immediately to Dorsai.'

Reyes stared at him in combined awe and amazement. 'But we'd planned a triumphal parade in case of victory ...' he began, uncertainly.

'Twenty-four hours,' said Cletus, brusquely. He turned on his heel and left the chancellor standing.

24

Landing back on Dorsai, Cletus phoned ahead to order Major Arvid Johnson, now acting field commander, to meet him at Grahame House. Then with Bill Athyer like a smaller, beak-nosed shadow at his side, he took a hired atmosphere craft to Foralie and Grahame House, still wearing his battle uniform.

Melissa, with Arvid and Eachan, met him just inside the front door. Athyer, diffident still in spite of his present rank, stood at the far end of the entrance hall as Cletus greeted Melissa and Eachan briefly before striding on toward the door to his office-study and beckoning Eachan and Arvid to follow him.

'You too, Bill,' he said to Athyer.

He closed the door of the office behind them. 'What's the latest word?' Cletus demanded of his father-in-law, as he walked around to stand behind the pile of message blanks on his desk and stare down at them.

'It seems deCastries was appointed to this position as Commander-in-Chief of the joint Alliance-Coalition troops on the new worlds several months ago,' answered Eachan. 'The Coalition and the Alliance just kept it secret while the two high commands built up a news campaign to get the common citizens of Earth on both sides ready for the idea. Also, Arthur Walco's here to see you. Seems like deCastries is already making trouble for him at those stibnite mines on Newton.'

'Yes, there'll be brush wars breaking out all over the new worlds now ... I'll see Walco tomorrow morning,' said Cletus. He turned to Arvid.

'Well, Arv,' he said. 'If the Dorsai had medals to give I'd be handing you a fistful of them right now. I hope someday you can forgive me for this. I had to have you thinking I'd shoved you aside into the field for good.'

'You didn't, sir?' asked Arvid, quietly.

'No,' said Cletus. 'I wanted a development in you. And I've got it.'

In fact, it was a different man who stood before them to answer to the name of Arvid Johnson. Not the least of the changes was that he looked at least five years older. His white-blond hair had darkened as though with age, and his skin was more deeply suntanned than it had been. He looked as though he had lost weight, and yet he appeared larger than ever, a man of gaunt bone and whipcord muscle, towering over all of them.

At the same time something was gone from him for good. A youthfulness, a friendly softness that had been a basic part of him before was vanished now. In its place was something grim and isolated, as though he had at last become coldly conscious of the strength and skill in him that set him apart from other men. A quality like the sheer, physical deadliness of Swahili had entered into him.

He stood without moving. When he had moved earlier, it had been almost without a sound. He seemed to carry about him now a carefulness born of the consciousness that all others were smaller and weaker than he, so that he must remember not to damage them without intent. Like someone more warrior than man, prototype of some line of invincible giants to come, he stood by Cletus' desk.

'That's good to hear,' he said softly, to Cletus, now. 'What do you want me to do?'

'Fight a campaign – if necessary,' said Cletus. 'I'm going to give you a world to defend. And I'm promoting you two grades to a new rank – vice-marshal. You'll be working in team with another officer also holding an entirely new rank – the rank of battle operator.'

He turned slightly to look at Bill Athyer. 'That'll be Bill here,' he said. 'As battle op, Bill will rank just below you and above any other officer in the field with you, except myself.'

Arvid and Bill looked at each other.

'Battle operator?' said Eachan.

'That's right,' Cletus answered him. 'Don't look so surprised, Eachan. This is something we've been headed toward from the start, with the reorganization and retraining of the men.'

He looked back at Arvid and Bill. 'The marshal, or vice-marshal, and the battle operator,' Cletus said, 'will form a general commander's team. The battle op is the theoretical strategist of that team and the vice-marshal is the field tactician. The two will bear roughly the same relationship to each other as an architect and a general contractor in the construction of a building. The battle op will first consider the strategical situation and problem, and lay out a campaign plan. And in this process he will have complete authority and freedom.'

Cletus had been watching Bill in particular as he spoke. Now, he paused. 'You understand, Bill?' he said.

'Yes, sir,' he replied.

'Then, however' – Cletus' eyes swung to Arvid ... 'the battle op will hand his strategical plan to the vice-marshal, and from that point on, it'll be the vice-marshal who has complete authority. His job will be to take the plan given him, make any and all alterations in it he thinks it needs for practical purposes and then execute it as he sees fit. *You* understand, Arv?'

'Yes, sir,' said Arvid, softly.

'Good,' said Cletus. 'Then you and Bill are released from your present duties as of now and you'll begin immediately on your new jobs. The world I'm giving you to start with is Dorsai here, and the first force you'll be working with will be made up of women and children, the sick, the injured, and the average men.'

He smiled a little at them. 'Then get at it, both of you,' he said. 'None of us has any time to waste nowadays.'

As the door to the office closed behind the two of them, a wave of the fatigue he had been holding at bay for a number of days and hours now suddenly washed over him. He swayed where he stood and felt Eachan catch him by the elbow.

'No – it's all right,' he said. His vision cleared and he looked into Eachan's concerned face. 'I'm just tired, that's all. I'll take a nap and then we'll hit things after dinner.'

With Eachan walking guardedly beside him, he walked out of the office-study, feeling as though he were stepping on pillows, and went up to his bedroom. The bed was before him; he dropped onto its yielding surface without bothering even to take off his boots ... And that was the last he remembered.

He awoke just before sunset, ate a light meal and spent half an hour getting reacquainted with his son. Then he closeted himself in his office with Eachan to attack the pile of paper work. They sorted the correspondence into two piles, one which Cletus had to answer himself and one which Eachan could answer with a few words per letter of direction from him. Both men dictated until nearly dawn before the desk was cleared and the necessary orders for Dorsai and off-world troops were issued.

The interview in the study next day with the Newtonian chairman, Walco, was brief and bitter. The bitterness might have gone into acrimony and the interview prolonged unduly if Cletus had not cut short Walco's scarcely veiled accusations.

'The contract I signed with you,' said Cletus, 'promised to capture Watershed and the stibnite mines, and turn them over to your own troops. We made no guarantee that you'd stay in control of the mines. Holding onto them was up to you, and to whatever agreement you could make with the Brozans.'

'We made our agreement!' said Walco. 'But now that they've suddenly been reinforced by fifteen thousand Alliance and Coalition troops, courtesy of this fellow deCastries, they're refusing to honor it. They claim they made it under duress!'

'Didn't they?' Cletus said.

'That's not the point! The point is, we need you and enough troops from Dorsai, right away, to match those fifteen thousand soldiers from Earth that the Brozans're holding over us like a club.'

Cletus shook his head. 'I'm sorry,' he said. 'I'm facing unusual demands on my available mercenaries right now. Also, I'm not free to come to Newton, myself.'

Walco's face went lumpy and hard. 'You help get us into a spot,' he said, 'and then when trouble comes, you leave us to face it alone. Is that what you call justice?'

'Was justice mentioned when you signed us to the original contract?' replied Cletus, grimly. 'I don't remember it. If justice had been a topic, I'd have been forced to point out to you that, while it was your funds and experts who developed the stibnite mine, that was only because you were in a position to take advantage of the Brozan poverty that was then keeping them from developing the mines themselves. You may have a financial interest in the mines, but the Brozans have a moral claim to them – they're a Brozan natural resource. If you'd faced that fact, you'd hardly have been able to avoid seeing their moral claim, which would have to be recognized by you, eventually—' He broke off.

'Forgive me,' he said, dryly. 'I'm a little overworked these days. I gave up long ago doing other people's thinking for them. I've told you that neither I, nor an expeditionary force of the size you ask for, is available to you right at the moment.'

'Then what will you do for us?' muttered Walco.

'I can send you some men to officer and command your own forces, provided you contract to let them make all the military decisions, themselves.'

'What?' Walco cried out the word. 'That's worse than nothing!'

'I'll be perfectly happy to let you have nothing, then, if that's what you prefer,' said Cletus. 'If so, let me know now. My time's limited at the moment.'

There was a second's pause. Gradually the lumpiness of Walco's features smoothed out into an expression almost of despair.

'We'll take your officers,' he said, on a long exhalation of breath.

'Good. Colonel Khan will have the contract ready for you in two days. You can discuss the terms with him then,' said Cletus. 'And now, if you'll excuse me ...'

Walco left. Cletus called in David Ap Morgan, one of Eachan's old officers, now a senior field commander, and gave him the job of herding up the officers to be sent to command the troops of the Associated Advanced Communities on Newton.

'You can turn the job down, of course,' Cletus wound up.

'You know I won't,' said David Ap Morgan. 'What do you want me to do?'

'Thanks,' said Cletus. 'All right. I'm going to give you about twelve hundred and fifty men, each one bumped up at least one rank from what he's holding now. You'll have ex-noncoms to be your force leaders. Use them to replace all the local commissioned officers – I mean *all*. And the contract's being written to give you sole command in military matters. Be sure you keep that command. Don't take any advice from Walco and his government, under any circumstances. Tell them if they don't leave you alone, you'll pull out and come back here.'

David nodded. 'Yes, sir,' he said. 'Any plan for the campaign?'

'Just make sure you don't fight any stand-up battles,' said Cletus. 'I probably don't need to tell you that. Your AAC troops wouldn't be any good in a stand-up battle anyway. But even if they would be, I still wouldn't want you to fight. Tease the Alliance-Coalition forces into chasing you – and then keep them chasing. Lead them all over the map. Hit them just enough to keep them hot after you and break up into guerrilla groups if they get too close. Do anything needed to keep them worried and your own casualties down as much as possible.'

David nodded again.

'I think' – Cletus looked at him seriously – 'you'll find you'll lose 70 or 80 per cent of your AAC troops through desertion in the first four to six weeks. The ones that hang on will be the ones who're starting to have faith in you. You may be able to start training them as they go to turn into fairly effective soldiers.'

'I'll do that,' said David. 'Anything else?'

'No. Just make it as expensive for the enemy as possible,' answered Cletus. 'Don't hit their troops when you can avoid it. Make their casualties light, but make it expensive for them in material. The more active duty soldiers they have, the more there'll be around to miss the food, equipment and other supplies I'm counting on you to destroy, every chance you get.'

'Got it,' said David, and went off, whistling, to his nearby home of Fal Morgan, to pack his gear for the campaign. Like all his family, he had a fine singing voice and he also whistled sweetly and intricately. Unexpectedly, hearing that tune fade away down his entrance hall and out the front door of Grahame House, Cletus was reminded of a song Melissa had played and sung for him once. It was a small, sad, beautiful tune made by a young member of the Ap Morgan family who had died in some campaign when Melissa had been even younger, long before Cletus had come to Dorsai.

He could not remember it all, but it dealt with the young soldier's strong memories of the house where he had grown up, remembered while he was waiting for an engagement to begin on some other world.

... *Fal Morgan, Fal Morgan, when morning is gray, Your wall stones and rooftree stand near me, today* ...

Cletus shook the emotional tag end of recollection from his mind. He turned to the task of picking out the men he would promote and send with David.

During the weeks that followed, the demand upon the Dorsai professional soldiers continued. Everywhere that Cletus had won a campaign, the combined Alliance-Coalition forces were in action, trying to reverse whatever situation his successful actions had created.

The efforts of the forces from Earth were ponderous and awesome. Together, the Alliance and the Coalition had better than half a million military people scattered out upon the new worlds. If the full half million could have been made effective in the campaigns Dow deCastries was trying to conduct, any opposition by the Dorsais or the attacked colonies could not have lasted more than a few days in each case.

As it was, however, nearly half the half million were engaged in military occupations other than those of a fighting soldier or officer. And of the more than two hundred and fifty thousand men that this left technically available for active duty in the field, more than a hundred and fifty thousand at any one time were rendered – or managed to render themselves – ineffective through a variety of means and for a variety of causes.

Among these were deep suspicions and old rivalries between former Alliance officers and their new Coalition partners; also, there was laziness and inefficiency among those of all ranks and political backgrounds, and the sheer blundering that inevitably resulted from the disorganization in such a large, hastily formed partnership of military units.

In spite of this, with all these subtractions, there remained a hard core of perhaps eighty thousand well-trained and superbly equipped troops from Earth to face a couple of hundred thousand almost useless and practically non-equipped local Colonial troops, plus a relative handful of Dorsais. Cletus could hardly have put twenty thousand Dorsai men in the field, even if he had scraped together every male from that small world, including walking cripples, between the ages of twelve and eighty.

Sending small contingents of Dorsais to officer Colonial troops was one solution; but only where the Colonial troops had at least a shred of training and effectiveness. Where this was not the case – as on Cassida – or where there simply were no native Colonial troops to officer – as on St. Marie – actual contingents of Dorsais had to be sent.

'But why don't we just stop?' demanded Melissa, anguished one day after she had come back from visiting a neighboring household that had lost yet another of the family's men. 'Why can't we just stop sending men out?'

'For the same reason the Coalition and the Alliance have combined to send men to reverse everything we've accomplished,' Cletus answered her. 'If they beat us at every point, they'll destroy our value as soldiers for hire to the other colonies. That's what Dow's really after. Then they'll come on to Dorsai and destroy us.'

'You can't be sure of that – that they're out to destroy us!'

'I can't be other than sure. Nor can anyone who's thought the matter through,' said Cletus. 'We were winning every campaign and proving ourselves superior to their own troops. A little more of that, and troops from the Alliance and the Coalition wouldn't be needed any more on the new worlds. And with the need gone for any military support from Earth, there'd go Earth's influence among the colonies. This way, if they win, they protect their hold on the new worlds. While if we win—'

'Win!' snorted Eachan, who was in the room at the time.

'If we win,' repeated Cletus, looking steadily at the older man, 'we break that hold for good. It's a battle for survival between us now – when it's over, either Earth or Dorsai are going to be counted out on the new worlds.'

She stared at him, her eyes unnaturally wide, for a long moment of silence. 'I can't believe that!' she said at last. She turned to her father. 'Dad—'

'Oh, it's true enough,' said Eachan flatly, from across the room. 'We *were* too successful – with Cletus' early campaigns on Newton and worlds like that. We scared the Alliance and the Coalition, both. Now they're out to make themselves safe. And they're very big, and we're very small ... And we've already sent out the last men we've got to send.'

'They haven't any left in reserve either,' said Cletus.

Eachan said nothing. Melissa turned back to Cletus.

'No,' said Cletus, although she had not spoken, 'I don't intend to lose.'

Eachan still said nothing. In the silence, distantly, the front door annunciator chimed. A second later, an aide opened the door.

'Rebon, Exotic Outbond to Dorsai, sir,' he said.

'Bring him in,' said Cletus. The aide stood aside and a slight man in blue robes entered the room.

His face held the eternal Exotic calm, but his expression was serious nonetheless. He came up to Cletus as both Cletus and Eachan got to their feet.

'I've got some bad news I'm afraid, Cletus,' he said. 'A military force of the Alliance-Coalition Peace Force has seized the Maran core-tap site and all the equipment and technicians there.'

'On what basis?' snapped Eachan.

'The Coalition has filed claims against the Associated Advanced Communities of Newton,' said Rebon, turning slightly to face Eachan. 'They've seized the core-tap site as an AAC asset pending settlement of their claim. Mondar' – he turned back to Cletus – 'asks your help.'

'When did this happen?' asked Cletus.

'Eight hours ago,' said Rebon.

'Eight hours!' exploded Eachan. The fastest spaceship – and there was no known swifter way of transmitting messages across interstellar space – required at least three days to cover the light-years between Mara and Dorsai. Rebon's eyes veiled themselves slightly.

'I assure you it's true,' he murmured.

'And where'd the troops come from?' demanded Eachan. He threw a glance at Cletus. 'They weren't supposed to have any more available!'

'From the Friendlies, undoubtedly,' replied Cletus.

Rebon lifted his gaze back to Cletus, slowly. 'That's true,' he said, on a note of surprise. 'You expected this?'

'I expected deCastries to hire help from Harmony or Association eventually,' said Cletus, brusquely. 'I'll leave right away.'

'For the core-tap site on Mara?' Relief sounded in Rebon's voice. 'You *can* raise men to help us, then?'

'No. Alone. For Kultis,' said Cletus, already striding out of the room, 'to talk to Mondar.'

Boarding the spaceship that would take him to Kultis, he encountered at the foot of the boarding ladder Vice-Marshal Arvid Johnson and Battle Operator William Athyer, who had been ordered to meet him there. Cletus stopped for a moment to speak to them.

'Well,' said Cletus, 'do you still have any notion I gave you a nothing job when I put you in charge of defending Dorsai?'

'No, sir.' Arvid looked calmly at him.

'Good. It's up to you then,' said Cletus. 'You know the principles behind whatever action you'll need to take. Good luck.'

'Thank you,' said Bill. 'Good luck to you, too, sir.'

'I make it a point not to know the lady,' said Cletus. 'I can't afford to count on her.'

He went up the boarding ladder and the entry port of the ship closed behind him.

Five minutes later it leaped skyward in thunder and was lost into space.

25

Mondar had changed in some indefinable way, since Cletus had seen him last, when they met again in Mondar's garden-enclosed residence in Bakhalla. There were no new lines in the calm face, no touch of gray in the Exotic's hair, but the blue eyes, like Melissa's, were becoming strangely deeper in color, as though the time that had passed had dredged new levels of understanding in the mind behind them.

'You can't help us on Mara, then, Cletus?' were the words with which he greeted Cletus on the latter's arrival.

'I don't have any more troops to send,' said Cletus. 'And if I had, I'd strongly suggest we not send them.'

They passed through the halls of Mondar's house, walking side by side, and emerged into an enclosure, half-room, half-arbor, where Mondar waved Cletus to a wide, basket-weave chair, and then took one like it himself. All this time Mondar had not spoken; but now he did.

'We stand to lose more than we can afford, if we lose our present investment in the core-tap,' said Mondar. 'We've still got a contingent of your Dorsais here in Bakhalla. Can't we use some of them to retake the core-tap site?'

'Not unless you want the additional Alliance-Coalition troops that have been put into Neuland to come boiling over the border into your colony, here,' said Cletus. 'You don't want that, do you?'

'No,' said Mondar. 'We don't want that. But what's to be done about the Friendly mercenaries occupying the core-tap site?'

'Leave them there,' said Cletus.

Mondar gazed at him. 'Cletus,' he said softly after a second, 'You aren't just trying to justify this situation you've created?'

'Do you trust my judgment?' countered Cletus.

'I've got a high regard for it,' Mondar answered slowly, 'personally. But I'm afraid that most of the other Outbonds here and in the Maran colonies of our people don't share that high regard at the moment.'

'But they still trust you to make the decisions about me, don't they?' asked Cletus.

Mondar gazed at him, curiously. 'What makes you so sure of that?' he asked.

'The fact that I've gotten everything I've ever asked the Exotics for, through you – up until now,' answered Cletus. 'You're the man who has to recommend me as a bad bet or a good one, still, aren't you?'

'Yes,' said Mondar, with something of a sigh. 'And that's why I'm afraid you won't find me as personally partial to you now as I might be, Cletus. I've got a responsibility to my fellow Exotics now that makes me take a harder view of the situation than I might take by myself. Also, I've got a responsibility to come to some kind of a decision between you and the Alliance-Coalition combination.'

'What's the procedure if you decide for them – and against us?' asked Cletus.

'I'm afraid we'd have to come to the best possible terms with them that we could,' Mondar answered. 'Undoubtedly they'd want us to do more than dismiss the troops we've now got in hire from you, and call in your loan. They'd want us to actively throw our support on their side, hire their troops and help them against you on Dorsai.'

Cletus nodded. 'Yes, that's what they'd want,' he said. 'All right, what do you need to decide to stick with Dorsai?'

'Some indication that Dorsai stands a chance of surviving the present situation,' said Mondar. 'To begin with, I've told you we face a severe loss in the case of the Maran core-tap, and you said just now, even if you had the troops to spare, you'd suggest doing nothing about the Alliance-Coalition occupation of the site. You must have some reasoning to back that suggestion?'

'Certainly,' said Cletus. 'If you stop and think for a moment, you'll realize the core-tap project itself is perfectly safe. It's a structure with both potential and actual value – to the Alliance and Coalition, as well as to anyone else. Maybe they've occupied the site, but you can be sure they aren't going to damage the work done so far by the men or machines that can finish it.'

'But what good's that do us, if it stays in their hands?'

'It won't stay long,' said Cletus. 'The occupying troops are Friendlies and their religious, cultural discipline makes them excellent occupying troops – but that's all. They look down their noses at the very people who hire them, and the minute their pay stops coming they'll pack up and go home. So wait a week. At the end of that time either Dow will have won, or I will. If he's won, you can still make terms with him. If

I've won, your Friendlies will pack up and leave at a word from me.'

Mondar looked at him narrowly. 'Why do you say a week?' he asked.

'Because it won't be longer than that,' Cletus answered. 'Dow's hiring of Friendly troops gives away the fact that he's ready for a showdown.'

'It does?' Mondar's eyes were still closely watching him. Cletus met them squarely with his own gaze.

'That's right,' he said. 'We know the number of the available field troops in the Alliance-Coalition force that Dow's put together. It can be estimated from what we already knew of the number of troops the Alliance and the Coalition had out on the new worlds, separately. Dow had to use all of them to start enough brush wars to tie up all my Dorsais. He hadn't any spare fighting men. But, by replacing his fighting troops with Friendlies, he can temporarily withdraw a force great enough, in theory, to destroy me. Therefore the appearance of Friendly troops under Dow's command can only mean he's forming such a showdown force.'

'You can't be sure his hiring of Friendlies as mercenaries means just that, and not something else.'

'Of course I can,' said Cletus. 'After all, I was the one who suggested the use of the Friendly troops in that way.'

'*You* suggested?' Mondar stared.

'In effect,' said Cletus. 'I stopped off at Harmony myself some time back, to talk to James Arm-of-the-Lord and suggest he hire out members of his Militant Church as raw material to fill uniforms and swell the official numbers of my Dorsais. I offered him a low price for the men. It hardly took any imagination to foresee that once the idea'd been suggested to him, he'd turn around as soon as I'd left and try to get a higher price from Dow for the same men, used the same way.'

'And Dow, of course with Alliance and Coalition money, could pay a higher price,' said Mondar, thoughtfully. 'But if that's true, why didn't Dow hire them earlier?'

'Because exposing them to conflicts with my Dorsais would have quickly given away the fact that the Friendlies hadn't any real military skills,' replied Cletus. 'Dow's best use of them could come only from putting them into uniform briefly, to replace the elite Alliance-Association troops he wanted to withdraw secretly, for a final battle to settle all matters.'

'You seem,' said Mondar slowly, 'very sure of all this, Cletus.'

'That's natural enough,' said Cletus. 'It's what I've been pointing toward ever since I sat down at the table with Dow and the rest of you on board the spaceship to Kultis.'

Mondar raised his eyebrows. 'That much planning and executing?' he said 'Still, it doesn't mean you can be absolutely sure Dow will do what you think he'll do.'

'Nothing's absolutely sure, of course,' said Cletus, 'But for practical purposes I'm sure enough. Can you get your fellow Exotics to hold off action on the occupation of the Maran core-tap site for seven days?'

Mondar hesitated. 'I think so,' he said. 'For seven days, anyway. Meanwhile, what are you going to do?'

'Wait,' said Cletus.

'Here?' said Mondar. 'With Dow, according to your estimate, gathering his best troops to strike? I'm surprised you left Dorsai to come here in the first place.'

'No need to be surprised,' said Cletus. 'You know I know that the Exotics somehow seem to get information of events on other worlds faster than the fastest spaceship can bring it. It merely seemed to me that information might reach me as fast here as it would any place. Would you say I was wrong?'

Mondar smiled slightly. 'No,' he answered. 'I'd have to say you weren't wrong. Be my guest, then, while you wait.'

'Thank you,' said Cletus.

Mondar's guest, then, he remained – for three days during which he inspected the Dorsai troops in Bakhalla, browsed in the local library that had been the scene of Bill Athyer's discovery of a new occupation and life and renewed his old acquaintance with Wefer Linet.

On the morning of the fourth day, as he and Mondar were having breakfast together, a young Exotic in a green robe brought in a paper, which he handed to Mondar without a word. Mondar glanced at it and passed it over to Cletus.

'Dow and fifteen shiploads of Coalition elite troops,' Mondar said, 'landed on Dorsai two days ago. They've occupied the planet.'

Cletus got to his feet.

'What now?' Mondar looked up at him from the table. 'There's nothing you can do now. Without Dorsai, what have you got?'

'What did I have before I had Dorsai?' retorted Cletus. 'It's not Dorsai Dow wants, Mondar, it's me. And as long as I'm able to operate, he hasn't won. I'll be leaving for Dorsai immediately.'

Mondar got to his feet. 'I'll go with you,' he said.

26

The shuttleboat, with the Exotic sunburst emblem inlaid on its metal side, was allowed to land without protest on Dorsai at the Foralie shuttleboat pad. But on emerging with Mondar, Cletus was immediately disarmed of his sidearm by competent-looking and obviously veteran troops in Coalition uniforms, with the white bands of the Alliance-Coalition Joint Force fastened about their right sleeves. The same soldiers escorted the three men through a Foralie town where none of the local people were to be seen – only the occupying soldiers – to a military atmosphere craft that flew them up to Grahame House.

Word of their arrival had obviously been sent ahead. They were escorted to the door of the main lounge of the house, ushered inside and the door closed firmly behind them. Within, seated with drinks in which they obviously had little interest, were Melissa and Eachan, in their stiffness and unnaturalness, like set pieces arranged to show off Dow deCastries, slim in the gray white Coalition uniform, standing beside the bar at the far end of the room with a drink also in his hand.

Across the room, Swahili, also in Coalition uniform, stood holding a heavy energy handgun.

'Hello, Cletus,' Dow said. 'I was expecting to find you here when I landed. I'm surprised you came on in when you saw my transports in orbit. Or didn't you think we'd have occupied all of Dorsai yet?'

'I knew you had,' said Cletus.

'But you came in anyway? I wouldn't have,' said Dow. He raised his drink and sipped from it. 'Or did you come down to trade yourself if I'd turn Dorsai loose? If you did, that was foolish. I'm going to turn it loose anyway. All you've done is save me the trouble of hunting you down on some other world. I've got to take you back to Earth, you know.'

'To be sure,' said Cletus. 'So I can have a trial – which will end in a death sentence. Which you can commute to life imprisonment – after which I'll be imprisoned secretly somewhere, and eventually just disappear.'

'Exactly right,' said Dow.

Cletus looked at the watch on his wrist. 'How long is it since your scanning screens picked up the approach of the spaceship I came in?' he asked.

'About six hours,' Dow put his drink down and straightened up. 'Don't tell me you came in here expecting to be rescued? Maybe the handful of officers you left here do have a screen that picked your ship up, and maybe they did know it was you aboard her. But Cletus, we've been chasing them twenty-four hours a day since I brought my troops in here. They're too busy running to worry about you, even if they had enough men and guns to do something.'

He stared at Cletus for a second. 'All the same,' he said, turning to Swahili, 'we won't take any chances. Go give the local commander my orders to set up a security cordon to the shuttleboat landing pad in Foralie. And order a shuttle down from one of the transports. We'll get Grahame aboard as soon as possible.' He looked back at Cletus. 'I'm not going to start underestimating you now.'

Swahili went out, handing his weapon to Dow and closing the door carefully behind him.

'You've never stopped underestimating me,' said Cletus. 'That's what brought you here.'

Dow smiled.

'No. What I'm saying is quite true,' said Cletus. 'I needed a lever to change history and I picked you. From the time I sat down at your table on the ship to Kultis, I was busy working you into this situation.'

Dow leaned the elbow holding the heavy handgun on the bar beside him, keeping its muzzle pointed steadily at Cletus.

'Move a few feet away from him, Mondar,' Dow said to the Exotic, who had been standing beside and a little behind Cletus all this time. 'I can't imagine you sacrificing yourself to give him a chance to escape, but there's no point in risking it.'

Mondar moved.

'Go on, Cletus,' said Dow. 'We've got a few moments to wait anyway. I don't believe what you're saying at all, but if there's even a slight chance you've been able to maneuver me, I want to know about it.'

'There's not much to tell,' said Cletus. 'I started out first by attracting your attention to myself. Then I showed you I had military genius. Then I began to make a name for myself on all the new worlds, knowing this would suggest an idea to you – the idea you could use what I was doing as an excuse to get what you wanted for yourself.'

'And what was that?' The gun in Dow's hand was steady.

'Personal control of both the Alliance and the Coalition – and through them the new worlds,' answered Cletus. 'You talked up my successes on the new worlds as a threat to both the Alliance and the Coalition, until they agreed to combine their outworld forces and put you in command of them. Once in command, you thought all you needed was to stretch the Dorsais out so thin you could defeat them. Then you'd capture me and use your popularity and military power to put military juntas in place of the political leaders at the head of both the Coalition and Alliance, back on Earth. Naturally, the generals you picked for the military juntas would be your men – and in time they'd be yielding up the government of all Earth to you.'

Swahili came back into the room. Dow handed him the handgun and, carefully covering Cletus all the while, Swahili crossed once more to his position on the other side of the room.

'How long?' Dow asked him.

'Twenty minutes,' Swahili answered. Dow looked thoughtfully back at Cletus.

'Maybe a trial would be too much of a risk after all—' He broke off.

There were shouts, and the sharp, chorused whistling of cone rifles outside the house, followed by the heavy sizzle of at least one energy weapon. Swahili ran toward the door of the room.

'No!' snapped Dow. Swahili checked and spun about. Dow pointed at Cletus. 'Shoot him!'

Swahili brought the energy handgun up and there was a sound like the snapping of a small stick. Swahili checked abruptly, turning toward Eachan, who was still sitting in his chair, but now holding the same flat little handgun – minus the long sniper's barrel – that he had used long ago from under the overturned command car in which he, with Melissa, Mondar and Cletus, had been trapped on the road to Bakhalla.

Swahili went suddenly, heavily, to his knees on the carpet. The energy pistol dropped from his grasp. He fell over on his side and lay there. Dow moved sharply toward the fallen weapon.

'Don't!' said Eachan. Dow stopped abruptly. There were more sounds of voices shouting outside the house.

Eachan got to his feet and walked across to the fallen energy weapon, still holding his own pistol. He picked up the fallen gun and bent over Swahili, who was breathing raggedly.

'Sorry, Raoul,' Eachan said, gently.

Swahili looked up at him and almost smiled. The almost-smile continued and did not change. Eachan reached down in an old-fashioned gesture and softly closed the lids over the unmoving eyes. He straightened up as the door burst open and Arvid, a cone rifle in one large hand, strode into the room closely followed by Bill Athyer.

'All right, here?' said Arvid, looking at Cletus.

'All right, Arv,' Cletus answered. 'How about outside?'

'We've got them all,' Arvid answered.

'You'd better start running in a hurry, then,' said Dow, dryly. 'All these detachments of mine are in constant open-channel communication with each other. There'll be other detachments moving in here within minutes. And where are you going to run to?'

'We're not going to run at all.' Arvid looked at him. 'All your troops on Dorsai are now captured.'

Dow stared at him. Black eyes locked with pale blue.

'I don't believe it,' Dow said flatly. 'There are nothing but women, children and old men left on this world.'

'What of it?' Cletus asked. Dow turned to look at him. Cletus went on: 'Don't you believe I could defeat a few thousand Coalition elite troops with a worldful of women, old men and children to help me?'

Dow regarded him for a few seconds without speaking. 'Yes,' he said at last. 'You, Cletus – I'll believe you could do it. But you weren't here.' He lifted his right hand and pointed his index finger at Cletus. 'The thing you forget—'

There was a small, momentary, soundless puff of white vapor from the sleeve of his jacket. What felt like a sledgehammer smashed into Cletus' upper right chest. He stumbled backward and the edge of a table stopped him from falling.

Arvid took one long, swift pace toward Dow, his nearer hand flinging up and starting to descend, edge-on.

'Don't kill him!' snapped Cletus, with what little breath was left in him.

Arvid's hand changed direction in midair. It came down to close on Dow's outstretched arm. He peeled back the sleeve and they all saw a dead-man's tube, a reflex single-dart thrower, strapped to Dow's wrist. Arvid broke the strap fastening loose and tossed the tube into a corner of the room. He caught up Dow's other arm and peeled the sleeve back, but the wrist was bare.

'Don't move at all,' Arvid said to Dow, and stepped back from him. Melissa was already at Cletus' side.

'You've got to lie down,' she said.

'No.' He shook his head, resisting the pull of her hands. He could not feel the extent of the damage from the shock-point of the dart, but his right upper body was numb and a weak dizziness was threatening to overwhelm him. He fought it back with all the strength of physiological discipline he had. 'There's something I've got to tell him.'

He leaned gratefully back against the supporting edge of the table top behind him.

'Listen to me, Dow,' he said. 'I'm going to send you back to Earth. We're not going to kill you.'

Dow looked at him fearlessly and almost curiously.

'If that's so, I'm sorry I shot you,' he said. 'I thought I was on my way out and might as well take you with me. But why send me back to Earth? You know I'll just raise another army and come back. And next time I'll beat you.'

'No.' Cletus shook his head. 'Earth's lost its influence on the new worlds. You'll tell them that, back there. From now on any colony can hire half the number of Dorsai troops that the Alliance or the Coalition supplies to their enemy – and defeat the Earth troops easily. The Dorsais will always win, and any colony can afford to hire them.'

Dow frowned. 'It's you that make Dorsais potent,' he said. 'And you won't last forever.'

'But I will.' Cletus had to pause to fight off the encroaching dizziness again. Barely, once more, he won the battle and went on. 'Just as you said – I wasn't here when you landed. And a planetful of women, children and oldsters beat you. That's because I was as good as here. You see these two?' He nodded weakly toward Arvid and Bill.

'They're the two parts of me,' he said, almost whispering now. 'The theoretician and the field general. The only orders I left them was to defend Dorsai. But they defended it just the way I would have – right down to being here, when I knew they would, to rescue me from you. There's no end to the Dorsais now. Earth won't ever have troops able to beat them.' The dizziness surged in on him and he forced it back.

'... Why?' he heard Dow saying. He looked about for the man and saw the lean face under the black hair and graying temples floating as if on a field of mist.

'It's time for the new worlds to go free,' Cletus said. 'They had to break loose from the Alliance, the Coalition – from all Earth – and make themselves into what they're meant to be. It was time. I did it.'

'... because of the books you wanted to write, you said,' Dow's voice faded out almost to nothingness and then roared like the sound of surf on his ears.

'That ... too ...' Cletus held hard to the table edge behind him with both hands, for the floor was threatening to dissolve under his feet. 'The last sixteen volumes will be tactics only as Dorsais-to-come can use ... no use to ordinary military, back on Earth. Only with a new sort of soldier ... with restraint ... obligation ... mind and body ...'

There was no more.

After what seemed many centuries of nothingness, he drifted back to fuzzy consciousness to find himself lying on a bed. A young commandant wearing medical insignia was just finishing a broad bandage across his upper chest, and behind the commandant stood Melissa and Mondar.

'I'm not dead ... then?' he asked, hearing the words come out in a whisper so weak it was ridiculous.

'Dow used the wrong weapon on you, Cletus,' said Mondar. 'Darts that trigger a state of physical shock and collapse are all right for killing ordinary men, but not one like you, who's trained his physiological processes to obey his will automatically. You're going to live – isn't he, Doctor?'

'Absolutely.' The medical commandant straightened up and stepped back from the bedside. 'He should have died on his feet within the first minute and a half after he was hit. When he got past that point, there was no place for his system to go but toward recovery.'

He handed a hypospray arm band to Melissa. 'See that he does a lot of sleeping,' he said. 'Come on, Outbond.'

The figures of the two men moved out from Cletus' field of vision. He heard a door close at a little distance. Melissa sat down in the chair the doctor had occupied and began to strap the hypospray around Cletus' sleeveless right arm.

'You don't have to do that,' he whispered to her. 'You can go now, to Earth or anywhere you want. It's all over.'

'Don't talk,' she said. 'It's all nonsense, anyway. If I'd wanted to go, I'd have gone right after you made me marry you. I could have dreamed up some excuse – to explain it to Dad. You know he'd believe anything I told him.'

He stared at her. 'Then why didn't—'

'Because you told me you loved me,' she said. 'That was all I wanted to know.'

He rolled his head a little, weakly and negatively, on the pillow. 'I said—'

She finished strapping the hypospray on his wrist and bent down and kissed him, stopping the words on his lips.

'You idiot!' she said, fiercely and tenderly. 'You magnificent, genius-idiot! Do you think I paid any attention to what you *said?*'

TIME STORM

During the 1930s and 1940s anyone writing science fiction did so almost exclusively for magazines. Then in the early 1950s the magazine market began to die and paperback books took over. But the paperback books were on the stand one week and gone the next. By the time an author's newest book came out his older books had disappeared.

As a result, during these later years, when the magazines were mostly gone and the paperback books were coming and going, there were only a few of us who could afford to be full-time writers of science fiction; and the fact that this was possible at all was only because libraries continued to be the only real market for hardcover science fiction. The libraries alone bought science fiction books on a regular basis, shelved them, and made them continuously available to readers; and in this way libraries kept both science fiction and those of us who wrote it, alive.

To librarians everywhere, therefore, this book – the youngest of my literary children to see the light of day – is dedicated.

1

The leopard – I called him Sunday, after the day I found him – almost never became annoyed with the girl, for all her hanging on to him. But he was only a wild animal, after all, and there were limits to his patience.

What had moved me to pick up first him, then her, was something I asked myself often without getting a good answer. They were nothing but encumbrances and no concern of mine. My only concern was getting to Omaha and Swannee. Beyond that point there was no need for me to think. But ... I don't know. Somehow out of the terrible feeling of emptiness that I kept waking up to in the mornings, I had gotten a notion that in a world where nearly all the people and animals had vanished, they would be living creatures I could talk to. 'Talk to,' however, had turned out to be the working phrase; because certainly neither of them was able to talk back. Crazy cat and speechless girl and with them, myself, who before had always had the good sense never to need anybody, dragging them both along with me across a landscape as mixed up and insane as they were. But, of course, without me they would have been helpless.

This time, the trouble erupted just as I pushed the panel truck over a rise in late summer wheat country, which I figured had once been cornland, a little below the one-time northern border of Iowa. All the warning I heard was a sort of combination meowsnarl. Not a top-pitch, ready-to-fight sound, but a plain signal that Sunday had had enough of being treated like a stuffed animal and wanted the girl to leave him alone. I braked the panel sharply to a stop on the side of the empty, two-lane asphalt road and scrambled over the seat backs into the body of the truck.

'Cat!' I raved at him. 'What the hell's got into you now?'

But of course, having said his piece and already gotten her to let him go, Sunday was now feeling just fine. He lay there, completely self-possessed, cleaning the fur on the back of his right forepaw with his tongue. Only, the girl was huddled up into a tight little ball that looked as if it never intended to come unwound again; and that made me lose my temper.

I cuffed Sunday; and he cringed, putting his head down as I crawled over him to get to the girl. A second later I felt his rough tongue rasping on my left ankle in a plea for forgiveness – for what he did not even understand. And that made me angry all over again, because illogically, now, I was the one who felt guilty. He was literally insane where I was concerned. I knew it, and yet I had taken advantage of that to knock him around, knowing I was quite safe in doing so when otherwise he could have had my throat out in two seconds as easy as yawning.

But I was only human myself, I told myself; and here I had the girl to unwind again. She was still in her ball, completely unyielding, all elbows and rigid muscle when I put my hands on her. I had told myself I had no real feeling for her, any more than I had for Sunday. But somehow, for some reason I had never understood, it always damn near broke my heart when she went like that. My younger sister had had moments of withdrawal something like that – before she grew out of them. I had guessed this girl to be no more than fifteen or sixteen at the most, and she had not said a word since the day I found her wandering by the road. But she had taken to Sunday from the moment I had led her back to the truck and she first laid eyes on him. Now, it was as if he was the only living thing in the world for her; and when he snarled at her like that, it seemed to hit her like being rejected by everyone who had ever loved her, all at once.

I had been through a number of crises like this one with her before – though the others had not been so obviously Sunday's fault – and I knew that there was nothing much to be done with her until she began to relax. So I sat down and wrapped my arms around her, cuddling her as close as her rigidness would allow, and began to try to talk her out of it. The sound of my voice seemed to help, although at that time she would never show any kind of direct response to it, except to follow orders.

So, there I sat, on the mattresses and blankets in the back of the panel truck, with my arms around her narrow body that was more sharp bones than anything else, talking to her and telling her over and over again that Sunday wasn't mad at her; he was just a crazy cat, and she should pay no attention when he snarled, except to leave him alone for a while. After a while I got tired of repeating the same words and tried singing to her – any song that I could remember. I was aware it was no great performance. I may have believed at that time that I was hell on wheels at a number of things, but I knew singing was not one of them. I had a voice to scare bullfrogs. However, that had never seemed to matter with the girl. It was keeping up the human noise and holding her that helped. Meanwhile, all the time this was going on, Sunday had crept up as close to us as he could and had his forepaws around my left ankle, his forehead butted against my knee.

So, after a while, illogically, I reached down and patted his head, which he took as forgiveness. I was a complete fool for both of them, in some ways. Shortly after that, the girl began to stir. The stiffness went out of her. Her arms and legs extended themselves; and without a word to me she pulled away, crawled off and put her arms around Sunday. He suffered it, even licking at her face with his tongue. I unkinked my own cramped muscles and went back up front to the driver's seat of the truck.

Then I saw it, to the left of the highway. It was a line of sky-high mist or dust-haze, less than a couple of hundred yards away, rolling down on us at an angle.

There was no time for checking on the two back there to see if they were braced for a racing start. I jammed the key over, got the motor started, and slammed the panel into motion down the narrow asphalt lane between the brown-yellow of the standing wheat, now gently wind-rippled by the breeze that always preceded a mistwall, until the plant-tops wavered into varying shades of gold.

2

No mistwall I had seen, with the time change line its presence always signalled, had ever moved faster than about thirty miles an hour. That meant that unless this one was an exception, theoretically, any car in good working order on a decent road should have no trouble outrunning it. The difficulty arose, however, when – as now – the mistwall was not simply coming up behind us, but moving at an angle flanking the road. I would have to drive over half the length of the wall or more – and some mistwalls were up to ten miles long – to get out of its path before it caught us, along with everything else in its way. I held the pedal of the accelerator to the floor and sweated.

According to the needle on the speedometer, we were doing nearly a hundred and ten – which was nonsense. Eighty-five miles an hour was more like the absolute top speed of the panel truck. As it was, we swayed and bounced along the empty road as if five more miles an hour would have sent us flying off it.

I could now see the far end of the mistwall. It was still a good two or three miles away; and the wall itself was only a few hundred yards off and closing swiftly. I may have prayed a little bit at this point, in spite of being completely irreligious. I seem to remember that I did. In the weeks since the whole business of the time changes started. I had not been this close to being caught since that first day in the cabin northwest of Duluth, when I had, in fact, been caught without knowing what hit me. I had thought then it was another heart attack, come to carry me off for good this time; and the bitterness of being chopped down before I was thirty and after I had spent nearly two years putting myself into the best possible physical shape, had been like a dry, ugly taste in my throat just before the change line reached me and knocked me out.

I remember still thinking that it was a heart attack, even after I came to. I had gone on thinking that way, even after I found the squirrel that was still in shock from it; the way Sunday had been later, when I found him. For several days afterwards, with the squirrel tagging along behind me like some miniature dog until I either exhausted it or lost it, I did not begin to realise the size of what had happened. It was only later that I began to understand, when I came to where Duluth should have been and found virgin forest where a couple of hundred thousand people had lived, and later yet, as I moved south, and stumbled across the log cabin with the bearded man in cord-wrapped leather leggings.

The bearded man had nearly finished me. It took me almost three minutes too long after I met him to realize that he did not understand that the rifle in my hand was a weapon. It was only when I stepped back and picked up the hunting bow, that he pulled his fancy quick-draw trick with the axe he had been using to chop wood when I stepped into his clearing. I never saw anything like it and I hope I never see it again, unless I'm on the side of the man with the axe. It was a sort of scimitar-bladed tool with a wide, curving forward edge; and he had hung it on his shoulder, blade-forward, in what I took to be a reassuring gesture, when I first tried to speak to him. Then he came toward me, speaking some kind of Scandinavian-sounding gibberish in a friendly voice, the axe hung on his shoulder as if he had forgotten it was there.

It was when I began to get worried about the steady way he was coming on and warned him back with the rifle, that I recognized suddenly that, apparently, as far as he was concerned, I was carrying nothing more than a club. For a second I was merely paralysed by the enormity of that insight. Then, before I could bring myself to shoot him after all in self-defence, I had the idea of trying to pick up the bow with my free hand. As an idea, it was a good one – but the minute he saw the bow in my hand he acted; and to this day, I'm not sure exactly how he did it.

He reached back at belt-level and jerked forward on the handle-end of the axe. It came off his shoulder – spinning, back, around, under his arm, up in the air and over, and came down, incredibly, with the end of its handle into his fist and the blade edge forward.

Then he threw it.

I saw it come whirling toward me, ducked instinctively and ran. I heard it thunk into a tree somewhere behind me; but by then I was into the cover of the woods, and he did not follow.

Five days later I was where the twin cities of Minneapolis and St. Paul had been – and they looked as if they had been abandoned for a hundred years after a bombing raid that had nearly levelled them. But I found the panel truck there, and it started when I turned its key. There was gas in the filling station pumps, though I had to rig up a little kerosene generator I liberated from a sporting goods store, in order to pump some of it into the tank of the truck, and I headed south along U.S. 35W. Then came Sunday. Then came the girl ...

I was almost to the far end of the mistwall now, although to the left of the road the haze was less than a hundred yards from the roadway; and little stinging sprays of everything from dust to fine gravel were beginning to pepper the left side of the panel, including my own head and shoulder where the window on that side was not rolled up. But I had no time to roll it up now. I kept pushing the gas pedal through the floor, and suddenly we whipped past the end of the wall of mist, and I could see open country clear to the summer horizon.

Sweating, I eased back on the gas, let the truck roll to a stop, and half-turned it across the road so I could look behind us.

Back where we had been, seconds before, the mist had already crossed the road and was moving on into the fields that had been on the road's far side. They were ceasing to be there as it passed – as the road itself had already ceased to be, and the farm land on the near side of the road. Where the grain had rippled in the wind, there was now wild, grassy hillside – open country sparsely interspersed with a few clumps of trees, rising to a bluff, a crown of land, less than a quarter of a mile off, looking so close I could reach out and touch it. There was not a breath of wind stirring.

I put the panel back in gear again and drove off. After a while the road swung in a gentle curve toward a small town that looked as normal as apple pie, as if no mistwall had ever passed through it. It could be, of course. My heart began to pound a little with hope of running into someone sane I could talk with, about everything that had happened since that apparent heart attack of mine in the cabin.

But when I drove into Main Street of the town, between the buildings, there was no one in sight; and the whole place seemed deserted. Hope evaporated into caution. Then I saw what seemed to be a barricade across the street up ahead; and a single figure crouched behind it with what looked like a rocket launcher on his shoulder. He was peering over the barricade away from me; although he must have heard the sound of the motor coming up the street behind him.

I pulled the truck into an alley between two stores and stopped it.

'Stay here and stay quiet,' I told the girl and Sunday.

I took the carbine from beside my driver's seat and got out. Holding it ready, just in case, I went up behind the man crouched at the barricade. Up this close I could see easily over the barricade – and sure enough, there was another mistwall, less than a mile away, but unmoving. For the first time since I had come into the silent town, I became conscious of a steady sound.

3

It came from somewhere up ahead, beyond the point where the straight white concrete highway vanished into the unmoving haze of the mist-wall – a small buzzing sound. Like the sound of a fly in an enclosed box on a hot July day such as this one was.

'Get down,' said the man with the rocket launcher.

I pulled my head below the top line of the makeshift barricade – furniture, rolls of carpeting, cans of paint – that barred the empty street between the gritty sidewalks and the unbroken store windows in the red brick sides of the Main Street building. Driving in from the northwest, I had thought at first that this small town was still living. Then, when I got closer, I guessed it was one of those places, untouched but abandoned, such as I had run into further north. And so it was, in fact; except for the man, his homemade barricade, and the rocket launcher.

The buzzing grew louder. I looked behind me, back down Main Street. I could just make out the brown, left front fender of the panel truck showing at the mouth of the alley into which I had backed it. There was no sound or movement from inside it. The two of them in there would be obeying my orders, lying still on the blankets in the van section, the leopard probably purring a little in its rough, throaty way and cleaning the fur of a forepaw with its tongue, while the girl held to the animal for comfort and companionship, in spite of the heat.

When I looked back through a chink in the barricade, there was something already visible in the road. It had evidently just appeared out of the haze, for it was coming very fast. Its sound was the buzzing sound I had heard earlier, now growing rapidly louder as the object raced toward us, seeming to swell in size, like a balloon being inflated against the white backdrop of the haze, as it came.

It came so fast that there was only time to get a glimpse of it. It was yellow and black in colour, like a wasp; a small gadget with an amazing resemblance to a late-model compact car, but half the size of such a car, charging at us down the ruler-straight section of highway like some outsize wind-up toy.

I jerked up my rifle; but at the same time the rocket launcher went off beside me with a flat clap of sound. The rocket was slow enough so that we could see it like a black speck, curving through the air to meet the gadget coming at us. They met and there was an explosion. The gadget hopped up off the road, shedding parts which flew toward us, whacking into the far side of the barricade like shrapnel. For a full minute after it quit moving, there was no sound to be heard. Then the whistling of birds and the trilling of crickets took up again.

I looked over at the rocket launcher.

'Good,' I said to the man. 'Where did you get that launcher, anyway?'

'Somebody must have stolen it from a National Guard outfit,' he said. 'Or brought it back from overseas. I found it with a bunch of knives and guns and other things, in a storeroom behind the town police office.'

He was as tall as I was, a tight-shouldered, narrow-bodied man with a deep tan on his forearms, and on his quiet, bony face. Maybe a little older than I; possibly in his late thirties. I studied him, trying to estimate how hard it would be to kill him if I had to. I could see him watching, doubtless with the same thought in mind.

It was the way things were, now. There was no shortage of food or drink, or anything material you could want. But neither was there any law, anymore – at least, none I'd been able to find in the last three weeks.

4

To break the staring match, I deliberately looked away to the gadget, lying still now beyond the barricades, and nodded at it.

'I'd like to have a look at it close up,' I said. 'Is it safe?'

'Sure.' He got to his feet, laying down the rocket launcher. I saw, however, he had a heavy revolver – possibly a thirty-eight or forty-four – in a holster on the hip away from me; and a deer rifle carbine like mine was lying against the barricade. He picked it up in his left hand.

'Come on,' he said. 'They only show up one at a time; on a staggered schedule, seven to ten hours apart.'

I looked down the road. There were no other wrecked shapes in black and yellow in sight along it.

'You're sure?' I said. 'How many have you seen?'

He laughed, making a dry sound in his throat like an old man.

'They're never quite stopped,' he said. 'Like this one. It's harmless, now, but not really done for. Later it'll crawl back, or get pulled back behind the mist over there – you'll see. Come on.'

He climbed over the barricade and I followed him. When we got to the gadget, it looked more than ever like an overlarge toy car – except that where the windows should be, there was a flat yellow surface; and instead of four ordinary-sized wheels with tyres, the lower halves of something like sixteen or eighteen small metal discs showed through the panel sealing the underbody. The rocket had torn a large hole in the gadget's side.

'Listen,' said the man, stooping over the hole. I came close and listened myself. There was a faint buzzing still going on down there someplace inside it.

'Who sends these things?' I said. 'Or what sends them?'

He shrugged.

'By the way,' I said, 'I'm Marc Despard.' I held out my hand.

He hesitated.

'Raymond Samuelson,' he said.

I saw his hand jerk forward a little, then back again. Outside of that, he ignored my offered hand; and I let it drop. I guessed that he might not want to shake hands with a man he might later have to try to kill; and I judged that anyone who worried about a nicety like that was not likely to shoot me in the back, at least, unless he had to. At the same time, there was no point in asking for trouble by letting any misunderstandings arise.

'I'm just on my way through to Omaha,' I said. 'My wife's there, if she's still all right. But I'm not going to drive right across that time change line out there if I've got a choice.' I nodded at the haze from which the gadget had come. 'Have you got any other roads leading south or east from the town?'

'Yes,' he said. He was frowning. 'Did you say your wife was there?'

'Yes,' I answered. For the life of me, I had meant to say 'ex-wife,' but my tongue had slipped; and it was not worth straightening the matter out now for someone like Samuelson. 'Look,' he said, 'you don't have to go right away. Stop and have dinner.'

Stop and have dinner. Something about my mentioning a wife had triggered off a hospitality reflex in him. The familiar, homely words he spoke seemed as strange and out of place, here between the empty town and the haze that barred the landscape to our right, as the wrecked gadget at our feet.

'All right,' I said.

We went back, over the barricade and down to the panel truck. I called to the leopard and the girl to come out, and introduced them to Samuelson. His eyes widened at the sight of the leopard; but they opened even more at the sight of the girl behind the big cat.

'I call the leopard "Sunday",' I said. 'The girl's never told me her name.'

I put out my hand and Sunday stepped forward, flattening his ears and rubbing his head up under my palm with a sound that was like a whimper of pleasure.

'I came across him just after a time change had swept the area where he was,' I said. 'He was still in shock when I first touched him; and now I've got his soul in pawn, or something like that. You've seen how animals act, if you get them right after a change, before they come all the way back to being themselves?'

Samuelson shook his head. He was looking at me now with some distrust and suspicion.

'That's too bad,' I said. 'Maybe you'll take my word for it, then. He's perfectly safe as long as I'm around.'

I petted Sunday. Samuelson looked at the girl.

'Hello,' he said, smiling at her. But she simply stared back without answering. She would do anything I set her to doing, but I had never been able to make her seem conscious of herself. The straight, dark hair hanging down around her shoulders always had a wild look; and even the shirt and jeans she was wearing looked as if they did not belong on her.

They were the best of available choices, though. I had put her into a dress once, shortly after I had found her; and the effect had been pitiful. She had looked like a caricature of a young girl in that dress.

'She doesn't talk,' I said. 'I came across her a couple of days after I found the leopard, about two hundred miles south. The leopard was about where the Minneapolis-St. Paul area used to be. It could have come from a zoo. The girl was just wandering along the road. No telling where she came from.'

'Poor kid,' said Samuelson. He evidently meant it; and I began to think it even more unlikely that he would shoot me in the back.

We went to his house, one block off Main Street, for dinner.

'What about the – whatever-you-call-them?' I asked. 'What if one comes while you aren't there to stop it?'

'The buzzers,' he said. 'No, like I told you, they don't run on schedule, but after one's come by, it's at least six and a half hours before the next one. It's my guess there's some kind of automatic factory behind the mist there, that takes that long to make a new one.'

Samuelson's house turned out to be one of those tall, ornate, late-nineteenth century homes you still see in small towns. Two stories and an attic with a wide screen porch in front and lilac bushes growing all along one side of it. The rooms inside were small, dark and high-ceilinged, with too much furniture for their floorspace. He had rigged a gas motor and a water tank to the well in his basement that had formerly been run by an electric pump; and he had found an old, black, wood-burning stove to block up in one corner of this spacious kitchen. The furniture was clean of dust and in order.

He gave us the closest thing to a normal meal that I'd eaten – or the girl had, undoubtedly – since the time storm first hit Earth. I knew it had affected all the Earth, by this time; not just the little part west of the Great Lakes in North America, where I was. I carried a good all-bands portable radio along and, once in a while, picked up a fragment of a broadcast from somewhere. The continuity – or discontinuity – lines dividing the time areas usually blocked off radio. But sometimes things came through. Hawaii, evidently, was unique in hardly having been touched, and I'd occasionally heard bits of shortwave from as far away as Greece. Not that I listened much. There was nothing I could do for the people broadcasting, any more than there was anything they could do for me.

I told Samuelson about this while he was fixing dinner; and he said he had run into the same thing with both the shortwave and long-wave radios he had set up. We agreed that the storm was not over.

'We've only had the one time change here in Saulsburg, though,' he said. 'Every so often, I'll see a line of change moving across country off on the horizon, or standing still for a while out there; but so far, none's come this way.'

'Where did all the people go, that were in this place?' I asked.

His face changed, all at once.

'I don't know,' he said. Then he bent over the biscuit dough he was making, so that his face was hidden away from me. 'I had to drive over to Peppard – that's the next town. I drove and drove and couldn't find it. I began to think I was sick or crazy, so I turned the car around and drove home. When I got back here, it was like you see it now.'

It was clear he did not want to talk about it. But I could guess some of what he had lost from the house. It had been lived in by more than one adult, and several children. There were a woman's overshoes in the front closet, toys in a box in one corner of the living room, and three bicycles in good condition in the garage.

'What did you do for a living?' he asked me after a moment.

'I was retired,' I said.

He frowned over that, too. So I told him about myself. The time storm had done nothing in my case to leave me with things I did not want to talk about, except for the matter of Swannee, down in Omaha; and somehow I was perfectly comforted and sure that she and that city had come through the time storm changes unharmed, though I had heard no radio broadcasts from there.

'I started investing in the stock market when I was nineteen,' I said, 'before I was even out of college. I struck it lucky.' Luck, of course, had nothing to do with it; but I had found I could not tell people that. Because the word 'stocks' was involved, it had to be luck, not hard research and harder-headed decision-making, that had made money for me. 'Then I used what I had to take over a company that made trailers and snowmobiles; and that did all right. I'd be there yet, but I had a heart attack.'

Samuelson's eyebrows went up.

'A heart attack?' he said. 'You're pretty young for something like that.'

'I was damned young,' I said. 'I was twenty-four.'

I discovered suddenly that I had been wrong about not having things I did not want to talk about. I did not want to tell him about my heart attack. He looked too much like a man who'd never had a sick day in his life.

'Anyway,' I said, 'my doctor told me to take it easy and lose weight. That was two years ago. So I sold out, set up a trust to support me, and bought a place up in the woods of northern Minnesota, beyond Ely – if you know that state. I got back in shape, and I've been fine ever since; until the time storm hit three weeks ago.'

'Yes,' he said.

The food was ready, so I helped him carry it into the dining room and we all ate there; even Sunday, curled up in a corner. I had thought Samuelson might object to my bringing the leopard into his house, but he had not.

Afterwards, we sat on his screened porch at the front of the house, with the thick leaves of the sugar maple in the yard screening us from the western sun. It was after six by my watch, but now in midsummer, there was at least another three hours of light left. Samuelson had some homemade white wine which was not bad. It was not very good either, but the town was apparently a dry town; and of course, he had not left it since he had first come back here and found his people gone.

'How about the girl?' he asked me, when he first poured the wine into water glasses.

'Why not?' I said. 'We may be all dead – her included – tomorrow, if the wrong sort of time change catches us.'

So he gave her a glass. But she only took a small sip, then put it down on the floor of the porch by her chair. After a bit, while Samuelson and I talked, she got out of the chair itself and sat down on the floor where she could put an arm around Sunday, who was lying there, dozing. Outside of raising a lazy eyebrow when he felt the weight of her arm, the leopard paid no attention. It was amazing what he would stand from her, sometimes.

'What is it?' Samuelson asked me, after we'd been talking for a while about how things used to be. 'I mean – where did it come from?'

He was talking about the time storm.

'I don't know,' I said. 'I'll bet nobody does. But I've got a theory.'

'What's that?' He was looking at me closely in the shadow of the porch. A little evening breeze stirred the lilac bushes into scraping their upper branches against the side of the house.

'I think it's just what we're calling it,' I said. 'A storm. Some sort of storm in space that the whole world ran into, the same way you could be out driving in your car and run into a thunderstorm. Only in this case, instead of wind and rain, thunder and lightning, we get these time changes, like ripples moving across the surface of the world, with everything getting moved either forward or back in time. Wherever a change passes over them.'

'How about here?' he asked. 'The town's just where it was before. Only the people ...'

He trailed off.

'How do you know?' I said. 'Maybe the area right around here was moved forward just a year, say, or even a month. That wouldn't be enough to make any change in the buildings and streets you could notice, but it might have been beyond the point where everybody living here, for some reason, decided to get out.'

'Why?'

'Those buzzers, as you call them,' I said. 'Seeing one of them come at the town would be pretty good reason to me to get out, if I was someone living here.'

He shook his head.

'Not everybody,' he said. 'Not without leaving some kind of message.'

I gave up. If he did not want reasonable explanations, there was no point in my forcing it on him.

'Tell me,' he said, after we had sat there without talking for a while, 'do you think God has something to do with it?'

So that was his hang-up. That was why he stayed here, day after day, defending a town with no people in it. That was why he had carefully adapted the well in the basement to the new conditions and set up a wood stove so that he could give a regular meal at a moment's notice to a complete family, if they should return unexpectedly, showing up at the front door, tired and hungry. I wanted to tell him neither God nor human had ever changed things much for me; but now that I knew what his question meant to him, I could not do it. All at once I felt the pain in him – and I found myself suddenly angry that someone I did not even know should be able to export his troubles to me, like that. It was true I had lost nothing, not like him. Still ...

'Who can tell?' I said, standing up. 'We'd better be going.'

He stood up also, quickly. Before he was on his feet, Sunday was on his, and that brought the girl scrambling upright.

'You could stay here overnight,' he said.

I shook my head.

'You don't want to drive in the dark,' he went on.

'No,' I said. 'But I'd like to get some miles under our belt before quitting for the day. I'm anxious to get to my wife.'

I led the leopard and the girl out to the panel, which I had driven over and now stood in his driveway. I opened the door on the driver's side, and the other two got in, crawling back into the body. I waited until they were settled, then got in myself and was about to back out, when Samuelson, who had gone in the house instead of following us to the truck, came out again, almost shyly, with a pair of large paper grocery sacks. He pushed them in through the open window at my left.

'Here,' he said. 'There's some food you could use. I put in a bottle of the wine, too.'

'Thanks.' I put the two sacks on the empty front seat beside me. He looked past me, back into the body of the van, where the girl and the leopard were already curled up, ready for sleep.

'I've got everything, you know,' he said. 'Everything you could want. There's nothing she could use – clothes, or anything?'

'Sunday's the only thing she wants,' I said. 'As long as she's got him, there's nothing else she cares about.'

'Well, goodbye then,' he said.

'So long.'

I backed out into the street and drove off. In the sideview mirror I could see him walk into the street himself so that he could look after us and wave. I turned a corner two blocks down and the houses shut him from view.

He had given me a filling station map earlier, with a route marked in pencil, that led me to the south edge of the city and out at last on a two-lane asphalt road rising and dipping over the land, with open, farmer's fields on either side. The fields had all been planted that spring; and as I drove along I was surrounded by acres of corn and wheat and peas no one would ever harvest or use. The sky-high wall of haze that was the time change line, holding its position just outside of Samuelson's town, now to the left and behind us, grew smaller as I drove the van away from there.

In a car we were pretty safe, according to what I had learned so far. These time lines were like lengths of rod, rolling across the landscape; but as I say, I had yet to encounter any that seemed to travel at more than thirty miles an hour. It was not hard to get away from them as long as you could stick to a road.

I had been keeping my eyes open for something in the way of an all-terrain vehicle, but with adequate speed. Something like a Land-Rover that could make good time on the roads but could also cut across open country, if necessary. But so far I had not found anything.

I became aware that the engine of the van was roaring furiously under the hood. I was belting us along the empty asphalt road at nearly seventy miles an hour. There was no need for anything like that. It was both safer and easier on the gas consumption to travel at about forty or forty-five; and now and then gas was not easily available, just when the tank ran low. It was true I had four spare five-gallon cans-full, lashed to the luggage carrier on the van's roof. But that was for real emergencies.

Besides, none of the three of us had anything that urgent to run to – or away from. I throttled down to forty miles an hour, wondering how I had let my speed creep up in the first place.

Then, of course, I realized why. I had been letting Samuelson's feelings get to me. Why should I cry for him? He was as crazy from the loss of his family as the girl was – or Sunday. But he had really wanted us to stay the night, in that large house of his from which his family had disappeared; and it would have been a kindness to him if we had stayed. Only, I could not take the chance. Sometime in the night he might change suddenly from the man who was desperate for company to a man who thought that I, or all of us, had something to do with whatever it was that had taken his people away from him.

I could not trust his momentary sanity. Samuelson had talked for a while like a sane man; but he was still someone sitting in a deserted town, shooting rockets full of high explosives at out-size toys that attacked at regular intervals. No one in that position could be completely sane. Besides, insanity was part of things, now. Sunday was the definitive example. I could have cut the leopard's throat, and he would have licked my hand as I was doing it. The girl was in no better mental condition. Samuelson, like them, was caught in this cosmic joke that had overtaken the world we knew – so he was insane too, by definition. There was no other possibility.

Which of course, I thought, following the idea to its logical conclusion, as I drove into the increasing twilight, meant that I had to be insane, too. The idea was almost laughable. I felt perfectly sane. But just as I had not trusted Samuelson, if I were him, or anyone else looking at me from the outside as I drove across the country with a leopard and a speechless girl for companions, I would not trust myself. I would have been afraid that there could be a madness in me too, that would overtake me sometime, suddenly and without warning. Of course, that was all nonsense. I put the ridiculous thought out of my head.

5

When the red flush of the sunset above the horizon to our right began to grow narrow and dark, and stars were clearly visible in the clear sky to the east, I pulled the van off the road into a comfortable spot under some cottonwood trees growing down in a little dip between two hills and set up camp. It was so warm that I had the tent flaps tied all the way back. I lay there looking out at the stars, seeming to move deeper and deeper in the night sky, becoming more and more important and making the earth under me feel more like a chip of matter lost in the universe.

But I could not sleep. That had happened to me a lot, lately. I wanted to get up and go sit outside the tent by myself, with my back to the trunk of one of the cottonwoods. But if I did, Sunday would get up and come out with me; and then the girl would get up and follow Sunday. It was a chain reaction. A tag-end of a line from my previous two years of steady reading, during my hermit-like existence above Ely, came back to me. *Privatum commodum publico cedit* – 'private advantage yields to public.' I decided to lie there and tough it out.

What I had to tough out was the replaying in my head of all the things that had happened. I had almost forgotten, until now, my last summer in high school when I started teaching myself to read Latin because I had just learned how powerfully it underlays all our English language. Underlays and outdoes. *'How long, O Cataline, will you abuse our patience?'* Good, but not in the same ballgame with the thunder of old Cicero's original: *'Quo usque, Catilina, abutere patienta nostra?'*

After the sweep of the first time change that I thought was my second heart attack come to take me for good this time – after I had found I was not dead, or even hurt – there had been the squirrel, frozen in shock. The little grey body had been relaxed in my hands when I picked it up; the small forepaws had clung to my fingers. It had followed me after that for at least the first three days, when I finally decided to walk south from my cabin and reach a city called Ely, that turned out to be no longer there. I had not understood then that what I had done to the squirrel was what later I was to do to Sunday – be with it when it came out of shock, making it totally dependent on me … Then, a week or so later, there had been the log cabin and the man in leggings, the transplanted Viking or whoever, who I thought was just anyone cutting firewood with his shirt off, until he saw me, hooked the axe over his shoulder as if holstering it, and started walking toward me …

I was into it again. I was really starting to replay the whole sequence, whether I wanted to or not; and I could not endure that, lying trapped in this tent with two other bodies. I had to get out. I got to my feet as quietly as I could. Sunday lifted his head, but I hissed at him between my teeth so angrily that he lay down again. The girl only stirred in her sleep and made a little noise in her throat, one hand flung out to touch the fur of Sunday's back.

So I made it outside without them after all, into the open air where I could breathe; and I sat down with my back against the rugged, soft bark of one of the big cottonwoods. Overhead the sky was perfectly clear and the stars were everywhere. The air was still and warm, very transparent and clean. I leaned the back of my head against the tree trunk and let my mental machinery go. It was simply something I was stuck with – had always been stuck with, all my lifetime.

Well, perhaps not all. Before the age of seven or eight, things had been different. But by the time I was that old, I had begun to recognize that I was on my own – and needed no one else.

My father had been a cipher as far back as I could remember. If some-one were to tell me that he had never actually realized he had two chil-dren, I would be inclined to believe it. Certainly I had seen him forget us even when we were before his eyes, in the same room with him. He had been the director of the Walter H. Mannheim private library in St. Paul; and he was a harmless man – a bookworm. But he was no use either to me or my younger sister as a parent.

My mother was something else. To begin with, she was beautiful. Yes I know, every child thinks that about its mother. But I had independent testimony from a number of other people; particularly a long line of men, other than my father, who not only thought so, also, but told my mother so, when I was there to overhear them.

However, most of that came later. Before my sister was born my mother was my whole family, by herself. We used to play games together, she and I. Also, she sang and talked to me and told me stories endlessly. But then, after my sister was born, things began to change. Not at once, of course. It was not until Beth was old enough to run around that the alteration in my mother became clearly visible. I now think that she had counted on Beth's birth to do something for her marriage; and it had not done so.

At any rate, from that time on, she began to forget us. Not that I blamed her for it. She had forgotten our father long since – in fact, there was nothing there to forget. But now she began to forget us as well. Not all of the time, to start with; but we came to know when she was about to start forgetting because she would show up one day with some new, tall man we had never seen, who smelled of cigars and alcohol.

When this first started happening, it was the beginning of a bad time for me. I was too young then to accept it, and I wanted to fight whatever was taking her away from me; but there was nothing there with which I could come to grips. It was only as if a glass window had suddenly been rolled up between her and me; and no matter how I shouted or pounded on its transparent surface, she did not hear. Still, I kept on trying to fight it for several years, during which she began to stay away for longer and longer periods – all with my father's silent consent, or at least with no objections from him.

It was at the close of those years that my fight finally came to an end. I did not give up, because I could not; but the time came when my mother disappeared completely. She went away on one last trip and never came back. So at last I was able to stop struggling; and as a result I came to the first great discovery of my life, which was that nobody ever really loved anyone. There was a built-in instinct when you were young that made you think you needed a mother; and another built-in instinct in that mother to pay attention to you. But as you got older you discovered your parents were only other humanly selfish people, in competition with you for life's pleasures; and your parents came to realize that this child of theirs that was you was not so unique and won-derful after all, but only a small savage with whom they were burdened. When I understood this at last, I began to see how knowing it gave me a great advantage over everyone else; because I realized then that life was not love, as my mother had told me it was when I was very young, but competition – fighting; and, knowing this, I was now set free to give all my attention to what really mattered. So, from that moment on I became a fighter without match, a fighter nothing could stop.

It was not quite that sudden and complete a change, of course. I still had, and probably always would have, absent-minded moments when I would still react to other people out of my early training, as if it mat-tered to me whether they lived or died. Indeed, after my mother dis-appeared for good, there was a period of several years in which Beth clung to me – quite naturally, of course, because I was all she had – and I responded unthinkingly with the false affection reflex. But in time she too grew up and went looking somewhere else for attention; and I became completely free.

It was a freedom so great I saw most people could not even conceive of it. When I was still less than half-grown, adults would remark on how strong-minded I was. They talked of how I would make my mark in the world. I used to want to laugh, hearing them say that, because anything else was unthinkable. I not only had every intention of leaving my mark on the world; I intended to put my brand on it and turn it into my own personal property; and I had no doubt I could do it. Free as I was of the love delusion that blinkered all the rest of them, there was nothing to stop me; and I had already found out that I would go on trying for what I wanted as long as it was there for me to get.

I had found that out when I had fought my mother's withdrawal from us. I had not been able to stop struggling against that until it had finally sunk in on me that she was gone for good. Up until that time I had not been able to accept the fact she might leave us. My mind simply refused to give up on her. It would keep going over and over the available data or evidence, with near-idiot, unending patience, searching for some crack in the problem, like a rat chewing at a steel plate across the bottom of a granary door. A steel plate could wear down a rat's teeth; but he would only rest a while to let them grow again, and then go back once more to chewing, until one day he would wear his way through to where the grain was. So it was with me. Pure reflex kept the rat chewing like that; and, as far as I was concerned, it was a pure reflex that kept my mind coming back and back to a problem until it found a solution.

There was only one way to turn it off, one I had never found out how to control. That was if somehow the knowledge managed to filter through to me that the answer I sought would have no usefulness after I found it. When that happened – as when I finally realized my mother was gone for good – there would be an almost audible *click* in my mind, and the whole process would blank out. It was as if the reflex suddenly went dead. But that did not happen often; and it was certainly not happening now.

The problem my mind would not give up on at the moment was the question of what had happened to the world. My head kept replaying all its available evidence, from the moment of my collapse in the cabin near Duluth to the present, trying for one solid, explainable picture that would pull everything together.

Sitting now under the tree, in the shade of a new-risen quarter moon and staring up at the star-bright sky of summer, I went clear back to reliving my college days, to the paper I had written on the methods of charting stocks, followed by the theoretical investments, then the actual investments, then the penthouse suite in the Bellecourt Towers, hotel service twenty-four hours a day, and the reputation for being some sort of young financial wizard. Then my cashing out and buying into Snowman, Inc., my three years as president of that company, while snowmobile and motor home sales climbed up off the wall chart – and my marriage to Swannee.

I had never blamed Swannee a bit for what had happened. It must have been as irritating to her as it would have been to me to have someone hanging on to her the way I ended up doing. The way I had decided to get married in the first place was that I had gotten tired of living in the penthouse apartment. I wanted a real house, and found one. An architecturally modern, rambling building with five bedrooms, on about twenty acres of land with its own small lake. And of course, once I had decided to have a house, I realized what I really needed was a wife to go along with it. And I looked around a bit and married Swannee. She was not as beautiful as my mother, but she was close to it. Tall, with a superb body and a sort of golden-custard coloured hair, very fine, that she wore long and which floated around her shoulders like a cloud.

By education she had been headed for being a lawyer; but her instincts for work were not all that strong. In spite of the fact that she had done well academically in law school, she had never taken her bar exams and was, in fact, working as a sort of ornamental legal assistant to a firm of corporation attorneys down in St. Paul. I think she was glad to give up the pretence of going to the office every day and simply take over as my wife. She was, in fact, ideal from my standpoint. I had no illusions about her. I had buried those with the memories of my mother years before. So I had not asked her to be anymore than she was; ornamental, good in bed, and able to do the relatively easy job of managing this home of mine. I think, in fact, we had an ideal marriage – until I spoiled it.

As I said, occasionally I would become absent-minded and respond as if other people really mattered to me. Apparently I made the mistake of doing this with Swannee; because little by little she drifted off from me, began disappearing on short trips almost as my mother had done, and then one day she told me she wanted a divorce and left.

I was disappointed, but of course, not much more than that; and I decided that trying to have an ordinary, live-in wife had been a mistake in the first place. I now had all my time to devote to work, and for the next year I did just that. Right up to the moment of my first heart attack.

At twenty-four. God damn it, no one should have to have a heart attack after only twenty-four years in this world! But again there was my rat-reflex mind chewing away at that problem, too, until it broke through to a way out. I cashed in and set up a living trust to support me in style forever, if necessary; and I went up to the cabin to live and make myself healthy again.

Two years of that – and then the blackout, the squirrel, the trek south, the man with the axe ... and Sunday.

I had almost shot Sunday in the first second I saw him, before I realized that he was in the same sort of trance the squirrel had been in. We ran into each other about twenty miles or so south of the Twin Cities, in an area where they had started to put together a really good modern zoo – one in which the animals wandered about almost without restriction; and the people visiting were moved through wire tunnels and cages to see the creatures in something like their natural wild, free states.

But there was no zoo left when I got there; only half-timbered country. A time-change line had moved through, taking out about three miles of highway. The ground was rough, but dry and open. I coaxed the panel truck across it in low gear, picking as level a route as I could and doing all right, until I got one rear wheel down into a hole and had to jack it up to get traction again.

I needed something firm to rest the jack base on. I walked into a little patch of woods nearby looking for a piece of fallen tree limb the right size, and literally stumbled over a leopard.

He was crouched low on the ground, head twisted a little sideways and looking up as if cringing from something large that was about to attack him. Like the squirrel, he was unmoving in that position when I walked into him – the time storm that had taken out the road and caught him as well, must have passed only minutes previously. When I stubbed my toe on his soft flank, he came out of his trance and looked at me. I jumped back and jerked up the rifle I had had the sense to carry with me.

But he stepped forward and rubbed along the side of my upper leg, purring, so much like an overgrown household pussycat that I could not have brought myself to shoot him, even if I had had the sense to do so. He was a large young male, weighing a hundred and forty pounds when I later managed to coax him onto a bathroom scale in an abandoned hardware store. He rubbed by me, turned and came back to slide up along my other side, licking at my hands where they held the rifle. And from then on, like it or not, I had Sunday.

I had puzzled about him, and the squirrel, a number of times since. The closest I had come to satisfying my search for what had made them react as they had, was that being caught by a time change jarred anything living right back to its infancy. After I first came to in the cabin – well, I had generally avoided thinking about that. For one thing I had a job to clean myself up. But I do remember that first, terrible feeling of helplessness and abandonment – like a very young child lost in a woods from which he knows he can never find his way out. If someone had turned up then to hold my hand, I might have reacted just like the squirrel or the leopard.

Then there had been our meeting – Sunday's and mine – with the girl. That had been a different kettle of fish. For one thing, evidently she had passed the point of initial recovery from being caught in a time change; but equally evidently, the experience – or something just before the experience – had hit her a great deal more severely than my experience with the time change had done.

But about this time, the stars started to swim slowly in a circular dance, and I fell asleep.

I woke with the sun in my eyes, feeling hot and itchy all over. It was a bright cloudless day, at least a couple of hours old, since dawn; evidently the tree had shaded me from the sun's waking me earlier.

Sunday lay curled within the open entrance to the tent; but he was all alone. The girl was gone.

6

My first reaction, out of that old, false, early training of mine, was to worry. Then common sense returned. It would only be a relief, as far as I was concerned, to have her gone; with her fits of withdrawal and her pestering Sunday until he, in turn, became a bother.

Damn it, I thought, *let her go.*

But then it occurred to me that something might have happened to her. It was open country all around us here, except for a screen of young popple, beyond which there was a small creek. I went down through the popple and looked across the creek, up over a swelling expanse of meadow lifting to a near horizon maybe three hundred yards off. There was nothing to be seen. I went down to look at the creek itself, the edges of which were muddy and marshy, and found her footprints in soft earth, going toward the water. A little further, one of her shoes was stuck in the mud and abandoned.

The creek was shallow – no more than knee deep for someone her size. I waded across, picked up the shoe, located her tracks in the mud on the far side and saw them joined by two other sets of footprints. Bare feet, larger than hers. I began to feel cold and hot inside at the same time.

I went back to the tent, strapped on the belt with the holstered revolver and took the carbine. The carbine held thirteen shells and it was semi-automatic. My first thought was of following the tracks up the hill; and then I realized that this would be more likely to alert whoever the other two people had been than if I drove. If they saw me coming in the panel, they might figure I'd given up the girl and left her. If they saw me coming on foot, particularly with Sunday, they wouldn't have much choice but to think I was chasing her down.

I packed the gear. It would be hard to replace, maybe; and there was no guarantee we'd be coming back this way again. Then I got into the panel, letting Sunday up on the seat beside me for once, but making him lie down out of sight from outside. I pulled out on the highway and headed up the road parallel to the way I had last seen the footprints going.

We did not have far to go. Just up and over the rise that belonged to the meadow across the creek, I saw a trailer camp with some sort of large building up in front of all the trailers. No one had cut the grass in the camp for a long time, but there were figures moving about the trailers. I drove up to the building in front. There were a couple of dusty gas pumps there, and a cheerfully-grinning, skinny, little old man in coveralls too big for him came out of the building as I stopped.

'Hi,' he said, coming up within about four feet of Sunday's side of the car and squinting across through the open window at me. 'Want some gas?'

'No thanks,' I said. 'I'm looking for a girl. A girl about fourteen, fifteen years old with dark hair and doesn't talk. Have you seen—'

'Nope!' he chirped. 'Want some gas?'

Gas was something you had to scrounge for these days. I was suddenly very interested in him.

'Yes,' I said. 'I think I'll have some gas. And . . .'

I let my voice trail off into silence. He came closer, cocking his left ear at me.

'What'd y'say?' He stuck his head in the window and came face to face with Sunday, only inches between them. He stopped, perfectly still.

'That's right,' I said. 'Don't move or make a sound, now. And don't try to run. The leopard can catch you before you can take three steps.' He didn't know that Sunday would never have understood in a million years any command I might have given to chase someone.

I jerked my thumb at the back of the panel. Sunday understood that. He turned and leaped into the back, out of the right hand seat in one flowing movement. The old man's eyes followed him. I slid over into the right hand seat.

'Now,' I said, 'turn around. Give me room to open the door.'

He did. I opened the door on that side of the panel a crack. The baggy coverall on his back was only inches away. Vertically in the centre of the back, about belt level, was a tear or cut about eight inches long. I reached in through it and closed my hand on pretty much what I expected. A handgun – a five-chamber .22 revolver – stuck in a belt around his waist under the coveralls.

'All right,' I said, picking up the carbine and getting out of the panel behind him. 'Walk straight ahead of me. Act ordinary and don't try to run. The leopard will be with me; and if I don't get you, he will. Now, where's the girl? Keep your voice down when you answer.'

'Bub-bu-bu—,' the old man stammered. Sounds, nothing understandable. Plainly, as his repeated offer of gas had shown, whoever lived in this camp had chosen one of their less bright citizens to stand out front and make the place look harmless.

'Come on, Sunday,' I said.

The leopard came. We followed the old man across the drive, past the pumps. The large building looked not only closed, but abandoned. Darkness was behind its windows, and spider webs hung over the cracked white paint of its door frame. I poked the old man with the carbine muzzle, directing him around the right end of the building and back into the camp. I was expecting to be jumped or fired at, at any second. But nothing happened. When I got around the end of the building, I saw why. They were all at the party.

God knows, they might have been normal people once. But what I saw now were somewhere between starving savages and starving animals. They were mostly late adolescents, rib-skinny every one of them, male and female alike barefoot below the ragged cuff-edges of the jeans they wore and naked above the waistband. Every one of them, as well, was striped and marked with black paint on face and body. They were gathered, maybe thirty or forty of them, in an open space before the rows of trailers began. It might have been a stretch of show lawn, or a volleyball court, once. At the end of it, tied to a sort of X of planks set upright and surrounded by burnable trash, paper and bits of wood, was the girl.

Whether she had come there willingly, I do not know. It is not beyond the bounds of possibility that she had finally despaired of ever having Sunday love her; and when she met those two other pairs of feet by the creek, she had gone off of her own free will with them. But she was terrified now. Her eyes were enormous, and her mouth was stretched wide in a scream that she could not bring forth.

I poked the old man with the gun muzzle and walked in among them. I saw no weapons; but it stood to reason they must have something more than the revolver that had been hidden on the old man. The back of my neck prickled; but on the spur of the moment the best thing I could think of was to put a bold front on it, and maybe we could just all walk out of here – the girl, Sunday and I – with no trouble.

They said not a word, they did not move as I walked through them. And then, when I was less than a dozen feet from the girl, she finally got that scream out of her.

'*Look out!*'

For a part of a second I was so stunned to hear her utter something understandable that I only stared. Then it registered on me that she was looking over my shoulder at something behind me. I spun around, dropping on one knee instinctively and bringing up the carbine to my shoulder.

There were two of them, lying on the roof of the house with either rifles or shotguns – I had no time to decide which. They were just like the others, except for their firearms. The girl's shriek must have startled them as much as it had me, because they were simply lying there, staring down at me with their weapons forgotten.

But it was not them I had to worry about, anyway, because – I have no idea from where – the crowd I had just passed had since produced bows and arrows; perhaps a bow for every five or six of them, so that half a dozen of them were already fitting arrows to their strings as I turned. I started firing.

I shot the two on the roof first, without thinking – which was pure foolishness, the reflex of a man brought up to think of firearms as deadly, but of arrows as playthings – because the two on the roof did not even have their guns aimed, and by the time I'd fired at them a couple of arrows had already whistled by me. They were target arrows, lacking barbed hunting heads, but nonetheless deadly for that. The rest of the ones being aimed would certainly not all have missed me – if it had not been for Sunday.

There was nothing of the Lassie-dog-to-the-rescue about Sunday. The situation was entirely beyond his understanding; and if the two on the roof or the bow-wielders had shot me quickly and quietly enough, probably he would merely have sniffed sadly at me as I lay on the ground and wondered why I had stopped moving. But the girl had screamed – and I must suddenly have reeked of the body chemicals released by fear and fury – so Sunday operated by instinct.

If I was frightened, he was frightened, too. And in wild animals, as in man himself once he is broken down to it, fear and fury are the same thing. Sunday attacked the only fear-making cause in view – the group of archers and their friends before us; and they found themselves suddenly facing a wild, snarling, pinwheel-of-knives that was a hundred and forty pound member of the cat family gone berserk.

They ran from him. Of course they ran. All but three or four that were too badly clawed or bitten to get away. I had plenty of time and freedom to get the girl untied from the planks and start to lead her out of the clearing. By that time Sunday was off in one corner of the open space, daintily toying, with one hooked claw, at a bleeding, moaning figure that was trying to crawl away from him. It was a little sickening;

but so was what they had planned for the girl. I called the leopard. He came – if reluctantly – and followed us back to the truck. We got out of there.

Half a mile down the highway I had to pull over to the shoulder and stop the car, again. Sunday was still prickly from the adrenaline of the battle. He wanted to lie in the back of the panel all alone and lick his fur. The girl, rebuffed by him, was suddenly sick. I helped her out of the car and held her head until it was over. Then I got her back into the front seat of the car, curled up there with a blanket over her.

'They were going to EAT me,' she whispered, when I covered her up.

It was the second time she had spoken, and all in one day. I looked at her, but her eyes were squeezed shut. I could not tell if she had been talking to me, or only to herself. I got the panel moving again and let her sleep. That evening when we camped, I tried talking to her myself. But she had gone back to being dumb. She would neither speak nor look at me. Foolishly, I even found myself feeling disappointed – even a little hurt at that. But of course that was just the wrong-headed early training at work in me again. I had been feeling good over the fact that she was coming out of her mental prison – as if that really mattered, one way or another.

The next day we headed south by west again. It was a bright, hot day, and I was feeling good. We had gotten off the asphalt on to a stretch of superhighway, and there was no one to be seen – not even anything on the road as inconsequential as an abandoned car. We were making good time; and Samuelson had helped me to fix myself on the map. We were close enough to the location of Omaha that, barring unforeseen delays along the road, we would reach it by sunset. When noon came, I picked a ramp and pulled off the freeway – just to be on the safe side in case someone unfriendly should be cruising it about the time we were having lunch – and found a patch of shade under some large, scraggly-limbed trees I could not identify.

We had hardly glimpsed the mistwall of a time change all morning – and the few we had seen had been far off, so far off that in the bright daylight it was impossible to tell whether they were standing still or moving. But obviously one had passed by where we were sometime, since the storms started. About four hundred yards from the exit ramp of the highway the cross road ended abruptly in a clump of tall mop-headed palms, the kind you find lining the street boulevards in Los Angeles.

The palms and the big scraggly-limbed trees signalled that we were into a different time-changed territory than we had been earlier. Now that I stopped to notice it, for some time there had been a different kind of dampness to the air than that which comes from midwestern, mid-summer humidity. The softness of the atmosphere was more like that of a seacoast; and the few white clouds that moved overhead seemed to hang low and opulent in the sky, the way they do in Florida, instead of being high and distant like piled up castles, as they are in temperate zone mid-continental skies during the warm months.

It was a hint, I thought, to be on our guard against strange company. As far as I had been able to determine, it was only everything below the animal level that got changed by the time storms when they passed. I had begun to add up some evidence in what I saw to reach the conclusion that much of what I came across was several hundred, if not several thousand, years forward from my own original time. There was some evidence of extensive storm damage and geological change, followed by considered reforestation in a majority of the landscapes I moved through. There must have been massive loss of life in most areas at the same time or another, which accounted for the scarcity of most warm-blooded creatures, except for birds. Certainly topography and vegetation changed when a time line passed; and I had noticed fish in lakes that had not been lakes before the time change. But just where on the scale of life the dividing line was drawn, I had no idea. It would pay to be watchful. If, for example, snakes were below the dividing line, then we might suddenly encounter poisonous varieties in latitudes or areas where such varieties had never existed before.

I spent part of the lunch hour trying to get the girl to talk; but she was back at being voiceless again. I kept chattering to her, though, partly out of stubbornness and partly out of the idea that if she had loosened up once, she could again; and the more I tried to wear down the barrier between us, possibly, the sooner she would.

When we were done with lunch, we buried the tin cans and the paper. The girl and I ate a lot of canned stuff, which made meals easy; and I had fallen into the habit of feeding Sunday on canned dog food or any other meat that could be found. He also hunted occasionally as we went along. But he would never go very far from me to do it, and this restricted what he could catch. We buried our trash just in case some one or something might find the remains and take a notion to trail us. We got back in the panel truck and headed once more down the superhighway.

But it was exactly as if stopping to eat lunch had changed our luck. Within five miles the superhighway disappeared – cut off by some past time storm line. It ended in a neat lip of concrete hanging thirty feet in the air with nothing in the shape of a road below or beyond it but sandy hills, covered with cactus and scraggly trees. I had to backtrack two miles to find an exit ramp that led down on to a road that appeared to keep going off at an angle as far as I could see. It was asphalt, like most of the roads we had been travelling earlier, but it was not in as good shape as the ones that had led us through Samuelson's small town and past the trailer camp. It was narrower, high-crowned, and weedy along the edges. I hesitated because, although the road angled exactly in the direction I wanted to go, there was something about it that filled me with uneasiness. I simply did not like the look of it. Here and there sand had blown across it, a smudge of gold on black – but not to any depth that would slow down the panel truck. Still, I slowed on my own and cruised at no more than thirty miles an hour, keeping my eyes open.

The road seemed to run on without end, which did nothing to allay that uneasiness of mine. There was something about it that was unfamiliar – not of any recognizable time – in spite of the fact that it looked like a backwoods road anywhere. The sandy hillscapes following us on either side were alien, too, as if they had been transported from a desert somewhere and set down here. Also, it was getting hotter and the humidity was worse.

I stopped the panel, finally, to do a more precise job of estimating our position on the map than I could do while driving. According to the compass I had mounted on the instrument panel on our vehicle, the asphalt road had been running almost exactly due west; and the outskirts of Omaha should be less than twenty miles southwest of us.

As long as we had been on the superhighway, I had not worried; because a road like that, obviously belonging to our original twentieth century time, had to be headed toward the nearest large city – which had to be Omaha. Just as on the asphalt road at first I had not worried either, because it headed so nearly in the direction I wanted to go.

But it was stretching out now to the point where I began to worry that it would carry me to the north and past the city, without letting me catch sight of it. Certainly, by this time we had gone far enough to intersect some other roads heading south and into the metropolitan area. But we had crossed no other road. For that matter, we had come across nothing else that indicated a city nearby, no railroad tracks, no isolated houses, no fences, no suburban developments in the bulldozer stage of construction ... I was uneasy.

Laying out the road map on the hood of the car, I traced our route to the superhighway, traced the superhighway to what I believed to be the exit by which we had come down off it, and along the road that exit tied into – headed west. The road was there; but according to the map, less than a dozen miles farther on, it ran through a small town called Leeder; and we had come twenty miles without seeing as much as a road sign.

I went through the whole thing twice more, checked the compass and traced out our route, and checked the odometer on the panel to see how far we'd come since leaving the superhighway – and the results came out the same. We had to be bypassing Omaha to the north.

I got back in the truck and started travelling again, driving slowly. I told myself I'd give myself another five miles without a crossroad before turning back. I drove them, and then another five. But I saw no crossroad. Nothing. Only the narrow, neglected-looking strip of asphalt which looked as if it might continue unchanged around to the Pacific Ocean.

I stopped the panel again, got out and walked off the road to check the surface of the ground to the south. I walked back and forth and stamped a few times. The surface was sandy, but hard – easily solid enough to bear the weight of the panel truck; and the vegetation was scattered enough so that there would be no trouble driving through it. Up until now I had been very careful not to get off the roads, for fear of a breakdown of the truck which would strand us a distance from any hope of easily finding another vehicle. On foot we would be at the mercy of the first moving time storm wall that came toward us.

But we were so close now – we were just a few miles away from getting back to normal life. I could see Swannee in my mind's eye so clearly that she was almost like a mirage superimposed on the semidesert landscape around us. She had to be there, waiting for me. Something inside me was still positive, beyond all argument, that Omaha had survived; and that along with it Swannee had survived in the sanity of a portion of the world as it had been before the time storm. In fact my mind had toyed a number of times with the idea that since Omaha, like Hawaii, had survived, it might mean there might be many other enclaves of safety; and the fact that there were such enclaves would mean there was a way of beating the time storm, by applying to all other places the special conditions or whatever unusual elements had kept these enclaves protected.

In those enclaves she and I could still lead the reasonable and normal life we could have had before the time storm hit; and somehow I felt sure that the experience of the time storm would have straightened her out on what had gone wrong between us before. Time would have brought her to the realization that it was simply an old reflex on my part that had made me act like someone literally in love with her. Also, she would know how tough life could be outside the enclaves like the one she now lived in – or even there, for that matter. She would have a new appreciation of what I could do for her, in the way of taking care of her. In fact, the more I thought, the more confident I was that by this time she would be ready to indulge these little emotional lapses of mine. All I had to do was find her and things would go well.

– But that was something to think about when there was time to think about it. The big question now was – should I take the panel cross-country, south, away from the road, to find a highway or street that would bring me to the city?

There was really no argument about it. I got Sunday and the girl back into the panel – they had followed me outside and wandered after me as I stamped on the ground to make sure it would not bog down the panel – then we got back in the truck, turned off the asphalt and headed due south by the compass.

It was not bad driving at all. I had to slow down to about five to ten miles an hour; and I kept the panel in second gear, occasionally having to shift down to low on the hills, but generally finding it easy going. It was all up and down, a roller coaster-type of going for about nine-tenths of a mile; and then suddenly we came up over a rise and looked down on a lakeshore.

It was just a strip of whitish-brown, sandy beach. But the shallow, rather stagnant-looking water beyond the beach stretched out as far as I could see and out of sight right and left as well. Evidently the time storm had moved this whole area into the northwest of the metropolitan area, pretty well blocking off access from that direction. The problem for me now was – which was would be the shortest way round the lake? Right or left?

It was toss-up. I squinted in both directions but for some reason, just while I had been standing there, a haze of some sort seemed to have moved in, so that I could not see far out on the water in any direction. Finally I chose to go to the right, because I thought I saw a little darkness through the haze upon the sun-glare off the water and sand in that direction. I turned the nose of the truck and we got going.

The beach was almost as good as a paved road to drive on. It was flat and firm. Apparently, the water adjoining it began to shelve more sharply as we went along, for it lost its stagnant, shallow appearance and began to develop quite a respectable surf. There was an onshore wind blowing; but it helped the heat and the humidity only a little. We kept driving.

As I watched the miles add up on the truck's odometer, I began gradually to regret not trying in the other direction. Clearly, I had picked
the long way around this body of water, because looking ahead I could
still see no end to it. When the small, clicking figures of the odometer
rolled up past the twelve mile mark, I braked the truck to a halt, turned
around and headed back.

As I said, the beach was good driving. I pushed our speed up to about
forty, and it was not long before we were back at the point where we
had first come across the lake. I kept pounding along; and shortly I
made out something up ahead. The dazzle of sunlight from the water
seemed to have gotten in my eyes so that I could not make out exactly
what it was – something like a handkerchief-sized island with a tree, or
a large raft with a diving tower out in the water, just a little way from
the beach. But there were the black silhouettes of two-legged figures on
the sand there. I could stop to get some directions, and we could still be
pulling into Swannee's driveway in time for dinner.

The dazzle-effect on my eyes got worse as the panel got close to the
figures; and the glitter of sunlight through the windshield was not
helping. I blinked, and blinked again. I should have thought to pick
up some dark glasses and keep them in the glove compartment of the
panel for situations like this – but I just had not expected to run into
water-glare like this. I must have been no more than thirty or forty feet
from the figures by the time I finally braked the panel to a stop and
jumped out of it on to the sand, blinking to get the windshield-glitter
out of the way between us – and I still could not see them clearly. There
were at least half a dozen of them on the beach, and I saw more out on
the raft or whatever it was.

I started toward them.

'Hey!' I said. 'I'm lost. Can you put me on the road to Omaha?' I want
to get to Byerly Park, there.'

The figures did not answer. I was within a few steps of them now. I
stopped, closed my eyes and shook my head violently. Then I opened
my eyes again.

For the first time I saw them clearly. They had two legs apiece all
right; but that was the only thing people-like about them. As far as
I could see, they wore no clothes; and I could have sworn they were
covered with greenish-gold scales. Heavy, lizard-like features with
unblinking dark eyes stared directly into my face.

I stared back at them. Then I turned and looked out at the raft and
beyond. All around were the beach and the water – nothing more. And
finally, finally, the truth came crashing in on me.

There was too much water. There was no way Omaha could still exist out there beyond the waves. I had been wrong all the time. I had been fooling myself, hugging to my mind an impossible hope, as if it was the fixed centre of the universe.

Omaha was gone. Gone completely. Swannee was gone. Like so many other things, she had been taken away forever. I had lost her for good, just as I had lost my mother ...

The sun, which had been high overhead, seemed to swing halfway around the sky before my eyes and turn blood red. The water seemed to go black as ink and swirl up all around me and the watching lizard-humans. My mind felt as if it was cracking wide open; and everything spun about me like liquid going down a drain, sucking water and beach and all, including me, away down into some place that was ugly and frightening.

It was the end of the world. I had been intending to survive anything for Swannee's sake; but all the time she had already been gone. She and Omaha had probably been lost in the first moment after the time storm hit. From then on, there had only been the illusion of her in my sick mind. I had been as insane as Samuelson, after all. The crazy cat, the idiot girl and I – we had been three loonies together. I had flattered myself that the mistwalls were all outside me; but now I could feel them breaching the walls of my skull, moving inside me, wiping clean and destroying everything over which they passed. I had a faint and distant impression of hearing myself howling like a chained dog; and of strong hands holding me. But this, too, swiftly faded away, into a complete and utter nothingness ...

7

The world was rocking gently underneath me. No … it was not the world, it was the raft rocking.

Waking, I began to remember that there had been moments of clarity before this. But they had been seldom. Most of the time I had been in a world in which I had found Swannee – but a changed Swannee – after all; and we had settled down in an Omaha untouched by the time storm. But, slowly, that world had begun to wear thin; and more and more often there had been moments when I was not in Omaha but here, seeing the raft and the rest of it from my present position. Now, there was no doubt which world I lived in.

So I was back for good. I could feel that; along with a grim, aching hunger in my belly. For the first time I began to wonder where the raft was going, and to worry about Sunday and the girl.

I looked around, identifying things from the hazy periods earlier. It was a beautiful, clear day at sea, or at whatever equivalent of a sea it was upon which we were afloat. A few inches from my nose were saplings, tree branches or what-have-you, that had been woven into a sort of cage about me. Beyond the cage, there was a little distance – perhaps ten feet – of open log surface to an edge of the raft, studded with the ever-sprouting twigs that tried to grow from the raft logs, though these had been neatly and recently bitten off for this day. Beyond the logs was the restlessly heaving surface of the grey-blue water, stretching away to the curve of the horizon.

I rolled over and looked out in the opposite direction, through another cage-side of loosely woven withes, at the rest of the raft.

It was about a hundred or so feet in length. At one end was a stand of – I had to call them 'trees' for want of any better name – their thick-leaved, almost furry-looking tops taking advantage of whatever breeze was blowing to push the raft along before it. Around their base grew the carefully cultivated stand of shoots from which my cage, and just about everything else the lizard-people seemed to make with their hands, had been constructed.

Behind the trees and the shoots were a couple of other cages holding the girl and Sunday, plus a pile of shells and stones that apparently had some value for the lizards. They looked all right. They were both perhaps a little thinner; but they seemed lively enough; and, in fact, the girl was looking brighter and more in charge of herself than I could ever remember seeing her. From her cage on back, except for piles of assorted rubble and junk – everything from sand itself to what looked like a heap of furs – were the various members of the crew. I found myself calling them a crew for lack of a better term. For all I knew, most of them may have been passengers. Or perhaps they were all members of one family; there was no way of telling.

But in any case, there were thirty or forty of them, most simply lying on their bellies or sides, absolutely still in the sunlight, but with dark eyes open and heads up, not as if they were sleeping. The few on their feet were moving about aimlessly. There were only four who seemed to have any occupation. One was an individual who was working his way down the far side of the raft on all fours, delicately biting off the newly sprouted twigs from the logs of the raft as he went, and three others at the rear of the raft. These three were holding the heavy shaft of a great steering oar, which evidently gave the raft what little directional purpose it could have while floating before the wind.

In the very centre of the raft, back about twenty feet from my cage, was a roughly square hole in the logs, exposing a sort of small interior swimming pool of the same water that was all around us. For several minutes, I stared at the hole, puzzled. The sight of it triggered off a nagging feeling in the back of my mind, as of something that ought to be remembered, but which, annoyingly, refused to surface from the unconscious. Something half-recalled from one or more moments of earlier temporary return to rationality. As I watched, one of the recumbent lizard-people got up, walked over to the pool and stepped into it. He splashed down out of sight and stayed invisible for what must have been at least four or five minutes before his head bobbed to the surface momentarily, and then he disappeared again.

There were several more splashes. A few of the others had joined him in the pool. I watched the water there for a while, but the lizard-people stayed mainly below the surface. After about fifteen minutes or so, one of them climbed back out and lay down on the bare logs once more, scales wet and glistening in the sun.

From my earlier brief moments of sanity, I remembered seeing a lot of this swimming pool activity, but without speculating about it. Now that my mind was back in my head for good, the old reflex in me to gnaw away at answers I did not have went to work. The most obvious reason for their continual plunges was to keep the outside of their bodies reasonably damp. They had the look of a water-living race; either one which had evolved in the sea, or whatever we were on, or humans who had returned to an aquatic environment. If it was the latter, then it could be that this part of the earth had been moved very far into the past or future indeed, either far enough back to find the great Nebraska sea – that shallow ocean that had occupied the interior of the North American continent in the Permian period, or far enough into the future to find a time when that sea had been geologically recreated.

A shift that far forward would have given time for humans to de-evolve and make a genetic shift to the form of these who had captured us. I studied them.

I had not really looked closely at them before, but now that I did so, I could see clearly that there were, indeed, two sexes aboard, and that the females had a mammalian breast development – although this was barely perceptible.

The genitals of both sexes were all but hidden in a heavy horizontal fold of skin descending from the lower belly into the crotch; but what I could see of these external organs was also mammalian, even human-like, in appearance. So it looked strongly as if a far futureward development of this area under the time storm influence was a good guess.

Outside of the slight bodily differences, the sex of the individual creatures around us seemed to make little difference in the ordinary conduct of their daily lives. I saw no signs of sexual response between individuals – no sign even of sexual awareness. Perhaps they had a season for such things, and this was not it.

They were clearly used to spending a good share of their time in water; and that perhaps explained their periodic dunkings in the raft pool. It could be that they were like dolphins who needed to be wetted down if they were out of water for any length of time.

It seemed strange to me, though, that they should go to the trouble of cutting a hole in the centre of their raft, rather than just dunking themselves over one of the edges, if that was their reason for getting in the water. I was mulling this strangeness over, when something I had been looking at suddenly registered on me as an entirely different object from what I had taken it to be.

Everybody has had the experience of looking right at an object and taking it for something entirely different from what it really is – until abruptly, the mind clicks over and recognizes its true nature. I had been staring absently at a sort of vertical plane projecting from the water alongside the raft and perhaps half a dozen feet off from the edge, and more or less half-wondering what usefulness it had, when the object suddenly took on its true character, and my heart gave an unusually heavy thump.

I had been allowing the plane's apparent lack of motion relative to the raft to deceive me into thinking it was a surface of wood, a part of the raft itself. Abruptly, I recognised what it really was – I had seen enough of the same things charter-fishing on my vacations to South America, back when I still owned Snowman, Inc. What I was watching was a shark's fin, keeping pace with the raft. There was no mistaking that particular shape for the fin of a sailfish, a tarpon, or any other sea denizen. It was the dorsal of a shark – but what a shark!

If the fin was in proportion to the body beneath it, that body must be half as long as this raft.

Now that I saw it clearly for what it was, I could not imagine what had led me to mistake it for a plane of wood. But now my mind had clicked over and would not click back. If monsters like that were about in these waters, no wonder the lizard-people wanted to do their swimming inboard.

On the other hand, it was odd … once one or more of them were in the water, the shark should be able to get at them as easily underneath the raft as alongside it. Unless there was some reason it would not go under the raft after them. Or did the lizard-people figure that by the time the shark started under the raft, they would have time to get back out of the pool and back up on top of the logs of which it was built? Now, that was a good theory. On the other hand, I had seen no evidence of unusual haste in those getting out of the pool.

Was it possible that in the water the lizard-people could out-swim the shark? That did not seem likely, although obviously, our captors were at home in the water, and obviously, they were built for swimming. They were thick-bodied and thick-limbed, their elbows and knees bent slightly so that they stood in a perpetual crouch; and both their hands and feet were webbed to near the ends of their fingers and toes. They looked to be very powerful, physically, compared to a human, and those teeth of theirs were almost shark-standard in themselves; although none of them were much more than five feet tall. But in relation to a shark that size, the strength of any one of them would not be worth considering.

I was puzzling about these things, when a change came in the schedule. One of the lizard people approached the cage holding the girl and opened up some sort of trapdoor in one end of it. The girl crept out, as if she had been through this before and knew the procedure, and, without hesitation, got up, walked to the pool, and jumped in. She stayed there, holding onto an edge.

The same lizard who had let her out was joined by another, and the two of them went over to the cage of Sunday, who snarled as they approached. They paid no attention to him but lifted up his cage easily between them – evidently I had been right about their strength – carried it to the edge of the pool and opened its end.

Sunday, however, showed none of the girl's willingness to leave his cage for the water. But evidently the lizards had encountered this problem before. After a moment's wait, one of them got down into the pool, reached up with a scaly arm, and pulled cage and Sunday under the surface with him.

For a moment there was no sign of leopard, cage, or lizard. Then the head of Sunday broke water in the exact centre of the pool, snorting, and swimming strongly. He swam directly to the edge of the pool by the girl, crawled out, and sat down in the sun to lick himself dry, looking as furious as only a wet cat can look. The lizard rose behind him, towing an empty cage and climbed out on the other side.

The two made no immediate attempt to recage him, and I was still watching him when a sudden squeaking sound behind me made me turn my head to look. A door in the far end of my own cage was being lifted. I turned around and crawled out. A lizardman was standing facing me, and I caught a sickish, if faint, reek of fish-smell from him before I turned and went toward the pool. But at the edge I stopped, looking once more to my right where the shark fin was still on patrol.

My escort picked me up and dropped me in the water. I came up sputtering, and grabbed hold of the edge to haul myself out. Then I saw the girl, still hanging on to a log, in the water near me, watching. Evidently, she considered it safe enough where we were.

I turned and tried to look down through the water; but the shadow of the trees at the front of the raft was on it and it made it took dark to see. I took a breath, stuck my head under the water and looked about. Then I saw why the shark was nothing to worry about when you were in the pool. The underside of the raft was a tangle of tree-growth; either roots or saplings of the same sort I could see growing upwards from the top of the logs.

It was growth that had run wild, a veritable nightmare jungle of straight and twisted, vine-like limbs, some of them almost half as thick as the logs of the raft itself. The roots grew everywhere but in towards the pool area itself, until about fifteen feet down or so, they curved in and came together in a mat, like the bottom of an underwater nest. I assumed the lizards kept the pool area clear underwater by biting off the new suckers emerging from the logs, as they did in the clean areas topside. Plainly, even something the size of the shark companioning this raft could not get at us through that tangle below.

So, the pool was safe territory after all. Not only that, it occurred to me now, but the heavy mass of vegetation underneath must act as a sort of keel for the raft. I pulled my head back up out of the water and looked around in the air.

The girl was still in the pool. Sunday was still out of it and licking his fur, undisturbed. The two lizards who had turned us out of our cages had wandered off and become indistinguishable from their companions. I wondered what would happen if I got out of the pool myself. I did so – the girl imitating my action a second later – and found that nothing happened. The lizards ignored us.

I was startled suddenly to feel a hand slip into mine. I turned and it was the girl. She had never done anything like that before.

'What is it?' I asked.

She paid no attention to the words. She was already leading me toward the back of the raft. I followed along, puzzled, until a nagging sense of familiarity about our actions sprang an answer out of my hazy memory of those earlier brief returns to consciousness. She was leading me – the two of us completely ignored by the lizards – to the back edge of the raft; and the back edge was what was available to us by way of sanitary conveniences on this voyage. Apparently, while I had been out of my head, she had acquired the responsibility of leading me back there to relieve myself, after each periodic dip in the pool.

When this memory emerged, I put on the brakes. She and I had been living under pretty close conditions from the moment we had met. But now that my wits were back in my skull, I preferred at least the illusion of privacy in matters of elimination. After tugging at me vainly for a while, she gave up and went on by herself. I turned back to the pool.

Sunday was nearly dry now, and once more on good terms with the world. When I got back to the pool edge, he got up from where he was lying and wound around my legs, purring. I patted his head and sat down on the logs to think. After an unsuccessful – because I wouldn't let him – attempt to crawl into my lap, he gave up, lay down beside me and compromised by dropping his head on my knee. The head of a full-grown leopard is not a light matter; but better the head than all of him. I stroked his fur to keep him where he was; and he closed his eyes, rumbling in sheer bliss at my giving him this much attention.

After a little while the girl came back, and I went off to the back of the raft by myself, warning her sternly to stay where she was, when she once more tried to accompany me. She looked worried, but stayed. When I came back, she was lying down with her arm flung across Sunday's back and was back to her customary pattern of acting as if I did not even exist.

I sat down on the other side of Sunday, to keep him quiet, and tried to think. I had not gotten very far, however, when a couple of the lizards showed up. The girl rose meekly and crawled back into her cage. I took the hint and went back into mine. Sunday, of course, showed no sings of being so obliging; but the lizards handled him efficiently enough. They dropped a sort of clumsy twig net over him, twisted him up in it, and put net and all in his cage. Left alone there, Sunday struggled and squirmed until he was free; and a little later a lizard, passing, reached casually in through the bars of the cage, whisked the loose net out and carried it off.

So, there I was, back in the cage – and it was only then that I realized that I was hungry and thirsty. Above all, thirsty. I tried yelling to attract the attention of the lizards, but they ignored me. I even tried calling to the girl for advice and help; but she was back to being as unresponsive as the lizards. In the end, tired out, I went to sleep.

I woke about sunset to the sound of my cage being opened again. Before I knew it, I was being dumped in the pool once more. This time, I got a taste of the water into which I had been thrown. It was not ocean-salty – it had a faint taste that could be a touch of brackishness, but it was clearly sweet enough for human consumption. If this was the Nebraska sea, it was open to the ocean at its lower end. But as I remembered reading, it had been very shallow; and like the Baltic in my time, this far north, inflowing rivers and underground springs could have diluted it to nearly fresh-water condition. I climbed out of the pool and went to the side edge of the raft to drink, just to avoid any contamination there might be in the pool. I could not remember water tasting quite so good.

I lay on the logs of the raft with my belly full until the liquid began to disperse to the rest of my dehydrated body, then got up and went looking for something to eat. A quick tour of the raft turned up coconuts, which I had no way of opening, some green leafy stuff which might or might not be an edible vegetable, and a stack of bananas – most of which were still green.

I helped myself to the ripest I could find, half expecting the lizards to stop me. But they paid no attention. When I had taken care of my appetite, I thought of the girl and took some back to her.

She gave me one quick glance and looked away. But she took the bananas and ate them. After she had finished, she got up and went a little way away from me and lay down on her side, apparently sticking her arm right through the solid surface of the raft.

I went over to her and saw that she had found a place where two adjoining logs gapped apart; and her arm was now reaching down through the gap into the water and the tangle of growth below.

Something about her position as she lay there struck an odd note of familiarity. I straightened up and looked around the raft. Sure enough, the lizards who were lying down were nearly all in just the position she had taken. Apparently, they too had found holes in the raft.

I wondered what sort of a game she and they were playing. I even asked her – but of course I got no answer. Then, just a few seconds later she sat up, withdrawing her arm and held out her closed fist to me. When she opened it up, there was a small fish in the palm of her hand – hardly bigger than the average goldfish in a home fishbowl.

She held it out to me with her head averted; but clearly she was offering it to me. When I did not take it, she looked back at me with something like a flash of anger on her face and threw the fish away. It landed on the raft surface only inches from Sunday. The leopard stretched out his neck to reach it and eagerly licked it up.

The girl had gone back to her fishing. But whatever she caught next, she put in her own mouth. Later on, she made a number of trips to feed Sunday with what she caught. Full of curiosity, I went looking for another gap in the logs, lay down and put my eye to it.

In the shadow under the raft I could at first see nothing. But as my vision adjusted, I looked into the tangle of growth there and saw a veritable aquarium of small marine life. So this was how the lizards provisioned themselves. It was like carrying a game farm along with you on your travels. The small fish and squid-like creatures I saw through the gap in the logs did not look all that appetizing to me, at first glance. But after my third day on bananas, I found myself eating them along with the girl and the lizards – eating them, and what's more, enjoying them. Protein hunger can be a remarkably powerful conditioning force.

Meanwhile – on the days that immediately followed – I was trying to puzzle out a great many things, including why we had been brought along on the raft. The most obvious answer that came to me was the one I liked least – that, like the bananas and the coconuts, we three represented a potential exotic addition to the ordinary lizard diet, a sort of special treat to be eaten later.

I also toyed with the thought that we had been picked up as slaves, or as curiosities to be used or traded off at some later time. But this was hard to believe. The lizards were clearly an extremely primitive people, if they were a true people at all, and not some sort of ant-like society operating on instinct rather than intelligence. They had shown no sign of having a spoken language; and so far I had not seen any of them using even stone tools to make or do anything. The extent of their technology seemed to be the weaving of the nets and cages, the gathering of things like coconuts (and the three of us) and the building of this raft; if, indeed, this raft had been deliberately built, rather than being just grown to order, or chewed loose from some larger mass of vegetation of which it originally had been a part.

No, I was forgetting the steering oar. The next time I was let out of my cage, I went back to the stern of the raft to look at it. What I found was on a par with the rest of the raft. The oar was not so much an oar as a thinner tree trunk of the same variety as those which made up the logs of the raft. It had no true blade. It was bare trunk down to the point where it entered the water, and from there on, it was mop-like with a brush of untrimmed growth. It was pivoted in a notch between two logs of the raft, tied in place there with a great bundle of the same flexible vine or plant with which the lizards had made the net they used to restrain Sunday. This tie broke several times a day, but each time, it was patiently rewrapped and reknotted by the nearby lizards.

Whatever their cultural level – in fact, whether they had a culture or not – they had clearly collected the three of us for their own purposes, not for ours. It struck me that the sooner we got away from them, the better.

But here on a raft in the middle of an unknown body of water, getting away was something easier to imagine than do. For one thing, we would have to wait until we touched land again; and there was no telling when that would be. Or was there? I puzzled over the question.

It was hard to believe that the lizards could be trying to follow any specific route with their clumsy sail of trees and their mop-ended steering oar. At best, I told myself, they could only impose a slight angle on the path of their drift before the wind. But, when I thought about this some more, it occurred to me that the wind had been blowing continually from the stern of the raft with about the same strength since I had gotten my senses back. We were, of course, still in the temperate latitudes of what had been the North American continent, well above the zone of any trade winds. But, what if here on this body of water, current climatic conditions made for seasonal winds blowing in a certain direction? Say, for example, winds that blew east in the summer and west in the winter, from generally the same quarters of the compass? Judging by the sun, we were now headed generally east. With a continuous directional breeze like that to rely on, even the crude rig of this raft could follow a roughly regular route depending only on the season of the year.

That evening I marked on one of the logs the angle of the sunset on the horizon to the longitudinal axis of the raft, by cutting marks in one of the logs under my cage with my pocketknife. It set almost due astern of us, but a little to the north. The next morning I again marked the angle of the sunrise – again, a little to the north of our long axis. A check of the angle of the steering oar confirmed this. The three lizards holding it had it angled to guide the raft slightly to the north from a true east-west line. It was not until then that I thought of checking the stars.

So I did, as soon as they came out that evening; but they were absolutely unfamiliar. I could not recognize a single constellation. Not that I was very knowledgeable about astronomy; but like most people, I was normally able to pick out the Little and the Big Dippers and find the pole star from the Big Dipper. Such a difference in the patterns of the heavens I saw could only be strong evidence that a time change had moved this part of the world a long way from the present I had known – either far into the future or far into the past.

If so … a new thought kindled in an odd back corner of my mind.

If it was indeed the Permian period, or a future one like it, through which this raft was now sailing, then one thing was highly likely. We were almost surely moving along roughly parallel to the northern shore of the inland sea since the beach where we had first run into the lizards had to be that same northern shore; and it now seemed probable we had been holding a steady northeasterly course ever since. I had seen a geology textbook map of the Great Nebraska Sea once, years ago. It had showed the land area of the southern and middle states depressed, and that part of the continent drowned, so that the Gulf of Mexico, in effect, filled most of the lower middle region of North America. That meant, almost certainly, we should be running in to land again before long. We were not, as I had originally feared, off on some endless voyage to nowhere, as we were perfectly capable of being, while an endless supply of food swam underneath us and water all around us that was drinkable.

The prospect of coming to land again before too long meant we ought to at least get a chance to escape. I cheered up at the thought and, with immediate anxieties out of the way, remembered the rest of what was still heavy in my mind.

The insane belief I had had in the survival of Swannee was, of course, still with me, like the mistwall of a time change line in the back of my thought.

But the rest of my brain recognized it for the illusion it was. Evidently, while I had been out of my head, what was left had been coming to terms with this matter. I was now ready to admit that there had been something more than a lingering knee-jerk reflex of the affection response operating in me. The plain truth of the matter was that I had flipped over Swannee. Not only had I flipped, but I had done it after I married her, not before; and the thing that had driven her off was the fact that I had tried to change the rules of the game after the game was started. I had let myself go with the idea that I loved Swannee; and made up in my mind a completely imaginary image of her as someone who was lovable. Of course she wasn't. She was an ordinary self-seeking human being like all the rest of us, and when she acted like one and took off to escape my trying to make her into something she was not, I literally set out to work myself to death, and almost succeeded with the heart attack.

I suppose, in a way, I had never really let go of Swannee – even then. So that when the time storm hit, the one thing I could not accept was that it could have touched her in any way.

But I now had met, and survived, the fact of her death. The madness, of course, was still back there in the recesses of my mind, and still virulent; but it was dying, and time would kill it off entirely. Just as time had healed my first sense of loss when she had gotten married. Now that it was dying, locked in my wooden cage most of the time and going nowhere, I had plenty of leisure to begin looking more sanely at the world around me. Out of that look came a couple of recognitions I had been refusing to make earlier. One was that we would have to work hard to survive on this raft. Sunday and the girl were not only thin, as I had noticed, but getting thinner. Sunday himself required the equivalent of four pounds of meat a day to keep him alive. I needed about two thousand calories, or nearly half that amount; and the girl, because she was not yet at her full growth, probably the same. We two, of course, could make use of carbohydrates – like the bananas – as well, as long as those lasted. But getting Sunday the equivalent of four pounds of protein daily through the cracks between the logs of the raft, was impossible; even with both the girl and I doing our best – which we did as soon as I realized what the situation was. The lizard-people showed no interest at all in providing food for us. We would need to reach land soon if we wanted to live.

The second recognition was that only a few people, relatively, had escaped the time change. A few people and a few animals. Apparently the changes had been like great rakes that swept away most of the population, but here and there let an individual like me, the girl, or Sunday, slip through their tines. Either that, or some of us simply were natural survivors – statistical immunes.

Whether the greater number of the population of my time had been carried off to some other continuum, or destroyed by the suddenly changed conditions, there was no telling. But one fact was becoming more apparent day by day – there was no reasonable hope of their ever coming back. *The moving finger writes* ...

I, and the girl, and Sunday, along with a relative handful of others, possibly including these lizard-people, were stuck with making what we could out of the world as it now was. What we had at the present, of course, was chaos, with the time lines still moving and different times coming into existence behind each of them. But maybe if I was right about some of us being statistical immunes, we would learn eventually to live with the lines, passing from zone to zone and becoming a new civilization which took constant time changes for granted.

Unless, that is, there was some new way of bringing the time changes to a halt ...

Now, that was a new thought. It exploded in me silently, one night as I lay there on my back, looking up through the bars of my cage at the unfamiliar star-patterns, while the raft rocked gently under me. I lay there, turning it over and over in my head, examining it. That relentless part of my mind had fastened on the idea the second it emerged, like the jaws of a boa constrictor on part of a prey the snake intended to swallow, and now I knew I could never let it go, until I had succeeded with it, or proved its impossibility.

8

Ten mornings later we saw land, and by noon it was obvious we would reach it the same day. I was ready to blow kisses at it from the first second it had appeared like a dark smudge on the horizon. Try as the girl and I might, we could not keep the three of us properly fed with the small underraft waterlife; and I had lived with a sharp-toothed fear that we would have grown too weak to try escaping by the time our chance for it came. Our goal was a curving bay with a wide beach shelving gently down to it, some hills hazy in the background, and one or two large rocks or small rocky islands just beyond the mouth of the bay.

Shortly after noon the lizards lined up along the side of the raft facing the shark fin and began to roll up the vegetable-like leaves I had seen and throw these small green balls at the shark. Where the balls of vegetable matter touched the water, a milky stain spread immediately and was still spreading, like the blossoming of some underwater flower, as the motion of the raft left the spot behind us. As the lizards continued to pelt the water around the fin with the balls of green stuff, a milky rime gradually gathered around the base of the fin itself.

Suddenly the fin moved, changed angle in the water and moved off rapidly until it was lost from sight. Looking back along the wake of the raft, I saw the shapes of small fish come to the surface belly-up through the whitened water where the green stuff had fallen.

So we half-drifted, half-steered at last into the bay without our overside companion. In the bay the water was as calm as a lake on a still day, and startlingly clear. I could look down at a sandy, plant-and-shell strewn bottom, finally, that must have been fifty feet below, although it looked much shallower.

I was able to estimate its true depth because the full extent of the growth on the underside of the raft was now visible; and it stretched down almost as far, if not as far, as the trees that were our 'sail' stretched up from the deck of the raft. A good two hundred yards or more from the beach we grounded, the lowest extensions of the growth under our raft touching against the bottom of the bay and stopping us from going further inshore.

The lizards immediately began diving for what seemed to be some sort of large shellfish. The shells were a good foot in length, and when I picked up one of the first that was brought on board, I was startled by the heaviness of it. The whole thing must have weighed twenty pounds.

In the sun and the air, the shells soon opened of their own accord; and the lizards scooped the interior creatures out and swallowed them more or less whole.

So did the girl, Sunday and myself. They were delicious; and we would have stuffed ourselves if I had not stopped, and made the girl stop, feeding herself as well as Sunday, for fear of intestinal upset in all of us after such a period of semi-starvation.

But beyond a few mild stomach cramps an hour or so later, I had no bad effects, and the girl and Sunday did not even seem to have that. So, I left them to eat or not as they wished; and during the next few days, we ate our persistent hunger out of existence through steady snacking on the shellfish.

We were free to do this around the clock, because Sunday, the girl and I had been let out of our cages some time before we came to anchor, so to speak; and since then, none of the lizards had bothered to put us back in. As my hunger diminished, I began to think less of that and more about escaping. I could stand on the edge of the raft and look at the sand of the beach. Only a couple of hundred yards away, as I said; but it might as well have been a couple of hundred miles away. There was no way to get ashore except to swim there. And even if the girl could, and Sunday would make it through the water with me, any one of the amphibious-looking lizard-people could probably let us get nine-tenths of the way to the beach and still reach us in time to bring us back before we could wade ashore. They shot through the clear underwater like green rockets. But there had to be a way. It was bad enough to have to figure out a way of escaping by myself. The headache would come in bringing the girl and Sunday safely with me. But I could not leave them behind. Neither one was able to survive alone. It had to be the three of us, together.

I was standing looking down into the water at them, even envying them in a way, when something like a swiftly-moving dark shadow suddenly intruded on the scene; and all at once lizards were literally leaping out of the water back on to the surface of the raft. All but one. Down in the transparent depths, that one was being swallowed. Either our original shark, or one just like it, had joined us; and once more we had a deadly companion alongside.

The lizards stood on the deck and stared down at the shark. I did not blame them. In the beautifully clear water the huge sea predator loomed like a nuclear submarine. It was patrolling the water about the raft now, in short runs and turns back and forth, as if impatient for another victim.

I looked at the still-large pile of green vegetation on the raft. But none of the lizards made a move toward it, and after a second I realized why. Clearly the stuff, in water, was a potent poison. They could safely throw it overside when they were moving before a breeze, away from the place where the poison would linger. But here in this bay, once the water was poisoned, they would not be able to return soon to their diving for shellfish.

I waited. The shark stayed. The lizards waited. I fumed. The shark's presence was one more obstacle in the way of escape for the girl, Sunday and myself. At the same time I was amazed at the apparent helplessness of the lizards. I had assumed without thinking that they would have some kind of plan to deal with a situation of this sort. But apparently not – unless their technique was to simply wait out the shark, sit on the raft until it got tired and went away.

However, if it was the same shark – or even of the same breed and temperament as the shark that had dogged the raft earlier – it was not likely to leave in any reasonable length of time. The fin that had followed us earlier had been with us for days on end.

The eerie part of the whole business was that there was no visible sign of an attempt at consultation among the lizards. From the beginning they had shown no indication of having a spoken language; and I had not been able to make out any other method of signs or signalling they might be using between themselves. But I had always assumed that in some way, if they had to, they could communicate with each other. Now it seemed they could not even do that. A handful of them stood and watched the shark for a while; but eventually, all of them went back to acting as if they were still out at sea, resting on the logs, hunting between them in the growth under the raft in search of small marine life to eat, and so on. The only sign that there was anything at all unusual about the situation was the fact that still none of them came to put us back in our cages.

Night came with no change. A day after that followed with the shark still waiting and the lizards still all on the raft. Around noon of the third day, however, something new began to happen.

Just before the sun was full overhead, one of the lizards lying near the edge of the raft, beyond which the shark was presently patrolling, got to his feet. He stood facing down at the shark in the water, and then he began to bounce as he stood, not moving his feet, but bending his knees slightly so that he bobbed up and down like someone on a diving board getting ready to dive.

Once started, he continued the bobbing steadily and with a sort of reflexive monotony of pace. The other lizards seemed to be paying no attention to him; but after perhaps half an hour, when I looked back over at where he was, after having my attention elsewhere for a while, I saw that another of the lizards, about ten feet from him, was now also on his feet and bobbing. The two of them matched their rhythms precisely, rising and falling together as if the same invisible spring was actuating them both.

An hour later, there were four of them on their feet and bobbing. Gradually, more and more of the others joined them in silent, continuous movement – until by mid-afternoon all the lizards on the ship were performing the same soundless, feet-in-place dance.

The shark, meanwhile, either having seen them on the edge of the raft, or – what is more likely – having been attracted by the vibrations of their movements through the logs and the water, was now patrolling in very short runs back and forth, almost within touching distance, it seemed, of the raft edge.

Suddenly, as the shark passed, one of the lizard figures leaped into the water upon its back ... and all at once the air was full of lizards taking to the water.

I ran to the side of the raft and looked out – and down. The shark was already at the bottom of the bay, moving rapidly away from the raft. But the lizards were all over him, like green-scaled dogs clinging to a bull. Their heavy jaws were tearing chunks out of the shark's incredibly tough hide; and a filmy cloud of blood was spreading through the underwater. Not merely shark's blood, either. I saw the huge selachian catch a lizard in its jaws and literally divide him in half.

Then the whole struggle moved away out of my sight, headed toward the open sea, as the shark evidently followed its reflex to go for deeper water.

For some moments I simply stood, staring – then the implications of the situation exploded on me. I ran to the girl and grabbed her by the arm.

'Come on,' I said. 'Come on, now's our chance! We can get ashore now, while they're all gone.'

She did not answer. She only stared at me. I looked over at Sunday.
'Come, Sunday!'

He came. The girl came also. She did not hang back; but on the other hand, she only let me pull her toward the shoreside of the raft, which was its forward end.

'We've got to swim for the beach!' I shouted at her. 'If you can't swim, hang on to me. You understand?'

I roared the last two words at her as if she was deaf; but she only stared back at me. She was not hindering, but neither was she helping. The cold thought came through me that, once more, I was being put in a concerned situation. Why didn't I go off and leave her – her and the leopard both, if it came to that? The important thing was that I live, not that I save other people's lives.

But, you know, I could not. Somehow, to go ashore by myself and leave both of them here was unthinkable. But she would have to do something more than just stand there, not making an active effort to get ashore. I tried to tell her this; but it was at once like talking to someone who was deaf and someone who had given up thinking.

I was reaching the desperation point. I was about to throw her bodily into the water when the first of the lizards started coming back aboard the raft, and our chance to escape was past.

I gave up and turned back to watch them climb out of the water onto the logs. Those who had been hurt were the first to return. They crawled back up into the sunlight, one by one, and dropped down, to lie as still as if each of them had been knocked on the head.

Lizards kept coming back over the next half hour or so. The last dozen or so to come aboard had been very badly bitten by the shark. Three of these later died, and the surviving lizards simply pushed the bodies overside. The tide took them out in the late afternoon, and in the morning they were gone. There would be plenty of scavengers waiting for them.

The lizards did not go immediately back to their shell-fishing when day broke the following morning. They had evidently won their battle with the large shark – though my guess was that it had cost them at least a dozen of their number. But they seemed exhausted by the effort; and as the sun rose, the clear water of the bay showed itself to be full of small sharks, not more than two or three feet long but dashing around madly as if still excited by the gore and torn meat of the day before. Sunday, the girl and I were still uncaged; and I began to hope that, possibly, this would become the permanent state of affairs. If so, I appreciated it; although of course, I could always have cut myself out of my woven cage with my pocketknife and then freed the girl and Sunday.

I could not decide what was keeping the smaller sharks around us. There was nothing for them to feed on that I could see. Then that night the first storm I had ever known to ruffle that sea blew up, a heavy, tropical rainstorm type of atmospheric explosion; and I found out why they were still with us.

The wind began in the afternoon, and the sky piled up with white clouds which crowded together and darkened until we had an early twilight. Then the breeze died and the water beneath us became viscid and heavy. The raft rocked, rubbing on the floor of the bay with its undergrowth, swayed by a swell that came in on us from far out on the airless water, even though we felt no wind where we were.

Then lightning and thunder began to flicker and growl – high up in the clouds above us, but also far out, over the open water. A new, cold breeze sprang up, blowing shoreward, strengthening as the daylight faded; and the sound and activity of the storm grew, approaching us and coming lower, closer towards the surface of the sea. As the last of the sun's illumination went, leaving us in a pitch darkness, the storm broke over us with its full power; and we clung in darkness to the now heavily pitching and rolling raft.

I had found a place to wedge myself among the trees of our 'sail,' with one arm around the girl and the other holding on to Sunday. The girl trembled and shivered as the cold rainwater poured down on us; but the leopard took it stoically, pressing close to me but never moving. Around us, also wedged in among the trees, were some of the lizards. Where the rest of them were, I had no idea. It was impossible to see someone in the total darkness unless they were right beside you. In the total darkness, vision came only in brief glimpses, every few seconds or so, when there would be a crack of thunder and a vivid lighting flash that lit up the whole surface of the raft, streaming with the rain and plunging like a tethered horse as the black waves all around us tried to drive us up on the beach, and the raft's undergrowth, grounded on the sand below, resisted.

The lighting flashes were like explosions in the mind. After the sudden brilliance of each was gone, the scene it revealed would linger for a second on the retina and in the mind before fading out. I got wild glimpses of the struggling raft – and wilder glimpses of the waters of the bay, not merely their surface but their depths, as sometimes the raft heeled over to hold us in a position staring almost directly down into the heaving sea.

The water was alive with marine life of all kinds, visible in the lightning flashes, dashing about in a frenzy. I had wondered what had brought all the small sharks into the bay after the fight with the big shark was over. Now I suddenly saw why. Like a great waterlogged mass bumping and rolling along the very floor of the bay, impelled by the storm and by the fly-like swarm of smaller fish tearing at its carcass, the huge shark, now dead, was with us again.

It could not have died at the time the lizards abandoned their fight with it, or its skeleton would have been stripped clean long before this. It must have survived, weakly fighting off the smaller members of its own species who were ready to devour it while it still lived, until just a few hours past, when loss of blood and strength had finally let it down into death.

Now, like a dead man returned to the scene of the crime, it was back with us, courtesy of the storm and the onshore wind. A freak of that wind and storm was bringing it back, not merely into the bay, but right up against the roots of our raft itself. Clinging to the tree-trunks on either side of me, looking down into the water with each flash of lightning, I was less than fifty feet or so in a straight line from where what was left of the carcass was being torn apart – now, by larger sharks and other fish up to fifteen or twenty feet long, still small compared to the sea corpse, but big enough from my point of view. I fretted over their presence. Even if another chance to escape should come, with all the lizards off the raft, we could not hope to make the swim ashore in safety, through those swarming shark jaws.

Then, suddenly, there was a lightning flash and the underwater scavengers were all gone. The half-eaten body of the large shark lay rolling to the sea-disturbance and the tearing it had just been getting by its devourers, but now it was alone on the floor of the bay. I blinked and waited for the next flash. I could not believe what I saw.

With the next flash came enlightenment; and with it, an end to shark carcass, raft, lizards, and everything. The next glare showed the shark overshadowed by a shape twice its size – a dark body, like an underwater cloud. And it also showed, out of the water and white against the black of the waves, a grey-white tentacle as thick as a cable used to tie up a superliner. The tentacle was out of the water. It stood erect in the air, like a telephone pole, twenty feet above the deck at the far end of the raft. A moment later the raft shuddered, as if to the blow of an unthinkably huge axe, and the end where we were began to rise in the air.

Another flash of lightning showed the great tentacle now gripping the whole far end of the raft and pulling it over, down into the waves.

There was no more time for waiting, nor any time to talk the two of them into coming with me. I yelled in Sunday's ear to come, pulled the girl after me, and jumped for the water. Its choking wetness closed over my head; but I came up still holding on to the girl, and taking a sight on the beach with the next flash, began to swim ashore.

I do not remember how I made it. It seemed I swam forever holding up the girl. But eventually the wet blackness that enclosed us threw us forward into a blackness that had no substance, and a split second later we slammed against hard, level sand. Even with most of the breath knocked out of me, I had the sense to crawl as much farther up the beach as I could, dragging the girl. Then I collapsed. I let myself drop on the beach, one hand still holding an arm of the girl. The damp, grainy surface beneath me went soft as a mattress and I fell into sudden, deep sleep.

I woke to daylight and warming air. The girl was only a few feet away. So was Sunday.

In the bay there was no sign of any raft, or anything, for that matter. We were as alone as if we had been lost in the desert for weeks. I lay there, slowly letting our new situation become real to me.

We were free again, but without food, weapons, or transportation. In addition, I felt as if I had been drawn through a whole series of knotholes, one after another. By contrast, the girl and Sunday looked as rested and cheerful as if the storm and all the rest of it had never happened. Well, their reactions were nothing to be surprised at, I told myself, grumpily. I was twice the age of the girl or nearly so and probably five times the age of Sunday. It didn't matter. By God, the three of us had made it!

The minute I tried to sit up, they noticed me. In a second they were all over me. Sunday gave one large leap to land beside me and started to rub himself up against my chest, knocking me flat. The girl reached me a split-second later and picked me up.

'Stop that,' she scolded Sunday, out loud, in actual and unexpected words. I was sitting up again now, but her arms were still around me, her head against my chest; and I got the strange impression that she was hugging me. This sort of response by the two of them made me feel absurdly warm inside; but when I tried to pat the girl on the head, she broke away at once, scrambling to her feet, turning her back and walking off a few steps. Sunday, purring loudly, was doing his best to knock me down again; but I was braced for him.

I leaned heavily on his back with one arm and pulled myself creakily to my feet. Seen from the shore, the place we had ended up had much less of the California look than the beach where we had first run into the lizards. Back from the stretch of open sand were some kind of pine-needle trees with a northerly look and a tree like a willow, with fairly thick-standing grass in the open spaces.

I patted Sunday on the head and spoke to the girl's back.

'We'd better look around,' I said, hoarsely.

I led the way and the other two followed. Behind the immediate fringe of trees there was a small bluff. We went up to the top of that and looked out at what seemed to be a stretch of midcontinental prairie spottily overgrown with clumps of trees. There were not quite enough trees to call it a forest and an almost total lack of undergrowth. In the open patches it was mainly high grass, green and brown, with just an occasional, scattered, lone sapling or bush.

Nowhere in sight was there any sign of civilization.

I stood on the top of the bluff and did some pondering. I did not like the semi-arid look of the country before me. We were on foot now, and we could survive without food for a few days, if necessary; but what I was looking at did not have the appearance of being either lake or river country, and drinking water was a constant need. Add to that the fact that we were now completely unarmed except for my pocketknife; and it might not be just wild animals we would have to worry about encountering out there.

In the end, I decided against leaving the only drinking water in view, which was the lake. We went east along the beach, the route in which the lizard raft had been headed anyway, for three days, living off shellfish and whatever small creatures we could find in the sand or shallow water just offshore. Our diet of small things from the underside of the raft had done my sensibilities a world of good in that area of diet. I could now eat anything that didn't look as if it would poison me – and eat it raw at that. The girl was equally open-minded, I noticed; and as for Sunday, he had never had a problem about the looks of his food to begin with.

The third day we hit the jackpot – well, a jackpot of sorts. It must have been somebody's lakeshore home, on a lake that had now become part of the inland sea. There were no people in sight around it, and no other lakeshore houses or cabins nearby. But this place must have cost someone a good deal of money. It had a large house, with attached garage and a separate pole barn – that is, a type of barn-size building, made of metal roof and siding that were literally hung on wooden posts the thickness of telephone poles, set in the earth. It also had a dock and a boat. A road that was dirt, but well-graded and well-kept, led from the house and the lake away into the country beyond the beach. The country here was treed thickly enough to be honestly called forested.

The home looked as if it had been abandoned less than a week before. Some of the food in the refrigerator still looked edible; and the food in the large, chest-type freezer in the double garage would probably have been edible if the electric power had stayed on. We must have crossed a former mistwall line, some way back; because this was the kind of trick the time storm played. A few miles off, we had been several geologic ages in the past, here we were only in yesterday. Tomorrow we might be in any future time, I supposed. As it was, I trusted none of it. But there was a wealth of canned goods on shelves – also bottled goods. It gave me a peculiar feeling to mix myself a scotch and soda – even an iceless scotch and soda – and sit sipping it in the overstuffed chair of a carpeted living room.

The only drawback to the place was that it had neither of the two things we needed most – weapons and transport – a car or truck in which we could travel.

I searched the place from dock to driveway. There was not even a canoe in the boathouse. There was, in the pole barn, a 1931 all-black Model A Ford roadster somebody had been restoring; but it was not in drivable condition, nor were there parts lying around that could be put in to make it driveable. It held only the block of a motor, with the head off and the cylinders, crankshaft and oil pan missing. There were a couple of bicycles in the garage, a girl's battered singlespeed, and a man-size three-speed Raleigh, which had been kept in only slightly better condition.

In one end of the pole barn, however, was a gasoline-driven electric generator, in beautiful condition under its protective coat of grease, and a good deal of wood and metal-working tools – power and other- wise – also in fine condition. I got the generator cleaned up and going; although after about fifteen minutes I shut it off again. The three of us were used to doing without the luxury of electric lights and appliances; and there was, I judged after measuring it with a stick, only ten or fif- teen gallons of gas left in a drum by the generator. I did not yet know exactly what I would use the gas for, but it was too useful a material to be wasted. Later, I found some empty pop bottles with screwtops and filled them with the gas, then tied rags around their necks, so that they could be turned into molotov cocktails in a hurry. That gave us one kind of weapon.

Meanwhile, the girl and Sunday were settling in. There were two bedrooms with closets holding women's clothes, and the girl, for the first time, began to show some interest in what she wore. She still stuck to shirt and jeans, generally, but I caught her a couple of times trying on things when I came into the house unexpectedly from outside.

Sunday liked the carpets. He slept and ate. We all ate – and gained back some of the weight we had lost on the raft.

I was determined that we would not stir from where we were without some means of protecting ourselves. I had two ideas about weapons I might be able to make. I had rejected the thought of a bow and arrows. I was a mediocre-to-poor archer; and no bowyer at all. Making a really effective bow was beyond me. Other alternatives were, first a home-made, muzzleloading gun using a length of metal water pipe wrapped with wire, if I could find any, and using match heads for the explosive element. In short – a zip gun. Second, a crossbow using a leaf from one of the springs of the Model A. There was enough gas to let me run the generator and get the wood and metal-working power tools operating in the pole barn.

In the end, I chose the crossbow, not because it was simpler, but because I couldn't find any wire; and I had a vision of the water pipe blowing up in my face. I found a dry chunk of firewood that looked to me to be maple or oak, sawed it roughly to shape and then worked it on the lath to an approximation of a stock and frame for the crossbow. I cut a slot across the frame, sank the leaf spring (the smallest of the leaf springs) into it crosswise and did as good a job of gluing it there as I could. Modern glues were miracle-workers, given half a chance. I glued a separate, notched bar of hard wood along the top of the frame for the cord of the crossbow, and set up a lever-crank to allow me to tighten the bow cord, notch by notch.

I had more trouble making the short, heavy arrows – quarrels – for the thing than I did putting together the crossbow itself. It was not easy to make a straight shaft from a raw chunk of wood, I discovered.

But the day came when I had both crossbow and quarrels. Both had been tested. There was no lack of power in the crossbow. The problem was with my quarrels. Their shafts broke too easily when they hit something hard. But, they would do on any flesh and blood target. The morning came when we mounted the two bikes, the girl and I – happily she had evidently ridden a bicycle before, and the skill came back to her quickly – and wearing backpacks, we started off down the empty road, away from the lake, with Sunday footing it alongside us.

The weather was pleasant, with the temperature in the high sixties, Fahrenheit, and the sky was lightly spotted with occasional clouds. As we got away from the water the humidity began to fall off sharply, until the day was almost like one in early autumn up near the Canadian border. We made good time, considering – considering Sunday, that was. Dogs are generally content to trot steadily alongside the bikers they belong to, but Sunday had a cat's dislike of regimentation. Sunday preferred that the girl and I travel at the equivalent of a slow walk, so that he could make short side excursions, or even take a quick nap and still catch up with us. When we did stop finally, to give him a break, he lay down heavily on top of the girl's bike and would not be moved until I hauled him clear by sheer muscle-strength and a good grip on the scruff of his neck.

In the end we compromised with him, riding along at hardly more than a walking speed. As a result, it was not surprising that I got more and more involved in my own thoughts.

The road we were on had yet to lead past any sign of civilization. But, of course, we were not covering ground at any great speed. Eventually our route must bring us to someplace where we could get the weapons and wheels I wanted. Then, once more mobile and protected, as it were, I meant to do a little investigating along the thought I had come to, lying on the lizard raft, nights ago. If the world was going to be as full of potential threats, as we had just seen it, it was high time we set actively about the business of learning the best ways to survive in it ...

We hit no signs of civilization that day, but late afternoon, we crossed a creek hardly larger than a trickle, running through a culvert under the road. In this open territory it looked as though it probably contained clean water; but I boiled it to make sure, and we set up camp for the night by it.

Midday through the next morning on the road, we rode past a chunk of a suburb. I mean exactly that – a chunk. It was some two hundred yards off our asphalt highway, a roughly triangular piece of real estate with lawns, garages, streets and tract houses looking as if it had been sliced off at random and dropped down here in the middle of nowhere.

There were no people about it any more than there had been people about the lakeshore home. But these buildings were not in the untouched condition of the house by the lake. The area looked, in fact, as if a tornado had passed through it, a tornado, or else something with the size of a dinosaur and a destructive urge to match. There was not one building that was whole and weather-tight, and some were all but flattened.

Nonetheless, they represented a treasure trove for us. I went through all the houses and turned up a sixteen gauge shotgun and a carbine-type .22 rifle. There were no shells for the shotgun and only one box of shorts for the .22. But the odds on picking up ammunition for these

two common calibre firearms were good enough to count on. The sub-
urb-chunk also contained eight cars. Five of these had been made useless by whatever had smashed the buildings. Of the remaining three,
all were more than a few years old, and one would not start at all. That
left me with a choice between a two-door Pontiac hardtop in relatively
good shape and a Volvo four-door sedan that was pretty well beaten up.

I chose the Volvo, however. Not only for its extra carrying capacity, but because the gas mileage should be better. There was no filling
station among the homes in the suburb, but I drained the gas tanks of
all the other cars that proved to have anything in them; and when we
started out in the Volvo, we had a full tank plus another fifteen gallons
in cans tied on to a makeshift rack on top of the trunk. Also, I had
found two three-speed bikes in good shape. They were tied to the top
of the car.

The suburb had a fine, four-lane concrete road leading out of it,
but that ended about two hundred yards from the last of the smashed
houses. I drove the Volvo, bumping and bucking across a lumpy open
field, to get it back on our familiar asphalt and turned left into the
direction in which we had been originally headed. We kept going; and
about an hour later, I spotted a mistwall to our right. It was angled
toward the road we were on, looking as if it crossed the asphalt somewhere up ahead of us.

9

My heart jumped when I saw it; but after watching it closely for a little while, I calmed down. Clearly, the wall was standing still. We continued on up along the road, with its vertical, white face getting closer and closer, until finally we were far enough along to see where it ended. It did indeed cut across the road at last, about a quarter mile ahead of where we were; but it only continued beyond that point of intersection for about a hundred yards. By going off the asphalt to the left just a short distance, we could get around the end of the cloud-high curtain. Not only could we bypass it safely; but after going a little further, we would be able to get where we could see what was behind it, without ever having to set foot in what might be dangerous territory. I kept us moving.

We stopped finally and left the road, a good fifty or a hundred feet short of the point where it was intersected by the mistwall. Up this close to the wall, we could see it seeming to reach clear out of sight above us; and we could feel the peculiar breeze and the dust that always eddied from it, like the peppering of a fine spray on our face and hands. We struck off into the trees and brush to the left of the road, with the car in low gear and moving along level with the face of the wall.

It did not take long to reach the end of it. I kept on a little further, however, not wanting to turn the corner until I could see behind it. But though we kept going further and further, we still did not seem to quite clear the end. Finally, I saw why. We were not going to be able to see behind that mistwall after all. Here at what I had thought was its point of termination, it had either bent to the right and continued, or run into another mistwall going off at an angle in that direction.

At first, all I felt was disappointment that I was not going to get a look behind it. Then it occurred to me that perhaps the reason neither mistwall nor mistwall section had been moving had been because each had butted up against the other; and the two time change lines coming together had somehow created an unusual state or condition that had halted them both.

The moment that I thought it, I was hungry to see what was behind the intersection of those two mistwalls. Ever since, lying on the lizard raft, I had come up with the idea that perhaps those of us who were still here on the earth might be individually immune to the time changes, I had been playing with the idea of not avoiding the next mistwall we met, but deliberately walking into it, to see if I could get through and survive. Now I had a double reason to try going through the one before me. It was not merely to find out if I could get through with nothing worse than the unconsciousness I had experienced the first time, but to discover if there was something special or strange about the situation where one time change line ran into another. I stopped the Volvo.

I got out and looked at the wall. I also looked forward along the other angle of the second, or continued, mistwall to see where the road emerged once more from it, only about a couple of hundred yards away. It occurred to me that all I had to do was get back on the road and keep going, and the three of us would continue to stay safe, united, and happy. Or, I could turn and go through the mistwall; and I might, just might, learn something – that is, if I made it through all right.

I stood there. And the longer I stood, the stronger grew the desire in me to try going through the wall. It was exactly the way it had always been, from my earliest childhood, when my mind fastened on to a question and would not let it go without finding the answer. The phenomenon was like every time since I'd first let that relentless mental machinery in my head get its teeth into a problem. I remembered perfectly the terrible feeling I had felt during the initial seconds of that first time change, when I had thought I was having another heart attack. I remembered the miserable, helpless, empty sensation all through me after I had come to. I remembered every bit and part that had been bad about it; and still ... still ... as I stood there the wanting to go through that wall and find out what I did not know was like a sharp, sweet taste on my lips and a hunger that used me up inside like fire.

I turned back at last to look at the girl and Sunday. If I went through the wall and never returned, what would happen to them? I told myself that I owed them nothing, and something inside me called me a liar. At the same time, the thought of any responsibility I might have toward either of them had about as much deterrent effect on the hunger that was eating me up as a cup of water tossed on a burning building. I had no real choice. I had to go through that wall if I – and they – died for it. I turned back to the leopard and the girl, both of whom were still sitting in the car.

'Stay here!' I said. 'You understand me? Stay right here. Don't take as much as one step after me. *Stay where you are!*'

They both stared at me silently. One of the girl's hands twitched – that was all. I turned and walked away from them, toward the mistwall, until I had to squint my eyes against the flying dust of it. Just before I reached the actual mist of the wall, I turned and looked back. The girl still sat with Sunday beside her, both watching me. Neither had moved a muscle.

I turned back again, closed my eyes to the sting of the dust, and walked blindly forward.

But the hard part was not the dust. The hard part was that it was like walking into an emotional tornado. It was bad. It was very bad. But, somehow, it was not as bad as I remembered it from the first time, outside my cabin. Maybe this was because my first time through had left me with a sort of immunity; as if I had been inoculated against the effects I felt. Maybe it was easier because I now had some idea what to expect and was braced for it. Basically, I felt as if my soul had been ripped out of my being. I felt naked, sick and frightened. But, you know, it was not the kind of fear I feared – if that statement makes any sense to you. I stayed on my feet and came out the other side, walking.

I was suddenly assaulted by the clamour of dogs barking not far in front of me. I opened my eyes and saw them – more than a dozen of them, all tied to short leashes, but all barking, snarling and leaping against their tethers to get at me. They were tied to leashes anchored to thick stakes driven into the earth, in front of a slice of a house about fifty yards away, a house sitting on a chunk of a lawn in the interior angle of the two mistwalls. Behind the house was forest, and the house itself was a two-storey frame building that looked as if it would be at home surrounded by a midwestern farmyard. As I looked, the door opened, and a woman came out with a rifle already at her shoulder, pointed at me.

'Drop your gun.' Her voice was a low, carrying soprano, soft but positive.

'Wait a minute,' I told her. 'How about talking about this?'

I had no intention of dropping my gun. She was standing behind the dogs, in the open, with no rest or other support for her rifle, but with the weapon up and aimed. If I had to shoot her to live myself, I would. At that distance, unless she was a natural markswoman, holding her gun steady enough to hit me would not be easy. Even from where I stood, I could see the end of the barrel waver slightly in the sunlight.

I was more concerned about her dogs; and I was not about to drop the one weapon that could defend me against them. In fact – the situation framed itself in my mind and produced its own inescapable conclusion – if she turned the dogs loose on me, I was going to shoot her first. They were dogs of all sizes, but the least of them must have gone at least forty pounds, which is heavy enough to be a potential man-killer. I could shoot three-quarters of them, and there would still be enough left to pull me down and finish me off. Nor did I think she would be able to pull them off in time to save my life, once she had set them on me.

'Listen!' I called to her. 'I'm just here by accident—'

'I said put down your gun!' she cried. Her rifle went off, and a bullet whistled wide of me into the mistwall beside me.

'Quit that!' I said, raising the .22. 'Or I'll have to start shooting back.'

She hesitated – or if it wasn't hesitation, at least she did not pull her trigger again. Perhaps the first shot had been more accidental than otherwise. I kept talking.

'Look,' I told her over the noise of the dogs. 'I don't want to bother you. I just happened to stumble on your place here, and I'll be glad to be on my way again. Why would I want to be any trouble to you anyway? You're armed, you've got your dogs; and I'm all alone. Now, why don't we just both point our rifles to the ground and talk for a moment—'

Her gaze, which had been focussed on me, shifted suddenly. Her rifle barrel changed its aim slightly.

'Alone?' she shouted back. 'Do you call that alone?'

I turned to look; and sure enough, her question was a good one. If there was one thing I could count on – if there was one damn thing under the sun that I could absolutely be sure of with Sunday and the girl – it was that they would do exactly what I had told them not to. Somehow they had worked up the courage to come through the mistwall on their own, and now they were standing right behind me.

Of course, this changed the situation entirely. The woman had three times as much target, now. She might not hit me, but her chances of hitting one of our group was tripled. I felt a touch of something not far from panic. Add to what was happening the fact that with Sunday in view and scent, the dogs were now really going crazy; while Sunday's own back was beginning to arch like the stave of a drawn bow. He did not like dogs.

But for all that, he would not leave me to face them alone. He pressed close against my leg and snarled softly in his throat, watching the dogs. It was magnificently touching and, at the same time, monumentally exasperating to know that the crazy cat would stay beside me, even if I tried to drive him back with a club.

I looked again at the woman – just in time. She had grown arm-tired of holding the rifle to her shoulder and was moving now to untie the nearest dogs. There was no time for me to debate the ethics of the situation. I put a shot from my own rifle into the dirt between her and the animal she was approaching. She froze.

'Don't try letting any of them go!' I called to her. 'I don't want to hurt you; but I'm not going to let us be chewed up by your animals. Step back now and put your own gun down.'

She backed up, but without letting go of her rifle. I put another shot from the .22 into the frame of the doorway behind her. She checked, hesitated, and let the gun slip from her hands to the earth at her feet.

'All right!' I said. 'Now, I'm not going to hurt you, but I've got to make sure you're not going to hurt us. Stay where you are and don't move.'

She stood still. I turned to the girl.

'Hold, Sunday!' I said. 'Stay right where you are, both of you. This time, I mean it!'

I went forward, holding the .22. The dogs had their tethers stretched taut, trying to reach me, so that it was possible for me to see where I needed to walk to stay out of reach of each one of them as I went through their pack. I came up to the woman, bent and picked up her gun. It was a 30.06, a good, clean, hunting rifle. With that in my hands, I felt more secure.

I knew what I had to do, then – and that was shoot the dogs while they were all still safely tied up. But when I raised her rifle I found I could not do it. It was not just that the woman would be vulnerable without them once I had taken her rifle and gone on. It was also the matter that I was still too civilized. I could not get over thinking of them as pets, instead of as the four-legged killers she had turned them into. I twisted about to face the woman.

'Look,' I said, 'I'm going to have to kill your dogs to make sure they won't hurt us, unless you can think of some way to fix things so I can trust them not to attack us.'

She sighed and shivered at the same time. It was as if all the strength in her had suddenly run out.

'I can do it,' she said, in a dead voice. She looked away from me, to the dogs. 'Quiet! Down – all of you. *Down!* Be quiet!'

They obeyed, to my astonishment. Their barking and snarling fell gradually into silence. They stared at the woman, licking their muzzles, and lay down one by one until they were all on the ground and silent, watching.

'That's pretty good,' I said to the woman.

'I used to run an obedience school,' she answered in the same dead voice. 'You don't have to worry. You can go now.'

'Sorry,' I said. 'But I don't know what else you have in the way of guns or dogs inside that house of yours. Let's go inside. You first.'

She stiffened.

'No!'

'Calm down, damn it!' I said. 'I just want to look around.'

She was still stiff.

'Just a minute,' she said. She turned her head and called back through the open doorway into the dark interior behind her. 'Wendy, come out here.'

'My daughter,' she said, harshly.

We waited, and after a second, a blonde-haired little girl of early grade school age came out and pressed herself up against the woman, who put her arm around the child.

'It's all right,' the woman said, 'We're just going to show this man our house.'

She turned then, and with one arm still around her daughter, led the way inside. I followed, carrying both rifles. There was not a great deal to see inside. A time change line had cut the house very nearly in half. A portion of the living room, all of the kitchen and bathroom, plus one bedroom and a half, remained. The bright sun coming in the uncurtained windows of the rooms that were still whole made the spartan existence that the two of them had been living here all very clear and plain. I went over the rooms carefully, but there were no other guns and only some kitchen knives that might have possibilities as weapons.

The woman said nothing all the time I was looking around. She stood by the living room window and glanced out from time to time. I thought she was checking on the dogs, because they stayed quiet. But I was wrong.

'Is that your wife out there?' she asked at last.

'Wife?' I said.

For a second, the question made no sense at all. I looked out the window where she was looking and saw only Sunday and the girl. Then, of course, I understood.

'No!' I said. 'She's just a kid. I picked her up after she'd just been through a time change; and it mixed her up pretty badly. She's not right yet, for that matter. I—'

I broke off. I had been about to go on and tell her about my previous conviction that Swannee had escaped the time changes, and a lot more that was purely personal. But it was none of her business. For that matter, the girl was none of her business, either. The fact of the matter was, I had long since drifted into ignoring any sexual quality in the girl; if I had ever paid any attention to that, in the first place. My mind had been full of my own personal problems. But I could hardly try to explain that to this woman without confusing the matter more than I would clear it up. I was a little surprised at the strength of the sudden urge in me to talk about it; then I realized that she was the first rational, adult human I had met since the beginning of the time storms. But it was still none of her business.

I looked once more around the living room of the house, ready to leave now. The woman spoke quickly, as if she could read my mind.

'Why don't you ask her to come in?'

'Ask her in?' I said. 'If she comes in, the leopard has to come in, too.'

She grew a little pale at that and held the young child closer to her side. But then she tossed her head back.

'Is he dangerous?' she asked. 'The leopard?'

'Not if the two of you stay well back from him,' I said. 'But if he comes in here, he's got to pass by those dogs of yours, and I can't imagine that happening.'

'I can,' she said, flatly. 'They'll obey orders.'

She walked with her daughter to the door, which was standing open, and through it. I followed her.

'Come on in!' she called to the girl and Sunday. Of course the girl neither moved nor answered, any more than Sunday did.

'It's all right,' I told the girl. 'You and Sunday come in.' I turned to the woman. 'And you'd better control those dogs.'

The girl had already started toward the house; but Sunday held back. Seeing he would not come, she turned back to him. I had to go out to both of them.

'Come on,' I said. I took a fistful of the loose skin at the scruff of Sunday's neck and led him with me toward the house. He came; a little reluctantly, but he came. The dogs tied nearest to his path shrank back from him as we approached, but those farther off whined and crawled forward to the limit of their tethers, white-toothed and panting.

'Down!' said the woman from the doorstep, and, hearing her, if I'd been a dog I would not have delayed doing what she said. The soft soprano now had a knife-edge to it. It lifted and cut. It carried clearly without her seeming to have to raise the volume. 'All of you – down!

Quiet!' The dogs followed the girl and Sunday with eyes and wet breath; but they neither got to their feet nor raised a clamour.

We all went back inside the house and the woman shut the door behind us. One lone bark sounded from the yard as the door closed. The woman opened it again and looked out. There was silence. She closed the door once more and this time the silence continued.

'Hello,' she said to the girl. 'I'm Marie Walcott, and this is my daughter, Wendy.'

The girl – my girl – said nothing. Her face had a look that made it appear merely as if she did not understand, but which I knew well enough to recognize as an expression of stubbornness.

'She doesn't talk,' I told the woman. 'I mean, she can talk, but she doesn't like to – part of the shock she went through, I suppose. But she hears and understands you, all right.'

The girl stepped to my side, at that, then went around me and knelt down on the other side of Sunday, putting an arm around the leopard's neck.

'Poor thing,' said the woman, watching her. The expression on the girl's face did not change. The woman looked back at me. 'What are you going to do now?'

'We'll move on,' I said. 'I told you that. And I'm taking this rifle of yours. I'll leave you my .22 rifle – I'll drop it about five hundred yards out, so we'll be well gone by the time you get to it. It's a lighter gun and it'll suit you better in any use you've got for a rifle. The dogs are your real protection, and I'm leaving you those, alive. But try to track us down with them, and I'll shoot every one of them that Sunday doesn't tear up.'

'I wouldn't come after you that way,' said the woman. 'Where are you going anyway?'

'Into the futuremost segment of time-changed country I can find,' I said. 'Somewhere there must be somebody who'll understand what's happened to the world.'

'What makes you so sure there's anyone like that?'

'All right,' I said, 'if there isn't we're still going to be looking – for the best piece of time to stay with, or some way of living with the time changes, themselves. I've been running away from the mistwalls; but now I'm going through any one I meet, so I can find out what's on the other side.'

She looked out her window toward the two mistwalls overshadowing her dogs and her home.

'What is on the other side out there?' she asked.

'You wouldn't like it,' I said. 'What's farther in?' I pointed through the back of the house toward the forest that crowded close upon her place.

'I don't know,' she said. 'There used to be a town of fifty thousand people – Gregory, Illinois – about ten miles down the road, there. But there's not even any road, now. I don't know.'

I looked closely at her.

'You haven't moved from this place since the time storms first started?'

'That's right.' She looked sombre. 'Wendy and I sat here and prayed, after the first time change came close. At first we prayed for Tim – for my husband to come back. But now for some time we've just prayed that the mistwalls will leave us alone.'

'Two of them are right on top of you,' I said. 'Didn't you think of getting away from them?'

'To what?' she said, shrugging. 'I've got half a year's supply of food in the basement here – had to, since we live out of town. If they move over us, then it's over, all at once. Meanwhile, we're safer here than some-place else. I ran a boarding kennel, so I had the dogs, here, to guard me. And there was – or we thought there was – always the chance my husband ...'

She shrugged again and stopped talking.

'All right,' I hefted both rifles and turned toward the door. 'Come on, Sunday, Girl. As for you, Mrs. Walcott, wait fifteen minutes and then follow us out. You'll find the .22 leaning against a tree, a little way into the woods, there.'

I opened the door. The woman's voice spoke from behind me to the dogs, commandingly.

'Quiet! Down!' Then her tone changed. 'We could go with you.'

I turned around. My first, unthinking reaction was that she was joking. I saw she was not. Then, suddenly, I saw and understood a great many other things.

I had been assuming, without really looking at her, that she was housewifely middle-aged. She was wearing slacks and a man's shirt, and of course she had on no makeup. Her hair was cut short – rather clumsily cut short; and there were dark circles of weariness under her eyes. By contrast with the girl, the only human member of the opposite sex I had seen since the first time storm, at first glance, Marie Walcott had looked maturely-fleshed and unremarkable. Now, suddenly, I real-ized that she was probably no older than I. In fact, given the conditions of civilization once more she would have been damned attractive. She was full grown, someone my own age, with the body of a woman rather than that of a half-grown girl, with a sane adult mind and capability of speech. Suddenly I remembered that it had been a long time since I and any woman ...

I noticed all this in a moment; and in the same moment, I realized that she had wanted me to notice – had set out to make me notice. It changed the whole picture.

'Go with us?' I said, more to myself than to her.

'We'd all be safer, in one large group,' she said. 'You could use another grown-up. And of course, there's the dogs.'

She was right about the dogs. A pack like that, properly trained, could really be valuable.

'There's your daughter,' I said. 'She's too young to be making long marches every day.'

'I've got a cart the dogs can pull her in – also, we'd be running into roads, and some kind of transportation sooner or later, don't you think? Meanwhile, I ... we'd both feel better with a man around.'

She was giving me all the practical reasons why our teaming up would work, and I was countering with all the practical arguments against it; and we both knew that we were talking around the one real reason I should or should not add her to my party, which was that I was male and she was female.

'Why don't you think it over?' she said. 'Stay here overnight and think about it. Maybe we can talk about it some more, later on.'

'All right,' I said. 'We'll stay until tomorrow.' I glanced out the window.

'I'd better camp off by the edge of the trees, there,' I said. 'Sunday isn't going to take to your dogs just like that – or they to him.'

'Sunday?' said the woman. 'Is that what you call him? I think you heard me say my name. I'm Marie Walcott and this is Wendy.'

'I'm Marc Despard,' I said.

'Marc, I'm pleased to meet you.' She held out her hand and I took it. It was a strange feeling to shake hands after the last few weeks. Her hand was small but firm, and there were callouses at the base of her fingers. 'Are you French?'

I laughed. 'The name's French-Canadian.'

She let go of my hand and looked at the girl.

'I didn't hear ...'

'She's never told me her name,' I said. I looked at the girl. 'How about it? Do you want to tell us now?'

The girl was absolutely silent. I shrugged.

'I've just been calling her "Girl."' I said. 'I guess you'll have to do the same.'

'Maybe,' Marie smiled at her, 'she'll tell us her name – later on, when she feels like it.'

The girl stood without a word.

'Don't count on it,' I said to Marie.

10

I had rigged a backpack-style tent for the girl and myself from some of the canvas in the boatdock before we left the deserted lakeshore house. I set this up at the edge of the trees, upwind of the dogs. Sunday had already begun ignoring the dog pack; and Marie rode herd on them through the afternoon, commanding them to be quiet any time they started to get worked up about Sunday or the rest of us. Once the camp was made, I left the girl with Sunday and went to the house alone.

Marie took me around and introduced me individually to each of the dogs. I spoke to each and petted each one briefly while Marie stood sternly over them to make sure that they behaved. Occasionally I got a brief tail movement by the way of acknowledgment but most of them merely rolled their eyes up at me and only endured both my touch and my voice. I guessed that I smelled too much of cat for any of them to be really comfortable; and I mentioned this to Marie. But she shrugged it off.

'They'll get used to you,' she said. The tone of her voice indicated that they had better.

She left me then, to get dinner ready. I spent a little time trying to make friends with her daughter. But Wendy was a quiet, shy child who – like the dogs – evidently found me too strange and potentially frightening to warm up to, on short acquaintance. She was obviously relieved when I left her at last and went back to camp.

Sunday was there, tied to the trunk of a large tree with a length of our heaviest rope, ending in a loop around his neck. He was lying down and, to my surprise, did not seem to mind being restricted this way. Since he was not objecting and it was convenient to have him anchored so, I left him the way he was. The girl must have tied him up so that she could wander off by herself, because she was nowhere to be seen.

She had not returned by the time Marie stuck her head out her door to call us to dinner. I waited a little while, but she still had not come back when Marie called a second time; and I decided not to worry about her. There was no counting on her, anyway. Sunday was still not objecting to being tied up – which was ideal from my point of view. He had dozed off kittenishly lying on his back with his paws in the air, as if there was no dog within a thousand miles. I got up and left; and all he did was open his eyes sleepily to look after me.

The good smell of cooking reached me before I opened the door and surrounded me as soon as I came in. Marie had produced a ham – it had to have been a canned one – heated and glazed it, and filled out the meal with what must have been home-grown tomatoes, potatoes and a salad made with some greens I didn't identify, but which, with a cheese dressing, tasted magnificent.

'She didn't come with you?' Marie asked, as she sat down at the table with Wendy and me.

'She's gone off somewhere. Sunday's tied up,' I said.

She nodded, evidently reassured. She did not know that Sunday was capable of chewing through any rope that tied him in no seconds flat, if the notion occurred to him. But he was not likely to wander off; and he had sense enough not to start trouble with the dogs, but to pick his way among them, if he got the urge to free himself and join me in the house.

It was a marvellous dinner. Marie had gotten rid of the slacks and shirt. She was wearing a soft, yellow dress that went well with the colour of her blonde hair, which – while still short – was smoothed out somehow and looked less as if it had undergone home barbering. She had used a touch of lipstick too, and possibly a hint of other makeup. The total result was enough to bring back the past in a way that the scotch and sodas I had made in the lakefront home never had.

I had been regretting all afternoon that I had not had the sense to bring at least one bottle from the liquor stock of the lakeshore home. But as it turned out, Marie had her own supply. She had not produced any wine with the meal; but afterwards she came up with a bottle of rum, after everything was over and Wendy had gone off to bed. It was not great rum, but it went well with the coffee.

We sat on the couch in her living room and talked, about our situations – and a lot else. Under the influence of the rum, I remember telling her more about myself than I had intended to ever tell anyone. But in the warmth and privacy of the living room, I was lulled into a sense of security. I knew very well that Marie was only out after her own advantage. I knew what was going on with both of us; but I did not give a damn. In fact, I remember thinking that I deserved something like this, after wet-nursing an insane leopard and a wild girl all these weeks. Somewhere along there with the rum and the coffee, I put my arm around Marie; and only a little later we turned the lights out.

I don't know how late it was. It was certainly sometime after mid-night when I left the house. Marie followed me naked to the door in the darkness to put her head out and hiss the dogs into silence when they roused on seeing me. I gave her a last kiss and went across the dark ground under a young moon to the camp.

Sunday was curled up under the tree to which he had been tied; and there was a lump on the ground beside him that was the girl, come back. The groundsheet out of our tent was a black pool under them on the semi-moonlighted ground; and some of our blankets were spread over both of them.

I shrugged, drunkenly. If the girl wanted to lie out there and get soaked through with the morning dew, that was up to her. I crawled into the tent and wrapped myself as well as I could in the remaining blankets. I was either not quite asleep and hallucinating, or else I was already asleep and dreamed the whole thing; but it seemed to me that just before I dropped into a deep well of unconsciousness, Sunday raised his head and looked me right in the eye, speaking to me.

'You stink!' he said distinctly, in the girl's voice. – And that was the last I remember.

When I woke, someone was standing over me. But it was neither Sunday nor the girl. It was Marie; and she handed me a cup of hot coffee.

'Sorry to wake you,' she said. 'But I can use your help if we're going to get off today.'

'Get off today?' I echoed stupidly. She stood there, looking down at me for a long second.

'That's what we talked about last night, wasn't it?' she said. 'Do you remember?'

I started to say I didn't. But then it came back to me. She was right, of course. That was, indeed, one of the things we had talked about last night. We had made plans to leave today – all of us, together.

'Yes,' I said. I lay looking at her, part of me hating myself and filled with self-contempt at letting myself be bought so easily; and part of me remembering last night and looking forward to tonight. 'I'll be along in a bit.'

'Good,' she said.

She went off. I got up and dressed. The girl and Sunday were not to be seen. During the period on the lizard raft, with no way to do anything about it, my beard had grown to a respectable length. But I had always liked the feel of being clean-shaven, and as soon as we found the lakeshore home, I had been happy to discover a razor and go back to being naked-faced once more. Normally, I liked shaving. It was part of the familiar ritual of coming awake in the morning – and I did not come awake in the morning easily. But this morning the habitual scraping actions did not clean off a layer of guilt left on me by the night before. In a sense, I had sold Sunday and the girl down the river for the selfish satisfaction of my own desires.

Sunday, of course, did not know what was going on. But he was not going to have the old freedom he was accustomed to, living with the dog-pack alongside him, whether he knew it or not. Also, he was going to have to share me with a couple of extra humans – and that was not going to make him happy, either. He had adjusted to the girl; but the girl loved him – Marie and Wendy did not, and there was no guarantee that they ever would. As for the girl, she had already made it plain how she felt about the situation.

I washed the last of the soap off my face and began to pump myself up with counter-arguments. We had been bound eventually to bump into other people with whom we would want and need to associate. Sunday had been destined to have to learn to share me with other people, finally. The girl, likewise. The three of us could not go on forever being exclusively insane together, as we had been until I faced the freshwater sea and the fact that Swannee was gone for good.

It was not going to be easy adapting, for me either, I told myself. But I was going to have to do it. So were the girl and Sunday. That was life – you could not always have what you wanted.

By the time I went over to get some breakfast from Marie and help her prepare to move out, I had the top layer of my mind – if nothing beyond that – thoroughly convinced that I was not only doing the best thing for all concerned, but being considerably self-sacrificing to boot.

It took us most of the day to get ready. Marie had two carts fitted with bicycle wheels, which she had trained certain of her dogs to pull. The carts themselves were obviously homemade, but remarkably well put together. Marie, apparently, had a definite mechanical talent. They were light and rolled easily. But they had one real drawback – no springs except the bicycle parts that supported the wheels. They would be all right on road surfaces, but I could not see them lasting more than a few days loaded and going cross-country, as we were going to be doing sooner or later. However, since we had nothing in the way of materials and tools around to provide them with springs, I decided not to say anything. There was no point in borrowing trouble.

We started out shortly after noon. The girl – she had showed up in time for breakfast, after all – Sunday, and I made up the advance guard, about fifty yards ahead of the rest. Behind us came Marie, walking, and the two carts, with Wendy riding one and the other loaded with food, water and gear for all of us, plus the .22, which I had given to Marie. Three dogs pulled each cart; and all the rest moved in a tight and disciplined patrol around the carts and Marie.

The others travelled at a fair walking speed for cross-country; but they did not make as good time as Sunday, the girl and I would have by ourselves, because they stopped more often for one reason or another – and often, the reason was Wendy. The original three of us, up in front of them all, however, could pretty well ignore the problems of these others. It was almost like being off on our own again. Sunday, of course, did not mind the slower pace at all. It gave him that much more time to explore things. He and the dogs, I noticed, had already solved the problem of coexistence in typical animal fashion – by ignoring each other. Once, when Sunday lagged behind, one of the forward dogs trotted past him at a distance of less than ten feet, and neither one so much as glanced at the other.

Several times I took advantage of being alone with the girl to try getting her to talk some more. But she was not in the mood, evidently. Nor would she look at me.

'All right,' I told her, at last. 'You work it out by yourself, then.'

I stepped out ahead, putting her from my mind and concentrating on scouting for our whole group. A few hours after we had left Marie's place, I ran across something like a logging road, or a farmer's tractor path among the trees, and followed it up until I could see through a thinning screen of forest to what was obviously a small town, down in a small cup-shaped valley area surrounded by open fields. It was about three hundred yards from the edge of the forest to the nearest buildings.

I turned about and headed back to contact Marie. Just in case there was anyone in that town, I did not want us to come strolling in followed by a leopard and a pack of dogs. Some nervous citizen was liable to take a shot – at Sunday, in particular. The rest were a fair distance behind me. Evidently, I had gained on them more than I had thought. At any rate, we got together once more and together came up to the edge of the woods to take a look at the town through some binoculars Marie had brought.

Through the binoculars, the town seemed deserted. There was no sign of movement, human or animal. I handed the binoculars to Marie, who was beside me.

'Take a look,' I said.

She did.

'That's Gregory, I take it?' I said, when she put the binoculars down.

'Yes,' she said. But she was frowning. After a short pause she added, but slowly and still frowning, 'It's got to be.'

'Got to be?' I asked. 'What do you mean?'

'I mean it *is* Gregory – I recognize it,' she said. 'But I don't know ... there's something different about it.'

'Nobody in sight,' I suggested.

'That, too,' she said. 'But something else. It looks changed, somehow. Only I can't say how.'

I took the binoculars back from her and studied the buildings I could see. Aside from their stillness in the late afternoon sun, there was nothing that struck me immediately as unusual about the town. Then I noticed a house with the blinds down on all of its windows.

I looked at the other houses. Those nearby did not have their blinds drawn. If all had, of course, it could simply have meant that a time change had come through the area at night and caught the inhabitants after they had settled to sleep. But the houses close to the one with the blinds drawn had theirs up – then, moving the glasses about, I found first one, and then four more houses where all the shades seemed to be down.

It could mean nothing, of course.

'Do they know you in Gregory?' I asked Marie.

'Oh, yes,' she said. 'We did all our shopping here.'

I turned to the girl.

'Hang on to Sunday. Keep him with you,' I said. 'Marie, you and I can take a walk in with a couple of the dogs – just a couple – and see if there's anyone there.'

I left my rifle behind, and made Marie leave hers. We stepped out into the sunlight and walked toward the buildings. It was all so ordinary that I felt a little ridiculous; and then, when we were about fifty feet out in the open, a figure came shambling around the corner of the house with the blinds down and faced us.

I did not get a good look at it. It was very big, either an unusually large man or woman all bundled up in loose furs, or something else. Even its face was furry, or hidden by a beard. But it came around the corner of the building and lifted one arm. There was a wink of light from the end of the arm; and the dog furthest in front of us – leading the rest of us by perhaps fifteen feet – leaped into the air with a howl that broke off abruptly as it fell back on its side in the grass, to lie there still.

I dove to the ground, pulling Marie down with me; and something sizzled over our heads as we lay there. A second later, there were sounds like rifle shots from the town and the singing of bullets over our heads.

'Back!' I said to Marie. 'Crawl! Back to the woods!'

We turned and went on our bellies. The shots continued, and once or twice I heard the sizzle overhead again; but nothing touched us. It seemed a long, long crawl. We were almost back when we came across the second dog we had taken with us, a lean German shepherd-type that had been named Buster, lying dead. In his case, it was a bullet from behind that had gone in at the back of his head and taken off half of his lower jaw when it came out. Flies were already buzzing around the corpse.

We crawled on, Marie and I, until the shadows of the trees were about us. Even then, we continued on hands and knees a little further before we risked standing up. Then we turned and went back to join the girl and Wendy for a look at the town.

But there was nothing to see. The fur-covered figure was no longer in sight; and the shooting had stopped.

'What was it?' said Marie. She was shaking and her voice was tight.

'I don't know,' I said. I turned to the girl. 'Did you get a look at it through the binoculars?'

The girl nodded.

'Was it a man or a woman?'

The girl shook her head.

'*Why won't you talk?*' Marie suddenly screamed at her.

'Easy,' I said to Marie. 'Easy.' I spoke to the girl again. 'Not a man or a woman either? You mean you couldn't tell?'

The girl nodded.

'You could tell?'

She nodded again.

'You could tell it wasn't a man or a woman?' I said. 'What was it then?'

'I don't know,' said the girl, unexpectedly. 'A thing.'

She turned and walked off. I went after her, but she would not even stand still to be questioned, let alone answer, after that. Defeated, I went back to Marie.

'Maybe something out of the future that wandered through its own mistwall into Gregory, here,' I said to her. 'Anyway, whatever it is, it doesn't seem to want to come after us – just seems to want us to leave it alone. I think we'd better go around this town. What's the next one up the line called? And how far is it?'

'Elton,' said Marie. 'And it's about five miles.'

'That's where we'll head, then,' I told her.

We stayed within the cover of the woods and made a circuit of Gregory. By the time we were around the town, the afternoon was fairly well advanced; but we pushed on, hoping to reach Elton. We never did, though. After nearly three more hours of travelling without a sight of a road or a town, we came to bluffs overlooking a river. A big river; easily a quarter of a mile across.

There was obviously no going farther that day. We set up camp on the bluff, and in the morning I went down to the river's edge to take a look at the situation.

The water was fresh and cold. The edge where I stood was overgrown with willows and seemed to drop off deeply; but a little farther downstream the river made a bend, and there was a sandy beach and shallow water. I explored that far, accompanied by Sunday and the girl. The current of the water seemed to slow, going around the curve, and there was plenty of driftwood on the beach to make into a raft. I went back to Marie on the bluff. She was making coffee and she gave me a cup.

'So you want to cross the river,' she said; after I had told her what it was like, there.

I shrugged.

'We don't have to,' I answered. 'We can go upriver, or downriver, and we may even run into a bridge, somewhere, crossing it. But summer isn't going to last forever; and the more I think about it, the more it seems to me that we ought to keep heading due east. It's our best chance to find some large civilized group that's survived the time storms.'

So it was settled – more or less. I did some planning, out loud, with Marie and the girl listening. The dogs could swim, of course. So could Sunday and we adults – or, rather, we two adults and the one near-adult, who was the girl. Wendy, the equipment and the supplies could be rafted over. Reducing the raft load to Wendy and our possessions meant we would need only a relatively small raft. Luckily we had a hammer and even some nails along, although, actually, I had decided to save the nails and chain the logs of the raft together with the dog chains, for maximum safety.

As I mentioned earlier, I had been looking forward to the evening – and Marie. However, it developed that Wendy was either coming down sick with something, or upset by the travel; Marie gave me to understand that, as far as that night went, she would be tied up with family matters. So as not to waste time, I took advantage of the long twilight to go down on the beach and make a start gathering the logs for the raft, then chopping them to length with Marie's axe.

Sunday and the girl went down there with me; and as things turned out, I built a fire and went on working by that, even after the sunset left us; so that we ended up making a separate camp down there. Just before I turned in for the night, something occurred to me.

'You know,' I said to the girl, looking across the fire to where she sat with Sunday, 'we left that raft of the lizards in one hell of a hurry, that night. I remember pulling you through the water; but I don't really remember how well you can swim – or even if you can really swim. Can you? Do you think you can make it across the river?'

I expected a nod or a shake of the head at the most. But to my surprise, she answered in words.

'I'm not going.'

I stared at her.

'What do you mean – you're not going?' I exploded. 'Do you think you can stay here on this side of the river, alone? Get that thought out of your mind. You're going.'

She shook her head, looking not at me, but at the fire.

I sat, staring at her, too angry for words. Then I took hold of my anger with both hands, figuratively speaking, and tried to talk calmly.

'Look,' I said, as reasonably as I knew how. 'We've been together for some time, you and I and Sunday. But nothing lasts forever. You must have known that sooner or later we were going to be meeting other people and joining them, or they'd be joining us ...'

I went on talking, calmly and persuasively, using all the arguments I had used to myself the day before, and doing, I thought, a good job of it. It was only common sense I was telling her; and I pointed this out to the girl. Aside from her youth and sex, any single person stood a much reduced chance of survival. What would she do with herself? Practical matters aside, Sunday would miss her. For that matter I would miss her, myself ...

I was talking away quite earnestly, and even beginning to think that I was getting through to her, when she got up suddenly and walked away out of the circle of firelight, leaving me in mid-sentence.

I stared after her into the darkness. Something cold came in out of the night and sat down on my chest. For the first time, it occurred to me that she could actually be meaning to do what she had just said she would.

11

An hour after sunrise, Marie, Wendy, our equipment, supplies, dogs and all were down on the beach watching me finish off the raft. Watching and helping, as much as they could. It was Marie who brought up the subject of the girl.

'I think,' said Marie, looking over to where the girl sat on a log, stroking Sunday at her feet, 'everybody should do their share.'

'She's not going,' I said.

Marie stared at me.

'She's not going?' Marie said. There was an odd note in her voice – a note which could have meant anything. I could not interpret it at all. 'You don't mean that?'

'I don't mean it,' I said. 'She does.'

'Oh?' said Marie. She looked over at the girl again. 'It's her idea?'

'That's right.'

Marie stood for a moment, watching the girl.

'No,' Marie said, finally. 'She'll go.'

I did not say anything more, myself. I concentrated on finishing the raft. When I was done, we launched it and loaded it with the contents of the two bicycle carts and the carts themselves. It floated well, a square of good-sized logs almost ten feet by ten feet in area; and there was plenty of room on it for Wendy – though the little girl was pale as moonlight and clearly frightened to death of riding across the river on the rocking log surface.

While Marie coaxed and soothed the child, I took six of the dog-leash chains I had set aside while I was making the raft. Three of these I put around Sunday's neck to make a choke-collar for him. I fastened the second three to the first and looped them around a log too big for the leopard to drag. Then I went to the raft and picked up the .22 rifle and its box of shells.

'What are you doing?' Marie interrupted her efforts with Wendy to stare at me. 'That's mine. You gave it to me.'

302

'I'm taking it back,' I said.

I walked away, not listening to what else she said. The girl had come to stand concernedly over Sunday and examine his chains – Sunday, himself, had hardly blinked when I had put them on him. He lay basking in the sun. I walked up to the girl and shoved both rifle and shells into her hands.

'You can learn to shoot this,' I said. 'Keep the shells dry and use them up only when you really need to. Whatever you do, make sure they're not dirty when you put them in the rifle. And make sure no dirt gets in the barrel of the rifle. If it does, take some string from your pack, and tie a clean patch of cloth on the end of it. Drop the string through the barrel and keep pulling the cloth through the barrel until it looks shiny from end to end, when you hold it up and look at the light through it, the way you've seen me do. Have you got that?'

She took the box and gun from me without a word.

'I'm leaving Sunday with you,' I said. 'Don't unchain him until we've been gone at least a day and a night. If I'm not around, I think he'll stick with you; and he'll be even more protection to you than the gun. Remember, winter's coming on in a few months. Try to find some place where you can settle in and be protected until it warms up again.'

She looked at me.

'Well,' I said. 'Goodbye.'

She did not move or speak. I turned and went back to Marie,

Marie had Wendy on the raft and was already stripped down to a yellow one-piece swimsuit. She looked good in it, as I would have expected since the night before last. I had not stopped to think about such niceties myself. Now, out of tribute to her own bathing dress, I left my shorts on – a foolish bit of male modesty which I had not planned on, earlier. But I had spare underclothing in my backpack, and I could hang the wet shorts outside the backpack to dry as I travelled, after we reached the other side.

I looked back once more at the girl and Sunday, and waved. Neither one responded, of course. I got into the cold river water, holding on to the raft along with Marie. The dogs took to the water on their own, after us; and we began the swim across.

As I said, the water was cold, in spite of it being midsummer. The current swept us farther downriver than even I had expected by the time we made the crossing; and by that time, in spite of considering myself a fairly strong swimmer, I was grateful to have the raft to cling to, and sympathetic to the dogs who had no such thing. One of them, indeed, got the idea at one point to try and climb up on the raft; but a sharp command from Marie made him drop back off it. All in all, though, we must have been in the water more than half an hour by the time we finally struggled ashore on a small sandy spot backed up by a space, about two house-lots in size, of sand and grass reaching back to the edge of a fairly thick wood.

I had gotten out, hauled the raft in close and lifted Wendy ashore, and was beginning to unload the raft when a tense word from Marie made me straighten up and turn around.

Five men had come out of the trees – about half-way out between trees and water. They stood perhaps twenty yards or so from us in a semi-circle, hemming us in against the river's edge. They were all well-dressed – dressed for the outdoors, that is. Each of them wore thick-soled country-style boots, with high tops disappearing up inside heavy trousers; and above the waist they all wore leather or firm-cloth jackets, with the collars of winter-weight shirts showing at the neck; and all but one of them wore some kind of hat. Every one of them had at least one handgun belted around his waist as well as a rifle in his hands.

The one without a hat stood a little forward of the rest and seemed to be the leader, though he was younger than any of the others, and even looked to be a good half-dozen years younger than I was. But he was as tall as I, and wider of shoulder, in his jacket. His face was heavy-boned; and like mine, it was clean-shaven – all the rest wore beards of varying lengths. He grinned at me as I reached for the rifle on the raft.

'Leave it lay,' he said. I stopped reaching.

'Guard!' snapped Marie. 'Point!'

Swiftly, the dogs fanned out around us, each facing one or more of the men, which in most cases meant that there were a couple of dogs on each; and each canine form went into its own version of a tense on-the-mark position, like a trained bird dog pointing quail. The rifles of the men came up.

'Hold it!' said the young man. 'Keep your dogs there if you don't want them shot!'

Marie said nothing, but the dogs stood still. The young man dropped the butt of his rifle to the ground and leaned on the gun in friendly fashion – though I noticed the rest of them kept their weapons ready to use. He smiled at us again.

'Well,' he said. 'What's it like on the other side of the river?'

'There's nothing much there,' I said. I was freezing to death, standing mid-thigh deep in the water, but I did not want to move out of arm's reach of the rifle on the raft. 'What's it like on this side?'

'Nothing much on this side, either,' the young man said. 'Couple of empty towns ...'

He was answering me, but he was watching Marie. They were all watching Marie. It was that yellow swimsuit. I had not been unaware that she had put it on with at least part of her mind on what it would do to me. Now, it was doing the same thing to these men; only with them it was, I thought, turning out to be a bit too much of a good thing. But yet, instead of doing something sensible, like taking a jacket or blanket from the raft to cover herself, and in spite of the fact that, like me, she had to be both wet and cold, she continued to stand where she was, deliberately inviting their stares. Not only that, but now she had to start talking, to draw that much more attention on herself.

'What do you think you're doing?' she cried, pulling Wendy to her. 'As if my child wasn't frightened enough, you have to come charging out of the woods like this with guns—'

She had begun to rub the little girl down with the towel Wendy had worn around her neck, as a seal to keep water spray from getting under the blanket in which she had been wrapped during the raft voyage. The activity may have been purely motherly, but it was almost as effective as if Marie had begun to do the dance of the seven veils in front of our visitors. A couple of them were grinning slightly.

'Well now, I'm sorry,' said the young leader. 'Awfully sorry.' His men grinned a little more widely.

'You ought to be!' said Marie, towelling away. 'Just because something's happened to the world doesn't mean the people can't be decent! Anybody with any brains would offer to help, instead of bursting out like that, like thugs—'

'We'll be glad to help,' said the young man. 'You don't understand us, that's why we came over, to help you—'

'I should think so!' snapped Marie. 'That's more like it. Here, when there's hardly any people left in the world, those that are left need to stick together. Well, maybe I shouldn't jump down your throat like that—' She was still continuing to towel Wendy vigorously in her almost-dance, in spite of the fact that Wendy now, plainly, wanted only to be released. 'But if you'd just had to swim an icy river like that, you'd be a little upset too, when a bunch of men with guns—'

'Mommy, I'm dry now!' Wendy was protesting, squirming in Marie's grasp.

'Hold still, dear!' Marie. 'As I was saying, a bunch of men with guns—'

I caught it then, out of the corner of my eye; just a flicker of movement.

Suddenly, I saw what was happening, and why Marie had been standing there, chattering and bouncing about to hold their attention.

While she had been putting on her little show, the dogs had been about their own business. Apparently she had trained them well. As long as the eyes of the man it watched was upon it, the dog guarding him stood tensely still, at point. But the moment that attention moved elsewhere for even a fraction of a second, the dog stole forward – one step, two steps, even half a step, as if it was stalking a rabbit lying still and hidden in a cornfield. To begin with, the dogs had been almost as far away from the men as Marie and I were. Now, they had halved the distance between them and our welcoming committee.

Now, it was no longer a case of the men being able to kill all the dogs before the dogs could reach them. They might kill a good half of the dogs, but the other half stood an almost equal chance of reaching them while they were doing that.

In the same moment that I saw the flicker of movement, the man with the gun, at which the movement had been directed, saw it too. Evidently the dog had gotten too far inside our fields of vision to move without being noticed.

'Tek—' shouted the man. 'The dogs! Look!' The young leader jerked his eyes from Marie and swept them around the semicircle of half-crouching canines. At the same time the others started to jerk their guns up. But I had already taken advantage of the fact that their attention was off me to sweep up the rifle off the raft into my own hands.

'Hold it!' I shouted.

I had the rifle to my shoulder, aimed at Tek's belt. The dogs were ready.

'Hold it – just like he says!' barked Tek – if that was the young leader's full name. He himself stood perfectly still.

His men froze.

'That's better,' he said, in a calmer voice. He looked once more at Marie and me and smiled; but I could see a little shininess of sweat on his face. A 30.06 slug through the intestines is not a happy prospect; and I was close enough so that even if I was a poor shot, I shouldn't miss. 'That's much better. You don't want to waste any of these good dogs, now do you, ma'am? We'll just back out of here and let you folks go your own way, since that's what you seem to want. If we can't be friends' – and he was smiling at Marie alone, now – 'then that's just how it'll have to be. Sorry, though. It'd have been nice to know you. Now, we'll just start backing up ...'

And he did start backing up. His men imitated him. The dogs

immediately followed, step for step, as if invisible threads connected each of them to the man on which the dog focused.

'Hold!' said Marie. The dogs stopped; and the men kept backing, each holding his rifle now in one hand, down by his side and out of the way. I kept my own rifle steady at my shoulder.

The men reached the edge of the trees and slipped back into their shadow, all but Tek, who stopped briefly.

'Keep going,' said Marie.

'Sure. See you sometime,' called Tek.

'Only if we don't see you first!' answered Marie, grimly.

Tek waved. He paused for a second and looked directly at me. He made a little gesture like tipping a non-existent hat.

'You're a lucky man!' he called to me. 'Don't anyone ever tell you you're not!'

There was no sneer in his voice. There did not have to be. His message was clear enough. I was negligible – it was Marie and her dogs who were driving him off. For a second I flared into a rage – and for a second I almost charged out of the water after him, to call him a liar to his face – then that answer-seeking reflex in the back of my mind pounced on his clear intent like Sunday pouncing on a scuttling fieldmouse. He was trying to get me to charge after him in just that fashion. The dogs were not dangerous from a distance without my rifle covering them from behind. If I got out in front they could shoot me, then kill the dogs safely from a distance they had now regained between themselves and the canines.

So I did not rush out, after all. Instead, I laughed. I laughed loudly, hoping he would hear me – but he was already gone into the shadows of the trees, and I could not tell if he was still within earshot or not.

I came out of the water then, but slowly, and handed the rifle to Marie.

'Watch the woods,' I said.

I turned back to haul the raft, safely, far enough out of the water so that the river current could not pull it away until we had unloaded it. Then I took the rifle back from Marie while she rubbed some life back into my body and towelled herself dry. Meanwhile, there had been no further sign of Tek and his men. Marie posted a couple of dogs at the very edge of the woods, on watch; and we turned to unloading the raft.

Once we were unloaded, I built a fire to warm us up. It was only after the fire was going well and Marie had some soup heating on its flames, that I thought to look back across the river to see if the girl and Sunday had witnessed our encounter with Tek and his men. But a glance showed me that we had drifted so far down river in our crossing, that the beach where I had left girl and leopard was now around the bend of the further shoreline, out of sight. I turned back to the soup, grateful for its filling heat, but feeling a little empty inside all the same.

After I dressed, I scouted with Marie and a few of the dogs to see if the neighbourhood was really clear of Tek and his companeros. We found that the woods into which they had gone was actually only a narrow fringe of trees, perhaps a couple of hundred yards in width, paralleling the river. The woods were clear of human life and beyond them rose a small slope to a sort of shallow river bluff, from which we could see over a fairly wide, open, grassy area. There was no sign of Tek and company there, either, and no sign of mistwalls, or anything else, moving. We went back and made camp by the river, where we had landed. Marie and I both figured we deserved a little holiday.

The next day we pushed on east, with me scouting well ahead. A few of the dogs were beginning to take to me, finally – perhaps the water had washed off enough of Sunday's smell to make me socially acceptable to them – and there were a couple I could trust to obey a few simple commands. Marie drilled them with me; and they responded well. One was a bitch – a sort of large cocker spaniel mix and the more intelligent of the two. The other was a lean, nervous, German shepherd type, male and looking half-starved. The bitch was called Merry and the German shepherd was Cox. They would heel, stand, guard and scout for me in a circle, at a sweep of my arm – and that was pretty good, considering our limited acquaintance.

So, they and I got along pretty well, moving perhaps four hundred yards or so in front of Marie, Wendy and the rest. I was off by myself, as I liked it; but travelling with two dogs was not like travelling with Sunday. They would obey commands; Sunday almost never had – except by accident. They travelled at my pace; I had been used to travelling more or less at Sunday's. They were deadly weapons I could control. Sunday had been almost uncontrollable and absolutely unpredictable.

But there was one great point of difference that outweighed all their virtues. The crazy cat had loved me – loved me for myself alone. It was a love induced by accident and the time change effect, but nonetheless it was there. And I – I had gotten used to it. Merry and Cox could have been as cheerfully working for Tek at this moment, if Marie had drilled them into obeying him instead of me.

So I put thoughts of Sunday out of my mind – I had not dared to think of the girl from the first. Now I allowed myself the thought that it was lucky she was on the far side of the river, and Tek with his men, on this. Hopefully she would run into some decent people on her side. People being naturally spread out over the spectrum of human character as they were, she had as good a chance of finding good people as she had of finding bad ones. I put her out of my mind, too. No man – and no girl – could have the world just the way they wanted it, always.

By noon of the second day after we had crossed the river, we moved out of the relatively open area beyond the river bluff on this side and began to come on rolling country covered by what was obviously farmland, scattered with deserted-looking farm houses. The change was gradual enough so that it was impossible for us to tell whether the change from open country to cultivated earth was natural or the result of a time change. But in any case, the appearance of the area did not jibe exactly with Tek's words about only a 'couple of empty towns' on this side of the river. We passed by the deserted-looking farmhouses at a healthy distance; and at no time did the dogs give any kind of alarm.

So three days of travel went by quietly with no sign of Tek and his group, or any other humans, and no sign of trouble. Then, on the morning of the fourth day we spotted a mistwall standing off to our right, and I changed our line of march to angle toward it.

12

Marie objected to the whole idea. Her own instinct was to head away from the mistwall; and I could not blame her.

'All right,' I said, turning away. 'You go on. I should catch up to you in a couple of days. If not, you'd better not wait for me.'

I took perhaps a half a dozen steps away from her before she made a sound; and then I heard her behind me.

'What can I do? *What can I do?*'

It was an aching, tearing sort of cry. I turned around and saw her, her eyes squeezed shut, her face white, her fists clenched at her sides, and all her body rigid. I went back to her.

Suddenly, I understood how it was with her. From her point of view, she had contributed to our partnership everything she had to contribute. She had abandoned what little security she still had left, following the time storm, to go with me – more for Wendy's sake, I suspected, than for her own. She had been adjustable, faithful and hardworking, a good partner by day and night. She had trusted her dogs, herself – and even her daughter – to me. And still, here on some reasonless whim, as it seemed to her, I was going to risk everything on a chance that could just as easily be avoided.

I put my arms around her and tried to get her to soften up; but she was as rigid as ever the girl had been in one of her states of shock. But I simply stood there and kept holding her, as I had kept holding the girl in those instances, and after a while, I thought I felt some yielding in her. She shuddered and began to cry, in great, inward, throaty, tearing sobs that were almost tearless.

However, after a while, even these began to quiet down; and I began to talk, quietly, into her ear while I held her.

'Listen to me,' I said, 'There only were three things I might not have gone along with you on; and now that Sunday and the girl are gone, there's only one. But that's something I've been stuck with all my life. Now that I've taken on the question of figuring out the time storm, I don't have any choice. I've got to go through any mistwalls I find and see what's on the other side of them – I've got to, you understand? There's no choice for me when I come to something like this. There never has been.'

'I know you don't love me,' she said into my chest. 'I never asked for that. But where will we go if you don't come back? What will we do?'

'You'll do just fine,' I said. 'All you have to do is sit down for half an hour and wait, while I step through the mistwall and take a look at what's beyond it before I come back out.'

'All!' she said.

'That's right. All,' I told her. 'You'll have to take my word for it; but with most of the mistwalls I've seen, the two sides of them were pretty much the same, front and back. The odds are against anything being there that's either very good or very bad. If it's bad, I'll duck back right away. If it's good, it could mean a new, safe future for all of us. You ought to be pushing me to go and look, not holding me back!'

'Oh, you'll do what you want,' she said and pulled away from me. But evidently it was settled; we set off for the mistwall.

At the point where we came up to it, the mistwall crossed a little hollow crowned by trees on both sides, so that there was a sort of natural trough some sixty yards wide and perhaps a hundred long leading to it. I had picked this point as one where Marie, Wendy and the dogs could stay more or less hidden from anyone observing from the higher level of land surrounding them. We had spotted the mistwall early, and we reached the trough, or hollow, perhaps an hour before noon. The mistwall itself was completely unmoving – now that I thought of it, I had never seen a motionless mistwall begin to travel, or a moving one stop. It could be that there were two different varieties of time lines involved ... now that was a new thought.

I got everyone down in the hollow and climbed back out to the surrounding level to make sure they were invisible from anyone looking across the outside plain. They were, and using the binoculars reassured me that there was no sign of movement between the clumps of trees on the plain itself. They should be perfectly safe for an hour or so while I was on the other side of the mistwall – certainly they would be safe for the time it would take me to go, turn around and come back, if I found something on the other side I did not like.

Going back down into the hollow, I found myself trying to remember if I had ever seen anyone or anything alive moving voluntarily through one of the mistwalls. But I could remember none.

Marie held me tightly for a long moment before she would let me leave them for the mistwall itself – and even Wendy clung to me. The little girl had been getting over her shyness where I was concerned, these last few days since the girl and Sunday had been gone. I felt a sudden touch of discomfort at the realization that I had not reacted to the small overtures the child had been making in my direction. It came to me suddenly and heavily that it was some obscure connection between her presence and the absence of the other two, the girl and Sunday, that had kept me cool to her. Now, suddenly, I felt guilty. It was not Wendy's fault that things were happening as they were.

At any rate, I broke away from Marie and her at last and walked into the dust and the mist, as tense as one of the dogs walking into a strange backyard. The physical and emotional feeling of upset took me before I had a chance to close my eyes against the dust – but again, as on that earlier time I had gone through the mistwall to find Marie's place, the sensations were less than I had felt before. I found myself wondering if it was possible either to build up an immunity to going through the walls, or else simply to get used to the reactions they triggered in living bodies.

I pushed ahead blindly, the ground becoming a little rough and uneven under my feet, until the lessening of the dust-sting against the skin of my face told me I must be coming out on the other side of the time change line. I opened my eyes.

I stood now in rugged territory. If I was not among mountains, then certainly I was in the midst of some steep hills. Directly ahead of me was some sort of massive concrete structure, too large for me to see in its entirety. The part I was able to see was a mass of ruins, with new grass sprouting at odd points among the tumbled blocks of what had evidently been walls and ceilings.

What had smashed it up so thoroughly was hard to imagine. It didn't look so much as if it had been bombed as if it had been picked up and *twisted*, the way you might twist a wet towel to wring it dry. About it, the steep slopes, covered with gravel and a few fir and spruce trees, looked deserted under the cloudless, midday sky. The air temperature was perceptibly cooler than it had been on the other side of the mistwall, as if I was now at a noticeably higher altitude – though I had not felt the elevator-sort of inner ear sensations that would suggest a sudden change to a lower air pressure. There were no birds visible and no sounds of insects. Of course, if this new land was high enough it could be above the flight zone of most insects.

However, whatever the structure before me had been at one time, now it was a ruin only. There was no sign of life anywhere. It was far-fetched to think that there could be anyone in that pile of rubble who might have a greater understanding of the time storm than I did, let alone ideas on how to live with it or deal with it. I might as well go back through the mistwall to Marie, Wendy and the dogs.

But I hesitated. There was a reluctance in me to cut short this business of being off on my own – almost as much reluctance as there was in me to face Marie and admit the whole experiment of going through the mistwall had been profitless. I compromised with myself finally; it would do no harm to go around the ruin and a little farther into this new territory, until I could see the whole extent of it and perhaps make some guess as to what it had once been. The concrete of what was left of it appeared as modern, or more so, than anything in my native time – it might even have come from a few years beyond my original present.

It was an odd feeling that was pushing me to explore farther – a small feeling, but a powerful one. There was something about that jumble of concrete that plucked at my problem-solving mental machinery and beckoned it.

I swung to the right, approaching the ruin and circling it at the same time. As I got closer, the building turned out to be larger even that it had looked at first, and it was not possible to see it all at once. After a while, however, I got to where I could get a sight down one long side line of it. I still could not really see it as a whole, because it curved away from me, following the contours of the hill on which it was built; but it seemed to become progressively less of a ruin as its structure receded from me, and its interest to me grew. It reminded me a little of my own life, beginning as a wreck and developing into something with a shape, purposeful, but too big to see and know as a whole. I felt almost as if the building was something familiar, like an old friend built out of concrete; and I prowled further on alongside it.

It continued to sprawl out and curve away from me as I went; and after I had gone perhaps a quarter of a mile, I realized that I never would be able to see the thing as a whole. It was simply too big, and it spread out in too many directions.

I might have turned back then; but I noticed that the building was relatively undamaged in the further area of it I had now reached. Facing me were some windows that were whole, in sections of grey concrete wall that looked untouched. Farther on, there was even a door that looked slightly ajar – as if it needed only to be pushed to open to let anyone into the interior.

I went towards the door. It was a heavy, fire-door type; and when I put my weight into it and pulled, it swung outward slowly. Inside was a flight of bare concrete stairs with black iron pipe railing, leading upward. I mounted the stairs slowly and quietly, the rifle balanced in my hands, ready to use, even while the sensible front of my mind told me that this was ridiculous. I was wasting my time on a deserted and destroyed artifact; and it was high time I was heading back to Marie and Wendy, who would be worrying about me by now.

Reaching the top of the stairs, I let myself through another door into a long corridor, with only a bare white wall and window to my left, windows through which the sun was now striking brilliantly, but aglitter with glass doors and interior windows to my right, through which I could see what seemed to be row on row of offices and laboratories.

I took a step down the corridor, and something plucked lightly at the cuff of my left pantleg. I looked down. What appeared to be a small black thread had been fastened to the wall of each side of the corridor and now lay broken on the floor where my leg had snapped it.

'Who's there?' asked a voice over my head.

I looked up and saw the grille of a speaker – obviously of some public address system that had been built into this corridor when the whole structure had been put up.

'Hello?' said the voice. It was tenor-weight, a young man's voice. 'Who is it? Just speak up. I can hear you.'

Cautiously, I took a step backward. I was as careful as I could be in picking up my foot and putting it down again. But still, when the sole of my boot touched the corridor surface, there was a faint gritting noise.

'If you're thinking of going back out the way you came in,' said the voice, 'don't bother. The doors are locked now. It's part of the original security system of this installation; and I've still got power to run it.'

I took two more quick, quiet steps back and tried the door to the stairway. The door handle was immovable and the door itself stood motionless against my strongest push.

'You see?' said the voice. 'Now, I don't mean to keep you prisoner against your will. If you want to leave, I can let you out. I just thought we might talk.'

'Can you see me?' I asked.

'No,' he answered. 'But I've got instruments. Let's see ... you're about one hundred and ninety centimetres tall and weigh eighty-two point five three plus kilos. On the basis of voice tone and body odours, you're male, blood temperature approximately half a degree above normal, heartbeat fifty-eight – cool-headed customer, plainly – blood pressure a hundred and eight over eighty-seven. You're wearing some synthetics, but mostly wool and leather by weight – outdoor clothes. My mechanical nose also reports you as carrying a combination of metal, wood, oil and other odours that imply a rifle of some kind, plus some other metal that may be a knife; and according to the other scents you carry, you've been outside this building only a little while after coming from some place with a lot of grass, few trees and a warmer, moister climate.'

He stopped talking.

'I'm impressed,' I said, to start him up again. I did not trust his promise to let me go just for the asking; and I was looking around for some way out besides the locked door. There were the windows – how many stairs had I climbed on the way up? If I could break through a window, and the drop was not far to the ground ...

'Thank you,' said the voice. 'But it's no credit to me. It's the equipment. At any rate, reading from what I have here, you're out exploring rather than looking for trouble. You aren't carrying equipment or supplies for living outdoors, even though the odours on you say that's how you've been living. That means such equipment and supplies you have must be elsewhere. You wouldn't be likely to leave them unattended – some animal might chew them up to get at whatever food you were carrying, so you probably have others with you. They aren't in view anywhere around the area outside the building, or I'd know about them, and you're the only one inside, besides me; so that means you just about had to come through that stationary line of temporal discontinuity, out there.'

I stopped looking for windows. Now I actually was impressed. The equipment had been remarkable enough in what it could tell him about me; but any idiot could sit and read results from gauges and dials, if he had been trained well enough. This kind of hard, conscious reasoning from evidence, on the other hand, was something else again.

'What did you call it – a temporal discontinuity?' I asked.

'That's right. Have you got another name for it?' said the voice. 'It really doesn't matter what it's called. We both know what we're talking about.'

'What do you call it when it moves?' I asked.

There was a long second of silence.

'Moves?' said the voice.

I damn near grinned.

'All right,' I said, 'now I'll do a little deducing. I'll deduce you haven't left this building since the time storm struck.'

'Time storm?'

'The overall pattern of your temporal discontinuities,' I said. 'I call that a time storm. I call individual discontinuities like the one out there, time lines. I call the haze in the air where one is, a mistwall.'

There was a pause.

'I see,' he said.

'And you haven't left this building since that mistwall appeared out there, or since whatever it was, first happened to this building?'

'That's not quite the way it's been,' he answered. 'I've gone outside a few times. But you're right, essentially. I've been here since the first wave of disruption hit, studying that discontinuity you came through. But you – you've been moving around. And you say there're discontinuities that move?'

'Some of them travel across country,' I said. 'Where they've gone by, the land's changed. It's either changed into what it's going to be sometime in the future, or into what it was, once, in the past.'

'Very interesting ...' the voice was thoughtful. 'Tell me, are there many people out there, where the moving dis – time lines are?'

'No,' I said. 'It's been some weeks and I've covered a lot of ground. But I've only found a handful. The Hawaiian Islands seem to have come through pretty well. You can hear broadcasting regularly from there on short wave and other stations on the radio, now and then—'

'Yes, I know,' the voice was still thoughtful. 'I thought it was the discontinuities cutting off most of the reception.'

'I doubt it,' I said. 'I think there just aren't many people still left in the world. What was this place?'

'A federal installation. Research and testing,' said the voice, absently. 'What's it like out there?'

'It's like a world-sized crazy quilt, cut up into all sorts of different time areas, marked off one from each other by the mistwalls – by the time lines or discontinuities. The big problem is the situation's still changing. Every moving time line changes everything where it passes.'

I stopped talking. His voice did not pick up the conversation. I was busy thinking about the words 'research and testing.'

'You said you'd been studying the time line, there,' I said. 'What have you learned so far?'

'Not much,' his voice was more distant now, as if he had moved away from the microphone over which he had been speaking, or was caught up in some other activity, so that he was giving me only a part of his attention. 'What you call the mistwall appearance seems to be a matter of conflicting air currents and temperature differentials between the two zones. But there doesn't seem to be any material barrier ... you say they sometimes move?'

'That's right,' I said. 'Any reason why they shouldn't?'

'No, I suppose ... yes,' he said. 'There's a reason. As far as I've been able to measure, these lines of discontinuity stretch out beyond the reach of any instruments I have. In other words, they go right off into space. You'd assume any network of forces that massive would have to be in balance. But if certain of the lines are moving, then it has to be a dynamic, not a static, balance; and that means ...'

'What?'

'I don't know,' he said. 'Maybe I'm just letting my human ideas of size and distance influence me. But I've got trouble imagining something that big, shifting around internally.'

He stopped talking. I waited for him to start up again. But he did not.

'Look,' I said. 'I just sort of ran from this overall situation, the way you'd run for shelter from a thunderstorm, for the first few weeks. But now I'm trying to find out if there isn't some way to get on top of the situation – to control it—'

'Control?'

I waited a second; but he did not say any more.

'What's the matter?' I asked. 'Did I say some kind of dirty word?'

'You don't understand,' he said. 'If the whole disturbance is bigger than our planet, possibly system-wide – and in some sort of dynamic balance, the idea of controlling it is ...' He hesitated. For the first time there was something like emotion in his voice. 'Don't you realize we never have been able to control even a hurricane – no, not even a thunderstorm like the one you were talking about – when this first hit us. Have you any idea of the magnitude of the forces involved in something like this, if it's stretching all over the solar system?'

'What makes you think it is?' I asked.

He did not answer.

'All right,' I said, after a moment. 'If you're not going to talk, let me out of here and we'll say goodbye. I was going to invite you to come along with me – out where you can study the moving lines as well as this static one. But I gather that's not the way you like to work.'

I turned on my heel, went back to the stairway door and pushed. But it was still locked.

'Wait,' he said. 'Do you have other people with you?'

'Yes,' I told him. 'How about you? Are you alone here?'

'That's right,' he said. 'There were a couple of hundred people in the installation here, when the disruption first hit. When I got my senses back, I was the only one left. I was in the hyperbaric chamber at the time – not that I can figure out why that should have made a difference.'

'I've got an idea about that,' I said. 'I think some of us are just naturally immune – statistical survivors.'

'Survivors.'

'Of the time changes. It's only a thought. Don't ask me for details.'

'An interesting thought ...'

The voice trailed off. Down the long inner wall of the corridor, one of the doors opened, and a short, lightly-boned figure in white slacks and white shirt stepped out and came toward me. He was so small that my first thought was that he could not be more than twelve or fourteen years old in spite of his adult voice; but when he got closer, I saw that his face was the face of a man in his late teens or early twenties. He came up to me and offered me his hand.

'Bill Gault,' he said. It was a strong name for someone that light.

I shook hands with him.

'Marc Despard,' I answered.

'I think I'd like to go with you, after all,' he said.

I studied him. He was in no way frail or abnormal, just light and small. At the same time, his lack of size and the spurious air of being half-grown about him, made me hesitate now at the thought of adding him to our party. I had just not expected anyone so ... so physically insignificant, to be the person behind the voice I had been talking with. For a moment I felt a touch of exasperation. All my life, until I had run into the girl and the crazy cat, I had gotten by nicely with no responsibility for anyone but myself. But since this damned time storm started, it seemed I had done nothing else but play guardian and protector – to girls, leopards, women and children – and from the look of Bill Gault, I now had another responsibility on my hands. I could imagine what would happen if this featherweight should try to stand up alone to one of Tek's men, for example.

'Well, you can't just walk out there like that,' I said. 'Haven't you got some heavier clothes and some hiking boots? And if you've got a gun of any kind around, bring that along, too, with whatever in the way of a pack and extra clothing you can scrape up.'

'Oh, I'm all prepared,' Bill Gault said. 'I've had things ready for some time, in case I did decide to leave.'

And you know – he had. He took me down the corridor to a room where he outfitted himself in synthetic wool and leather gear that filled me with envy. Evidently, this installation had been testing, among other things, various kinds of special-duty outer-wear for the armed services. When he was done, he looked like an officer in the ski troops, lacking only the skis. The well-stuffed backpack he wore was a marvel; and he had both a revolver and the latest in army lightweight, automatic rifles.

I looked at the rifle particularly.

'You don't have another one like that lying around, do you?' I asked.

'This is the only one,' he said. 'But there's a machine pistol, if you'd like it.'

I looked at him. He had looked so ready in his outdoor garb, it had been hard for me to remember that he had been boxed up here since the time storm had started. But one good innocent sentence like that brought back the realization in a hurry.

'You've got ammunition for it?'

'Lots of ammunition,' he said.

'And,' I said, 'you were actually going to let us walk off without it? You were going to leave it behind?'

'Well, you've already got a rifle,' he said, nodding at the 30.06. 'And a machine pistol's not very practical for hunting.'

I shook my head.

'Get it,' I said, 'and as much ammunition for it as you think I can reasonably carry.'

He did. It was an Uzi. And the damn fool would have left it behind.

'Let's go,' I said, loading my pockets and belt with the spare clips he had brought, until I felt heavy enough to walk bow-legged. 'That is, unless you've got some other useful surprises to spring on me.'

'Nothing I can think of,' he said. 'Food—'

'Food's no real problem,' I said. 'There seems to be canned goods enough to last the few of us who're left for the rest of our lifetimes. Come on.'

He led me out. The door opened this time when I pushed on it. We went down the stairs and out of the building; and I led him back to the mistwall.

'What should I expect?' he asked, as we came up to it.

His tone was so casual that, for a second, I did not understand. Then I looked at him and saw that his face was pale. Calm, but pale.

'You're thinking of how it was when the time storm first caught you?' I said. He nodded. 'It won't be that bad. It seems to get easier with experience. Hang on to my belt, though, if you want; and if I feel you let go, I'll put down the rifle and lug you through myself. But try and stay on your feet if you can, because we can use both these guns if we can get them out.'

He nodded again and reached out to hook fingers in my belt.

'You'll have to close your eyes against the dust when we get close,' I said. 'Just concentrate on keeping on your feet, and staying with me.'

We went into the mistwall then. It was not bad at all for me, this time; but I could imagine how it might be for him. I was so undisturbed by the passage through that I had attention to spare when I heard Marie's voice on the far side of the mistwall, as we started to come out of the far side of it.

'... shoot it!' Marie was crying, almost hysterically.

'No,' said another voice. 'If you make them hurt him at all, I'll shoot *you!*'

It was the girl talking and making the longest speech I had ever heard her utter.

13

I took a few more steps forward out of the dust and opened my eyes. There was a regular convention in session in the hollow where I had left just Marie, Wendy and the dogs. They, of course, were still there; and all the dogs were on guard position, not making a sound. Wendy was holding tight to her mother, and Marie was facing away from me.

Beyond Marie were the girl and Sunday. The girl sat cross-legged on the ground, with the .22 rifle aimed at Marie. The girl's back was against the back of Sunday. He also was seated, on his haunches, and looking bored – but the tip of his tail was twitching ominously. He faced outward at a half-ring of figures, all with their rifles facing in Sunday's direction but looking momentarily baffled. Tek and his gang had come visiting us again and, apparently, encountered a problem.

The appearance of myself and Bill Gault out of the mistwall did nothing to make their problem any easier. In fact, clearly it came as a severe jolt. They stared at us as if Bill and I were ghosts materializing before their eyes; and a sudden intuitive conclusion clicked into place in the back of my mind. Just as I once had, obviously they were in the habit of avoiding mistwalls. No doubt, everybody still on the face of the earth today avoided them, instinctively, remembering the emotional upset and discomfort of their first experience with any part of the time storm. And here were Bill and I, strolling out of this particular mistwall as casually as walking from one room into another.

Hard on the heels of that bit of understanding came another. The scrap of overheard conversation I had heard suddenly resolved itself. Clearly, the 'it' Marie had been telling Tek and his men to shoot had been Sunday; and, just as clearly, Sunday and the girl had come here hunting me – which meant that Tek and company had probably been following them, as well as the dogs and us, all this time.

I had gotten this far with my thoughts, when the frozen moment in which the girl and Tek's gang stared at me was abruptly and joyously smashed asunder by Sunday. Plainly, he heard, smelled, or otherwise recognized me in spite of his back being turned. He jumped to his feet, turned about, and came bounding at me like a kitten, purring like an outboard motor and stropping himself up against me with unrestrained enthusiasm.

I had a second to brace myself, but being braced did not help much. When a hundred and forty pound leopard throws an affectionate shoulderblock into your midsection, you realize the advantages of four legs over two. At least when one cat makes loving demonstrations to another, the recipient has a couple of spare feet to prop himself upright with. I staggered and nearly went down. Meanwhile, Marie had turned around to see what was going on and saw me.

'Marc!' she cried.

There was so much desperate relief in her voice, I was almost ready to forget that she had seemed on the verge of entering into partnership with the enemy to get rid of Sunday and the girl. But our difficulties were not at an end, because now she also came to throw her arms around me.

'You've been gone for hours!' she said.

I had no time to point out that I had not even been gone one hour, at the most; because Sunday, seeing her coming, had already classed her as a potential attacker and finally decided to do something about her. I fended her off with one arm, while just managing to slap Sunday hard on the nose to check the lethal paw-swipe with which he would have turned our little reunion into a very real tragedy.

I succeeded – but of course, success left me with a rebuffed woman and a rebuffed leopard at once, on my hands. Marie was hurt that I should shove her off. Sunday was destroyed. I tried to soothe the leopard with my hands and the woman with my voice at the same time.

'Marie – no!' I said. 'Bless you! I love you – but stand back, will you? Sunday's likely to claw you in half.'

'Then what are you doing petting the animal?' cried Marie.

'So he won't get loose and claw somebody else! For Christ's sake—' I yelled at her, 'stand back, will you? Keep Wendy back—'

I was running out of breath. Sunday had forgiven me and was once more trying to throw frantic, affectionate shoulder blocks into me.

'Down, Sunday!' I managed, finally, to wrestle the leopard to the ground and lie on him while he licked cheerfully and lovingly at any part of my person that was within tongue-reach. I looked up and glared at the girl.

'What are you doing on this side of the river?' I snarled.

'He pulled himself loose!' she said.

I went on glaring at her. She was an absolute, bare-faced liar. Sunday would have choked himself to death on those chains I had used to restrain him, before he would have been able to pull himself free. Of course, the girl had turned him loose herself, deliberately, so that they could both follow me. I knew it, and she knew I knew it; and I could see she didn't care a hoot that I knew it.

Girl, leopard and woman – I could not do a thing with any of them. I looked around for something in my own class to tie into; and my gaze lighted on Tek. The man was two axe-handles across the shoulders and besides being six years or more younger than I, had that easy, muscular balance of movement that signals the natural athlete. He could, almost undoubtedly, have held me off with one hand while beating me to death with the other; but just at that moment, if I had not been occupied with the absolute necessity of keeping Sunday flattened out, I would have picked a fight with Tek for the simple joy of having something legitimate to hit.

I had dropped both the machine pistol and the rifle, necessarily, needing both hands to handle Sunday and Marie. But the pistol was only a short arms-length from me. I scooped it up, now, pointing it at Tek, and noticed that Bill Gault had maintained enough presence of mind to lift his army automatic rifle into firing position under his arm. In terms of sheer firepower, we two more than matched up to the hunting rifles carried by Tek and his men, and the dogs could mop up any other difference that existed. But then, Tek took me completely by surprise.

'Hold it!' he shouted, before I could say anything more. 'Hold it – I'm with you!'

To my astonishment, he threw his rifle toward Marie and walked unarmed up to us and turned around to face his former crew. He grinned at Marie and nodded pleasantly to me.

'Just give the orders,' he said to me. 'I won't pick up my gun unless you say so.'

There had been a moment of frozen disbelief on the part of his men when he had switched sides. But now there was a general outcry from them.

'Tek!'

'Tek, you bastard – what are you doing to us?'

'Tek, damn it!'

'Tek ...'

'Sorry,' he said, shrugging his shoulders and smiling at them. 'I can tell when I've run into a better team, that's all. If you're bright, you'll come over on their side, too. If you're not, don't blame me.'

Three of the five of them began to argue with him all at once. He said nothing, though, and gradually their voices died down. One of the two men who had not tried to argue him out of it finally spoke. He was a narrow-bodied, balding man in his late thirties or early forties, with a sharp, hard face.

'That was all pretty quick and easy,' he said. 'Almost like it was planned, the quick way he went over to them. Come on, the rest of you. Let's clear out and leave Tek with them, if that's what he wants.'

The men shifted uneasily. I looked at Tek, but he was staring off at the horizon, ignoring the whole matter with an indifference as sublime as Sunday's could be on occasion. But the other man who had not argued with Tek now spoke up.

'Sure, Garney,' he said. 'Let's all go off and let you run things instead of Tek – is that it? I'm sticking with him. Come on, everybody.'

He walked across to us and laid his rifle down beside Tek's. But I noticed he laid it down carefully. It was a bolt action, and he had the bolt uppermost; and when he stepped back from it, he was only a couple of feet away from a quick grab to regain it.

Slowly, one by one, the others came over. All except the man called Garney, who had suggested they leave Tek behind. When at last they were all standing with us, leaving Garney alone, Tek took his eyes off the horizon slowly and gazed at him.

'Well,' he said, gently. 'So long then, Garney. Maybe you better head off in a different direction from where we're going.'

'All right, Tek,' said Garney, 'that's all right. I wouldn't want to have anything more to do with any of you.'

He backed up a few steps, watching us. Then, evidently deciding that it was simply not practical to back the long distance it would take to get him out of our rifles' range, he turned his back and walked swiftly away. He went off, up over the lip of the hollow and disappeared.

Tek's men who had joined us moved to pick up their rifles.

'Leave them lay!' said Tek.

They stopped, staring at him; and he nodded in my direction. 'Leave them, until the chief here tells us what to do.'

I became suddenly conscious of the fact that they were all staring at me; and that I was still lying sprawled out on Sunday, trying to control him with one hand, while I clung to the Uzi and attempted to keep it pointed, with the other. Sunday had quieted down somewhat by this time; so I scrambled to my feet, cuffed him lightly when he tried to recommence his greetings to me and faced Tek with his men.

'All right,' I said, 'Let's talk about this. I don't remember hanging out any sign asking for volunteers.'

Tek shrugged.

'All I can do is try,' he said.

'Marc!' said Marie, sharply. She looked at me for a second as if she was going to say something then and there, then closed her mouth and crossed the little distance between us. This time, I was glad to see, she made it a point to approach me on the opposite side from Sunday. She came up to me and took hold of my arm, whispering in my ear.

'Marc, are you crazy?' she demanded. 'Isn't it better to have these men as friends, instead of enemies?'

I was about to answer sharply, when I thought better of it. I nodded to Tek.

'Ask him how he'd answer that,' I said out loud. 'Go ahead.'

Something like a dark shadow seemed to pass across Marie's face; and she looked at me oddly. But she stepped back from me without a word and turned to face Tek.

'I asked Marc if it wasn't better to have you as friends instead of enemies,' she said, loudly and clearly. 'He said to ask you how you'd answer that.'

'Sure,' said Tek, 'if I was him, I'd want to know how you'd know you could trust us.'

She stared at him. He smiled back.

'You see, now,' he said, 'I'm not trying to put anything over on anybody. I volunteered to join you all on my own. It's up to chief there – what did you say his name was? Marc? It's up to Marc.'

'And up to me, too!' said Marie, sharply.

'And you, too, of course, ma'am,' said Tek. 'But – no offence to you and your dogs – but I'd worry a bit more about Marc, here, if it came right down to picking one of you over the other to have trouble with. Him, his pet leopard, and his friend there.'

He nodded to Bill Gault. I had almost forgotten Bill. Now, I called him over and introduced him to Marie, Wendy, and the girl, while still keeping a cautious eye on Tek and the others. All the time, the back of my mind was working. The truth of the matter was, if Bill and I were to dig into this business of the time storm seriously, we would need troops to take the ordinary work and fighting off our hands. Plus the fact that we might well be adventuring through a mistwall into a situation where a number of people with guns were needed.

Also, something Tek had just said had sparked off a notion in the back of my mind. While listing the things that might worry him about having me for an enemy, Tek had specified Sunday as one of them. I had grown so used to Sunday that I had almost forgotten how unnatural it was to other people to see a full grown leopard tagging after me like a kitten. The tendency was for the watchers to assume I had a lot more control over him than I actually did – as well as to assume that he was a great deal brighter and more responsive than his cat brain would ordinarily allow. There was a bluff I could run.

'All right,' I said, 'I'll tell you what we can do. We can take all of you on a probation, and see how you'll do. Leave your guns piled where they are; and if any of you have to go someplace away from the camp, where you might run into trouble, one or two of the dogs can go with you. Meanwhile, I'll set the leopard to watch you. He may not be able to tell me what you talk about; but if any of you make any move that looks as if you mean to hurt one of us, he can tear you apart before you'll know what hit you.'

I looked them over.

'Well?' I said. 'How about it? Want to join us on those terms?'

They looked at me hesitantly – all but Tek. Then they looked at Tek.

'Marc—' began Marie, and then checked herself.

'What?' I looked at her.

'Nothing,' she said. I looked back at the men.

'How about it?'

'Speaking, just for myself, of course,' said Tek, 'I think that's fine – real fine. I've got no intentions of being anything but a good friend to you all anyway, so your leopard doesn't worry me a bit. But that's just me. The others are going to make their deals with you on their own.'

'All right,' I said. 'Suppose the seven of you find a place to sit down together over there about ten yards away from your guns and the rest of us. I've got some things to do.'

Tek led off agreeably. He sat down, and the rest followed.

I turned my attention to the girl, who was now getting to her feet. She had been holding her rifle grimly aimed at Marie, all the while, but now she lowered it.

'Are you all right?' I asked her. 'You haven't been hurt or anything? Have you been getting enough to eat?'

She looked at me with a very strange expression. For a moment I swore she was going to answer me. But habit took over. She turned without a word and walked away from me to where Sunday was, a few steps away, and began petting him, with her back to me.

'I take it that means "yes"!' I called after her. She did not reply, of course. The voice of Marie spoke in low, but tight, tones in my ear.

'Marc, she's not staying, she or that leopard, either.'

I turned to stare at her. She looked ready to fight.

'Of course they're staying,' I said.

'Then I'm leaving, with Wendy and the dogs.'

'And Tek and his men right behind you,' I said. I had not meant to put it that bluntly; but I was just about out of patience. 'Go ahead.'

She glared at me fiercely for a moment, then turned and went to Wendy. But she made no move to begin a departure.

I looked around for Bill Gault, saw him standing waiting a little distance away and beckoned him over to me. He came and I led him off out of low-voiced earshot of the rest.

'I didn't mean to lead you into a touchy situation like this,' I said. 'You can go back to your installation, if you feel like it, and I won't blame you.'

'No,' he said. 'You were right. I couldn't really learn anything more, shut up there. The only way to study the situation is to look at as many of the discontinuities as I can find. We ought to keep on the move and, every time we get near one, have a look at it.'

'Good,' I told him. 'By the way, you never did tell me what your field is. Were you a research scientist, a lab man, or what?'

'Well, no,' he said. 'I do have a degree in physics ... but actually, I was just technical editor for the installation.'

He gazed at me uncomfortably.

'Technical editor!' I said.

'That's right.'

'Well, what the hell can you do, then?' I demanded. I was about at the end of my temper, anyway; and this last disappointment threatened to cut me loose. I had taken it for granted he was some sort of scientific expert, at least.

'I can do a lot!' Bill said, swiftly. 'I can observe, make tests and record – and I know something about physics, as I said. Also, I've been up to my eyebrows in everything we worked on at the installation for the five years I've been there. I'm not helpless.'

'All right,' I answered. 'But you're going to have to show me.'

He did. During the two weeks that followed, my opinion of him, starting from the sub-basement level of that moment, went steadily up. He had brought with him in his backpack some remarkably small, but durable instruments to measure temperature, air pressure, wind velocity and humidity, plus a few less common things like electrostatic levels and magnetic flows. He also designed a number of long rods for pushing these into and through a mistwall, while we stood safely outside.

This is not to say we did not enter the walls. In the final essential, it was necessary to go through them. As we moved across country in the days following the addition of Tek and his men to our group – to say nothing of Bill himself, and the rejoining of the girl and Sunday – we ran into at least one, and sometimes more, mistwalls a day. We would make all the tests on them that Bill could think of; but once he had the results noted down, it was a matter of he and I going through them, that is, unless it were a moving mistwall we were investigating, in which case we spotted them early through binoculars and moved to outflank and see behind them.

We did not go into them as blindly as I had gone into earlier ones. Among other designs of Bill's were rod or rope devices to be thrown through the mistwall and dragged back, to give us an idea of the ground situation and atmosphere beyond. The third time we used them, what we learned kept us from walking off a cliff on the far side of the mistwall, before we would have had a chance to open our eyes. But, in the end, in almost every instance, we still had to go through personally.

We found a number of different situations, from raw desert to empty city, on the far sides of these walls; and we profited from what we found. Fourteen days after our group had come to its full size, we were riding in a sort of motorcade, all of us, including the dogs. Our vehicles consisted of a couple of brand new motor homes for sleeping and living quarters, preceded by a couple of jeep carryalls and followed by a pickup truck, all three smaller vehicles with four-wheel drive, carrying the armed members of the party while we were on the move. With wheels under us, outflanking the moving mistwalls became not only easier, but more certain.

There were four of us who carried weapons to start with – myself, Marie, Bill, and also the girl. She had become attached to that .22 of hers. In fact, she refused to give it up, and when I had her fire it for me, I found that she had not merely kept it in good condition, she was developing into a good shot. At short to medium range in rough country, a light gun like a .22 could be as effective as an elephant gun, in every way but impact, if the person shooting it was accurate enough; and I was glad to have her able to use it.

By the end of the first week we added a fifth gunner – Tek. The man had worked hard to do anything that was asked of him; until he had begun finally to make a believer even out of me. The conclusion I came to at last was that whatever it was he wanted, for the moment, at least, it included cooperation with the rest of us. I walked him off a short distance from our night camp on the end of our seventh day together and asked him a lot of questions about himself.

The answers were unhesitating and interesting. His full name was Techner, pronounced 'Tek-ner,' Wilson Ambervoy – he had been named for a couple of grandparents. He had been good enough as a high school football player to get a scholarship to the University of Indiana – and Indiana had fielded a Big Ten team which did not play mediocre football. However, he had not taken the study end of college seriously and had flunked out midway through his sophomore year. Luckily – he was usually lucky, Tek told me frankly – he got a job immediately with an uncle who owned a paint store. The uncle was in poor health and inside of half a year, Tek was managing the store. About that time, he got into real estate. With the cosignature of his paint store uncle, Tek swung a mortgage and bought a twelve-unit apartment building. To run it, he brought in a friend named Ricky, a drinking buddy the same age as himself, who had a knack for card games and was in the habit of having a poker session in his former bachelor apartment every night after the bars closed.

He and Tek remodelled two of the apartment units of their building into one large one to make, as Tek put it, 'a pretty impressive-looking cave'; and the after-hours card games expanded. Meanwhile, they made it a point to rent the rest of the units to girl friends of Tek's; and a number of these would also drop in on the card game after hours to make sandwiches, pour drinks and watch the game. If the supply of these girls ran short, Tek went out prospecting and found some more.

The result was that there were always a number of good-looking girls around the card game, and young male strangers began dropping in for a hand or two, just to meet them. Tek's buddy did well with his cards. He paid Tek a percentage of his winnings as rent for the apartment; and the other units became very much in demand among Tek's girl friends, so that he was able to raise the rent several times and still keep every unit filled.

'… You understand,' Tek said to me. 'Nobody cheated in the card games. There was nothing professional about the girls. Just everybody had a good time, and Ricky and me had it for free – well, maybe we came out a little bit ahead, but when we did, we just spent it on more good stuff …'

And then the time storm had come along; Tek had been taking a nap. When he woke, he was alone in the apartment building. Alone in an empty town. He ended up going out adventuring, and one by one, he ran into the other men of his gang, whom he recruited out of a sort of pack-instinct for leadership.

'But that wasn't really what I was after,' Tek said to me as we walked together, with the camp and the fire we always built for it distant in the twilight before the small town on the outskirts of which we had stopped for the night. 'You know, even before this time storm, or whatever you call it, came along, I was beginning to get a little filled up on the apartment, the fun and games, and all the rest of it. I was beginning to want to do something – I don't know what. I still don't know. But just roaming around, living off the country, isn't it either.'

Tek stopped and looked at me in the growing dimness.

'They're not bright, you know,' he said, 'those five back there I picked up. Garney was the brightest of them all; and he was nothing you could build on. Now, little old Bill Gault there, he's bright; and you are, too. Someday maybe you'll tell me what you did before this happened and where you came from; and I'll bet it'll be interesting. And this business of yours with the mistwalls – it might lead to something. That's what I want. Something.'

He stopped talking.

'All right,' I said. 'Let's head back.'

Halfway back to the camp, I came to a conclusion.

'You can start carrying a rifle tomorrow,' I told him. 'But don't forget you're still under orders. Mine.'

'Right,' he said. 'But I'd be on your side anyway.'

'For now, you would,' I said dryly.

He laughed.

'Come on, man,' he said. 'Anything can happen if you look far enough into the future. If anything comes along to change the situation that much, you'll know about it as soon as I will.'

So we moved on with five gunners instead of four, and things went almost suspiciously well. The plan Bill and I had evolved was based on our theory that our best chance to get on top of the time storm was to keep looking for the most advanced future segment we could find. Hopefully the more advanced an area we could hit, the more likely we were to find the equipment or the people to help us deal with the time storm. If we were going to be able to do something about it, that was where we were most likely to find the means. If we were going to be forced to live with it – perhaps we could find the techniques and patterns we needed in something beyond our present time slot.

As I had discovered earlier, however, the time changes seemed to be weighed toward the past, rather than toward the future. We found three futuristic-looking segments behind mistwalls; but they were either apparently stripped of anything or anyone useful, or else their very futureness was in doubt. It was two weeks and two days before we found a segment that was undeniably part of a city belonging to a time yet to come – a far future time, we thought at first. Though of course, there was no way we might tell how much time would have been necessary to make changes.

This particular segment was behind the second mistwall we had encountered that day. The first had showed us nothing but unrelieved forest, stretched out over descending hills to a horizon that was lost in haze, but which must have been many miles off. Such a landscape might be part of a future segment, but it was not passable by our wheeled vehicles, and it promised nothing. We pulled back through the mistwall – it was then about ten in the morning – paused for an early lunch and went on.

About 2:30 P.M., we saw a second, stationary mistwall and moved up to it. We were travelling along a gravel road at the time, through what seemed like an area of small farms. The mistwall sliced across a cornfield and obliterated the corner of what had once been a tall, white and severely narrow farmhouse – an American Gothic among farmhouses.

We left our motorcade in the road, and Bill and I walked up the farm road into the farmyard, carrying most of the instruments. The rest straggled along behind us but stayed back, as I had repeatedly warned them to, a good twenty yards from where we were working.

I said the rest stayed back – I should have said all the rest but Sunday. The leopard had put up with seeing me go through mistwalls for about two days after he and the girl had rejoined us and had contented himself with overwhelming me with pleased greetings when I returned. Like all our humans, he obviously had a powerfully remembered fear of the time lines, in spite of having crossed one at Marie's place. But after Bill and I had penetrated through the third wall we had encountered, I had heard something odd behind me and looked to see Sunday coming through the mistwall behind us, tossing his head, his eyes closed and mewling like a lost kitten. He broke out and came to me – still with his eyes closed and evidently depending on nose alone – and it had taken me fifteen minutes to soothe him back to quietness. However, going back through the mistwall later, he had been much less upset; and two days later he was accompanying us with the indifference of a veteran. Of course, as soon as he started coming through the mistwalls after us, the girl did too. But it was possible to order her not to; Sunday could not be kept back.

So, in this case, as had become his habit, Sunday followed Bill and me up to the mistwall and waited while we made our measurements and tests. These showed it to be little different from the many other walls we had tested. But when we finally went through this time, we found a difference.

We came out in a – what? A courtyard, a square, a plaza ... take your pick. It was an oval of pure white surface and behind, all about it, rose a city of equal whiteness. Not in the whiteness of new concrete, but the whiteness of veinless, milk-coloured marble. And there was no sound about it. Not even the cries of birds or insects. No sound at all.

14

'... *We were the first*,' wrote Samuel Taylor Coleridge in his *Rhyme Of The Ancient Mariner*—
'*Who ever burst,*
'*Into that silent sea ...*'
If you know that bit of poetry, if you love poetry the way I do, you will be able to feel something like the feeling that hit Bill and me when we emerged from the mistwall into that city. Those lines give it to you. It was with us and that city beyond our time, as it had been with that sea and Coleridge's Mariner. It was a city of silence, silence such as neither of us had ever heard, and such as we had never suspected could exist – until that moment. We were trapped by that silence, held by it, suddenly motionless and fixed, for fear of intruding one tiny noise into that vast, encompassing and majestic void of soundlessness, like flower petals suddenly encased in plastic. It held us both, frozen; and the fear of being the first to break it was like a sudden hypnotic clutch on our minds, too great for us to resist.

We were locked in place; and perhaps we might have stood there until we dropped, if it had been left to our own wills alone to save us.

But we were rescued. Shatteringly and suddenly, echoing and reechoing off to infinity among the white towers and ways before us, came the loud scrape of claws on a hard surface; and a broad, warm, hard, leopard-head butted me in the ribs, knocking me off my frozen balance to fall with a deafening clatter to the pavement, as my gun and my equipment went spilling all around me.

With that, the spell was smashed. It had only been that first, perfect silence that operated so powerfully on our emotions, and that, once destroyed, could never be recreated. It was an awesome, echoing place, that city – like some vast, magnificent tomb. But it was just a place once its first grip on us had been loosed. I picked myself up.

'Let's have a look around,' I said to Bill.

He nodded. He was not, as I was, a razor addict; and over the two weeks or more since I had met him, he had been letting his beard go with only occasional scrapings. Now a faint soft fuzz darkened his lower face. Back beyond the mistwall, with his young features, this had looked more ridiculous than anything else; but here against the pure whiteness all around us and under a cloudless, windless sky, the beard, his outdoor clothing, his rifle and instruments, all combined to give him a savage intruder's look. And if he looked so, just from being unshaved, I could only guess how I might appear, here in this unnaturally perfect place.

We went forward, across the level floor of the plaza, or whatever, on which we had entered. At its far side were paths leading on into the city; and as we stepped on one, it began to move, carrying us along with it. Sunday went straight up in the air, cat-fashion, the moment he felt it stir under his feet, and hopped back off it. But when he saw it carrying me away from him, he leaped back on and came forward to press hard against me as we rode – it was the way he had pressed against me on the raft during the storm, before he, the girl and I had had to swim for shore.

The walkway carried us in among the buildings, and we were completely surrounded by milky whiteness. I had thought at first that the buildings had no windows; but apparently they had – only of a different sort than anything I had ever imagined. Seeing the windows was apparently all a matter of angle. One moment it seemed I would be looking at a blank wall – the next I would have a glimpse of some shadowed or oddly angled interior. It was exactly the same sort of glimpse that you get of the mercury line in a fever thermometer when you rotate the thermometer to just the proper position. But there was no indication of life, anywhere.

Around us, over us, the city was lifeless. This was more than a fact of visual observation. We could feel the lack of anything living in all the structures around us like an empty ache in the mind. It was not a painful or an ugly feeling, but it was an unpleasant feeling just for the reason that it was not a natural one. That much massive construction, empty, ready and waiting, was an anomaly that ground against the human spirit. The animal spirit as well, for that matter; because Sunday continued to press against me for reassurance as we went. We stepped off the walkway at last – it stopped at once as we did so – and looked around at a solid mass of white walls, all without visible windows or doors.

'Nothing here,' said Bill Gault after a while. 'Let's go back now.'

'No,' I said. 'Not yet.'

I could not have explained to him just why I did not want to give up. It was the old reflex at the back of my head, working and working away at something, and feeling that it was almost on top of that missing clue for which it searched. There had to be something here in this empty city that tied in with our search to make reason out of the time storm, the time lines, and all the business of trying to handle them or live with them. I could feel it.

'There's no one here,' Bill said.

I shook my head.

'Let's get inside,' I said. 'Any one of these buildings will do.'

'Get inside? How?' He looked around us at the marble-white, unbroken walls.

'Smash our way in somehow,' I said. I was looking around myself for something to use as a tool. 'If nothing else, the machine pistol ought to make a hole we can enlarge—'

'Never mind,' he said, in a sort of sigh. I turned back to look at him and saw him already rummaging in his pack. He came out with what looked like a grey cardboard package, about ten inches long and two wide, two deep. He opened one end and pulled out part of a whitish cylinder wrapped in what looked like wax paper.

The cylinder of stuff was, evidently, about the same consistency as modelling clay. With its wax paper covering off, it turned out to be marked in sections, each about two inches long. Bill pulled off a couple of sections, rewrapped the rest and put it away, back in his pack. The two sections he had pulled out squeezed between his hands into a sort of thin pancake, which he stepped over and pressed against one of the white walls. It clung there, about three feet above the ground.

'What is it?' I asked.

'Explosive,' he said. 'A form of plastic—' He pronounced it plas-*teek*, with the emphasis on the second syllable – 'but improved. It doesn't need any fuse. You can do anything with it safely, even shoot a bullet into it. Nothing happens until it's spread out like that, thin enough so that sufficient area can react to the oxygen in the air.'

He moved back from the wall where he had spread out the pancake, beckoning me along with him. I came, without hesitating.

We stood about thirty feet off, waiting. For several minutes nothing happened. Then there was an insignificant little *poof* that would hardly have done credit to a one inch firecracker; but an area of the white wall at least six feet in diameter seemed to suck itself inward and disappear. Beyond, there was a momentary patch of blackness; and then we were looking into a brightly lit chamber or room of some sort, with

335

several large solid-looking shapes sitting on its floor area, shapes too awkwardly formed to be furniture and too purposelessly angular to seem as if they were machinery.

Like the room, like the walls, they were milky white in colour. But that appearance did not last long.

Without warning, the damaged wall blushed. I don't know how else to describe it. From white it turned blood-red, the reddishness most intense around the edges of the hole blown in the wall and toning down from there as it spread outward. And it spread with unbelievable speed. In a moment, the colour change had swept over all the walls and pavement around us and raced on to turn the city, the whole city, to red.

Far off among the buildings, a faint, siren sound began. It was uncomfortably as if the city was a living thing we had wounded, and now it was not only bleeding internally but crying.

But this was just the beginning of the change.

'Look!' said Bill.

I turned back from gaping at the city to see Bill pointing once more at the hole in the wall. The red around the ragged rim of broken material had darkened and deepened until it was almost black – a thick and angry colour of red. But now, as I watched, that dark-red edge began to develop a hairline of white – glowing white-hot-looking brightness beyond the edge of darkest red. And this tiny edge of white thickened and widened, tinged with pink where it came up against the dark red, but continuing to thicken in whiteness on its other, broken edge that touched only air.

'It's healing itself,' said Bill.

I had not realized it until he put it into words, but that was exactly what was happening. The white that was appearing was new wall surface, growing down and inward, beginning to fill the hole that we had blown in the wall.

I took a step forward as soon as I realized this, then stopped. The hole was already too small for me to go through, easily; and those white-glowing edges did not look like anything I would want to brush up against on my way past.

'All right,' I said to Bill, 'let's try it someplace else, and next time be a little quicker about going through, once we've opened it up.'

'No. Wait,' he said, catching hold of my arm as I started off to a further section of the wall. 'Listen!'

I stopped and listened. The distant, wailing, siren-sound had been continuing steadily, but without any indication of coming any closer to us and the scene of the action. But now that Bill had my attention,

I heard another sound superimposed on the first. It was the noise of a faint, dull-toned but regular clanking. The sort of thing you might hear from a large toy tractor, if it had been constructed, with its movable parts, out of plastic rather than metal. And this sound was coming toward us.

I had the machine pistol up and aimed without thinking; and Bill had his gun also pointed, when the source of the noise came around the corner of the same building where we had blown the opening in the wall. It came toward us, apparently either not understanding, or understanding but ignoring, the menace of our guns. I stared at it, unbelievingly, because I had a hard time making up my mind whether it was creature or machine.

By the time I had reluctantly concluded it was a creature, it was less than a dozen feet from us and it stopped. A machine I might have risked pumping a few slugs into. A creature was another matter entirely. Aside from the fact that killing another living thing has some emotional overtones to it, there were a great many more dangerous possibilities involved for us if it was alive, and our hostile response was not successful. So we simply stood and looked it over, and it looked us over.

It looked – it's hard to say how it looked in that first minute. Something like a Saint Bernard-sized, very short-limbed, very heavy-headed, bulldog shape, with a clump of three tails or tentacles, about two feet in length, sprouting from each shoulder. The whole body was covered with rectangular bony plates about a couple of inches at their widest, which flexed at their jointures with the plates surrounding them to allow the body beneath them to move. Smaller plates even covered most of the massive head. The two eyes were brown and large.

'Don't shoot!' I said to Bill, without taking my eyes off the creature.

I don't know what movement of his, if any, triggered off that reaction in me. At the moment, I only know two things. I had been searching from the very beginning, for an x-factor, a Game Warden, a missing piece to the puzzle of the time storm; and the old reliable search-reflex in the back of my mind now was practically shouting at me that this might be it. And – second, but no less important – the whole improbable being radiated an impression of non-enmity. That impressive armour, that ferocious head, somehow added up, not so much to something threatening, as to something rather clumsy and comic – even lovable, like the bulldog it faintly resembled.

Still, I would have had trouble convincing Bill of any of that alone – but luckily, just at that moment, I got corroborative testimony from a completely unexpected source – Sunday. Up until now the leopard had not moved; but now, suddenly, he strolled past me, right up to the creature, and proceeded to strop himself in a friendly manner up one side of it and down the other. He then sniffed it over a few times and gravely returned to me. That did it. Bill lowered his gun.

'Hello,' I said to the creature. The word sounded almost ridiculous in the context of our confrontation, here in this silent, strange place. The creature said nothing.

'I'm Marc Despard,' I said. 'This is Bill Gault.'

Still no answer.

'Marc,' said Bill, in a strained, thin voice. 'Let's start backing up, slowly. If it lets us go, we can back right into the mistwall, and maybe it won't follow us—'

He broke off because some sounds were finally beginning to come from the creature. Sounds that were something like a cross between the internal rumblings of indigestion and the creaking of machinery that had not been used in a long time.

'Due ...' said the creature, in a deep-tone, grating voice. 'Yanglish.'

It fell silent. We waited for more sounds, but none came.

'Start backing if you want,' I answered Bill, still keeping my gaze, however, on the creature. 'I'm going to stay and see if I can't find out something about this.'

'I ...' said the creature, loudly, before Bill could answer me. There was a pause while we waited for more.

'I am ...' it said, after a second. Another pause. Then it continued, in jerks, almost as if it were holding a conversation with itself, except that the pauses between bits of conversation became shorter and shorter until they approached ordinary sentence-length human speech.

'I am ...' said the creature again.

'... Porniarsk.'

'Porniarsk. I am ... an of ...'

'I am Porniarsk Prime Three ... of ... an ...'

'I am Porniarsk Prime Three, an ... avatar ... of Porniarsk ...'

'... Expert in Temporals General. I am the ... third ... avatar of Porniarsk ... who is an ... expert on the Temporal Question.'

'It's a robot of some sort,' said Bill, staring at Porniarsk's avatar.

'No,' it said. 'I *am* Porniarsk. Avatar, secondarily only. I am living – ... alive. As you are.'

'Do we call you Porniarsk?' I asked.

There was a pause, then a new sort of creaking, unused machinery noise; and the heavy head was nodding up and down, so slowly, awkwardly and deliberately that the creature called Porniarsk looked even more comic than before. It broke off its head-movements abruptly at the top of a nod.

'Yes,' it said. 'Porniarsk Prime Three is ... a full name. Call me Porniarsk. Also, *he*. I am ... male.'

'We'll do that,' I said. 'Porniarsk, I'm sorry about damaging your city here. We didn't think there was anyone still around.'

'It is not ... it isn't my city,' said Porniarsk. 'I mean it's neither mine as avatar, nor is it something that belongs to me as Porniarsk. I come from ...'

He had been going great guns, but all at once he was blocked again. We waited, while he struggled with his verbal problem.

'I come from many ... stellar distances away,' he said, finally. 'Also from a large temporal ... time ... distance. But I should say also that, in another measure, I am ... from close to here.'

'Close to this world?' Bill asked.

'Not ...' Porniarsk broke off in order to work at the process of shaking his head this time, 'to this world, generally. Just to ... here, this place, and a few other places on your Earth.'

'Is this place – this city or whatever it is ...' asked Bill, 'from the same time as the time you come from?'

'No,' said Porniarsk. 'No two times can be alike – no more than two grains of sand be identical.'

'We aren't stupid, you know,' said Bill. For the first time I'd known him, there was an edge in his voice. 'If you can tell us that much, you can do a better job of explaining things than you're doing.'

'Not stupid ... ignorant,' said Porniarsk. 'Later, perhaps? I am from far off, spatially; from far off, temporally; but from close, distance-wise. When you broke the wall here, this city signalled; I had been for a long period of my own time on the watch for some such happening at any one of the many spots I could monitor; and when the city signalled, I came.'

'Why is the city so important?' I asked.

'It isn't,' said Porniarsk, swinging his heavy head to look at me. 'You are important. I believe. I'll go with you now unless you reject me; and at last, perhaps we can be of use to ourselves and to the universe.'

I looked at Bill. Bill looked at me.

'Just a minute,' I said. 'I want to look this place over. It's from out of our future, if my guess is right. There may be a lot of things here we can use.'

'Nothing,' said Porniarsk. 'It is only a museum – with all its exhibits taken away long since.'

He made no visible move that my eyes could catch, but suddenly, all the walls about us seemed to suck themselves in and produce circular doorways.

'If you would like to look, do so,' Porniarsk said. He folded his short legs inward under him and went down like a large coffee table with its four supports chopped away by four axemen at once. 'I will wait. Use-time is subjective.'

I was half-ready to take him at his words that the 'city' was no use to us; but Bill was beckoning me away. I followed him away and around a corner, with Sunday trailing along after me, out of sight of Porniarsk. Bill stopped, then, and I stopped. Sunday went on to sniff at an open doorway.

'Listen,' whispered Bill, 'I don't trust it.'

'Him,' I said, absently. 'Porniarsk – he said he was male.'

'He also said he was an avatar,' said Bill. 'The incarnation of a deity.'

Bill's carping pricked me the wrong way.

'– Or the incarnation of an idea, or a philosophy, or an attitude!' I said. 'Why don't you read all of the entry in the dictionary next time?' Abruptly, I realized that he was scared; and my jumping on him was the last sort of move likely to help matters. 'Look, he's just the sort of thing we've been hunting for. Someone out of the future who might be able to help us handle this time storm business.'

'I don't trust ... him,' said Bill stubbornly. 'I think he's just planning to use us.'

'He can't,' I said, without thinking.

'Why not?' Bill stared at me.

He had me, of course. I had responded out of my feelings rather than out of my head – or, to be truthful, out of my reflex for pattern-hunting, which was still yelling that I might have found the missing piece necessary to complete the jigsaw puzzle. I did not know why I was so unthinkingly sure of the fact that while we might be able to use Porniarsk, he could not use us. I had thought that the end result of my certainty about Swannee's survival had taught me some healthy self-doubt. But here I was, certain as hell, all over again.

'I've just got a hunch,' I said to Bill then. 'But in any case, we can't pass him up. We've got to, at least, try to get the information we need out of him. Now, you can see the sense of that, can't you?'

He hesitated in answering. I had hit him on his weak side – the side that believed in scientific question and experimentation.

'Of course you can,' I went on. 'There's no point to anything if we throw away the first good lead we've found to making sense out of things. Let's go back now and take Porniarsk along with us to the rest of them. There'll be plenty of time to find out what he's after personally, once we've got him back in camp. Whatever he's got, I'll feel a lot safer when he's got the dogs, Sunday and the rest of our guns all around him – don't you agree?'

Bill nodded reluctantly.

'All right,' he said. 'But I want to look into a few of these buildings, anyway.'

'We'll do that, then.' I could afford to give in on a small point, now that he'd yielded on the large one. 'But I've got a hunch Porniarsk's right, and there's nothing to find.'

So, accompanied by Sunday, we searched through a couple of the now-open buildings. But it was just as I'd thought. Porniarsk had not been lying so far as we could discover. The buildings were nothing but a lot of empty rooms – in immaculate condition, without a trace of dust or damage – but empty. Echo-empty.

In the end we went back and collected Porniarsk. He clattered to his feet as we came up and fell in step with us when I told him we were headed back through the mistwall to the rest of our people. However, I stopped when we came to the nearer edge of the wall.

'I'd like you to wait here, Porniarsk,' I told him, 'while Bill and I go through first. Give us a chance to tell the rest of our people about you and tone down the surprise when you show up. Is that all right with you?'

'All right,' said Porniarsk, clunking down into lying position again. 'Call when you want me to come after you.'

'We will,' I said.

I led Bill and Sunday back through the mist. When we opened our eyes on the other side, it was to find a deserted, if cozy-looking, farm-yard. The cooktent had been set up in the yard and Marie had both charcoal grilles going, but no one was on duty except the dogs. Clearly, the others were all inside the farmhouse – the very sort of place I had ordered them never to go into unless I told them it was safe, and only after a couple of us had done a room-by-room search with guns, first. There were too many nasty surprises, from booby traps to ambushes, that could be set up in a place like an abandoned building.

'Get out here!' I shouted. 'Get out here, all of you!'

I had the satisfaction of seeing them come scrambling out of the door and even out of a couple of windows, white-faced, possibly thinking we were under attack from somewhere, or perhaps another mistwall was bearing down on us. It was not the best of all possible times to rub a lesson in; but I took a few minutes once they were outside to read them out for what they had done.

'Well, it's ridiculous!' said Marie. 'It isn't as if we walked in there blind. Tek and the girl took their guns and checked it out first.'

Of course that put a different face on the matter, but I was hardly in a position to admit so at the moment. I looked over at Tek and the girl. He, of course, had been too smart from the beginning to make his own excuses; while the girl, of course, was simply following her usual practice of not talking. But I met her eyes now; and grim, angry eyes they were.

'They did, did they?' I said. 'And who ordered them to do that?'

'I asked them to,' said Marie.

'You did?'

'Yes, I did!' said Marie. 'For God's sake, Marc, the rest of us have to start doing things on our own, sooner or later, don't we?'

I was finding myself slipping into a public argument with my people – not the best thing for a leader, if he wants to hold his position.

'Right! And I'll tell you when. Meanwhile—' I went on before she, or any of the rest of them could say something more, 'Bill and I brought back someone for you all to meet. Brace yourself – he's not human. Bill, do you want to call him?'

'Porniarsk!' shouted Bill, turning to the mistwall.

Marie and the rest also turned toward the mistwall, with a swiftness that cheered me up somewhat. I had meant what I had said to Porniarsk about preparing them for the shock of meeting him. Now the thought in my mind was that a little shock might have a salutary effect on them. We were not an army of world-conquerers, after all. Half a dozen determined adults with decent rifles could wipe us out, or make slaves of us at a moment's notice, if we took no precautions.

Porniarsk came clanking through the mistwall into view and stopped before us.

'I am Porniarsk Prime Three,' he announced, in exactly the same tones in which he had introduced himself to Bill and me. 'The third avatar of Porniarsk, an expert in temporal science. I hope to work together with you so that we all may benefit the universe.'

'Yes,' said Bill dryly. 'Only, of course we've a little more interest in helping ourselves first.'

Porniarsk swivelled his heavy head to look at Bill.

'It is the same thing,' Porniarsk said.

'Is it?' said Bill.

Porniarsk creaked off a nod.

'What you've observed as local phenomena,' he said, 'are essentially micro-echoes of the larger disturbance, which began roughly half a billion years ago, according to your original time pattern.'

'Oh?' said Bill. He was trying to be indifferent, but I could catch the ring of interest in his voice that he was trying to hide. 'Well, just as long as it can be fixed.'

'It cannot be fixed,' said Porniarsk. 'The knowledge is not available to fix it.'

'It isn't?' I said. 'Then what's all this about helping the universe?'

'The whole problem is beyond my time pattern and any other time pattern I know,' said Porniarsk. 'Yet, our responsibility remains. Though we cannot solve, we can attack the problem, each of us like the ants of which you know, trying to level a mountain such as you are familiar with. With each micro-echo, each infinitestimal node attacked, we approach a solution, even if it is not for us to reach it.'

'Wait a minute—' began Tek.

He had not liked my blowup over their going into the house without my orders, even though he had said nothing. And now, the note of potential rebellion was clear in his voice.

'Hold it!' I said, hastily. 'Let me get to the bottom of this first. Porniarsk, just how far does the whole problem extend – this problem of which our troubles here are a micro-echo?'

'I thought,' said Porniarsk, 'I had made clear the answer to that question. The temporal maladjustments are symptoms of the destruction of an entropic balance which has become omnipresent. The chaos in temporal patterns is universal.'

None of us said anything. Porniarsk stood waiting for a moment and then realized he had not yet reached our basic levels of understanding.

'More simply put,' he said, 'all time and space are affected. The universe has been fragmented from one order into a wild pattern of smaller orders, each with its own direction and rate of creation or decay. We can't cure that situation, but we can work against it. We *must* work against it; otherwise, the process will continue and the fragmentation will increase, tending toward smaller and smaller orders, until each individual particle becomes a universe unto itself.'

... And that's all of what he said then that I remember, because about at that point my mind seemed to explode with what it had just discovered – go into overdrive with the possibilities developing from that – on a scale that made any past mental work I had ever done seem like kindergarten-level playtime, by comparison. At last, my hungry rat's teeth had found something they could tear into.

15

They tell me that, after a while, I came to and gave everybody, including Porniarsk, orders to pack up and move on; and I kept the avatar and all of us moving steadily for the better part of the next three weeks. Just moving, not stopping to investigate what was beyond the mistwall, or in any of the buildings or communities we passed. Pushing forward, as if I was on a trek to some far distant land of great promise.

Moments of that trek, I dimly remember. But only moments. I was too full of the end result of all the speculations I had been making about the time storm – now paying off all at once. I did have flashes of awareness of what I was doing, and of what was going on around me. But it was all background, unimportant scenery, for the real place I was in and the real thing I was doing, which was The Dream.

In The Dream I was the equivalent of a spider. I say 'the equivalent of,' because I was still myself; I was just operating like a spider. If that doesn't make sense, I'm sorry, but it's the best I can do by way of explanation. As description, it hardly makes sense to me either; but I've never found another way to describe what that particular brain-hurricane was like.

In The Dream, then, I was spider-like; and I was clambering furiously and endlessly about a confusion of strands that stretched from one end of infinity to the other. The strands had a pattern, though it would have taken someone infinite in size to stand back enough to perceive it as a whole. Still, in a way I can't describe, I was aware of that pattern. My work was with it; and that work filled me with such a wild, terrible and singing joy that it was only a hairline away from being an agony. The joy of working with the pattern, of handling it, sent me scrambling inconceivable distances, at unimaginable speeds, across the strands that filled the universe, with every ounce of strength, every brain cell engaged in what I was doing, every nerve stretched to the breaking-point. It was a berserk explosion of energy that did not care if it destroyed its source, that was myself, as long as things were done to the pattern that needed

344

doing; and somehow this was all associated with my memories of my first determination to put my brand on the world about me; so that the energy sprang from deep sources within me.

Actually, what I was experiencing was beyond ordinary description. The pattern was nameless. My work with it was outside definitions. But at the same time, I knew inside me that it was the most important work that ever had been and ever would be. It carried an adrenalin-like drunkenness that was far beyond any familiar self-intoxication. People talk, or used to talk, about drug highs. This high was not a matter of chemistry but of physics. Every molecule of my body was charged and set vibrating in resonance with the pattern and the work I was doing upon it.

Meanwhile, I continued, with some detached part of my consciousness, to lead and direct my small band of pilgrims; effectively enough, at least, so that they did not depose me as a madman and set up some new leader in my place. Not – as I found out later – that they did not all notice a difference in me and individually react to, or use, that difference to their own purposes. When I returned wholly to myself, I found that a number of things were changed.

It may have been sheer accident that I was able to return at all, but I don't think so. I think I was ready to back off from the pattern, at least for a while; and what triggered my return was only a coincidence, or the first summons able to reach over the long distance to that part of me that was out there on the web-strands of the universe.

It was Sunday – I almost said, 'of course' – who brought me back. Apparently, he had been sticking to me like a paid attendant all through this three week period. I would guess he had sensed enough of the fact that a major part of my mind was missing, to make him worried. Most of the time I must have paid him no attention. But during my brief flashes of awareness of those about me, I remember being annoyed by the fact that I was literally tripping over him every time I turned around.

In this instance, I was momentarily partway back in my full senses, and I had deliberately left the others, gone off out of sight and sound of the others to find a place where I could sit on a rock and be alone for a bit. Sunday had followed me; and he pushed himself on me after I was seated, almost crawling into my lap. I shouted at him to go away; and in exasperation, when he paid no attention, I cuffed at him with my open hand.

It was not a hard blow. I had never hit Sunday hard; but sometimes, swinging at him was the only way to get across the idea that I was serious about what I wanted. Still, as I struck at him, that little part of my mind that was back, apart from the pattern, was beginning to feel a twinge of guilt for hitting him. Only, abruptly, that guilt was lost in a much deeper feeling of shock, and suddenly, I was stone-cold sober, free of the web-pattern for the first time in three weeks.

Because I missed him. My hand swung through nothing but empty air, and I almost fell off the stone.

Sunday had dodged – and that was all wrong. I don't mean wrong, physically, of course. Naturally, his cat reflexes made my human ones look silly. If he had wished, at any time in all the while we had been together, he could have seen to it that no finger of mine ever came close to him. But he never had. He had never dodged before. It was one of the effects of the time storm upon him. When I would lose my temper and slap him, he only closed his eyes, flattened his ears, and crouched down like a kitten before an annoyed mama leopard.

But this time, he had dodged. And he sat now, just out of arms' length, gazing at me with an expression that, for the first time in our months of being together, I could not read.

'Sunday?' I said wonderingly.

He came to me then, with a bound, pushing against me, licking at my hands and face and purring like a motorboat. Just as he evidently had known I was gone, now he knew I was back. Indeed, indeed I was back – and it was wonderful from my point of view as well. I hugged the old son of a bitch and came close to crying over him, in return.

It was at this moment that a shadow fell across us both; and I looked up to see the girl. Where she had come from – whether she had been standing off at a distance, watching Sunday and me – I don't know. But there she was; and the look on her face was like the look now on Sunday's. I almost reached out my arms to her also, as naturally and instinctively as I was hugging and punching Sunday; but just as I was about to do so, the back of my mind said, '*Hold it! What're you doing? She's no crazy leopard!*' And I hesitated.

It was only a second's hesitation, but apparently it was enough. The look went out of her face, and the next thing I knew, she was gone. For a wild moment I thought of going after her; then I told myself there was no point in it until she got over whatever had made her leave.

Her going like that had left me with an empty place inside me and just above my belt buckle, though. I sat where I was, fondling Sunday until I felt normal again, then got to my feet; and the two of us headed back toward the others, who were at a noon camp just over a rise to our left. I joined them; and nobody seemed to notice anything different about me.

However, beginning at once, and through the three days that followed, I quickly began to discover differences in them. It dawned on me that those in my inner circle of people had been as aware of my abnormal mental state as had Sunday and the girl and had gone on pretending to everybody else that I was perfectly normal, for reasons of their own.

The reason in Marie's case was obvious. As the consort of the leader of our little band, she had a self-interest in seeing that I was not deposed for reasons of mental incompetence. Tek, apparently, liked the position of follower for some strong reason of his own. I got the impression that he was waiting for something, and the time was not yet ripe for whatever it was. Bill volunteered *his* reason.

'Thank God you're all right again,' he said to me, the first time we were off together out of earshot of the others, on an advance patrol in the pickup. 'If you'd gone on that way, with your mind a thousand miles off most of the time, for another week, this outfit would have fallen apart.'

'Oh, I don't think so,' I said. 'Tek and Marie would probably have worked out some kind of agreement to keep the tribe together.'

He looked at me, I thought, a little oddly.

'Even if they had,' he said, 'that'd be as bad as falling apart. We're not out here just to survive. We're out here to find out what makes the temporal discontinuities operate. With you not in charge, any hope of that'd be lost.'

'Not necessarily,' I said.

'Necessarily. I can't control them, and you're the only other intelligent person here.' He was serious.

'Don't underestimate Tek,' I said.

'He's smart,' said Bill grimly. 'He's not intelligent. He can't appreciate the value of going after knowledge for its own sake. If he ever tries to take over from you, I'll kill him. I told him so.'

I stared at Bill. Evidently, he meant what he had said.

'There's no danger,' I said. 'Anyway, you'd better wait until I call for help, before you go thinking of killing anyone. We don't want anybody shot by mistake.'

'All right,' said Bill. Exactly as if he was agreeing not to pass the salt at breakfast until I asked for it.

'Good,' I said. 'Now everything's just the way it has been. Let's forget it.'

Only it wasn't – just the way it had been, I mean. For one thing, Marie had gone away from me in a manner that's hard to describe. She acted no differently than she ever had, but it was almost as if she had given up hope that there could be anything more than an alliance of convenience between us. Put that way, it doesn't sound like anything too important. But it left me feeling guilty in spite of the fact that I was fully convinced that I owed her nothing; and, in addition, I was helpless to do anything to mend the situation.

Tek had also changed. He was as much at my orders as ever, but I found him taking charge of the other men whenever there was a vacuum of command, quite as if I had appointed him my lieutenant. And finally, there was the girl ...

For one thing, she had evidently acquired a name while my mind was off on the web. It sounded like 'Elly' when the others used it; but Marie, when I asked her, told me that it was actually Ellen and that Tek had given it to the girl. Well, at least, that made more sense. It was unlikely she had suddenly remembered her name, when she had gone this long time without remembering anything else. But when I asked Tek what made him think he could name her, he denied he had.

'I had to call her something,' he said. 'I asked her what she wanted for a name, and that's the one she picked for herself.'

Ellen was a pretty enough name in its own way; I wondered where she had gotten it. But 'Elly,' or however they might have spelled its contraction, was ugly, I thought. I could not bring myself to use it. As far as I was concerned she was still 'the girl'; but I was plainly a minority of one in that.

Tek was paying a good deal of attention to her, and she was spending most of her time in his company. For no particular reason, I found I didn't approve of that either. She had developed more than I had noticed – I now noticed – since those first days when the only things that looked human on her were a shirt and jeans. She wore dresses now that, possibly with Marie's help, had been altered to fit her; and her hair was always clean, tied in a ponytail at the back of her head. She was even starting to develop a few curves.

All this was to her credit, of course. She was as sparing with words as ever, but the change in her made her seem a good deal older; and possibly that was what had attracted Tek's interest in her. As I say, I found that I didn't approve – although there seemed no specific reason I could nail down for going to him and telling him to leave her alone.

In the first place, even if he agreed, I knew her better than to think *she* would leave him alone, particularly if I was the one who ordered it.

In the second place, I had been ready to abandon her behind me on the bank of that river, so who was I to assume any responsibility for her? Finally, what did I have against Tek, anyway? Since he had been with us, he had been a model of propriety and obedience to orders; and she was only somebody born yesterday. So why make it any of my business?

I still didn't like it. I was stuck with the irrational feeling that he was nowhere near good enough for her. Unfortunately, I couldn't even get her alone to tell her so. I had been wrong about thinking she would get over what had put her off when I had hesitated in reacting to her, back on the rock where Sunday had returned me to my complete self. As far as she seemed to be concerned, I was invisible and inaudible.

To hell with her, I thought, and put my mind to deciding what our tribe should aim for next. We had evidently been travelling with no goal at all, being kept moving by my half-minded, but compulsive, determination. The evening of the day I made up my mind to put the whole question of the girl and Tek out of my mind for good, I waited until after dinner and then got Porniarsk and Bill together.

'Come along with me in one of the jeeps,' I said. 'It's time we had some discussion about this whole business of the time storms. I want to talk to the two of you, alone.'

'No,' said Porniarsk. 'You want to talk to me, alone.'

Bill looked startled and then bleak. He was not much at giving away his feelings through his expressions, but I had learned to read him fairly well by this time; and what I now read was that Porniarsk's words were like a slap in the face to him.

'Sorry, Porniarsk,' I said. 'I'm the one who decides how many of us are going to talk, and when.'

'No,' said Bill. 'You talk to him alone. It may be important.'

He turned around and walked off.

I opened my mouth to call him back and then closed it again. Inside that boy-sized body and behind that innocent face was the identity of a mature and intelligent man; and he had just shown himself capable of thinking in larger terms than I, in my reaction against Porniarsk's words.

I turned to look at the alien. It was still early evening and the whole landscape around us was softened and gentled by the pinkening light. Amidst all that softness, the bony-plated, uncouth form of Porniarsk looked like a miniature dinosaur out of a brutal and prehistoric age. Porniarsk said nothing now, merely stood looking at me and waiting. There was no way I could guess whether he had understood my reaction and Bill's and was simply unconcerned with our human feelings, or whether he had understood neither of us at all.

I had been pretty well ignoring Porniarsk during the last few weeks of my involvement with The Dream; and in fact, there seemed little to be learned from him unless he chose to inform us. His speech by this time was as human as that of the rest of us; but the thoughts behind his words, when he did speak, remained indecipherable. He moved from one statement to another by a logic mostly invisible to our human thinking.

And yet – he was not without some kind of emotion, even some kind of warmth. There was no more sentiment to be read in the tones of his voice, or in his actions, than in those of a robot; but he seemed ... likeable. I don't know what other word to use. He seemed to radiate a sort of warmth that we all, including the men we had acquired along with Tek, felt and responded to. Even the animals seemed to feel it. I had seen how Sunday had taken to him at first sight. The dogs also, in their rare free moments when they were not under command or tied up, would seek him out, wagging their tails and sniffing him all over each time as if this was a first meeting, before ending by licking at his armour-plated hide. Porniarsk paid them no more attention than he did Sunday or one of us humans when he was not exchanging specific information on some point or other. He seemed not to need to eat. Whenever he had no place in particular to move to, he would fold up and drop into a lying position with a clatter like that of a dumped load of bricks. But whether he ever slept in this position, I had never been able to find out. Certainly, I had never caught him with his eyes closed.

So – Porniarsk was a conundrum. He usually left us no choice but to accept him pretty much as he was. And now, with Bill having walked off, I found myself about to do just that, one more time.

'All right, Porniarsk,' I said. 'It's you and me then. Come on.'

I climbed into the jeep beside which we had been standing as we talked. Porniarsk made one of the astounding leaps he seemed to be capable of with only a slight flexing of his post-like legs, and crashed down into the seat beside me, on his haunches. The jeep rocked sideways on its springs – I had estimated before this that if Porniarsk weighed an ounce, he must weigh well over three hundred pounds – but recovered. I started the vehicle up and we drove off.

I did not go more than a few hundred yards, just enough to put us out of earshot of the rest of the camp. Then I killed the motor and turned to Porniarsk. It was an odd feeling to find myself almost nose to nose with that massive, bulldog-like head. For the first time I noticed his eyes were not just brown in colour, but so deep a brown as to be almost black. This close, I could see their pupils contract and expand in cat-fashion, while we talked.

'All right, Porniarsk,' I said. 'I need your help. You evidently know a lot more about the time storm effects than we do. I want to stop this random moving around just in hopes we'll run into a piece of country that's future enough for us to be able to do something about the mist-walls and the rest of it. I need you to help me figure out where to head.'

'No,' said Porniarsk.

'No?' I said.

'You do not need me to help you find a trigger area,' said Porniarsk.

'What's that supposed to mean?' I said. This, coming on top of his rejection of Bill, was enough to stir my temper again.

'It's supposed to mean that my assistance is not required to set you on the road to the destination you wish. You've already set yourself on that road.'

I took rein on my emotions. I reminded myself that I had to stop anthropomorphizing him. He was probably only trying to tell me something, and the fact that he was not built to think like a human was getting in the way.

'Since when?' I asked, as calmly as I could.

'Since your temporary abstraction, and during your partial involvement with the overall problem, ever since the moment in which my words caused you to visualize the magnitude of it. Am I making myself—' Porniarsk broke off uncharacteristically in mid-sentence. 'Am I talking sense?'

'I don't know,' I said. 'How'd you know why I collapsed, or about how I've been since?'

'I've been watching you,' he said, 'and drawing conclusions from what you do. The conclusions are those I just stated.'

'What've I been doing, then?'

'Going,' he repeated, with no hint of impatience in his voice, 'toward a trigger area.'

I felt a sort of delicate feeling – an instinct to caution. There was no way he could have known what had been working in the back of my mind with The Dream, these last few weeks; but he was talking one hell of a lot as if he had read my mind.

'That could be an accident,' I said. 'What makes you think it's any-thing more than an accident?'

'You withdrew,' he said. 'But then you recovered enough to guide your party, if not in a straight line, in a consistent direction by the most travellable route, toward the location of an area I know to contain devices of assistance at a technological level, which might achieve a first step of halting the moving lines of temporal alteration – temporal discontinuities, as Bill calls them, or mistwalls, as you say.'

I stared at him.

'If you know about a place like that,' I said, 'why haven't you done something about the temporal – oh, hell, whatever you want to call them – before now?'

'The devices are devices of assistance, but not of a design which will assist me. I'm an avatar, as I told you, an avatar of Porniarsk Prime Three. The devices would be of assistance to Porniarsk himself, but he's otherwise engaged.'

'Tell him to drop whatever's otherwise engaging him then, and get over here.'

'He wouldn't come,' said the avatar. 'This planet is your problem. The problem of Porniarsk is a larger one. It involves many planets like this. Therefore, he has such as I who am his avatar, so he can have several manipulative sets of himself at work. But all I am is an avatar. Alone, I can't manipulate the forces involved here, no matter how competent the device of assistance available to me.'

I shook my head.

'All right, then, Porniarsk – or Porniarsk's avatar—' I began.

'Porniarsk is fine,' he interrupted. 'You'll never meet Porniarsk himself, or any of his other avatars, so there's no danger of confusion.'

'I don't know about that,' I said. 'You've got me pretty confused right now. I don't understand any of this.'

'Of course,' said Porniarsk, agreeable. 'You're uneducated.'

'Oh? Is that it?'

'How could you be otherwise? You've never had the chance to learn about these forces and their effects. I can't educate you, but I can explain specific elements of the situation as you run across them. Trying to explain them before you encounter them won't work because you don't have either the vocabulary or the concepts behind the vocabulary.'

'But I will when I run into these elements?' I said. 'Is that it?'

'On encountering the experience, you'll see the need for the appropriate terms, with which you might then be able to understand enough of the underlying concepts to work with.'

'Oh?' I didn't mean to sound sarcastic, but this kind of conversation with Porniarsk had a habit of driving me to it. 'My understanding's not guaranteed then?'

'Be reasonable,' said Porniarsk; and this kind of appeal in colloquial, uninflected English from the genial gargoyle sitting next to me, had to be experienced to be believed. 'How can *I* guarantee *your* understanding?'

How, indeed? He had a point, there.

'I give up,' I said, and I meant it. 'Just tell me one thing. How did I happen to know enough to head in the right direction?'

'I don't know,' Porniarsk answered. 'I'd expected that, sooner or later, you'd ask me if there were any future areas containing the means to do something about the time storm effects locally, that is, here on this world. Then I could have directed you to such an area. However, you've directed yourself to one without me. I don't understand how. Porniarsk himself wouldn't understand how, though perhaps he could find the answer. I'm only an avatar. I can't.'

'All right, tell me what to do now, then,' I said.

Porniarsk's head creaked in a negative shaking.

'There's nothing I can advise you on until you've experienced the immediate future area of the assistance device technology,' he said. 'Now that I've seen you do this much by yourself, I'd be cautious about advising you in any case. It might be that you'll learn more, and faster, on your own.'

'I see,' I said. 'That's fine. That's just fine. Then tell me, why did you stop Bill from coming out here with us, if you weren't going to tell me anything anyway?'

'Bill wouldn't believe me,' said Porniarsk. 'He doesn't trust me.'

'And I do?'

The gargoyle head leaned slightly, almost confidentially, toward mine.

'You've learned something you shouldn't have been able to learn by yourself,' said Porniarsk. 'You've touched the greater universe. Of course, you don't trust me, either. You're too primitive to trust an avatar of another kind, like myself. But in your case, trust isn't necessary.'

'Oh?' I said. 'Why?'

'Because you want to believe me,' said Porniarsk. 'If what I'm saying is true, then you're headed toward something you want very much. That's not the same thing as trust; but trust can come later. For now, your wanting to believe will do.'

16

So we drove back to camp in the last of the twilight and in silence. I only asked him one question on the way back.

'Do you really give a damn about any of us?' I said. 'Or are you just interested in the time storm?'

'Porniarsk cares for all life,' his steady voice answered. 'If he didn't, he'd have no concern with the time storm. And I am Porniarsk, only in an additional body.'

It was cold comfort. I believed him; but at the same time, I got the feeling that there was something more he was withholding from me.

In any case, there was nothing to do now but keep going. Oddly, I trusted him. Something had happened to me since The Dream; and that was that, in a strange way, I had come to feel an affection and responsibility for him, along with all the others. It was as if a corner of my soul's house had put up a blind on one window to let in a little sunshine. I did take Bill aside the next day and gave him a rough briefing on my conversation with Porniarsk. Bill fulfilled Porniarsk's prediction by being highly sceptical of the avatar's motives and implications.

'It sounds to me like a con game,' he said. 'It's part of a con game to flatter your mark. Did you feel you were headed any place in particular, these last three weeks?'

I hesitated. Somehow, I didn't get the feeling that Bill was ripe right now for hearing an account of The Dream, and how it had been with me. But there was no way to answer his questions fully without telling him about my back-of-the-brain spiderwork.

'I had a feeling I was tied into something important,' I said. 'That's as far as it went.'

'Hmm,' said Bill, half to himself. 'I wonder if Porniarsk's telepathic?'

'That's as far-fetched as me supposed to be knowing where we're going, when I didn't know where we're going,' I said.

Bill shrugged.

'If we hit this trigger area place soon, you'll have known where we're

354

going,' he said. 'No reason there shouldn't be as much truth to telepathy. When did Porniarsk say we'd reach the area?'

Of course, wound up as I had been by what he'd had to say about me personally, I'd forgotten to ask him.

'I'll find out,' I said and went off to look for the avatar.

Porniarsk politely informed me that we should hit the trigger area in about a day and a half the way we were travelling; and, yes, it would be behind a mistwall like all the other mistwalls we'd seen. As to what was inside, it was best I experienced that for myself first, before Porniarsk did any explaining.

He was not wrong. Late in the afternoon of the following day, we spotted a stationary mistwall dead ahead; and two hours later we set up evening camp a couple of hundred yards from it.

The countryside here was open pastureland, rolling hills with only an occasional tree but small strands of brush and marshy ponds. Here and there a farmer's fence straggled across the landscape; and the two-lane blacktop road we had been following, since its sudden appearance out of nowhere ten miles before, ran at an angle into the mistwall and disappeared. The day had been cool. Our campfires felt good. Autumn would be along before long, I thought, and with that began to turn over ideas for the winter; whether to find secure shelter in this climate or head south.

I made one more attempt to get Porniarsk to tell me what lay on the other side of the mistwall; but he was still not being helpful.

'You could at least tell us if we're liable to fall off a cliff before we come out of the wall, or step into a few hundred feet of deep water,' I growled at him.

'You won't encounter any cliffs, lakes, or rivers before you have a chance to see them,' Porniarsk said. 'As far as the terrain goes, it's not that dissimilar from the land around us here.'

'Then why not tell us about it?'

'The gestalt will be of importance to you later.'

That was all I could get out of him. After dinner, I called a meeting. Porniarsk attended. I told the others that Porniarsk believed that, beyond this particular mistwall, there was an area different from any we'd run into so far. We might find equipment there that would let us do something about the time storm and the moving mistwalls. Bill and I, in particular, were interested in the chance of doing so, as they all knew. For one thing, if we could somehow stop the mistwalls from moving, we could feel safe setting down someplace permanently. Perhaps we could start rebuilding a civilization.

It was quite a little speech. When I was done, they all looked at me, looked at Porniarsk, who had neither moved nor spoken, and then looked back at me again. None of them said anything. But looking back at them, I got the clear impression that there were as many different reactions to what I had just said as there were heads there to contain the reactions.

'All right then,' I said, after a reasonable wait to give anyone else a chance to speak. 'We'll be going in, in the morning. The ones going will be Bill, me, and three others, all with rifles and shotguns both, in one of the jeeps. Anybody particularly want to be in on the expedition, or shall I pick out the ones to go?'

'I'll go,' said Tek.

'No,' I said. 'I want you to stay here.'

I looked around the firelit circle of faces, but there were no other volunteers.

'All right then,' I said. 'It'll be Richie, Alan, and Waite. Starting with the best shot and working down the list.'

The fourth man, Hector Monsanto, whom everybody called 'Zig,' did not look too unhappy at being left out. He was the oldest of the four men we had acquired along with Tek, a short, wiry, leathery-featured individual in his late thirties, who looked as if most of his life had been spent outdoors. Actually, according to Tek, he had grown up in a small town and had been a barber who spent most of his time in the local bars.

He was the oldest of the four and the least agile. The other three were in their early to mid-twenties and could move fast if they needed to.

So, the following morning we tried it. It took about an hour or so for Bill to satisfy himself, by throwing a weighted line through the mistwall and pushing pipe lengths screwed together to beyond the mistwall's far edge, that the terrain beyond was both level and safe. Then we brought the jeep we were going to use up to the wall and got in with our weapons. I climbed in behind the wheel with Bill on the other front seat. Alan, Richie, and Waite got into the back. We made a pretty full load.

Then Sunday, purring loudly, as if congratulating us all on a permission no one had given him, leaped up into Bill's lap and settled down for the ride; and, before I could shove him out, the girl began to climb into the back seat holding a rifle.

'Hold it!' I roared. 'Everybody out!'

We off-loaded, everybody except the girl and Sunday, who took advantage of the available empty space to settle down that much more firmly.

'Now, look—' I began to the girl.

'I'm going,' she said. Sunday purred loudly and cleaned the fur on top of one of his forepaws. It was a double declaration of insubordination.

Of course, there was no way I could stop them. I could put them out of the vehicle, but they could walk in right behind us. Sunday had proved that, unlimited times. In fact, I had known – everybody had known – that he would be coming along. I had not counted on the girl.

I glared around me. This particular expedition was sorting itself out in exactly the wrong way. I don't know what made me so convinced that there might be danger beyond this mistwall. I'd gone into a number of others confidently enough. Perhaps it was Porniarsk's refusal to tell me exactly what was beyond the wall. At any rate, I felt the way I felt; and for that type of feeling, I was taking all the wrong people and leaving all the wrong people behind.

An ideal expeditionary group would have been myself, Tek, and a couple of the men, none of whom meant a great deal to me – except myself; and I was too much of an egotist to think that I couldn't survive whatever mystery lay in front of me. Sunday, the girl, Bill, even to a certain extent, Marie and little Wendy, were people I cared about to one degree or another and would just as soon have kept safely in the rear area.

But Bill could not be left behind, in justice. The quest to understand the time storm was as much his as mine. Sunday could not be kept out, in practice; and now the girl had proclaimed her intention to go in with us whether I wanted her to or not. Meanwhile Tek, who outside of myself was the one person fit to take charge of those left behind, if enemies of some kind suddenly appeared over the horizon behind us, could, by no stretch of common sense, be taken. Ever since Marie, Wendy, and I had run into him and his group, I had been half-expecting that any day, we might bump into another such armed and predatory gang.

'All right!' I said. 'If everybody's going to go, we'll have to use the pickup. Let's get it cleared out!'

The pickup was our main transport. In the back, it had all our camping equipment, food, fuel, and other supplies. We had unloaded part of what it contained to set up camp the night before; but if it was to be used as a battle wagon, the rest of the box had to be cleared. We moved back and went to work.

Twenty minutes later, we once more approached the mistwall; this time in the pickup, in low gear. The girl and Bill and I were in the front seat with the windows rolled up, with me as driver. In the open box behind were Alan and Waite and Richie, holding a disgruntled Sunday on a leash. I'd shut the leopard out of the cab by main force and snapped his leash around his neck when he tried to join the three of us in the cab. As I pushed the nose of the pickup slowly into the first dust of the mistwall, there was a heavy thud on the roof of the cab. I stopped, rolled down the window and stuck my head out to glimpse Sunday, now lying on the cab top. I rolled the window back up and went on.

The mist surrounded us. The dust hissed on the metal of the pick-up's body, as the motor of the truck grumbled in low gear. We were surrounded by an undeviating whiteness in which it was impossible to tell if we were moving. Then the whiteness lightened, thinned, and suddenly we rolled out into sunlight again. I stopped the truck.

We were in a rocky, hilly section of country. The thin, clear air that made everything stand out with sudden sharpness signalled that we were at a higher altitude, and the sparseness of vegetation – no trees and only an occasional green, spiny bush – suggested a high, desert country, like the *altiplano* of inland Mexico. The landscape was mainly rock, from hard dirt and gravel, to boulders of all sizes. Rough, but not too rough for the jeeps to get through; and, if a clear route could be found between the boulders, probably even the pickup could be nursed along.

The ground before us was fairly clear and level, but boulder-strewn slopes rose sharply to the right and left of us. Directly ahead, the level space dipped down into a cup-shaped depression holding what appeared to be a small village. The buildings in the village were odd; dome-shaped, with floorless, front-porch extensions, consisting simply of projecting roofs upheld at each end by supporting poles. Under those roofs, out in the open, there seemed to be a few machines or equipment – mechanical constructs of some kind. No human beings were visible. Beyond the village, the ground rose sharply into a small mountain – it was too steep to be called a hill – wearing a belt of trees halfway up its several hundred feet of height. On one side of the mountain, the bare peak sloped at an angle the jeeps could possibly manage. But the other slopes were all boulder-strewn and climbable only by someone on foot.

On top, crowning the peak, was a large, solid, circular building, looking as if it had been poured out of fresh white concrete ten seconds before we appeared on the scene. That was as much as I had a chance to notice, because then everything started to happen.

A number of objects hit loudly on the body and cab of the truck, one shattering the window next to Bill. At the same time, there was a yowl of rage from Sunday and I caught sight, fleetingly, of the leopard leaping off the roof of the cab to the right, with his leash trailing in the air behind him. Suddenly the rocks around us were speckled by the visages of dark-furred, ape-like creatures.

The guns of the men in the box were firing. The girl, who had been seated between Bill and myself, scrambled over Bill crying out Sunday's name, opened the door of the pickup on that side, and disappeared. Bill exited after her; and I heard the machine pistol yammering. I jerked open the door on my side, rolled out on to the hard-pebbled earth, and began firing from a prone position at any furry head I could see.

There was a timeless moment of noise and confusion – and then without warning, it was over. There were no longer any creatures visible to shoot at, except for perhaps four or five who lay still, or barely stirring, on the ground. I fired a few more rounds out of reflex and then quit. The other guns fell silent.

I got to my feet. Sunday stalked back into my line of vision, his tail high in self-congratulation. He headed for one of the two furry figures that still moved. I opened my mouth to call him back; but before he could have reached the creature, a rifle in the box behind me began to sound again, and both the moving bodies went motionless.

'Quit that!' I shouted, spinning around. 'I want one alive—'

I broke off, suddenly realizing I was talking to a man who wasn't listening. Richie, his round face contorted, was kneeling behind the metal side of the pickup box, firing steadily at the dark-furred shapes; and he kept at it until his rifle was empty.

I climbed into the box and took the gun away from him as he tried to reload it.

'Simmer down!' I said.

He looked at me glassy-eyed, but sat without moving. There wasn't a mark on him.

But the other two were hit. Alan had one side of his face streaming blood from what seemed to be a scalp wound. He was holding up Waite, who was breathing in an ugly, rattling way with his face as white as the building on the peak. His right hand was trapped behind Alan; but he kept trying to bring his left hand up to his chest, and Alan kept holding it away.

My head cleared. I remembered now that the barrage that had come at us had contained not only thrown rocks but a few leaf-shaped, hiltless knives. One of the knives was now sticking in Waite's chest low on the left side. It was in perhaps a third the length of its blade; and evidently it had slid in horizontally between two ribs.

Waite coughed, and a little pink froth came out the corners of his mouth.

'He wants to get the knife out,' said Alan, pleadingly to me. 'Should we just pull it out, do you think?'

I looked down at Waite. It did not matter, clearly, whether we took the knife out or not. The blade had gone into his lungs and now they were filling up with blood. Waite looked back up at me with panic in his eyes. He was the quiet one of Tek's four men and possibly the youngest. I had never been sure if he was really like the others, or whether he had simply gotten swept up and tried to be like them.

There was nothing I or anyone else in our group could do for him. I stood looking down at him, feeling my helplessness, like something in my own chest being raggedly cut. This was one of the people I had been thinking meant little or nothing to me and would be easily expendable. I had not stopped to realize how close a group like ours could come to be, living together like a family, moving together, facing a possibly dangerous world together. Maybe he would die more quickly without the knife blade in him and removing it would be the kindest thing we could do for him.

'If he wants it out, he might as well have it out,' I said.

Alan let go of Waite's arm. The arm came up, and its hand grasped the handle of the knife but could not pull it out. Alan half-reached for the knife himself, hesitated, tried again, hesitated, and looked appealingly at me.

I reached down and took hold of the handle. The blade stuck at first, then slid out easily. Waite yelled – or rather, he tried to yell, but it was a sound that ended in a sort of gargle. He pulled away a little from Alan and leaned over forward, face tilted down intently toward the bed of the box, as if he was going to be sick. But he was not. He merely hung there sagging against the grip of Alan's arms, his gaze calm and intent on the metal flooring; and then, as we watched, he began to die.

It was like watching him dwindle away from us. His face relaxed and relaxed, and the focus in his eyes became more and more general, until all at once there was no focus at all and he was dead. Alan let him down quickly but softly on the bed of the box.

I turned and climbed out of the box back on to the ground. I saw Bill standing on this side of the truck now and Sunday nosing curiously at one of the bodies. Suddenly, it struck me.

'Girl!' I shouted at Bill. 'The girl! Where is she?'

'I don't know,' said Bill.

I ran around the front of the truck and the bouldered slope on the side I'd seen her disappear.

'Girl!' I kept shouting. '*Girl!*'

I couldn't find her. I found one of the dead ape-creatures, but I couldn't find her. I started threading back and forth among the rocks as I worked up the slope; and then, suddenly, I almost fell over her. She was in a little open space, half-sitting up with her back against a boulder and a torn-off strip of her shirt tied around one leg above the knee.

For a moment I thought she was already dead, like Waite – and I couldn't take it. It was like being cut in half. Then she turned her head to look at me, and I saw she was alive.

'Oh, my God!' I said.

I knelt down beside her and wrapped her up in my arms, telling myself I would never let go of her again. Never. But she was as stiff and unresponsive in my grasp as a wild animal caught in a trap. She did not move; but she did not relax either, and finally, this brought me more or less back to my senses; I didn't want to let her go, but I stopped holding her quite so tightly.

'Are you all right?' I said. 'Why didn't you answer me?'

'My name's Ellen,' she said.

'Is that all!' I hugged her again. 'All right! You'll be Ellen from now on. I won't ever call you anything else!'

'It doesn't matter what you call me,' she said. 'I'm not going to be here anyway.'

She was still stiff and cold. I let go of her and sat back on my knees so that I could see her face; and it was as unyielding as the rest of her.

'What do you mean, you aren't going to be here?' She was talking nonsense. She had evidently been hurt or wounded in the leg, but that could hardly be serious.

'Tek and I are going away by ourselves. It's already decided,' she said. 'We were just waiting to make sure you got through this last mistwall all right. You can keep Sunday. He only gets in the way all the time anyway.'

She turned, grabbed hold of the boulder against which she had been leaning, and pulled herself up on one leg.

'Help me back to the pickup,' she said.

My head was whirling with that crazy announcement of hers. I stared down at her bandaged leg.

'What happened to you?' I said, automatically.

'I got hit by a rock, that's all. It scraped the skin off and bled a little, so I wrapped it up; but it's only a bruise.'

'Try putting your weight on it.' Something automatic in me was doing the talking. 'Maybe it's broken.'

'It's not broken. I already tried.' She took hold of my arm with both her hands. 'It just hurts to walk on it. Help me.'

I put an arm round her, and she hopped back down the slope on one leg, by my side, until we reached the cab of the pickup, and I helped her up on to the seat. I was operating on reflex. I could not believe what she had said; particularly, just now, when I had just realized how important she was to me. It was the way I had found myself feeling about Waite, multiplied something like a million times. But there were things demanding decisions from me.

Richie and Alan were still in the back of the truck with the body of Waite. I looked at them. Somebody had to take the pickup back through the mistwall with the girl and Waite. Richie was the unhurt one, but his eyes still did not look right.

'How badly are you hurt?' I asked Alan.

'Hurt?' he said. 'I didn't get hurt.'

'You could fool me,' I said dryly. He didn't seem to get it. 'Your head! How bad's the damage to your head?'

'My head?'

He put up a hand and brought it down covered with blood. His face whitened.

'What is it?' he said. 'How bad ...' His bloody hand was fluttering up toward the head wound, wanting to touch it, but afraid of what it might feel.

'That's what I want to know,' I said.

I climbed into the cab and bent over him, gingerly parting the hair over the bloody scalp. It was such a mess I couldn't see anything.

'Feel anything?' I asked, probing with my fingertips.

'No ... no ... *yes!*' he yelped.

I pulled my hands away.

'How bad did that feel?' I asked him. He looked embarrassed.

'Not too bad – I guess,' he said. 'But I felt it, where you touched it.'

'All right,' I told him. 'Hang on, because I'm going to have to touch it some more.'

I probed around with my fingers, wishing I'd had the sense to bring bandages and water with us. He said nothing to indicate that I was giving him any important amount of pain; and all my fingers could find was a swelling and a relatively small cut.

'It's really not bad at all,' he said sheepishly, when I'd finished. 'I think I just got hit by a rock, come to think of it.'

'All right,' I said. My own hands were a mess now. I wiped them as best I could on the levis I was wearing. 'Looks like a bump and a scratch, only. It just put out a lot of blood. If you're up to it, I want you to stay.'

'I can stay,' he said.

'All right, then. Richie!'

Richie looked at me slowly as if I was someone calling him from a distance.

'Richie! I want you to drive the pickup back through the mistwall. You're to take the girl and Waite back, then pick up some bandages, some antibiotics and a jerry can of drinking water and bring it back to us. Understand me?'

'Yeah ...' said Richie, thickly.

'Come on, then,' I said.

I climbed out of the box of the pickup and he came after me. I saw him into the cab and behind the wheel.

'He'll take you back to the camp,' I told the girl and closed the door on the driver's side before she could answer – assuming, that is, that she had intended to answer. The pickup's motor, which had been idling all this time, growled into gear. Richie swung it about and drove out of sight into the mistwall, headed back.

I looked around. Bill was standing about twenty yards ahead of me. Beside him was Porniarsk, who must have followed us through the mistwall at some time when I wasn't looking. They seemed to be talking together, looking down into the village, the machine pistol hanging by its strap, carelessly, from Bill's right arm. It was incautious of him to be so relaxed, I thought. We had driven off one attack, but there was no way of knowing we might not have another at any minute.

I went toward them. As I did, I had to detour around the body of one of the attackers, who had apparently been trying to rush the pickup. It lay face-down, the apelike features hidden, and it reminded me of Waite, somehow. For a moment I wondered if there were others among its fellows that were feeling the impact of this one's death, as I had felt that of Waite. My mind – it was not quite under control right then, my mind – skittered off to think of the girl again. Of Ellen – I must remember to think of her as Ellen from now on.

It was so strange. She was small and skinny and cantankerous. How could I love her like this? Where did it come from, what I was feeling? Somehow, when I wasn't paying any attention, she had grown inside me, and now, she took up all the available space there. Another thought came by, blown on the wandering breeze of my not-quite-in-control mind. What about Marie? I couldn't just kick her out. But maybe there was no need for worry. All Marie had ever seemed to want was the protection inherent in our partnership. It might be she would be completely satisfied with the name of consort alone. After all, there were no laws now, no reason that I couldn't apparently have two wives instead of one. No one but us three need know Marie was a wife in name only ... of course, the girl would have to agree ...

I stopped thinking, having reached Bill and Porniarsk. They were still looking down at the village. I looked down, too, and, to my surprise, saw it populated and busy. Black, furry, apelike figures were visible all through its streets and moving in and out of the dome-shaped houses. Most, in fact, seemed to be busy with whatever objects they had under the porch-like roofs before the entrances of their buildings. But a fair number were visible simply sitting in the dust, singly or in pairs, doing nothing; and a small group were in transit from one spot to another.

They were within easy rifle shot of where we stood, and the three of us must have been plainly visible to them; but they paid us no attention whatsoever.

'What the hell?' I said. 'Is that the same tribe that hit us just now?'

'Yes,' said Bill.

I looked at him and waited for him to go on, but he nodded at Porniarsk instead.

'Let him tell you.'

Porniarsk creaked his head around to look sideways and up at me.

'They're experimental animals,' Porniarsk said, 'from a time less than a hundred years ahead of that you were in originally when the time storm reached you.'

'You knew about them?' The thought of Waite made my throat tight. 'You knew about them waiting to kill us, and you didn't warn us?'

'I knew only they were experimental animals,' said Porniarsk. 'Apparently part of their conditioning is to attack. But if the attack fails, they go back to other activities.'

'It could be ...' said Bill slowly and thoughtfully, 'it could be their attack reflex was established to be used against animals, instead of the people of the time that set them up here; and they just didn't recognize us as belonging to the people level, as they'd been trained to recognize it.'

'It's possible,' said Porniarsk. 'And then, if they attacked and failed, they might be conditioned to stop attacking, as a fail-safe reflex.'

'That's damned cool of the both of you,' I said, my throat free again.

'Waite's dead and you're holding a parlour discussion on the reasons.'

Bill looked at me, concerned.

'All right, all right,' I said. 'Forget I said that. I'm still a little shook up from all this. So, they're experimental animals down there, are they?'

'Yes,' said Porniarsk, 'experimental animals, created by genetic engineering to test certain patterns of behaviour. Up there on the height behind their community is the laboratory building from which they were observed and studied. The equipment in that structure that was designed for working with this problem is equipment that, with some changes and improvements, may be able to aid in controlling the effects of the time storm, locally.'

Bill was staring straight at me. His face was calm, but I could hear the excitement under the level note he tried to speak in.

'Let's take a look, Marc.'

'All right,' I said. 'As soon as the pickup comes back, we'll go get a jeep and try that long slope on the right of the peak.'

17

The only vehicle-possible route to the peak led down through the main street of the village. When Richie got back with a jeep, we left him there; and Porniarsk, Bill and I drove down the slope and in between the buildings. We had perhaps twenty feet to spare on either side of us as we went through the village, for the central street – if you could call it that – was twice the width of the other lanes between buildings. The furry faces we passed did not bother to look at us, with a single exception. A slightly grizzled, large, and obviously male individual – none of them wore anything but a sort of Sam Browne belt, to which were clipped the sheaths that held their knives and some things which looked like small hand tools – sat in front of one building and stared from under thick tufts of hair where his brows should be, his long fingers playing with the knife he held on his knees. But he made no threatening moves, with the knife or anything else.

'Look at that old man,' said Bill, pointing with the muzzle of his machine pistol at the watcher.

'I see him,' I said. 'What do you want me to do about him?'

'Nothing, I'd suggest,' said Porniarsk. My question had not really called for an answer, but perhaps he had not understood that. 'That one's the Alpha Prime of the males' community. The name "Old Man" fits him very well. As Alpha Prime, his reflexes, or conditioning, dictate a somewhat different pattern of action for him alone. But I don't think he or the others will act inimically again, unless you deliberately trigger some antagonistic reaction.'

'What are they all doing?' Bill asked.

I looked in the direction he was staring. There were a number of porches along the left side of the street, each with one or two of the experimentals under them. I picked out one who was operating what was clearly a spinning wheel. Another was cutting up a large sheet of the leathery material their harnesses were made out of, plainly engaged in constructing Sam Browne belts. But the rest were working with machines I did not recognize and either getting no visible results, or results that made no sense to me. One, in particular, was typing away energetically at a sort of double keyboard, with no noticeable effect, except for a small red tab that the machine spat out at odd intervals into a wire basket. The worker paid no attention to the tabs he was accumulating, seeming to be completely wound up in the typing process itself.

'They're self-supporting, after a fashion,' said Porniarsk. 'Some of what they do provides them with what they need to live. Other specific activities are merely for study purposes – for the studies of the people who put them here.'

'Where are those people?' I asked. 'Can we get in touch with them?'

'No.' Porniarsk swivelled his neck once more to look at me from the seat beside me. 'They are not here.'

'Where did they go?'

'They no longer exist,' said Porniarsk. 'No more than all the people you knew before your first experience with the time storm. You and Bill and the rest of you here, including these experimental creatures, are the ones who have gone places.'

I took my attention off the street for a second to stare at him.

'What do you mean?'

'I mean you, and those with you, are people the time storm has moved, rather than eliminated,' Porniarsk answered. 'I'm sorry, that can't be explained properly to you yet, by someone like me, not until you understand more fully what has been involved and is involved in the temporal displacements. Remember, I told you that this disturbance began roughly half a billion years in your past?'

I remembered. But it had only been a figure to me at the time. Who can imagine a time-span of a half a billion years?

'Yes,' I said.

'It also began several million years in your future,' said Porniarsk. 'Perhaps it might help you to think, provisionally, of the time storm as a wave-front intersecting the linear time you know – the time you imagine stretching from past to future – at an angle, so that your past, present and future are all affected at once by the same action.'

'Why didn't you tell us this before?' demanded Bill.

'Unfortunately, the image I just gave you isn't really a true one,' said Porniarsk. 'You forget the matter of scale. If the time storm is like a wave-front on a beach, we and our worlds are less than individual atoms in the grains of sand that make up that beach. What we experience as local effects appear as phenomena having very little resemblance to the true picture of the wave-front as a whole. I only mention this because it's now become important for Marc to be able to imagine something of the forces at work here.'

The front wheels of the jeep jolted and shuddered over some small rocks. We were moving beyond the end of the village street and up over open ground again. I gave my attention back to my driving.

The drive up even the easy side of the peak was rough enough, but the jeep was equal to it. With enough foresight, it was possible to pick a route among the really heavy boulders that would otherwise have barred our way. A little more than halfway up, we hit a relatively level area of hard earth, surrounding the basin of a natural spring coming out of the cliff; and we stopped to rest and taste the water, which was cold enough to set our teeth on edge. I had not been conscious of being thirsty, except for a fleeting moment when I told Richie to bring back a jerry can of water with the other things. He had; and I had forgotten to get a drink then. Now I felt a thirst like that of someone lost in the desert for two days. I drank until my jaws ached, paused, drank, paused, and drank again.

After a bit we went the rest of the way up to the top of the peak, where the building was. Seen up close, it turned out to be a structure maybe sixty feet in diameter, with only one entrance and no windows. Like a blockhouse at a firing range, only larger.

The entrance had a door, which slid aside as we came within a stride of it. We had a glimpse of darkness beyond, then lighting awoke within, and we stepped into a brightly illuminated, circular interior, with a raised platform in the centre and open cubicles all around the exterior wall, each cubicle with a padded chair, its back toward the centre of the room and its cushions facing a sort of console fixed to the wall.

'What is it?' asked Bill, almost in a whisper. He was standing with Porniarsk and me on the raised platform but, unlike us, turning continually on his heel as if he wanted to get a view of all hundred and eighty degrees of the room at once.

'It is,' said Porniarsk, 'something you might think of as a computer, in your terms. It's a multiple facility for the use of observers who'd wish to draw conclusions from their observations of the inhabitants in the village.'

'Computer?' Bill's voice was louder and sharper. 'That's all?'

'Its working principle isn't that of the computers you're familiar with,' said Porniarsk. 'This uses the same principle that's found in constructs from the further future, those I've referred to as devices-of-assistance. You'll have to trust me to put this construct into that future mode so it'll be useful in the way we need.'

'How'll we use it?' Bill asked.

'You won't use it,' said Porniarsk. 'Marc will use it.'

They both turned their heads toward me.

'And you'll teach me how?' I said to Porniarsk.

'No. You'll have to teach yourself,' Porniarsk answered. 'If you can't, then there's nothing anyone can do.'

'If he can't, I'll try,' said Bill tightly.

'I don't think the device will work for you if it fails for Marc,' said Porniarsk to him. 'Tell me, do you feel anything at this moment? Anything unusual at all?'

'Feel?' Bill stared at him.

'You don't feel anything, then,' said Porniarsk. 'I was right. Marc should be much more attuned. Marc, what do you feel?'

'Feel? Me?' I said, echoing Bill. But I already knew what he was talking about.

I had thought, at first, I must be feeling a hangover from the fight with the inhabitants of the village. Then I'd thought the feeling was my curiosity about what was inside this building, until I saw what was there. Now, standing on the platform in the centre of the structure, I knew it was something else – something like a massive excitement from everywhere, that was surrounding me, pressing in on me.

'I feel geared-up,' I said.

'More than just geared-up, I think,' Porniarsk said. 'It was a guess I made only on the basis of Marc's heading for this area; but I was right. Porniarsk hoped only that a small oasis of stability might be established on the surface of this world, in this immediate locality. With anyone else, such as you, Bill, that'd be all we could do. But with Marc, maybe we can try something more. There's a chance he has an aptitude for using a device-of-assistance.'

'Can't you come up with a better name for it than that?' said Bill. His voice was tight – tight enough to shake just a little.

'What would you suggest?' asked Porniarsk.

I turned and walked away from them, out of the building through the door that opened before me and shut after me. I walked into the solitude of the thin, clean air and the high sunlight. There was something working in me; and for the moment, it had driven everything else, even Ellen, out of my mind. It was like a burning, but beneficent, fever, like a great hunger about to be satisfied, like the feeling of standing on the threshold of a cavern filled with treasure beyond counting.

It was all this, and still it was indescribable. I did not yet have it, but

I could almost touch it and taste it; and I knew that it was only a matter of time now until my grasp closed on it. Knowing that was everything, I could wait now. I could work. I could do anything. The keys of my kingdom were at hand.

18

Then began a bittersweet time for me, the several weeks that Porniarsk worked on the equipment in what we were now calling the 'round-house.' It was sweet because, day by day, I felt the device-of-assistance coming to life under the touch of those three tentacle-fingers Porniarsk had growing out of his shoulders. The avatar had been right about me. The original Porniarsk had not suspected there would be anyone on our Earth who could use the device without being physically connected to it. But evidently I was a freak. I had already had some kind of mental connection with this place, if only subconsciously, during the days of The Dream in which I had pushed us all in this direction and to this location. I said as much to Porniarsk one day.

'No,' he shook his head, 'before that, I'd think. You must have felt its existence, here, and been searching for it from the time you woke to find your world changed.'

'I was looking,' I said. 'But I didn't have any idea what for.'

'Perhaps,' said Porniarsk. 'But you might find, after the device is ready and you can look back over all you've done, that you unconsciously directed each step along the way toward this place and this moment, from the beginning.'

I shook my head. There was no use trying to explain to him, I thought, how I had never been able to let a problem alone. But I did not argue the point any further.

I was too intensely wrapped up in what I could feel growing about me – the assistance of the device. It was only partly mechanical. Porniarsk would not, or could not, explain its workings to me, although I could watch him as he worked with the small coloured cubes that made up the inner parts of seven of the consoles. The cubes were about a quarter the size of children's blocks and seemed to be made of some hard, translucent material. They clung together naturally in the arrangement in which they occurred behind the face of the console; and Porniarsk's work, apparently, was to rearrange their order and get them to cling together again. Apparently, the rearrangement was different with each console; and Porniarsk had to try any number of combinations before he found it. It looked like a random procedure but, evidently, was not; and when I asked about that, Porniarsk relaxed his no-information rule enough to tell me that what he was doing was checking arrangements of the cubes in accordance with 'sets' he already carried in his memory centre, to find patterns that would resonate with the monad that was me. It was not the cubes that were the working parts, evidently, but the patterns.

Whatever he was doing, and however it was effective, when he got a collection of cubes to hang together in a different order, I felt the effect immediately. It was as if another psychic generator had come on-line in my mind. With each addition of power, or strength, or whatever you want to call it, I saw more clearly and more deeply into all things around me.

– Including the people. And from this came the bitter to join with the sweet of my life. For as, step by step, my perceptions increased, I came to perceive that Ellen was indeed intending to leave with Tek as soon as my work with the device had been achieved. She was staying for the moment and had talked Tek into staying, only so that he and she could hold down two of the consoles; as Porniarsk had said all of the adults in our party would need to do when I made my effort to do something about the time storm. After that, they would go; and nothing I could say would stop her.

The reasons why she had turned to Tek as she had, I could not read in her. Her personal feelings were beyond the reach of my perception. Something shut me out. Porniarsk told me, when I finally asked him, that the reason I could not know how she felt was because my own emotions were involved with her. Had I been able to force myself to see, I would have seen not what was, but what I wanted to see. I would have perceived falsely; and since the perception and understanding I was gaining with the help of the device were part of a true reflection of the universe, the device could give only accurate information; consequently, it gave nothing where only inaccuracy was possible.

So, I was split down the middle; and the division between the triumph and the despair in me grew sharper with the activation of each new console. After the fourth one, the avatar warned me that there was a limit to the step-up I could endure from the device.

'If you feel you're being pushed too hard,' he said, 'tell me quickly. Too much stimulus, and you could destroy yourself before you had a chance to use the device properly.'

'It's all right,' I said. 'I know what you're talking about.' And I did. I could feel myself being stretched daily, closer and closer toward a snapping point. But that point was still not reached; and I wanted to go to the limit no matter what would happen afterwards.

It was the pain of Ellen's imminent leaving that drove me more than anything else. With the device beginning to work, I was partly out of the ordinary world already. I did not have to test myself by sticking burning splinters in my flesh to know that the physical side of me was much dwindled in importance lately. It was easy to forget that I had a body. But the awareness of my immaterial self was correspondingly amplified to several times its normal sensitivity; and it was in this immaterial area that I was feeling the loss of Ellen more keenly than the amputation of an arm and a leg together.

There was no relief from that feeling of loss except to concentrate on the expansion of my awareness. So, psychically, I pushed out and out, running from what I could not bear to face – and then, without warning, came rescue from an unexpected direction.

It was late afternoon, the sunlight slanting in at a low angle through the door to the roundhouse, which we had propped open while Porniarsk worked on the last console. Bill and I were the only other ones there. We had opened the door to let a little of the natural breeze and outer sun-warmth into the perfectly controlled climate of the interior; and in my case, this had brought the thought of my outside concerns with it, so that for a moment my mind had wandered again to thinking of Ellen.

I came back to awareness of the roundhouse, to see Bill and Porniarsk both looking at me. Porniarsk had just said something. I could hear the echo of it still in my ear, but without, its meaning had vanished.

'What?' I asked.

'It's ready,' said Porniarsk. 'How do you feel – able to take this seventh assistance? You'll remember what I told you about the past increases not being limited? They each enlarge again with each new adaptation you make to the device. If you're near your limit of tolerance now, the effect of this last increase could be many times greater than what it is presently; and you might find yourself crippled in this vital, non-physical area before you had time to pull yourself back from it.'

'I know, I know,' I said. 'Go ahead.'

'I will, then,' said Porniarsk. He reached with one of his shoulder tentacles to the console half behind him and touched a coloured square.

For a second there was nothing. Then things began to expand dramatically. I mean that literally. It was as if the sides of my head were rushing out and out, enclosing everything about me ... the round-house, the peak, the village, the whole area between the mistwalls that now enclosed me, all the other areas touching that area, the continent, the planet ... there was no end. In addition, not only was I encompassing these things, but all of them were also growing and expanding. Not physically, but with meaning – acquiring many and many times their original aspects, properties, and values. So that I understood all of them in three dimensions, as it were, where I before had never seen more than a single facet of their true shape. Now, seen this way, all of them – all things, including me – were interconnected.

So I found my way back. With the thought of interconnection, I was once more in The Dream, back in the spider web spanning the universe. Only now there were patterns to its strands. I read those patterns clearly; and they brought me an inner peace for the first time. Because, at last, I saw what I could do, and how to do it, to still the storm locally. Not just in this little section of the earth around me, but all around our planet and moon and out into space for a distance beyond us, into the general temporal holocaust. I saw clearly that I would need more strength than I presently had; and the pattern I read showed that success would carry a price. A death-price. The uncaring laws of the philosophical universe, in this situation, could balance gain against loss in only one unique equation. And that equation involved a cost of life.

But I was not afraid of death, I told myself, if the results could be achieved. After all, in a sense, I had been living on borrowed time since that first heart attack. I turned away from the patterns I was studying and looked deeper into the structure of the web itself, reaching for understanding of the laws by which it operated.

Gradually, that understanding came. Porniarsk had used the word 'gestalt' in referring to that which he hoped I would perceive if I came to the situation here with a free and unprejudiced mind; and the word had jarred on me at the time. The avatar, we had all assumed, came from a race more advanced than ours – whether it was advanced in time or otherwise. I had taken it for granted that any twentieth century human terms would be inadequate to explain whatever Porniarsk dealt with, and that he would avoid them for fear of creating misunderstandings.

– Besides, 'gestalt' came close to having been one of the cant words of twentieth century psychology; the sort of word that had been used and misused by people I knew, who wanted to sound knowledgeable about a highly specialized subject they would never take the time to study properly and understand. Granted, the avatar was probably using the human word nearest in meaning to what he wanted to say, I had still felt he could have explained himself in more hard-edged technical or scientific terms.

But then, later, he had also used the word 'monad'; and, remembering that, I now began to comprehend one important fact. The forces of the time storm and the device he was building so I could come to grips with them, belonged not so much to a physical, or even a psychological, but to a *philosophical* universe. I was far from understanding why this should be. In fact, with regard to the whole business, I was still like a child in kindergarten, learning about traffic lights without really comprehending the social and legal machinery behind the fact of their existence. But with the aid of the device, I had finally begun, at least, to get into the proper arena of perception.

Briefly and clumsily, in the area in which I would have to deal with the time storm, the only monads – that is, the only basic, indestructible, building blocks or operators – were individual minds. Each monad was capable of reflecting or expressing the whole universe from its individual point of view. In fact, each monad had always potentially expressed it; but the ability to do so had always been a possible function, unless the individual monad-mind had possessed something like a device-of-assistance to implement or execute changes in what it expressed.

Of course, expressing a change in the universe, and causing that change to take place, was not quite as simple as wishing and making it so. For one thing, all monads involved in a particular expression of some part of the universe at a particular moment were also involved with each other and had to be in agreement on any change they wished to express. For another, the change had to originate in the point of view of a monad capable of reflecting all the physical – not just the philosophical – universe as plastic and controllable.

The time storm itself was a phenomenon of the physical universe. In the limited terms to which Porniarsk was restricted by our language, he had explained to me that it was the result of entropic anarchy. The expanding universe had continued its expansion until a point of intolerable strain on the network of forces that made up the space-time fabric had been reached and passed. Then, a breakdown had occurred. In effect, the space-time bubble had begun to disintegrate. Some of the galaxies that had been moving outward, away from each other and the universal centre, producing a state of diminishing entropy, began, in spot fashion, to fall back, contracting the universe and creating isolated states of increasing entropy.

The conflict between opposed entropic states had spawned the time storm. As Porniarsk had said, the storm as a whole was too massive for control by action of the monads belonging to our original time, or even to his. But a delaying action could be fought. The forces set loose by the entropic conflict could be balanced against each other here and there, thereby slowing down the general anarchies enough to buy some breathing time, until the minds of those concerned with the struggle could develop more powerful forces to put in play across the connection between the philosophical and physical universes.

I was a single monad (though, of course, reinforced with the other seven at their altered consoles), and not a particularly capable one basically. But I was also something of a freak, a lucky freak in that my freakiness apparently fitted the necessity of the moment. That was why I could think, as I was privately doing now, of creating an enclave in the time storm that would include the whole earth and its natural satellite, instead of merely an enclave containing just the few square miles surrounding us, which had been Porniarsk's hope.

'I'll need one more console adapted,' I said to Porniarsk. 'Don't worry, now. I can handle it.'

'But there's no one to sit at it,' said Bill.

'That's correct,' said Porniarsk patiently. 'There are only seven other adults in your party. I haven't any effectiveness as a monad. Neither has the little girl.'

'She hasn't?' I looked hard at the avatar.

'Not … in effect,' he said, with a rare second of hesitation. 'A monad is required to have more than just a living intelligence and a personality. It has to have the capability of reflecting the universe. Wendy hasn't matured enough to do that. If you could ask her about it, and she could answer you, she'd say something to the effect that to her the universe isn't a defined entity. It's amorphous, unpredictable, capable of changing and surprising her at any moment. For her, the universe as she now sees it is more like a god or devil than a mechanism of natural laws – something she's got no hope of understanding or controlling.'

'All right,' I said. 'I'll settle for the fact she's at least partially a monad.'

'There's no such thing,' said Porniarsk. 'A monad either is, or is not. In any case, even if she was a partial monad, a partial monad is incapable of helping you.'

'What about when it's combined with another partial monad?'

'What other partial monad?' Bill asked.

'The Old Man, down at the village.'

'This is even worse than your idea of using Wendy,' said Porniarsk. For the first time since we'd met him, the tone of his voice came close to betraying irritation with one of us. 'The experimentals down below us are artificially created animals. The very concept of "universe" is beyond them. They're only bundles of reflexes, conditioned and trained.'

'All but one of them,' I said. 'Porniarsk, don't forget there're a lot of things I can see now with the help of the seven sets you've already produced, even if they don't have monads in connection with them yet. One of those things is that the Old Man may have been bred in a testtube – or whatever they all came from – but he's got some kind of concept of "universe," even if it's limited to his village and a mile or so of the rock around it. When we first came in here and passed the initial test of their attack, all the rest of them immediately took us for granted. Not the Old Man. By design or chance, he's got something individual to measure new things against, plus whatever it takes to make new decisions on the basis of that measurement. And you can't deny he's adult.'

No one said anything for a moment.

'I don't think,' said Bill at last, 'that Marie's going to like Wendy being hooked up to something like the Old Man.'

'Wendy won't be. They'll both just be hooked in with all the rest of us. Anyway, I'll explain it to Marie.'

'How'll you get the Old Man to cooperate?'

'He doesn't have to cooperate,' I said. 'I'll bring him up here, connect him to one of the consoles and chain him to it with Sunday's chain. Then give him a day or two to get used to the feel of assistance, and his being in connection with my mind. Once he feels the advantages these things give him, my bet is he'll get over being scared and become interested.'

'If you use force to bring him up here,' said Porniarsk, 'you'll undoubtedly trigger off the antagonisms of his fellow experimentals.'

'I think I can do it without,' I said. 'I've got an idea.'

With that, I left the two of them and went back down to our camp, which was set up at the foot of the peak. I unchained Sunday and went looking for Marie. Sunday could only be trusted to stick around the camp when I was there. He had shown no particularly strong hunting instincts before in all the time I had known him; but for some reason the experimentals seemed to fascinate him. Since the first day of our camp at the foot of the hill, when I had caught him stalking one of the village inhabitants who was out hunting among the rocks, we had kept him chained up when I was up on the peak. It was possible he might not have hurt the experimental, but the sight I had had of him, creeping softly along, belly almost dragging the ground and tail a-twitch, was too vivid to forget.

At any rate, now I let him loose, and he butted his head against me and rubbed himself against my legs all the time I was looking for Marie. I found her, with Wendy, down at the creek by the foot of the peak, doing some washing.

It was not the time to mention that I wanted Wendy at one of the consoles. The little girl had come to trust me; and – I don't care how male and solitary you are – if a small child decides to take to you, you have to carry your own instincts somewhere outside the normal spectrum not to feel some sort of emotional response. Anything unexpected or new tended to frighten Wendy; and any concern or doubt about it by her mother made the fright certain. The idea would have to be presented to Wendy gently, and with Marie's cooperation. I spoke to Marie now, instead, about the other matter I had in mind.

'Have you got any of that brandy left?' I asked.

She put down in a roaster pan some jeans of Wendy's she was wringing out and shook her hands to get the excess water off. She had her own slacks rolled up above her knees and her legs and feet bare so that she could wade into the creek. The work had pinkened her face and tousled her hair. She looked, not exactly younger, but more relaxed and happy than usual; and for a second I felt sad that I had not been able to love her after all, instead of Ellen.

'What's the occasion?' she asked.

'No occasion,' I said. 'I'm hoping to bait the Old Man in the village down there, so I can get him up to the roundhouse. We want to try him with the consoles. You do have some brandy left?'

'Yes,' she said. 'How much do you want?'

'One full bottle ought to be plenty,' I said. 'Is there that much?'

'I've got several full bottles,' she said. 'Do you want it right away, or can I finish up here first?'

'I'd like to get down to the village before dark.'

'I'll be done in five minutes.'

'Fine, then,' I said and sat down on a boulder to wait. It took her closer to fifteen than five minutes, as it turned out, but there was still at least an hour or so of sunset left. We went back to the camper; she got me an unopened bottle of brandy, and I walked down to the village with it.

The whole thing was a gamble. I had no idea what kind of body chemistry the experimentals had. From what Porniarsk had said, they had evidently been developed by future humans from ape stock; chimpanzee at a guess. The larger part of their diet seemed to be some sort of artificially prepared eatable in a cube form that came from inside one of the dome-shaped buildings. But since the building was small, and the supply of the cubes seemed to be inexhaustible, I had guessed that there was some kind of underground warehouse to which the building was merely an entrance. However, in addition to the cubes, the experimentals were at least partly carnivorous. They went out into the rocks around the village in the daytime to hunt small rodent-like animals with their throwing knives; and these they either ate raw on the spot or carried back into their buildings at the village to be eaten at leisure.

All these things seemed to add up to the strong possibility that they had digestive systems and metabolisms pretty similar to a human's. But there was no way of being sure. All I could do was try.

The Old Man was not out in the open when I first walked into the village, but before I was half a dozen steps down the main street, he had emerged from his dwelling to hunker down in front of his doorway and stare at me steadily as I approached. I detoured along the way to pick up a couple of handleless cups or small bowls that one of the local workmen was turning out on his machine. I'd thought earlier of bringing a couple of containers from our camp, then decided the Old Man would be more likely to trust utensils that were familiar to him. I came up to within ten feet of him, sat down cross-legged on the hard-packed, stony dirt of the street, and got my bottle from the inner jacket pocket in which I had been carrying it.

I put both cups down, poured a little brandy into both of them, picked up one, sipped from it and started staring back at him.

It was not the most lively cocktail hour on record. I pretended to drink, pouring as little as possible into my cup each time, and putting somewhat more into the other cup, which slowly began to fill. The Old Man kept staring at me; apparently, he was capable of keeping it up without blinking as long as the daylight lasted. Eventually, even the small amounts of liquor with which I was wetting my tongue began to make themselves felt. I found myself talking. I told the Old Man what fine stuff it was I was drinking, and I invited him to help himself. I speculated on the interesting discoveries he would make if he only joined me and became friendly.

He continued to stare.

Eventually, the other cup was as full as it could safely be, and the sun was almost down. There was nothing more I could do. I left the cups and the bottle with the top off and got to my feet.

'Pleasant dreams,' I said to him, and left. Back once more in the rocks a safe distance from the village, I got out my field glasses and peered down in the direction of his building. It was almost dark, and one thing the experimentals did not have was artificial lighting. They all disappeared into their buildings at dusk and only reappeared with the dawn. But by straining my vision now, I was able to make out a dim figure still in front of the Old Man's building. I squinted through the binoculars, my eyes beginning to water; and, just as I was about to give up, I caught a tiny glint of light on something moving.

It was the bottle, being upended in the general area of the Old Man's head. I gave an inward, silent whoop of joy. Unless he had decided to use the brandy for a shampoo, or unless he turned out to have a body that reacted to alcohol as if it was so much branch water, I had him.

I waited until the moon came up, then got the pickup and drove by moonlight down through the main street of the village to the Old Man's building. I took an unlit flashlight and went in the building entrance. Inside, I turned the flashlight on and found the Old Man. He was curled up in the corner of the single room that was the building's interior on a sort of thick rug. He reeked of brandy, and was dead drunk.

He was also no lightweight. I had not thought it to look at him, for all the experimentals looked small and skinny by human standards; but apparently they were nothing but bone and muscle. Still, I managed to carry him out to the pickup and get him inside the cab. Then I drove back out of the village to the camp.

At the camp, I took him out of the pickup, unchained Sunday and put him in the pickup, put the chain and collar on the Old Man and lifted him, still snoozing, into one of the jeeps. By this time, I was surrounded by people wanting to know what I was doing.

'I want to try him out on the equipment up at the roundhouse,' I said. 'He drank almost a full bottle of brandy, and he ought to sleep until morning, but with all this noise he may just wake up. Now, will you let me get him put away up there? Then I'll come down and tell you all about it.'

'We already had dinner,' said Wendy.

'Hush,' said Marie to her, 'Marc'll have his dinner when he gets back. You're coming right back down?'

'In twenty minutes at the outside,' I said.

I turned on the lights of the jeep and growled up the hillside in low gear. The partitions between the consoles had supports that were anchored in the concrete floor of the roundhouse; and I chained the sleeping Old Man to one of these. As an afterthought, I took from the jeep the canteen of drinking water we always kept with each of the vehicles and left it beside him. If he got drunk like a human, he was likely to have a hangover like a human.

Then I growled my way back down again to the camp to turn Sunday loose, answer questions, and have my dinner.

To everybody except Porniarsk and Bill, who already knew what I had in mind, I explained my capture of the Old Man with a half-truth, saying I wanted to see if he could be useful as a partial monad when we tried to use the equipment in the roundhouse, the day after tomorrow. It was not until later that evening, in the privacy of the camper, after Wendy was asleep, that I talked to Marie about using the little girl at one of the consoles. Surprisingly, Marie thought it was a very good idea. She said Wendy had no one to play with but the dogs, and she had been wanting badly to get in on what the adults were doing.

19

I slept that night, but I did not rest. As soon as I closed my eyes I was off among the strands of the spider web, riding the shifting forces of the time storm about our world. I scuttled about, studying them. I already knew what I would have to do. Every so often, for a transitory moment, the forces in this area I had chosen came close to a situation of internal balance. If, at just the right moment, I could throw all the force controlled by the eight other monads and myself against the tangle of conflicting forces that was the storm, hopefully I could nudge this tiny corner of the storm into a state of dynamic balance.

Why do I say 'hopefully'? I knew I could do it – if only Wendy and the Old Man, under the assistance of the device, would give me amplification enough to act as an eighth monad. For it was not power I needed but understanding. As clearly as I could see the forces now, I needed to see them many times more clearly, in much finer detail. Close in, focused down to the local area which was all that Porniarsk had envisioned me bringing into balance, my vision was sharp enough. But on wider focus, when I looked further out into the time storm, the fine detail was lost. One more monad and I could bring those distant, fuzzy forces into clarity.

It was merely a matter of waiting until morning, I told myself, finally, and made myself put the whole problem out of my head. At my bidding, it went; which was something such a problem would never have done a week before. But then another thought came to perch on my mind like a black crow.

I was aware I had never been what the world used to call a kind or moral man, a 'good' man, as my grandfather would have said. I had always let myself do pretty much what I wanted, within practical limits; and I had never been particularly caring, or concerned for other people. But ethical laws are a part of any philosophical universe; they have to be. And was it entirely in agreement with those laws, now, my carrying these eight other people – nine, if you counted the Old Man as being in the people category – into a joust with something as monstrous as the time storm, only because of my own hunger to know and do?

Granted, I could not see any way in which they could be hurt. The only one I was putting on the line, as far as I knew, was myself. But there are always understandings beyond understandings. Perhaps there was some vital bit of information I did not have.

On the other hand, perhaps that was not really what was bothering me. I looked a little deeper into myself and found the real fishhook in my conscience; the unanswered question of whether, even if I knew there was real danger to the others, I would let that be reason enough to stop me. Perhaps I would go ahead anyway, prepared to sacrifice them to my own desires, my own will.

This question was harder to put out of my mind than the time storm problem, but in the end, I managed. I lay, open-eyed and without moving, until the dawn whitened the shade drawn over the window on the side of the camper across from the bunk on which I lay with Marie.

I got up and dressed quietly. Marie slept on, but Wendy opened her eyes and looked at me.

'Go back to sleep,' I told her. She closed her eyes again without argument. (Probably only humouring me, I thought.)

Dressed, I glanced at Marie, half-tempted to wake her and say a few words to her. But there was no good reason for that, I realized, unless I only wanted to leave her with some enigmatic, but portentous, statement she could remember afterwards and worry over, wondering if she could have done something more for me in some way; and things might have been different. I was a little ashamed of myself and let myself out of the camper as softly as I could.

Outside, the morning air was dry and cold. I shivered, even under the leather jacket I was wearing, and fired up the coleman stove to make a pot of coffee. All the time I was making it, I could feel the Old Man's presence in the back of my mind. He was connected to the console, which meant he was in connection with me. I could feel that he was awake now and suffering from the hangover I had anticipated. The discomfort was making him savage – I could tell that, too. But underneath the savagery he was beginning to wonder a little at what his mind could now sense of me, and through me, of the larger universe.

I made my coffee, drank it, and drove one of the jeeps to the roundhouse. Inside, around where the Old Man had been, it was a mess. He had been sick – I should have thought of the possibility of that. In addition, he had urinated copiously.

I cleaned up, cautiously. Now that he was awake, I had enough respect for those ape-like arms of his not to let him get a grip on me. But he let me work on until I was right next to him, without making any move in my direction. He was still staring at me all the time, but now there was a speculative gleam in his brown eyes. He had now realized who it was his mind connected to. I could feel him in my head, exploring the connection and the situation. I had guessed right. Now, he was interested. But his mind was still alien to me, much more alien than Porniarsk's.

I took a chance, disconnected him from the console, unhooked his chain from the stanchion, and led him outside, to ensure that any further eliminations he was moved to would take place somewhere else than in the roundhouse. I found a boulder too heavy for him to move and with a lower half that was narrower than the top, so that the loop of chain I locked around it could not be pulled off over the top. I rechained him to this. The boulder was on the far side of the roundhouse, so that he could neither see his village nor be seen from it, assuming that his fellows down there had distance vision good enough to pick him out. Then I left him with some bread, an opened can of corned beef and a refilled canteen of water, and went down to my own breakfast. He let me go without a sound, but his eyes followed me with their speculative look as long as I was in sight. All the way down the mountain, I could feel his mind trying to explore mine.

Once back at the camp, I got out the binoculars and looked over the village. Its inhabitants were out of their homes and about their daily activities. None of them seemed to be missing the Old Man or showing any curiosity about the lack of his presence. That much was all right, then. I went back, put the binoculars away and ate breakfast. All the others were up and also breakfasting; but there was a tension, a taut feeling in the very air of the camp.

I did not feel like talking to anyone; and the rest seemed to understand this. They left me alone while I was eating – all but Sunday, who clearly sensed that something unusual was up. He did not rub against me in his usual fashion, but prowled around and around me, his tail twitching as if his nerves were on fire. He made such an ominous demonstration that I was alarmed for Bill, when at last, he started to come toward me.

But Sunday drew back just enough to let him get close, although he circled the two of us, eyeing Bill steadily and making little occasional singing noises in his throat.

'I don't want to bother you,' Bill said. His voice was hardly more than a murmur, too low for any of the others to overhear.

'It's all right,' I said. 'What is it?'

'I just wanted you to know,' he said, 'you can count on me.'

'Well,' I said, 'thanks.'

'No, I really mean *count* on me,' he insisted.

'I hear you,' I said. 'Thanks. But all you'll have to do today is sit at that console and let me use you.'

He looked back at me for a second in a way that was almost as keyed-up and strange as Sunday's present behaviour.

'Right,' he said and went off.

I had no time to puzzle over him. There was Sunday to get into the cab of the pickup and the doors safely closed on him; and the leopard was just not agreeable to going in this morning. In the end I had to haul him in as a dead weight, swearing at him, with one fist closed on the scruff of his neck and my other arm around his wedge-shaped cat chest below his forelegs. I didn't dare have any of the others help me in the mood the leopard was in – even the girl. Though, in fact, she was busy at the moment, doing something in the motorhome with Marie – and she probably would not have come anyway if I'd called.

I finally got Sunday in and the door closed. Immediately he found himself trapped, he began to thrash around and call to me. I closed my ears to the sounds he was making and got my party into the jeeps and headed up the side of the peak. I was already at work with the back of my head, monitoring the present interplay of the forces in the storm, as far as I could pick them out. A real picture of the pattern out as far as the Moon's orbit would have to wait until the others were all at their consoles and connected with me. I thought I was gaining some advantage from them already, which was a very good sign. Either I had been building psychic muscle since the last two consoles had been finished, or the Old Man was proving to be even more useful than I had hoped. Actually, in one way, he had already exceeded expectations; because I was still as strongly linked to him as I had been when he had been connected to the console and chained inside the roundhouse.

Wendy, who had been chattering away merry and bright in the back of the jeep I was driving, fell into dubious silence as we pulled up to the level spot where the roundhouse stood and she saw the Old Man staring at us. But he only gave her and the others a single surveying glance and then came back to concentrate on me as I got out of the jeep and came back toward him.

He knew where I was going to take him. He came along almost eagerly when I unlocked the chain and led him to the roundhouse door. It slid aside automatically as we got within arm's length of it, and he went over the threshold ahead of me with a bound, headed toward his console. I took him to it and chained him on a short length of the chain, so that he could not reach around the partition to whoever would be at the console next to him.

Bill followed me in and blocked the door open to the outer air, as we had got in the habit of doing. The others followed him. They began to take their places under Porniarsk's direction and let themselves be connected to their consoles. The dark material clung to itself when one end of it was loosely wrapped around the throat. The further end of it reached through the face of the console to touch the pattern of blocks inside. It was so simple as to seem unbelievable, except for the fact that the strap had a mild, built-in warmth to it. It was a semi-living thing, Porniarsk had told me. All the connections in the roundhouse were made with such semi-living objects. They operated like psychic channels. If you imagine the tube through which a blood transfusion is being given, as being alive and capable of making its own connection with the blood systems of the two people involved in the transfusion, you have an analogous picture.

The straps were vaguely comforting to wear, like a security blanket. I noticed Wendy brighten up for the first time since seeing the Old Man, when hers was wrapped around her throat by Bill. There was one waiting for me at the monitoring station in the middle of the room; but I wanted to try seeing what kind of connection I could have with the other monads without it, before I strapped myself in.

Bill and Porniarsk strapped in the others, then Bill strapped himself in, and Porniarsk went to the monitoring station. He reached with one tentacle for the coloured square on the console there that activated all connections. His tentacle flicked down to touch the square, and the connection already established between myself and the Old Man suddenly came alive with our mutual understanding of what would happen when activation took place.

The Old Man howled.

His vocal capabilities were tremendous. All of us in the roundhouse were half-deafened by the sound, which rang like a fire siren in our ears, and broadcast itself outward from the propped-open door. In that same second, Porniarsk's tentacle touched the surface of the square, and the connections were activated. Full contact with all the other monads there erupted around me; and full perception of the time storm forces out of Moon orbit distance smashed down on me like a massive wall of water. The Old Man's howl was cut off in mid-utterance. I found my body running for the roundhouse door.

For with contact had come full understanding of what the Alpha

Prime had done, and what he had been trying to do. I burst out of the roundhouse and looked down the steep, bouldered face of the peak that fell towards the village. The lower edge of it was alive with black, climbing bodies.

How the Old Man had contacted them, I did not know. His connection with me and the console had made it possible, that was obvious; but he had used channels of identity with his own people that were not part of my own, human machinery. The most I could understand was that he had not actually called them, in a true sense. He had only been able to provoke an uneasiness in them that had sent most of them out hunting among the lower rocks, in the direction of the peak.

But now they had heard him. Lost somewhere in the gestalt of the monad group of which he and I were a part – Porniarsk had been right in his use of that word, for the group, myself and this place were all integrated into a whole now – the Old Man's mind was triumphant. He knew that he had called in time, that his people had heard and were coming.

I whirled around and stared back into the roundhouse through the open door, though I already knew what I would see. Inside, all the figures were motionless and silent. There was not even a chest-movement of breathing to be seen in any of them, for they were caught in a timeless moment – the moment in which we had contacted the storm and I had paused to examine the pattern of its forces. Even Porniarsk was frozen into immobility with his tentacle-tip touching his activation square on the monitor console. The square itself glowed now, with a soft, pink light.

I was still unconnected and mobile. But the Old Man's people would be here in twenty minutes; and all our weapons were down at the camp.

I watched my body turn and run for the nearest jeep, leap into it, start it, turn it, and get it going down the slope toward camp. I had the advantage of a vehicle, but the distance was twice as much, down to camp, than it was up the slope the experimentals were climbing, and twice as far back up again. The jeep bounced and slid down the shallower slope on this side of the peak, skidding and slewing around the larger boulders in the way. My body drove it; but my mind could not stay with it, because I had already seen enough of the present moment's pattern to locate the upcoming pressure point I searched for. That pressure point would be coming into existence in no more time than it would take the villagers to climb to the roundhouse, possibly, even in less time. I had that long only to study all the force lines involved and make sure that my one chance to produce a state of balance was taken exactly on the mark.

20

It was not the pattern of forces in the time storm itself I studied; but the image of this pattern in the philosophical universe during that fractional, timeless moment when I had first tapped the abilities of our full monad-gestalt. That image was like a three-dimensional picture taken by a camera with a shutter speed beyond imagination. Already, of course, the configuration of the forces in the storm had developed, through a whole series of changes, into totally different patterns, and they were continuing to change. But with the gestalt and the device to back me up, I could study the configuration that had been and calculate how the later patterns would be at any other moment in the future.

In any such pattern – past, present, or future – the time storm forces of any given area had to have the potential of developing into a further state of dynamic balance. The potential alone, however, was not good enough. To begin with, the forces had to be very close to balance, within a very small tolerance indeed; otherwise, the relatively feeble strength of my gestalt would not, be able to push them into balance.

But first, the imbalances to be corrected must be understood in detail. Balance was an ideal state; and the chances of it occurring naturally were as small as the total time storm itself was large. The only reason it was barely possible to achieve it artificially lay in a characteristic of the time storm itself; the storm's tendency to break up progressively into smaller and smaller patterns and for these to break up in turn, and so on. This was the same characteristic that Porniarsk had mentioned as presenting the greatest danger of the storm if it was not fought and opposed. The continuing disintegration would continue to produce smaller and smaller temporal anomalies until, at last, any single atomic particle would be existing at a different temporal moment than its neighbour. But in this case, it offered an advantage in that the disintegration process produced smaller temporal anomalies within larger ones, like miniature hurricanes in the calms that were the eyes of larger ones; and so, by choosing the right moment to act, it was possible to balance the forces of a small, contained anomaly, without having to deal with the continuing imbalanced forces of a larger disturbance containing it.

Of course, the word 'hurricane' did not really convey the correct image of a temporal anomaly. In its largest manifestation, such an anomaly represented the enormous forces released in intergalactic space along the face of contact between an expanding galaxy and a contracting one. Here on earth, in its smallest – so far – manifestation, it was an area such as the one we and the experimentals were inhabiting now, with the conflicting forces existing where the mistwalls marked their presence. Temporally, the mistwalls were areas of tremendous activity. Physically, as we had discovered, they were no more than bands of lightly disturbed air and suspended dust, stretching up from the surface of the earth until they came into conflict with other forces of their same 'hurricane.'

In my philosophical image of the apparent walls that were time storm force-lines, I saw them in cross-section, so that they seemed like a web of true lines filling a three-dimensional space, the interstices between lines being the chunks of four-dimensional space they enclosed. Seen close up, the lines looked less like threads than like rods of lightning frozen in the act of striking. Whatever this appearance represented of their real properties in the physical universe, the fact was clear that they moved and were moved by the other force-lines with which they interacted; so that they developed continually from one pattern to another, in constant rearrangement, under the push of the current imbalance.

I already knew in what general direction the patterns in the area I was concerned with were developing. But now I projected these developments, studying the parade of succeeding configurations for specific details, looking for one that would give me a possibility of forcing a balanced pattern into existence before the experimentals arrived at the roundhouse. I could not do this until I had returned with weapons and driven off the figures now climbing the peak, for the good reason that the pattern showed me the development of affairs here, as well as the larger picture. I alone, even with guns, would not be able to drive off those who were coming. There were more than a hundred of them; and this time they would not give up as easily as they had before. They had been conditioned to ignore the roundhouse. Now, somehow, the Old Man had managed to break that conditioning. The only thing that would stop them would be fright at some great natural event. A volcanic eruption, an earthquake – or the meteorological reaction when the mistwall through which we had entered went out of existence, and the atmosphere of the area on its far side suddenly mixed with the atmosphere on this.

I must get down, get weapons, get back up, and hold them off long enough to use the gestalt successfully to produce balance in the pattern. My mind galloped past the developing patterns, checking, checking, checking; and as it went, the jeep under me was skidding and plunging down the slope to our camp.

I slid in between our tents, at last, in a cloud of dust and stopped. I jumped out of the jeep, unlocked the door of the motorhome, and plunged inside.

Warm from the hot, still atmosphere within, the guns were where we always kept them, in the broom closet, with the ammunition on a shelf above. I grabbed two shotguns and the two heaviest rifles, with ammo. But when I reached for the machine pistol, it was not there.

I spent, perhaps, a couple of frantic minutes looking for it in improbable places about the motorhome, before I finally admitted to myself that it was gone. Who could have managed to get into the vehicle, which Marie and I kept locked religiously except when one of us was in it, was something there was no time to puzzle about now. With its extendable stock collapsed, the weapon was light and small enough to be carried under a heavy piece of outer clothing by either man or woman – and most of us going up to the roundhouse this morning had worn either a jacket or a bulky sweater. I got out of the motorhome in a hurry, not even bothering to lock it behind me. I made the driver's seat of the jeep in one jump, gunned the still-running motor and headed back up the slope of the peak.

I was perhaps a hundred and fifty yards from the camp when the dead silence that had existed there registered. Sunday had been back there all the time I was getting the guns, locked up in the cab of the pickup. But I had not heard a sound from him, in spite of the fact that he must have heard the jeep arrive, and seen, heard, and possibly even smelled me. He should have been putting up as much racket as he could, in an effort to make me come and let him out. But there had been no noise at all.

I drove another twenty yards or so before I gave in to the suddenly empty, sick feeling inside me. Then, I wrenched the jeep around and roared back down to the camp to the pickup.

I did not need to get out of the jeep to look at it. I did not even need to get close. From twenty feet away, I could see the wind-shield of the pickup lying on the hood of the vehicle like a giant's lost spectacle lens. Somehow, Sunday had managed to pop it completely out of its frame. And he was gone.

I knew where he was gone. I got the field glasses and looked off up the steep slope leading directly to the roundhouse, where the tiny black figures of the experimentals could now be seen more than halfway up. Down below them, I saw nothing for a moment – and then there was a flash of movement. It was Sunday, headed to join me on top, where he must have believed me to be, not travelling by the roundabout, easy slope I had come down in the jeep, but directly up the mountainside on a converging route with those from the village below.

He would keep coming. If the experimentals did not get in his way, he would simply pass them up. But if they tried to stop him, he would kill as long as he could until he was killed himself. But he would keep coming.

The idiotic, loving beast! There was nothing but death for him where he was headed; but even if he had known that, it would not have stopped him. There was nothing I could do for him now. I could not even take time out to think of him. There were eight people and a world to think of.

I ripped the jeep around and headed up the slope. The best I could do; the longer distance before me would make it a tossup whether I could get back to the roundhouse before the experimentals arrived.

I had the upcoming patterns of the time storm in my head now. I could see the one I wanted developing. It was not an absolutely sure thing, so far; but it was as close to a sure thing as I could wish for in limited time, such as we had now. It would form within seconds after I made the top of the peak and the roundhouse.

There was nothing more I could do now but drive. In the round-house the others were still immobile – even the Old Man – caught up in the gestalt. I gave most of my attention to the ground ahead.

It was the best driving I had ever done. I was tearing hell out of the jeep, but if it lasted to the top of the peak that was all I asked of it. I did not lose any time, but what I gained – the best I could gain – was only seconds. When I did reach the level top and the roundhouse at last, the experimentals were not yet there.

I skidded the jeep to a stop beside the door of the roundhouse and tossed one rifle, one shotgun, and most of the ammunition inside. Then I pulled the block that was holding the door open – and all this time, the storm pattern I was waiting for was coming up in my mind – stepped back, and the door closed automatically. The experimentals did not have doors to buildings. Perhaps they did not know what a door was and would think, seeing this one closed, that there was no entrance into the roundhouse. If they did by accident trigger the door to opening, those inside would have the other two guns which, one way or the other, they would be awake and ready to use; for in a moment I would either win or lose, and the gestalt would be set free again.

I watched the door close and turned just in time to see the first round, ape-like head come over the edge of the cliff-edge, some forty yards away. I snatched up the rifle and had it halfway to my shoulder when I realized I would never fire it. There was no time now. The moment and the pattern I waited for were rushing down upon me. I had no more mind to spare for killing. Still standing with the rifle half-raised, I went back into the pattern; meanwhile, as if through the wrong end of a telescope, I was seeing the black figure come all the way up into view and advance, and other black figures appear one by one behind him, until there were four of them coming steadily toward me, not poising the knives they held to throw, but holding them purposely by the hilt, as if they wanted to make sure of finishing me off.

It was the final moment. I saw the pattern I had waited for ready to be born. I felt the strength of my monad-gestalt; and at last, I knew certainly that what I was about to try would work. The four experimentals were more than halfway to me; and now I could understand clearly how the indications I had read had been correct. I would be able to do what I had wanted; and with the windstorm that would follow the disappearance of the mistwalls, the experimentals would panic and retreat. But the cost of all this would be my life. I had expected it to be so.

I stood waiting for the experimentals, the pattern rushing down upon me. In the last seconds, a different head poked itself over the edge of the cliff, and a different body came leaping toward me. It was Sunday, too late.

The pattern I awaited exploded into existence. I thrust, with the whole gestalt behind me. The fabric of the time storm about me staggered, trembled and fell together – locked into a balance of forces. And awareness of all things vanished from me, like the light of a blown-out lamp.

21

The world came back to me, little by little. I was conscious of a warm wind blowing across me. I could feel it on my face and hands; I could feel it tugging at my clothes. It was stiff, but no hurricane. I opened my eyes and saw streamers of cloud torn to bits scudding across the canvas of a blue sky, moving visibly as I watched. I felt the hard and pebbled ground under my body and head; and a pressure, like a weight, on the upper part of my right thigh.

I sat up. I was alive – and unhurt. Before me, out beyond the cliff-edge where the experimentals had appeared, there was no more mist-wall – only sky and distant, very distant landscape. I looked down and saw the four black bodies on the ground, strung out almost in a line. None of them moved; and when I looked closer I saw clearly how badly they had been torn by teeth and claws. I looked further down, yet, at the weight on my thigh, and saw Sunday.

He lay with his head stretched forward to rest on my leg, and one of the leaf-shaped knives was stuck, half-buried in the big muscle behind his left shoulder. Behind him, there was perhaps fifteen feet of bloody trail where he had half-crawled, half-dragged himself to me. His jaws were partly open, the teeth and gums red-stained with blood that was not his own. His eyes were closed. The lids did not stir, nor his jaws move. He lay still.

'Sunday?' I said. But he was not there to hear me.

There was nothing I could do. I picked up his torn head, somehow, in my arms and held it to me. There was just nothing I could do. I closed my own eyes and sat there holding him for quite a while. Finally, there were sounds around me; I opened my eyes again and looked up to see that the others, released now that the gestalt was ended, had come out of the roundhouse and were standing around looking at the new world. Marie was standing over me.

Tek and Ellen were off by themselves some thirty yards from the roundhouse. He had turned the jeep around and evidently pulled it off

393

a short distance in a start back down the side of the peak. But for some reason he had stopped again and was now getting back out of the driver's seat, holding one of the rifles, probably the one I had thrown into the roundhouse, tucked loosely in the crook of his right elbow, barrel down. Ellen was already out of the jeep and standing facing him a few steps off.

'You go,' she was saying to him. 'I can't now. He doesn't even have Sunday now.'

I remembered how much Sunday had meant to her in those first days after I had found her. And how he had put up with her more than I ever would have expected. But she had always been fond of him. And I – I had taken him for granted. Because he was mad. Crazy, crazy, insane cat. But what difference does it make why the love's there, as long as it is? Only I'd never known how much of my own heart I'd given back to him until this day and hour.

Ellen was walking away from Tek and the jeep now.

'Come back,' Tek said to her.

She did not answer. She walked past me and into the roundhouse through the door that was once more propped open. In the relative shadow of the artificially lit interior, she seemed to vanish.

Tek's face twisted and went savage.

'Don't try anything,' said Bill's voice, tightly.

I looked to the other side of me and saw him there. He was pale-faced, but steady, holding one of the shotguns. The range was a little long for accuracy with a shotgun; but Bill held it purposefully.

'Get out if you want,' he told Tek. 'But don't try anything.'

Tek seemed to sag all over. His shoulders drooped; the rifle barrel sagged downward. All the savageness leaked out of him, leaving him looking defenceless.

'All right,' he said, in an empty voice.

He started to turn away toward the jeep. Bill sighed and let the shotgun drop butt-downward to the earth; so that he held it, almost leaning on the barrel of it, wearily. Tek turned back, suddenly, the rifle barrel coming up to point at me.

Bill snatched up the shotgun, too slowly. But in the same second, there was the yammer of the machine pistol from inside the roundhouse, and Ellen walked out again holding the weapon and firing as she advanced. Tek, flung backward by the impact of the slugs, bounced off the side of the jeep and slid to the ground, the rifle tumbling from his hands.

Ellen walked a good dozen steps beyond me. But then she slowed and stopped. Tek was plainly dead. She dropped the machine pistol as if her hands had forgotten they held it; and she turned to come back to me.

Marie had been standing unmoving, close to me all this time. But when Ellen was only a step or two away, Marie moved back and away out of my line of vision. Ellen knelt beside me and put her arms around both me and the silent head I was still holding.

'It'll be all right,' she said. 'It's all going to be all right. You wait and see.'

22

We had won. In fact, the world had won, for the freezing of the movement of the time lines into a state of dynamic balance was complete for the immediate area of our planet. But for me, personally, after that there followed a strange time, the first part of which I was not really all there in my head and the second part of which, I was most earnestly trying to get out of my head.

It was left to the others to pick up the pieces and deal with the period of adjustment to the new physical state of affairs, which they did by themselves. Of the months immediately following the moment of change at the station, I have no clear memory. It was a period of time in which days and nights shuttered about me, light and dark, light and dark, like frames on a film strip. Spring ran into summer, summer into fall, and fall into winter, without any real meaning for me. When the cold months came, I would have still sat outside in jeans and tank top if the girl or Marie had not dressed me to suit the temperature; and I would probably have starved to death if they had not put food in front of me and stood over me to see that I ate it.

My reality during that time was all inside my skull, in a universe where the grey fog of indifference only lifted to a sharp awareness of psychic pain and guilt. Sunday had loved me – the only thing in the world that ever had – and I had killed him.

Porniarsk had worked a piece of technological magic almost immediately, out of knowledge from time and place of his original avatar; but it did not help the way I felt. He had created some kind of force-field enclosure, in which Sunday's stabbed and slain body was held in stasis – a sort of non-cryogenic preserving chamber. He could not bring Sunday back to life, Porniarsk told me; but as long as time had become a variable for us, there was always the chance that, eventually, we would contact someone with the knowledge to do it. He told me this many times, repeating himself patiently to get the information through the fog about me. But I did not believe him; and, after the first time, I refused to go anywhere near the black-furred body lying still, inside its glasslike energy shell.

The core of my guilt, though none of the rest suspected it, lay in the knowledge of my responsibility for Sunday's death – and something more. The further element was part of the knowledge that I had always failed with any person or thing who had tried to get close to me. It was a fact of my experience; and, buried behind it all this time, had been the darker suspicion that when I could not turn love away from me, I would always at least manage to destroy its vehicle. Now, in my awareness of my own responsibility for the death of Sunday, I had confirmed that suspicion.

The confirmation was my own private purgatory. No one, not even Porniarsk, seemed to suspect that I might have, subconsciously, used the moment of coming to grips with the time storm to rid myself of the one creature who embarrassed me with an affection I lacked the personal machinery to return. But I myself knew the truth. I knew – and I woke fresh to the knowledge every morning. I sat with it through days of the months that followed and went to sleep with it at night.

As I saw it, my sin was not one of simple, but of calculated, omission. Which made it one of commission instead. It printed itself as a damning question on the clouds above me in the daytime and glowed, invisible to all eyes but mine, on the darkness of the ceiling above me, at night. If I could read the factors of the time storm, the question ran – and I had been able – then why hadn't I also taken a moment to puzzle out the factors of human and animal interaction that had led to the deaths of Tek and Sunday?

I had not done so, the whisper inside me repeated night and day, because I had wanted them dead. Particularly, I had wanted Sunday dead; for if he continued to exist and follow me about, eventually the other humans would discover that there was an emptiness in me where a heart ought to be. Then it would strike them that I could never care two cents for them either; and they would turn on me because who could be safe with someone like me around?

So, I told myself all this through something like a year and a half following the time storm; and in the telling I skirted the grey edge of insanity, because I could not stand myself as I now knew myself to be. It was a grim trick of fate that had sent me into life lacking the one necessary, invisible part that would have made me human, rather than some flesh and blood robot. Inside my mind, I pounded on walls, screaming at the unfairness of circumstances, that had taken me out of a situation where I had not known what an emotional cripple I was and brought me face to face with the fact of it.

For that was what had happened. Beginning with my mental explosion, when I had found out that Swannee was gone – dead and gone, gone forever – there had been a string of small confrontations. A series of little turns which gradually turned me about one hundred and eighty degrees, until at last I saw myself full-on in the mirror of my mind and stared at the metal bones shining through my plastic skin, the glow of the light bulbs artificially illuminating the polished caverns of my eyesockets. It was then that I realized what had been going on in my unconscious all along.

Only Swannee had known me for the essentially nonhuman I was. Her reaction to that had been a sort of proof that I was human; but with all hope of finding her gone, I ran the risk of being recognized. At first, I had believed that the two with me – the crazy girl and the insane cat – were no threat to my secret. No one could expect me to have to prove myself to them. But then had come Marie and the unrecognized, but nagging, suspicion that she sensed the lack in me. Then Bill, another real person to watch me and draw conclusions. Then Porniarsk, who, perhaps, was too alienly knowledgeable; and after him, the experimentals, who, by definition, must also be creatures without souls, so that at any moment any one of the other people, the real people, might say to themselves – *look at the way he acts with Sunday! Doesn't that strike you as being like the way you'd expect the experimentals to respond to any affection or kindness?*

But the greatest danger had come from the girl outgrowing her craziness after all. She had known me too long; and she had known Sunday. There had been signs in her to show that she knew me better than I had thought she did. I wanted to keep her around; but unless I did something, she would be the very one who would watch me with Sunday and put two and two together – after which she would have no use for me, and I would lose her forever.

Of course, Tek had threatened to take her away anyway, which would have solved things in a way I did not want. But deep inside me, I knew Tek was no match for me. He had never really been a threat. There were a dozen ways in which I could have eliminated him from the situation, right down to following him and the girl, killing him and bringing her back by force. No, Sunday had been the one to eliminate, and now I had taken care of him. Sitting around by myself as the days and nights went past, I mourned – not for him, but for the bitterness of having to face what I was, when I had been so successful at hiding it from myself before.

The others were very patient with me. I would have shot me, dug a grave, tumbled myself in and got rid of the extra mouth to feed, the extra clothes to wash. But they were different. So they endured me, letting me roam around as I liked, only coming to collect me when it was time for a meal or bedtime; and I had the privacy I wanted.

Or at least, I had it for a long time. But then my isolation began to be invaded. I don't know when I first became conscious of it; perhaps I had been seeing his dark, lean figure around, but ignoring it for some time. But the day came when I noticed the Old Man sitting watching me, hunkered down in the shade of a boulder (it was summer again by that time) about thirty yards off along the hillside where I sat by myself.

I remember wondering then how he had gotten loose. In the back of my mind, he had been still chained up, all this time, in the station. Possibly, I thought, they had turned him loose some time since to go back down with his fellow experimentals. I did not want to come out of my grey fog to the effort of asking any of the others about him, so I decided to ignore him. He was simply sitting, watching me; and his limited mind, I thought, should get tired of that after a while, and I would be rid of him.

I decided to ignore him.

But he did not grow tired of watching and go away. Gradually, I began to be aware that he would always be around somewhere close, even if he was not plainly visible. Not only would he be there, but after some weeks, it became obvious that he was gradually lessening the distance at which he sat from me.

I had no idea what he was after; but I wanted him gone. I wanted to be left alone, even by imitation subhumans. One day – he was now in the habit of sitting less than twenty feet from me – I let one hand that was hidden from him by my body drop casually on a stone about the size of a medium hen's egg, gathered it in, and waited. Some time later, when I thought I saw his attention distracted for a moment – as it turned out I was wrong – I scooped it up and threw it at him as hard as I could.

He lifted a hand and caught it before it reached him.

The catch he made was so effortless that I never tried to throw another thing at him. Nothing except his arm had moved, not even his shoulder. His long, skinny arm had simply lifted and let the stone fly into the palm of it. Then he had dropped it, discarding it with a disinterested opening of his fingers; and all the while, his eyes had stayed unmoving on mine.

Sour fury boiled in me at that; and it was enough to bring me partway back to life. My first reaction was that I would tell Bill or one of the others to take him away and chain him up again. But then, it struck me that if I betrayed the fact that I was no longer pretty much out of things, the others would want me to come back to being human with them again – which would put me once more on the way to having my secret discovered.

I decided I would have to get rid of the Old Man myself; and I began to plot how to do it. Eventually, I worked out a simple, but effective, plan. I would take one of the handguns when no one was looking and hide it in my shirt until I had a shot at him that a blind man could not miss. Then when the others came to find out who had fired, I would tell them he had made threats of attacking me for some time now; and finally, I had been forced to kill him in self-defence.

The business of getting the gun was simple enough. The handguns and most of the rifles were still kept in the motor home where I lived with the girl, Marie and little Wendy. I helped myself to a Snubnose .32 revolver the morning after I had concocted my scheme and tucked it inside my shirt into the waistband of my slacks. The shirt was loose enough so that it hid any outlines that might have shown through. Then I went about my daily business of leaving the others as soon as I had eaten breakfast and going off to sit among the rocks of the hillside about half a mile from camp.

I had been tempted to go even farther than usual from the camp – far enough so that the sound of my shot could not be heard. But, now that I had made up my mind to kill the Old Man, I was afraid of doing any-thing out of the ordinary that might make him suspicious. Therefore, I went to my usual place and sat down in the morning sunlight. Shortly I spotted him, squatting less than thirty yards off in a patch of shadow.

I sat where I was, ostensibly ignoring him. After a little while, I made an excuse to glance in his direction and saw that he was a good deal closer than before – perhaps half the distance. It was curious, but I had never been able to actually catch him in the process of moving. Whenever I looked, he was always seated and still, as if he had been there for several hours.

The morning wore on. He came close – but close was still not close enough. He was less than fifteen feet from me at last and would come no closer, but he was off to my left side behind me, so that I would have to turn about to face him and pull the gun at the same time – two movements that, I was sure, would startle him into leaping for protec-tion behind one of the large boulders that were all around us.

That particular day ended with nothing happening. I sat. He sat. The only difference from the many days we had spent together but apart, before was that for the first time, my mind was not concentrated on my inner fog, but on stealthily observing him and calculating the possibility of luring him within certain range of my weapon.

However, he did not cooperate. The next day, it was the same thing. The next day, again the same. I finally realized that he was either too wary or too diffident to approach me except from an oblique angle. I would have to resign myself to waiting until he came almost close enough to be touched, or otherwise put himself in some other completely vulnerable position.

I consoled myself with the fact that all I needed was patience. He would be bound to come close eventually, since every day he inched a little nearer. In fact, it took him nearly three weeks before he did come near enough to provide the target I wanted; and in those three weeks, something strange began to happen to me. I found myself actually enjoying the situation we were both in. I was still trapped in my own miseries like a fly in a forest of flypaper, but at the moment, I was navigating between the sticky strands under the impetus of the excitement of the hunt. I was reminded one day of a poem I had not thought of for years, or read since I was a boy, by Rudyard Kipling and called 'The Ballad Of Boh Da Thon.' It was about a bandit who had been chased by an English army unit weeks on end, and it had a pair of lines that applied nicely to the Old Man and me:

And sure if pursuit in possession ends,
the Boh and his trackers were best of friends ...

For the first time I found myself beginning to like the Old Man, if for no other reason than that he was giving me something to want.

However, the day finally came in which – glancing out of the corners of my eyes – I felt, rather than saw, him squatting almost within the reach of one of my arms and certainly within the reach of one of his.

There was no way I could miss with the revolver or he could dodge, at this distance. But, strangely enough, now that I had him exactly where I wanted him, I was more than ever fearful of frightening him off, of missing him somehow. I was as shy as a kid on his first date. I wanted to turn and look at him; but it took all my will to do so. For a long time I could not manage to turn my head towards him at all. Then, as the sun began to climb higher in the sky, I began to swivel my head on my neck so slowly that it felt like the movement a stone statue might make over centuries. When the sun was directly over our heads, I was still not looking squarely at him, although now I was conscious of his dark shape as a sort of cloud, or presence, at the corner of my left eye.

All this time I had been sliding my hand gradually in between the two lowest buttons of my shirt. I slid it in until my cold fingers lay flat on the warm skin of my belly, and the tips of those same fingers touched the hard curve of the polished butt of the revolver.

It was now noon, lunchtime; but I was afraid of breaking the spell. So I continued to sit without going back to camp, and the Old Man continued to sit, and the sun moved on while the slow, agonizing, almost involuntary turning of my neck continued. I was like someone under a spell or curse. I began to be afraid that the day would end, and I would have not turned enough to catch his eyes with my own, to hold his attention for the seconds I would need to draw the gun and shoot him. Strangely, in this moment, I had finally lost all connection with my reason for killing him. It was simply something to which I was committed, as a tightrope walker might be committed to cross a narrow wire stretched from one cliff to another.

Then – I don't know why – but there was an abrupt snapping of the tension. Suddenly, I was free to turn my head as swiftly as I wanted.

I turned and looked directly at him.

It was a shock. I had completely forgotten that I had never looked closely into his features before. The black-haired anthropoid face, with something of the immutable sadness of the gorilla, looked back at me. It looked back at me from as close a distance as the features of some human companion might face me across a table in a restaurant. But the Old Man's face was all black fur, red nostrils, yellow teeth and yellower eyes – eyes as yellow as Sunday's had been.

For a moment, those eyes froze me. They placed a new paralysis upon my soul, one that, for a moment, I did not believe I could throw off. Then, with a fierce effort, I told myself that this was not Sunday or anything like him; and I felt my hand reaching automatically for the revolver.

My fingers closed upon the butt. I pulled it loose from the pressure of the waistband of my pants – and all the time I was looking directly into his face, which did not alter its expression, but gazed steadily back at me.

It was a moment outside of time. We were caught together in a tableau, flies in amber both of us, frozen and incapable of movement – except for that gun-hand of mine which continued to move with a life of its own, closing about the gun butt and lifting it to clear the muzzle toward the face before me. There was something inevitable about its movements. I could have felt no more trapped by circumstances if I had been tied down in the path of a juggernaut.

In a second it would have been over – but in that second, the Old

Man reached out and placed a hand on both my shirt and the hand holding the gun, arresting my movement.

The pressure of his hand was a calm, almost a gentle touch. I could feel the unexerted strength behind his fingers; but he was not gripping my hand, merely laying his own top of it, just as, once, I might have stopped some business guest reaching for the check of a lunch to which I had just taken him. It was not the kind of touch that could have checked me from continuing to draw the gun and shoot him if I had decided to. But somehow, I was stopped.

For the first time I looked directly into – deeply into – those eyes of his.

I had gone to zoos once and looked into the eyes of some of the animals there. There were no more zoos now, nor was it likely that there would ever be again. But once there had been; and in their cages, particularly in the cages of the big cats, the apes, and bears and the wolves, I had looked into wild animal eyes from only a few feet of distance. And there had been something in those eyes that was not to be found in the eyes of my fellow humans. There were eyes that looked at me from the other side of the universe. Perhaps they could be loving, perhaps, under stress, they could be filled with fury and anger; but now, to me, a human, they were remote – separated from me by a gulf neither man nor beast could cross. They looked at me, without judgment and without hope.

If they lived and it was their fate to encounter me in the open, they would deal with me as best their strength allowed. If I died they would watch me die, simply because there was nothing else they could do; whether I was their deepest enemy or their dearest friend. Their eyes were the eyes of creatures locked up alone in their own individual skulls all the hours and minutes of their life. As animals, they neither knew nor expected the communication every human takes for granted, even if he or she is surrounded by mortal foes.

The eyes of the Old Man were like that – they were the fettered eyes of an animal. But mixed in with that, there was something more – for me alone. It was not love such as Sunday had had for me. But it was something in its own way, perhaps, as strong. I recognized it without being able to put a name to it – although suddenly, I knew what it was.

The Old Man and his tribe, who had been born from test tubes, had been created on the brink of humanity. They teetered on the nice edge of having souls. Of these, the most aware was the Alpha Prime, Old Man himself, because he was the most intelligent, the strongest and the most questioning. Also, he had shared the monad with me in that moment in which we had brought the local effects of the time storm to a halt. In fact, he had shared it alone with me, before any of the other humans had joined in. He had been exposed then to communication for the first time in his life; and it must have awakened a terrible hunger in him. I realized that, all this time, he had been trying to get back into communication with me.

So, that is why as soon as he had been let free again – whenever that was – he had begun to search me out, to approach me little by little, day by day, until now, at last, he sat an arm's length from me. He not only sat at arm's length from me, but with his hand in a gesture that was almost pleading, arresting the gun with which he must know I had planned to kill him.

My own soul turned over in me. Because I suddenly understood what he had understood. From the beginning, because of what we had shared in the moment of the taming of the time storm, he had been much more understanding of me than I had suspected. He had known that I did not want him near me. He had known that my desire to be free of him could be murderous. And he had known what I was doing when my hand went inside my shirt.

I had had enough experience with him to know that my strength was like a baby's compared to his – for all that we probably weighed about the same. It would have been no effort for him to have taken the gun from me. He could have easily broken the arm that held it or throttled me with one hand. But he had done none of these. Instead he had merely come as close as he ever must have come in his life to pleading with someone to spare him, to accept him, to be his fellow, if not his friend.

In that same moment I realized that he – strange as it seemed and incredible as it was that he should have the capability, just from that solitary shared moment in the monad – understood better than any of them how Sunday had felt about me, and how I had felt about Sunday. In his animal-human eyes I read it, how I had *really* felt about Sunday; and at last – at last – I fell apart.

I had been right both ways. I had been right in that I was someone who did not know how to love. But I had been wrong, in spite of this, when I told myself I had not loved the crazy cat. All this I understood suddenly, at last, in the moment in which the Old Man squatted before me, with one long hand still laid flat against my shirt, over the spot where my fist and the revolver that was to have killed him were concealed. The floodgates within me went down suddenly and I was washed halfway back again once more to the shores of humanity. Only halfway, but this was farther than I had ever been before.

23

I sat there and cried for a long time; and the Old Man waited me out as he might have waited out a storm, squatting in a cave in the hills. When it was over, I was sane again; or at least as close to sanity as I could expect to be, under the circumstances. Together we went back to the camp, and from then on, he was openly at my side most of the daylight hours.

What he had done, of course, was to crack the protective shell I had grown about myself in reaction to the massive internal effort of controlled power that had been involved in using the monad. In doing that, I had discovered muscles of the inner self that I had not known I owned, and I had also tuned myself up emotionally with a vengeance. In self-defence, with Sunday's death, my mind had closed itself off until it could heal the psychic tearings these stresses had created. Now that I was back in my skull, however, these things were suddenly very obvious to me; and some other things as well. Chief of these was that there was a great deal I needed to do with myself if I wanted to continue my joust with the time storm and the universe.

Meanwhile, I was faced with reentering the world of the living. To my pleasure and to the feeding of a new humbleness inside me, the others had been doing very well without my guiding hand. I found that I was now ruler of what might well be called a small kingdom – and that was only the beginning of the discoveries awaiting me.

A great deal had happened in the year and a half that I had been obsessed with myself. For one thing, the world was a world again. With the interference from the moving time lines ended, shortwave radio communication had tied the continents back together, to the mutual discovery of all us survivors that there were more of us than we had suspected. The North American continent was now a patchwork of relatively small kingdoms, like my own, with the exception of the west coast, from Baja California northward halfway into British Columbia, Canada. That west coast strip, as far east as Denver and in some cases beyond, was now a single sovereignty under a woman who called herself the Empress. The Empress was from the Hawaiian Islands – which appeared to have suffered less than any other part of the world from the moving mistwalls and the time changes of the time storm. The islands had lost no more than two-thirds of their population, as opposed to a figure that must be much closer to ninety-eight or ninety-nine per cent for most of the rest of the world. The Empress was a woman from the island of Hawaii itself, who had seized control there with a ragtag, impromptu army, and then gone on to take over the other islands and the west coast of North America.

England and Ireland, apparently, were nearly deserted. Most of northern Europe also was a wasteland because of a brief ice age that had come with some of the time changes and covered most of that continent with an ice sheet from the Arctic Circle as far south as the middle of France. This ice sheet was now gone; but the human life that was left was now all below the former ice line. Stretching around the Mediterranean and into the north of Africa were essentially nothing more than scattered, single family households. The rest of Africa, like South America, was largely noncommunicating, from which Bill assumed that those areas had been pretty well depopulated by the time storm also.

Russia, India and the whole Oriental area had also been hard hit. As a result they appeared to have fallen back into a sort of peaceful medieval, agricultural condition, with small villages scattered sparsely across the immensity of land. Australia and New Zealand had lost almost all of their cities, but had a surprising number of families surviving pretty much as they always had in the interior and on the rest of that island continent. However, these people, although articulate and largely supplied with their own radios, were so widely scattered that they were also, in effect, no more than individual families living in isolation.

Bill had made a large map on one wall of the rambling, continually building structure that my group had come to call the summer palace. The place was a strange construction, being composed partly of lumber, partly of native rocks cemented together, and partly of cement blocks trucked in from a half-obliterated town thirty miles away, that had owned a cement block factory. The place had poured concrete floors and bare walls for the most part; but Bill had been a good enough architect to see that it was adequately wired and equipped with ductwork, not only for heating, but for summer air conditioning. I think that I had been conscious of the existence of his map in it, during my nonparticipating period; but I had never looked at the map with any degree of interest until the Old Man cracked me out of my shell. Now that I did,

I found myself marvelling that what was left of the world could have gotten its scattered parts back into contact with each other in such a short time.

I discovered something else, as a byproduct of reawakening to what was going on around me. This was that our new world was a world hungry for news, and I myself was a piece of that news. By this time, all the people on earth who had radio receivers knew who it was who had brought the local effects of the time storm into balance. They knew what I looked like, who my lieutenants were, and what our local situation here was. I was, I discovered, regarded as a sort of combination of Einstein and Napoleon – and the planet's number one celebrity. This attention might ordinarily have given me a large opinion of myself. However, under the circumstances, it had a hollow ring to it. It was rather like being crowned King of the Earth on the stage of the empty Hollywood Bowl, while an audience of five sat in the middle of the front row seats and applauded energetically. After discovering what it was like, I put my position in the world-wide, public eye out of my mind and concentrated on matters close to home.

It was curious that I, who had once believed that I could never endure to be married, now had two wives. Of course, legally, I was married to neither one of them; but wives they were in every practical sense of the word, and particularly in the eyes of the community surrounding us. Marie and Ellen – I would have bet anyone that if there were ever two women likely not to get on with each other at all, it would be those two. Marie was talkative, conventional and probably – she had never told me her age – older than I was. The girl was certainly still well under twenty, closemouthed to an almost abnormal degree, and recognized no convention or rules but her own. What the two of them could have in common was beyond me. I puzzled over it from time to time but never succeeded in getting an answer.

But they joined forces magnificently when it came to lining up in opposition to me. One of the typical examples of this appeared directly after I had come back to my senses and rejoined the world of the living. All the time that I had been more or less out of my head, they had taken care of me as if I had been three years old. Now that I had my ordinary wits back, rather than just getting back to normal ways, they both apparently decided, without a word, that I should get it through my head that my days of being waited upon were over.

This would have been all right if they had merely returned to the normal pattern of affairs that had existed before we got the time storm forced into balance. But they now moved as far in the direction of leaving me to my own devices as they had gone previously in watching over me. In fact, the whole matter went to what I considered ridiculous limits.

For example, during the time I had been obsessed with my inner problems, I had been, except for rare intervals, as sexless as a eunuch. When I came back to myself, of course, that changed. The day the Old Man helped me break me loose, I found myself waiting for the evening and the hours of privacy in the motorhome. I had never been one to want more than one woman in my bed at a time; and I was not at all sure whether it was the girl or Marie I wanted that night. But I definitely knew that I wanted one or the other. I gave them time to get settled first; but when I came to the motorhome, Ellen was nowhere to be seen and Marie was a mound under covers on her own bed, her back toward me.

I blew gently into her ear to wake her up and get her to turn toward me. She came to, but not satisfactorily.

'Not tonight,' she murmured sleepily, and pulled the blanket up to where it almost covered her head.

Annoyed, I left the motorhome and went out to look for Ellen. I found her after some search, in a sleeping bag at the foot of a tree, with her rifle leaning up against it in arm's reach. The rebuff from Marie had taken some of the rosy glow off my feelings. I poked the sleeping bag and her eyes opened.

'What are you doing out here?' I said.

'Sleeping,' she said. 'Goodnight.'

She closed her eyes and pulled her head down into the sleeping bag.

Angry, and not a little hurt, I wandered off. Was this all the two of them cared for me after all? Here I was back to normalcy and neither one seemed to give a damn. It was almost as if they had preferred me as the mindless near-idiot I had been for the past eighteen months.

I went back into the motorhome, opened the cupboards that held our bottled goods and took out a bottle of sour mash bourbon. I made myself a solitary campfire off into the woods, at the edge of the clearing holding the motorhome and the half-finished shape of the summer palace, and set out to get myself drunk by way of solitary celebration. But it did not work. I got thickheaded without feeling any better and finally gave up, going back to the motorhome and falling into my own lonely bunk without bothering to do much more than take off my boots.

If that was all they cared for how it had been with me this past year and a half, I thought resentfully as I dropped off.

It was not until late the next morning, when I woke up to a dry mouth, a headache and the sunlight streaming through the windows of the motorhome, that it occurred to me to think how it might have been for them too. If I had been essentially without a woman all that time, they had been essentially without a man. Or had they? That was a question I found I really didn't want to consider, although I made a mental note to find the answer sometime later. (I never did find out as a matter of fact.) I got up, washed, shaved, changed clothes and went out.

Not only had they forsaken my bed, there was no sign of any breakfast made for me. Not that I was incapable of cooking for myself, but I had gotten used to having the spoon all but put in my mouth, and I felt the transition to the present state of neglect to be unnecessarily harsh and abrupt. However, the motorhome refrigerator, run from the standby oil generator outside it, had cold juice, eggs and canned sausage. I made myself a pretty decent meal, scrupulously washed up after myself – just to rub their noses in the fact that I could be independent too – and went outside to see what was going on.

There was no one around outside the summer palace, not the girl or Marie – not even Wendy. Now that I began to think of it, I had a vague impression from the past months that Wendy was ceasing to be the timid little creature she had been when I first saw her and was beginning to develop into a lively young girl, busy every hour of the day all over the place.

I went into the summer palace, prowled through its rooms and discovered Bill busily at work at a large draughtsman's table in the same room that had the map on the wall. Besides those two items, the room had three large filing cabinets, a regular desk covered with papers, and one wall entirely in bookcases.

'Hello,' I said to Bill.

He glanced at me over the top of whatever it was he was drawing, put down his pen and ruler and got off the high stool he had been sitting on. We shook hands with awkward formality.

'How are you?' he asked.

'Fine,' I said. 'Just fine.'

I glanced around the room.

'You've all been pretty busy,' I said.

'Oh well,' answered Bill, 'there's always a lot to do.'

'And you've been doing most of it, I'd guess,' I said.

'Oh, no,' he shook his head, 'I couldn't have carried most of the responsibility here if I'd wanted to. Actually, all I've been doing is handling the instruction, the maintenance and supply, and things like that.

Marie and Ellen have been doing most of the everyday work of running things. Marie's a natural manager, and Ellen—'

He paused.

'Go on,' I said, interested. 'You're about to say that Ellen is—'

'Well, I was going to say – sort of a natural general,' he said awkwardly. 'Maybe I ought to say, a natural war leader. She's been the one who's been making sure that all our people know how to use their guns and that none of our neighbours think they can walk in here and help themselves to anything we've got.'

'Neighbours? What neighbours?' I asked.

'Well,' he said, 'to the north and northwest of us it's the Ryans, and the TvLostChord. To the west, it's Wallinstadt. South and moving around to the east, it's Billy Projec and his tribe. Not that we've anything really to worry about, even if they all took it into their heads to combine against us.'

He shot me a quick glance.

'We've now got over six hundred people,' he said.

'Six hundred people!'

I was rocked back on my heels. I had vaguely gathered during the last year and a half that the numbers of my small community were growing; but I had guessed that, at the most, we would have somewhere between thirty and fifty people. Six hundred under these conditions was a small nation.

'Where did they all come from?' I asked.

'Some of them knew about us back when the mistwalls were still operating,' said Bill. 'Or they heard about us from others they ran into. We were a pretty good-sized party – and a well-equipped party – to be moving around back then. After the time changes stopped locally, they began gradually to drift in, either out of curiosity or because they'd always wanted to join us.'

He waved a hand at the filing cabinets.

'I've got each one down on the census rolls,' he said. 'In fact, if you'd like, you can read each one's life history up to the time they've joined us. About nine months ago, I made everybody fill out a complete file on themselves; and now we make every new person do that before we accept them here. I've got not only the facts of the life, but bloodtype, medical history, occupational skills and everything else that might be useful information for us.'

I shook my head. His mind and mine were two different constructs. The last thing I would have thought about with a group that size would be getting into their former occupations and bloodtypes. It had probably been the first thing that Bill had thought of. He had an orderly brain.

'You don't need me,' I said. 'From what I can see you've all been doing fine on your own.'

Now he shook his head.

'All we've been doing is keeping the machinery running, idling, waiting for you to do something with it,' he said. 'Do you want to look around at things?'

'Yes,' I said.

He led me out of the room and down a corridor of the summer palace that I had not been in before – or if I had, I didn't remember having been through it – and out another door. A jeep and a station wagon were parked there. He got in behind the wheel of the jeep and I climbed in beside him.

'Porniarsk's got his working area back here behind the summer palace,' Bill said as he started up the motor of the jeep and backed it away from the building, to swing it around to head down the hillside. 'But I thought we'd end up with him. Let me show you the rest of it first.'

We drove down through the belt of trees into the lower area where the village of the experimentals had stood. I had not been down here since we had halted the effects of the time storm, and what I saw was startling. The village of the experimentals was still there; although it was now enclosed in cyclone fencing and the gates wide enough to drive a truck through were standing ajar. Sprawling out on the open space beyond and slightly downhill from the village was what could only be described as a town – a new town of everything from prefab houses to tents.

'Eventually,' Bill spoke in my ear over the noise of the motor as we negotiated the now clearly marked, if unsurfaced, road downward from the tree belt, 'we'll set up some uniform construction. For the present, however, we've been giving anyone who's accepted here a free hand, provided their housing and their habits conform with our sanitary regulations and local laws.'

'Who enforces our local laws?' I asked, bemused.

'Everybody belongs to the militia, and everybody who belongs to the militia pulls police duty on a regular rotation,' said Bill. 'That's Ellen's department. You should ask her about it. She's on top of it all the time; and she makes it work without a hitch. From what I can gather, we've got a much more organized community here than they have almost any-place else in the world. Of course, the people who are here badly want to be here. They all think that you're going to go on pulling miracles out of your hat and that they'll end up, either on top of things, or with all the luxuries of former civilization back again.'

'All that, just because we managed to stop the time storm?' I said.

'It's a function of the situation,' Bill said, with his precise pronunciation of each word. 'Think of it this way. You're the sorcerer. Porniarsk's your demon assistant.'

'You're my Grand Vizier, Ellen's General of the Armies and Marie's the Number One Queen – is that it?' I asked.

Bill laughed.

'Yup,' he said.

24

By this time we were almost down level with the gates of the experimentals' village.

'How come you've got them penned up?' I said.

'They're not penned,' Bill answered. 'That fence is there for their own protection, in case some of our newcomers don't have the sense to leave them alone. Or in case there's a sudden surprise attack on us from somewhere. They can lock their gates and have a certain amount of protection until we drive the attackers off. They seem to understand that perfectly well.'

He looked at me briefly.

'I think the Old Man can communicate with them all right,' he said. 'Anyway, things have gone pretty smoothly with all of them since we stopped the effects of the time storm.'

There were a few of the experimentals out in front of their buildings; and these watched us solemnly as we passed, but made no move either to come towards us or to retreat inside. The jeep roared on and we drove down what seemed to be a sort of centre street between the heterogeneous buildings of the human community. Eight or nine young children were flying kites in a clearing half-surrounded by trees, just beyond the village. The picture they made was so normal and so pre-time storm that it jolted me.

'Where did all the kids come from?' I asked.

'Some of the people coming in had them,' Bill said, braking the jeep to a halt before one large quonset hut. 'And we've had several babies born here during the past year. Of course, those are too young to play yet. Still, the proportion of children to adults isn't that large. I don't think we've got more than twenty of them.'

I shaded my eyes and tried to make out a familiar figure among the darting young bodies.

'Is that Wendy out there?' I said.

'I don't think so,' said Bill without turning around. 'She's probably out with the dogs somewhere. She handles them now most of the time, instead of Marie; and they've gotten so that they follow her wherever she goes. Generally, Marie thinks it's a good thing; and I agree. The dogs are good protection for her. This is our government building here. Come on in.'

He got out of the jeep. I followed him and we went up three wooden steps and in the front door of the quonset. It was like stepping into any busy office. Behind a low barrier of wooden fencing, there were five desks at which three men and two women were sitting, typing or engaged in other paperwork. File cabinets occupied one wall and there was a large copying machine in a corner.

'Where are you getting the power to run all this?' I asked Bill. For the typewriters were all electric, and the copier looked as if it had to require at least a 220 volt line.

'We put in a much larger gas generator,' said Bill, leading me through a gate in the wooden fence. 'Before fall, we ought to finish a dam on the river and have a waterpowered generator that'll take care of all our needs for the next five years.'

He led me into a corridor with two doors on each side and opened the first one on the right briefly.

'Supplies,' he said.

I looked in. It was, as he had said, a supply room. Most of the supplies were clerical; but I saw some stacks of blankets and other material for household living. A chained and locked gunrack against the far wall of the room held rifles, and there was a rack of handguns below it, also chained and locked. I shut the door again and turned open the door across the way.

'Communications,' he said briefly, and let me into a radio room containing two women, one young and one middle-aged. It was filled with radio equipment that even to my amateur eye seemed impressive.

'Bebe, Jill,' Bill said, 'this is Marc Despard.'

The two looked up from their panels, smiled and nodded to me. Bill led me out of the room again.

'Now,' said Bill, moving down to knock on the second door on the left, 'this is—'

'Come in,' said Marie's voice.

Bill smiled at me and led me in. Marie was seated behind a large desk in a very businesslike office, with papers in front of her. She was looking over the papers at a lean, big-boned man who must have stood about six feet six when he was on his feet. Right now he was sitting down, dressed in a white shirt and what seemed to be white duck pants.

'I'll be right with you, Marc,' she said, and picked up what was apparently an interrupted conversation with the man in white.

'What you've got to make them understand, Abe, is that if they want to draw supplies and cook their own meals, they have to do it according to our rules. At our convenience, not theirs. I'm not going to put up with anyone either wasting food or not eating adequately – any more than I'd put up with their breaking any of the other laws. That means they submit their menu for the week in advance to you, you approve it, and then – only then – you authorize one of your own people to give them supplies for just exactly what they've planned to serve. You understand?'

'Sure,' said Abe, in a deep slow voice. He had a touch of some Eastern European accent.

Marie looked away from him over to me again.

'Marc,' she said, 'this is Abe Budner, our Director of Food Services and chef for the community kitchen. I'm hoping we can train people to take the chef's job off his hands before long.'

Abe Budner got up as slowly and solemnly as he had spoken, shook hands with me and sat down again.

'We're just looking around,' Bill said.

'Good,' said Marie briskly. 'Because I really don't have time to stop and talk now. I can tell you all about this work this evening, Marc.'

We were dismissed. Bill and I left.

'And this,' said Bill, knocking on the remaining door in the corridor, 'is Ellen's.'

We waited, but there was no answer to his knock.

The door at the far end of the corridor opened behind us.

'Something?' said a voice. We turned and I saw what looked like a boy of about eighteen, wearing dark pants and a khaki shirt with two brass buttons pinned on the left side of his shirt collar.

'Ellen's out checking the Ryan boundary,' this individual said. 'Is there anything I can do for you?'

He looked questioningly at me.

'This is Marc Despard, Doc,' said Bill.

'Marc Despard? I'm really glad to meet you, sir,' said Doc flusteredly and energetically, shaking my hand. 'I've looked forward to meeting you.'

'Well, now you have,' I said. I was not exactly taken with him.

'Doc is Ellen's second in command,' said Bill. 'His full name's Kurt Dockwiler, but we all call him Doc. His militia rank is captain.'

'Oh?' I said.

'I was just going to show Marc Ellen's office,' Bill added.

'You bet. Come in,' said Doc, stepping past us, throwing open the door and leading us in. I followed him and Bill brought up the rear.

I don't know what I had expected; but Ellen's office was simply a tidy, utilitarian place with the usual filing cabinets, a perfectly clean desk and a few extra chairs facing the desk as if she had been holding a conference recently.

'If you'd like to wait,' said Doc, 'she ought to be back in about twenty minutes. I can send over to the kitchen for coffee – or anything else.'

'No, I'm just looking around,' I said. 'I'll see her tonight.'

'Of course!' Doc followed Bill and myself back down the corridor and out through the outer office. 'If I can ever be useful in any way, Mr. Despard, the message centre can reach me at any time.'

'I'll remember that,' I said getting in the jeep.

Bill started up and we drove off.

'How old is he, anyway?' I said.

'I don't know exactly,' answered Bill. 'Twenty or twenty-one, I think.'

'He looks more like Ellen's age.'

'Nothing wrong with that,' Bill said.

I looked at him. But his face was perfectly innocent of any particular expression.

'I'm just surprised there aren't any older men around to hold down a job like that,' I told him. 'That's all.'

'We've got older men, of course,' said Bill. He was heading the jeep back up into the trees in the direction of the summer palace. 'Most of them have families, or at least somebody, who make them a bad choice for a high risk occupation. Then again, none of them have Doc's qualifications.'

'Qualifications?'

'His father was career army,' Bill said. 'He absorbed a lot of the military art, just by growing up in various bases. That and other things. He's a black belt in judo and he's taught survival classes. Also he's a mountain climber.'

There was not much to say to that. I sat quiet during most of the ride back up to the summer palace, and in that time I came around to feeling that I might have been a little unfair to Doc.

'We'll go see Porniarsk now,' Bill said, stopping the jeep once more at the palace. 'I didn't take you to him right away because I thought either Marie or Ellen might have things they'd want to show you in their areas; and their schedule is pretty well tied in with other things. Porniarsk, you can see any time.'

I felt a warmth of old affection at the thought of the alien avatar.

Porniarsk, with his ugly bull-dog shape and unemotional responses, was a particularly stable point in my pyrotechnic and shifting universe. I followed Bill into the palace, thinking with surprise that, in all the last year and a half, I had not sought out Porniarsk once and had seen him in total perhaps no more than half a dozen times.

The room in the summer palace that Bill led me into, eventually, must have had as much floor space as the quonset hut down in the village we had just left. It was a rectangular room with floor, walls and ceiling painted white and a row of windows all down one side. The other walls were occupied mainly by equipment that had once been in the station. Apparently, Porniarsk had had it all transported down here.

However, what caught my eye immediately was not this, nor even the friendly sight of Porniarsk himself, but a box shape with transparent sides perhaps twenty feet long by six wide and three deep, almost filled with some greyish-blue substance. When I got closer, I saw that whatever it was seemed to be a liquid. There was a noticeable *meniscus*, and a black tube running over the edge of one of the sides and down into the box showed the apparent angular distortion at the surface that a stick does, poked down into water. Porniarsk had been doing something with the tank; but he turned and came to meet us as we entered.

'How are you, Marc?' he said as we met, his easy speech at odds, as always, with the curious mechanical sound of his voice, and his manner of speaking.

'I'm fine – now,' I said. 'How've you been?'

'There's been no reason for me to be other than I always am,' Porniarsk said.

'Of course,' I said. 'Well, then, how have things been going?'

'I've been getting a few things done,' Porniarsk said. 'But nothing with any great success. But then, real progress isn't often dramatic, being a matter of small steps taken daily that add up to a total accomplishment over a period of time.'

'Yes,' I said. I thought of the experience it had taken me a year and a half to come to terms with. 'There's a lot of things I'd like to talk to you about.'

'I'm glad to hear it,' said Porniarsk. 'On my part, I've been looking forward to talking to you. I can progress much more rapidly if I've got a primary mind to work with; and the only primary mind we've produced so far is you.'

'Only me?' I said. It jarred me slightly to hear it – at the same time I felt a small ego-pleasure.

'Primary minds can only be developed or uncovered by monad

activity,' he said. 'All the other minds involved in the gestalt only reso-
nated and amplified yours, without developing. So I've been restricted to
doing what I can with the resonating minds. In fact, I've been restricted
to the one resonating mind that had no other duties to occupy it.'

He turned his head and nodded ponderously toward a corner. I
looked and saw the Old Man, perched on the seat before one of the
consoles taken from the station, the helmet on his head.

'The Alpha Prime,' said Porniarsk. 'He's been my main subject.
Happily, he seems eager for the experience of being connected with the
equipment here. Daytimes, he's generally unavailable. I understand he's
been with you most of the time. But at night, he often comes here on his
own initiative to work with me.'

I gazed at the Old Man. He squatted utterly still on the chair before
the console, with a curious assurance – almost as if it was a throne and
he was a king.

'What could you learn from him?' I asked.'

'It's not what I can learn *from* him,' said Porniarsk deliberately, 'but
what I could learn *through* him. Just as I want to learn and discover
matters through you – though since you're a primary mind, I'd expect
that you'd also learn, and be able to add the knowledge you personally
gain to what I can gain.'

He stopped speaking for a second, then started again.

'In fact,' he said, 'I ought to point out that what I can learn is limited
by the kind of instrument I am, myself – personally. As an avatar of
Porniarsk I've got only so much conceptual range. On the other hand,
Marc, your conceptual range is something I don't know. It could be
less than Porniarsk's – that is to say, mine – or it might be a great deal
greater. It could be limitless, in that you might be able to go on increasing it, as long as you want to make the effort to extend its grasp. Which
brings me to an important point.'

He stopped again. But this time he did not continue immediately.

'What point?' asked Bill, finally.

'The point,' said Porniarsk in his unvarying accent, 'of whether Marc,
after his one experience with the monad, really wants to explore further into an area where mind becomes reality and where it's impossible
to draw a line where the definitive change occurs.'

'I'll answer that,' I said.

It came to me suddenly, that while I'd never really come to doubt
that I wanted to dig deeper into the time storm and everything
connected with it, for the last year and a half, I'd been hiding from
the fact that I'd eventually have to get back to that work.

'I don't have any reverse gear.' I said. 'The only way for me to go is straight ahead. Even standing still doesn't work.'

'In that case,' said Porniarsk, 'you and I have a big job ahead of us.'

'Fine with me,' I said.

'I guessed so from the beginning,' said Porniarsk. 'So, in that case, maybe we might talk right now about the basic principles involved here, and how you can be involved also.'

'Absolutely,' I said. I meant every word I said. 'This all ties in with something I want to do – something I'm going to do.'

'If you'll forgive me,' said Porniarsk, 'I felt that about you from the first time we met. However, it's a bit bigger universe than you, or the entities of your time, seem to realize. If you were anything else than a rather unusual individual, I'd have to say you're presumptuous to have the ambition I think you're entertaining.'

'I told you I've got something to do,' I said. 'In any case, we both want the same thing, don't we? To control this runaway situation with time?'

'Quite correct. But remember what I said – if you weren't an unusual individual, I wouldn't be devoting this much energy to you. Not because I wasn't interested; but because it'd be a waste of time. By your own standards, Marc, you're arrogant. Partly, this is simply because you recognize your own ability. Part of it is a prickliness, what you'd call a chip on the shoulder, because other people don't see what you see. I can sympathize with this. But it's still something you'll have to overcome, if you're going to achieve the full primary identity you'll need.'

'We'll see,' I said.

I had been looking forward to talking to him. I had a great deal, I had thought, to tell him. What I most wanted to talk about was how it could be that, just as it had been back in the days when I had been playing the stock market, I could almost taste – almost *feel* – what it was I wanted to take hold of in the time storm. But his sudden criticism put me off.

'You said this was some sort of representation of the storm?' I said, turning to the tank.

'Yes,' he answered.

'I don't see anything.'

'It's not operating right now,' said Porniarsk. 'But I can turn it on for you.'

He went to a control panel on the far wall and touched several studs and dials there with the tips of his shoulder tentacles.

'What you'll see,' he said, coming back to Bill and me, 'isn't actually a view of the time storm. What it is, is a representation produced by the same equipment that was in the station. Look into the tank. Not at it, into it.'

I'd already been looking – but now I realized my error. I had been staring the same way you might stare at a fish tank from entirely outside it. But what this piece of equipment apparently required – and require it did, for it was evidently already warming up, and I could feel it drawing my attention psychically the way a rope might have pulled me physically – was for an observer to put his point of view completely inside it.

There was nothing remarkable about the first signs of its activation. All I saw were little flickerings like miniature lightning, or, even less, like the small jitterings of light that register on the optic nerves when you close your eyes and press your fingers against the outside of the eyelids. These small lights will-o-the-wisped here and there through the blueness of whatever filled the tank; and I suddenly woke to the fact that what I had taken to be a sort of blue-grey liquid was not liquid at all. It was something entirely different, a heavy gas perhaps. Actually, I realized, it had no colour at all. It was any shade the subjective attitude of the viewer thought it was. For me, now, it had become almost purely black, the black of lightless space; and I was abruptly, completely lost in it, as if it was actually the total universe and I stood invisible at the centre of it.

The little flickerings were the forces of the time storm at work. They had been multiplying to my eye as my point of view moved their centrepoint; and now they filled the tank in every direction, their number finite, but so large as to baffle my perception of them. I understood then that I was watching all the vectors of the full time storm at work at once; and, as I watched, I began slowly to sort their movements into patterns.

It was like watching, with the eyes of a Stone Age savage, a message printing itself on a wall in front of you; and gradually, as you watched, you acquired the skill of reading and the understanding of the language in which the message was set down, so that random marks began to orient themselves into information-bearing code. So, as I watched, the time storm began to make sense to me – but too much sense, too large a sense for my mind to handle. It was as if I could now read the message, but what it told was of things too vast for my understanding and experience.

Two things, I saw, were happening. Two separate movements were characteristic of the patterns of the still-expanding storm. One was a wave-front sort of motion, like the spreading of ripples created by a stone dropped in a pond, interacting and spreading; and the other was like the spreading of cracks in some crystalline matrix. Both these patterns of development were taking place at the same time and both were complex. The wave-fronts were multiple and occurring at several levels and intensities. They created eddies at points along their own line of advance where they encountered solid matter, and particularly, when they encountered gravitational bodies like stars. Earth had had its own eddy, and it had been only the forces within that eddy that we had been able to bring into dynamic balance.

The crystalline cracking effect also intensified itself around gravity wells. It was this effect that threatened the final result of the storm that Porniarsk had first warned us about – a situation in which each particle would finally be at timal variance with the particles surrounding it. The cracking extended and divided the universe into patterns of greater and greater complexities until all matter eventually would be reduced to indivisible elements ...

So much I saw and understood of what the tank showed. But in the process of understanding so much, my comprehension stretched, stretched, and finally broke. I had a brief confused sensation of a universe on fire, whirling about me faster than I could see ... and I woke up on the floor of the room, feeling as if I had just been levelled by an iron bar in the hands of a giant. The heavy, gargoyle head of Porniarsk hung above me, inches from my eyes.

'You see why you need to develop yourself?' he asked.

I started to get up.

'Lie still,' said the voice of Bill, urgently; and I looked to see him on the other side of me. 'We've got a real doctor, now. I can get him on the radio from the communications room here and have him up here in twenty minutes—'

'I'm all right,' I said.

I finished climbing to my feet. Looking beyond Porniarsk, I saw a huddled mass of black fur at the base of the console, a helmet still on its head.

'Hey – the Old Man!' I said, leading the way to him. Porniarsk and Bill followed.

He was still on the floor by the time I reached him and took the helmet off; but apparently he, too, was coming out of it. His brown eyes were open and looked up into mine.

'Yes,' said Porniarsk, 'of course. He'll have been in monad with you just now.'

The Old Man was all right. He continued to stare at me for a second after I took his helmet off; then he got to his feet as if nothing had happened. I thought that if he really felt as little jarred as he looked,

421

by what had decked us both, he was made of stronger stuff than I. My knees were trembling.

'I just want to sit down,' I said.

'This way,' Bill answered.

He led me out of the room and down a corridor, the Old Man tagging after us. We came to a solid, heavy-looking door I had never seen before in the palace. He produced a key, looked at me for a second with a shyness I'd never seen in him before, then unlocked the door and pushed it open.

'Come in,' he said.

I stepped through, feeling the Old Man crowding close behind me – and stopped.

The room Bill had opened for us was narrow and long; and one of its lengthier walls was all windows. They were double windows, one row above the other so that, in effect, that wall of the room was almost all glass; and the view through them was breathtaking. I had seen what was to be seen through them, but not from this particular viewpoint.

From where I stood in the room, my gaze went out and down the open slope just below the palace, over the tops of the tree belt below to a familiar view, the village of the experimentals and the human town beyond. But then it went further – for the angle of this room looked out, between a gap in the lower vegetation, to the open land beyond, stretching to the horizon and divided by a road that had not been there a year and a half ago. Now this road stretched like a brown line to where earth and sky met, with some small vehicle on it a mile or so out, moving toward us with its dust plume, like a squirrel's tail in the air behind it.

'How do you like it?' I heard Bill asking.

'Wonderful!' I said – and meant it.

I turned to talk to him, and for the first time focused in on the interior of the room itself. There was a rug underfoot and a half a dozen armchairs – overstuffed armchairs, comfortable armchairs. I had not realized until now that I had not seen a comfortable piece of furniture in months. The kind of furniture that we tended to accumulate was that which was most portable, utilitarian straight chairs and tables of wood or metal. Those in this room were massive, opulent things meant for hours of comfortable sitting.

But there was more than furniture here. Most of the available floorspace was stacked with books and boxes containing books. All in all, there must have been several thousand of them, stacked around us. The piles of them stretched between the armchairs and right up to a massive stone fireplace set in the middle of the wall opposite the windows. There was no fire in the fireplace at the moment, but kindling and logs had been laid ready for one. At the far end of the wall in which the fireplace was set, I saw what the ultimate destination of the books would be, for the first two vertical floor-to-ceiling shelves of built-in bookcases were completed and filled with volumes, and framing for the rest of the shelves stretched toward me what would eventually be three solid walls of reading matter.

'Sit down,' said Bill.

I took one of the armchairs, one that faced the windows, so that I could gaze at the view. The small vehicle I had seen – a pickup truck – was now close to the town. Without warning, the music of The Great Gate of Kiev from Moussorgsky's *Pictures At An Exhibition* poured forth around me into the room.

'I thought,' said Bill from behind me, 'that we ought to have some place just for sitting ...'

He was still being shy. The tones of his voice carried half an apology, half an entreaty to me to like what I saw around me.

'It's really magnificent, Bill,' I told him and turning, saw him standing at one end of the windows, looking out himself. 'Who's been building all this for you?'

'I've been doing it myself,' he said.

I took a long look at him. I had known he was a good man in many ways; but I had never thought of him as a carpenter, mason, or general man of his hands. He looked back at me stiffly.

'I wanted to surprise people,' he said. 'Only just now you seemed jolted by what happened, so ... I actually wasn't going to tell anyone until I had it all finished, the books on the shelves, and all that.'

'Look. This room's the best idea you could have had,' I told him.

I meant it. God knows, if anyone ever loved reading, it was me. I was no longer looking at the view now, I was looking at the books, beginning to feel in me a stirring of excitement that I would not have guessed was still possible. The books were suggesting a million things to me, calling to me with a million voices. Maybe only a handful of those voices had anything to tell me about the things I really needed to know; but the possible smallness of their number did not matter. It was me against the time storm and I was humankind; and what was humankind was locked up in those codes of black marks on white paper that had once filled libraries all over the earth.

Suddenly, I wanted to know a million things, very strongly. There was the dry ache in my throat and the fever in my head of someone athirst and lost in a desert.

25

I was reading the last paragraph of Joyce's short story 'The Dead' in his collection *Dubliners*:

'*Snow was general all over Ireland. It was falling on every part of the dark central plain, on the treeless hills, falling softly upon the Bog of Allen and, farther westward, softly falling into the dark, mutinous Shannon waves. It was falling, too, upon every part of the lonely churchyard on the hill where Michael Furey lay buried. It lay thickly drifted on the crooked crosses and headstones, on the spears of the little gate, on the barren thorns. His soul swooned slowly as he heard the snow falling faintly through the universe and faintly falling, like the descent of their last end upon all the living and the dead.*'

There was something there I told myself, tight with certainty. There was something there. A certain part of humankind and the All. A tiny something; but something.

I put down that book and went to find the words of Ernest Hemingway, in the first paragraph of *A Farewell to Arms*:

'*In the late summer of that year we lived in a house in a village that looked across the river and the plain to the mountains. In the bed of the river there were pebbles and boulders, dry and white in the sun and the water was clear and swiftly moving and blue in the channels. Troops went by the house and down the road and the dust they raised powdered the leaves of the trees. The trunks of the trees too were dusty and the leaves fell early that year ...*'

Something ... I went looking further.

Hui-Nan Tzu, in the second century before Christ, had written:

'*Before Heaven and Earth had taken form all was vague and amorphous. Therefore it was called the Great Beginning. The Great Beginning produced emptiness and emptiness produced the universe ... The combined essences of heaven and earth became the yin and yang ...*'

Sigmund Freud:

'No one who, like me, conjures up the most evil of those half-tamed demons that inhabit the human breast...'

Tennyson, in *The Passing of Arthur*:

'Last, as by some one deathbed after wail
Of suffering silence follows, or thro' death
Or deathlike swoon, thus over all that shore,
Save for some whisper of the seething seas,
A dead hush fell; but when the dolorous day
Grew drearier toward twilight falling, came
A bitter wind, clear from the North, and blew
The mist aside, and with that wind the tide
Rose, and the pale King glanced across the field
Of battle, but no man was moving there ...'

Einstein, *What I Believe*:

'It is not enough that you should understand about applied science in order that your work may increase man's blessings. Concern for man himself and his fate must always form the chief interest of all technical endeavours ... that the creations of our mind shall be a blessing and not a curse to mankind. Never forget this in the midst of your diagrams and equations...'

'Do you feel it?' I asked, looking at the Old Man as the two of us sat alone in Bill's library. 'Do you feel it, too, there – someplace?'

He looked back at me out of his fathomless, savage brown eyes without answering. He was not my companion in the search for what I sought. Only a sort of trailer or rider who hoped I would carry him to the place which would satisfy his own hunger for understanding – that hunger which being part of the monad had awakened in him. It was his curse not to be quite human – but still not to be a simply a beast, like Sunday, who could love, suffer and even die, unquestioningly. It was something I could see, like a heavy load on him; how he knew he was dependent on me. After a second, he put a long hand lightly on my knee, in a nearly beseeching gesture that had become habitual with him lately and stirred my guts each time he did it.

So we continued; he with me, and I poring over the books in the library, along with many more Bill had since brought me from the surrounding territory. What I was after was still undefined, only a feeling in me of something that must be there, hidden in the vast warehouse of human philosophy and literature. But I kept finding clues, bits and pieces of thought that were like gold dust and stray gems spilled from the caravan of knowledge I tracked.

I had not concerned myself about it during the first few days of this.

But after a week or two, it occurred to me to wonder that no one, not Marie, or Bill, or even Ellen, had been after me to take charge of our community, once more. The wonder brought with it both a touch of annoyance and a sneaking feeling of relief. I was bothered that they did not miss my help more; but at the same time, I felt in my guts that what I was doing was by all measures more important than being an administrator. So, the summer colours outside the window dried and brightened to fall ones, then faded to the drab brown of winter grass and the occasional white of snow, with only the different hues of ever-green to relieve the scene; and I came to understand that my presence was required, so to speak, only on state occasions.

One of these was called Thanksgiving, although for convenience it was held on the tenth of December and began three weeks of general celebration that ended with New Year's Day. At Thanksgiving dinner that year we had as guests in the summer palace the leaders and chief-tains of the surrounding communities Bill had listed for me.

The leaders themselves were a mixed bunch. Merry Water of the TvLostChord was in his early twenties, thin, stooped, black, and intense. He had the look of someone about to fly into a rage at a word; and in fact, the three wives and five children he brought with him walked around him, so to speak, on tiptoes. He was the only really young man among the leaders present, and the rest of his semi-communal group, Bill told me, were about the same age.

Bill Projec was in his late thirties. He claimed to be preblooded Sioux from the Rosebud Reservation in South Dakota; but he did not have the look of the Sioux I had seen around Minnesota, although otherwise he looked undeniably Indian. He had a face that looked as if he could walk through a steel wall without a change of expression. Actually, he was almost exclusively a political leader for his colony, of whom only a few were also Indian. Petr Wallinstadt was in his mid-fifties, a tall post of a man with iron grey hair, large hands and a heavy-boned face. He was a limited-minded man whose quality of leadership lay in an utter stead-fastness of attitude and purpose. Whatever Wallinstadt said he would do, he would do, Bill had told me in the briefing he had given me on the leaders before their arrival, and calling him stubborn was a weak way to describe him. Once he had made up his mind, it was not merely no use to try to argue further with him, he literally did not hear you if you tried to talk about it.

Old Ryan – otherwise called Gramps – was the patriarch among the leaders, and the patriarch of his own group as well. He may have been only a few years older than Wallinstadt, or he may have been as much as twenty years older. He was white-haired, as wide as a wall, bright, tricky, domineering, and explosive. He and Merry Water did not hide their intentions about steering clear of each other; and there had been bets made in the other communities for some time now as to when the two would hit head on and over what. One possible reason why this had been avoided so far may have been the fact that the young Ryans (anyone in Gramps' group was labelled a Ryan, whether he or she was one by blood or not) sneakingly admired the more esoteric freedoms of the TVLostChord people; and there was a good deal of fraterniza-tion – and sororization, to coin a word – going on. Meanwhile, the two leaders stayed close to home and ran into each other in person only on occasions such as this Thanksgiving bash at our place.

There had been considerable jockeying by the four leaders from the moment they showed up to see who could get the most of my attention. Not surprisingly, Old Man Ryan was the clear winner. He could not monopolize my time, but he could and did get half again as much of it as anyone else. I found myself with a sneaking liking for the old bas-tard, a title he came by honestly both in the ancestral and moral sense and was, if anything, rather proud of. For one thing, he had both brains and experience; and he was not the monomaniac that Merry was, the taciturn farmer that Petr Wallinstadt was and had been before the time storm, or the suspicious chip-on-the-shoulder character that Billy was. Ryan could talk about many things and did, and his sense of humour was well-developed, though raunchy to the point of unbelievability.

It was he who brought up the matter of The Empress, after about a week or so of celebrating. We were standing in the library, brandy snifters half-full of beer in our hands, looking down the slope in the late-winter afternoon sunlight to the river, where a skating party was in progress on the ice that stretched out from the banks to the black, open water of midchannel.

'What'll you do if she comes?' Ryan asked, without warning, in the midst of a talk about spring planting.

'Who?' I asked, absently.

My attention and my mind were only partly on the discussion we had been having about storing root vegetables; and it seemed to me I had missed something he had said. Actually, I had been concentrating on the skaters. In the early twilight, some of them had put on hard hats with miner's lamps attached to them and these, now lit, were glinting like fireflies in the approach of the early twilight. The little lights circled and wove figures above the grey of the ice. Patterns of all kinds had been a fascination to me from my beginning. It had been the patterns

I saw in the movements of the stock market that had been the basis of my success there. Similarly, with the management of my snowmobile company and everything else right up to our duel with the time storm, in which my ability to see the force-patterns was crucial. Now, I was beginning to make out a pattern in the encircling lights. It was a fragile, creative pattern, built as it developed, but determined by the available space of ice, the social patterns of the occasion, and the affections or dislikes of the individuals involved. I felt that if I could just study the swirl of lights long enough, I would finally be able to identify, by his or her movements, each invisible individual beneath a light source.

'Who?' I asked again.

'Who? The Empress! Beer getting to you, Despard? I said, what'll you do if she comes this way? And she'll be coming, all right, if she lives that long; because she's out to take over the world. You've got a pretty good little part-time combat force but you can't fight three hundred full-time soldier-kids, equipped with transports, planes, helicopters and all sorts of weapons right up to fly-in light artillery.'

'What'll *you* do if she comes?' I asked, still not really with him.

'Christ! Me? I'll wheel and deal with her, of course,' he grunted into his glass, drinking deeply from it. 'I know I can't fight her. But you might be sucker enough to try.'

He tickled me. I finally pulled my attention entirely from the skater patterns on the ice.

'So?' I said, mimicking his own trick of argument. When he got serious like this, he talked with the explosiveness of a nineteen-twenties car backfiring. 'I better not plan to ask you for help if I'm crazy enough to take her on, then? That it?'

'Damnright!' He stopped backfiring suddenly, turned full or to face me, and switched to purring like an asthmatic alley cat. 'But you're smart. You know well as I do how many ways there are to peel a grape like that. Now, if you'd just let old Gramps do the talking – for your bunch and mine only – I tell you I can deal with someone like her ...'

'Sure you can,' I said. 'And with you dealing with her for your people and mine, all the other groups would be forced into joining us, in their own self-defence. Which would leave her with the idea – particularly since you could help it along while you were doing the dealing – that you were the real power in this area, the man to settle with; and, like all the rest, I was in your pocket.'

'Screw you!' He swung away from me to stare out the window at the skating party. The cold afternoon was darkening fast; and his fat profile, against the dimming light, showed panting and angry. 'Let her take your balls then. See if I make you a neighbourly offer like that a second time!'

I grinned. He could not help himself. It was simply in him to push for an advantage as long as he had the strength to do it. If I ever really needed an alliance with him, I knew he would jump at the thinnest offer. From what Bill had told me, we would have had very little trouble conquering all our neighbours, including Gramps and his clan, if we took the notion.

But all this did not alter the facts that the Empress was nothing to grin about and that the old man had a head on his shoulders. I sobered.

'What's this about her having three hundred full-time soldiers, aircraft and artillery?' I asked. 'Where'd you hear that?'

'One of my boys came back from the west coast,' he said.

'*Back* from the west coast?' I said. 'When did any one of your people go out there?'

'Ah, it's some time back,' he said, taking a drink from his snifter. He was lying and I knew it, but I couldn't waste half an hour pinning him down to the truth. 'The point is, he was in San Luis Obispo. There's an old army camp outside that town, and she's been using it as a training area. All the people in town know about the planes and the helicopters and the guns. And the soldiers come into San Luis Obispo every night to hit the bars. They've got four actual bars in there.'

'She's got half the world to go after down to the top of South America, and the other half clear up to Alaska,' I said. 'What makes you think she'd be coming this way?'

'Don't be a jerk,' grunted Ryan. 'It's not country you take over nowadays. It's people. The important places. And this place is important enough. It's got you here.'

Unfortunately, he was right. It had gradually begun to dawn on me, since I came from living exclusively inside my own skull, how much I was considered some sort of post-time storm wizard, not only among the people of our own community, but generally around the globe. Why they had settled on me and not on Porniarsk – or even on Bill, for that matter – puzzled me. Possibly Bill was not colourful enough to make good myth and legend; and Porniarsk could be considered too inhuman to be judged the wizard rather than the wizard's familiar. But it was a fact that this impression of me seemed to be spreading all over the world, according to the shortwave talk we heard, no doubt growing more wild and hairy the greater its distance from anyone who had ever seen me in person.

That being the case, it suddenly made sense why the Empress might mount an expedition in my direction. She could hardly lose. If I was as magical as rumour had it, she would be acquiring a valuable sort of Merlin. If I was not, she could still keep me close under wraps and maintain the legend, threatening people with my powers, and gaining the sort of credit anyone acquires by owning a pet sorcerer.

A corner of that situation suddenly opened up into innumerable corridors of possibilities; and the pattern-seeking portion of my mind began to gallop along them to map out the territory to my own advantage.

Ryan was still talking to me.

'What?' I asked.

'Got through to you with that, didn't I?' he said.

'That's right, Gramps,' I told him, 'you got through to me.'

I turned to face him.

'I want to talk to that boy of yours,' I said. 'I want to hear him tell me about everything he saw.'

'Well, now I don't know ...'

'We can dicker over your price for letting him talk to me later. Is he here with the people you brought along?'

'No,' said Ryan, frowning. 'Now, where did he say he was going? Seems to me he said something about going east this time...'

But, of course, this was only his way of making sure he gave nothing away for nothing. I had to promise him I'd send someone over to do welding for him on a windmill generator he was putting up – none of his group could weld for sour apples; and then of course, it turned out that the relative who'd been on the west coast was out on the ice right now, together with the others we were watching from the window.

I had the boy in – he was only eighteen – and with Ryan, Bill, and Ellen standing by, we shook him down for everything he could remember about the Empress and her armed forces. He was a little reticent about why he had gone away to the Pacific coast in the first place. I got the impression he had had a fight with Gramps and run off before the old man could have him beaten up by some of the more loyal sons and daughters of the clan. He kept moving because he ran into no one who particularly wanted him to stay; and so he had ended up somewhere around San Bernardino, where he found work as a wagon-driver (the west coast was short of petroleum products, and horse breeding was becoming a way of life). As a teamster he had eventually driven a load of freight north to San Luis Obispo and spent a week or so in the town before selling his freight goods to someone other than the person he was supposed to deliver them to, and cutting and running with the sale price.

Once safely away from San Luis Obispo, he had decided to head home. Not only because San Bernardino was now an unhealthy place for him, but because he thought he could probably buy his way back into Gramps' favour with the stories he had to tell, if not with his newly acquired possessions. For he had used the value of the goods he had stolen to buy himself the best horse, saddle and rifle he could find. Besides, as he told us, he was more than a little homesick by that time.

It turned out, however, he did not have that much more of value to add to what Gramps had already told me, except that his description of the planes used to transport the Empress' troops revealed them to me to be VTOL's, vertical-take-off-and-landing craft. That bit of information explained how the Empress could plan to airlift her soldiers into potential battlefields around a world where airports and landing strips were either no longer in existence or in bad states of repair. With VTOL's, she would be able to land just about anywhere.

But – there was a joker in the deck at the same time. My mind went *click* and put the matter of the petroleum shortages and the horse breeding together, in a military context. Her aircraft would need fuel to operate. That meant that to come as far east as we were, she either had to be sure of finding refuelling spots along the way – the remains of cities with fuel still in storage somewhere – or carry her fuel along. To carry it along in the aircraft themselves would leave no room for the troops. It was an equation in supply that had only one sensible solution. Before she went anywhere, she would need to send the fuel ahead of her overland, for which horse-drawn wagons were the only answer. Not only that, but her soldiers must necessarily hoof it to within a few miles of their objective. Meanwhile, the pilots of the aircraft would undoubtedly fly them empty, except perhaps for the Empress herself and her immediate staff, to a rendezvous with the soldiers on foot, when those were at last within striking distance of their objective.

I sent Gramps and his wandering relative away and laid the matter, as I saw it, before Bill and Ellen.

'What it means,' I told them, 'is that we've got a cushion of a few months between the time when she decides to come this way and when she actually gets here. Not only that, but we ought to be able to set up some sort of agreement with communities west of us to warn us when her soldiers and wagons start to come through. Is there someone around here we could send off to do that for us?'

Bill looked at Ellen.

'There's Doc. He'd be good at it,' Bill said, 'if you could spare him for a couple of weeks.'

'Doc?' I echoed; and then I saw them looking at me. 'All right, all right. I just can't get over how young he is.'

That was not the right thing to say. Ellen's face did not change an inch, but I could feel her reaction.

'Once they get to know him,' Bill said, 'Doc can command a lot of respect. And it isn't exactly like taking a stroll in the park, travelling around like that these days. The number of things that still might have kept somebody like young Ryan from coming back alive might surprise you, Marc. With Doc, we'd have the best possible chance of getting our envoy back.'

'All right,' I said. It was a time for giving in. 'I was just thinking how he'd strike other people who'd see him the way I see him. But you know better than I do. I suppose I ought to get to know him better myself.'

Ellen grinned, a thing she did rarely.

'You'll learn,' she said.

I was left with the feeling that while I was forgiven, I had lost a point to her, nonetheless.

Well, as I told myself after they left, all that was mainly in her, Bill and Marie's department. My department, right now, was tracking down that something I searched for in the library and in my own head. I had not been able to do much while the holiday season was still on, with the guests around; but as soon as all that nonsense was over, I went back to work.

The search I returned to kept producing the same results as it had before, only more of them. I kept picking up clues, bits, indications, twingles – call them what you like. What they all really added up to was evidence that what I searched for was not just in my imagination. At the same time, they were no more than evidence. I began to lie awake nights, listening to the breathing of the woman-body beside me, staring at the moon-shadowed ceiling over the bed and trying to stretch my mind to form an image of what I was after. But all I could come up with was that whatever its nature, it was something of a kind with the time storm. Not *akin* to the time storm, but something belonging to the same aspect of the universe.

What I searched for had to deal with the total universe, no matter what else it did. If nothing else, the track of its footsteps was undeniably there, like the track of some giant's passing, all through the thought and creativity of the literary world.

I became avaricious, impatient to close on the quarry I hunted. My reading speed, which had been fast to begin with, increased four or five times over. I galloped through books furiously, swallowing their information in huge gulps, making a pile of unread volumes at the right of my chair in the library every morning, mentally ripping out the information they contained in chunks, and dropping the empty to the left of the same chair, in the same second that I was picking up the next book. As the winter wore on toward spring, I became like an ogre in a cave – I turned into a blind Polyphemus, made drunk by Ulysses, bellowing for books, more books.

Nonetheless, I did not lose myself in this, the way I had lost myself after Sunday's death. I continued to dress, shower, shave, and eat my meals on time. I even pulled myself out of my search now and then when there was an administrative or social matter that needed the attention of Marc Despard. But, essentially, the winter snows and the waking year that took place around me this year were like some scene painted fresh daily on a wall at which I barely looked; and it came as a shock to me one morning to look out on the fields of April and see that the snow was gone and there was a fuzz of new green everywhere.

I had made a fresh stack of books at the end of the previous day on the right side of my chair; but the morning I first noticed the new green of the landscape, I did not reach out, as usual, to pick up the top volume and start devouring it. For some reason the Old Man was not keeping me company that day. Lately the sun, through the wall of windows, had been so warm that I had gotten out of the habit of making the fire in the fireplace. That morning a curious stillness and peace seemed to hold all the room, piled and cluttered and jumbled as it now was with the books I had demanded and discarded until it looked like a warehouse.

But out beyond the window was warm yellow sunlight; and where I sat was like a small bubble of timelessness, a moment out of eternity where anyone could catch his breath, without the moment wasted being charged against his life. Instead of reading, I found myself just sitting, looking out down the slope and over the town and the plain beyond.

I had been reading a great deal of writing on religion in the past few weeks, on yoga and Zen and all the martial arts, trying to pin down what the Chinese called *Ch'i* and the Japanese *Ki*, and which was usually translated by the English word 'spirit.' As I sat staring out the window, a male cardinal flew down and perched on a feeding platform for birds which Bill had set up during the winter without my hardly noticing it. I stared at the cardinal; and it came to me that I had never seen such a beautiful colour in my life as the rich red of his body feathers leading up to the black ones at his throat. He balanced on the feeder, pecked at some seeds Bill had put there, then lifted his head and was perfectly still against the high blue sky of spring.

Something happened.

Without warning, the timeless moment that enclosed me also reached out through the glass pane of the window to encompass the cardinal as well. It was not a physical thing happening, it was a moment of perception on my part – but all the same it was real. Suddenly I and the cardinal were together. We were the same, we were identical.

I reached down and picked up not one of the unread books, but the last volume that had been in my hands the evening before. It fell open near the beginning, where I had laid it face down, open, for a minute yesterday; and under the influence of the timeless moment, the words I had read before stood forward to speak to me with a voice as large as the world. They were the words of the opening paragraph of Chapter 2: THE VALUE OF OUR EXISTENCE, in the book *Aikido in Daily Life* by Koichi Tohei, who had founded Ki Society International, and who had himself studied under Master Morihei Ueshiba, the founder and creator of the art of Aikido.

'*Our lives are a part of the life of the universal. If we understand that our life came from the universal and that we have come to exist in this world, we must then ask ourselves why the universal gave us life. In Japanese we use the phrase* suisei-mushi, *which means to be born drunk and to die while still dreaming, to describe the state of being born without understanding the meaning of it and to die still not understanding ...*'

With that it all came together; not suddenly, but at once, so that it was as if it had always been together. I had been like someone born drunk, doomed to die drunk – and now I was sober. The cardinal was still on the feeder; the timeless moment still held the library; but it was as if a strange golden light had come out to flow over everything. All at once I understood that what I had been after was not just in the scraps of lines I had read in the books that had passed so hotly through my hands. It was not the fragments of ideas, the shards of wisdoms I had studied that alone were precious bits of what I sought; but that everything I had read, everything I had experienced, the world and all in it – all time and all space – were what I hunted and needed to grasp. And now I could grasp it, not by making my hands big enough to cup the universe in my palms, but by taking hold anywhere, in anything as small as a moment, a sentence, or the sight of a bird on a feeder.

With that understanding, it seemed to me that the golden light was suddenly everywhere; and I was abruptly aware of life around me as far as my mind could stretch to picture it. I could feel the rapid beating of the heart of the cardinal on the feeder. I could feel the beating hearts of the experimentals and the humans at the foot of the slope. I could feel the slow, true life in the firs and the oaks and the grasses and flowers. I could feel the blind stirring of the earthworms in the newly warmed earth. My new sensitivity ranged on and out without limit, beyond the horizon and over the whole world. I could feel life stirring everywhere, from the shark cruising the hot tropical seas, to the Weddell seal sun-bathing on the south Polar ice. The whole globe beat to the rhythms of existence, and below that beat were the quieter, more massive rhythms of the inanimate, of the soil, rock, water, wind, and sunlight. Gravity pulled. The Coriolis force spun, clockwise to the north, counterclockwise to the south. The intermixing patterns of weather sounded together like the disciplined instruments of an orchestra rendering a symphony.

I do not remember the golden light leaving and the sensitivity it had brought me. Just, after a while, it was gone and the cardinal had vanished from the feeder. I was back to feeling with merely the ordinary sensitivities of my body and mind; but within those I felt alive as I never had before. Everything seemed as if seen under a very bright light, clear and sharp. My mind was racing. I seethed with energy. I could not wait to put what I had just found to practical use. I bolted from the chair and went out of the summer palace by the entrance where the vehicles stood. There was a jeep sitting in the parking area. I climbed behind its wheel and sent it bouncing down the slope toward the town. I did not quite know where or how I was going to take hold of the universe in the new way of doing so that had just become clear to me; but now it seemed impossible that I could not find a place and a means.

But oddly, as I got close to the flat ground and the houses, a strange shyness came over me. I had been down there only briefly before on half a dozen separate occasions, and each time I had gone directly to City Hall to see Ellen, Marie, or someone else, then left again in less than an hour. It came home to me that I really had never met those who lived in the town; and I was abruptly as conscious of my stranger status as a grade school child on a first day at a new school.

I parked the jeep in some bushes that hid it several hundred yards from the closest of the buildings, got out and went ahead on foot.

The first building I found myself heading for was a temporary one with a platform floor, plank walls and a canvas tent roof. To this was being added a more permanent structure of cement block walls and gable roof, already shingled. There was no glazing as yet in the window opening, and outside the door aperture, a white pickup truck was parked, from which a man in blue jeans and sweater was carrying in various lengths of lumber.

I reached the pickup while he was still inside and waited by it until he came out again. He was a lean, black-haired type in his late twenties or early thirties with a long, straight nose.

'Hi', I said.

He glanced at me indifferently.

'Hullo,' he said, went to the truck, and began pulling off some twelve-foot lengths of two by four.

'Can I give you a hand?'

He looked at me again, not quite so indifferently.

'All right,' he said. 'Thanks.'

I went over to the truck as he backed off from it with his two by fours, picked up several of my own and followed him through into the building.

There was no light inside except what came through the window openings, but this was enought to see that the building would be illuminated well enough with natural light, even on dark days, once it was finished. The two by fours were apparently for wall studs, for he had several partitions already framed up.

I carried my load over to where he was piling his. A cement floor had been poured, but not professionally finished, and the footing was both gritty and a little uneven. But it, like the wall framing and the block laying of the outer shell was good enough for security and use. We worked together at unloading the truck for some time without saying anything to each other.

I found myself getting an odd pleasure out of being useful in this ordinary way. The feeling was above and in addition to the pleasure of the physical exertion which, once I warmed up to it, was body-enjoyable, the way such efforts usually are. I was conscious of the house-builder eyeing me as we worked, but that was as much reaction as he showed until we had finished getting all the two by fours into the building. I came out from carrying in the last two lengths of lumber and found him standing, considering what was left on the truck – mostly nails and odds and ends of hardware.

'What next?' I asked him.

'I forgot to pick up conduit for the wiring,' he said, without looking at me. 'Well, let's get the rest of it in. You and I better take the nail cartons together, one by one. They're heavy.'

We pulled a nail carton to the open tailgate, took it each on a side and carried it in. As we went toward the door opening, he spoke.

'You're Marc Despard, aren't you?'

'Yes,' I said.

He stared hard at me for a second.

'No, you're not,' he said, as we stepped into the semigloom of the interior.

'I'm afraid I am.'

'You can't be.'

'I'm afraid I am.'

'Look, he's got a long beard and he's six inches taller than you are.'

We laid the carton of nails down and went out after another.

'I tell you,' he said, as we went in carrying the second carton, 'you can't be. I know. I know what Despard looks like.'

I grinned. I couldn't help myself.

'So do I,' I said.

'Then you admit you aren't him.'

'No,' I said. 'I'm him. What makes you think I've got a beard and I'm six inches taller?'

'Everybody knows that. Besides, you never come down from that mountain.'

'I do now.'

'Shit!'

We carried in the other cartons without words. It occurred to me suddenly that he might think I had been laughing at him and that all this was some sort of practical joke on my part. I was distressed.

'If I don't look like Marc Despard,' I asked him, 'why'd you ask me if that's who I was?'

He did not answer me immediately. It was not until we had made one more delivery inside and were back out in the sunlight that he spoke again, without looking directly into my face.

'I don't know why you'd want to help me.'

'You had this truck here to be unloaded,' I said. 'It goes faster with two people than with one.'

'There's got to be more to it than that.' He stopped dead and faced me. 'What's up? What is it? What's going on? Is there some kind of law here or something like that I've broken?'

'Man—' I began, and then broke off. 'Look, I don't even know your name.'

'Orrin Elscher.'

'Orrin—' I held out my hand. 'Marc Despard. Glad to meet you.'

He stared at my hand as if it had a mousetrap in it, then slowly put out his own hand and we shook.

'Orrin,' I said, 'it was just such a fine day I thought I'd come down, and when I got here I saw you unloading the truck, so I thought I'd offer you a hand. That's all there is to it.'

He said nothing, only took his hand back.

We finished unloading the truck. It was strange, but once upon a time it would have bothered me that he was bothered. I would have geared up emotionally in response to his emotions. But now all I could think of was what a nice day it was and the enjoyment of using my body to some practical and useful purpose. I was getting the same sort of pleasure from unloading that truck that I might have gotten from engaging in a favourite sport; and I was grateful to Orrin Elscher for providing me with the opportunity for that pleasure. As far as his puzzle about me went, I felt no pressure to explain it. In his own time he would understand; and if that time never came, it would not make any real difference to the world. All that really mattered was that his truck was unloaded, he had been saved some work, and I had enjoyed myself.

I had gotten this far in my thinking when I remembered I had left the summer palace intending to put my new insight to work; and here I had forgotten about it completely.

But of course I hadn't. I saw the connection now between the insight and what I was presently doing. I had set out to take hold of the universe; and I had done that. There was no such thing as an unrelated action; and the act of my helping Orrin to unload his truck connected with the necessary completion of his house, the development of the whole town, the future of the people here, plus their effect and interrelation with all the rest of the people in the world. In fact, it connected with the whole future pattern in a way I could see building and stretching out until it became part of the great spider web of interacting forces that contained the time storm itself. As for me, in enunciating that connection by being part of it and recognizing it, I had expanded my own awareness that I needed to stretch before I could take the next step against the storm.

We finished unloading the truck.

'Well, take care of yourself,' I said to Orrin and turned away.

I was perhaps five steps from him, headed back toward where I had hidden the jeep, when I heard him call me.

'Mr. Despard—'

I turned to find him right behind me.

'I – thank you,' he said.

'Nothing to thank me for,' I answered. 'I enjoyed the workout. I suppose I'll be seeing you around?'

'Sure,' he said – and then, more strongly, added, 'Sure. You will!'

'Good.'

I turned and went. I had gotten a good echo from him, like the unblurred ring of uncracked metal when you tap a bronze vase with a fingernail. I went back to the jeep, got behind the wheel, and after a moment's thought headed on into City Hall.

But there was no one around when I got there. Even the typists were not at their desks. I looked at my watch and saw it was just after ten in the morning. Coffee break time, perhaps. I went out, got back in the jeep and headed back up toward the summer palace, enjoying the bright day, the sight of the buildings and people I passed, as if the whole world was something marvellous invented yesterday that I had never seen before.

When I got to the summer palace there were eight vehicles of various kinds parked in the parking area. As I climbed out of the jeep, Bill came out of the door with a rush.

'There you are,' he said. 'We've been looking all over for you. The Empress is on her way. We just got word.'

26

We were not surprised to see the helicopters ignore the town and head directly toward the summer palace. There were three of them, all the size of aircraft I had flown in between airports like LaGuardia and Kennedy in New York. They could each hold at least thirty people comfortably.

We stood in the parking area and watched them come – a baker's dozen of us, including the Old Man and Porniarsk. There was nothing much else we could do. Our advance warnings from the communities farther west had earlier confirmed the fact that Paula Mirador, the Empress, was indeed moving toward us with at least five hundred armed bodies (about one-third of them women) plus three .155 millimetre howitzers. She had apparently merely passed through these other communities, pausing just long enough to accept their formal submissions on her way. Wisely, no one had tried to oppose her, and we ourselves were hardly in a position to do so, even though we were probably the strongest single social unit between our territory and the Rockies.

According to her usual battle plan, which our scouts had confirmed, she had the main body of her troops standing off just over the horizon, with the VTOL transports ready and waiting. The howitzers were with them, ready to be moved in close to pound flat any property we owned before the troops followed to mop up any still-living defenders. It was a strong military argument she proposed.

We had not given in to it – yet. Our town was evacuated, except for a half-dozen fortified positions with .50 calibre machine guns, hidden among the buildings. These, if they survived the artillery, could make it something less than a picnic for the troops advancing on the wreckage. Whether the Empress knew about our machine guns was a question. She apparently knew a good deal about us, but possibly not the full extent of our weapons and supplies.

The rest of our noncombatants were scattered, back in the hills, with a light force to guard them and weapons of their own, as well as enough food and other basic supplies to last a year. She could not hunt them all down, even if she wished to spend the time trying. Aside from all this, there were three more heavy machine guns and gun crews camouflaged and dug in to cover this parking area from the surrounding rocks and trees – and one other machine gun nest hidden inside the palace. Even if she were bringing as many as sixty or eighty soldiers in her helicopters, it would not be a wise idea for her to simply try and make the thirteen of us prisoners by head-on force.

But of course all this was beside the point. She did not really want to waste trained people and ammunition on us, any more than we wanted to fight a small war with her. She and we were both lining up our resources face-to-face for a bargaining session. The helicopters sidled in, looking very dramatic against the blue sky with its few patches of high clouds, and settled to earth with a good deal of noise and raised dust.

The doors of the two furthest from us opened, and uniformed men with rifles and mortars and a couple of light machine guns jumped out and set up a sort of perimeter, facing the surrounding country. They did not, however, move too far away from their planes and seemed to be making the point that they were there to protect the helicopters and themselves primarily.

After they had settled down, there was a wait of two or three more minutes, then the door to the helicopter closest to us opened, the steps were run down, and a dozen men and women in civilian clothes came out to range themselves like an honour guard in a double line ending at the foot of the steps.

Another brief wait, and a single figure came out. There was no doubt that this was Paula Mirador, even if the rest of the proceedings had been designed to leave any doubt. I stared, myself. I had not seen anything like this since before the time storm; nor had any of us, I was willing to bet. We had grown so used to living and dressing with practicality and utility in mind that we had forgotten how people had used to wear clothes, and what sort of clothes they might wear.

Paula Mirador was a page out of some ghostly fashion magazine, from her dainty, high-heeled, cream-coloured boots to an elaborately casual coiffure. She looked like she had just walked out of a beauty shop. In between was a tall, slim woman who only missed being very beautiful by virtue of a nose that was a little short and a little sharp. Besides the boots and the warm brown hair of her coiffure, she wore a carefully tailored white pants suit over an open-throated polka-dotted blouse, with the wide collar of the blouse lying over the collar of the suit. A grey suede shoulderbag with an elaborately worked silver clasp hung from one shoulder.

She took my breath away – and not by virtue of her band-box perfection alone. Her hair was not that blonde, her face was not that perfect, but something about her rang an echo of Swannee in my mind.

She walked down the steps, not looking at us yokels, and gazed around at the general scenery, then said something to one of her civvies-dressed attendants, who popped to and turned away to peel off an escort of eight armed troopers to come toward us.

Once upon a time, I would have credited the attendant with a prior knowledge of what I looked like, seeing him come directly toward me, alone. Lately, however, I had begun to realize how much the way in which human beings instinctively position themselves gives out signals. The group pattern of those standing around me amounted to a sign with an arrow pointing to me and the words *here is our leader*.

At any rate, the envoy, a round-faced young man in his mid-twenties, who looked something like a taller version of Bill, came up within a dozen feet of me and stopped. His troopers stopped with him.

'Mr. Despard?' he said. 'You are Mr. Despard, aren't you, sir? I'm Yneho Johnson. The Empress would like to speak to you. Will you follow me, please?'

I did not move.

'That makes two of us,' I said. 'I'd like to talk to her. I'd like to know what the hell she's doing here on my property without my invitation. I'll wait here five minutes. If she hasn't come personally to explain by that time, I'll blow the whole batch of you apart. You're parked on top of enough buried industrial dynamite to leave nothing but dust.'

He blinked. Whether because of my tone and attitude, or because of the information about the dynamite, was hard to tell. Probably both. The dynamite, of course, was a bluff. It would have taken twenty truckloads of that explosive to mine the whole parking area even sparsely. But there was no way he and the rest of Paula's party could be sure we did not have that much; and in any case, I had nothing to lose by bluffing since they outgunned us anyway.

He hesitated. I turned away.

'Bill,' I said, 'see he doesn't waste time.'

I walked back a few steps toward the palace, hearing Bill's voice behind me.

'You've lost fifteen seconds already,' Bill was saying. 'Do you want to try for more?'

I turned around and saw Johnson, with his escort, retreating at a fair pace toward his mistress. He rejoined her and spoke animatedly. She, on the other hand, as far as we could tell from this distance, was the picture of cool indifference. She waved a hand gracefully on the end of one slim wrist, and he came back to us with his bodyguards.

'Mr. Despard,' he said. 'The Empress warns you. If you're bluffing, you'll be shot down by our escort troops as soon as the five minutes are up. If you're not bluffing, whether you kill us or not, her troops, who love her, will catch you and roast you over a slow fire. She, herself, never bluffs.'

I turned toward Doc.

'Doc,' I said, 'shoot him.'

Doc unslung the machine pistol he had hanging from his right shoulder.

'Stop. Stop—' shouted Yneho Johnson. 'Don't! Wait a minute. I'll be right back.'

'Just under two minutes left,' I reminded him, and watched him gallop back across to his Empress.

They were still talking a minute later.

'Four minutes up,' said Bill, behind me.

'Let it get down to thirty seconds,' I told him.

We waited.

'Coming up on four and a half minutes,' Bill said.

I stepped out in front of the others and made an elaborate show of looking at my watch.

'Now,' I said to Bill, under my breath.

He had a small detonator switch in his pocket, with a wire running from it back into the palace and from there out again to a spot in the parking area near its west edge. He reached into the pocket, pressed the detonator button; and a fountain of dirt exploded very satisfactorily to about thirty feet in the air, thereby cleaning us out of dynamite almost completely – and not industrial dynamite at that, but the sort of explosive that used to be available in hardware stores in mining areas. I made a large show of looking at my watch again.

'Maybe they won't realize it's a warning,' said Marie, tightly.

'They'll realize,' Ellen said.

They had. The Empress was at last on the move toward me – not by herself, but with her whole entourage surrounding her. Mentally, I docked her a couple of points for not coming sooner. It should have been obvious to her that if there was one patch of ground in the parking area not likely to be mined, it would be the space where I and my own people were standing. She came on until her group merged with mine, and she walked up to stand face to face with me, smiling.

'Marc,' she said, 'you and I have to have a private talk.'

'I can talk out here,' I said.

'*You* probably can.' She was very pleasant. 'I find it works better for me if I don't take my own staff into my confidence exclusively. But don't you think we could both be a little more relaxed and free if it was just the two of us chatting?'

It was not an unreasonable argument; and I had already made my point – which was that I was not about to make any deal behind the back of my associates. I could afford to give in gracefully.

'All right. Come inside,' I said.

I took her into the palace. On the still air indoors, I could catch a hint of perfume about her that had not been noticeable outside. I was suddenly very conscious of her physically – both of her female presence and her band-box costuming. The ghost of Swannee moved momentarily between us, once more. On impulse I took her to the library, cleared the books off one of the other chairs for her, and we sat down facing each other.

'You must have somebody around who cares about preserving information,' she said, looking about the room.

'Yes,' I said. 'What did you want to talk about?'

She crossed one leg over the other.

'I need your help, Marc.'

'You could have written me a letter, Paula.'

She laughed.

'Of course – if it'd just been a matter of you and me. But I'm the Empress and you're Marc Despard, the man who controls the time storm. When two people like us get together, it has to be a state visit.'

'Aside from the fact that I don't begin to control the time storm,' I said, 'what about this state visit of yours? A state visit with an army and three howitzers?'

'Don't pretend to be something other than the intelligent man I know you are,' she answered. 'All this show of force is an excuse for you, Marc – an excuse for you to agree to work with me because that's the only way you can keep the people you have around you now from being hurt.'

'I'm that valuable?'

'I said, don't pretend to be less bright than you are. Of course you're that valuable.'

'All right. But why should I take advantage of your excuse? Why should I want to work with you, in any case?'

'Wouldn't you rather have the resources of the whole world at your fingertips, than just what you can reach here, locally?'

'I don't need any more than I have here,' I said.

She leaned forward. There was an intensity, a vibrancy about her that was very real, unique. She had to know I knew she was using it deliberately to influence me.

'Marc, this world still has got a lot of people in it who need putting back together into a single working community. Don't tell me you don't want to have a hand in that. You're a natural leader. That's obvious, aside from the time storm and what you've done with it. Can you really tell me you'd turn your back on the chance to set the world right?'

She either had a touch of the occult about her, or she was capable of reading patterns from behaviour almost as accurately as I might have myself. My deep drive to defeat the time storm reached out with its left hand to touch the basic human hunger to conquer and rule. Mentally, I gave her back the two points I had docked her earlier – and a couple more besides. But I did not answer her right away; like a good salesman, she knew when to close.

'Say you'll at least talk it over with me in the next few days,' she added.

'I suppose I can do that,' I told her.

So it turned out that her appearance became a state visit in reality. The main body of her troops and the howitzers stayed out of sight over the horizon, although none of us, including me, ever forgot they were there; and she, with her immediate official family, slipped into the role of guests, as old Ryan and the others had been over the Thanksgiving holidays.

She was a good deal more entertaining than my neighbours had been, and much more persuasive. She had a mind like a skinning knife. But the most effective argument she brought to bear on me in the next five days was the pretence that she was putting her military strength aside and trying to convince me by argument alone. I knew better, of course. As I just said, none of us could forget those troops and the artillery just beyond field glass range. But her refusal to bring her military muscle directly into the discussion left me to argue silently with my own conscience over whether it was not just personal pride or stubbornness on my part that made me so willing to expose my wives and friends to death or maiming rather than join forces with her.

She had another lever to use on me, although at the time I did not rate its effectiveness with that of the argument-only ploy. She was reputed to have the kind of legendary sexiness that made her troops dream of her at night and consider all other women as watered-down substitutes;

but I got no such signals from her at all. Except for the odd moments in which she reminded me of Swannee, she was good company and interesting, that was all. At the same time, by contrast, she did seem to make Marie look limited and unworldly, and Ellen juvenile.

Of course, she and I had very little time out of each other's company. We were the two heads of state and if she was to be entertained by us, I usually had to be on stage myself. The time I had with my own people was what was left over, usually either the early hours in the morning, before Paula had put in an appearance from the several rooms – suite was too pretentious a word for them – we had turned over to her and her several personal attendants – or late at night after she had tired out.

It was a situation that put both Ellen and Marie, particularly, at some distance from Paula and myself, but perhaps this was not a bad arrangement. It developed that neither of them liked her or saw anything but serious trouble coming from any extended association with her.

'She really doesn't like you, either, you know,' Marie told me, the evening of the third day Paula had spent with us. 'She doesn't like anyone.'

'She can't afford to,' I said. 'She's a ruler. She's got to keep her head clear of likes and dislikes for individuals so she can make her decisions strictly on the basis of whether something is a good thing for her people, or not.'

'A good thing for her or not, you mean,' said Marie.

That was unusually outspoken for Marie. But the more I thought over what I had said to her, the more I liked the ring of my own words. I went to Ellen's room and tried the same speech on her.

Ellen snorted.

'Is that supposed to be an answer?' I said. 'All right, tell me. Exactly what is it that's wrong with Paula?'

'Nothing's wrong with her,' said Ellen.

'Well, you must think something's wrong or you wouldn't be acting this way. What is it?'

'You.'

'Me?'

'You want to be a damn fool, go ahead and be one.'

I lost my temper.

'How can I be a damn fool? I've got to find some way to deal with her and do it with gloves on. She can wipe us all off the map if I don't!'

Ellen got up out of bed, put on her clothes and went for a walk – at three in the morning. Nobody but she could have done something like that with such finality and emphasis. Her back was an exclamation mark going out the door.

Bill did not like her either. Neither did Doc. For that matter, neither did the Old Man, who always disappeared when Paula came on the scene. I began to feel like the tragic hero in a Greek play with the chorus in unison warning me of disaster at every step. I did not mention any of this to Paula; but she evidently sensed some of it at least, because along about the end of the week she got off on a subject that was particularly timely in view of the situation.

'... It *is* a lonely life,' she said, apropos of something I had said. We were taking a stroll through the woods below the summer palace early in the morning. 'Rank does more than isolate you socially. Do you realize, Marc, you're essentially the only person in the world I can talk to on the level, so to speak? With everyone else, I have to remember I'm the Empress. But it's not even *that* so much as having to put myself in the balance sometimes against everyone around me when it comes to making decisions. Every so often, all the advice I get is one-sided; and sometimes I have to brace myself to turn it all down and go just the opposite way, because when it gets down to it I have to trust my own decision more than all of theirs or else I'm not a fit ruler.'

'I know what you mean,' I said.

'Sure you do.' She glanced at me for a moment, then looked ahead the way we were walking. 'You can't take on responsibility without taking on everything else that goes with it.'

She stopped and turned to face me. I stopped also, necessarily, and turned toward her.

'That's why it would mean so much to have you with me, Marc,' she said. 'I know you've got your own work with the time storm. I've only just begun to realize these last few days how important that is. But what you're needed more for, now, is to help me unify this torn-up Earth we've got and put it on a single, working community basis. That's your higher responsibility, at the moment.'

'And if I'm not with you, I'm against you?'

'Oh, Marc!' she said, sadly. 'I'm not a monster.'

I felt slightly ashamed of myself. It was a fact that, so far, I had seen nothing in her that was not reasonable to the point of being admirable. The only evidence I had ever had that contradicted this was contained in the large body of rumour about her; and I had some experience with rumours, having heard some of the ones that circulated about me.

'Well,' I said, 'how much time are you asking me to invest?'

'A couple of years at the most.' She looked sideways at me as we walked. 'Certainly no more than that.'

'You think you can take over the world in two years? That's better than Alexander's record, and he was only thinking about the Asian continent.'

'There aren't that many people nowadays. You know that as well as I do,' she said. 'And it's a matter of contacting just the large population centres. Once those are organized, the small communities in each area and the individuals will want to adjust to the situation on their own.'

'Two years . . .' I said. All at once, it seemed like a long time away from here, away from the library and Porniarsk's workroom.

'Look,' she said, stopping again. Once more we faced each other and, for the first time since I had known her, she touched me, putting a hand lightly on my arm. 'Let's forget about it for today. Why don't we do something different? You let me entertain you for a change.'

'How?'

'We'll fly to my base camp and have lunch there. You can see for yourself what my regular soldiers are like and why I think it won't take even two years to bring order to the world.'

'I don't know,' I said. 'The others may worry . . .'

'Even if they do, it'll do them good,' she said. 'When they see you coming back safe and sound after going off alone with me, they'll understand I'm no one to be afraid of.'

'All right.'

We went back up to the palace. I did not quite feel like telling Ellen or Marie I was taking a solo jaunt into Paula's armed camp, so I looked for Bill or Doc. Doc was the one I found first; and he took the idea of my going calmly enough. In fact, it seemed to me his eyes even lit up a bit at the idea.

'Want me to come?' he asked.

'It's not necessary—' I checked myself. 'Come to think of it, why not? You may be able to see some things there I won't.'

I sent him to tell Bill we were both going and went back to explain to Paula that there would be two of us, feeling somewhat smug with the notion that I had taken some of the force out of the objections the others would have to my going entirely alone.

'Of course, bring him,' said Paula graciously, when I mentioned that I couldn't come after all, unless I had someone like Doc along with me. It had occurred to me that, just as I had, she might be underestimating Doc because of his youth. I had learned better during the past few months; but if she was making the same initial error, it could do us no harm and might turn out to our advantage. On the helicopter ride to her camp, accordingly, I watched her closely for any sign that this was the case, but saw no clear signals either way. She was friendly but a little condescending to him, which could mean that she did not, in fact, recognize his worth, or simply that she lumped him in with all those human bodies she looked down on from her status as Empress.

The camp, when we got there, was impressive enough. Paula's soldiers might or might not love her, as rumour had it, but they were well-uniformed, well-armed, and under good discipline. Their field tents were pitched in a hollow square with Paula's clump of larger tents at the centre, so that these were protected on all sides. The helicopter that brought us put us down in the open space outside this interior clump of tents and within the camp area. If Paula had been intending to make me prisoner once she had me here, she would have had no difficulty once we had landed. There were armed guards ten deep around me in all directions.

But as it was, our visit was nothing but pleasant. Paula evidently travelled with a full complement of personal servants – I estimated at least two full helicopter-loads worth, which meant that she might not have needed to be so saving of fuel as I had guessed – including a number of younger women, none of them quite as good-looking as she was, but close enough. These were dressed as impractically as she was, with an eye to appearance rather than practicality; and this puzzled me until I began to realize that their primary job, or at least their highly important secondary job, was to act as ornaments and geishas. They were all over Doc and me while we were having cocktails before lunch, and they both served and joined us at the meal itself.

I did not at all mind being fussed over by these attendants; and I could all but see Doc's ears wiggling. I say, I could all but see his ears wiggling. What I saw, of course, was that they did not wiggle at all, and he was so poker-faced and determinedly indifferent to the attentions he was getting that it was almost painful to watch. Being a little more case-hardened by years than Doc, I had a corner of my mind free to note that it was a shrewd move of Paula's to provide herself with such courtiers. Not only did they act as a setting to show her off and emphasize her authority, they added an extra level between her and ordinary female humanity. Perhaps her troops did worship her, after all, seeing her set off this way, in the same way that they might worship a god or a demigod.

After lunch, Paula called in the commander of her soldiers, a small, lean, grey-haired man named Aruba with three stars on each shoulder strap of his impeccable uniform. General Aruba and Paula together took us out to look over the camp and observe her troops. Those in uniform were all young. I saw some boys and girls I could swear were no more than fourteen or fifteen years old. They were all cheerful, bright-looking and had the air of individuals aware of themselves as members of an elite group. There was a curious uniformity among them, too, which puzzled me for a while before I realized that I saw no tall bodies among them, either female or male. Like the general, they were short, and most tended to squareness of body.

Aside from their size, though, they were impressive. They were apparently spending their time in active training while awaiting the results of Paula's negotiations with us. They had set up an obstacle course outside their camp, and we watched as some thirty or forty of them ran through it, looking like trained athletes. They were, as Gramps Ryan had hinted, a far cry from my part-time militia.

After the inspection tour, we stepped into Paula's largest tent once more for drinks and then were flown back to the summer palace. I was itching to know what Doc's reaction was to everything we had seen; but I was back in host position again and could not abandon Paula to plunge immediately into conference with one of my staff. So it was nine that night before I had a chance to get together with him and the others. We held a staff meeting down in the City Hall, safely away from the summer palace and the view or hearing of any of Paula's attendants.

'Well,' I said to Doc, when we were at last gathered over the coffee cups in Ellen's office – he and I, Ellen, Marie, and Bill – 'how about it? What did you think of those soldiers of hers?'

'Well,' Doc scratched his right ear, 'they're in good shape physically. They're well-trained. They're young and bouncy and they've learned to obey orders. I'd guess they know their jobs—'

'Tough as we've heard they are, then,' said Ellen.

'Maybe,' said Doc.

'Why maybe?' I demanded.

'Well,' said Doc, 'they're not veterans. My dad and the other officers used to talk a lot about that; and it was a fact. I mean, I could see it too. The ones who'd actually been shot at somewhere along the line knew what it was like; but there was no way the ones who hadn't been shot at could know what it was like. My dad and the others used to say there was no telling what a man who hadn't been shot at was going to do the first time he was.'

'What makes you so sure the ones we saw haven't been shot at?' Bill asked.

Doc shrugged.

'They just look like they haven't. I mean, it shows.'

'How?' I said. 'For example?'

'Well …' he frowned into his coffee cup for a second, then looked back at me. 'They're too bright-eyed and bushy-tailed. Too gung ho. You understand? If they were veterans, they wouldn't be wasting energy except when they had to. For example, when they were off duty, you'd see them off their feet, sitting or lying down somewhere. That sort of thing.'

We thought about it for a moment.

'You try to remember,' Doc said, 'when it was you last heard of the Empress actually fighting anyone. Maybe on the Islands, where she started, there was some fighting. But ever since she landed on the west coast, it seems she just shows up with all those guns and whoever she's dealing with surrenders.'

'Then you think we might have a chance, fighting her?' Bill asked. 'Is that it?'

'We might have a chance,' Doc said. 'One thing for sure, the people we've got carrying guns are going to use them and keep on using them when the fighting starts.'

There was another short silence, full of thought.

'I don't like it,' said Marie finally. 'There's still too many of them compared to us.'

'I think so too,' I said. 'Even if we were sure of winning, I don't want our town wrecked and even one of our people killed. Now, Paula's been after me to join her for the next year or two while she brings the rest of the world under control—'

They all started to talk at once.

'All right, now just hang on there for a moment!' I told them. 'If I do decide to go with her, it doesn't necessarily mean I'm going to stay for two years, or even one year. But if that's the best way, or the only way, to get her to leave everybody else alone here, then my spending some time with her is a cheap way to buy her off.'

'But what sort of a place will this be without you?' said Marie fiercely.

'Come on, now,' I said. 'The rest of you run everything here. All I've been doing is sitting around and reading books. You can spare me, all right.'

'Marc,' said Bill, 'you aren't needed here because you've got duties. You're needed here because you're the pivot point of the whole settlement.'

'Let him go,' said Ellen. 'It's what he wants to do.'

451

Bill looked at her quickly.

'You don't mean that.'

'All right, I don't,' said Ellen. 'But it gripes me.'

She folded her arms and looked hard-eyed at me.

'And what about the time storm?' Bill said to me. 'How can you keep on working toward a way to do something permanent about that, if you go off with Paula? What if the balance of temporal forces we set up breaks down sometime in the time you're gone? What if it breaks down tomorrow?'

'If it breaks down tomorrow, I can't do a thing more about it but try to reestablish the balance again, the way I did the first time.'

'You can't do that if you're not here,' Marie said.

'Don't talk nonsense, Marie,' I said to her. 'Paula needs a stable Earth as much as we do. She'd send me back in a hurry to reestablish a balance of forces if that balance broke down and mistwalls started moving again.'

'It might not be so easy to reestablish next time, Porniarsk says,' Bill put in. 'What about that?'

'If it's not as easy, it's not as easy,' I told them all. 'I tell you I'm not yet ready to take on the time storm again to produce any more permanent state of balance than I did before.'

For a second, nobody said anything. The silence was as prickly as a fistful of needles.

'Anyway,' said Ellen, 'have you checked with Porniarsk? You owe him that much before you do anything like going off.'

As a matter of fact, I had completely forgotten about Porniarsk. The avatar was never concerned or consulted in any of our purely human councils about community matters; and as a result, I had fallen out of the habit of thinking about him when decisions like this were to be made. Ellen was quite right. I could not do anything with the time storm if I lost the help of Porniarsk. If I simply went off with Paula and he should think I'd given up on the storm ...

'I haven't checked with him yet,' I said. 'Of course I will. I'll go talk to him now. I suppose he's in the lab?'

'I think so,' said Bill.

'Yes, he is,' said Ellen. 'I was just in there.'

That bit of information caught at my attention. As far back as I could remember, Ellen had never paid any particular attention to Porniarsk. I went out and down the corridors toward the lab. On the way, I passed the little interior courtyard where Sunday lay preserved; and on impulse I checked, turned, and went in to look at him.

I had not come to see him in months. It had been a painful thing even to think of him for a long time; and while now the pain was understood and largely gone, the habit of avoidance was still strong in me. But at this moment, there was a feeling in me almost as if I should let the crazy cat know that I was going – as if he was still alive and would worry when I did not come back immediately. The roofless courtyard was dark, except for starglow, when I stepped into it, and cold with the spring night. I closed the door by which I had come out and reached out to thumb on the light switch controlling the floodlights around the walls. Suddenly the courtyard was illuminated so brightly it hurt my eyes; there, to my right, was the transparent box in which Sunday lay.

It was like a rectangular fish tank a little longer than the leopard and perhaps three feet deep, set up on a wooden support about coffee table height and dimensions. Within, it held that same fluid-looking stuff that filled Porniarsk's universe viewing tank and which he had given me to understand was actually something like an altered state of space – if you could picture nothingness as having variable states. At any rate, what he told me it did was to hold Sunday's body in a condition outside of the movement of time, any time. As a result, his body was even now in exactly the same condition it had been in less than two hours after his death, when Porniarsk had surrounded it with a jury-rigged version of this non-temporal space tank.

Nearly two hours, of course, was far too long for him to have been dead if we had been hoping for any sort of biological revival. If it had been possible to mend his wounds and start his life processes in the present state of his dead body, there would have been nothing to bring to life. His brain cells had died within minutes without oxygen, and the information contained in them was lost. A body in perpetual coma would have been all we could have achieved.

But what Porniarsk had hopes of was something entirely different. It was his expectation that, if we could learn to control the time storm even a little, we might be able to either acquire the knowledge directly, or contact others farther up the temporal line who had it, so that we could return the temporal moment of Sunday's body back to a few seconds before he had been wounded. It was a far-fetched hope and one that I, myself, had never really been able to hold. But if Porniarsk could believe in it, I was willing to go along with him as far as his faith could take us.

Perhaps at that, I thought to myself as I stood looking at Sunday's silent form lying there with its eyes closed and its wounds hidden under bandages, I had indeed had some secret and sneaking hope of my own, after all. I needed to hope. Because Sunday was still there in my mind like a chunk of jagged ice that would not melt. He represented unfinished business on my part. He had died before I could show him that I appreciated what he had given me – and the fact that the gift was an unthinking animal's one did nothing to lessen the obligation. What I owed to the others, to Ellen, to Marie perhaps, and Bill – or even to Porniarsk himself – I still had time to pay, because they were still alive and around. But the invoice for Sunday's love, and his death, which had come about because he had rushed to rescue and protect me, still hung pinned to the wall of my soul with the dagger of my late-born conscience.

No – it was not because of how he had died that I was in debt to him, I thought now, watching his motionless body in the floodlights. It was what he had done for me while he was alive. He had cracked open the hard shell that cased my emotions, so that now I walked through the world feeling things whether I wanted to or not; which was sometimes painful, but which was also a part of living. No, regardless of what happened with Paula, I could never be diverted permanently from work with the time storm, if only for my hope of seeing Sunday alive again, so that I could let him know how I felt about him.

I turned off the lights. Suddenly, in the dark and the starlight, I began to shiver, great shuddering, racking shivers. I had become chilled, standing there in the raw spring night in my shirtsleeves. I went back to the warmth inside and down the hall a little farther to Porniarsk's lab.

He was there when I stepped through its door and the Old Man was with him, squatting silently against one of the walls and watching, as the avatar stood gazing into the universe tank. They both turned to me as I came toward them.

'I thought I'd drop by,' I said; and the social words sounded foolish in this working room, spoken to the alien avatar and the experimental, near-human animal. I hurried to say something more to cover up the fatuous sound of it. 'Have you found out anything new?'

'I've made no great gain in knowledge or perception,' Porniarsk said, quite as if I had last spoken to him only an hour or two before, instead of something like months since.

'Do you think you will?' I said.

'I have doubts I will,' he said. 'I'm self-limited by what I am, as this one here—' he pointed to the Old Man, who turned to gaze at him for a second before looking back at me, 'is self-limited by what he is. Porniarsk himself might do a great deal more. Or you might.'

'You're sure there's no hope of getting Porniarsk here?' I asked. I had asked that before; but I could not help trying it again, in the hope that this time the answer would be different.

'I'm sure. There's a chance of something large being accomplished here. But there's a certainty of something not so large, but nonetheless important, being accomplished where Porniarsk is now. He will never leave that certainty for this possibility.'

'And you can't tell me where he is, even?'

'Not,' said the avatar, 'in terms that would make any sense to you.'

'What if things change? Could you then?'

'If things change, anything is possible.'

'Yes,' I said. I was suddenly very aware that we were at the end of a long and full day. I would have sat down just then if there had been a chair nearby; but since neither Porniarsk nor the Old Man used chairs, the nearest one at the moment was at a far end of the room, and it was not worth my going and bringing it back.

'I haven't been getting anywhere myself, I'm afraid,' I said – and immediately, having said it, remembered that this was not quite true. I hesitated, wondering if my experience of several days past with the cardinal that had come to perch on the bird feeder, and all that had followed, would mean anything to the avatar. 'Well, there has been something.'

He waited. The Old Man waited. If they had been two humans, at least one of them would have asked me what that something had been.

'I've been doing a lot of reading for some time now ...' I went on after a moment; and I proceeded to tell Porniarsk how the Old Man had cracked me loose from the mental fog I'd been in ever since Sunday's death, and how I had started on my search through everything I could lay my hands on between book covers. I had never told him this before; and, hearing the words coming from my mouth now, I found myself wondering why I had not.

Porniarsk listened in silence, and the Old Man also listened. How much the Old Man comprehended I had no way of telling. He certainly understood a fair amount of what we humans said to each other, apparently being limited, not so much by vocabulary, as by what was within his conceptual abilities. Certainly he knew I was talking about him part of the time, and almost certainly, he must have understood when I was talking about that moment on the mountainside when I was ready to kill him and the touch of his hand stopped me.

Porniarsk let me go through the whole thing, right down to the description of the golden light and my helping Orrin Elscher unload his pickup truck. When I was finally done. I waited for him to say something, but still he did not.

'Well,' I said, at last. 'What do you think? Did I really break through to something, or didn't I?'

'I've no way to answer that question,' Porniarsk said. 'Any discovery can be valuable. Whether it's valuable in the way we need it to be, valuable toward learning how to control the time storm, I've no way of knowing. Basically, I'd say that anything that expands your awareness would have to be useful.'

I found myself less than happy with him. It had been a great thing to me, that episode with the cardinal and the golden light and the passage with Elscher; and the avatar's treating it so calmly rubbed me the wrong way. I was on the edge of snapping at him; then it came to me that I was having one of the suspect emotions – anger.

So – why was I angry? I asked myself that, and the answer came back quickly and clearly. I was angry because I had been expecting to be patted on the back. Subconsciously, I had been cooking in the back of my head all this time a neat little argument for him, to the effect that I had made this large step forward, working on my own; so going off with Paula would not waste any time, since I could continue working toward more large steps while I was away. But now Porniarsk had shot the whole scheme down by not showing the proper astonishment and awe at my accomplishment; and I was left without the necessary springboard for my argument.

All right. So it was a case of going back and starting over again – with honesty this time.

'We're up against a situation,' I said. 'I may have to leave here for a time. I don't know how long.'

'Leave?' Porniarsk asked.

I told him about Paula.

'You see?' I said, when I was done. 'The only safe way for the people here – and for that matter, for what you have in this room and any work with the time storm – is for me to go along with her, for a while anyway. But it's temporary. I'll only be gone for a while. I want you to know that.'

'I can understand your intentions,' said Porniarsk. 'Can I ask if you've weighed the importance of what you want to protect here against the importance of what you may be able to do eventually in combating the time storm? If nothing else, an accident could destroy you while you're away from here.'

'Accident could destroy me here.'

'It's much less likely to do so here, however; isn't that so? With this Paula, you'll be moving into an area of higher physical risk?'

'Yes, I guess so,' I said. 'No. No guess about it. You're right, of course.'

'Then perhaps you shouldn't go.'

'God help me, Porniarsk!' I said. 'I've got to! Don't you understand? We can't fight her and survive. And we've got to survive first and get our work with the time storm done after, because there's no way to do it the other way around.'

'You're sure we couldn't survive if you stayed?'

'As sure as I am of anything.'

He stood, the heavy mask of his features facing me silently for a second.

'Do one thing, please,' he said. 'It's been some time since you looked into the viewer here. Will you look again now, and tell me if there's any difference in what you see?'

'Of course,' I told him.

I stepped up to the tank and looked into it. Now that I focused in on the space contained by it, I once more saw the myriad of tiny lights moving about in it. I looked at them, feeling a strange disappointment; and it took me a second or two to realize the reason. I had unconsciously bought my own story about having accomplished some breakthrough in understanding, the moment with the cardinal. I had really expected to see something more than I ever had, the next time I looked into this device; and now came disappointment.

Identified, the disappointment grew to a sharp pang. It was against all reason. I did not want to discover evidence that would be against my going with Paula. I wanted evidence that I should go, and it was exactly that sort of evidence that I was getting. But I realized that this was not what I really wanted – it was not what my heart wanted.

I reached into my memory to recapture the moment with the cardinal and the golden light that had been everywhere. But it slipped away from my imagination. I could not evoke it. A bitter anger began to rise in me. My mind beat against the iron bars of its own inability, and what I reached for went further and further from me.

I may have said something. I may have snarled, or sworn, or made some sound. I think I remember doing something like that, though I am not sure. But suddenly, there was a touch on my left hand. My mind cleared. I looked down and saw the Old Man beside me. He had taken hold of my fingers, and he was looking up at me.

My mind cleared. Suddenly, Sunday and the cardinal and all things at once came back together again. All the angry emotion washed out of me and I remembered that it was not by pushing out, but by taking in, that I had finally found the common pattern that connected me with all things else. I let go then, opened up my mind to anything and everything, and looked into the universe tank once more.

There were the lights again. But now, as I watched, I began to pick up rhythms in their movements, and identify patterns. Forces were at work to shift them about, and those forces were revealed in the patterns I saw. As I identified more and more of them, their number grew until they began to interact, until larger and larger clusters of lights were locking together in interrelated movements. There was no golden illumination around me this time; but there was an intensity – not a tension, but an intensity – that mounted like music rising in volume until it reached a certain peak, and I broke through. All at once, I was there.

I was no longer standing looking into a viewing device. I was afloat in the actual universe. I was a point of view great enough to see from one end of the universe to the other and, at the same time, able to focus in on single stars, single worlds. Now I observed not the representation, but the reality; and for the first time I perceived it as a single, working whole. From particle to atom, to star, to galaxy, to the full universe itself, I saw all the parts working together like one massive living organism moving in response to the pressure of entropy ...

'*My God!*' I said – and I heard my own voice through the bones of my skull, very small and far away, for I was still out there in the universe. 'My God, it's collapsing! It's contracting!'

For it was. What I looked at were the patterns of a universe that had been uniformly expanding, all its galaxies spreading out from each other, creating an entropy that was running down at a uniform rate. But now the pattern had been expanded too far. It had been stretched too thin, and now it was beginning to break down in places. Here and there, galaxies were beginning to fall back into the pattern, to reapproach each other; and where this was happening, entropy had reversed itself. In those places, entropy was increasing, side by side and conflicting with those still-expanding patterns in which entropy continued to decrease.

The result was stress; a chaos of laws in conflict, spreading like a network of cracks fracturing a crystal, spreading through the universal space, riding the tides of movement of the solid bodies through space. It was stress that concentrated and generated new fractures at the points of greatest mass, primarily at the centres of the galaxies; and where the fracture lines ran, time states changed, forward or back, one way or another.

Four billion years ago, the first stress crack had touched our galaxy. My point of view turned time back to that point and I saw it happen. An accumulation of entropic conflict near the galaxy centre. A massive star that went nova – but unnaturally, *implosion* nova.

There was a collapse of great mass. A collapse of space and time, followed by an outburst of radiating time faults, riding the wave patterns of the stellar and planetary movements within the galaxy, until at last the time storm reached far out into the galactic arms and touched our own solar system.

What had gone wrong was everything. What was falling apart was not merely this galaxy, but the universe itself. There was nothing to tie to, no place to stand while the process could be halted, the damage checked and mended. It was too big. It was everything, all interconnected, from the particles within my own body to the all-encompassing universe. There was no way I or anyone else could stop something like that. It was beyond mending by me, by humanity, beyond mending by all living intelligent beings. Facing it, we were less than transitory motes of dust caught up in a tornado, helpless to even dream of controlling what hurled us about and would destroy us at its whim ...

27

I woke in my own bed and with the feeling that I had been through this once before. For a moment, I could not remember when; then I recalled my earlier experience with the universe tank and how I passed out after getting caught up in what I saw there. I felt a momentary quirk of annoyance. If I was going to fold up every time I tried to see things in that tank ...

But the annoyance faded as I remembered what I had seen. Here, lying in the familiar bed in the familiar room with everything simple and usual about me, the memory seemed impossible, like nothing more than some bad dream. But it was not a bad dream. It was reality; and in spite of the comfortable appearance of everyday security that surrounded me, the fact of the time storm as I had seen it loomed over us all like some giant, indifferent mountain that might crumble and bury us at any moment, or might let us live a thousand years in peace.

But still ... for all that I could feel the shadow of the storm still dark on me, I was not quite as destroyed by it as I had been when I had first seen it in its full dimensions, imaged in the tank. A reaction had taken place inside me, a stubborn reflex against utter despair and hopelessness. There was no way I could even begin to dream, as I had for so long, of controlling the storm. And still ... and still ... something inside me was refusing to give up. Some strange and snorky part of my being was insisting that the situation could still be fought and perhaps overcome.

It was impossible. Perhaps a thousand more individuals like myself, armed with powers beyond the powers of gods, might have stood a chance of achieving control, but I was alone and had no such powers. Only, there it was. I could not let go. Something in me refused to do it.

Ellen came in, carrying a glass of water.

'How are you?' she asked.

'I'm all right,' I said.

The shade was pulled down on the bedroom's one window and a

light was on. But now that I looked, I saw the paler, but brighter, gleam of daylight around the edge and bottom of the shade.

'How long have I been here?' I asked, as she came over to me. She handed me the glass of water and also, two white pills.

'Take these,' she said.

'What are they?' I asked, looking at the pills in my hand.

'She didn't tell me, but Marie said you should take them when you woke up.'

'Now damn it, I'm not taking some medication I don't know about just because you say Marie says I should take them.'

'I think they're only aspirin.'

'Aspirin?'

I looked at them closely. Sure enough, they had the little cross stamped on one side that was the trademark of the brand we had been able to get our hands on locally; and when I held them close to my nose, I could catch a faint whiff of the acid smell that was the sign of aspirin when it was getting old. Overage drugs were one of our problems since we were restricted to stocks from time periods all antedating at least the time when we had balanced the forces of the time storm. These two tablets were really fresher than most of their kind that I had encountered in the last half year. Marie must have been hoarding these against some emergency. I felt ashamed of myself. I did not need the pills, but they would only keep on aging toward uselessness if I did not take them, while swallowing them would do me no harm and make Marie feel her efforts had not been wasted.

I took them.

'Porniarsk wants to talk to you if you're up to it.'

'I'm up to it, all right.' I threw the covers back and sat up on the edge of the bed. They had undressed me. 'Where are my pants?'

'Closet,' said Ellen. 'Maybe you'd better not get up.'

'No, I'm fine,' I said. She looked unconvinced and I decided to lie a little. 'I had a headache but it seems to be getting better already.'

'If you're sure,' said Ellen. 'I'll go tell him then.'

She went out, and I had time to get dressed before Porniarsk trundled into the room.

'Are you well?' he asked me.

'Fine,' I said. 'No problems. I'm not even particularly tired.'

'I'm glad to hear that. Do you remember what you said before you collapsed?'

'I'm not sure ...'

'You said "My God ..." and then you said "It's impossible. I can't do

461

it. It can't be done ..." Can you tell me what you meant and what made you say that?'

'What I saw in the tank,' I said.

I told him what that had been. When I was through he stood for a second, then creaked off one of his heavy-headed nods.

'So you believe now that further effort to control the storm is useless?' he asked.

'That's the way those patterns looked,' I said. 'But now ... I'm not sure. I still don't see any hope in them, but at the same time, I don't seem to be able to bring myself to give up.'

'I'm glad of that,' said the avatar. 'With no will to succeed, you'd fail even if there was good reason to expect success. But with will, there's always hope. Porniarsk himself has always believed that the apparent is only the possible. Therefore failure, like success, can always be only a possibility, never a certainty.'

'Good,' I said. 'But what do we do now?'

'That's my question to you,' said Porniarsk. 'My earlier guess was right. Your capabilities are far beyond mine. It's up to you to find the answer.'

For the next three days I tried, while holding Paula in play as well as I could. But the evening of the fourth day her impatience came out in the open.

'I'll need an answer tomorrow, Marc,' she said, as she went back to her own rooms. 'I've spent more time here now than I planned.'

It was the eleventh hour, clearly. I thought of calling Porniarsk, Ellen, and Marie together for a brainstorming session and rejected the notion. There was nothing they could do to help me. As Porniarsk had said, it was up to me – alone.

I isolated myself in the library, paced the floor for a while, and came up with absolutely nothing. My mind kept sliding off the problem, like a beetle on a slope of oily glass. Finally, I gave up and went to bed alone, hoping that something might come to me in my sleep.

I woke about three hours later, still without a solution. My mind was spinning feverishly; but only with worries. What was to become of Ellen and Marie, and for that matter, our whole community, if I went off as Paula's captive-servant and either died or did not come back? What could help the world if the local forces of the storm broke out of balance again? There was no answer anywhere except the hope of doing something with the storm after all and using control of its forces to somehow break the hold that Paula's superior army gave over us all.

And I could not find such a hope. Every possibility seemed bleak and dry and worn out. There was only one way to unlock the door confronting me – with some kind of a key; and there was no key. My thoughts had spun around in a circle so long they were exhausted. I threw on the topcoat that I used as a bathrobe and went back to the library to get away from my own circular idea-dance.

Under the artificial lights, the library was still and comfortless. I sat down in one of the overstuffed chairs and closed my eyes. My mind skittered off at all angles, throwing up pictures of everyone for whom I felt responsible ... Marie, Wendy, Ellen, the avatar ...

Their images chased each other before the vision of my imagination, like movie film played on the inner surfaces of my closed eyelids. Even the shapes of people who were not around any more. I watched Tek, going down from the bullets of the machine pistol in Ellen's hands; Samuelson, waiting with his rocket launcher for the outsize toy-like attackers of his small town; Sunday, as I had first seen him; Sunday again, with Ellen, back when I had called her only 'the girl'; Sunday ...

Sunday.

Suddenly, with the thought of him, it all came together. My mind opened up like a flower at sunrise, and life flowed back into me. The light and all things in the still room seemed to change. Once more, I felt my identity with all my people and the cat who slumbered; and I saw at once what could perhaps be done if there was time enough. I got to my feet with my idea still in me and went as quickly as I could to Porniarsk's lab.

Porniarsk was standing immobile beside the vision tank, his eyes fastened on nothing, when I turned the lights on in the dark room. It was impossible to tell whether he slept at times like this, or whether in fact he slept at all. We had all asked him about that at one time or another, and he had always answered that the question was meaningless in his terms and unanswerable in ours. Now, when the lights went on, he stayed as he was for a second, then turned his head to look at me.

'What is it, Marc?' he asked.

'I think I might have it!' I said. 'It just came to me. Look, you can run this tank like a computer, can't you? I mean you can extrapolate the storm forward and back?'

'Yes.'

'How far forward?'

'Until extrapolation's no longer possible,' he said. 'Until the time storm destroys the universe, or the capacity of the tank's logical sequencing is exceeded.'

'Look,' I said. My vocal cords were tight and my voice bounced loudly off the bare, white-painted concrete walls. 'There's always been the chance we might be able to get help with the storm up forward, but I've never thought about that in terms of a really long way forward. I remember now, when I was seeing the patterns in the tank, I thought that if I could find a thousand like me something might, just might, be done. We'd never find anything like that in the reasonably near future. But, if we went as far forward as we could – maybe way up there there really are a thousand others like that. Away up there. As far into the future as we can reach.'

'And if there were,' said Porniarsk. 'How could we contact them?'

'We might be able to go to them.' The words were galloping out of me and my brain felt wrapped in flames. 'If I could just see what the storm patterns were, up in that time – just the patterns affecting this immediate area, the area right around this house, maybe just even around this lab – I might be able to unbalance the present forces enough so they'd correspond. I might be able to produce a time change line; one single mistwall to move just us, far down the future-line to them.'

He neither moved nor made a sound for five or six seconds, while my heart beat heavily inside me, shaking my chest.

'Perhaps,' he said.

The breath I had not realized I was holding went out of me in something like a grunt.

'We can do it?'

'I can show you the ultimate pattern possible to this device – perhaps,' he said. 'Are you sure you can make use of it, if I do?'

'No,' I said, 'I can try, though.'

'Yes,' he said. His head went up, his head went down, in one of his nods. 'I'll need time to work out the storm patterns that far forward.'

'How much time?'

He looked at me steadily.

'I don't know. Maybe days. Maybe, some years.'

'Years!' I said. But then the sense of what he was saying sank into me. The furthest pattern perceivable by the vision tank could only be reached by going through all preceding patterns.

'When I've reached the limits of the device's capacity,' he said, 'I can call you in to see it.'

'Then we need to buy whatever time that takes,' I said. 'That settles it. I'll tell Paula I'll go with her.'

'Probably that's best. But you'll have to be able to come back here when I've found the final pattern.'

'I'll get back,' I said. 'Don't worry about that.'

I felt wonderful. All my frustration had vanished in a burst of energy and certainty. I would not have gone back to bed even if I could have slept. I looked at my wristwatch, and it was five-thirty in the morning.

'I'll wake up everyone who needs to know and tell them,' I said, 'right now. Will you come along?'

'You don't need me,' he said, 'and any time wasted from now on delays the final moment of achievement.'

'All right.'

I went out and started waking up the others. A little under an hour later I had them all sitting around the dining room of the summer palace, drinking coffee to get their eyes open and waiting for an explanation. I had rung into the meeting all those whom I thought must know what would be going on, but nobody else. At the table were Ellen, Marie, Bill, Doc, and Wendy – Wendy looking particularly sullen. She was grown up enough now to have a fourteen-year-old boyfriend – or thought she was. I thought ten years old ridiculously young for anything like that, though it was a fact she was beginning to develop physically; and she had asked to have him take part in this council as well. Naturally, I had spiked the notion. It was merely the last in a series of efforts she had made recently to get her mother and the rest of us to adopt the boyfriend into our inner family.

For the rest, Doc looked unperturbed, as if he was the only person there, besides myself, who was wide awake. Ellen looked concerned, Marie looked drawn and older than I had ever seen her look, and Bill was still white-faced and shrunken-looking from interrupted slumber.

'I'm going to tell Paula today I'll go with her,' I said, without preamble. 'We'll probably take off later today.'

I told them about my hope, my talk with Porniarsk and about what he was already at work on at this moment.

'... The point is,' I wound up, 'Porniarsk and the rest of you are probably safe here as long as Paula still considers me a friend and coworker. If that changes, she might think of keeping me under control by picking up some of you as hostages for my good behaviour. So, if things get prickly between the two of us I'll send you warning of it; and I want you all to clear out of here immediately and scatter. Scatter all over the place, each one by yourself – and don't let the rest of the community know you're going.'

Wendy looked grim.

'I mean that,' I said, looking her in the eye. 'Nobody. Wendy, you can stay with your mother; but everybody else take off alone.'

'Marc,' said Marie, 'do you really need the rest of us to go into the far future with you, if this works? Can't you just go alone, tell the people there what you want to tell them, and then come back?'

'How can I?' I said. 'You know I need a monad-gestalt to control the storm forces; and that'll take all of you. So, listen. What I'll do is take the Old Man with me. If I send him back to you or if he comes back under any conditions, that's your signal. Take off and scatter.'

'Marc,' said Doc, 'you'll need some way of getting the message from us in a hurry when Porniarsk finds what he's after. How's about I make regular runs to you, just to bring in letters from the home folks and a box of cookies and such, so Paula's people won't think anything of it when I pop in with the word?'

I looked over at him gratefully. It was nice to hear a sensible mind at work around the table that morning.

'Good,' said Ellen. 'Then if you need help getting away from wherever you are, Doc can help you.'

Another sensible mind.

'Fine idea, Doc,' I said. 'You're right, Ellen. Anybody else have any suggestions?'

'How long will you be gone altogether?' Marie asked.

'I can't tell,' I said. 'It depends on how fast Porniarsk can reach the ultimate configuration in his tank. Why?'

I knew why. She was having more and more trouble controlling Wendy and leaning on me more and more for that task.

'Maybe Wendy could go with you. She could see something of the rest of the world that way.'

'No!' said Wendy and I, simultaneously. That was all I needed, to have Wendy on my hands, while I was trying to keep Paula happy and unsuspecting. I thought quickly. 'Too dangerous for her.'

'I don't want to,' whimpered Wendy, who was no slouch herself at picking up cues. Marie looked from the girl to me, helplessly. She knew she was being doubleteamed, but she was helpless to do anything about it.

'All right,' I said. 'Then, if nobody's got any more suggestions, you can get busy putting together what I'll need to take with me and spreading the word that I'll be going. I'll break the news myself to Paula over breakfast in an hour or so.'

28

Paula took the news coolly. Whether this was because some of her people had already picked up the word of it that was spreading rapidly through the ranks of our own people, or simply because it was a strategy on her part to act as if her enlisting me had never been in doubt, was impossible to tell. In either case, it made no difference to me, who was going with her for my own private reasons.

'All right,' she said, over the breakfast table. 'How soon can you be ready?'

'Six hours, maybe,' I said.

'In that case, I'll wait for you and you can join my staff right here. If you hadn't been able to move quickly, I'd have needed to let you catch up with me. I'll send word to my officers. No offence to your kitchen help, Marc, but I'll be glad to get back to my own headquarters and have some decent coffee.'

There was only one small incident of interest in our leaving. Paula's people had already climbed aboard the helicopters that had been sitting parked and waiting for them, and I was not yet aboard the one carrying Paula herself. The Old Man, as I said, had shown no liking for Paula; and now he had made himself scarce. Doc had found him, finally, about half a mile from the summer palace among the rocks of the hillside and literally held an automatic pistol at his head to get him to come along back to the takeoff point. The Old Man knew what human weapons were and came, but not happily.

When I finally saw him approaching, squatting ominously beside Doc in the front of the jeep, I changed my mind about taking him.

'Look,' I said to Doc, under my breath, when the jeep drove up and stopped by the entrance ladder of the 'copter, 'this isn't going to work. If he's going to bolt the minute I take my eyes off him, this'll never work. Leave him here and you come along instead while we figure things out. Then I can send you back with word.'

'All right,' said Doc, climbing out of the jeep. 'Do I have time to pick up any gear, or—'

But at that point, the Old Man solved the problem for us. He had been staring at the 'copter, and at me, all the while the jeep was driving out to us on the open area. He was not unintelligent and he must have finally realized that I was actually going, with or without him. At any rate, he took a sudden leap out of the jeep directly onto the first step of the ladder, caught my hand and pulled me toward him and the steps.

'That's all right, then,' I said to Doc. 'But why don't you come along anyway, at least until I've had a chance to settle down. No, you won't have time to bring anything. Got any kind of weapon with you?'

'Pistol.'

'All right. I can shake down Paula's people for what you'll need beyond that, and what you'll need to get back here from wherever she's headed next. Let's get inside.'

He followed me up the ladder, the Old Man preceding us.

'What's this?' said Paula when we were inside and the ladder was being taken in, the entry hatch being shut behind us. She looked from Doc to me.

'There's some unfinished business,' I said. 'I've got some decisions yet to make. He can carry word back from wherever we stop, a couple of days from now – if that's all right with you?'

'Certainly. Why not?' She turned her attention to the Old Man who still clung to my hand. 'This is the creature? I thought I saw it around earlier. Is it housebroken?'

'Since long before I met him,' I said. 'All his people learn to live like human beings while they're growing up, just as our children do.'

'People?' She smiled. 'Well, keep him out of the way. Find your seats now.'

She turned away.

Apparently, we were not to return to where her camp had been when I had visited. Her orders had already gone out, and her troops and wagons had been on the move from an hour after I had broken the news to her over our breakfast table. We flew on eastward and put down by a river about twenty-five miles further on, where the motorized section of Paula's transport had already arrived and set up her personal tents. Later, that evening, the main body of her wagons and infantry arrived.

I kept Doc with me for four days, mainly so he could prowl around and get acquainted with the way Paula's people did things; then I sent him home before they saw through the bright-eyed, teenage image he had been careful to wear anywhere near her and them. The Old Man stayed close in the tent I had assigned to me for my exclusive use and was no problem. I found myself happy to have him there. He was, after all, a small touch of home.

We continued to move steadily eastward. In open country, between objectives, the pattern seemed to be for Paula's headquarters to stay comfortably put for three days while her army marched forward. Then her motorized division would move the headquarters tents and equipment forward one short day's trek in their jeeps and trucks. Meanwhile Paula, her general, and a handful of us who were at the top of the table of organization took it easy for most of the day, then struck the pavilion tent and made a half to three-quarters of an hour hop in a single 'copter to the new site, while the other two aircraft followed empty except for pilots and copilots.

It was a pleasant life, but monotonous; particularly when it began to be obvious that Paula had no real need for services from me, but was only carrying me along as a satellite to impress possible enemies and reluctant allies. I had a great deal of time on my hands; but it turned out this had been provided for by Paula's foresight. I discovered one of the main duties of her large staff of women clerks and attendants.

Briefly, they were there to keep everyone happy, from me down to the lowest officer in the army; and also to keep us out of Paula's way and off her mind, except when she had a need for us. A good share of this, I picked up from my own observation; but it was General Pierre de Coucy Aruba who dotted the i's and crossed the t's for me.

The general was a drinker. That is, he could not yet be called a drunk because he held his alcohol without visible sign and never seemed to prolong his drinking beyond three or four drinks. But those drinks came at every lunch, dinner, cocktail hour and late supper at which I ever saw him.

'You could call me a philosopher,' he told me one evening in his tent, after a post-dinner planning session with his staff had concluded. His officers were gone and he had invited me in for a private chat with just the two of us.

'You might think that I could probably set up with my own army and carve out a nice little empire for myself,' he went on. 'And I could – I could. But I'm not the kind who wants an empire for himself. *"Everybody's a little mad except thee and me, and I even have my doubts about thee."* People intrigue me. I like to be comfortable and watch them. So I'm the perfect commander for our Empress. She knows she never needs to worry about a military coup as long as I'm in control.'

'I can see she'd appreciate that,' I said.

'Yes, indeed.' He smiled at me – and it was a smile, not a grin, with the sun-wrinkles deepening at the corners of his eyes and the tidy, little grey moustache quirking upwards at the corners. 'Wouldn't you, in her shoes?'

'I gather she makes a good boss?' I said.

'A good Empress, you mean.' He waggled a forefinger at me. 'Always remember that. An Empress has to be an Empress, at all times. That's why the young ladies.'

'The young ladies?'

'Of course. Familiarity breeds contempt.' He smiled again. 'And there's no familiarity like that in bed, eh?'

'That's true enough,' I said soberly, thinking of my own two women.

'Most queens had trouble out of getting laid,' he said. 'Most empresses, too. Queen Elizabeth … Catherine of Russia … notice none of the girls around here, though, are quite as good-looking as the Empress?'

'I had,' I told him.

'Obviously. The art of controlling a man with your female presence is to be just out of reach, but out of reach. You understand?'

I did. Not only did I understand, but a certain near-demonic impulse moved in me, and my trader's instinct was challenged. During the days when Paula had been talking to me about coming with her on her road of conquest, she had sent up clear signals that she was attracted to me personally. I had taken for granted, that part, if not all of this was calculated, to gain her own ends. But, as it turned out, she had wanted me neither for my services as a magician nor myself; she had simply bought herself a show piece at the cost of nothing more than promises, rather than having to spend her troops and materiel to get it. Again, it had been a case of 'seller beware'; so I really had no kick coming if I had taken counterfeit currency for what I had sold. But for her to assume that, after having been sharped, I would cheerfully reconcile myself, given the equivalent of two cents on the dollar, was something of an insult.

Accordingly, I played the game with the female staff, so as not to arouse any suspicions; but privately, I set my sights on Paula after all. I was patient. I had my ability to see patterns working for me. Success would be along, down the line there, somewhere.

Meanwhile, in the patterns, I had found another hobby to occupy my time. Now I had broken through twice to the oneness of the universe, and there was no longer any doubt in my mind that such a state of mind existed; and if that was so, anything was possible, even the destruction of the time storm. I made it an invisible exercise to look around me for patterns constantly, and to develop my perception of them to the point where that perception and recognition and understanding of the patterns would be simultaneous.

The work paid off. The patterns were there, all about me all the time. They were there in the interactions of people, in their physical movements, their speech, their reactions, and their thinking; and in all else about fauna, flora, earth, and sky. Little by little, my knowledge of such patterns became deeper and surer, until it began to approach eerily close to the true magic of telepathy and second sight. I could have played chess now, better than anyone I had ever encountered; but the chess patterns, for all that they were fascinating and innumerable, were dead patterns. I preferred the live patterns created by my fellow men and women.

So I observed and learned; and, curiously, I could feel the Old Man learning through me.

Meanwhile, we were marching to the Atlantic seaboard. The points we searched out were sometimes the fragments of cities or towns that still held supplies or needed equipment; or sometimes they were population centres like my own community, which had not existed before the time storm forces had been balanced, but which had sprung up since around some acquired communication equipment or military force.

In every case, however, these places and the people in them were plainly inferior to the armed strength of the Empress. They sometimes bluffed for a day or two before yielding, but in the end they all acknowledged her as their overlady. Then, at last, we ran into opposition.

We had reached the ocean and a place that called itself Capitol, which once had been half Washington International Airport, and was now half that and half something else, because deep-water ocean lapped up against the base of cliffs that abruptly cut off the main road into the airport. On the ocean, moored out a little distance from a jerry-built wharf, were a number of small ocean-going craft. Still hangared about the airport were a number of 1980 commercial passenger jets and – on the land area of that part that now opened to the ocean – some light, five-passenger craft, that were like flying bubbles with stubby wings, and a tiny power plant that seemed permanently fuelled with an inexhaustible, built-in supply of energy.

These were from some time later than the twentieth century; and these also were the real prize from Paula's point of view. The craft, in their own right, were almost as famous as I was in mine. For, although there were still large cruise ships and other massive watercraft to be found up and down the Atlantic coast, there was no way now to either maintain or operate them. It was still possible to cross the Atlantic in boats up to the size of small yachts. But the trip would be uncomfortable and a matter of some weeks. With these light aircraft out of the post-twentieth century, the ocean could be crossed in hours.

Once more, Paula moved in, going gutsily herself with a small guard to negotiate, while readying her armed forces and artillery behind her. But this time, the target did not yield; and she was forced to fight for what she wanted.

Not only that, but these people fought hard. It took nearly a week for Aruba and his soldiers to take the place and subdue its inhabitants; and it cost them over half of their strength in casualties. Replacements would have to be marched across the continent from the west coast, since she could not trust any of the recently subjugated communities in between to furnish her with loyal fighters. That meant months. Fall and winter would be upon us before they were here and trained. Paula herself, and her inner staff officers, could cross the ocean by air at any time; but the small boats available could not ferry her army across the Atlantic in bad weather. We were stuck where we were until spring.

I saw the pattern of this situation evolving ten days before the rest of them did. It solidified in my mind on the first day of hard fighting in which they pounded the enemy positions with artillery and confidently advanced afterwards, only to be cut to pieces by machine gun fire. I saw it; and I raged inside at the inevitable delay it implied for Paula's plans of world conquest. Doc was overdue for one of his periodic visits, and for the first time, I found myself fearing, rather than hoping, that he would bring me word that Porniarsk had found the ultimate universe pattern possible to the viewing tank. If the avatar had found it, I had no choice. I could not delay going home, with the risk that, in the meantime, some chance here might kill me, cripple me, or somehow prevent me from returning at all.

On the other hand, I told myself, I did not want Paula still on the North American continent when I left her, without leave, and headed once more for my own territory. I wanted her on the other side of the world, by preference; or at least across the Atlantic, so that the trouble and expense of sending forces after me to bring me back would be so great she would delay as long as possible in doing so. It was, I believed, a reasonable reason for wishing her success. Therefore, as the week of fighting went on and casualties mounted, I looked grim along with everyone else in the Empress' camp – but for my own private reasons.

About Thursday, Doc finally arrived.

'Porniarsk's found it?' I said, the moment we could get off someplace where we were safe from being overheard. In this daylight instance, that meant a training area behind the field hospital, where we could see there was no one else within earshot.

'No,' he said. 'Not yet.'

'Good!' I said. He stared at me for a fraction of a second.

'Never mind,' I told him. 'I'll explain later. What's the rest of the news?'

'I was going to say,' he said, 'Porniarsk doesn't have it yet, but he thinks he's close—'

'Hell's bloody buckets!'

This time he really did stare at me, his tanned young face stretched smooth-skinned with puzzlement.

'I've got a reason.' I said. 'Go on.'

'I was saying, Porniarsk hasn't found the furthest possible future configuration the device can show; but he did find a sort of sticking point – some point where he got hung up for some reason. He's pretty sure he can get the tank to go beyond it, with a little more work; but he says to tell you he thinks this sticking point is some kind of sign he's close to the ultimate.'

I took a deep breath.

'All right,' I said. 'If he has, he has. I'll talk to you about that in a minute. Anything else important? How's everybody? The community running the way it should?'

'Nothing else. I've got some letters for you of course.' He tapped the leather wallet that hung from one of his shoulders. He always brought me a bundle of personal mail, that being the ostensible reason for his coming. 'But everyone's fine. And the place's running, like always, on the button.'

'Fine. Let's go back to my tent.'

We headed toward it. It was a matter of elementary caution not to talk to him for more than a few seconds as we were now, for fear of triggering off suspicions. Given the important and general news, we could do a fairly good job of discussing matters in hyperbole while I went through the home mail, even if there might be ears listening.

At the tent the Old Man leaped up to seize my hand, then turned to grasp one of Doc's as well. He walked with us to a pair of armchairs, still hanging on, and hunkered down between us. Since he and I had been away from home, he had become more dependent, not only on me, who had been the only human, originally, he would get close to, but on Doc during Doc's brief visits.

'Make yourself a drink,' I said to Doc now, 'while I go through these letters.'

'Thanks,' he said enthusiastically. He pried his hand loose from the Old Man's and went over to the table that did duty as my liquor cabinet. Doc was, in fact, a nondrinker as well as a nonsmoker. But he always carried cigarettes with him, and he was expert at making a show of both smoking and drinking, these being only two of a large number of casual acts he had perfected, apparently on the off-chance that the misdirection in them might prove useful someday. I ripped open my letters and read them.

They were perfectly ordinary, personal mail from home; and in spite of the fact that they were intended primarily as camouflage, I found myself going through them as eagerly as anyone else would, away from home and family against his will. Marie was still worried about Wendy, who herself had written me a few lines of pure prattle – under duress probably. Ellen had written almost as brief a note, saying that things were fine, just the way I'd left them, and there was no need to worry about anything. I read the last line as a hint to take Marie's motherly concern with a certain amount of advisement. Ellen's language could not have been any more spare and stiff if she herself had been a soldier in the field; so that the word 'love' at the end looked incongruous. But I knew her.

Bill wrote he was pleased with the way things were going. From him, this would be a reference to Porniarsk's work. Also, he mentioned that he had finally refined the 'emergency harvest plans,' which would be a reference to my orders that they all split up and scatter if Paula suddenly decided to take some of them hostage as insurance against my noncooperation. Porniarsk sent no message.

'Good,' I said to Doc, when the last letter had been read. 'Things seem all right at home.'

'They are,' he answered. 'Have you got letters for me to take back?'

'Over on the writing table, there,' I said. He went to get them. 'Were you planning on heading back right away?'

'Unless there's something to keep me here.'

He tucked the letters I had written into his wallet, came back and sat down. The Old Man took his hand again.

'I was just thinking – why don't you stick around a day or so until we've taken this local area? They're putting up quite a fight, and if you stay you'll be able to go back and tell the women personally that I didn't get hurt in the process.'

'Glad to,' said Doc. 'You've got a good life here. Far as I'm concerned, it's a vacation with all expenses paid.'

He had a nice, light tone to his voice as he said it; but his eyes were sharp on mine, ready to read why I was asking him to stick around. I shook my head very slightly, to tell him *not now*, and started to talk about the situation, saying nothing that wasn't highly complimentary to Paula and confident about her eventual achievements here, but filling him bit by bit with data on the actual state of affairs militarily. When I was done, he knew what the facts were, but not what the connection was between these and the reason I wanted him to stick around.

That was the third day of the battle for control of the area. It was not until Sunday that Paula's soldiers overran most of the strong points of the opposition and not until Monday afternoon that they finished mopping up.

'As long as you've stayed this long, you might as well stay for the victory celebration, too,' I told Doc.

'Suits me,' he said. His voice sounded a little thickly from one of the couches in my tent where he sprawled with a glass in his hand; but his eyes were as clean and steady as the eyes of a sniper looking along the sights of his rifle.

I was more glad to have him there than I had thought. I had seen the pattern of the battle's consequences building all week. Paula and Aruba, in particular, must be seeing the same thing themselves, now that the fight was over and the returns were in. So, while the rank and file survivors whooped it up in celebration, Paula herself and her immediate staff would now be biting into the bitter fruit of a win that had cost so highly. The way they would react, I had told myself, could tell me a lot more about their patterns; and part of what I might learn might be useful information to send home with Doc.

Paula had already had to face one particular ugly truth; that there was a point beyond which her well-trained soldiers would not obey her. From dressed-up recruits they had turned into veterans in the blood-bath of the last seven days; and commanders back to the dawn of history could have told her what would happen when such soldiers were finally allowed to overrun an enemy who had bled them heavily in preceding days. Her kids had turned into killers. They slaughtered right and left on that Monday afternoon as they subjugated the conquered people.

It was Paula's first setback. There were aircraft mechanics and boat mechanics, as well as other experts, among her former enemies that were worth regiments to her; but there was no way she could hold her blood-high soldiery back long enough to weed out such valuable individuals from the otherwise killable chaff of the local population. Monday cost her dearly.

Nonetheless, she had to put a good face on it and appear to encourage the wild celebration that ensued that night. It began at late afternoon and went on until dawn, by which time all but a few rarely tough individuals had collapsed. It was at dawn that Aruba came for me.

That he came himself for me, rather than sent for me, was an index of his upset. He stepped into my tent, peered for a second at the still form of Doc, who appeared to be asleep on one of the couches, and then looked back at me. In the early daylight coming through the plastic windows of the tent, his face was sallow, the shade of new liverwurst.

'She wants to see you,' he said.

'Paula?' I asked.

He nodded. I got to my feet. I was still dressed. Anything could have happened in that night just past and I had not felt like trying to sleep.

'What about?' I asked, as I went with him out into the cool morning. A breeze was blowing from the ocean.

'She'll want to tell you herself,' he said and licked his lips. He had been badly shaken and I could see him reaching for a bottle the minute he was alone in his own quarters.

I nodded indifferently enough, but inwardly I braced myself. On this morning, her purpose in wanting to see me would not be good. I walked alongside Aruba to the entrance of the pavilion tent, where two of her officers – colonels – now stood with machine rifles, doing sentry duty. He stopped at the tent flap.

'Go in,' he said, 'she's waiting for you.'

I went in alone. Paula was alone also, wearing a filmy yellow dressing gown as if she had just risen from bed; but her face was hard and weary with the look that comes from being up and tensely awake for hours.

'Marc,' she said, and her voice was pure industrial diamond in tone, 'there's a paper over there on the desk. Sign it.'

'Sign ...?' I went across to the desk and looked down. It was a neatly typed letter, several pages long, beneath the letterhead she had given me as one of her staff.

'Just sign it,' she said.

'Not until I read it,' I answered.

Our eyes clashed. Then she shrugged and turned away; but I could almost see the note her memory made of this, my balking at her command. It would be recalled when the hour was right.

'Of course,' she said.

I bent my head to the letter again and read. It was like being unexpectedly hit in the stomach. Or, more accurately, it was like a sickening collision in the dark, running full tilt into a concrete wall you had known was there all the time, but whose existence you had put out of mind – an impact so unexpected and brutal it left you nauseated; because suddenly I understood Paula, saw her complete and naked in the glaring, fluorescent light of what she was planning to set me up for.

I read that I had been shocked by the irresponsible behaviour of some of her soldiers in taking over the enemy area. But, over and above my shock, I had been aghast to see the criminal murder of certain innocent individuals among the defenders; artisans and mechanics, as well as other trained personnel, who had only been in the enemy camp under duress. The slaughter of these innocents was not only a heinous crime against them as individuals, but amounted to treason against the Empire, since the Empress was now deprived of the willing services of these people and many of her subjects would suffer because of that lack. Consequently, I called upon her formally to take action against the criminals responsible and see that they were brought to justice, since I, with the skills that had allowed me to halt the ravages of the time storm, could see more deeply and clearly than anyone into the terrible cost we must all bear because of the deaths of these innocents.

Suddenly, reading this, the pattern I had been building on Paula was complete. I saw the hell she had in mind not only for the soldiers responsible for delaying her here over the coming winter, but for anyone who had been around to witness this happening to her; and that told me more about her than she might have betrayed to me in two more years of my observing her.

I signed.

'I'm proud to do this,' I said, taking the letter over to her. 'It doesn't say anything I didn't feel myself. No wonder you're the Empress, Paula. You can even read minds.'

She smiled and took the letter. I was by no means forgiven for wanting to read before signing, but for the present small moment, the smile was genuine. I would never have risked flattering her so grossly before I had stepped through the flap of this tent; but now I knew when and where she was vulnerable.

'Dear Marc,' she said. 'You understand.'

She looked at me; and I understood, all right. Ironically, suddenly the moment I had patiently waited for, in which I could gain control over her by securing her physically, was with me. In this devastated moment she was available, if I had still wanted her. But the fact was, after reading that letter, I now would not have touched her with a shark-stick.

'More than ever before,' I said. 'Do you want me to let other people know I've written you this letter?'

She hesitated, but it was only the habit of caution operating in her. Again, if she had been herself, I myself would have hesitated to show her such rapid agreement. But she was not herself. That was the crucial truth that had broken out into the open, with the completing of her pattern in my mind just now. She had a flaw I had never really appreciated until now, a deep flaw that would cost her the rulership of the world that had seemed so possible up until now. Already, she was adapting to my own hint that I was eager to accept the authorship of the letter she held. Already she was beginning to make herself believe the attractive idea that I had indeed written it on my own initiative.

'If I just drop the letter with you and go out to spread the word, I know your officers'll be eager to back me up. I know they will,' I said. 'Then we can arrest the guilty ones and bring them to justice before they have time to fill the minds of their fellow soldiers with lies.'

'Yes.' She laid the letter softly down on the end-table beside her. 'Of course. You've got my permission to tell what you've written me. Justice should be speedy.'

'I'll go right now, then,' I said. 'Wait a second, though. Maybe if you give me a written order to do what's necessary, I can make sure none of them escape. Or, for that matter, with that kind of authority I could do anything necessary in connection with the matter ...'

She smiled dazzlingly, seeing me setting the noose of responsibility for this so firmly around my own neck.

'Of course,' she said.

She crossed to the desk, wrote on the top sheet of an order pad sandwich, tore off the top sheet and pushed the carbon copy to the back of the desk.

'There you are.'

'Thank you.' I took it without looking at it and moved toward the door. 'Probably I shouldn't waste time ...'

'No. No, you shouldn't. I have to rest now; but – see me after lunch, Marc. Dear Marc ... What would I do without you?'

'Come on, now. You're the Empress. You can do anything.'

She smiled dazzlingly.

I went out. Aruba was gone, as I had expected him to be; and I went directly back to my own tent. Doc was off the couch and on his feet the second the tent flap fell behind me.

'We're leaving for home right away,' I said. 'I'll explain as we go. You armed?'

'My rifle's with the jeep,' he said. He patted his shirt at belt level before and behind. 'Belly gun and knife.'

'Right. I want your help in bringing some blood-soaked criminals to justice,' I said. 'The Empress has given me special authority to corral the soldiers who committed atrocities on certain innocent people among the civilian population opposing us until tonight.'

His eyebrows went up ironically. I reached into my shirt pocket where I had put the order after folding it up, still without having read it. I unfolded it and read it now, then passed it to him.

'"*Marc Despard has asked for authority from me, and I have given it to him, to do whatever is required ...*"' he nodded slowly. 'All riiight!'

I took the order back from him and replaced it in my pocket.

'The first thing I want to do is check those future-built aircraft we captured,' I said, 'to make sure none of those responsible for the atrocities are planning on using them for escaping. They may even have explosives to destroy the aircraft they can't use. You're an expert on explosives. What kind do you think they might be able to get hold of for something like that?'

He grinned and patted himself at belt level again.

'Primer cord,' he said. 'It wouldn't take much to do a lot of damage – particularly if they know what they're doing.'

'That's what we'll search the area for, then. Come along.'

We headed out the door. The Old Man came with us.

'Want me to put him back inside?' Doc asked, as we stopped just beyond the tent.

'Why, no,' I said. 'Seeing him with us, they won't think I'm doing anything important. It'll serve to allay suspicions – Major!'

I called out to a short, swarthy block of an officer in his mid-twenties who was passing by. The fact that he was on his feet at all this morning meant that he had not been deeply involved in the celebrations of the night before. He came closer and I recognized him. There were only so many majors in Paula's army, in any case.

'Major Debrow? Sorry to interrupt whatever you're doing; but I've got a special job and I'm going to have to ask you to help. Take a look at this.'

I passed him Paula's authorization.

'You see,' I said, while he read it, 'we want to move before these criminals take off on us – don't we, Major?'

His face did not agree. Someone who was unprejudiced might have found a trace of loathing in it for me, a civilian who called combat-battered soldiers 'criminals.'

'Yes, Mr. Despard.'

'Good. I knew I could count on you, Major. We've got an idea that some of them might be trying to get away in some of the valuable future aircraft these people had. We're going to go and check. I want you to come along with us.'

'Those planes are locked up, as well as being under guard,' Debrow said. 'Nobody could get away with one of them.'

'Let's make sure.'

We walked toward that part of the former airport where the post-twentieth-century planes were kept. It was not a short distance, but eventually we clambered over a low barrier of sandbags and found ourselves not more than forty feet from the entrance to a separate hangar, around which perhaps a dozen apparently sober and competent male soldiers stood guard.

'Go get their officer and bring him here, quietly, so we can explain things, will you, Major?'

'Just what is it you want?' Debrow asked. 'What do you want him to do?'

'I want to check the men on guard and have a look inside,' I said. 'And I want the officer with us when we do that.'

Debrow went forward to the two soldiers on guard at the hangar door and was challenged. As he answered, I turned to Doc and saw him looking at me questioningly.

'I want you and me to take off from here in one of those planes inside,' I said in a low voice. 'I don't want the other planes left behind to be workable; and I want the soldiers on guard here out of action. I'll try to arrange it to give you a chance at them, one at a time.'

'Just the two of us to leave. Not the major?'

'Not the major.'

Doc nodded. Debrow came back, led us forward to the hangar doors and in through a small personnel door set in one of them. Inside was the large, dim, echoing interior of the hangar with small, pearly glowings in the gloom that were the future aircraft. To our right was a glassed-in office brightly lit with self-powered battle fluorescents, standing in for the built-in fluorescent lights in the ceiling, now dark for lack of power from the community's central supply.

Inside at a desk was a single thin, young officer with first lieutenant's silver bars on the straps of his uniform leather jacket. He got to his feet as we came in.

'Major?' he said.

'Lieutenant,' said Debrow. 'This is Marc Despard.'

'I know Mr. Despard,' said the lieutenant.

'And his ...' Debrow glanced at Doc and the Old Man, 'servants. Mr. Despard has some special authority from the Empress for you to see.'

I passed Paula's authorization to the lieutenant. The light blond eyebrows jumped several times while he was reading it, although the rest of his narrow face remained calm.

'Yes sir,' he said passing the letter back to me. 'What is it you want, Mr. Despard?'

'First,' I said, 'I want to check the future aircraft, without making a fuss about it. Just you, the Major and I, and Doc here.'

I nodded at Doc.

'Doc,' I said, 'has had some experience in handling sabotage. If we find one or more of the aircraft has been booby-trapped, he may be of help to us in disarming it. This Experimental with us is called the Old Man. His sense of smell, particularly, is much more acute than ours, and he works well with Doc on jobs like this. Now, how many of the future planes are there?'

'Nine,' said the lieutenant.

'Does anyone here know how to fly them?'

'Nobody's tried so far,' said the lieutenant. 'I believe the plan is to talk first to these people who had them.'

'It seems to me I heard they weren't hard to operate,' I said. 'The criminals we're looking for may have heard that, too. These planes would buy them anything they wanted, anywhere in the rest of the world, if they could successfully steal them from the Empress.'

I saw both officers looking at me oddly and wondered if I'd been laying on my image of self-importance too thickly.

'All right,' I said. 'Let's go then. Major, Lieutenant, we'll take three planes apiece. We won't take the Experimental on this first search. I'll keep Doc and the Experimental with me until they're needed. Do you have flashlights?'

'You mean hand torches?' said the lieutenant. 'Yes, sir.' He went to a locker across the office and came back with flashlights for Debrow and myself. Leaving the Old Man in the office, we went out into the hangar proper and split up.

I took the three planes closest to me, forcing the two officers to take the ones further over. In the illumination of the flashlight, the first aircraft I came to seemed to glow with an inner gleam of its own. It was made of some milky, semi-transluscent plastic and looked light enough to float up in the air if it was breathed on too heavily. But in spite of appearances, it was solid and firm when I pulled open the door in its curving side and stepped in. Within, possibly because of the almost egg-shaped hull, there was more room than I would have guessed. I went forward to the control panel.

It was a simple-looking affair, a single small television-like screen inset in the panel and a five-key keyboard just below it. I pushed down one of the keys at random and the lights went on; not only on the panel but all over within the aircraft.

'*Ready*,' said a voice.

I grinned. There had been no pattern at all to what I was looking at; and now, suddenly, there was very nearly a complete one.

'How do I take off?' I asked.

'*You may pilot yourself, or instruct a takeoff and flight.*'

'Thanks. Go back to sleep.' I punched the same key again and the lights went out. Experimentally, in the glow of the flashlight, I punched another of the keys.

'*Ready*,' said a voice, as the lights went on once more.

'Go back to sleep.'

So, that was it. The secret to flying these things. It was that there was no secret at all. I punched off again, the lights went out and I beckoned Doc to follow me. Together, we left the plane.

'All right,' I whispered to him, 'get busy taking out those other planes. I'll take my time with the two I've still got to look at. Meet you at the last one, the third one up straight ahead near the back of the hangar. I'll go as slow as I can, but don't let those two officers see you'

'They won't,' said Doc and he evaporated in the gloom.

I took the Old Man and went on to the next plane and let myself in, then sat down before the control panel and turned it on. I had quite a little conversation with the computer, or whatever it was, on this second aircraft; and by the time I had finished asking questions, I had as good a general knowledge of this kind of craft as if I had kept one around for some years. They were ridiculously, child-level foolproof, and operable.

After I had wasted as many minutes as I thought I reasonably could, I went on to the third craft, poked about inside for a while, and then stepped out again. Neither Doc nor the other two men were in sight. I stepped around to the far side of the plane to wait; and a finger tapped me on the shoulder.

I whirled, stepping back instinctively as I did so, and found Doc grinning at me.

'All set,' he said.

'Good. Come on then.'

We walked toward the next plane over and found the lieutenant there, conscientiously examining the craft's undercarriage with his flashlight.

'Did you find anything, Lieutenant?'

He got to his feet.

'No sir. You, sir?'

'No luck for me, either. Maybe Major Debrow's found something. Shall we go see?'

We all moved over and found Debrow inside his last aircraft. After a moment he came out.

'Nothing,' he said.

'I'm greatly relieved,' I said. 'Now, if you don't mind, Lieutenant, I'd like to examine the men you've got on guard here?'

'But why, sir? We didn't find anything.'

'For that very reason. We want to be sure. The Empress wants us to be sure. Doesn't she, Major?'

'Lieutenant,' said Debrow with a tight throat.

'Yes, Major. Yes, Mr. Despard. If you'll come up to the office, I'll bring in the men on the doors first—'

'You'll bring them in one at a time, Lieutenant,' I said. 'Is there another door to this hangar besides those in the front?'

'There's a small service entrance in the back wall.'

'Good.' I turned to Doc. 'After we examine each one, I'd like you to take him out the back way and back to his post. See he doesn't talk to any of the others, particularly not to any who haven't been examined yet. You go out with the lieutenant here, so you'll know where to bring them back to. Lieutenant?'

'Mr. Despard?'

'I imagine you'll be taking the place of each of your guards as you relieve them. If Doc should come for you without returning the man he last took – if he comes for you alone – it'll mean we've found one of them. I'd like you to come back with Doc as naturally as possible, so as not to alarm any of the others we may find.'

The lieutenant opened his mouth, glanced at the Major and closed it again.

'Perhaps,' said Debrow, 'it might be better if the lieutenant simply stayed here, Mr. Despard. It's a little unusual, his filling in for one of the enlisted men on post; and—'

'If you don't mind, Major?' I said.

'No sir,' said Debrow slowly. 'I don't mind, sir.'

'Then we'll do it this way, I think. Lieutenant, will you take Doc out so he can get the first guard?'

They went off. I turned to Debrow.

'Major, how well do you know the lieutenant?'

'I've known him for several years. More than three years, I'd say.'

'But do you know him well?'

Debrow looked at me with sudden caution. After a second he answered, slowly.

'I couldn't say ... *well*, Mr. Despard.'

'Yes,' I said.

I left it at that. After a few minutes of silence on both our parts, Doc came back with the first guard, a chunky lance corporal five and a half feet tall and looking about the age of the lieutenant.

'Your name?' I asked.

'Lance Corporal Charles Onash, sir. Third Platoon, Fourth Company, Blue Regiment.'

'Have you ever ridden a motorcycle, Corporal Onash?'

'No, sir.'

'Good. You can go. Take him back, Doc.'

The next man had never ridden a motorcycle either. No more had the three after that. The fifth man we questioned had. I had to reach for some other mysterious question.

'Ever fly a sailplane, Private Mahn?'

'As a matter of fact, yes, sir.'

'How about drive a hydroplane?'

'Yes, sir.'

Debrow shifted uneasily in the seat he had taken behind one of the desks. I was beginning to feel a little trapped.

'How are you on reading Sanskrit?'

'Sir?'

'I said, can you read Sanskrit?'

'No sir.'

'All right,' I said, with inner relief, 'take him back, Doc.'

'Sir?' said Debrow, almost a little timidly, after Private Mahn had left. 'I'm afraid I don't understand ...'

'You will, in due course.'

He sat back without saying anything more. The seven more enlisted men on duty there came through and I managed to send them all back after getting each one to admit he didn't know how to do something or other.

'Mr. Despard,' began Debrow, after the final one had left. 'That's all the men on duty here. Does that mean—'

'It means this situation is a good deal more serious than I thought. Are you armed, Major?'

'No sir.'

'That's unfortunate. Well, we'll have to do what we can. I'll stay here. Will you go quietly to the personnel door we came in by, and stand just inside it. Lock it if you can, and listen for any sounds you can hear on the other side. If anyone tries to force it open, let them; but stand back out of sight and when they're through, go for help.'

'Yes sir. But for Christ's sake, Mr. Despard, what's supposed to be going on here?'

'I can't tell you quite yet. I've my duty to Paula – to the Empress – to think of,' I said. 'Get going now. I'm going to step off into the shadows just outside this office and be ready to warn you if anyone who shouldn't comes from the other end of the building.'

He went. I took the Old Man by the hand and followed the Major out, moving off to where the shadows hid us from him, but where we would be in line to intercept Doc, coming back from returning the last soldier to his post. From where we were, I could see the thin line of daylight showing around the personnel door, blocked out now and then by an uneasily shifting body standing just this side of it. Eventually, this occultation ceased, and a second or two later, Doc emerged alone from the dimness in front of us.

'All set,' he said under his breath.

'All taken care of?' I asked.

He nodded.

'The lieutenant?'

'I saved him until next to last.'

'All right. The Major's over by the personnel door.'

'Was. I've taken care of him, too. He was the last of them.'

I wanted to ask how many of them were dead, but the words stuck in my throat. It was a lifesaver to have a young timberwolf like Doc for a friend, but it was a little illogical to demand he be wolf and harmless at the same time.

'How about the aircraft?' I asked.

'The first one you looked at, I didn't touch,' Doc answered. 'The rest are set to blow any time you want.'

'All right. I've got to see if we can get the hangar doors open easily. Otherwise, you may have to blow a hole in them—'

'No sweat there either. They're supposed to be electrically operated, but there's a chain block-and-tackle type dingus to use if the power's off. Can you fly that thing, Marc?'

'I can fly it. Or rather, I can tell it to fly itself and it will.'

'Just checking,' he said; and I could barely see his grin in the gloom.

'I don't blame you. I would too,' I told him. I was very tired, suddenly. 'Why don't you rig the other planes to destruct as soon as we're safely out of here, and I'll move the one we're taking up to this side of the doors? Then you open the door, hop in, and we'll move.'

'Right.'

He moved off. I turned on my flashlight and led the Old Man toward the aircraft Doc had specified as untouched. We climbed in, shut the door, and I depressed one of the keys.

'*Ready.*'

'Move up slowly on the ground to the inside of the doors to this building. Or – to put it another way – move slowly forward along the ground and I'll tell you which way to turn and when to stop.'

The craft stirred and seemed to slide rather than roll forward.

'Left,' I told it. 'Left maybe ten degrees. Now maybe five degrees more. All right, straight ahead ... stop!'

We halted just inside the hangar doors. I opened the door of the craft and waited. In a moment, there was a faint, rattling sound to be heard through the opening; and the big doors slid apart to either side of the opening they guarded, and bright sunlight blinded us.

'That's good enough!' I called softly into the brilliance after a moment. But the doors had already stopped parting with just enough room for us to go through. I heard a faint thud and Doc was in the cabin, shutting the aircraft door behind him.

'All set,' he said.

'Go!' I told the craft. 'Straight ahead, out on the ground through this opening, take off and climb to three thousand metres. Head west.'

It slid forward through the doors into the full sunlight. Without any run, it leaped suddenly skyward. There was a sound like a paper bag popping below and behind us. I glanced back and down to see smoke coming from the open doorway of the hangar building, dwindling rapidly to toy size below us. A second later, we were up where the roads looked like thick pencil lines and the landscape was starting to move backwards beneath us toward the sun half way up in the clear sky.

'That takes care of everything, I guess,' Doc said. He came forward and pushed the Old Man off the seat next to mine – a move the Old Man took without complaint. It was surprising what the Old Man would take from Doc, nowadays. Almost as much as Sunday used to take from Ellen. Doc seated himself where the Old Man had been.

'Need any help flying, or anything like that?' he asked.

I shook my head.

'Then I'll get some sleep,' he said, imperturbably. 'This gadget's better than a locked door. No one's going to break in and surprise you in the middle of the air.'

He curled up in the seat, closed his eyes, and dropped off.

I was not so lucky.

29

The aircraft out of the future did not seem to need any serious attention. I asked it for a map of the country, and it was displayed on the screen in front of me. On the map, I picked out the general area of our community, asked to have it enlarged for me, and so continued zeroing in and enlarging until I could identify our destination to the craft. Once this was done, I simply told it to take us there and land by the summer palace – which I described – and my duties were done. I would have liked, then, to curl up and sleep like Doc; but I could not. I could not even imitate the Old Man, who was half-dozing, opening his eyes every so often to blink at me, as if to make sure I was still there.

Instead, I just sat, watching the empty, clean sky and the slowly moving landscape far below. There was no sound of passage inside the plane and I felt like a fly trapped under an overturned water glass.

As long as we had been working to escape, my mind had been clear and sharp and purposeful. But now, the effect of the body adrenalin began to die out in me, leaving me feeling empty, dull, and ugly. The thought of the soldiers on guard who had undoubtedly died so the three of us could go free came back to my mind whether I wanted to think of them or not. God knows I had never wanted to be the cause of anyone's death, particularly now, since I had found that at least part of myself could blend with the rest of the universe. It was, in fact, that specific, blendable part of myself that I now felt I had betrayed, misused like a fine-edged tool put to some wrong purpose.

But what else could Doc and I and the Old Man have done, I kept asking myself? We had to escape, and the only route open to us lay over the dead or incapacitated bodies of at least some of Paula's warriors.

Did it? a jeering little voice in the back of my mind nagged at me.

All right, I told myself, what other way was there?

You tell me. You're the man who can see patterns.

I couldn't see one here that didn't involve violence.

Then you're not much good, are you?

Leave me alone, I told it. Get out of my head.

How can I leave you alone? I'm you. You're stuck with me.

There's a way out, I thought. And I became very cold when I thought it.

You haven't got the guts. And even if you did, what about Ellen and Marie and all the rest you'd be leaving for Paula to take her revenge on? You want their deaths on your conscience, too?

Paula – I forced myself to think of Paula instead. But that brought no relief either. Her image summoned up another sort of sick feeling inside me. Because I had been attracted to her. I actually had. The fact that she had challenged me with her unavailability had been a cloak for the fact that I wanted her anyway, had wanted her, in fact, from the moment I had first seen her getting out of her helicopter looking like a page out of a fashion magazine in a world now vanished forever. Having her would have been almost like getting that world back again.

Of course, I had known she had dressed like that deliberately, that the whole matter of her entrance on the scene had been cool-headedly calculated to produce the effect on all of us that it had. But knowing this didn't alter the emotional leap I had felt. Seeing her like that, I had been lifted out of the raw and dusty reality of my present into a gilded dream of a memory. I had suddenly been reminded of the tawdriness of the little world I was about to defend with my life. I had felt suddenly embarrassed by the workaday plainness of the two women who shared my life with me, and my handful of loyal friends. They were like coarse brown bread compared to angel food cake. They were like flat home-brew beer compared to champagne.

I had been attracted to Paula all right – from that moment. I could have convinced myself I was in love with her, given time. Given enough time, time enough to hang myself with, I could even have gradually forgotten my duty to go back and finish what I had begun with the time storm. Maybe, I thought now, there had been the thought of not returning in the back of my mind all along. So that when I raged at the possibility of Paula not being able to get her army – and me – across to Europe this fall, I was really raging against the delay of the excuse that being on the other side of the Atlantic would have given me, the excuse to put off escaping from Paula if and when word came that Porniarsk had succeeded in accomplishing the very large task I had set him to do.

Yes, it had all been there, hidden inside me, the impulse to throw away the golden light I had found for the gaining of an enamelled tin ring. How purely tin, I had finally discovered when I had seen her in her tent that dawn, and she had directed me to sign the letter she had written for me.

At that moment, the last piece of her personal pattern had clicked into place for me; and I was forced to see her as she innately was. I had thought that there must be at least a touch of something Napoleonic under the display brightness that was her surface. After all, she conquered the larger part of the North American continent. She had a government, a standing army, and more accumulated resources than any other half-dozen communities in the world combined. Above and beyond this, she had an Alexandrian dream of conquering the whole world. There must, I thought, be something there that was unique and powerful.

But there was not. When I had stepped into her tent that morning, when I saw her appearance and the letter she had for me to sign, her pattern had been completed for me; and I realized that what I was looking at was an individual who momentarily, at least, had gone irrational under the pressures of defeat and disappointment. With the evidence of that irrationality, everything about her had fallen into place. She was neither Napoleonic nor Alexandrian. She was a borderline psychotic who had fallen into a chain of circumstances which allowed her to ride forward triumphantly on the crest of a mounting wave – as long as everything went her way. While luck was with her, she appeared to be inspired by genius. But when things went wrong, she had no plan.

Literally.

Those who were on her side were people. Those who were not were rag dolls to be thrown at the wall or have the sawdust ripped out of them if she was in a temper. She could wade in blood up to her elbows and it would not matter; because, of course, it was not real blood. It could not be real blood, because it belonged to those who were against her. That was the psychotic side of her; that was what had hit me like a swinging barn door in the face when I had stepped into her tent.

All the communities who had given in to her on her way here were composed of real people, of course. But Capitol had chosen to refuse her. Therefore, its population were not real people and she told her soldiers to kill them. But some of her soldiers had not distinguished between those she wanted killed and those she did not, and so obviously those soldiers were not real people either. Therefore, she would have Marc Despard find them and kill them. But Marc Despard would know that the idea to kill had come from her in the first place, which might make him think wrong things about her – things no real person would think. Therefore, it should be arranged so that it looked as if the soldiers' punishment were Marc's own idea, and then later she would use some new soldiers to kill him for doing such a thing. Then everyone would be happy again; because there would be nobody left but people who agreed with her. Real people.

Of course, this pattern explained why she had never let me or anyone else get close to her. Experience would have taught her that anyone she let get too close to her might end up disagreeing with her about something or other. I had thought I was beyond the point where any other single human being could scare the hell out of me; but she had done that, this morning in the tent. It had been like finding myself locked in a cage with a wounded tiger.

So it was someone like Paula that I had been willing to trade the universe for – the universe and everything else I thought I loved. I was sick: sick at heart and sick at mind. And to cure a bad situation I had now gone out and caused bloody deeds to be done myself. I who had seen the golden light had done my own wading in blood. I had sent Doc to kill ...

The pain of it was more than I could stand. I groped desperately for the unity – the golden light – and could not find it. I scrabbled and clutched for self-justification and found nothing. Nothing, but the wrong-end-to excuse of saving the lives of the few people that meant something to me. I had killed that they should not be killed. *Nature, red in tooth and claw* ... wrote Tennyson. The books I had drowned in during earlier weeks danced in my head; but there was no comfort in them. The only small, slim reason I could find for my living was to defend what I loved. At least, if there was no justification in doing that, there was no agony. Perhaps I could be simply pagan, and simply simple.

And how can man die better
Than facing fearful odds,
For the ashes of his fathers,
And the temples of his gods?

I had no ashes of my fathers, no temples and no gods. I was not Horatius, the ancient Roman of whom Macaulay had rhymed in these lines from his *Lays of Ancient Rome*. I only had my little tribe of one-time strangers to guard against all things human, temporal and infinite; and I wanted some comfort, some prayer to cling to. Like an overboard passenger hanging on to a life preserver, I clung now to Macaulay's four lines and the idea of a finish in battle, to end all, to wash all out; and I went whirling down into darkness, into dreams and final forgetfulness ...

I woke suddenly, it seemed a long time later, staring up into two close, concerned faces. One was the smooth face of Doc and the other the hairy face of the Old Man.

'Marc! said Doc. 'Are you all right? Were you dreaming?'

'Why? What?' My tongue was thick and dry. 'What is it?'

'Your eyes were closed and you kept saying, "*I can't do it – I can't do it*—" and we couldn't wake you up,' Doc said.

The Old Man nuzzled my face in relief. I got a noseful of his hair and realized he badly needed a bath. That brought me back to normality faster than anything else.

'Where are we?' I said, sitting up.

'I think we're almost home,' said Doc. 'You take a look. You know how this plane works. I don't.'

I turned to the control panel and depressed one of the keys.

'Where are we?' I asked. 'Show me with a mark on a map.'

Obediently, the screen gave me the image of the last enlargement of the map I had asked it for earlier. A tiny image of the aircraft appeared on this and I peered at it for a second or two before I could see that it was actually in motion across the map lines.

'Looks like we're not more than a few minutes out,' I said, 'depending on how fast we're travelling.'

I looked out and down. We still seemed to be at the same altitude; and, surprisingly, the sun seemed no higher above the horizon behind us than it had been when we took off. That would seem to indicate that we had been matching the earth's rotational speed – which was a good rate of travel, to be sure.

'I've told it to go in and land by the summer palace,' I told Doc. I turned back to the control panel and spoke to it. 'Land slowly. I don't want any of our own people shooting at us. And I don't want to scare anybody.'

The craft took me literally. It came in over the summer palace at exactly three thousand metres of altitude and then descended vertically, and slowly. We took about twenty minutes to actually touch ground in the landing area, and by the time we did, most of the population of the community was on hand, standing off about fifty feet from our touch-down spot, with the community leaders in the front rank.

I opened the door of the future plane and stepped down to the earth – and they all just stared at me, as if I were a man from Mars. Then Doc and the Old Man came scrambling out behind me; and everyone poured in on us with a rush. I was surrounded, picked up and carried, literally, almost all the way to the summer palace entrance before I could make them put me down on my feet.

When I finally did get a semblance of quiet, I climbed up in one of the jeeps parked there, stood on the back seat and told them, as briefly as I could, that I had escaped from Paula, that she would be after me eventually, but should not be showing up for some weeks at least, and I would have more details for them tomorrow. But right now, I had to sort myself out and talk things over with the other leaders.

They were a little disappointed not to hear the whole story at once; but they dispersed to their various activities eventually, after I had promised a community-wide celebration for that evening. Finally, I got to go inside the palace with Ellen, Marie, Bill and the rest.

Over food in the same dining room in which I had told them I was going with Paula, I broke the news to them, bluntly.

'She's not completely sane,' I said. 'I don't mean she's out of her head all the time; she'd be less dangerous if she was. I mean that when it comes to certain things she'll do exactly what she wants, regardless of the consequences. Because when she gets to that point, nothing matters except doing what she wants. That's why I left; because sooner or later, she would want something and find me in the way; and that would be the end of me.'

I told them about the letter she had me sign.

'The point was to hit back at the soldiers who had killed the experts,' I said, 'and to saddle me with the blame for doing it. Sooner or later, she would have used that blame to get rid of me. That's why I had to get out of there without wasting time. Because it could have been sooner. It could have been the minute the men she wanted executed were executed.'

'But what'll she do now?' Marie asked.

'She'll send a force to bring me back,' I said. 'But maybe not right away, because she's understrength now. That's one reason leaving her now was good timing. Here, I can work with Porniarsk and maybe we can find a way to make the move forward before her people can show up here. I've been working on pattern recognition. I'm stronger in that area than I was. It's a fighting chance, anyway.'

I looked over at Porniarsk, who had not been outside with the others when we landed, but who had come into the dining room since we had been sitting there.

'I should have sent word to you sooner,' he said. 'The fact is, I ran into this sticking point over a month ago, but I thought that it was something I could get through. Now, I don't know. Maybe the two of us can get through it.'

'I'll come to the lab with you as soon as we're finished here,' I said, between bites of the home-cured ham I was digging into. 'But in any case—'

I looked back at the rest of them.

'In any case, everyone in the community who won't be needed for the monad-gestalt, when and if we're ready to use it, better start making preparations to scatter, now. If Paula can't get me back, she'll raise bloody hell – and I mean bloody hell literally – with anyone connected to me she can get her hands on. Bill, Marie—'

They both looked at me, from farther on down the table.

'You'd better start making plans as to how supplies are to be portioned out, and where to, and how people are to take off. Also, Doc—'

'Yo.'

'We're going to need a fast, a really fast warning system to give us as much notice as possible when we learn Paula or some of her people are headed this way. Maybe you can figure out something using that aircraft we came in.'

'I think so, Marc.' He looked at Ellen. 'Right, Ellen?'

Ellen nodded.

'All right.' I finished the ham and pushed my plate back. 'Anyone have any suggestions or comments, before I head out to the lab with Porniarsk?'

'You need some sleep,' said Marie. 'You look dead. So does Doc.'

I looked at her. The words were Marie-type words, but there was a difference about her which found an echo in the way she said them. However, I had no time to investigate such things now.

'I slept on the flight coming in,' I said. 'Doc probably could use some sleep.'

'I slept last night,' said Doc.

'Whatever,' I said, getting to my feet. 'Anyway, I'll catch up on my sleep later. Porniarsk? Ready to go?'

'Yes,' he said. We went out of the dining room together, leaving the others behind us.

'It's an unusual situation,' said Porniarsk, once we got to the tank in the lab. 'It's the kind of stoppage as if the extrapolative element of this device – what you've been calling the computer – had encountered a logical contradiction, so that further extrapolations from this point would result in increasing error. But attempts on my part to find out what such a contradiction might be have produced no results.'

'Let me look at where it stopped,' I said.

He activated the tank. Once more I stared into the blue-greyness, with the little firefly points of light flickering through the space of it. For a moment, a small crawling fear woke inside me, a fear that in my step aside with Paula I had lost whatever had given me the ability to see patterns in the tank before. But then, slowly, the little points of light began to relate and group themselves into associations.

The pattern took shape. It was a strange and unfamiliar pattern, which was to be expected. But when I tried to go one step further and change my perception from that of small lights in a tank to the actual universe envisioned, as I had done once before, I could not do it. The small crawling fear came back, stronger.

'I can see what you've got there,' I said to Porniarsk, finally. 'But I can't seem to make it mean anything to me. I don't know what's wrong.'

'You may just be tired,' said Porniarsk. 'Or perhaps you've been away from the device long enough to feel unfamiliar with it.'

'Maybe.'

I gave up and withdrew my attention from the pattern in the tank. Suddenly, I was dead tired. Tired right down to the marrow of my bones.

'You're right about one thing,' I told Porniarsk. 'I need sleep. I'll go lie down.'

I went back to my own room, part of the suite I shared with Marie and Ellen. But neither of them were there now. It was only early afternoon, and they, with the rest of the community, would be hard at work. I felt a child's loneliness for someone to sit with me while I fell asleep; but I pushed the emotion away from me. I undressed, lay down on the bed, pulled a blanket over me and stared at the white ceiling, lightly shadowed now and then by the clouds outside reflecting from the window.

I was still dead tired; but I began to wonder if I would sleep. I lay there.

I woke to someone shaking me. For a second, I thought I was back on the future plane again and being woken by Doc and the Old Man. Then I saw it was dark outside the window and dark in the room, and the shape bending over me was female.

'Marc—' It was Ellen's voice. 'I hate to wake you, but the whole community's waiting for you. If you can just come out and show yourself for a little while, you can come back after that and sleep as long as you want.'

'Sure,' I said. 'All right.'

I levered my wooden body up to a sitting position on the edge of the bed and she began to massage my neck, standing in front of me and reaching around behind my head. I leaned my forehead gratefully against the human softness of her belly, feeling myself come alive again to the warm pressure of her fingers kneading the stiff cords and muscles running up from my shoulders into the area behind my ears. She felt and smelled delightful; and I wanted to stay there for the rest of my life, getting my neck rubbed.

But she stopped after a while.

'You're awake now,' she said. 'Get dressed.'

She was right. I was awake; and there was nothing to do but get dressed. I was standing on one leg, putting on my pants, when it came to me suddenly that what I had felt was second cousin to what makes dogs and other animals enjoy being petted and stroked by humans. Not the physical sensation alone, but the implications of affection and concern. For a second, I could almost feel what an animal might feel in such case – and there, for a second, the universe-identity almost was with me again. But the second passed, and it was gone.

I finished dressing. Ellen had already gone ahead. I followed down the corridors, out through the door, and stepped into the warm, early evening dark of outside. A barbecue pit had been dug in the landing area, and I could smell roasting meat. There were several other large fires, throwing sparks high in the air so that they seemed to mingle with the stars overhead; and the open space around them was filled with moving silhouettes and the hubbub of voices. For some reason, it reminded me of a small town in Mexico I had happened to go through once on vacation on an evening of a fiesta. I could not remember the name of the saint who was the cause of the fiesta; but it had been night, and fireworks were exploding high in the air over the town, their sparks raining down into the dark streets. Lights and voices had been all over the place, with people coming and going in the narrow streets, so that it all had a sort of incredible richness to it. I had wondered then where that feeling of richness came from; but of course now I knew where. Unconsciously, I had been reading the patterns of the fiesta around me the way those who lived in the area read them. I was picking the rich feeling up from them; and now I was doing the same thing, picking up the magic and warmth of the moment from the rest of the community, gathered here to celebrate the fact that Doc and I, and even the Old Man, were back safe.

I went forward into the crowd, and was recognized. The faces and bodies swirled around me, drink was shoved into my hand. I was mobbed and hustled and questioned and patted on the back and kissed until my head started to spin. Between that spinning and the fatigue I had, measured by the little sleep I had just had, I was not to remember most of the events of that evening. It was merely one long happy blur that ended when I finally groped my way back into my dark room and fell on my bed again, some hours later.

Ellen was there and I hung on to her.

'Where's Marie?' I asked after a while.

'She's still outside,' Ellen said. 'Sleep, now.'

I slept.

I did not come to until late the next day. But in spite of that long, exhausted slumber, it was three days before I was really back in proper body and mind again. The night of the celebration with the crowd had healed me somewhat, in a way I could not quite pin down, but I felt more whole and healthy generally. I went back to Porniarsk's lab on the third day and tried the pattern of the tank again.

The first time I tried it, I was no more successful than I had been the first day I had come home. Still, my failure did not leave me with the sensation of being so helpless as before, and after a rest I tried again. This time I was also unsuccessful, but I got the impression I had come closer to actually envisioning the universe; and so I continued, trying and trying again, feeling that I got a little closer with each try – and a couple of weeks later I broke through.

Whatever barrier I had been pushing against went down all at once. Without warning, I was suddenly in the universe of galaxies and stars – and what I saw leaped at me so hard that I was jarred out of it, back into the conscious reality of the lab and myself standing there, staring into the tank.

'Why, hell!' I said. 'It's wrong!'

'Wrong?' Porniarsk said. 'In what way?'

I turned to the avatar.

'I don't know,' I said. 'I mean, I do know; but it doesn't matter! Don't you see? Your device here shut itself down because it began to turn up inconsistencies within the patterns it was evolving from the patterns it had evolved previously. Logically, there couldn't be any inconsistencies, but there are!'

'I don't understand,' said Porniarsk.

'Don't you? Look,' I said, 'this tank has been extending previous patterns that were correct and getting one that is incorrect.'

'Then you're saying the device has broken down? I don't see how it could,' said Porniarsk.

'No. It hasn't broken down – that's the point. *It's* not wrong! What's wrong is reality. One of the factors the device takes into account is the human – pardon me, I mean the intelligent life – factor; and that factor logically evolved is creating inconsistencies with the purely physical evolution of the other factors considered. Don't you see what that means?'

'I do not,' said Porniarsk.

'It means somewhere up there in the future – at the time we're looking at right now – intelligent life is doing something about the time storm. Doing something at least effective enough to produce inconsistencies with what would have happened if the storm had just been allowed to run its course. We've found them, Porniarsk! We've found a time when they're able to do something about the time storm!'

The avatar stood perfectly still, looking at me. He was so motionless and his silence went on so long that I began to entertain the outrageous thought that he had not heard me.

'I see,' he said, speaking just as I opened my mouth to repeat to him what I had just said. 'Then our search is over.'

'That's right. All we have to do now is figure out how the monad needs to shift the immediate small factors so that at least this lab can move forward to that time.'

'Is it possible?'

I had never actually stopped to doubt that it was possible; and his question took half the joy out of me at one blow.

'Of course it is,' I said. 'It has to be. We're away down at the end of the chain of storm changes. The forces dealing with this area have to be relatively light ...'

I ran down.

'We'll have to check and see, of course,' I said, 'maybe we'd better do that first before I tell everyone what we've found and start getting their hopes up.'

We were still checking several days later when Doc came into the lab one morning.

'I've just made a swing east in the plane,' he said. He had become used to the craft now and he flew daily patrols. 'There's a force of about a hundred and fifty of Paula's soldiers, about half on foot and half on horseback, about a hundred and twenty miles east of here. No motorized transport or anything more than carry weapons. They aren't wearing her uniforms, but they can't be any other troops. No one else on this continent can put together that many people and get them to move in formation like that.'

'How did they get so close?' Porniarsk asked.

'They must have started out individually or in small groups,' Doc said. 'That's the only way I can think of. Then they rendezvoused someplace

498

last night, so that this was the first day they've been all together. I'd have spotted them from the air otherwise. At the rate they're marching, they'll be here in less than a week.'

I looked at Porniarsk.

'That ends the checking,' I said. 'All we can do now is go, and hope we make it.'

30

There was something wrong in the atmosphere around the summer palace. I could feel it, but I could not take the time to pin it down. I set the rest of the community to packing up, ready to get out, and with Porniarsk, got down to the choosing of an optimum target nanosecond on the day before the soldiers were due to arrive. We wanted a time when the pattern of storm forces concerned with our small area would be as close as possible to the conformation I was going to try to force them into with the monad. My original idea had been to deal with as small an area as possible – probably only the lab itself and everything inside it. But as the situation developed, it turned out that the difference between restructuring the forces dealing with just the lab and those dealing with an area including the summer palace, mountain section and enough of the plain to contain the town and a couple of square miles outside it, was essentially no difference at all, in terms of the size of the forces to be dealt with.

This put a new complexion on things. It was the first good news I could remember finding in a long time. Now I could take along everybody, if they wanted to go. I was tied to the work in the lab, but I sent Doc out to tell the rest of the community that as things had turned out, they didn't need to run and hide from the soldiers unless they wanted to. Those who wanted to come along with the monad and myself into the future could simply stick around.

Having sent the word out I got back to work. Matters, for once, seemed to be all going in the right direction. The more I pinned down the force-changes to be made, the more possible they looked. Even setting aside the fact that I was much more pattern-experienced and more developed and mature than I had been when I had balanced the forces in the immediate area of the planet, what I now looked at was a much simpler job.

This, in spite of the fact that we would be moving an unguessable distance of time into the future. There was no way to measure how

far, but thousands of years anyway in terms of the old temporal yard-
sticks we had used before the time storm. The reason for this was that,
even taking in the area including the town, I was dealing with a very
small patch of space compared to that which enclosed the immediate
neighbourhood of the Earth. What it amounted to was that I would
be making a much larger temporal change – but in a very, very much
tinier area than I had the time before. It was as if I multiplied by a factor
of a few thousand, but then divided the result by millions.

So, matters in the lab progressed well; but nothing goes with complete smoothness. It was a good thing that Porniarsk and I were, if anything, ahead of our schedule for charting all the parameters of the shift
as I had laid it out; because I found myself called away from the lab to
deal with the human side of the move.

Without realizing it, I had hit everyone in the community harder
than I had planned when I had sent out word with Doc that those who
wanted to come with me could do so. Living with the time storm as I
had been all this time, I had forgotten that only those who had been
with me at the time of the balancing of forces originally would have
any idea of what to expect from involving themselves in what I planned
to do. Nor did they look on going far into the future as calmly as I did.

Accordingly, they were seething with questions that needed some
kind of answers if they were to come up with their individual decisions.
I found I had to call a meeting of the community as a whole to explain
matters and answer those questions. We were too many to crowd into
even the largest quonset hut, so the meeting was held outside on the
landing area, with a public address system rigged by Bill for the occasion, with extra microphones on long cords, so that everybody could
hear the questions as well as the answers.

I began by explaining the mechanism of the time storm as well as I
understood it, and how this mechanism had affected us here on Earth.
Porniarsk stood beside me in the jeep I was using for a speaker's platform, ready to answer questions himself; but no one asked him any. I
think they were still a little wary of Porniarsk, whom few besides those
in the summer palace had, in fact, ever seen.

When I finished that part of my explanation, I called for questions,
but there were none. So I went on to explain how I believed that up
ahead in the future, people – not merely human people, but 'people' in
the larger sense, including intelligent, civilized life like that represented
by Porniarsk's race – would finally come to grips with the time storm
and find some way of stopping it. Finally, I repeated what I was sure
they must know already, that I thought I had located such a time and I

planned to go there. Those who wanted to go with me, could.

Once more I asked for questions. This time I got them – three hours or more of them, mostly unanswerable, by me or anyone else there at least.

Basically, they were unanswerable because what they all wanted most to know was what it would be like for them up there in the future. This was, naturally, something about which I had no more idea than they had themselves. It began to sink in on me as I stood there doing my best to answer them, what an unimaginable gulf exists between those who are obsessed by a goal and those who simply want to live as best they can. In a manner of speaking, I wanted only to arrive in Samarkand, and anything short of the moment when I got there was unimportant. The others were concerned with the possibility of tigers and robbers on the way, the availability of wells along the route, the quarters they would occupy once they arrived and the marketplace where they would eventually vend their wares.

I could not help them. Without realizing it, I had discounted myself completely from the price I was willing to pay to get what I wanted. They had not. They could not think like me; and – God help me – I could no longer think like them.

But I did what I could. I gave them words, explanations, until my throat was hoarse, and they went away discussing what I had said, sure that I had told them something of importance, but finding themselves still unsatisfied, and unreassured.

Porniarsk and I went back to the lab. With or without the extra people, I had to close with the storm forces when the proper moment came; and the moment was marching inexorably toward us.

We finished going over all possibilities by mid-afternoon of the day before the soldiers were due in. Doc had been checking the progress of our invaders from the air, at heights of ten to fifteen thousand feet. Whether they noticed him – the milky-coloured aircraft was all but invisible to the ground at that altitude – or not, they continued to come on steadily, neither slowing nor increasing their first observed rate of travel. If they had been the total force that Paula could bring against us, it would have been a temptation to go out and meet them. A night raid or two on their camp, led by some of our people who had picked up special skills from Doc, plus a few good daytime ambushes, could have cut their strength to a point where we would have been able to defend against them quite handily. But Paula could keep after us forever, and there was no use wasting lives.

I had been worrying about what to do with the experimentals, now that some of us were moving forward in time and the rest taking to the hills. Paula was just the sort of person to kill them all on sight when she found out I had escaped, if they were left behind and undefended.

That problem, however, I found no longer existed. Apparently, when the Old Man had taken his interest in me, the rest of the village had started to disintegrate socially. Except for a few of the others who had formed alliances with some of the human families and were either going forward with these families or taking to the hills with them, the rest had long since wandered away from the village on their own and disappeared. It was a sad sort of diaspora to think about, because there was nothing away from here for them but the lives of solitary, intelligent animals; but there was nothing I, or any of our people, could do about it now. It could be, I told myself, that there was a consciousness in them that their race, as a race, had no future – just as it had had no past beyond a test tube. But that thought did not make me feel any better.

In any case, I had no time to think about experimentals now. This afternoon was the afternoon that had been picked for saying goodbyes. I made myself available out in the landing area; and they came up by individuals and families and groups to say farewell, not only to me, but to the rest of us who were going. I was surprised, and even a little secretly unhappy, to see the number who had decided to take their chances running from Paula the rest of their lives, in preference to following me forward. But, it was their decision; and better they make it now while they had the chance than regret that they had not made it, later.

Dinner time was to be the end of the farewells. We broke off finally and went inside. I had wanted to hold a meeting of the people who would be with me in the monad before we settled down to eat; but when we all gathered in the dining room there were some extra faces. One of these was merely Wendy, who had never shown any interest in being part of the time storm work, but who was welcome to the monad if she wanted to join. Also, there were her gangling young boyfriend, who was not welcome under any circumstances, and Abe Budner, our big, slow-moving Director of Food Services and former chef, whom I liked personally, but whom I had never thought of as being monad material.

'Abe,' I said, as I sat down at the table, 'no offence, but we're just about to start a business meeting. You and—'

'Marc,' said Marie.

My mind suddenly became alert. By which I mean that it came out of the whole problem of the move into time and back to the everyday present of the dining room and the people now in it. I woke to the fact that

Marie, Wendy, the boyfriend and Abe were all in hiking gear, rough clothes and heavy boots. I also became aware that there was a silence in the room, a tense silence on the part of everybody else that said that all of them there had known for some time about what I was just now recognizing.

I looked at Marie.

'You're not going?' I said.

'That's right, Marc,' she said. Now that I really examined her for the first time in a very long, long period, I was a little shocked at what I saw. Her face was tired, and definitely now showed the signs of middle-age, the crow's-feet at the corners of the eyes, the sagging of the chin line. I had never really looked at her in all these months. I had never thought to look.

'Get out of here, the rest of you,' I said, hoarsely. I did not specify who the rest were, but they all left the room except the four who were dressed to travel, and Ellen.

'Wendy and Walter don't want to go into the future, Marc,' Marie said. 'And I've decided to go along with them and Abe.'

'Marie …' I said. The words would not come. Patterns flashed and clicked through my mind; and I saw what I did not want to see. If Marie stayed here, Paula would find her sooner or later; and Paula would remember that Marie had been one of my two wives. It was inevitable – no, it was not inevitable. Did I think I was a deity to deal in inevitability? But it was so overwhelmingly probable that the chances it might not happen were too insignificant to consider.

'Marie,' I said. 'Don't you understand? Unless you go with me, you'll land right in Paula's hands. Believe me, I know. You will.'

'Even if I do,' she said.

'Look …' I made an effort to get the emotion out of my voice and talk reasonably. 'There's no point in throwing yourself away just because Wendy wants to stay. I know, she's young, and—'

'You don't understand,' Marie said. 'I don't want to go with you. I *want* to stay here myself.'

Understanding suddenly struck me like a numbing blow. I had not fooled anyone, it seemed, except myself. I realized now that she and Ellen had known all along how I had reacted to Paula, and what at least part of my reason was for going off with her.

'Listen to me,' I said. 'About Paula and me—'

'Marc,' Marie said. 'You're going to have to understand. It's me who doesn't want to go into the future. It's me. I can't take this moving any more. I'm sick of it. I want to settle in one place and stay.'

'With Paula hunting you down?' I couldn't believe what I heard.

'That doesn't matter. I'll be here, in this world, not in some other. Not starting all over again. I can't keep starting over and over again, Marc. You can. All right, you go ahead. But I want a little ordinary life for as long as I can have it, here, before the end comes.'

I shook my head. It was all crazy. Vaguely, I became aware that even the ones who had stayed behind before had gone – Wendy and the boyfriend and Abe. All except Ellen, and she was standing far back now in a corner of the room, almost lost in shadow. Marie came around the table to me.

'You never did understand me, Marc, did you?' she said. 'You didn't understand me from the first; and you didn't love me.'

'Maybe not at first,' I said; and my voice had gone hoarse again. It was part of the general craziness that I should be standing here now telling her this while the other woman I loved stood back listening. 'It's different now.'

'Not different enough,' she said. 'Not to the point where you'd move one inch out of your way for me. Or anyone.'

'That's not true.'

'Then prove it. Stay here yourself. Don't go forward.'

'Marie! For Christ's sake, talk sense!'

'I am talking sense. But you can't even hear me.' She stopped and said nothing for a moment; then, surprisingly, she reached up and stroked my cheek with her fingers, very gently. 'It's all right, Marc. You don't have to hear. You can't change for me, I know that. But there's a point beyond which I can't change for you. Nobody can make all the changes you'd like them to make, don't you know that?'

'I just want you to live,' I said. 'I don't want Paula to get you.'

'I know, dear,' she said. 'But it won't work. I've got to stay; and even if you wanted to stay too, you couldn't protect me.'

'Don't be so damn sure about that!' I said; and for an insane, small second, hope of straightening this out after all flickered alive in me. 'If I decided to take Paula and all her army apart, it might take some time; but—'

'You'd be throwing yourself away on something other than what you're built to do,' she said. 'If things went that way, I'd have held you prisoner here, instead of you taking me prisoner into the future.'

I didn't know what to tell her.

'Marc,' she said, raising her face to me. 'Say goodbye to me.'

The ghost of some giant hand took me by the neck and bent my head down to hers. I kissed her and her lips felt dry and strange, as if I had never known them before. She hugged me, and I hung on to her in return until she used strength to break herself loose.

'There,' she said, stepping back a pace, 'it'll be all right. A big part of it is you just can't bear to lose anything, Marc. But it'll be all right in the long run. Goodbye now; and be careful.'

She went out. I watched the doorway through which she had gone, and when I looked around not even Ellen was in the room. I went out into the shadows of the evening and walked by myself for a long while.

When I came back inside, it was nearly ten o'clock and there were a great many things to be done. I called together the monad, which now consisted of the Old Man, Ellen, Bill and myself. Doc had volunteered to join us; and with Marie missing, I now more than wanted him, I needed him there. I went over the patterns with them, as best I could describe them. Not so much because the patterns would mean anything particular to them; but the more their minds could identify with mine once we were in action together, the stronger we would be as a unit, and the more certain I could be of doing what I had set out to do.

Most of the people in the community who were leaving had already gone by midnight, when the meeting broke up. I sent Doc out to check that everyone was clear of the area who did not want to be transported forward with the rest of us. It was one of those coffee nights, when everything is due to happen with the next day's sunrise, and the nerves feel stretched to the point where they sing like guitar strings at a touch. A warm weather front had moved in early in the evening, and the dark outside was still and hot. Only a faint rumble of thunder sounded from below the horizon, from time to time; and the lights among the buildings down below were fewer even than they might be at this hour on an icy winter night, so that already the community looked like a ghost town.

Doc came back.

'Everyone gone but the Mojowskis,' he said, 'and they were just leaving as I came up. Be clear of the area in another twenty minutes.'

'Fine,' I said. 'Go on into the lab. Porniarsk's getting everybody into helmets and set to go. Tell them I'll be along in twenty minutes.'

He went. I took one more turn around outside. The night air was so dark and still it could almost be felt by the fingers; and the mutter of distant thunder seemed to sound halfway around the horizon of the plain below. I had a vision of Paula's soldiers night-marching through the gloom to take us by surprise. But even if they had started to move the moment the sun was down, they could not get here in time. No one was moving in the streets of the town below. Those going with us would be in their homes, waiting.

I went into the summer palace and took a final tour of the building. The rooms seemed oddly empty, as if they had been abandoned for years. I stepped into the courtyard where Sunday lay for a moment, but without turning on the lights. As I stood there; a cicada shrilled suddenly in the darkness at my feet and began to sing.

I went back inside, with the song of the cicada still trilling in my head. It stayed with me as I went down the halls and into the brightly lit lab. Everybody was in place, with helmets already on. Only Porniarsk stood by the directing console, which he had moved out into the centre of the room by the tank. I went to the tank myself, to make one last check of the patterns, for we had it set on the pattern of our moment of destination. There was no change in what I saw there.

I seated myself and took a helmet. As I lowered it over my head, the cicada sound was still ringing in my ears, so that it was like being trapped under there with it. I felt my strength flow together with the strength of the others in the monad and the memory of the cicada sound was lost in the silent song of blended identities as I opened myself to the time storm forces in balance around us.

They were there. They had been there all this time, waiting, quivering in balance like a tangle of arrested lightnings. I read their pattern at a glance this time and laid the far future pattern that I wanted like a template upon them. There was matching and overlap and disagreement between the two patterns. I reached out with the strength of the monad, pushed, and the two slid together. It was suddenly done, and over. There had been nothing to it.

I took off my helmet and looked around. The others were taking off their helmets also and, under the fluorescent lights, their faces looked pale and wondering, like the faces of children.

'We're there?' said Ellen. 'But where are we?'

'I don't know,' I said.

Then I noticed that around the corners of the drawn shades of the windows, the gleam of full daylight was showing.

31

We put up the shades; and the sunlight, which looked no different than any sunlight we had ever known, poured in. But outside the windows, all we could see was the same inner courtyard that held Sunday. Overhead, it was a half-cloudy day with thick white cloud masses and clear blue alternating.

We went down the corridors and out into the parking area. Below us, the empty village of the experimentals and the town were unchanged; but beyond a short distance of plain that surrounded these, high grasses now began. The stalks looked to be six feet tall at least and stretched to the horizon like an endless field of oversize wheat. The road was gone. What now was on the other side of the mountain behind us, we could not, of course, see.

Down in the town, there was still no one stirring. This was not surprising, since many of them might not yet have realized that the move had been made. There had been no sound, no feeling of physical movement when it had happened. It was difficult even for me to realize that this was the far future I had talked about.

'Shall I go tell them, below?' Doc asked.

'Go ahead,' I said.

He hopped into one of the jeeps and drove off. I stood where I was with Ellen beside me, and the others, including Porniarsk, not far off. A moment later, we could see Doc's jeep emerge beyond the trees and drive in among the buildings of the town, stopping here and there while he jumped out and went inside.

Each time he came out again, he was followed by people from inside a building. Soon the streets were swarming, and the figures below were starting to stream back up the slope toward us. Half an hour later, there was an impromptu celebration underway on the landing area.

It struck me, caught up in it as I was, that I had had more shocks, and more large gatherings recently than in any time since before the time storm. Nonetheless, this last one – this arrival party, as it was named

508

almost immediately – vibrated with something neither the welcome home blast, nor the information session had possessed. There was a relaxed feeling of peace about this occasion that I had not noticed before. It was a warm, almost a cosy, feeling. Moving about among my fellow time travellers, picking up patterns, I finally zeroed in on the reason for it. There was something held in common by all the people now around me that I had not thought to look for in them, before we made the move.

In a sense, those who had come with us were the adventurers among our community, the true pioneers. Those particular words all rang a little off-note, applied to the situation we were in. But what I mean is that, to an individual, those who had come forward with me were men, women, and even children who did not want to be any further back down the line of history than they had to be. In all of them, there was an urge to be at the very front of the wave, up where the race as a whole was breaking new ground.

Realizing this, something new and unsuspected in me warmed to them. It was a corner of myself that I had not even realized existed before. It was, in fact, the part of me that felt just the way they did. Even if I had known before we started that what we would all find up here would be the hour of Armageddon and the final end for our kind, I at least would have wanted to go anyway, to be part of even that, while it lasted, in preference to living out my life in any previous time, no matter how comfortable.

Now, here I was with perhaps a hundred and eighty people who felt the same way I did. Under the most unlikely set of conditions that could be imagined, I had unconsciously put together my own special tribe. I was so elated with this discovery that I had to talk about it with someone. Ellen was busy helping organize the food and drink aspect of the gathering, so I went looking for Bill.

I found him also busy. He had set up a table with some sheets of paper and was asking everybody to sign up so that we could have a complete and correct list of who had actually come through with us, since there were people at the last moment who had changed their minds either for or against the move. The sign-up table, however, was essentially self-operating, now that word of it was being passed through the crowd, and I managed to pull him aside.

We walked off a little way from the rest, and I told him my discovery about the pioneer element in those who had come and my pleasure in it.

'I can't get over striking gold like that,' I said. 'Stop and think how small the whole North American population was after we got the mistwalls halted. And out of that small population we've gathered nearly two hundred people who really belong up here, thousands of years ahead in time.'

'That's true, of course,' he said.

His handsome, small face had been tanned by several years of outdoor weather, and the same amount of time seemed to have thickened and matured even the bones of it, so that he now looked more competent and mature. I realized that it was with him as it had been with Marie. Just as I had not really looked at her for a long time, so I had not really looked at him either; and he had been changing under my nose.

'... it shouldn't be such a surprise, though,' he was going on to say, even as I was noting the changes in him. 'Stop to think that the ones who gathered around us in the first place were survivor types. You had to be a survivor type to stay alive while the mistwalls were moving. Even if you were one of the few who were lucky enough to stay put and have no mistwalls come near you, contact with the survivor types around you afterwards either made you like them in a hurry, or buried you.'

'My point, though,' I checked and glanced around to make sure that none of the others were close enough to overhear me discussing them in this clinical fashion, 'my point is that these people are a lot more than simple survivors.'

'Right,' said Bill, his brown face serious. 'Look what happened, though. After the time storm, our group began to attract a particular type of people – those who had heard of us and thought they'd like to be associated with us. The ones we attracted were the ones who saw the same sort of things in us they saw in themselves. So they came – but they didn't all stay. Those who didn't fit went off again. The community was a sort of automatic self-filter for a common type. Then, when it came down to a question of who wanted to make the jump forward in time or not, that decision shook out the last of the chaff.'

I winced inside; though I was careful to make sure no sign of it showed on my face. He had labelled Marie with a tag I neither agreed with, nor would have wanted to hear applied to her even if I had agreed with it. At the same time, I had to admit he had laid out a good argument. I said as much.

'Time will tell, of course,' he answered. 'I'll say one thing, though.' He turned and met my eyes directly with his. 'I've never felt happier in my life than when I realized that it was a settled thing, an unchangeable thing, that I was coming forward like this.'

'Well,' I said, a little lamely. 'I'm glad.'

'I think even if Bettijean hadn't wanted to come along, I still wouldn't have hesitated.'

I opened my mouth to ask who Bettijean was, and then closed it again. One more thing had evidently been going on under my nose without my noticing. I would ask Ellen later.

'I'd better get back to the others,' I said.

After the celebration had begun to settle down a bit, I got up on my customary jeep-rostrum to tell them what we would be doing in the next few days. I said that we would start setting up the community again, here. Meanwhile, Doc would be flying surveys to locate other human settlements in this future world. He would, in fact, fly a spiral course out of this area; and the navigating equipment of the plane could be used to map the ground he covered, in the sense that it would store up information about it, which could later be recalled on the view screen of the control panel.

'How soon do you think we'll find other people?' some male voice I did not recognize, somewhere toward the back of the crowd, asked.

'I can't make any guesses,' I said. 'Actually, if I was betting, I'd bet they'd find us first.'

There was a silence; and I suddenly realized they were waiting for me to expand on that.

'This is the future,' I said. 'Porniarsk and I found evidence that up here they may be doing something about the time storm. If that's the case, they have to be pretty competent technologically. I'm assuming that sooner or later, and probably sooner, the fact that we're here will register on whatever sort of sensing equipment they've got. For one thing, if they're aware of the time storm, they're going to know that a chunk of their real estate suddenly got exchanged by the time storm forces for a chunk from the past.'

There were a lot more questions after that, some serious, some not so, covering everything from what future humans would look like to whether we should post guards – against animals, if not humans – until we learned that this was unnecessary. I turned that suggestion over to Doc, who thought it was a good idea. The session ended with Bill climbing into the jeep and making himself somewhat unpopular by saying that he wanted to start tomorrow morning getting a complete inventory of everything we had left after those leaving had taken what they wanted; and he wanted everybody to cooperate by listing their own possessions.

I broke away from the gathering before it finally ended and got together with Porniarsk in the lab. The view we had in the tank was essentially the same as the one that had been in it before our move. The difference was that now it was real rather than extrapolated; and there were minor corrections in its display because of that.

'Try it now,' I said to Porniarsk. 'See if we can extrapolate forward from here, now that it's the present.'

He worked with the equipment for perhaps twenty minutes.

'No,' he said. 'It's still hesitating over inconsistencies.'

'Then we've landed in the right place – or time, I mean,' I said. 'To tell the truth, I've been a little worried. Between you and me, I half-expected the people from this time to be waiting for us when we appeared.'

'You were assuming that our activity of time forces would at once attract their attention? I would have thought so, too.'

'And that they'd have means of getting here the moment they saw it,' I said. 'If they don't, how can they be advanced enough to do anything about the time storm generally?'

'I don't know,' said Porniarsk. 'But I think there are too many unknowns here for either of us to speculate.'

'I hope you're right.'

'About that, I believe I am. Beyond that, it's anyone's guess.'

'All right,' I said. 'But if no one shows up within twenty-four hours, I'm going to begin to worry.'

No one did show up in the next forty-eight hours. Nor within the forty-eight hours after that, nor in the week that followed. Meanwhile, Doc was coming back from his daily mapping flights and reporting no sign of other human existence. No habitations, no movement. We were evidently at the far eastern end of a mid-continental area of plains uniformly covered by the tall grass, like central North America in the time of the buffalo; though there were none of the bison breed to be seen now.

However, both the grasslands and the hardwood forest that began about sixty miles west of where our chunk of territory had landed, were aswarm with other game. Deer, elk, wolf, bear, moose … and the whole category of familiar smaller wildlife. The hardwood forest gave evidence of stretching to the east coast and had been in existence long enough to kill off most of the undergrowth beneath it, so that it had a tidily unreal look about it, like a movie set for a Robin Hood epic. Doc had landed in an open section of it and reported great-trunked oaks and elms with level, mossy ground beneath them, so that there was a cathedral look to the sunlight streaming down between the lofty limbs overhead.

I kept to myself my concern over the fact we were not being approached by the other intelligences of this future time. Our community was digging in, literally. Just as we had arrived here in daylight when we had left our former time period at night, so we had also arrived here in the spring; although it had been fall where we had left. A fair amount of planted crops had been lost behind us; and even without Bill's urging, a number of our people were eager to get seeds in the ground in this place. There would be no stores of pre-time storm goods to plunder for additional food and supplies in the time where we were now.

So the first week became the second, and the second the third, with no sign of other intelligent life to be found on the continent around us and no futuristic visitors. Gradually we began to adjust to the fact that we might, indeed, be completely alone on this planet of the future; and the life of our own community began to take up most of our attention.

It was a strenuous time. In addition to coping with the fact that here we would have to supply our own necessities, there was evidence that the climate in this future time and area would have colder winters than we had endured, back where we had been. Possibly, much colder winters. There was a good deal of work to be done to insulate buildings and expand the capacity of their heating units, whether fireplaces or stoves.

With the move, we had lost the small river from which we had powered our electric generator. Bill had said he could get some windmill structures built in a few weeks to give us at least intermittent current; but this depended on having the hands available to do the work. More immediate was the need for firewood. Right now the only wood available was on our section of a mountain that had come forward in time with us. One hard winter would deforest this completely. It was almost an imperative that we arrange somehow to bring fuel from the forested area sixty miles to our east, or move the community to it; and we had too big a stake in fixed property here to make that move in one short summer.

The result was that everybody worked time and overtime, including me. In a way, this was something I was grateful for; because it kept my mind off the fact that no one had contacted us. Doc had by now flown as far as the east coast and for some hundreds of miles north of what had once been the Canadian border. He had seen absolutely no sign of civilization. Everywhere, there was only wilderness visible from the muskeg conifer forest of the north, through the now-distorted pattern of the Great Lakes, down to the flat country north of the former Mexican border. A cold worry had begun to nibble at me that possibly Earth at this time was completely uninhabited and forgotten; and if that was so, how in my lifetime was I ever to contact time storm fighters who were light-years – possibly hundreds to millions of light-years – away?

So I was grateful for the hard work, in one way. In another way, it kept me from coming to grips with a second worry, one that was like acid eating away deep within me. With Marie's leaving, something in her had come out into the open that I had never suspected she felt. Now, I was aware of it in Ellen as well. Ellen was still there during the days; she was there beside me at night; but I could sense now that not all of her was there. Some part of her was being withheld from me. There was a wall between us, as there had been between Marie and myself, although I had never realized it.

I wanted to talk to her about it; but there was no time. In the morning we only had time to rise, dress, eat, and run. During the day there was no rest, no pause in which to talk. At night, there was only time for another meal, and sleep would threaten to claim us before we had finished refuelling the weary, empty engines of our bodies. We fell into bed, opened our eyes – it seemed – a moment later; and another day's cycle was already rushing us inexorably onward.

But there had to be a break sometime. It came at the end of the fifth week, when the first of Bill's windmills began to power the generator, and a trickle of electricity came to make our lighting fixtures glow faintly against the ceilings and walls behind them. It was as good an excuse as any to give people a breather, and I declared a night and a day off.

For all the wonders of artificial light refound, there was little celebrating that first evening. All that most of us wanted to do was to sleep; and sleep we did, until late the next day. Then, in the noon sunlight, we gradually came out of our sleeping quarters to sit or move around slowly in the sun, either doing nothing at all, or turning our attention at last to something that had long gone neglected, that we now had time to check, clean, mend, or build.

It was the second of these activities that concerned me. When I woke, Ellen was already up and out of the summer palace. I got up, drank a couple of cups of black coffee and went looking for her.

I found her hanging out a wash on the upsloping hillside that lay on the opposite side of the summer palace from that which held the landing area. Coming around the corner and seeing her from a distance, I woke to the fact that she had necessarily taken over all of Marie's household obligations in addition to her own. I had been so used to having both of them around and being selfishly immersed in my own problems, that it had never occurred to me that Ellen would now be doing double duty in addition to her outside work with the rest of the community. Nor had it ever occurred to me to help either her or Marie before. I came around a corner of the building and saw her from a little distance. I stopped, and for a moment I simply watched her, for she had not yet seen me. Then I went forward, picked up a pair of my own jeans from the basket and joined her in hanging up the rest of the wet stuff.

We worked side by side in silence.

'Look,' I said, when we were done. 'Why don't you sit down for a moment? I'll take the basket in, bring out a card table and some chairs and fix us a lunch. You just sit still. How about it?'

She looked at me. I had never been able to read the deep thoughts behind her face, and I could not now. But I noticed again, as I had come to notice since Marie had left, how Ellen had also changed with the years in between. She was still young – what had I figured out once, that she could not be any older than Doc and was perhaps even younger? But there was nothing of a girl left about her now; not even the ghost, it seemed, of she whom I had picked up in the panel truck long since. The Ellen I looked at now was a mature woman and another person entirely.

'All right,' she said.

She sat down on the grass of the hillside, took off the scarf she had tied around her head and shook her hair out. She was wearing some old, autumn-brown slacks and a dark green shirt, open at the throat. Her neck rose in one straight column from the spread collar of the shirt, and under her dark hair, now loose about her head and shoulders, her eyes were blue-green and brilliant.

I took the basket and went into the house. I rummaged around the kitchen, trying to remember what she had shown a liking for, in the way of food. I had become a halfway decent cook in my years alone in the north woods before the time storm hit; but there was not much available here in the way of foodstuffs. We were all living off stored goods until fall, when the crops of our recent planting would hopefully be in.

I finally found a small canned ham, and with this, some canned new potatoes, and three of the highly valuable eggs from our community's small flock of chickens, managed to make a sort of ham and potato salad, moistened with a spur-of-the-moment, homemade mayonnaise I whipped up from the yolk of one of the eggs and the corn oil we had in fair quantity. I also hunted around the palace and found a bottle of Liebfraumilch that was not overage. There was no way to cool it, lacking electricity for our refrigerator; but salad and wine, once I had the card table and chairs set up outside with a tablecloth of sorts on it, looked reasonably festive.

'That's good,' said Ellen, about the salad, as we ate; and I warmed clear through.

'Glad to hear you say so,' I told her. 'Do you realize I really don't know that much about what you like to eat?'

'I like everything,' she said.

'That's good. Because it'll be a long time before we have anything like what we were used to before,' I said; and I went on about what we could expect in the way of diet that winter, even if the crops went well.

I was talking around and about, trying to get her to give me some sort of conversational lead from which I could get onto the topic I wanted to bring up. She said nothing, however, to help. Nonetheless, with the relaxation of the food and wine in me, I finally began to drift on the tide of my own words into the area I wanted.

'There's two chances that might help protect Marie and the others,' I said. 'One's that when Paula's soldiers arrived and found the country changed where we'd been, they figured I'd magicked everybody safely forever beyond their reach, and Paula bought that idea when they told her—'

'Do you really think she would?'

I hesitated.

'No,' I said. 'If she was completely normal, mentally, I'd think she might. But part of her mind is never going to rest, where I'm concerned; and sooner or later, word is going to reach her of people who've met and recognized some of our people who stayed behind. Then her hunt'll be on again. All we can really hope for is a delay.'

'What's the other chance?'

'That's the long one. If I ever do get into contact with the time storm fighters here and get to work with them, maybe I can learn some way to go back and make Marie and the rest permanently safe from Paula – maybe by shifting Paula herself to a different time.'

Ellen said nothing. There was a little silence between us; and a fly that had discovered the empty wine bottle circled it, droning.

'God help her!' I said; and the words broke out of me, all of a sudden. 'God help them all!'

'It was her decision,' said Ellen.

'I know,' I said. 'But I—'

I looked at her.

'How much did Paula have to do with her going?' I asked.

'Not much,' said Ellen.

'You both knew how I reacted to – to Paula. Believe me, I didn't even know it myself. I didn't even realize it until after I caught on to what she actually was, headwise, and then I knew I had to get out of there.'

'Paula wasn't that important to Marie.'

'You say that? If it hadn't been for Paula and how I felt about her, we'd still have Marie and Wendy with us.'

'I don't think so,' Ellen said.

'How can you say you don't think so? Marie never talked about leaving before.'

'Not to you. She did to me, lots of times.'

I stared at Ellen.

'She did? Why?'

'She told you why, when she left. Marc,' Ellen said, 'you don't listen. That's one of the reasons she went.'

'Of course I listen!'

She said nothing.

'Ellen, I loved Marie!' I said. 'Why wouldn't I listen to someone I loved? I loved Marie – and I love you!'

'No.' Ellen got up from the table, picked up the empty plates and silver and started in toward the house. 'You don't, Marc. You don't love anyone.'

'Will you come back here!' I shouted after her. She stopped and turned. 'For once will you come back and say more than three words in a row? For Christ's sake, come and sit down and talk to me! There's something here, in the air between us. I can feel it. I bump into it every time I turn around. And you're telling me that there was something like that between Marie and me and I didn't know about it. Come back and tell me what it was. Come back and *talk* to me, damn it!'

She stood facing me, holding the dishes.

'It wouldn't do any good.'

'Why not?'

She did not answer.

'Do you love me?' I said.

'Of course. So did Marie.'

'She loved me and she wanted to leave me? I didn't love her and I want to keep her? What kind of sense does that make? If you loved me the way you say you do, you'd explain it to me, so I could do something about it, about me, or whatever was necessary.'

'No,' she said. 'You've got things the wrong way around. I love you without your doing anything.'

'All right, then!'

'But you're asking me to change. Talk doesn't come easily to me. You know that. If I have to talk before you can love me, then you don't love me. You wanted Marie to change, too, but she couldn't. I can, but I won't. It's up to you, Marc, not me.'

I stared at her; but before I could say anything more, a stranger walked around the corner of the summer palace and came up to us. He was a startling figure, a good four inches taller than I was, completely bald, and wearing only a sort of kilt of white cloth around his waist. Even his feet were bare. His features looked something like those of an eskimo's but his skin was brown-dark, and the muscles stood out like cords under the skin. He looked as if he had spent his lifetime exercising, not with barbells, but on the parallel rings and other gymnastic equipment. He came up to me.

'Marc Despard?' he said. He had no accent that I could put my finger on, but the timbre of his voice was somehow different from that of any other human voice I'd heard. 'My name's Obsidian. Sorry we took so long to come forward and meet you, but we had to study you for a while, first.'

32

He was offering his hand in ordinary fashion. I took it and shook it automatically. I had been expecting him, or at least someone like him; but the delay had been long enough, and he had appeared so suddenly that he had managed to knock me off balance with his appearance, in spite of all my expectations. I found myself going through the social routine.

'... my wife, Ellen.'

'Ellen,' and he shook hands with Ellen, 'my name's Obsidian.'

He had a round, friendly face, a little flat-looking and mongoloid; and this, with the hairless skull, gave him something of a tough look.

'Hello,' said Ellen. 'Where did you come from?'

'We're perhaps two hundred miles from you.'

'Just a couple of hundred miles away?' I echoed.

'We had to keep you from finding us while we were studying you,' he answered. 'You have to understand that we had to gather a lot of data on you in order to work out your language and customs. And, of course, we wanted to collect data towards understanding the accident that brought you here.'

'Accident?' I said. 'We came here deliberately.'

He stared at me for a long second.

'You did?'

'That's right,' I said. 'I'd probably better take you down to see the lab and Porniarsk. Sorry, maybe I'm getting the cart before the horse. But after expecting you every day from the moment we landed here, and not having you show up until now—'

'Expecting me when you arrived?' Obsidian said.

We seemed to be talking at cross purposes.

'That's right,' I said. 'We came here because I wanted to contact you people who were doing something about the time storm—'

'Just a moment,' he said. 'Excuse me.'

He disappeared.

He did not come back in a moment, either. He did not come back the rest of that day, nor the day after. It was nearly a week later that I stepped outside from the door of the summer palace that opened onto the parking area, and found him standing there, bright with the morning sun on his bare shoulders. Ellen stepped out just behind me.

'Excuse me for not getting back before this,' he said. 'But possibly I got off on the wrong foot when I first visited you. I've talked the matter over with a number of others, and we've decided that our data was much more insufficient than we thought. Would you be willing to sit down with me and tell me the whole story of how you came to be here, so that we can have that information to work with?'

'I'll be glad to,' I said, turning back toward the door. 'Do you want to step inside?'

'No. If you don't mind, no,' he said. 'Later on, I'd like very much to have the chance to look inside your summer palace, but not just yet. Can we talk out here?'

'Certainly.'

'Good.' He dropped into a sitting position, cross-legged on the grass.

'If you don't mind, I'll use a chair,' I said.

'I don't mind,' he said. 'I'm very interested. Is it actually comfortable for you, sitting on that piece of furniture?'

'It's more comfortable than sitting the way you are,' I said. 'I can sit like that, but not for any length of time.'

'I see.'

I went inside and came out with chairs for myself and Ellen. We sat down.

'The chair was more a product of western culture in my time, though,' I said. 'In the east, even then, people would be perfectly comfortable sitting the way you sit.'

'Thanks,' he said. 'That's the sort of data we appreciate.'

'All right,' I went on. 'Where do you want me to start?'

'Any and all information you can give us will help,' he said.

'Suppose I start with the time storm then,' I said. 'We're together on that, aren't we? You know what I mean when I talk about the time storm?'

'Oh yes,' Obsidian said. 'We're aware of the time storm.'

'Well, we weren't,' I said, 'until it hit us without warning one day. I was up in a northern, wild area of a state called Minnesota in the north central part of this continent ...'

I picked up my own history from the moment when I had thought I was having a second heart attack and proceeded to tell it. I had thought it was something I could cover in an hour or so; but I had badly under-estimated what there was to tell, and I had come nowhere near begin-ning to estimate how many things Obsidian would need explained. We began with the matter of my heart attack, which took some thirty minutes or so of explanation by itself, and went on from there, fre-quently dropping into what must have sounded like a vaudeville act built around the idea of two blind men meeting in the middle of the Sahara desert at midnight.

'But there's no evidence of any damage to your heart, now.'

'There isn't?'

'You mean you don't know there isn't?'

... And so on, far into the night. After a little while, Ellen sensibly got up and left us to bring Porniarsk out to join us, and to call Doc to let the rest of the community know what was going on. Within a few hours Obsidian and I had a quiet, attentive audience seated in a semicircle around us and consisting of everyone able to get from the town up to the landing area.

The talk went on for four days. Obsidian had clearly come with the intention of getting information, but giving little or none himself; but it proved impossible for us to communicate unless he explained something of his own time and civilization. He and I had nothing in common but the language his people had deduced from the first weeks of recording and then taught him to speak accentlessly, and by the end of the first hour, we were both realizing how inadequate this was by itself.

The words alone meant little without their connotative referents, and his connotative referents and mine were separated by thousands, possi-bly hundreds of thousands, of years. It was a curious sensation to hear a sentence made up of nothing but the old, familiar sounds and, at the same time, realize that I had not the slightest idea of what Obsidian meant as he uttered them. Luckily he was an intelligent person; and above and beyond this, he had a sense of humour. Otherwise the talks would have broken down out of sheer exasperation on the parts of each of us.

But he was bright enough and sensible enough to adapt, in spite of the consensus he had been sent out with, that he should listen but not talk. By the end of the third day, he was telling us as much about his people as we were telling him about us, and from that point on, the information exchange began to work, to a point, at least.

By this time we were once more talking privately; but with a tape recorder powered by a stepped-down automobile battery that had been charged by Bill's windmill generator. The tapes were duplicated and made available to the rest of the community. To hit the high points of the information they gathered, Obsidian and his associates here on Earth numbered under a thousand individuals belonging to a race of latter-day humans that were primarily scattered, very thinly indeed, across the habitable worlds of this galaxy.

These humans did not think of themselves, however, so much as members of a race, but as members of a larger community, including representatives of some millions of other civilized races with whom they intermixed. Individuals of these other races were also thinly spread across the same habitable worlds; and some of them, as well as some of the humans, were to be found as well in other galaxies or elsewhere in the universe – although when this happened it was because of special circumstances Obsidian had not yet explained.

The reason for all these individuals being scattered so widely was apparently that (a) the time storm had cut populations on inhabited worlds to the point where there were several habitable worlds for each individual of intelligence; and (b) apparently there were means of travelling not merely faster than light, but many times faster than light, so that even visiting other galaxies was not impossible. Obsidian shied away from my questions when I tried to find out more about this means of travel. Evidently faster-than-light did not describe it directly in his terms; and he was clearly unsure of his ability to explain it to me at our present level of communication.

We had encountered a number of such points of noncommunication. The main problem was the complete dissimilarity of our referents, so that often we found ourselves talking at cross purposes. Some cultural differences only emerged more or less by accident. For example, it turned out that Obsidian was not his name – not at least in the way we think of 'names.' In the way we used that word he had no specific name. This was because he had a certain unique identity, structure, or value – there was no way to express it properly in *our* terms – which was recognized as *him* by his fellow humans and other race individuals who had met him and experienced this unique identity of his.

For reference purposes, in the case of those who had never met him, he was referred to by a code word or symbol that essentially told where he had been born and what he had been doing since. But this was never used except for that sort of reference. For ordinary communicative purposes he had a number of – nicknames is not the right word for them, but it is the closest I can come – depending on how the individual referring to him associated him. The most common of these nicknames, the one he favoured himself, and the one generally in use here among his fellows on Earth, was a name that compared him to the mineral we call 'obsidian' and since it had been established, during the month or so they had been recording our speech, that we would recognize that word, he had identified himself with it when he first met Ellen and me.

It was not just an arbitrary difference from us, this matter of names, it seemed. It was something much more important than that. The whole name business had to do with the different way he and his community of humans and nonhumans thought and worked; and until I could understand why they did their naming that way, a vital chunk of their culture would remain a mystery to me. Accordingly, I struggled to understand and to make him explain himself so that I could understand.

The name business had something to do with identity in that word's most basic sense, which was tied to occupation among them much more than it would be with us, which was, in turn, tied to a different sort of balance between individual and group responsibilities – which was all somehow connected with the fact that they had not approached us the moment we had appeared here, but had hid and studied us instead.

It had not been because they were in any way afraid of us. Fear seemed to have a more academic quality to Obsidian than it did to me. They had been obligated to be able to communicate with us before they could appear. Consequently, they had stayed out of sight of Doc in the plane – which was apparently not as hard as it might seem, since they used structures much less than we did. In fact, our buildings were almost a little forbidding to Obsidian, which was why he had refused my invitation to come inside the summer palace. Apparently, he was about as attracted to the interior of the summer palace as I might have been to the idea of a neighbourly crawl through the tunnels and dens of a human-sized mole. Obsidian's people built observatories and such, but these were generally constructed without walls or roof.

Apparently they did not need as much protection from the weather as we needed. When I asked about this, Obsidian demonstrated how he could envelop himself in a sort of cushion of invisible warmth, apparently just by wanting to do it – although he insisted that the heat was generated by mechanical, not mental, means. But beyond this, it was obvious to me early in our discussions that he had a far greater tolerance for temperature extremes and the discomfort of his physical surroundings than I did. In spite of the chilliness of the spring mornings or the heat of the afternoon, he showed the same indifference to the temperature and wore the same kilt, no more, no less. It was not until the third day that I discovered he was only wearing that out of courtesy to us, it having been established by them that we had some kind of clothing taboos.

It was about the third day, also, that a great many other things began to make sense. Surprisingly, my ability to communicate improved much more swiftly than did his; so much so, in fact, that he commented on it with unconcealed awe. The awe was almost more unsettling to me than the other mysteries about him. It gave me an uneasy feeling, mentally, to think that these people of the far future might not be so superior to us after all; that they might, in fact, be inferior in some ways. Obsidian and I worried over the communication discrepancy together and finally concluded that, paradoxically, Obsidian was in a sense being inhibited by the fine command of the spoken language he had exhibited the first time he appeared.

It emerged that his group was not used to translating concepts. Sounds and symbols, yes. These varied from race to race among them in infinite variety. But, just as they could agree on the unique identity of any single individual, they were apparently able to agree on the perfect value of any concept, so that translation, in that sense, was never necessary. When we first appeared, they had set up recording devices to pick up every sound made in our community and channelled these into a computer-like device which had sorted them out and deduced the rules and vocabulary of our language, with the observed or implied denotative values of each sound. With this done, they had pumped the information into the head of Obsidian and set him to talk to us, confident that he could now communicate.

Only, he had run into trouble. The sounds he used turned out to have had meanings over and above what the language computer had deduced. In short, Obsidian and his fellows were in the uncomfortable position of people who have grown up with a single set of concepts, thinking there was no other, and who had then run into an entirely different set – ours. They were like the person who grows to adulthood before he discovers that there are other languages than the one he knows, and then has to struggle emotionally with the concept that anybody else can prefer some outlandish sound to what he knows in his heart of hearts is the only 'real' sound for a thought or thing.

Because of this, his plans had gone awry. It had been planned that he would drop in on us, pump us dry of all other relevant data on us, feed that also into the computer, and come up with patterns of us in all departments, from which it could be figured how to adjust us to the culture of their time, if this was possible. Instead, here he was floundering at absorbing my patterns while I was picking up his, hand over fist.

Well, not exactly hand over fist. His patterns, unlike ours, were all logical and logically interrelated, which gave me a great advantage. But there were also abilities and concepts in his area that he took for granted and I could not get him to talk about because I had no way of describing what I was after.

It was not until the fourth day that I finally achieved a breakthrough in that respect; and it happened for a strange reason. That mind of mine, which could never leave a problem alone but must keep worrying at it and chewing it over until either mind or problem cracked wide open, had been at work on the two enigmatic conversations I had had with Marie, just before she left, and Ellen, the day that Obsidian had appeared.

I still could make no sense of what they said. For all my efforts to understand, my comprehension slid off the memories of their words to me as if both had been encased in glass. At the same time I had a reason to keep working at them, now. There was something in me which I evidently could not see, as I could not see my own eyeballs, except in a mirror, or the back of my head. There must be something in me, I thought, like a dark area, a shadow cast by the sensing mechanism itself, that was keeping me from the closeness I wanted to have with other people – and of all people, Ellen. I had been trying all sorts of approaches to the problem, trying to find some way of sneaking up on the unseeable, so to speak; and it occurred to me suddenly as I was talking to Obsidian that there might be a similarity between this problem and my problem of communication with him.

I had tried evoking the golden light as a means of reaching an understanding of Ellen. But I had found that when I tried to reach for the feeling of unity with all things for that reason, it was as it had been in the plane after leaving Paula's camp – I could not evoke the state of unity. It came to me now that it would do no harm to try for it once more in the case of Obsidian and his people, where the emotional roots concerned did not go so deeply into the dark of my own soul.

So I tried. It helped that I had grown to like Obsidian in the last few intense days of talking. I thought I could almost grasp what he described as that unique identity element by which all other beings of his time recognized him. So I picked a moment when he was trying to explain to me what among them took the place of family structure, as we in our community knew it. I watched him as he talked, seated cross-legged on the ground. His face was animated and his hands wove patterns in the air. He had the attribute of seeming to be alive with energy even while he was obviously without tension and relaxed. It was an ability I had seen before in casual encounters with professional athletes in top condition.

I was hardly listening to what he said. That is, my mind was making automatic note of it, but I was comfortably aware of the fact that the tape recorder was catching his words and I would be able to review them again this evening in the quiet of the summer palace library. Most of my attention was concentrated on him as a complete entity; a sound-making, limb-moving individual extending energy to me in the form of sound and gesture. I squinted, mentally, to focus in on him in this sense; and when I had him in focus, slid on top of his image before me the emotional/intellectual gestalt that was my friend Obsidian, as I knew him.

The two melted together; and as they did I was able for the first time to take a step back from him and the present moment. I kept my point of view at that distance and slowly let the rest of the day soak into me.

We sat just outside the summer palace and I had my back to it; so that I looked past Obsidian, across the open stretch of the landing area and out over the descending slope of the trees to the town below and the tall grass marching in all directions to the horizon. It was, for once, a perfectly clear day; there was not a cloud in sight. But a small, cool wind was wandering back and forth across the mountainside where we sat.

I saw the treetops moving to it and felt the intermittent light touch of it on my face and hands, cancelling out now and again the warmth of the steady afternoon sunlight. It was too early for insects; but down on the wooded slope below me, a cloud of specks that were small birds burst up unexpectedly as I watched, to swarm dark against the far bright sky for a moment like a cloud of gnats, and then settled back down out of sight into the dark mass of the leaves below them again.

High up, another single speck swam against the cloudless sky. A hawk? My vision went out to the horizon and beyond. Slowly, I became conscious of a rhythm that was the beating of my own heart and at the same time the breathing of the world. Once again, the golden light began to grow around me and, once more, I felt myself touching all things in the earth, sky, and water, from pole to pole. I was touching all things, and I reached out to touch Obsidian.

I looked at him without moving my eyes and saw him in full dimension for the first time. For he was a part of the universe, as all these other things were a part of it; and that was what was at the core of his community's difference from ours. They were aware of the universe of which they were a part, while we thought of ourselves as disparate and isolated from it. That was why Obsidian's identity was unchangeable and instantly recognized by his fellows. It was because the dimensions of that identity were measured by the universe surrounding him, in which he was embedded, and of which he was a working part. All at once the gestalt formed, and I understood without words, without symbols, the different, fixed place he and all other thinking minds of his period had in this, their own time and place.

I had produced the golden light again and it had helped me find what I had been seeking. I sat, just feeling it for a moment – then let it go. The light faded, I came back into my ordinary body and smiled at Obsidian.

But he did not smile back. He had stopped talking, and he was staring at me with a startled expression.

'Obsidian—' I began, about to tell him what I now understood.

He vanished.

33

Once again, he did not come back for a while. He was missing all the rest of that day and through the next two days. Under the conditions applying up until five minutes before he left, I would have worried that I had somehow damaged the relationship building between the two of us, and between our people and his interstellar community. Following the moment of light and my sudden access to understanding, I was sure this was not the case; and I tried to reassure the other members of our group who were inclined to worry about his non-appearance.

'It's not explainable in our words,' I told Ellen, Bill, Doc, Porniarsk and about five others of the community who had been emerging as leaders during the past few weeks. We were all sitting around the fireplace in the library on the second evening, with the windows open to the courtyard and the night sky outside. 'But I'm sure I didn't step on his toes in any way. I can't tell you how I know it, but I know it.'

'Why did he take off, then?' Bill asked. 'Can't you give us some idea, Marc?'

'He recognized what I was doing – this universe association trick I've told you about. I've explained that the best I can, and I won't try to explain it any more now. You'll have to learn how to do it yourselves if you really want to understand.'

'You'd better start giving us lessons, then,' said Doc. They all laughed.

'I will,' I said. 'Seriously, I will. When we've got the time.'

'Go on, Marc,' said Bill. 'Finish what you were saying. He knew what you were doing ... and that's what disturbed him?'

'Not exactly disturbed, I'd say,' I told them. 'He was just surprised. He's gone back to check with his friends. The way they are – the way I now *know* they are – that sort of checking's a responsibility on his part.'

'So that's why you're sure he'll be back?' Bill asked.

'Isn't that what I've been saying?'

'Porniarsk,' said Bill, turning to him, 'can't you help explain any of this? You're from a more advanced race than we are.'

'By comparison with Obsidian and his associates,' said Porniarsk, 'I'm essentially of the same primitiveness as the rest of you. Also, you'll remember, I'm only an avatar. I've no creativity, and no imagination beyond what I acquired when I was produced in the image of Porniarsk. I'm not equipped to speculate or interpret.'

'Well,' said Bill. 'Anyway, we've all got plenty of work to do while we're waiting for him to come back. Marc, you'll speak to him as soon as you can, about whether we can count on them for supplies or assistance in case we need it?'

'Yes,' I said. 'I can talk to him about that as soon as he comes back. I was afraid earlier that I couldn't explain what we wanted without muddying up the idea we intend to be independent here. We still do want to be independent and self-supporting, don't we?'

I looked around the room. I did not really need the murmurs of agreement from all of them. I only wanted to remind them we were all together on that one point.

'If it's only a station they've got here,' said Leland Maur, a thin, black man in his mid-twenties who was an architect and our construction and mechanical engineering expert, 'my feeling's that this world is ours by right of settlement anyway. Not theirs. We don't want to start off owing any piece of it to someone else.'

That comment ended the business of the evening. We sat back to drink coffee and compare notes on how things were going with our individual work projects to get ready for winter; and after about an hour of this, most of us were ready to fold for the night.

The next day, Obsidian had still not come back. That morning happened to be the half-day a week we had begun to take off as a rest period, following the good effect of our one day holiday after the first windmill generator had been put into operation. We had found that there was a limit to the efficiency involved in working seven days a week. After several weeks of unbroken work, we ended up going through the motions of our labours, but getting less done in total than if we had taken a break and started in fresh again. Accordingly, that morning I could stay home with a clear conscience, instead of lending my strength to one of the work jobs down in the town. Ellen was also home and busy doing something with her clothes in one part of the summer palace. I took advantage of the chance to dig once more into the books I had been neglecting lately. But they did not seem to hold my attention, after all. The urge had been growing in me to try for the golden light state again and, once more, to try to reach towards Ellen as I had reached toward Obsidian.

I was encouraged in this by my success with Obsidian, and also by the fact I began to believe I was at last zeroing in on my inner search. The outer search had always been the time storm; but the inner search, I now began to suspect, went back to my relationship with Swannee – and my mother.

I put the book I was holding aside and looked out into the courtyard feeling once more for a unity with the universe. It did not come easily this time. It was almost as if it knew why I wanted it and was reluctant to help me in that direction. But slowly, as the minutes went by, first the room and then the courtyard and the sky I looked out on took on greater values of reality, as if I was seeing them with a dimension added, a greater depth, a *beyondness*, in addition to the ordinary height, depth and width of normal vision. My body slowed its breathing and its heartbeat and began to blend with the movements of the planet.

The light changed, the gold moved in, and once more, I had it.

I held where I was for some little time – perhaps as much as ten or twenty minutes, although in that state of concentration time seemed almost suspended – to make sure that my hold on the state I had evoked was firm. Then I reached out to feel Ellen, elsewhere in the palace.

My touch went out like a wave spreading up on a sloping beach. I reached her, felt her there, lightly, and started to enfold her – and something far out in myself jerked back, so that the wave of my feeling was sucked away again, abruptly and my touch against her was lost. All at once, the golden light was gone and the unity was destroyed. I was alone and isolated, in my armchair in the room, looking out through the glass window panes at a world I could no longer feel.

I sat there, dulled and numbed by my failure. But after a few moments, a miracle happened; because the door opened, Ellen walked in, bent over the chair and kissed me. Then, without a word, she turned and went back toward the door.

'Why?' I managed to croak as she opened it.

She looked back and smiled.

'I just felt like it,' she said.

She went out, closing the door behind her; and I sat there with my heart rising like a rocket. Because now I knew. I had not succeeded in fully touching her; but I knew that I was going in the right direction now; because she had felt me trying. If I lived, I would reach her eventually.

Our half-day holiday ended with noon. I put on work clothes and left the summer palace to go down and help the people who were insulating and expanding our largest quonset, so that it could become a combination dining hall, hospital, and living quarters for those of us who might turn out to be too young, too old, or too feeble to live out the winter cold in the other, flimsier, buildings of the town. I had just shut the door of the summer palace behind me when Obsidian appeared in front of me.

'Can we talk?' he said.

'Of course,' I said. He came first before any rough carpentry of which I was capable.

'We've come to an important decision, my colleagues and I,' he said. 'You remember I told you our original plan was to gather enough information on you so that we'd know how to educate you into adjustment with civilization? At least, educate you enough so that you could stay with us, here?'

'I remember,' I said.

'I'm afraid I didn't tell you everything,' he said. 'There was an alternative I didn't mention. If it turned out you people couldn't be adjusted to a civilized pattern, we were intending to send you back to your own time, the time you left to come here.'

'No, you didn't tell me that,' I said. 'But you didn't have to. We primitives can think of those sort of alternatives without being prompted, you know.'

'Yes. Well,' Obsidian looked uncomfortable, 'as it happens, you've turned out to be in some ways more than we guessed; in fact, more than we bargained for. In particular, you're different, yourself, from anything we imagined. So, now we've come up with a third alternative. But for this we're going to need your agreement.'

'Oh?' I said. He did not answer immediately, so I prompted him. 'Agreement to what?'

'To an alternative that ties in to this desire of yours to get into the work of controlling what you call the time storm. Logically, it's unthinkable to expect someone from as far back in the past as you are to be capable of learning to do a kind of work that's done only by unusual, highly qualified individuals in our time. But because of certain anomalies about you, we'd like to test your aptitude for such work.'

'Fine,' I said. And for the second time that day my heart went up like a rocket.

'You understand,' Obsidian said, 'this testing in no way changes the fact that by no stretch of the imagination could we expect you to actually be able to work in the temporal area. It's simply a means of supplying us with data by which we can decide best what to do with all your group, here.'

'All right,' I said.

'Are you sure you understand? Our interest in whether you have any ability for temporal work is only academic.'

'I hear you,' I said. But my heart was still high inside me. Explain it any way he might, Obsidian could not hide from me the fact that, in offering me such tests, they were letting me come one step closer to the goal I had been working toward.

'Well, then,' said Obsidian, 'even if you're willing, there's a further question. Ordinarily, there'd be no need for you to leave your area, here. But in this particular case some special conditions are involved; so that to be tested you have to be willing to go some distance across the galaxy. Now, if you want time to consider this—'

'Thanks. It's not necessary. I'll be happy to go wherever being tested requires.'

He gazed across the jeep at me for a full second.

'Are you sure you understand?'

'I think so,' I said. 'You want to know if I'm willing to be tested for abilities in time storm fighting. I am. You also want to know if I'm agreeable to going a large chunk of light years to wherever I have to go to be tested. I am.'

'You understand this means travel between the stars, through space?'

'Well, I'd gathered that,' I said. But he did not echo my grin.

'I'm a little surprised,' he said. 'I understood from what you told me that you'd never been off this one world in your life.'

'That's right.'

'But you're willing to go, without thinking it over? Without talking it over with the rest of your people?'

'I'll check with them, of course,' I said. 'But they've been getting along without my immediate help while I've been talking to you. They ought to be able to get along without me for a bit longer. How long would I be gone?'

'In terms of time here, not more than a couple of your weeks. Probably considerably less. It may be a single simple test will give us an answer, once you've reached your destination. It's possible we might have to test further, but probably not more than a day or two.'

'I see,' I said. 'The more ability I show, the more you'll go on testing?'

'Essentially. But Marc,' said Obsidian, 'if you've got hopes of our tests finding you to have very great ability in that area, I wish you'd temper those hopes. Believe me—'

'I believe,' I said. 'I'm also willing to go. We're agreed?'

'Yes,' he said, slowly.

'Good. The thing you have to understand about me, friend Obsidian,' I said, 'is that I'll do whatever I decide is best. I'm not going to leave the other people here in a bind because I didn't bother to check. I'll check first. But I said I want to go, and I'm going.'

'Forgive me,' he said.

'There's nothing to forgive,' I said. 'It's just that this isn't a matter of group discussion. This is me, saying what I choose to do.'

'All right,' he said. 'But it's not quite what I'm used to. You understand that? We have—'

'I know,' I said. 'You people've got a pattern of responsibility. So've I. And I won't violate my pattern any more than you'd violate yours. But I tell you, Obsidian, I want to go where your people will test me. The fact it's across space doesn't matter; because I'd go cross-universe as quickly as I'd go around this jeep to get that done.'

I had gotten a little warm on the subject; and I was braced to have him react with equal emotion. Instead he only looked at me, a long, questioning look. Then he nodded.

'This means more to you than we'd thought,' he said.

I stared back at him. Something other than the golden light was moving me now; a surge of feeling that was more like a tide, a running tide carrying me irresistibly forward.

'You don't understand me at all,' I said, 'do you?'

'No.' He shook his head.

'All right,' I told him. 'See if it has meaning for you this way. I don't know who my remote ancestors were; but what moves me as far as the time storm goes, must go as far back as they do. There's something in me that's certain about one thing; that anything can kill me, but until I'm killed I'm what lives. And as long as I live, I'll fight. Come and get me out to face my special enemy, whoever that is; and while I can still move, I'll stay after it. When I'm finally done for, I'll still be happy; because I wasn't deprived of my chance to do something. All I want is that chance – nothing else matters; and here you come asking me if the fact I have to cross some space to be tested might make me decide against going!'

I had really moved off the high end of the emotional scale this time, but I saw now that at last I had gotten through to him. I do not think even then that he understood what I was talking about, but he had registered the charge of the emotion that had ridden on top of my words.

'How much time do you need before you'll be ready to go?' he said.

'Two – three hours, say.'

'Good. One more thing. We'd like, since we're moving you this distance, to take advantage of the opportunity to do some testing of the avatar, as well. Do you think he'd be willing to come? He's had experience in cross-space travel, I understand.'

'He has,' I said. 'I'll ask him. I think he'll want to come.'

'Then I'll be back in three of your hours.'

He vanished.

I turned back into the summer palace and went to find Porniarsk. It had not occurred to me until now to wonder what had been occupying him since we had arrived at our destination here in the future; and it struck me suddenly, now, that he had been busy in the lab all that time. But at what, I wondered? When I arrived, I found him working with the vision tank; and I asked him that question.

'I've been doing some charting,' he said, waving a stubby tentacle at the tank. 'I thought perhaps if I could establish specifically what the inconsistencies were that we noted, I might be able to evolve a picture of what's happening with the time storm at this future moment.'

'What did you find out?'

'I discovered that, except for certain areas where the force lines of the storm still seem to be breeding, the universe in general has been brought pretty much into the same sort of temporary, dynamic balance that we achieved around this planet back in our earlier time.'

'What about the breeding areas?' I asked.

'That's interesting. Very interesting,' he said. 'The force lines seem to be both breeding and healing – both increasing and decreasing in these areas. By the way, the areas I'm talking about are all out in the midsections of the galaxies. There's none of them down in the very centre of a galaxy – in what might be called the dead core area.'

'Dead core?'

'I thought you knew?' he glanced at me. 'The centre of most galaxies, like this one, is an area of very old stars, immersed in a dust cloud.'

'Where's the closest activity to this solar system?'

'The blue-white supergiant star,' said Porniarsk, 'that you call Rigel seems to be one of the near loci. But the main activity close to us is centred on the star you call S Doradus in the lesser Magellani Cloud, outside this galaxy, about a hundred and forty thousand light-years from us here.'

'S Doradus is a big, hot star, too, isn't it?' I said.

'Like Rigel, one of the brightest.'

'Sounds like a large, bright star is necessary. Can you tell why?'

'No,' said Porniarsk. 'All I know is that the lines of time storm activity in the area in question seem to centre on S Doradus. And, then, there's the matter that S Doradus has stopped radiating.'

'Stopped what?'

'It's no longer radiating. It's gone dark,' Porniarsk said. 'I mean by that, that if you were in the immediate neighbourhood of that star, it would no longer appear to be radiating. From our distance here, of course, it still seems to be shining; since we're getting light that left it thousands of years ago.'

My head began to spin. The distances, the star sizes, and the rest of the information involved was on such a scale that my imagination struggled to get a grip on it.

'I've got a message for you,' I said, to shift the topic of conversation.

I told him about Obsidian taking me to be tested, and his question as to whether Porniarsk would be willing to go also.

'Of course,' said Porniarsk. 'I'd be very interested to see how they do such testing.'

34

Three hours turned out to be less time than I thought in which to get hold of Ellen and the other leaders, explain what Porniarsk and I were going to be doing, and pack a suitcase. When Obsidian reappeared outside the summer palace at the landing area, he found about forty people – all who could possibly get up there to see Porniarsk and myself off. But it was not at the others he stared, or even at Porniarsk and I, but at the suitcase at my feet.

'Can I ask ...' he began.

'My bag,' I said. I guessed what was puzzling him. 'Personal necessaries. Remember, I wear clothes, shave every morning, and things like that.'

'Oh,' he said. I had discovered by the end of our first day of acquaintance that the humans of his time had no body hair to speak of. 'Of course.'

Following this conversation, there was a great deal of kissing and handshaking all around. In fact, our community nowadays was more like one large family than anything else. I almost spoiled the occasion by laughing out loud at the spectacle of Porniarsk solemnly promising people that he would be careful and take good care of himself. It was rather like a battleship assuring everyone that it would keep a wary eye out for sharks and take care not to get bitten.

But even the saying of goodbyes had to run down finally.

'We're all set,' I told Obsidian.

'All right,' he said. 'Then, if you'll just stand close to me, here.'

Porniarsk and I moved in until we were almost nose to nose with him, leaving a ring of unoccupied ground about ten feet wide around us. All at once, we were standing elsewhere, in a little open space between the trunks of massive elms spaced about thirty feet apart. We stood on something that looked like a linoleum rug, but felt underfoot like deep carpeting, a solid dark green in colour. About us were some walls at odd angles, several large puff-type cushions ranging up to a size that would have made a comfortable queen-sized bed, and several of what looked like control panels on stands apparently connected to nothing.

I looked around.

'This is your living area and working quarters?' I asked Obsidian.

'Yes,' he said. 'I think you'll find it comfortable for the three of us. I can arrange the walls so that you can have separate rooms for privacy, if you like.'

'Don't bother,' I said. 'I assume we won't be here long in any case, will we?'

'About the equivalent of five days of local time.'

'Five days?' I said. 'I thought we'd be leaving for wherever it is in a matter of hours, if not minutes?'

'Oh, we've already left,' he said. He waved his hand and something like a picture window appeared between us and the trees to our left. The view in the picture window, however, was a view of black space, bright pinprick stars as thick as pebbles on a beach, and a blue and white earth-globe nearly filling the lower right-hand corner of the view.

I stared at the earth-globe and confirmed my first impression that it was visibly shrinking in size as I watched.

'I thought you said this was your working and living area?'

'It is.'

'It's a spaceship, too?'

Obsidian waved a hand.

'I suppose you could call it that,' he said. 'Actually, it's more accurate to say it's simply living quarters. The process of travelling between the stars isn't much more cumbersome if we bring it along, however; and it's a lot more comfortable if we do so.'

I turned about in a circle, on my heel.

'The trees and all,' I said. 'That's just an illusion?'

'Out here, yes,' Obsidian said. 'Back when we first arrived, of course, you were looking at the actual surrounding forest.'

'When did we take off?'

'As soon as we arrived. But to call it a takeoff—'

'I know,' I said, '– doesn't exactly describe what happened. Never mind. I'm not really interested in the mechanics of it, right now. All right then, if we really are going to be here for five days, I believe I'd appreciate a room of my own, after all; and I'd imagine Porniarsk would too.'

'It makes no difference to me,' said Porniarsk. 'But I am interested in the mechanics of your space flight. Can I examine those control panels?'

'By all means,' said Obsidian. 'If you like, I'll explain them to you. They're for work back on the planet we just left, actually. Our trip will be handled automatically.'

'I'm interested in all things,' said Porniarsk. 'This is the effective result of being the avatar of an individual, Porniarsk, who has always been interested in all things—'

He checked himself.

'– I should probably say, was interested in all things.'

'Do you miss him?' Obsidian asked. 'This individual of whom you were an avatar?'

'Yes,' said Porniarsk, 'in a sense I do. It's a little like realizing that part of myself is gone, or that I had a twin I now know I'll never see again.'

The tone of his voice was perfectly calm and ordinary; but suddenly I found myself looking at him closely. I had never stopped to think of Porniarsk as having emotions, or stopped to consider what he might have lost in a personal sense by going forward in time with us.

'I should have asked you if you wanted to come with us,' I said.

'If you had, I'd have answered yes,' said Porniarsk. 'The process of discovery and learning is what I was constructed for.'

'Yes,' I said.

I was suddenly very tired, with an almost stupefying feeling of fatigue. Part of it, undoubtedly, was the work schedule we had been keeping in the community these last few weeks. But the greater part was something more psychological and psychic than physical. In spite of Obsidian's insistence that the testing I was about to take was that and no more, I was at last certain that I had reached the last arena, the moment of final confrontation.

I was like someone who had trained physically for months and years for one battle. I felt loose, light and ready, but drained and empty inside, hollow of all but the inevitability of the conflict toward which I was now marching inexorably. Not even enthusiasm was left – only a massive and silent acceptance of what would be.

'I think,' I said to Obsidian, 'I'd like that private room now, if you don't mind. I think I'd like to get some sleep.'

'To be sure,' he said.

Suddenly, the white walls were around me. I had not moved, but now I was enclosed, alone with the picture window, or screen, showing the innumerable stars and the shrinking Earth. I turned to the largest of the cushions and fell on it. For a second the lighting was still daylight strong, but just before I closed my eyes, it dimmed to nonexistence; and the space in which I now rested was lit only by the star-glow from the window.

I slept.

When I woke, the stars in the picture window were different. Not merely a little different; they bore no relationship to anything I had ever seen in the skies of Earth. Puzzled, I lay there looking at them while gradually I came to full alertness; and either automatically, or in response to some way of sensing my urge for better visibility, the lighting in the room slowly increased, back to the level of sunlight. I got up, explored, and found a doorway that let me into a bathroom, which was too good a replica of what I was familiar with to be anything but a construct created expressly for me by Obsidian.

Still, I was grateful for the fact that it looked so familiar. Part of my waking up had always been a morning routine involving a sharp razor blade, soap and a good deal of hot water. This out of the way, I left my private quarters and found Obsidian sleeping quietly on one of the larger cushions of the main area, Porniarsk busy doing incomprehensible things with one of the control consoles.

'Good morning, Marc,' he said, turning to look at me as I came up.

'Morning, if that's what it is—' I lowered my voice, glancing at Obsidian. 'Sorry, I forgot about him sleeping there.'

'I don't think you need worry,' said Porniarsk at ordinary conversational volume. 'I don't believe he hears any noise he doesn't want to hear until he wakes at the time he wants to wake.'

I looked at Obsidian curiously.

'Good trick,' I said. 'What's the breakfast situation?'

'There's food of various kinds in a room there,' said Porniarsk, pointing a tentacle at a doorway in one of the walls that had been there when we arrived.

I went to look and found he was right. It was a pleasant, small room, apparently surrounded completely by the illusion of the forest in forenoon sunlight. There were chairs, my style, and a table, my style; and a piece of furniture that looked like a heavy, old fashioned wooden wardrobe.

When I opened the door of this last piece of furniture, however, I found it filled with shelves full of all kinds of fresh earthly fruits and vegetables. There were fruit juices in transparent vessels, milk, and a pitcher of black liquid that turned out to be hot coffee; although what was keeping its temperature up was a mystery. There were no meat or eggs; and although I looked around carefully, I could not find a stove or any means of cooking any of the other foodstuffs. Well, at least the coffee was hot. I found a small empty vessel to pour it into and settled down to eat.

It was an interesting meal. There were no shocks, but some surprises. For one thing, the already-sliced loaf of bread I discovered turned out to be hot. Not toasted. Hot, like the coffee. The glass of what I had assumed was orange juice turned out to be slightly fizzy, as if it had been carbonated. There was no sugar and the honey tasted as if it had been spiked with vodka.

I finished up and went back into the other room. Obsidian was still asleep and Porniarsk was still at work.

'Have you eaten?' I asked Porniarsk. I knew he did eat; although Porniarsk and nutrition were something of a puzzle; because apparently he could go for weeks at a time without food. He had told me once that his bodily fuelling system was almost as much a mystery to him as it was to the rest of us; since that was an area of information in which Porniarsk, the original Porniarsk, had no interest whatsoever. Apparently our Porniarsk, at least, had some way of getting a great deal more energy out of the sustenance he took in than we humans did. I had played with the picture of a small stainless steel fission engine under the thick armour plating of his body – although he had assured us he was pure animal protein in all respects.

'No,' he said now. 'There's no need. I'm greatly interested in this equipment.'

'It looks like we built up quite a velocity while I was asleep,' I said. 'Where are we now?'

'That's the fascination of this,' he said, nodding heavily at the control console. 'Apparently, as Obsidian said, our trip's completely under automatic control. But this console, since he showed me how to operate it, has been furnishing me with information on our movements as we make them. Right now we're something like three million years in the past, and consequently, far displaced from your solar system—'

'Displaced?' I said. But even as I said it, even as he began to explain, my mind was jumping ahead to that explanation.

'Why, yes. Obsidian and his community,' said Porniarsk, 'have evidently done a superb job of, first, balancing the large areas of time forces; and second, an equally excellent job of charting specific force lines in between the balanced areas. In fact, I'm inclined to think that the process of balancing was designed to leave just the network of working force lines that remain. The result has been that, although they can't actually cross space at more than light speeds, by using the force lines they can jump distances equivalent to some hundreds or even thousands of light years, and arrive at their destination in a matter of hours, or even days. Watch the present stellar arrangement.'

He touched the console in front of him with a tentacle tip. Another picture window appeared, showing the starscape beyond. My memory for patterns now was too good to be deceived. This was a different view again of the galaxy than the one I had seen in the other room on waking up.

'We should be coming up on another transfer, momentarily . . .' said Porniarsk. 'There!'

The starview abruptly changed, without jar, without sound, and so instantaneously that I did not even have the sensation of having blinked at the scene.

'We've gone down the ladder in time in order to make large shifts through space,' said Porniarsk. 'In the smaller node of forces on Earth, the time jumps were also much smaller and the physical displacement was minor. Here, of course, when we take a large step forward or backward in time, the surrounding stars and other solid bodies move around us. What's that phrase I once learned from Marie about Mahomet not being able to go to the mountain, therefore, the mountain must come to him? Obsidian's people have learned to use the time storm to bring their mountains to them, instead of themselves making the journey to the mountains—'

He glanced at me. Porniarsk could not be said to have the most readable facial and body expressions in the universe; but I knew that hang of his tentacles well enough by now to tell when he was being apologetic.

'– I mean, of course,' he said, 'to refer to the stars and other solid bodies of the universe as "mountains".'

'I'd guessed you did,' I said.

'I'm afraid I'm sometimes a little pedantic,' he said. 'So was Porniarsk himself, of course. It's a failing that often goes with an enquiring mind.'

'Don't let it bother you where I'm concerned,' I said. 'One of my worst habits is telling other people what the situation is, at great length.'

'That's true, of course,' he answered, with gentle unconcern for my feelings. 'Nonetheless, two wrongs do not – I believe our host is waking up.'

He had creaked his head to one side as he spoke, to gaze at Obsidian, who now opened his eyes and sat up cross-legged on his cushion, all in one motion, apparently fully alert in the flicker of an eyelash.

'Are you rested, Marc?' he asked. 'I finally had to take a nap, myself. Apparently Porniarsk needs very little sleep.'

'Damn little,' I said.

'We'll have a little more than four days more before we reach our destination,' said Obsidian. 'I'm looking forward to doing a lot more talking with you, Marc. I gather you've already come to a better understanding of the present time.'

'I think so,' I said. 'Tell me if I'm wrong, but as I see it, all the intelligent races in the galaxy have joined together to fight for survival. Animate organisms against the inanimate forces that otherwise might kill you all off.'

'That's a lot of it,' Obsidian said. 'We're concerned with survival first, because if life doesn't survive, everything else becomes academic. So the first job is to control the environment, right enough. But beyond survival, we're primarily interested in growth, in where life goes from here.'

'All right. But—' I checked myself. 'Wait a minute. I ought to give you a chance to get all the way awake before I tie you up in a discussion like this.'

'But I am awake,' said Obsidian, frowning a little.

'Oh. All right,' I said, 'in that case, suppose you start filling me in on the history of everything. How did this brotherhood of civilized entities start? What got it going?'

'As a matter of fact,' he answered, 'what began the getting together of races that later became the present civilized community was what you call – excuse me, I'll just use your word for it from now on – the time storm, itself. This was paradoxical; because it was the time storm that threatened the survival of all life, and here it made real civilization possible ...'

With that, he was underway with a flood of information almost before I had time to find myself a seat on a nearby cushion. In the next four days, while his house, so to speak, flitted through space from time force line to time force line, and Porniarsk watched that process fascinatedly with the control console, Obsidian drew me a picture of some forty-odd thousand years of known history – on the time scale of our galaxy – and an unknown amount of time before that in which life was nearly destroyed by the time storm, but in which the foundation of a universal community was discovered and erected.

'The process was instinctive enough,' he said. 'We tried to adapt to an environment that included the time storm and, in the process, learned to manipulate that environment, including the time storm, as far as we could. Right now the time storm makes possible a number of things we couldn't have unless it existed. At the same time, by existing, it continues to threaten to kill us. So, we're doing our best to control it. Note, we no longer want to wipe it out; we want to keep it, but under our domination.'

'Like taming a tiger,' I said, 'to be a watchdog.'

He frowned for a second. Then his face cleared.

'Oh,' he said. 'I see what you mean. Yes. We want to tame and use it.'

'So do I,' I said.

He looked unhappy.

'I was hoping,' he said, 'that you'd be beginning to appreciate the difference between someone of your time and people of the present. We'll be arriving shortly, in a matter of hours in fact; and I thought that, maybe, with the chance we've had to talk on the way here, you'd be seeing the vast gulf between what you know and are, and what anyone from the present would have to know and be.'

'It's not that vast,' I said. 'Now, wait a minute—'

He had opened his mouth, ready to speak again. When I held up my hand, he closed it again – but not with a particularly comfortable look on his face.

'All right, look,' I said. 'You've evolved a whole science. But anyone born into this time of yours can learn it in that person's lifetime, isn't that so?'

'Oh, of course,' Obsidian said. 'I didn't mean to sound as if the hard knowledge itself was something more than you could learn. In fact we've got techniques and equipment which could teach you what you'd need to know in a matter of days. But the point's that the knowledge by itself wouldn't be any use to you; because to use it requires the sort of understanding of the time storm that only growing up and being educated in the present can give you.'

'What you're saying,' I told him, 'is that aside from the intellectual knowledge that's necessary, I'd need the kind of understanding that comes from knowing a culture and a philosophy. And the cultural part is simply the same philosophy expressed on a non-symbolic level. So, what it boils down to is understanding your basic philosophy; and you've just finished telling me that that's been shaped by contact over generations with the time storm. All right, I've had contact with the time storm. I've had some contact with you. And I tell you that your culture and your philosophy isn't that much different from what I've already understood myself where the time storm forces are concerned.'

He shook his head.

'Marc,' he said, 'you're aiming right at a disappointment.'

'We'll see,' I answered.

'Yes.' He sighed. 'I'm very much afraid we will.'

Just as there had been no sensation of taking off when we had left Earth, so there was no sensation of landing when we got to our destination. Simply, without warning, Obsidian broke off something he was saying about the real elements of art existing fully in the concept of the piece of artwork alone – a point with which I was disagreeing, because I could not conceive of art apart from its execution. What if the statue of Rodin's Thinker could be translated into a string of symbolic marks? Would the intellectual appreciation of those marks begin to approach the pleasure of actually seeing, let alone feeling, the original statue with whatever microscopic incidentals of execution had resulted from the cuttings of the sculptor's tools and the textural characteristics of the original material? The idea was absurd – and it was not the only absurd idea that I had heard from Obsidian, for all his personal likeableness and intelligence, during the last five days.

At any rate, he broke off speaking suddenly and got to his feet in one limber movement from the cushion on which he had been seated cross-legged.

'We're here,' he said.

I looked over at the picture window and still saw only a starscape in the picture window. Just one more, if once again different, starscape – with only a single unusual element about it, which was a large, dark area just to the right and below the centre of it. Porniarsk was also watching the window from his post near one of the control consoles, and he saw the direction of my attention.

He trundled across the room and tapped with a tentacle at the screen surface over the dark area.

'S Doradus,' he said.

Obsidian turned his head a little sharply to look at the avatar

'Aren't we down on some planetary surface?' I asked Obsidian.

'Oh yes,' he said. The starscape winked out, to be replaced with a picture of a steep hillside littered with huge boulders. The sky was a dark blue overhead and what looked like beehives, coloured a violent green and up to twenty or thirty feet in height, were growing amongst the rocks. 'The scene you were just looking at is of space seen from the vantage point of this landing spot. Haven't I mentioned that we nowadays have a tendency to surround ourselves with the type of scene that suits us at the moment, no matter where we are in a real sense?'

'You like the Earth forest scene yourself, then, Obsidian?'

'Not primarily,' he answered me, 'but I supposed you did.'

'Thanks,' I said. I felt gratitude and a touch of humbleness. 'I appreciate it.'

'Not at all. May I introduce—' he turned abruptly to face the several individuals who were now joining us from somewhere outside the illusion of the Earth forest.

There were only four of them; although my first impression when I saw them entering was that there were more. None of them wore anything resembling clothes or ornaments. In the lead was what I took to be a completely ordinary, male human, until I saw there was a sort of bony ridge, or crest, about three inches deep at the nape of his neck, running from his spine at midback up to the back of his head and blending into his skull there. He was somewhat taller than Obsidian. Next was a motley-coloured individual with patches of skin almost as light as my own intermixed with other patches of rust-red and milk chocolate darkness. This one was less obviously humanoid, but seemed plainly female, and of about Obsidian's size. The third was something like a squid-crab hybrid, with the squid growing out of the back shell of the crab – and he, or she – or for that matter, it – entered the room floating on a sort of three-foot high pedestal. I would have guessed this third individual's weight at about a hundred pounds or so, Earthside.

The fourth was a jet-black, pipestem-limbed humanoid about three feet tall, with a sour face and no more hair than Obsidian. I was secretly relieved to find that everybody with a generally human shape, nowadays, was not someone I had to get a stiff neck looking up to. As they all came into the room, its area expanded imperceptibly until we stood in the middle of a space perhaps thirty by forty feet. The illusion of Earth forest now only occupied a portion of the perimeter about us. In the remaining space were four other scenes, ranging from a sort of swamp to a maroon-sand desertscape with tall, whitish buttes sticking up dramatically out of the level plain below.

I was so interested in watching all this that I almost missed the fact that Obsidian was trying to introduce me.

'Sunrise—' this was the individual with the neck crest. 'Dragger—' (the particoloured female); 'one of the Children of Life—' (the squid-crab) and 'Angel—' (the sour-faced, little black individual).

'It's a remarkable thing to be able to meet you,' I told them. 'I'd like you to know I appreciate the chance.'

'Compliments are unnecessary,' said Dragger, in a somewhat rusty voice. 'I suppose we can call you Marc without offending you?'

'Certainly,' I said. 'You speak my language very well.'

'It wouldn't have been practical to have you learn ours,' Dragger said. She seemed to be the speaker for the group. 'If you don't mind, we'll get on with the test. Would you give your attention to that panel just behind you?'

I turned. The panel she was pointing at was about three feet high by five feet long, sitting on top of a boxlike piece of equipment that had appeared with their entrance. As I looked, an elliptical pool of blackness seemed to flood out and cover the corner areas of the slab. I stepped close to it and found myself looking into, rather than at, the darkness, as if it had depth and I was looking down into a three-dimensional space.

As I focussed in, deeper into the darkness, I saw that it was alive with shifting, moving fans of lights, something like the aurora borealis with its successions of milky colours spreading out over the northern sky at night. These lights I watched now moved much faster than the northern lights I was used to, and their pattern was much more complex. But, otherwise, they were remarkably similar.

They were similar to something else, too. I stared at them, unable to quite zero in on what they reminded me of. Then it burst on me.

'Of course!' I said, turning to Dragger and the others. 'Those are time storm force line patterns, extremely slowed, but still force line patterns in action.'

The four of them looked at me. Then Dragger turned to Obsidian.

'Thank you, Obsidian,' she said. She looked back at me. 'Thank you, Marc.'

She turned around and began to lead the rest out.

I stared after her, and at the rest of them.

'Wait a second!' I said.

'Marc,' said Obsidian behind me. 'Marc, I said you might be working yourself up for a disappointment—'

'Disappointment!' I said. 'The hell with that! I said they're force line patterns, and they are. Come on back here – Dragger, the rest of you. You can't just walk out. You owe me an explanation, if I want one. I've picked up enough about your time to know that!'

They slowed and stopped. For a moment they stood in a group, and I had the strong impression that a discussion was going on, although I could not hear a word or see a lip movement. Then they turned back into the room, Dragger still leading, and came to face me again.

'There is no explanation to give,' Dragger said. 'We wished to test you for a sensitivity we feel is necessary, if you and your group are to be allowed to stay in the present. Unfortunately, you don't seem to show that sensitivity.'

'And how do you figure that?' I said. 'You showed me a pattern of time storm forces in action, I told you what they were – where's the indication of a lack of sensitivity on my part?'

'Marc,' said Dragger, 'I'm sorry to say that what you looked at was not what you said it was.'

'Not a pattern of force lines from the time storm?'

'No. I'm sorry.' Once more she turned to go and the others shifted with her.

'Damn it, come back here!'

'Marc—' It was Porniarsk, now, trying to interpose.

'Porniarsk, stay out of this! You too, Obsidian! Dragger, you others, turn around. Come back! I don't know what the idea is, your trying to lie to me like this. But it's not working. You think I don't know time storm forces when I see them? Obsidian's been told what I've done and been through with Porniarsk here. You must know what I told him – or didn't you do your homework? If you do know what I told him, you know you can't get away with showing me a pattern of the storm lines and claiming it's something else.'

The four stood facing each other in silence. After a second, Obsidian took three quick steps across the floor and joined them. They stood motionless and voiceless, facing each other for a long minute. Then they all turned to face me.

'Marc,' said Obsidian, 'I assure you, that was not a representation of lines of force from what you call the time storm. It was a projected pattern of conceptual rhythms common to all minds in our present-day culture. If you had shown a capability for responding to those rhythms, the pattern would have evoked some common images in your mind – water, gas, star, space ... and so on. Apparently, it didn't; so we have to conclude that you don't have the capability to respond in modern terms. That's all. You don't gain anything by this insisting that you were looking at a representation of temporal force lines.'

'I *see!*' I said.

Because suddenly I did. And suddenly I was so sure I was right that I went ahead without even bothering to check the words out in my head before I said them.

'In fact,' I said, 'I see a lot of things. One of them is that I understand you better than you understand me – and I'm going to prove that right now. You see, I know you can't sluff me off and send me back with that answer, if I say the proper words. Your responsibility reflex won't let you; and I'm going to say the proper words now. The words are – you and these people here, and everyone else you know, have one galloping cultural blindness. You're dead blind in an area where I'm not; and I can see it where you can't, because I'm standing outside your culture and looking in at it. Your whole set of rules is based on the fact that you can't deny me a hearing on that point. Now that it's been raised, you have to settle conclusively whether I'm right about what I'm saying, or wrong. If I'm wrong, then you can get rid of me. But if I'm right, then you, all of you, are going to have to learn different – from me. Am I right?'

I stopped speaking and waited. They merely stood there.

'Well?' I said. 'Am I right, or aren't I?' Am I entitled to a hearing or not?'

They looked at each other and stood for a moment longer. Then they all turned back to me.

'Marc,' said Obsidian, 'we'll have to consult about this. In theory at least, you're right. You'll get your hearing. But now we have to talk the whole matter over, and that's going to take a little time. Meanwhile, because of the importance of your challenge to us, it seems you're going to have to learn our way of communicating after all.'

35

It developed that the reason they had not tried to teach me, and Porniarsk for that matter, how to communicate in their way was because of an assumption on their part that, conceptually, we were not up to such education. But since I had now told them that I believed the shoe was on the other foot, and that I knew things of which they couldn't conceive, their original reason for not teaching me had become indefensible. In short, whether I could actually handle their language effectively, or not, I had to be given a chance to explain myself in it, so that the accusation couldn't arise that I had failed to make my point because I had not been given the chance to state it in fully understandable terms.

That much established, the actual process of learning turned out to be easy. As Obsidian had said, they had devices and techniques for teaching. Within twenty-four hours, Porniarsk and I could handle all four modes of their communication. These were sound; signal (limb-waving, etc.); attitudinal (which was really another form of signal, since it meant communicating with physical attitudes – body language); and modification-of-surroundings, which essentially meant communicating by playing games with the surrounding scenery, whether illusory or real.

These four modes actually duplicated each other. That is, they had each been single, exclusive methods of communication originally, and had been combined as amplifying redundancies. Actually, I would be able to make my argument completely in the verbal mode. But if I should be questioned on a particular verbal statement, I could now nail down what I meant by repeating what I had said in one or more of the other modes. In theory, any statement made in as few as two modes established its message beyond any possibility of ambiguity.

So, I was ready for argument in twenty-four hours. The debate was not called to order, however, for the equivalent of three more Earth days. I was not too unhappy about that because it gave me time to do some thinking. Under pressure, I had jumped to a conclusion, there in that moment when Dragger and the others had turned to walk out; and that jump had been genuine inspiration. But now I needed to build that inspiration up into a solid, cohesive argument.

When the meeting was finally called to order once more, the number of the universal community's members present had grown from five individuals to thirty-two. The space that arranged itself around us, consequently, was large and had sloping sides around the flat central area; so the spectators looked down on Dragger and me as if they were a crowd in a small arena or a lecture hall.

Dragger began by replaying what had happened on our first meeting. It was a little strange to stand there and see myself, in apparently solid replica, demanding that the five come back and listen to me. When this reached an end with Obsidian's last words to me, the illusory figures of our former selves winked out and Dragger turned to me.

'You're going to point out a cultural blindness to us, Marc,' she said. 'Go ahead.'

'All right,' I said. 'As briefly as possible, then – the first evidence I noticed of a cultural blindness was during the first few days that Obsidian and I talked. We found out then that he had trouble under-standing what I meant, in spite of the fact that he'd been trained by your equipment. On the other hand, I was understanding him fairly well, in spite of the fact that he was trying to gather information on my culture, rather than teaching me about yours. You might want to check your records on that, sometime, to see what I mean.'

'We can show it,' put in Dragger.

The illusory figures appeared again. This time, they were Obsidian and myself talking back outside the summer palace. This was a bit of assistance I had not figured on. I stood there, as my image pointed out to Obsidian that he was like someone who had grown up thinking every-one spoke only one language and was having difficulty entertaining the idea that there might be other words possible for a familiar object.

The second set of figures disappeared.

'This started me thinking,' I went on. 'From the beginning, in your contact with us, you've assumed the only possible solution to my group existing in the same time with you people would be for us to adopt everything that was part of your culture and discard anything of ours that didn't fit. As with the language situation, your thought seemed to be that there was one, and only one, *right* way of doing things.'

I stopped and looked at Dragger, giving her a chance to argue this point. But she said nothing and seemed to be merely waiting. I went on.

'As far as I can gather,' I said, 'you wouldn't have had any intention of testing me for present-day abilities, even to this small extent you tried here a few days ago, except that Obsidian had turned up a couple of anomalies in the characters of me and my people that – because it's a cultural imperative on you to base your conclusions on certainties – made it necessary to check. The first anomaly was that I said we had moved ourselves to your present time deliberately, using the time storm forces to do so.'

I stopped again and looked at Dragger.

'Would you like to replay that particular conversation?' said Dragger. 'Very well.'

The figures of myself, Ellen, and Obsidian appeared before us.

'*... And, of course, we wanted to collect data toward understanding the accident that brought you here,*' Obsidian was saying.

'*Accident? We came here deliberately.*'

'*You did?*'

'*That's right,*' I answered. '*I'd probably better take you down to see the lab and Porniarsk. Sorry, maybe I'm getting the cart before the horse. But after expecting you every day from the moment we landed here, and not having you show up until now—*'

'*Expecting me when you arrived?*'

'*That's right. We came here because I wanted to contact you people who were doing something about the time storm—*'

'*Just a moment. Forgive me,*' said the figure of Obsidian; and he disappeared.

The figures of Ellen and me also winked out of existence.

'That bit of conversation,' I went on to Dragger and the rest of the audience, 'shook Obsidian up, because here I was talking about deliberately making use of time storm forces back in a time long before anyone was supposed to be able to make use of them. The second anomaly, and the one that made it imperative that you test me, was the fact that Obsidian caught me making what I call a universal-identification – I note, by the way, that this is one area of my vocabulary in your languages that you haven't filled in for me. You have to have a term for it yourselves—'

'We have,' said Dragger. 'You just used it. We term it "universal-identification".'

'Sorry,' I said. 'My apologies. So you didn't deliberately leave that part of my vocabulary out, then. At any rate, the point is, once more Obsidian had discovered that I could do something that I shouldn't be able to do, being from as far back in prehistory as I was. But, making use of time storm forces to move in time or space, and the concept of the individual being able to share the identity of the universe or vice versa, are things you've believed belong to your time, not mine.'

'So far,' said Dragger, as I paused to look at her, 'I hear nothing to disagree with. You must have more to say than this, though, I assume?'

'I have,' I said. 'Let's call me fish and you mammal, in the sense that I'm, in effect, your prehistoric ancestor. When you found I could breathe air the same way you did and had legs rather than fins, you had to classify me and those with me as something more than fish. So you thought you'd check me out to find if I was mammalian. But your first check turned up the fact that I'm an egg-laying creature. Since mammals, in your experience, don't lay eggs, you assumed I must be a fish, after all. It didn't occur to you that I might be something like a platypus.'

I had used the human word for 'platypus'; because there was no alternative in their four communication modes. It was true their spoken language gave me the building blocks to construct an equivalent word; but from their point of view, that equivalent would have been a nonsense noise. Dragger and the rest stared at me in silence.

'Platypus,' I said. 'An animal from my planet. A *monotreme*—' Now there was a word that was translatable into some sense in their language. Dragger spoke up.

'Just a minute, Marc,' she said.

There was a delay while the audience got a thorough briefing on the fauna of Earth in general, and that of Australia in particular.

'It's understood, then?' I said, when this was over. 'The platypus lays eggs, but nonetheless it's a hair-wearing, lactating mammal.'

'Primitive mammal,' said Dragger.

'Don't strain my analogy,' I said. 'The point is, there was a possibility of my people and me belonging in a category which your culture had made you blind to.'

'That's an assumption,' said Dragger.

'No,' I said. 'It's not. It'd be an assumption only if I was wrong about what you showed me having anything to do with the movement of time storm forces. Now, you were right in saying there was no connection between what you showed me and the storm. But in the overall sense, I was the one who was right, and you were wrong. Because the connection *is* there; and you're so culturally blind to it that I'm willing to bet that, even in these last three days, none of you have checked out the possibility that that connection might actually be there.'

There was a second – only a second – of silence.

'You're correct. There hasn't been any check made of a possible connection,' said Dragger. 'On the other hand, we've nothing but your guess that the connection exists.'

'I told you the last time I saw you,' I said, 'it's no guess. I'm neither fish nor fowl. I'm a monotreme. I've learned to use the time storm and to make a personal identification with the universe entirely without and apart from the history, culture, and techniques that you people have developed. I can read the time storm by reading patterns of movement. All movement falls into patterns.'

I looked around the room at the spectators.

'You're probably not aware of it,' I said, 'but the ways you've grouped and sorted yourselves around me, here, show certain patterns; and from those patterns, with what I now know about your culture and language, I can see a habit of social sorting by individual specialities or abilities.'

'If I didn't have that cultural information, I'd still be seeing these patterns, I just wouldn't know what they implied. In the case of your groupings here, I now do know; and in the case of the time storm forces also, I do know.'

'This is assertion only, Marc,' said Dragger.

'No. It's a case of my being on the outside of your culture, so I'm able to see clearly something you're refusing to see. You people have struggled with the time storm for hundreds of generations. That struggle literally created your community the way it is now and dominated every element of it. It's quite true the panel you showed me was supposed to be showing patterns of conceptual rhythms common to your time and culture; and that I didn't recognize them as such because my own conceptual rhythms aren't like that.'

I looked around at them.

'Marc,' said Dragger, 'have we waited these several days and gathered together here only to hear you admit that we were right to begin with?'

'No!' I said. 'Because you're wrong. What I saw, and recognized, *were* time storm force patterns. You, all of you, couldn't realize that because you don't recognize how much the time storm's become a part of you over this long struggle – part of your body, mind, and culture. Your conceptual rhythms *are* time storm rhythms. You don't see that because they're so much a part of you; you take them for granted. I can see it, because I'm standing outside your culture, looking at you. I'm the most valuable mind you've got in this present time of yours; and you'd better appreciate that fact!'

I was almost shouting at them now. This was a strong statement in their terms; but I needed to wake them up, to make them *hear*.

'Don't take my word for it!' I said. 'Check those conceptual rhythms on your instrument against the patterns of the time storm forces and pick up the identity between them for yourselves!'

I stopped talking. In my own past time, a moment of this would have provoked a buzz of unbelief from the spectators, or outcries against my idea or myself – anything but the way these individuals reacted, which was in a thoughtful silence. There was no visible evidence that I had attacked the very base of the culture they had always taken for granted.

But I knew what was happening in their minds. I knew, because I now knew more than a little about how they thought and about their obligation to consider any possibility for truth which that same culture put upon them. I knew they had been jarred, and jarred badly, by what I had just told them. But my knowledge of that was about all the emotional satisfaction I was likely to get from the situation. As far as appearances went, they showed no more reaction than they might have if I had told them that I planned on not shaving when I got up tomorrow.

The meeting was breaking up. Some of the figures in the stands were simply disappearing, some were walking off through visible doorways, some were simply melting into the illusions of surrounding scenery. I found myself alone with Porniarsk, Obsidian, and Dragger.

'We'll check, of course,' said Dragger to me. 'Tell me, Marc, what is it exactly you want?'

'I want to fight the time storm. Myself. Personally.'

'I have to say I can't see how that can be anything but a complete impossibility,' she said. 'On the other hand, there are always new things to be learned.'

36

'They're a great people, Marc,' said Porniarsk, once we were alone again in the ordinary configuration of Obsidian's quarters – which Obsidian had, by now, largely given over to our own private use. 'You shouldn't forget that.'

'You think they are?' I said.

I heard him as if from a middle distance. I was once more as I had been when we had just left Earth on the way here in Obsidian's quarters; like someone who had trained years for a single conflict. I was light and empty inside, remote and passionless, hollow of everything but the thought of the battle that would come, which nothing could avert or delay.

'Yes,' he said, 'they've survived the time storm. They've learned to live with it, even to use it for their own benefit, and they've made a community of innumerable races, a community that's a single, working unit. Those are great achievements. They deserve some honour.'

'Let other people honour them, then,' I said. It was still as if I was talking to him from some distance off. 'I've got nothing left except for what I've still got waiting for me.'

'Yes,' he said. He sounded oddly sad. 'Your foe. But these people aren't your foe, Marc. Not even the time storm's your foe.'

'You're wrong there,' I told him.

'No.' He shook his ponderous head.

I laughed.

'Marc,' he said, 'listen to me. I'm alive, and that alone surprises me. I'd expected I'd stop living, once I was taken from the time in which Porniarsk existed. But it seems, to my own deep interest, that in some way I've got an independent life now, a life of my own. But even if this is true, it's a single life only. I was constructed, not engendered. I can't have progeny. My life's only this small moment in which I live it; and I'm concerned with what and whom I share that moment. In this case, it's you, Ellen, Bill, Doc, and the rest.'

'Yes,' I said. At another time, what he had said might have moved me deeply. But at the moment, I was too remote, too concentrated. I heard and understood what he told me; but his words were like a listing of academic facts, off somewhere on the horizon of my existence, shrunken by their distance from what obsessed me utterly.

'Because of this,' he said, 'I'm concerned with what you're planning to do. I'm afraid for you, Marc. I want to save what I've got no other words to call but your soul. If that's to be saved, sooner or later, you'll have to reconcile yourself with things as they are. And unless you do it in time, you'll lose your battle. You'll die.'

'No,' I said. The need for sleep was deep in me and I only wanted to end the talking. 'I won't lose. I can't afford to. Now I've got to get some rest. I'll talk to you after I wake up, Porniarsk.'

But when I finally woke up, Dragger was standing over the cushion on which I lay.

'Marc,' she said, 'your training as a temporal engineer is going to begin at once; and if you can absorb that, you'll be taken out to where the line of battle runs with the time storm forces.'

I was suddenly fully awake and on my feet. She was going on, still talking. Porniarsk was also to be given the training. This was a bonus, because, in no way, had I dared to hope I could win for him also what I had wanted for myself. But now he, too, would have the chance. There was a comfort for me in the sight of his ugly, heavy bulldog shape. He was like a talisman from home, a good omen.

Obsidian took us far across space again. For the first time we came to another vehicle. It was like a raft the size of a football field, with some sort of invisible, impalpable shield, like a dome, over it to keep in an atmosphere that would preserve workable temperatures and pressures for the massive engineering equipment it carried. Barring the star scene that arched over us in every direction, it was like nothing so much as being in the engine room of an incredibly monstrous battleship.

All the way out to this star raft in Obsidian's quarters, and for nearly two weeks of Earth time after we got there, Porniarsk and I were force-fed with information from the teaching machines Obsidian had talked about. It was an unnerving process. We were like blank cassette tapes in a high speed duplicator. There was no physical sensation of being packed with instruction; and in fact, the information itself did not become usable until later, when contact with some of the actual engineering work going on aboard the raft tapped it, the way a keg of wine might be tapped. But at the same time, there was a psychic consciousness of mental lumber being added to our mental warehouses that was curiously exhausting in its own way. The sensation it produced was something like that which can come from weeks of overwork and nervous strain, to the point where the mind seems almost physically numb.

How Porniarsk reacted to it was something I had no way of knowing, because we were kept separated. Emotionally isolated by my own purpose, I was generally indifferent to what was being done to me, physically or mentally; and when, in due time, the process of information-feeding ended, I fell into a deep sleep that must have lasted well beyond the six hours of my normal slumber period. When I woke, suddenly, all the knowledge that had been pumped into me exploded from the passive state into the active.

I had opened my eyes in the same unstressed state of thoughtlessness that normally follows a return from the mists of sleep. I was at peace, unthinking – and then, suddenly the reality of the universe erupted all about me. I was all at once bodiless, blind, and lost, falling through infinity, lifetimes removed from any anchor point of sanity or security.

I tumbled; aware – too much aware – of all things. Panic built in me like a deep-sea pressure against the steel bulkhead of my reason, threatening to burst through and destroy me. There was too much, all at once, crowding my consciousness. Suddenly I had too much understanding, too much awareness ...

I felt the pressure of it starting to crack me apart; and then, abruptly, my long-held purpose came to my rescue. Suddenly I was mobilized and fighting back, controlling the overwhelming knowledge. I had not come this far in time and space and learning to disintegrate now in an emotional spasm. The universe was no bigger than my own mind. I had discovered that for myself, before this. I had touched the universe, not once, but several times previously. It was no great frightening and unknowable entity. It was part of me, as I was part of it. A thing did not frighten itself. An arm did not panic at discovering it was attached to a body.

I surged back. I matched pressure for pressure. I held.

But my mind was still far removed from my body, back on the raft. It felt as if, at the same time, I was floating motionless, and flying at great speed through infinity. My vantage point was somewhere between the island universes, out in intergalactic space. In a sense, it was as if I stood on the peak of a high mountain, from which I could see the misty limits of all time and space. Almost, it seemed, I could see to the ends of the universe; and for the first time, the total action of the time storm activity became a single pattern in my mind.

'So, Marc,' said a voice – or a thought. It was both and neither, here where there were no bodies and no near stars – 'you survived.'

It was Dragger speaking. I looked for her, instinctively, and did not see her. But I knew she was there.

'Yes,' I said. I was about to tell her that I had never intended anything else, but a deeper honesty moved me at the last second. 'I had to.'

'Evidently. Do you understand the temporal engineering process, now?'

'I think so,' I said; and as I said it, the knowledge that had been pumped into me began to blend with what I was now experiencing, and the whole effort they were making unrolled into order and relationship, like a blueprint in my mind.

'This isn't the way I imagined it,' I said. 'You're actually trying to stop the time storm, by physical efforts, to reverse its physical effect on the universe.'

'In a sense.'

'In a sense? All right, say in a sense. But it's still physical reversal. To put it crudely, in the sort of terms you're most familiar with, the normal decay of entropy began to stop and reverse itself when the universe stopped expanding. Then, when the farther stars and the outer galaxies started falling back here and there, they set up areas where entropy was increasing rather than decaying. Isn't that right, Dragger? So it had to be these stresses, these conflicts between the two states of entropy in specific areas, that spawned the nova implosions and triggered the time faults, so that on one side of a sharp line, time was moving one way, and on the other, a different way. So that's what made the time storm! But I assumed you'd be attacking the storm directly to cure it.'

'We're after the root cause.'

'Are you, Dragger? But this way – this is using sheer muscle to mend things.'

'Do you know of a better way?'

'But – using energy to reverse the falling back of these physical bodies, to force them to move apart again? There ought to be some way that wouldn't require tapping another universe. Isn't that what you're doing – and tapping a tachyon universe at that? You're working with forces that can tear this universe apart.'

'I asked you,' repeated Dragger, 'do you know a better way?'

'No,' I said. 'But I've got to see this for myself. I can't believe you can control something that powerful.'

'Look, then,' said Dragger. 'S Doradus is only a thought away from us here.'

It was true. Merely by thinking of it, we were there, with no time spent in the movement. Bodiless, with Dragger bodiless beside me, I hung in space and looked at the great spherical darkness that was the massive engine enclosing the young blue-white giant star called S Doradus. It was an engine that trapped all the radiation from that vast sun, to use it as a focus point, a lens in the fabric of our universe, through which then flowed the necessary jet of energy from the tachyon universe that was being tapped for power – to push not only stars, but galaxies around.

A coldness took my mind. Through that lens, we were touching another place where every physical law, and time itself, was reversed from ours. As long as the lens aperture was controlled, as long as it remained small and unvarying, the reaction between the two universes was under command. But if the lens should tear and open further, under the forces it channelled, the energy flow could flash to proportions too great to be constrained. The fabric between the universes would break wide open; it would be mutual annihilation of both – annihilation in no-time.

'You see now,' said Dragger, 'why we didn't think it was possible for you to do this work. In fact, if you hadn't been able to make the conceptual jump that set you free to survey the situation, like this, there'd have been no point in even considering it.'

'Made the jump? Just a minute,' I said. 'This isn't something I've done all on my own. I must be getting some technological assistance to let my point of view go wheeling through infinite distances, like this.'

'Of course you are,' said Dragger. 'But the only person who could make it possible for your mind to endure such assistance was you, yourself. You're strong enough to endure the sense of dislocation involved. We didn't think you were. I didn't think you were. I was wrong.'

'I've got work I want to do,' I said. 'That helps.'

'A great deal, evidently. At any rate, Marc, you're one of a select group now. Less than a millionth of one per cent of all our people have the talent to do this work and endure the conditions under which it's done. Are you surprised we doubted that you could? An individual has to be born with the talent to be a temporal engineer. Evidently, you *were* born with it – millenia before there was such work.'

'I didn't know about this,' I said. 'That's true enough. But there were other things that called for the same kind of abilities.'

I was thinking of the stock market, of that part of me which could never rest until it had tracked down what it searched for; also, of that other part of me that had immediately recognized, in the time storm, an opponent waiting for me ...

My mind boggled suddenly and strangely, and shied away from

finishing that particular thought. Puzzled, I would have come back to it; but Dragger was talking to me again.

'Are you listening to me, Marc?'

'I'm listening,' I said. I returned my full attention to the moment, and our conversation, with an effort. 'Something bothers me, though. If it's pure technology at work, why is it talent's needed at all? Why is it only a few can do this? There must be more than a few who can endure the conditions, as you say.'

'There are,' she answered. 'And that's why you've got one more strength you have to demonstrate. We need people with a special talent because when we move stars, and more than stars, we make gross changes in the time storm forces. We don't have any technological device quick enough to safely measure and assess the effect of those changes on the stresses by which we control the flow of energy from the tachyon universe. If the pressure against which we're exerting our energy flow changes suddenly, the flow can increase, the lens may dilate, and you must have guessed what can happen then, before any adjustment can be made.'

'You mean the lens tearing open,' I said.

'That's right. Only minds able to read the pattern of the time storm forces, directly, can see danger coming fast enough to correct for it. We who are temporal engineers have to direct our stream of extra-universal energy and, at the same time, make sure that it doesn't get out of our control.'

She stopped speaking. Eyeless, I hung in space, watching the great darkness that was the engine, the dyson sphere enclosing S Doradus. My imagination pictured the unbelievable holocaust within that shell of collapsed matter and the Klein bottle forces, that made the core of a star millions of times the mass of our sun into a tiny rent in the fabric of a universe. I had thought I was equal to any dimensions that might exist in the battle I wanted to join; but the dimensions here were beyond imagination. I was less than a speck of dust to that stellar nucleus; and in turn, it was infinitesimal, to the point of nonexistence, compared to the two great opposed masses of energy between which it formed a bridge and a connection.

And I was going to share in the control of that bridge?

My courage stumbled. There was a limit, even to imagination; and here that limit was exceeded. I felt my view of the space around me growing obscured and tenuous. I was aware of Dragger, watching, judging me; and with remembrance of her presence, my guts came back to me. If she could stay and work here, so could I. There was nothing any life born in this universe could do, that I could not at least attempt.

The view of the space before me, and the mighty engine in it, firmed. It grew clear and sharp once more.

'You're still with us?' asked Dragger.

'Yes,' I said.

'Then there's only one more step to take,' she said. 'We'll test you on the line. If you don't succeed there, no one can help you. There'll be no way out.'

'I'm ready.'

We went forward, toward the dyson sphere. Bodiless, we passed, like thought through its material shell, through the Klein bottle forces, down into the sea of radiation beyond any description that was the enclosed star. We approached the core that was the lens. Here, ordinary vision was not possible. But with the help of the information that had been pumped into me, the lens area rendered itself to my mental perception as an elliptical opening, dark purple against a wall of searing blue-white light. The energy stuff of the other universe pouring through that opening, was invisible, but sensible. It rendered itself as a force of such speed and pressure that it would have felt solid to the touch, if touch had existed in that place and it had been safe to use it upon that inflow.

Dragger led me almost to the lip of the lens.

'Do you feel anything?' she asked.

'Yes,' I said.

There was an odd counter force at work here. In spite of the tremendous outflow, I felt something like an undertow, as well, sucking us toward the lens. From where I felt it, it was nothing I could not resist; but I did not want to get closer.

'The downdraft,' said Dragger – the word she used in her communication form was not a precise or scientific term, but a casual one, almost a nickname for what I felt, 'does it bother you?'

'Yes,' I said; for the touch of its pull toward the open lens filled me with uneasiness. 'I don't know why.'

'It bothers us all,' she said, 'and none of us is sure why. It's no problem here, but out at operations point it becomes something you'll need to watch out for. Now, meet the others working in this area.'

She spoke in turn to at least a couple of dozen other identities. My stored information recognized the symbols that were their personal identification as they answered her and spoke to me. Our conversation seemed to be mind to mind, here in the heart of the star. But actually, as I knew, we were talking together through the purely technological communications centre of the space raft where my body and Porniarsk's were. Most of those I spoke to had been at my full-dress argument session, previously. I was a little surprised to realize how many, there, had been temporal engineers; although, now that I thought of it, it was only logical that most of them should have been, since they would be the ones most concerned with me.

'Marc is going on line with us, out at operations point,' Dragger said. 'If he works out, there, we've got another operator. Marc, are you ready to go?'

'Yes,' I said.

We withdrew from the lens, from the star and the engine. I had expected that I, at least, would be returning to my body on the raft, from which I would then go by ordinary, physical means to the operations point. But our identities instead started moving out along the energy projection from the engine, through interstellar space from the lesser Magellanic Cloud, where S Doradus was, toward our own galaxy.

'Your bodies will be sent back,' she said.

'Bodies?'

I woke to the fact that the identity of Porniarsk had just joined us.

'Porniarsk!' I said. 'You're going on the line, too?'

'Only as an observer, I'm afraid,' he answered. 'As I think I've said to you in the past, I lack creativity. And a certain amount of creativity is required for direct work in temporal engineering. But in all other respects, I'm qualified; and our instructors thought you, at least, might find me useful to have with you.'

'Dragger?' I said.

'Yes?'

'Thank you.'

'The decision wasn't mine,' she answered. 'But I think it's a good one. In spite of the fact you've passed all tests, Marc, you're still very much an unknown quantity to us. Aside from whatever advantage it'll be to you to have your friend with you, it'll make the rest of us feel more secure to know that there's an observer ready to tell us what happens if you do have trouble.'

'Enlightened selfishness,' I said.

'Of course.'

The trip we were now taking was a curious one. My newly educated memory told me it would have been thoroughly possible to make an immediate jump over the hundred and forty thousand light-years of distance from the neighbourhood of S Doradus to our own galaxy. But Dragger evidently had a reason for taking me over the distance slowly, following the route of the energy being sent from the engine to the retreating matter of our galaxy; and now I began to understand what that reason was.

The energy from the tachyon universe was not projected in the form it was received, like a light beam aimed over a hundred and forty thousand light-years of distance. Instead, it was converted to a time force line, itself – an extension across space of form without mass, which would not be converted back into energy until it touched the solid material at its destination; and even then, it would be absorbed, rather than felt, as an outside force, by that material.

The form in which it was extended, however, was designed to increase in cross section until it was as wide as the galaxy to which it was being sent. Crudely, then, the energy flow could be represented as a funnel shape, with the small end at the lens of S Doradus and the width of the funnel increasing over the light-years of intergalactic distance between lens and galaxy, until the large end could contain our whole galaxy, including its spiral arms.

We were following, then, alongside this expanding funnel; and as we travelled, I became acutely conscious of its steady growth, and of a corresponding increase in the uneasiness I had felt about the downdraft. And this was ridiculous; because here, with the energy converted into a massless form, there was no downdraft to be felt. Dragger's reason for moving Porniarsk and me this slowly along the route of the projected energy was becoming apparent.

I set my teeth against the reaction. It did not let itself be beaten down easily, because there was something very old about it; as if I had suddenly come face to face with a dire wolf out of prehistory, lurking among the shadows of some well-groomed, civilized park, at sunset. But it was only one more enemy to conquer; and gradually, as I faced it, it ceased to gain against me and then finally retreated. It was all but gone when Dragger spoke.

'How do you feel, Porniarsk?'

'I'm filled with wonder,' said Porniarsk.

'Outside of that, nothing?'

'Nothing,' he answered.

'And you, Marc?'

'Something,' I said. 'But I think I've got it licked.'

She did not say any more until we came, at last, to the edges of our own galaxy and moved in among its stars, ourselves now within the mouth of the funnel.

'When possible,' she said, 'we give the individual engineer a sector of work that includes their own home world. Your sector, Marc and Porniarsk, will include the world from which Obsidian brought you to us. Just now, there's no work going on in it. For the moment, no changes in the temporal forces are appearing here, although the earlier forces aren't balanced fully except in the local area of your world where you balanced them yourself, we understand, back before we have records of the storm. But there are going to be forces building up farther in toward the galaxy's centre in about nine months of your local time. You'll have that many months to study your sector. Your bodies are being returned there and you'll be able to spend some time in them. Obsidian's returning them and bringing in the equipment you'll need individually to work in this sector.'

We were in sight of Sol, now; and to my eyes, the star scene had a familiar look that moved me more deeply than I would have expected it could.

'I was told of one more test to be passed back here,' said Porniarsk.

'There's one,' said Dragger, 'but not for you – for Marc. Marc, in the final essential, the only way we'll ever know whether you can work with the time storm is to see you work with it. Only, if it turns out you can't, it'll almost certainly destroy you. That's why this is the last test; because it's the one that can't be taken under other than full risk conditions.'

'Fencing with naked weapons,' I said.

I had not meant to say it out loud, for one reason because I did not think Dragger would know what I was talking about; but she surprised me.

'Exactly,' she said. 'And now, I'll get back to my own work. Marc, Porniarsk, watch out for the downdraft, now that you're sensitized to it. It seems diffuse and weak out here; but don't forget it's always with you, whether you're in space like this, or down on a planet surface. Like any subtle pressure, it can either wear you down slowly, or build up to the point where it can break you.'

'How soon will Obsidian return, so we can have our bodies back?' Porniarsk asked.

'Soon. No more than a matter of hours now. Perhaps, in terms of your local time, half a day.'

'Good,' said Porniarsk. 'We'll see you again.'

'Yes,' she said. 'Before the next buildup of forces that affects this sector.'

'Goodbye, Dragger,' I said. 'Thanks.'

'There's no reason for thanks. Goodbye, Marc. Goodbye, Porniarsk.'

'Goodbye, Dragger,' Porniarsk said.

She was suddenly gone. As we had been talking, we had drawn on into the Solar System, until we now hung invisibly above the Earth at low orbit height of less than two hundred miles above its surface.

'I'd like to go down, even without our bodies and make sure everything's been going well,' said Porniarsk.

'Yes,' I said; then checked myself. '– No.'

'No?'

'Something's sticking in my mind,' I said. 'I don't like it. Dragger was talking about this sector being affected by a buildup of time forces farther in toward the centre of the galaxy, in about nine months.'

'If you'll consult the same information I had impressed on me,' said Porniarsk, mildly, 'you'll see that the area of space she was talking about is quite large. It'd be reasonable to assume that the chance of our own solar system being strongly affected by that buildup should be rather small—'

'I don't like it, though,' I said. 'I've got a feeling...'

I stopped.

'Yes?' said Porniarsk.

'Just a feeling. Just a sort of uneasy hunch,' I said. 'That's why I didn't say anything about it to Dragger – it's too wispy an idea. But I think I'd like to take a look at the forces of that full area from close up, out here, before I go down to Earth. You go ahead. It won't take me much longer to do that than the few hours we have to kill, anyway, before Obsidian gets here with our carcasses; and nobody's going to realize we're around until then. You go ahead. I'll be along.'

'If that's what you want,' said Porniarsk. 'You don't need me with you?'

'No reason for you to come at all,' I said. 'Go ahead down. Check up on things. You can check up for both of us.'

'Well, then. If that's what you want,' said Porniarsk.

I had no way of telling that he had gone; but in any case, I did not wait to make sure he was. Even while I had been talking to him, the uneasy finger of concern scratching at my mind had increased its pressure. I turned away from the Earth and the solar system, to look south, east, west, and north about the galactic plane at the time storm forces in action there.

37

It was not just the forces themselves I wanted to study. It was true that they would have progressed considerably since I had last viewed them in the tank of Porniarsk's lab; but that tank had still given me patterns from which I could mentally extrapolate to the present with a fair certainty of getting the present picture of matters, in general. But what concerned me was how those patterns would look in the light of my new knowledge; not only of the engine around S Doradus and the lens there, but of the downdraft as well. The downdraft worried me – if only for the fact that it had had the capacity to disturb me, gut-wise as well as mentally, when I had encountered it.

The situation I found in the area when I examined it was one in which the sectors were established within force lines that had been stabilized by the universal community, so that they might be used by members of that community in physical travel amongst stars. I was now able to trace with no difficulty the first twenty-nine force line time shifts Obsidian's quarters had used in carrying us to the testing by Dragger and the others. I could have continued to trace them all the way to our destination; but right now, I was concerned only with the situation in the area to which Dragger had assigned me.

Between the force lines, stability did not exist – except in our own area around Earth where we had produced it ourselves. Struck by a sudden curiosity, I checked the Earth's balance of forces with what I now knew about the time storm and satisfied myself that the present balance was not my doing. My original balance had evidently lasted far longer than I had expected – in fact, for several hundred years. But since that time, it had been periodically renewed by an outside agency. I was puzzled for a second that Porniarsk had not picked up this evidence of outside time storm control earlier than the present period. Then I remembered that the search had been made by the computer mind of the tank; and undoubtedly Porniarsk, like myself, had never bothered to instruct it to consider a continuing state of inaction, in what was already a nonstorm area, as an anomaly.

Within the fixed boundary lines of the stabilized force lines set up to be used for cross-space transportation, the time storm had gone on in its normal pattern of developing and spreading temporal disintegration, until about three thousand years ago, when there began to be evidence of periodic checking of areas threatening to set off large-scale disturbances throughout the general, galaxy-wide pattern. This checking had apparently been so minor as to be essentially unnoticeable, until the cumulative effect of a number of such incidents began to show evidence of anomaly on the large, general scale; and the tank picked them up.

I studied the stabilized force lines; and I studied the earlier, smaller evidence of disturbance checking. What was gnawing at me, I finally decided, was the fact that corrections which were too small to be important, taken singly, could pile up to have a much more serious cumulative effect on the stress situation of the galactic area as a whole.

Moreover, this could kick back against the flow through the lens and cause exactly the sort of tearing and enlargement that was the everpresent danger there.

It was all very iffy. It was a chain reaction of possibilities, only – but I did not like the look of it. I swung back and forth mentally over the force line stress pattern in my sectors, trying to make it all add up in some other way than it had just done; but I kept getting the same answer.

What I was hunting for were those elements of patterns that would point me toward the evolution of one particular pattern, less than a year from the present moment. It was difficult and frustrating because, so far, I had no idea what kind of ultimate pattern it was I was after. All I had to go on was a subconscious reaction to something I did not like; as when someone who spends his life in the open, in the woods or on the sea, will step out of doors on a morning, sniff the air, feel the wind, look at the sky and say – 'I don't like the looks of the weather.' The day might even be bright, sunny and warm, with no obvious hint of change about it; and still, some deep-brain sensor, conditioned by an experience consciously forgotten, sends up an alarm signal.

I thought of calling Dragger and immediately saw the pitfall on that path. Dragger had warned me that the only way, in the end, to prove I could work with the time storm was for me to work with it. My starting at shadows, if indeed that was what I was doing now and there was nothing really for me to worry about, might strike her as just the sort of sign she had been talking about, that I could not deal with the storm.

She might even be right in thinking that. She had given me no reason to think there was any dangerous situation building up here; in fact, she had deliberately reassured me this was not the case.

Maybe, I thought, the best thing for me was to put it out of my mind and follow Porniarsk back down to Earth's surface. I had been paying little attention to time, but now I realized that at least as many hours had gone by as Dragger had said it would take before Obsidian was due back on Earth with Porniarsk's body and mine. I should go to his station now, pick up my body and go back to my own clan.

I turned and went. Mentally, it was only a single stride to Obsidian's quarters, in the forest east of our community. Obsidian himself was not there when I arrived, nor was the body of Porniarsk, which meant that the avatar must already be back home. But my own body was waiting for me; and I sat up in it on the edge of the cushion on which it had been lying, feeling the strangeness of experiencing the weight and mass of it under the pull of gravity once more.

As I sat up, the illumination of the room increased around me, responding to my increased heart beat, temperature, and half a dozen other signals picked up by its technology from my now activated body. I stood up and moved to one of the two consoles that still stood in roughly the same places they had stood on our voyage out.

I knew how to use these now. I touched the keys of one of them and stepped from the room in Obsidian's quarters to the spot on the landing area, outside the door of the summer palace, where Obsidian had always appeared.

The darkness about me when I arrived came as a small shock. Waking in the room at Obsidian's, I had not realized I might have come home during the hours when that face of my planet was away from our sun. For a second after appearing there, I felt oddly as if I had not come home in the body, after all, but as if I was still only a point of view, hovering there, as I had hovered in space a few moments past, overlooking the whole galaxy and all the stars that were now shining down upon me.

The drawn shades on the windows of the summer palace were warm with light. Everyone there would be celebrating Porniarsk's return and expecting me at any moment. I turned and looked away, down the slope to the town below; and under the bright new moon of midsummer, I saw the buildings down there had their windows also warmly lit against the night. I had been intending to turn to the door immediately, and go on into the palace; but now I found myself caught where I was.

The small, cool wind of the after sunset hours wrapped itself around me. I could hear it moving also in the distance, whistling faintly amongst the trees on the slope below. No night bird called; and the chill and the silence held me apart from the light and the talk that would be indoors. Out of the avalanche of printed words I had read during my mad period crept something more for me to remember. Not a quote this time, but a story – the French-Canadian legend of La Chasse Galerie. It was a myth about the spirits of the old voyagers who had died away from home, out on the fur trade routes, coming back in a large ghost canoe on New Year's Eve for a brief visit with their living families and the women they had loved.

Standing alone in the darkness, strangely held from going inside, I felt myself like one of those returned ghosts. Inside the lighted windows there were the living; but no matter how much I might want to join them, it would be no use. Like the ghosts of the voyagers, I was no longer one of them, within. I had become something else, part of another sort of place and time. It seemed to me suddenly that the small cold breeze I felt and heard no longer wrapped around me, but blew straight through my bones, as it did through the tree limbs below me; and I thought that all my life I had been outside, looking at lighted windows, thinking how good it would be to be inside.

Once, I might have made it to there. God knows I had tried, with my mother, with Swannee ... but now it was too late; and that was no one's fault. It was not even my fault, in a sense. Because at each fork in the road along the way, I had made the best choice I knew to make; and all those choices had led me here. If here was outside forever, still, getting here had led me to many good things, beginning with Ellen and the crazy cat and continuing to this same moment, which was also, in its own way, good. For if I was lonely out here in the dark, looking at the lighted shades of the windows and knowing I could not be behind them, I was less lonely knowing who and what were there, and that their lives, which were part of me now, could be warm and bright.

Thinking this, I felt some of the warmth come out and enter me, after all. I remembered that I had discovered before this, that there was no real separateness. I was all things and all things were me ... and, with that bit of remembering, I began to move again into touch with the universe. I flowed out to be part of the breeze around me, the ground under me and the trees beyond me, part of all the houses below with their lights and separate lives. I felt the summer palace behind me and reached into it to touch everyone there. There was no light, but the gold came into everything again. I saw them all behind the walls at my back, the eternally-sleeping Sunday, Doc, Bill, Porniarsk and Ellen. I saw Ellen and I touched her; and she was the key to all the rest between the walls of infinity and all infinities beyond those walls. I had a larger picture of this universe and all others now. I went out and out ...

'Marc!'

I turned to vanish, to step back into Obsidian's quarters; and even as I turned, I knew it was already too late. I came all the way around to face the summer palace and saw, darker shadow within shadow, Ellen there.

'Ellen,' I said, 'how did you know I was here?'

She came toward me.

'I know where you are,' she said, stopping in front of me. I could barely make out her face. 'I always know where you are. Porniarsk was back, and when you didn't come in, you had to be here.'

'Go back inside,' I said. My voice was a little hoarse. 'Go back in. I'll be along in a moment.'

'No, you won't,' she said. 'You were going to leave and not come in.'

I said nothing.

'Why, Marc?'

Still, I could not answer. Because suddenly, I knew why. What had been niggling at me all the time I had been studying the force lines now suddenly rearranged itself from a possibility to a certainty, from a suspicion to a knowledge, as the absolute vision of my unity with the universes took hold.

I had been turning away because I knew I would not be coming back.

'Why?'

I realized, then, that she was not asking me why I had been leaving. She already knew it was because I would not be back. She was asking me why I would go to something from which I would never return.

'I have to,' I said.

She put her arms around me. She was very strong, but we both knew she could not hold me there. The whole damn universe was pulling me in the other direction. There always was Doc for her, I thought bleakly, looking down at her. I had seen the way he felt about her. But I was wiser now than I had been; and I knew better than to mention that to her now.

'I do love you, Ellen,' I said.

'I know you do,' she said, still holding me. 'I know you do. And you don't have to go.'

'I do,' I said. 'It's the time storm.'

'Let somebody else do it.'

'There isn't anyone else.'

'That's because you've made it so there isn't.'

'Ellen, listen.' I felt terribly helpless. 'The whole universe is going to blow wide open unless I do something.'

'When?'

'When?' I echoed.

'I said, when? Ten years from now? Ten months? Two weeks? Two days? If it's two days, take the two days – the first two, real days of your life – stay here and let it blow.'

'I can't do that.'

'Can't?' she said. She let go and stepped back from me. 'No, that's right. You can't.'

'Ellen ...' I said. I stepped toward her; but she moved back again, out of reach.

'No,' she said. 'You go now. It's all right.'

'It isn't all right,' I said.

'It's all right,' she repeated. 'You go.'

I stood there for a second more. But there was no way I could reach her, and I had no more words to say that would do any good. She already knew I yearned to stay. She knew I wouldn't. What was there to tell her beyond that?

I went. It was like tearing myself down the middle and leaving the larger half behind.

I stepped back into Obsidian's quarters and turned to the console to put in a call to Dragger. There was a little delay, and then Dragger's voice spoke to me out of the air of the softly lit room, with its cushions and its nighttime trees all around.

'Forgive me, but I'm working now and can't be disturbed. Leave word if you want me to call you back.'

It was a canned message.

'This is Marc,' I said. 'Call me as soon as you get this message. It's critical.'

I sat down on the cushion I had gotten up from earlier and set my mind back out among the stars.

The forces of the time storm were still out there, waiting for me. Now that I came back to them with the additional insight of my momentary contact with the universe, outside the summer palace, what I had only suspected before showed as not only certain but unavoidably obvious. But whether I could convince Dragger and the other engineers of its obviousness was by no means certain. My conviction rested on my own way of interpreting the forces, which was different from theirs.

The time storm was too much in their blood and bones for them to hate it and love it the way that I did. For I did, I realized now, both hate and love it. I hated it for what it had done, for the millions of lives it had swept out of existence. Or perhaps they were all still in existence somewhere else – locked up in little dead end universes – my wife; Swannee; and all those Ellen had known; Marie's husband; Samuelson's family; and the countless others erased by moving mistwalls, not only on Earth but all through the universe. But I loved it, even as I hated it, for being my opponent, for giving me an enemy to grow strong in fighting.

So it was because of both the love and hate that I could see where it was trending now; and it was because they saw it only as a technological problem that I feared the temporal engineers like Dragger would not. I traced the lines of my suspicion again now, through the network of forces, out beyond my sector, out beyond the galaxy and the influence of the one lens I had seen, until I had checked it out against the storm across all the viewable universe. What I feared was there, all right. I could trace the paths of my suspicions, I could see the connections to my own satisfaction, but I could not turn up any solid evidence to present to the engineers.

I was still searching for something to prove what I believed when Dragger called me back.

'Marc?' her voice sounded in my mind. 'You had something critical to talk to me about?'

'The time storm's going to get out of hand,' I said. 'It's going to get out of hand right here in our own galaxy, and possibly in a number of others throughout the universe, at the same time. The pattern's already evolving out of the patterns of the last thousand years. You've already got evidence of it. You told me there'd be increased activity here in nine months or so, my local time. That isn't just going to be increased activity. It's going to be activity that's quadrupled, sextupled, a hundred or a thousand times increased, all at once.'

'What makes you say so, Marc?'

'The character of the patterns I see evolving.'

There was a little silence.

'Marc, can you describe what you mean by "character"?'

'The colour, the feel, the implications of the patterns in the way they form and change.'

There was another silence.

'None of these words you mention have any precise meaning for me, Marc,' she said. 'Can you describe what you're talking about in hard concepts? Failing that, can you give me the concepts you're talking about in more than one mode?'

'No,' I said, 'because these verbal symbols of your language only approximate my personal meanings. I'm translating verbal symbols from my own language. Symbols that have special value derived out of my experience, my experience with all sorts of things outside your experience, my experience with buying and selling shares of stock in a market, with painting pictures in varied colours, with understanding what is written and carved in the name of art, with thousands of things that move intelligent and nonintelligent life, and make it the way it is.'

'I think I understand,' Dragger said. 'But to convince me you're right about this coming emergency you're talking about, you'll need to give me evidence in terms and symbols I can value and weigh exactly as you do. The only symbols like that are in my language, which you now also know.'

'I can't explain things your language hasn't any symbols for.'

'Then you're saying that you can't convince me of what you guess is going to happen.'

'Not guess. *Know.*'

'If you know, show me how you know.'

There was an emptiness of desperation in me. I had known it would be like this, but I had hoped anyway. Somehow, I had hoped, the gap would be bridged between our two minds.

'Dragger, don't you remember how I explained to you how I'd learned about the time storm by a different route than the rest of you? That route gave me a view of it you others don't have; and that view gives me insights, knowledge, you don't have. Don't you remember how I convinced you I had a right to be tested? And didn't I pass those tests?'

'But have you actually passed the last part of that test, now?' Dragger said. 'Or are you finding some incapability in yourself in actual practice, an incapability which you hide from yourself by imagining there's an emergency condition building, that none of the rest of us can see and you can't substantiate?'

'Dragger,' I said. 'I *know* this is going to happen!'

'I believe you think you know. I don't yet believe you're correct.'

'Will you check?'

'Of course. But if I understand you, my checking isn't likely to turn up any evidence that agrees with you.'

'Check anyway.'

'I've said I will. Call me again if you find something more to prove what you say.'

'I will.'

She said no more. She had gone then. I said no more, either, merely hung there, a point of nothingness in open space. The conclusion was the conclusion I'd feared. I was alone, as I had always been, as I still must be.

Dragger would check, but find nothing to convince her I was right. It was up to me either to find something she could understand, or stop the time storm myself.

It was the latter that I'd come to, eventually – I might as well face that now. It had been inevitable from the first, that the time storm and I should come to grips at last, alone, like this. I had come this far forward in time to find the tools to fight it and the allies to help me. I had not found the allies after all; but I had found some tools. Thanks to Dragger and the others, I knew that the storm could be affected by massive use of energy. Thanks to myself, I now knew that all things, all life, all time, were part of a piece; and if I could just reach out in the right way, I could become part of that piece and understand any other part as if it was part of me.

The thought was calming. Now that there was no hope of outside help, the solitary and abandoned feeling began losing its edge in me. It was ironic that I had come this far forward to find help who could handle a time storm I believed was too big for me to handle alone, only to discover that, while the help was here, it would not aid me. But now the irony no longer mattered. All that did was that I was back at ground zero, alone; and there was no need to waste any more effort on false hopes.

If anything was to be done, I would have to do it, by myself; and if nothing could be done, nothing could be done.

I felt more at peace than I could have dreamed I would, at this point. The unity with the universe came on me without my reaching for it, and I hung bodilessly in the midst of the galaxy that had produced my race and myself, sensing and touching all things in it. I had thought of failure as inconceivable. Nothing was inconceivable. Ellen had said to let the universe blow and take what time remained for myself, even if it was only a couple of days. It would be more than a couple of days, of course. It would be months, at least; and each day of that could be a lifetime if I lived it touching everything around me.

Ellen had been right in her own way, and I should have told her so. I thought of going back now and saying it – and then I realized that she was reaching for me.

'Ellen?' I said; as I might have spoken to Dragger.

No words came back. She could not speak to me in symbols, because she did not have access to the technological equipment of the engineers.

But across the touch between us, I could feel her thought, even though it was not in words.

I shouldn't have let you go like that, she was telling me.

'It's all right,' I told her. 'I'll come back.'

No, she told me, *you mustn't come back. Not as long as you still think you can do something and want to do it. I want you to do what you want to do. I just didn't want to cut you off; I didn't want to be separated from you.*

'You don't have to be,' I said. 'You never have to be separated from anything as long as you can really hold it in your mind. I didn't know that before; but I know it now.'

A sudden discovery moved in me.

'Ellen,' I said, 'where are all the short words, and the short speeches? You're thinking just the way everybody talks.'

It just always came out the other way, she answered. *But I talked to you like this, in my head, from the very beginning, from the first day you picked me up.*

'I should have known,' I said. 'Anyway, I know now, Ellen, I'm coming home.'

No, she told me. *You mustn't unless you're sure you don't want to stay at all. Are you sure?*

We no longer talked in a place where there were any rooms to hide what I did not want her to know.

'No,' I said. 'You're right. There may not be anything at all I can do, but I want to try. I've got to try.'

Then try, she said. *It's whatever you want, because I'm with you now. Aren't I with you?*

'Oh, you are,' I said. And I reached, forgetting how I was bodiless, to hold her.

With that she came to me, like a wraith but real, across the light-years of space from our little planet, to where I now floated. And with her came another wraith, a bounding, furry shape that bounced against me and sandpapered my face and hands with its rough tongue and crowded between our legs as we clung together.

'Sunday!' I said.

Of course, Ellen told me, *he was always there if only you'd reached for him.*

With them both there, with the three of us – we three ghosts – together once more, my heart broke apart with happiness and out of the broken pieces rose a strength that spread and towered in me like a genie let loose from a bottle when the Solomon's seal is snapped. There was no universe or combination of universes that I was not now ready to attack, to save what I now held; and I reached to the ends of all time and all spaces. So – at last – by the one route I had never dreamed existed, understanding dawned to me.

'I should have realized it,' I said to Ellen. 'It's one and the same thing, the time storm and what's always been inside me, what's always been inside all of us.'

38

'What's been inside you?' Ellen echoed. She was still not speaking to me by the physical route Dragger had used; but what she said was now so clear to me that my mind supplied her voice as if both it and my ears were physically present.

'The storm,' I said, 'the struggle. The fight to understand, and be understood by everyone else in the face of the equally strong need to be yourself and yourself only, that unique and completely free identity that never was before this moment in time and will never be again, once you're gone. "I've got to do that, say that" the identity says, "otherwise I can't grow, I can't make." "No, you can't do that," say the other identities outside your skull, all also struggling to grow and be free. "If you do that, I won't understand why. I'll take it as a threat. I'll isolate you; or I'll fight you." So, before each action, along the road to each goal, there are all the interior battles to find a way of compromising what you want, and need to do, with what others will accept your doing. The storm within. Everyone has it; and the time storm without is its analogy.'

'I don't see that,' said Ellen. 'Why?'

'Because both storms are the result of conflict between two things that ought to be working together. Like a couple of millstones, badly adjusted, chewing each other up, throwing off stone chips and sparks instead of joining to mill the grain between them.'

'But even so,' said Ellen, 'why's that important, here and now, and with you, particularly?'

'Because I never knew how to quit, to give up,' I said. 'When I ran into the inner storm I couldn't stop trying to conquer it; but because it was inside me, because it was subconscious, instead of conscious, I couldn't get at it. So I made everything else a surrogate for it – the stock market, the business, my heart attack . . . and at last, the time storm.'

'Even so, what good could it do to fight other things?'

'It could teach me how to fight. It could help me discover and forge

577

weapons to fight my inner storm with. And it did! By God, it did! I've found the answer to the inner storm.'

'Not fighting,' said Ellen, very positively.

'All right. That – yes. But there's more to it than just not fighting. The full answer's in the unity of everything. Reaching out and becoming part of everyone and everything else. It was you and Sunday who first broke me in to being a part of someone else without struggle. You were both completely dependent on me, so it never occurred to me that I had to adjust myself to suit you.'

'There was something besides that,' said Ellen. 'We cared for you.'

'I know,' I said. 'I know. I took that for granted too. I'm sorry, I didn't know any better than to take it for granted, then. I didn't begin to know any better until Sunday was gone and I suddenly found the big hole in myself where he'd been. I didn't realize then why it hit me as hard as it did; but actually, something of myself had just become suddenly dead. If Sunday hadn't been killed, just then—'

I broke off, looking instinctively for her face before I remembered she was not there in the body to be seen.

'Would you have gone off with Tek, then, if Sunday hadn't been killed?'

'I don't know,' she said. 'If I had, though, I think I'd have come back. I never loved Tek. But I couldn't make you hear me or see me.'

'I remember—' The wraith of Sunday jumped up to hug my bodiless spirit with nonexistent forepaws and tried to lick my face that was not there. 'It's all right, Sunday. Down, cat! I'm not feeling bad now; I was just remembering something ...'

'But the time storm's still there. You mean you can give up on it, now?' Ellen asked.

'I think I could – now.'

'But you don't really want to.'

'No,' I said. 'The truth is, no. If I give up, nothing'll be done; and that means the end, for all of us.'

'You're sure it does?'

'Yes. There's been a situation building up for a few thousand years now, ever since the temporal engineers started working with the storm. They've been trying to cure an imbalance between energies in this universe by importing more energy from another universe, to shore up the weaker of the two energies here. It's worked for a while, but it's also been creating the potential of a bigger imbalance if the scale should suddenly tip the other way, and the weak side become the strong one, with all that extra, imported energy added to its natural advantage.

And I think it's about to tip – in this universe at least – in about nine months.'

'The engineers don't know this?' Ellen asked. 'You're sure about that?'

'They know it, but they don't realize how great the reaction can be.'

'In any case, what can you do by yourself?'

'I don't know. I need to think. Quiet, cat. Leave me alone for a few minutes.'

Sunday stilled. His ghost body lay down with crossed paws, on nothingness, and resigned itself to patience. I still held my vision of unity with the universe, that had come on me after I had finally faced the fact that there was no hope from Dragger or her colleagues. I had found what I had stumbled toward and struggled for all this time; and now I wanted to live, as even more I wanted Ellen, Sunday, and my universe with everyone in it to live. It went against reason that I could have come this long journey through life and time without picking up the skill and knowledge to do something about the situation. Somewhere, there had to be a chance; and if there was a chance, my blessing/curse of being unable to turn away from an unsolved problem should keep my mind hunting until I found it.

'If I'm right about the parallel ...' I began at last, slowly.

'What parallel?' said Ellen.

'The parallel about the time storm being an analogy of the inner storm. If I'm right about that, and I had to get outside myself to find the key to my inner storm, then ...'

Ellen said nothing.

'Then,' I went on, after a moment, 'the answer to the time storm has to be outside too. Outside the universe – outside *this* universe. If I go outside this universe, I ought to be able to see it.'

'But how can you do that?' asked Ellen.

I did not say anything.

'There's no way you can do that, is there?'

'Yes,' I said, slowly, 'there is. There's the lens.'

'What lens?'

I told her.

'Marc!' said Ellen. 'Are you crazy?'

'It's the only way to get outside.'

'But it's the centre of a star – and worse than that. You'd be burned up before you got into the lens.'

'I'm not material at the moment, remember. It's my mind only that'd be going.'

'But even if you could go through this lens without being destroyed, there's the problem of getting back. How could you do that?'

'I don't know.'

'Why don't you check the idea out, first, with the temporal engineers?'

'They might want to stop me; and maybe they could,' I said. 'They can't help me, Ellen. The time storm's too much inside all of them, just like my inner storm was too much inside me. I'm the only one who can do anything; and the only thing I can think of to do is go through the lens.'

She said nothing for a moment. The wraith of Sunday lay waiting, trusting, leaving it all up to me.

'If you don't, we all die?'

'I believe so.'

She sighed.

'Then you do have to go. There actually is no choice,' she said. 'All right. I'm going along.'

'I don't think you can,' I said. 'Where are you? Back down in the summer palace asleep?'

'I'm in my own bedroom at the summer palace,' said Ellen, 'lying on the bed. But I don't think I'm asleep.'

'You're there, though. I'm here. Tell me, can you feel the downdraft?'

'The what?'

I explained what it was. She was quiet for a little while after I finished. Finally, she spoke.

'No,' she said.

'I thought so,' I said. 'I'm probably reaching down to you, as much as you're reaching up to me. You see, I really am out here – in a sense. I'm an energy pattern projected by the engineering devices of the temporal engineers. I can go from place to place at faster than light speeds only because I can turn off my projection in one spot and turn it on at another.'

'If you're a pattern of energy, then the energy coming through the lens *can* destroy you! Or at least, change you. Energy *is* material.'

'Maybe. I've got to try it, anyway.'

'There has to be some way I can go with you!'

'I don't think so; and that's good. Because then I couldn't stop you from coming; and there's no sense in both of us ... going.'

'Let's try and find a way. Wait a bit. You said we had nine months.'

'Nine months before the axe falls; but it may be already too late to stop its swing. I can't wait. I've got to go, now.'

'Wait just a little bit. Come back home for a couple of days, or even one, so we can talk it over first.'

'If I did that, I might not go after all. Particularly not now, with the two of you around. Ellen, I've got to go. I've got to go now!'

We flowed together, we ghosts. She held me. Sunday held me. I held them.

'All right, go then,' she said at last. 'Go now.'

'Goodbye,' I said. 'I love you. I love you both. I'll be back.'

'You'll be back,' said Ellen.

I pulled away from them and shut them out of my mind. I was alone among the stars; and, by reaching out for it, I could feel the funnel of energy and also the downdraft – weak, as Dragger had said, way out here, but unceasing, relentless.

I let the pull of the downdraft fill my mind. I let myself go with it. At first there was nothing; it was like floating on a lake. Then I noticed a slight movement, a drifting, and I became aware of the fact that I was dropping down below the galactic plane. I revolved and saw the direction of my movement, toward the Lesser Magellanic Cloud and a darkness there enclosing a young, blue-white giant star, a darkness I was still too far off to distinguish.

I let myself drift ...

The plane of the galaxy receded above me. I was in intergalactic space. There was nothing to measure the speed of my movement now, but I sensed that it was increasing. I was falling faster and faster, down the funnel of extra-universal energy, reaching from the lens at S Doradus to our galaxy.

I fell a hundred and forty thousand light-years; and time became completely arbitrary. It may have been minutes, and it may have been months, that I fell with steadily increasing velocity until I must have been travelling faster than any pulsar measured in my early, original time. I think it was probably minutes rather than months, or at least hours rather than months, because I could feel that my acceleration was not merely steady, but steadily increasing all that time. I had no ordinary way to measure this – I only knew it, with some measuring back part of my mind.

It became plain to me, finally, that I would not see the lens before passing through it. By the time I would be close enough to make out the dark circle of the engine among the lights of the Lesser Magellanic Cloud, I would be only a fractionless fraction of a second from entering the tachyonic universe, too small a moment of time for perception. I relaxed, letting myself go ...

And it happened.

There was a shock that felt as if the subatomic particles of the energy pattern that was my identity were being torn apart and spread through endless spaces. Following that, incomprehensibility.

I was afloat in darkness, streaked by lines of light that shot past me on every side almost too fast to see. Other than these, there was nothing. But the darkness had a value and the lights had a value – even if I could not read them. Feeling stricken and dismembered, I floated helplessly, watching the shooting lights.

I had no power of movement. I had no voice. I could find no means by which I might measure the time, the space, or anything else about me. If I had indeed come into the tachyon universe, I had arrived completely helpless to learn what I needed to know, and helpless to take the knowledge back with me. Look about as best I might, I could see nothing left to me but to give up; and the only reason I did not do so immediately was because I was not sure if I was even able to do that.

I floated; and gradually, like a shocked heart starting to beat again, my ancient weird woke again in me. I could not give up, because even here, I was still lacking the reverse gear I had been born without. Alive, dead, or in living pieces less than electron size, I was still committed to chewing at any cage that held me until I could gnaw a way out.

But what way was there? Where do you begin when there is no starting point on which to stand? A journey of a thousand miles may begin with a single step; but where to begin – if you are not standing still, but skating across eternity in total darkness, with meteor-like lights flashing all around you? I hunted through myself for something to hang to, and found nothing. Then Ellen came to my rescue.

'Remember?' she said. 'When you first found me, I was lost like that; and I found a way back.'

She was not speaking out loud to me. She was not even talking in my mind, as she had as I hung in space, normal space, just before I had come here. It was the Ellen which had become a part of me, speaking to me out of a corner of myself, as Sunday had come bounding back from death to hug me with nonexistent paws, out of a corner of myself where he had been all this time, without my realizing.

'If I did it, you can do it,' Ellen-that-was-me said. 'Do it the way I did it before. Take what there is, and build from there.'

She was right, of course; and I drew strength from her. If she had been able to do it once, she was able to do it again. Therefore, I could do it, as long as she was part of me. I drew certainty from her and looked about once more at what I had.

I had the darkness and the lights. The lights were totally incomprehensible; but with Ellen's certainly that I could build with them, I

started to watch them. They were too momentary to form patterns ...
or were they?

I floated, watching; and the watching became a studying.

All that underwent change fell into patterns of alteration, eventually.
It was a long time resolving to my understanding, but finally, I began
to see the elements of patterns in the streaking lights. They were not
entirely random after all.

If they had patterns, they were part of a larger identity in which such
patterns could be held, a larger identity which was the universe of their
context – whether that universe was as small as an atom of an atom, or
larger than all other universes put together. If this was so, then there
was a relationship between the universe that held them and the patterns that it held.

What I had learned in my own universe could be the key here, also.
Incomprehensible as this place was, the unity of every part of it with the
whole, the identity of every part of it with the whole, might be certain
here, as it had been where I came from. If this was so, I had to be a part
of this universe and it had to be a part of me, simply because I was now
in it. Therefore, its patterns had to be part of me also, as understandable
as my own physical speech in action when I was back in my old body,
because a part of the whole cannot be either strange or alien to the
whole, as I had found.

'Now you see,' said Ellen-that-was-me. 'And, since you see, all you
have to do now is reach out and touch.'

She was right again. There was no cardinal here, perched on a bird
feeder; and the golden light was lost and left behind in another infinity.
But she was still right; there was nothing to stop me from reaching out
and trying to touch, to connect with, that of which I was now a part.

I reached. I felt outwards for my identity with this place surrounding
me, just as I had felt in my home universe. Identity was slow coming;
but in the end, it turned out to be only one step more than I had needed
to make in reaching out for identity with Obsidian and his peers.

I touched something. It was something, or some things, with an
ability to respond. After that, it was only a matter of mastering the
necessary patterns to communicate with them; and in this they met
me halfway. Apparently – I say apparently, because the situation does
not translate into words easily if at all – the distinction between living
matter and nonliving matter was not the sharp division existing in our
own universe. Instead, the important division was between those, or
that, which had finite lifetimes and those who, or that which, did not;
and the lights I had been watching were each a single lifetime, lighting

up from the apparently brief moment of its birth until the moment of extinguishment at its death.

But what seemed so brief was not necessarily so. Looked at from another viewpoint, what seemed to me a momentary lifetime could have existed the equivalent of billions of years in our universe. Also, to live here was to communicate; so that, in the end, I myself lived to communicate and communicated by living. It was a long moment for me, because I had a large job in making them understand what I wanted them to know about us and our situation.

But the time came when I got through; and after that, no more time was needed. I was left, with my mission accomplished, but myself isolated.

The only way I had of telling that I had gotten the message to them was by the change I could observe in their patterns. For, of course, there was no way they could speak directly to me any more than I had been able to speak to them. Actually, the most I had been able to do had been to signal crudely in their direction; like someone on a hilltop waving flags to people in a valley far below, to direct their attention to a distant danger. It was not just the mechanism of communication that was lacking between them and me – it was the fact that not merely our thinking processes, but our very existences, were too different.

So, there I was successful, but stranded. I had no conception of what might now be left to me; for I had no conception of what I might be, here, in this different universe. It was possible that, here, I had an incredibly long life before me; a slow, almost imperceptible decay into extinction like that of some radioactive element with a half-life measured in millions of years. It might be that I was only seconds from extinction, but that the vastly different perception of time would make this into a practical eternity. It might be that I was truly immortal here and would exist forever, observing and apart from a universe filled with a life for which 'alien' was an insignificant, inadequate word, but unable to end.

Curiously, none of these prospects bothered me. I had done what I had set out to do and, in the larger measure, I was content. The only sadness left in me was because I could not tell my own people that the message had been carried, the battle won. Battles, I ought to say; because in coming here, in managing to get my message through to the life of this place, I had finally got outside myself, finally seen myself in full reflection, and come to the inner understanding I had been trying to find all along.

My hunt had been nothing more than the human search for love. Only I had been afraid of finding it even while I was pursuing it. So I had made sure to create masks for all those I encountered, so that if I became attached to any of them, my attachment would be to the mask and not to the real being behind it. That way, if the person betrayed me, it did not matter, because I had never really known them anyway. There was no way the living person behind the mask could sink emotional hooks into my soul because it was to the mask I had committed myself. In retrospect, I had put a mask on my mother and sister. I had put masks on Swannee and Marie and Paula. Those whom I feared I might love I gave unlovable masks. Only to those I was sure were unable to love me did I give masks that I could love.

It was a fail-safe system. It was only when I forgot to use it that I got tripped up. The crazy cat and the idiot girl – who would have suspected in the beginning that either of them would be able to reach through and tear me up inside? True, I had wakened to the danger in the girl and tried to put a mask on her, but by that time, it was too late. Meanwhile, the crazy cat had already got to me. When he was killed, for the first time in years, I hurt; and, hurting, I came back to life, whether I wanted to or not.

Now I was grateful for that return to life, because what I had been doing was wrong. It was against instinct and could only have led me nowhere finally, but to a dessicated hell of sheer loneliness that was at the opposite end of the spectrum from the contented isolation in which I now hung. This way I was alive. The other way, I would have been dead. The golden light had been first to give me the answer; but then, I had still struggled against it.

39

I was in my own bedroom of the summer palace. For a moment, the terrible thought came that the whole thing had only been some sort of dream. But then, I knew better.

I looked around and saw Ellen, standing beside my bed with Porniarsk and Dragger.

'Hello,' I said to Ellen, and my own physical voice echoed strangely in my ears. 'I'm back.'

'Yes,' she answered.

It was the sort of answer I would have expected from her. I lay there, savouring the familiar goodness of it, feeling warm and comfortable, while the three of them stood watching me with a careful concern, as if I were some sort of carefully brooded egg which was about to hatch and which might produce something strange. I thought over half a dozen things to say; decided against all of them and simply held out my arms to Ellen, who came and hugged me.

'How did I get back here?' I asked, finally, when she let me go. Outside of feeling as weak as dishwater, I seemed to be fine.

'We brought your body here right away,' said Dragger, speaking twentieth century English now, as well as Obsidian ever had. 'Just as soon as we caught you. We were barely in time to keep your identity from going through the lens.'

I stared at her.

'No, you weren't,' I said.

At that, Dragger looked embarrassed, like someone caught in a lie, which surprised me. I would not have thought it possible for her to show that particular reaction; and I would not have expected myself to be able to interpret it, if she had. But there was no doubt about what I was seeing now.

'At any rate,' she said, almost defensively, 'we trapped your mental energy pattern in time to keep it from going through. Something else *could* have gone through, that was a part of you, though what it would be, there's no way of telling.'

'His soul,' said Porniarsk, firmly and clearly.

'Call it that, for the moment, then,' said Dragger. 'At any rate, it's been some eight of the local days here, since then.'

'Eight days? Is that all?'

'That's plenty,' said Ellen.

'It felt like ...' I began, and ran out of words.

'Temporal differences,' said Dragger, more briskly, 'or possibly differences in temporal perception? It'll take a great deal of study.'

'But you did it, Marc,' said Ellen. 'Whoever they are in the other universe, they've been sending messages in through the lens. The engineers here understand now. They're cutting off the inflow of differential energy and doing something with the downdraft instead. It's going to work out. It's all going to work out.'

'You were right in the first place, Marc,' said Dragger. 'We were too much a part of the time storm ourselves to realize the forces that were building up.'

'It's interesting,' put in Porniarsk. 'When you get down to it, there's nothing in such great supply that it's inexhaustible, no container so large it can't be filled.'

'And that's true for a universe as well as boxes, bags, oceans, and galaxies,' said Ellen.

'I should say, however,' Porniarsk corrected himself, 'it may be that the human spirit is inexhaustible. Time and work will tell.'

'You were right, as I said, Marc,' Dragger repeated. She was apparently determined to make her apology, or say her piece, whichever it was. 'We were too close to the problem to see it properly. Are you interested in the details?'

'You could say that,' I answered. I pulled the pillow up behind me and propped myself up against it. I got it crooked, but Ellen straightened it out.

'Essentially,' Dragger said, 'you were right in assuming that it was a mistake to import energy into this universe from another one – Ellen told us what you told her, before you tried to go through the lens.'

'The energy already stored in the increase of entropy by matter falling back in toward itself,' I said, 'can be tapped to push it out again, instead of using the energy flow from the other universe.'

'They told you about it over there, then?' Dragger asked.

'They didn't tell me,' I said. 'When you've seen both universes it becomes obvious. Theirs is the opposite of ours. There, something travelling at the speed of light is standing still. When you started tapping the differential in energy between their universe and ours, you triggered off the equivalent of an entropic decrease in their universe, where normality was a continually increasing entropy and a collapsing universe.'

'Ah,' said Dragger, 'that explains it.'

'Explains why you've got to work with them to pump back the energy you've taken from them?' I said.

'No,' said Dragger, 'we're already doing that, of course. It becomes possible if we use the downdraft to trigger the release of energy stored on this side, as you said. No, I'm talking about a message we got from them, thanking us for solving their problem.'

'Oh,' I said.

'Apparently,' said Dragger, 'they don't realize that you weren't deliberately sent to them as our representative, and that your concern was to solve the problem here, rather than altruistically offering to aid them with their problem.'

'I see,' I said.

'All this is rather embarrassing to us,' said Dragger. 'There's little we can do to set the record straight with them – at least until communications between the two universes becomes more sophisticated and we understand their conceptual processes better. In time, no doubt, we can make it clear to them they owe us no gratitude. But that still leaves us overwhelmingly obligated to you.'

'I don't know what you can do about that,' I said. 'I was interested in saving this universe for myself and those I now know I care for. Wait—'

'Yes?' Dragger said.

'There's one thing,' I said. 'One of the things that Porniarsk and I hoped for from the beginning was that you could do something for a leopard who used to be a friend of mine. He was killed, and Porniarsk put him in a state of timelessness, hoping that, up here in our future, you people would know how to reverse time for him back before the moment he was hurt and killed. If you could do that for me—'

'Oh, yes,' said Dragger. 'Ellen and Porniarsk both told me about this; and we've looked at the body of the creature. I'm afraid there's absolutely nothing we can do with that.'

'I see,' I said.

'Life isn't something that can be created simply by an alteration of the temporal matrix, forward or back. You have to have noticed,' said Dragger, 'that when you passed through a time line – a mistwall, as you called it in the past – and through time lines in travelling with Obsidian to your testing, that your movement in external time did not change your apparent age or state of health—'

'All right,' I said. 'Yes. I understand. All right. Let it go then.'

'But what I was going to say,' went on Dragger, 'is that life is apparently a concept; and, given the concept, the rest isn't difficult. As you discovered yourself at the time you had your conversation with Ellen, in space, before you went to pass through the lens—'

'Oh, for God's sake!' said Ellen, exasperatedly.

She went to the door of the bedroom, opened it, and put her head out into the corridor.

'Doc!' she called.

'— you were able to summon up a complete conceptual gestalt of your leopard, probably largely thanks to your developed ability to recognize and think in patterns. We've theorized that what you did was to put together in your mind a critical number of behaviour patterns of the leopard and this triggered off a creative whole. Now, given this, of course, it's simple for us—'

'I should have thought of it myself, of course,' said Porniarsk. 'I'm ashamed that I didn't.'

'— to build a duplicate of the physical body to which that conceptual gestalt belonged. As Porniarsk says, this much was possible even in his culture, back in that early time. So, we took the completed pattern from your unconscious several days ago—'

Doc appeared in the open doorway. A black, furry thunderbolt shot past him, flew through the air and landed on top of me, stropping my face with a file-rough tongue. The bed collapsed.

'Oof!' I said.

I had intended to say, 'Will you get the hell off me, you crazy cat?' but I didn't have the wind. He had knocked it all out of me. It didn't matter.

THE DRAGON AND THE GEORGE

Thus boke us for
Bela of Eastmarch,
who hath in hus own time
known a dragon or two

1

At 10:30 A.M., sharp, James Eckert pulled up in front of Stoddard Hall on the Riveroak College campus, where Grottwold Weinar Hansen had his lab. Angie Farrell was not, however, ready and waiting at the curb. Of course.

It was a warm, bright September morning.

Jim sat in the car and tried to keep his temper under control. It would not be Angie's fault. That idiot of a Grottwold undoubtedly had dreamed up something to keep her working overtime in spite of – or perhaps because of – the fact he knew she and Jim were supposed to go home-hunting this morning. It was hard not to lose his temper with someone like Grottwold, who was not only one of the world's non-prizes but who had been very patently trying to take Angie away from Jim and get her for himself.

One of the two big doors on the front of the Stoddard Hall opened and a figure came out. But it was not Angie. It was a stocky young man with bushy reddish hair and mustache, carrying an overstuffed brief-case. Seeing Jim in the car, he came down the steps over to the car and leaned on the edge of the opened window on the curb side of the front seat.

'Waiting for Angie?' he asked.

'That's right, Danny,' said Jim. 'She was supposed to be out here to meet me, but evidently Grottwold's still hanging on to her.'

'That's his style.' Danny Cerdak was a teaching assistant in the Physics Department. He was the only other Class AA volleyball player on campus. 'You're going out to see Cheryl's trailer?'

'If Angie ever gets loose in time,' said Jim.

'Oh, she'll probably be along any second now. Say, do the two of you want to drop over to my place after we play tomorrow night? Nothing special, just pizza and beer and a few other people from the team with their wives and so forth.'

'Sounds fine,' said Jim, glumly, 'if I'm not stuck with some extra work for Shorles. Thanks, in any case, though; and we'll certainly be there if we can make it.'

'Right.' Danny straightened up. 'See you tomorrow for the game, then.'

He went off. Jim returned to his own thoughts.

At the same time, he told himself, maturity dictated that he should not lose his emotional control over something like this – even though they only had two hours to get to the trailer court and return and have lunch before getting Angie back to her part-time job as Grottwold's lab assistant. He must remember that frustration was a part of life. He had to learn to live with the whole business of selfish department heads, inadequate salaries and an economy that was pinching Riveroak College here, like all other educational institutions, to the point where it seemed that about all you could do with a doctorate in medieval history was use the diploma to shine your shoes, before going to apply for a job as a grain shoveler –

Jim hauled himself up in his thoughts at this point, having noticed that, far from calming him down, this rehearsing of things to be endured had his fists white-knuckled and beginning to bend the ancient steering wheel of the Gorp. Nothing about the Gorp was strong enough to ignore that kind of treatment. For a ten-year-old Fiat, it was still a faithful little car, but no honest person could call it in good shape. On the other hand, Jim himself – like many Class AA volleyball players – was in shape with a vengeance. He stood a shade under six feet, but even professional weight-guessers usually underestimated by twenty or more his two hundred and ten pounds, which he carried mostly in bone and hard muscle. Unfortunately, that sort of physical engine, matched with an instinct for taking direct action when challenged – which was useful on the volleyball courts with the caliber of opponents Jim had been facing in tournament play for some years now, but not perhaps the best thing socially – gave Jim reason to consider that he had cause for concern about himself.

Thank heaven for Angie. The beautiful thing about her was that she could get results from people without becoming at all annoyed with them, in situations when Jim would have sworn that the other persons were deliberately looking for a fight. How she managed it, Jim had never been able to figure out. As far as he could see, all she did was to explain matters in a level, friendly voice. Whereupon, for some reason, the other people immediately stopped doing whatever they had been doing that was antagonistic and became friendly and helpful. Angie was really rather special; particularly for someone hardly bigger than a minute. Look at the way she handled Grottwold ...

Jim woke to the fact that time had been sliding away as he had been sitting here thinking. He looked at his watch and scowled. Nearly a quarter to eleven. This was too much. If Grottwold didn't have the sense to let her go, Angie herself ought to have broken away by this time.

He pushed open the car door on his side, and was just getting out, when one of the two big front doors swung open again and Angie came running down the steps to the car, pulling on her light beige topcoat as she ran. Her brown eyes were bright and her cheeks pink with her hurry.

'Oh, there you are,' said Jim, getting back in.

'I'm sorry.' Angie got into the Gorp on her side and slammed the door behind her. 'Grottwold's all excited. He thinks he's right on the verge of proving astral projection is possible—'

'Whichjection?'

Jim keyed the Gorp to life and pulled away from the curb.

'Astral projection. Setting the spirit free to wander outside the body. What with the results he's been getting using advanced input on bio-feedback circuitry to duplicate certain forms of sleep states—'

'You aren't letting him experiment on you, are you? I thought we got that settled.'

'Don't get all worked up, now,' Angie said. 'I'm not letting him exper-iment *on me*, I'm helping him with his experiments. Don't worry, he's not going to hypnotize me, or anything like that.'

'He tried it once.'

Jim pulled the Gorp out of the college grounds onto West Street and turned down on the ramp leading to Highway Five.

'He only tried. *You* were the one who hypnotized me, if you'll remem-ber – after Grottwold taught you how.'

'Anyway, you're not to let anyone hypnotize you again. Me or Hansen, or anybody.'

'Of course,' said Angie, softly.

There she went, doing it again – just what he had been thinking about, Jim told himself. Now *he* was the one she'd just handled. All of a sudden there was no more argument and he was wondering what he had gotten excited about in the first place. He was also feeling half guilty for making a fuss over something that probably had not been that important to begin with.

'Anyway,' he said, heading out along Highway Five toward the trailer court Danny Cerdak had told him about, 'if this trailer for rent turns out to be the deal Danny said it was, we can get married and maybe, living together, we can get by cheaply enough so you won't have to work for Grottwold as well as holding down your assistantship in English.'

'Jim,' said Angie, 'you know better.'

'We could.'

'We could not. The only reason the co-op can get by charging us a hundred twenty apiece per month for food and board is that it makes slop food in quantity and beds us all down in double-decker bunks in dormitories. Any place we find for ourselves is going to put our living costs up, not down. I can't manage meals for us as cheaply as the co-op can. No, I can't quit my work with Grottwold. But at least having a place of our own will make it seem worth while to go on. We've got to have a place of our own – but let's not fool ourselves about the expense.'

'We could sort of camp out in the new place, the first few months.'

'How could we? To cook and eat, we've got to have utensils, and a table to eat on. We need another table so we can each have one to correct tests on and so forth for our jobs at the college. And chairs. We need at least a mattress to sleep on, and something like a dresser for the clothes that can't be hung up—'

'All right. I'll get an extra job, then.'

'No, you won't. I had to stop work on my thesis. You're going to stick with writing papers for the academic journals until you publish something. Then see Shorles keep you out of that instructorship!'

'Oh, hell,' said Jim. 'I'll probably never get anything published anyway.'

'You better not mean that!' For once Angie sounded almost angry.

'Well, actually, no,' Jim said, a little shamefacedly. 'Actually, this last paper was going pretty well this morning before I headed off for class.'

Professor Thibault Shorles, head of the History Department, liked his assistants to sit in on all of his classes, in addition to doing the usual work of correcting tests, reserving reference books for the students in the course, and so forth. It was a neat little whim that added eight hours a week to the time Jim otherwise required to put in to earn his hundred and seventy-five dollars a month.

'How was he?' Angie asked. 'Did you ask him about the instructorship again?'

'He wasn't in the mood.'

'He wasn't? Or you weren't?'

Jim winced internally. Shorles had interviewed Jim at the History Association meeting last year in Chicago; and as good as promised him a recently created instructorship just added to the history department Shorles headed at Riveroak. With this prospect, Angie had tried for, and to the happiness of both of them, got, a teaching assistantship in the English Department. She was still working for her doctorate in English literature, Jim having been three years ahead of her at Michigan State, where they met as graduate students. With both of them set for jobs at the same academic institution, it had looked as if they had the future taped. But then when they had gotten here, Shorles broke the news that because of last-minute budget problems, Jim could not be given his instructorship until the spring quarter at the earliest. Meanwhile, Shorles had a teaching assistantship open.

It had taken Jim less than a month to find out the real nature of the 'budget problem.' Like academic departments in many colleges and universities, the staff teaching history at Riveroak College was riddled with internal politics. Two established factions in the department opposed each other on almost every point. Shorles, independent of both, had gotten by for years by playing them against each other. But an additional instructor added at this time could cause a reshuffling of allegiances and a resultant upset in the neat balance of power. On the other hand, Professor Theodore N. Jellamine, the outspoken, motorcycle-riding vice-chairman of the department, was thinking of retiring this coming spring. His leaving would mean promotions for those under him; and by controlling these, Shorles could then absorb a new instructor into a fresh balance of power hand-tailored by himself.

'I'm sorry, Angie,' said Jim, contritely. 'I had to sit through that class for a hour with nothing to do but look interested and think of what he's done to us; and by the time the bell rang, I didn't dare talk to him for fear I'd put one in his teeth when he turned me down again.'

There was a moment's stark silence in the car as they drove along; then Jim, staring straight ahead out the windshield, felt his arm squeezed gently.

'That's all right,' Angie told him. 'If you felt like that, you did the right thing. You'll catch him sometime when you're able to talk calmly about it.'

They drove on for a little while longer without talking.

'There it is,' said Jim, nodding to the right, off the highway.

2

The Bellevue Trailer Court had not been laid out with an eye to attractiveness and none of its owners in the past twenty years had done anything to amend the oversight. Its present proprietor, in his fifties, was as tall and heavy as Jim Eckert, but his skin was now too large for his long face. The flesh had fallen into folds and creases, and the Prussian blue shirt he wore ballooned loosely about him. His faded maroon pants were drawn into deep puckers at his waist by a thin black belt. His breath smelled as if he had just been snacking on overripe cheese, and in the sun-hot interior of the empty mobile home he showed Jim and Angie this aspect of him was hard to ignore.

'Well,' he said, waving at the mobile home walls about them, 'this is it. I'll leave you to look it over. Just come back to the office when you're ready.'

He took his breath outside, leaving the door open behind him. Jim looked at Angie, but she was running her fingers over the cracked varnish on one of the cupboard doors above the sink.

'It's pretty bad, isn't it?' Jim remarked.

It was. Obviously the mobile home was in the last stages of its life. The floor canted visibly behind Jim and as visibly canted toward the trailer's other end, where Angie now stood. The sink was stained and gritty, the dusty windows sat loosely in their framing, and the walls were too thin to give anything but minimum insulation.

'It'd be like camping out in the snow when winter comes,' Jim said.

He thought of the ice-hard January of a Minnesota winter, both of them twenty-three miles from Riveroak College and the Gorp running on threadbare tires plus a worn-out motor. He thought of summer sessions at the college and the baking heat of a Minnesota July as they both sat in here with endless test papers to correct. But Angie did not answer.

She was opening and shutting the door to the trailer's shower-and-toilet stall. Or, trying to shut it. The door did not seem to latch very well.

Her shoulders in the blue jacket were small and square. He thought of suggesting they give up, go back and check the listings at the Student Housing Bureau once more for an apartment around the college. But Angie would not admit defeat that easily. He knew her. Besides: she knew he knew it was hopeless, their trying to find anything the two of them could pay for close in.

Some of the dreary grittiness of the mobile home seemed to blow through his soul on a bleak wind of despair. For a moment he felt a sort of desperate hunger for the kind of life that had existed in the European Middle Ages of his medievalist studies. A time in which problems took the shapes of flesh-and-blood opponents, instead of impalpable situations arising out of academic cloak-and-dagger politics. A time when, if you ran across a Shorles, you could deal with him with a sword, instead of with words. It was unreal that they should be in this situation simply because of an economic situation and because Shorles did not want to disturb the political balance of his department.

'Come on, Angie,' Jim said. 'We can find something better than this.'

She wheeled around. Under her dark hair, her brown eyes were grim.

'You said you'd leave it up to me, this last week.'

'I know ...'

'For two months we hunted around the campus, the way you wanted. Staff meetings for the fall semester start tomorrow. There isn't any more time.'

'We could still look, nights.'

'Not anymore. And I'm not going back to that co-op. We're going to have a place of our own.'

'But ... look at this place, Angie!' he said. 'And it's twenty-three miles from the campus. The Gorp could throw a rod tomorrow!'

'If he does, we'll fix him. And we'll fix up this place. You know we can do it if we want to!'

He yielded. They went back to the trailer park office and the manager.

'We'll take it,' Angie told him.

'Thought you'd like it,' said the manager, getting papers out of a drawer in his littered desk. 'How'd you happen to hear about it, anyway? I haven't even advertised it yet.'

'Your former tenant was the sister-in-law of a friend of mine,' Jim answered, 'guy I play volleyball with. When she had to move to Missouri, he told us her mobile home was available.'

The manager nodded.

'Well, you can count yourself lucky.' He pushed the papers across to them. 'I think you told me you both teach at the college?'

'That's right,' said Angie.

'Then, if you'll just fill in a few lines on these forms and sign them. You married?'

'We're going to be,' said Jim, 'by the time we move in here.'

'Well, if you aren't married yet, you've either got to both sign or one of you has to be listed as sub-renting. It's easier if you both sign. Then that'll be two months rent, the first and the last, as a deposit against damage. Two hundred and eighty dollars.'

Angie and Jim both stopped handling the papers.

'Two-eighty?' Angie asked. 'Danny Cerdak's sister-in-law was paying a hundred and ten a month. We happen to know.'

'Right. I had to raise it.'

'Thirty dollars more a month?' said Jim. 'For that?'

'You don't like it,' said the manager, straightening up, 'you don't have to rent it.'

'Of course,' Angie said, 'we can understand you might have to raise the rent a bit, the way prices are going up everywhere. But we just can't pay a hundred and forty a month.'

'That's too bad. Sorry. But that's what it costs now. I'm not the owner, you know. I just follow orders.'

Well, that was that. Back in the Gorp once more, they rolled down the windows and Jim turned the key in the ignition. The Gorp gorped rustily to life. They headed back down the highway toward the college.

They did not talk much on the way back in.

'It's all right, though,' Angie said as Jim pulled into the parking lot next to their co-op and they went in together to lunch. 'We'll find something. This chance opened up all of a sudden. Something else is bound to. We'll just keep looking until it does.'

'Uh-huh,' said Jim.

They cheered up a little over lunch.

'In a way,' Angie explained, 'it was our own fault. We got to counting on that mobile home too much, just because we'd been the first ones to hear about it being vacant. From now on, I'm not going to count on anything until we've moved into it.'

'You and me both.'

By the time they had eaten, little time was left. Jim drove back to Stoddard Hall and let Angie out.

'You'll be through at three?' he asked. 'You won't let him keep you overtime?'

'No,' she said, closing the car door and talking to him through the open window. Her voice softened. 'Not today. I'll be out here when you pull up.'

'Good,' he said; and watched her go up the steps and vanish through one of the big doors.

Putting the Gorp in gear, he pulled away and around to the other side of the campus to park in his usual space behind the History Building. He had said nothing to Angie, but over lunch a decision had crystallized inside him. He was going to confront Shorles with the demand that he give him his instructorship without any further delay – by the end of spring quarter and the beginning of the first summer session at latest. He ran up the three flights of the back set of stairs and came out into the long, marble floor corridor where most of the top staff members in the department had their offices.

Shorles was one step above anyone else in the department. He had a secretary in his outer office, who doubled as secretary to the department itself. Jim came through the door now and found her retyping something that looked suspiciously like the manuscript of Shorles' latest paper on the Etruscan roots of modern civilization.

'Hi, Marge,' Jim said. 'Is he in?'

Jim glanced toward the door leading to Shorles' separate office as he spoke, and saw it closed. So he knew Marge's answer almost before she gave it.

'Not just now,' said Marge, a tall, sandy-haired girl in her mid-thirties. 'Ted Jellamine's with him. They shouldn't be more than a little while, though. Do you want to wait?'

'Yes.'

He took one of the hard seats for visitors in the outer office; and, at her desk, Marge resumed typing.

The minutes crawled slowly by. Another half-hour passed and another quarter-hour on top of that. Suddenly the door burst open and out came Shorles, carrying his ample belly energetically before him and closely followed by Ted Jellamine in cowboy boots and a checkered houndstooth jacket. As they headed for the outer door without pausing, Shorles spoke to his secretary.

'Marge, I won't be back this afternoon. We're headed for the Faculty Club. If my wife calls, she can find me there.'

Jim had got to his feet automatically as the door opened and taken half a step in pursuit of the two men as they snailed through the room.

Noticing him now, Shorles gave him a cheerful wave of a hand.

'Marvelous news, Jim!' he said. 'Ted, here, is going to stay on another year!'

The door slammed behind both men. Jim stared at it, stunned, then turned to Marge, who looked back at him with sympathy.

'He just wasn't thinking. That's why he broke the news to you that way,' she said.

'Ha!' said Jim. 'He was gloating and you know it!'

'No,' Marge shook her head. 'No, really, you're wrong. He and Ted have been close friends for years; and Ted's been under pressure to retire early. But we're a private college with no automatic cost-of-living increases in the pensions, and with this inflation Ted wants to hang on to his job for the present if he still can. He really was just happy for Ted, when it turned out Ted could stay on; and he just didn't think of what that meant to you.'

'Mmph!' said Jim, and stalked out.

He was all the way back to his parking spot before he calmed down long enough to check his watch. It was almost two-thirty. He had to pick up Angie again in half an hour. He had no time to do much of anything before then, either on his essay, or in the way of his duties as assistant to Shorles – not that he felt overwhelmingly like doing work for Shorles right now. He got into the Gorp, slammed the door and drove off, hardly caring where he went as long as it was away from the campus.

He turned left on High Street, turned left again on Wallace Drive, and emerged a few minutes later on the Old River Road alongside the Ealing River: two-lane asphalt strip that had been the old route to the neighboring town of Bixley, before Highway Five had been laid over the rolling farmland on a parallel route.

The old road was normally free of traffic and today was no exception. It was even relatively free from houses and plowed fields, since most of the ground was low-lying and inclined to be marshy. Jim drove along with no particular destination in sight or mind, and gradually the peace of the riverside area through which he was passing began to bring him back to some coolness of mind.

Gradually he brought himself to consider that possibly Marge had been right and that Ted Jellamine might in his own way have been as concerned about *his* future and *his* livelihood as Jim was himself. It was a relief to come around to this point of view, because Ted Jellamine was the one other member of the History Department whom Jim liked personally. Like Jim, he was an individualist. It was only the factors of their situation that made them competitors.

But, outside of this crumb of comfort, Jim gleaned little happiness out of this new development. Perhaps it was not Ted who was to blame, but the tight economic situation which squeezed them all. Nonetheless, once again Jim caught himself wishing that life and the problems it produced were more concrete and in a position to be attacked more directly.

He glanced at his watch. It was fifteen minutes till three. Time to head back to Angie. He found a cross-road, turned the Gorp around and drove back toward the campus. Luckily, he had been driving slowly along the river road and was not that far from town. It would not do to have her standing and waiting for him, after all his insistence that she not let Grottwold keep her overtime and make him wait outside.

He pulled up in front of Stoddard Hall, actually with a couple of minutes to spare. Turning off the motor, he waited. As he sat, he put his mind to work to decide on the best way of breaking the news of his latest blow to Angie. To come up with news of this kind on the same day their hopes of renting the mobile home had been dashed was the worst possible timing. For a short while he played with the notion of simply not saying anything about it today at all. But of course that would never work. She would want to know why he had not told her immediately; and she would be quite right in asking. They would get nowhere if they fell into the habit of hiding bad news from each other out of a mistaken idea of kindness.

Jim glanced at his watch and was startled to see that while he had been sitting thinking, nearly ten minutes had gone by. Angie was staying overtime, after all.

Something popped inside Jim. Suddenly he was completely angry – cold angry. Grottwold had pulled his delaying tactics once too often. Jim got out of the Gorp, closed the door and headed up the front steps to the Hall. Inside the big double doors was the main staircase, its shallow stair treads capped with gray granite which had been worn into hollows by student's feet over a number of years. Jim went up them two at a time.

Three stories up and thirty feet down the hall on the right was the frosted-glass door to the laboratory section in which Grottwold had a ten-foot-square cubicle. Jim went through, saw the door to the cubicle was closed and strode in without knocking.

Grottwold was standing before what looked like some sort of control panel to Jim's right; and he looked around startledly as Jim burst in. Angie was seated against the far wall in what looked like a dentist's chair, facing Jim, but with her head and the upper part of her face completely covered by what looked like the helmet of the hair dryer in a beauty shop.

'Angie,' Jim snapped.

She disappeared.

Jim stood for a timeless moment, staring at the empty chair and the empty helmet. She could not be gone. She could not have just winked out like that! What he had just seen was impossible. He stood there waiting for his eyes to disavow what he had just seen and return him sight of Angie, still before him.

'*Apportation!*'

The strangled yell from Grottwold jarred Jim out of his half-stunned condition. He swung about to face the tall, shock-haired psychology graduate, who was himself staring at the empty chair and helmet with a bloodless face. Life and purpose came back to Jim.

'What is it? What happened?' he shouted at Grottwold. 'Where's Angie?'

'She apported!' stammered Grottwold, still staring at the place where Angie had been. 'She really apported! And I was just trying for astral projection—'

'What?' Jim snarled, turning on him. 'What were you trying?'

'Astral projection! Just astral projection, that's all!' Grottwold yelped. 'Just projecting her astral self out of her body. I wasn't even trying to get her to experience an actual projection. All I was hoping for was just enough astral movement to register on the microammeters connected to the plant ganglia I'm using as response indicator. But she *apported* instead. She—'

'Where is she?' roared Jim.

'I don't know! I don't, I swear I don't!' the tall young man's voice climbed the scale. 'There's no way I can tell—'

'You better know!'

'I don't! I know what the settings on my instruments are; but—'

Jim took three steps across the room, picked the taller man up by the lapels of his lab jacket and slammed him back against the wall to the left of the instrument panel.

'GET HER BACK!'

'I tell you I can't!' yelled Grottwold. 'She wasn't supposed to do this; so I wasn't prepared for it! To get her back I'd first have to spend days or even weeks figuring out what happened. Then I'd have to figure out some way of reversing the process. And even if I did, by that time it might turn out to be too late because she'd have moved out of the physical area she's apported to!'

Jim's head was whirling. It was unbelievable that he should be standing here listening to this nonsense and shoving Grottwold against the wall – but far more believable, at that, than that Angie should really have disappeared. Even now, he could not really believe what had happened.

But he had seen her disappear.

He increased his grip on Grottwold's lapels.

'All right, turkey!' he said. 'You get her back here, or I'll start taking you apart right now.'

'I tell you I can't! Stop—' Grottwold cried as Jim pulled him forward from the wall preparatory to slamming him back against it – or through it, if that was possible. 'Wait! I've got an idea.'

Jim hesitated, but kept his grip.

'What is it?' he demanded.

'There's just a chance. A long chance,' Grottwold babbled. 'You'd have to help. But it might work. Yes, it might just work.'

'All right!' Jim snapped. 'Talk fast. What is it?'

'I could send you after her—' Grottwold broke off at something that was almost a shriek of terror. 'Wait! I'm serious. I tell you this might work.'

'You're trying to get rid of me, too,' said Jim between his teeth. 'You want to get rid of the only witness that could testify against you!'

'No, no!' said Grottwold. 'This will work. I know it will work. The more I think about it, the more I know it'll work. And if it does, I'll be famous.'

Some of the panic seemed to go out of him. He straightened up and made an effort – an unsuccessful one – to push Jim away from him.

'Let me go!' he said. 'I have to get my instruments, or I can't do Angie or anyone else any good. What do you think I am, anyway?'

'A murderer!' said Jim, grimly.

'All right. Think what you want! I don't care what you think. But you know how I felt about Angie. I don't want anything to happen to her, either. I want to get her back safely here as much as you do!'

Cautiously, Jim let go of the other man but kept his hands ready to grab him again.

'Go ahead, then,' he said. 'But move fast.'

'I'm moving as fast as I can.' Grottwold turned about to his control

panel, muttering to himself. 'Yes, that's the way I thought I set it. Yes ...
Yes, there's no other way ...'

'What are you talking about?' Jim demanded.

Grottwold looked back at him over one boney shoulder.

'We can't do anything about getting her back until we know where
she's gone,' he said. 'Now, all I know is I asked her to concentrate on
anything she liked and she said she'd concentrate on dragons.'

'What dragons? Where?'

'I don't know where, I tell you! It could be dragons in a museum, or
anyplace! That's why we have to locate her; and why you've got to help
or we can't do it.'

'Well, tell me what to do, then,' said Jim.

'Just sit down in the chair there—' Grottwold broke off as Jim took a
menacing step toward him. 'All right, then, don't do it! Take away our
last chance to bring her back!'

Jim hesitated. Then, slowly, reluctantly, he turned back to the empty
dentist's chair at which Grottwold had been pointing.

'You'd better be right about this,' he said.

He walked over and seated himself gingerly.

'What are you going to do, anyway?' he asked.

'There's nothing to worry about!' said Grottwold. 'I'm going to leave
the control settings just the way they were when she apported. But I'll
lower the voltage. That must have been what made her apport in the
first place. There was just too much power behind her. I'll reduce the
power and that way you'll project, not apport.'

'What does that mean?'

'It means you won't go anywhere. You'll stay right there in the chair.
Only your mind'll reach out and project in the same direction Angie
went.'

'You're sure about that?'

'Of course I'm sure. Your body will stay right in the chair. Just your
astral self will go to join Angie. That's the way it should have worked for
her in the first place. Maybe she was concentrating too hard—'

'Don't try to blame it on her!'

'I'm not. I just – Anyway, don't you forget to concentrate, too. Angie
was experienced in this sort of concentration. You aren't. So you'll have
to make an effort. Think of Angie. Concentrate on her. Concentrate on
her in some place with dragons.'

'All right,' Jim growled. 'Then what?'

'If you do it right, you'll end up wherever she apported to. You won't
really be there, of course,' said Grottwold. 'It'll all be subjective. But

you'll fed feel as if you're there, and since Angie's on the same instrument setting, she ought to be aware of your astral self being there, even if no one else there is.'

'All right, all right!' said Jim. 'But how do I get her back?'

'You'll have to get her to concentrate on returning,' Grottwold answered. 'You remembered how I taught you to hypnotize her—?'

'I remember, all right!'

'Well, try to hypnotize her again. She's got to become completely oblivious to wherever her present surroundings are before she'll be able to apport back here. Just put her under and keep telling her to concentrate on the lab, here. When she disappears, you'll know she's come back.'

'And what,' said Jim, 'about me?'

'Oh, it's nothing for you,' Grottwold said. 'You just close your eyes and will yourself back here. Since your body never left here to begin with, you'll automatically return the minute you don't want to be someplace else.'

'You're sure about that?'

'Of course I'm sure. Now, close your eyes – No, no, you've got to pull the hood down over your head ...'

Grottwold stepped over and pulled the hood down himself. Jim was suddenly in a near-darkness faintly scented with the perfume of Angie's hair spray.

'Remember now,' Grottwold's voice came distantly to him through the open bottom of the helmet, 'concentrate. Angie – dragons. Dragons – Angie. Close your eyes and keep thinking those two things ...'

Jim closed his eyes and thought.

Nothing seemed to be happening. There was no sound from outside the helmet, and with the thing over his head he could see nothing but darkness. The scent of Angie's hair spray was overwhelming. Concentrate on Angie, he told himself. Concentrate on Angie ... and dragons ...

Nothing was happening, except that the hair-spray odor was making him dizzy. His head swam. He felt huge and clumsy, sitting under the hair dryer with his eyes closed this way. He experienced a thudding in his ears that was the sound of his heart, beating along the veins and arteries of his body. A slow, heavy thudding. His head began to swim in earnest. He felt as if he were sliding sideways through nothingness and in the process expanding until he bulked like a giant.

A sort of savagery stirred in him. He had a fleeting desire to get up from where he was and tear something or someone apart. Preferably

Grottwold. It would be sheerly soul-satisfying to take hold of that turkey and rip him limb from limb. Some large voice was booming, calling to him, but he ignored it, lost in his own thoughts. Just to sink his claws into that george—

Claws? George?

What was he thinking about? This nonsense was not working at all.

He opened his eyes.

3

The helmet was gone. Instead of into hair-spray-scented darkness, he stared at rock walls leading up to a ceiling also of rock, high above his head and flickeringly lit by reddish light from a torch blazing in a wall sconce.

'Blast it, Gorbash!' roared the voice he had been trying to ignore. 'Wake up! Come on, boy, we've got to get down to the main cave. They've just captured one!'

'One ... ?' Jim stammered. 'One what?'

'A george! *A george!* WAKE UP, GORBASH!'

An enormous head with crocodile-sized jaws equipped with larger-than-crocodile-sized fangs thrust itself between Jim's eyes and the ceiling.

'I'm awake. I—' What he was seeing suddenly registered on Jim's stunned mind and he burst out involuntarily, 'A dragon!'

'And just what would you expect your maternal grand-uncle to be, a sea lizard? Or are you having nightmares again? Wake up. It's Smrgol talking to you, boy. Smrgol! Come on, shake a wing and get flapping. They'll be expecting us in the main cave. Isn't every day we capture a george. Come on, now.'

The fanged mouth whirled away. Blinking, Jim dropped his eyes from the vanishing apparition and caught sight of a huge tail, an armored tail with a row of sharp, bony plates running along its upper surface. It swelled larger as it approached him—

It was his tail.

He held up his arms in front of him. They were enormous. Also, they were thickly scaled with bony plates like those on his tail but much smaller – and his claws needed manicuring. Squinting at the claws, Jim became aware of a long muzzle stretching down and out from where his formerly 'invisible' nose had been. He licked dry lips and a long, red, forked tongue darted out briefly in the smoky air.

'*Gorbash!*' thundered the voice once more; and Jim looked to see the other dragon face glaring at him from a stone doorway. It was in fact, he saw, the entrance to the cave he was in. 'I'm on my way. Catch up or not – it's up to you.'

The other disappeared and Jim shook his head, bewildered. What was going on here? According to Grottwold, no one else was supposed to be able to see him, let alone—

Dragons?

Dragons who talked … ?

To say nothing of his being – he, Jim Eckert – himself a dragon …

That was the absolutely ridiculous part. He, a dragon? How could he be a dragon? Why would he be a dragon, even if there *were* such things as dragons? The whole thing must be some sort of hallucination.

Of course! He remembered, now. Grottwold had mentioned that what he would seem to be experiencing would be entirely subjective. What he was apparently seeing and hearing must be nothing more than a sort of nightmare, overlying whatever real place and people he had reached. A dream. He pinched himself.

—And jumped.

He had forgotten noticing that his 'fingers' had claws on them. Large claws, and very sharp ones. If what he was experiencing was a dream, the elements of that dream were damned real!

But, dream or not, all he wanted was to find Angie and get out of here, back to the ordinary world. Only, where should he look for her? He had probably better find someone he could describe her to, and ask if she'd been seen. He should have asked whoever it was he had been 'seeing' as the 'dragon' trying to wake him up. What was it the other had been saying? Something about 'capturing a george … ?'

What could a george be? Or was it George with a capital G? Maybe if some people here appeared as dragons, then others would appear as St. George, the dragon-slayer. But then, the other dragon had referred to 'a' george. Perhaps the dragons called all ordinary, human-looking people by that name, which would mean that what they had really captured was probably—

'Angie!' Jim erupted, suddenly putting two and two together.

He rolled to all four feet and lumbered across the cave. Emerging through its entrance, he found himself in a long torchlit corridor, down which a further dragon shape was rapidly receding. Concluding this must be the – what it had called itself – grand-uncle of the body Jim was in, Jim took after him, digging in his memory to turn up the name the other had used for himself.

'Wait for me, uh – Smrgol!' he called.

But the other dragon shape turned a corner and disappeared.

Coming up rapidly in pursuit, Jim noticed that the ceiling of the corridor was low, too, low for his twitching wings, which he could now see out of the corners of his eyes evidently trying to spread themselves in reflexive response to his speed. He turned the corner himself and emerged through a large entrance into a huge, vaulted chamber that seemed jammed to overflowing with dragons, gray and massive under the light of a number of wall torches that cast large shadows on the high granite walls. Not watching where he was going, Jim ran squarely into the back of another dragon.

'Gorbash!' thundered this individual, jerking his head around and identifying himself by this cry as the maternal grand-uncle again. 'A little respect, blast you, boy!'

'Sorry!' boomed Jim. He was still not used to his dragon-voice and the apology came out like the explosion of a signal cannon.

But apparently Smrgol was not offended.

'That's all right, that's all right. No harm done,' he thundered back. 'Sit down here, lad.' He leaned over to rear in the ear of the dragon next to him. 'Make room for my grand-nephew, here.'

'What? Oh, it's you, Smrgol!' bellowed the other dragon, turning his head to look. He shifted over about eight feet. 'All right, Gorbash, squeeze in. We're just getting down to discussion on the george, now.'

Jim pushed his way between the two of them, sat down and began to try to make sense of what was going on around him. Apparently the dragons in this world all spoke modern English ... Or did they? Now that he listened closely to the verbal tumult around him, the words that his ear was hearing seemed to disagree with the sense that his mind was making out of it. Maybe he was talking 'dragon' and didn't know it? He decided to file that question for examination at a more leisurely moment.

He looked about. The great sculptured cave in which he found himself had seemed at first to be aswarm with literally thousands of dragons. On closer look, the idea of thousands gave way to hundreds, and this in turn resolved itself to a saner estimate of perhaps fifty dragons of all sizes. Size-wise, Jim was pleased to note, he was not among the smallest there. In fact, no dragon close to him at the moment, with the single exception of Smrgol, could compare to him in size. There was, however, a monster across the room, one of those who seemed to be doing most of the talking, gesturing now and then to a box-like shape of about dragon size, placed beside him on the stone floor and covered with a richly worked piece of tapestry that looked far beyond the capability of dragon claws to produce.

As for the discussion – verbal brawl was perhaps a better description of it. A discussion among dragons appeared to consist of all of them talking at once. Their voices were tremendous in volume and the stone walls and ceiling seemed to shiver under the resonances of the titanic bellowing. Smrgol lost no time in getting into it.

'Shut up, you – Bryagh!' he exploded at the oversize dragon beside the tapestry-covered object. 'Let someone get a word in edgewise who's had more experience with georges and the rest of the upper world than everyone else of you put together. When I slew the ogre of Gormely Keep there wasn't a dragon here that was out of the shell yet.'

'Do we have to listen to your battle with that ogre one more time?' roared the oversize Bryagh. 'This is important!'

'Listen, you inchworm!' Smrgol thundered. 'It takes brains to beat an ogre – something you haven't got. Brains run in my family. If another ogre cropped up nowadays, me and Gorbash here'd be the only two tails seen above ground for the next eighty years!'

The argument between the two gradually dominated the lesser bellowings that were going on. One by one, Jim noticed, the other dragons shut up and sat back to listen, until only his grand-uncle and Bryagh were left shouting at each other.

'. . . Well, what do you want to do about it, then?' Bryagh was demanding. 'I caught it right above the main cave entrance. It's a spy, that's what it is.'

'Spy? What makes you think it's a spy? Georges don't go spying on dragons, they come looking for a fight. Fought a good many in my time that way.' Smrgol expanded his chest.

'Fight!' sneered Bryagh. 'Ever hear of a george nowadays out to fight without its shell? Ever since the first george we've known, when they were looking for a fight they had their shells on. This one was practically peeled!'

Smrgol winked ponderously at the dragons near him.

'Sure you didn't peel it yourself?' he boomed.

'Does it look like it? Look!'

And, reaching down, Bryagh twitched off the tapestry from the box-like shape, revealing an iron cage. In the cage, crouching miserably behind its rough bars, was—

'ANGIE!' Jim cried.

He had forgotten the tremendous capabilities of the dragon-voice. Or, rather, he had not yet had a real chance to test them out. He had instinctively called Angie's name at the top of his lungs, and a shout at the top of a dragon's lungs was something to hear – provided you had earplugs and were safely over the horizon.

Even that oversize assembly in the cave was shaken. As for Angie, she was either blasted flat flat on her back or fainted.

Gorbash's grand-uncle was the first to recover from the shock.

'Blast it, boy!' he bellowed, in what Jim now unhappily realized were normal dragon conversational tones, 'you don't have to burst our eardrums! What do you mean – "hanchee"?'

Jim had been thinking fast.

'I sneezed,' he said.

A dead silence greeted this remark. Finally Bryagh retorted.

'Who ever heard of a dragon sneezing?'

'Who? *Who?*' snorted Smrgol. '*I* heard of a dragon sneezing. Before your time, of course. Old Malgu, my mother's sister's third cousin, once removed, sneezed twice on one day a hundred and eighty-three years ago. Don't tell me you never heard of a dragon sneezing. Sneezing runs in our family. It's a sign of brains.'

'That's right,' put in Jim hastily. 'A sign my brains are working. Busy brains make your nose itch.'

'You tell 'em, boy!' Smrgol rumbled, in the second dubious silence following this remark.

'I'll bet!' roared Bryagh. He turned to the rest of the assembly. 'You all know Gorbash. Mooning around aboveground half the time, making friends with hedgehogs and wolves and what all! Smrgol here's been talking up his grand-nephew for years, but Gorbash's never showed anything yet that I know of – least of all, brains! Shut up, Gorbash!'

'Why should I?' Jim shouted, hastily. 'I've got as good a right to talk as anyone else here. About this – uh – george, here—'

'Kill it!' 'Burn it alive!' 'Hold a raffle, and the winning diamond gets to eat it,' a roar of suggestions interrupted him.

'No!' he thundered. 'Listen to me—'

'*No*, is right,' trumpeted Bryagh. '*I* found this george. If anybody gets to eat it, it'll be me.' He glared around the cave. 'But I got a better use for this george. I say, let's stake it out where the other georges can see it. Then, when some of them come to get it back, we'll jump them when they aren't expecting it and grab the lot of them. Then we'll sell them all back to the rest of the georges for a lot of gold.'

When Bryagh said the word 'gold,' Jim saw all the dragon eyes around him light up and glitter; and he also felt a hot bite of avarice warming his own veins. The thought of gold rang in his head like the thought of a fountain of water to a man dying of thirst in the desert. Gold ... A slow, swelling murmur of approval, like the surf of a distant sea storm, rose up in the cave.

Jim fought down the gold hunger in his own dragon-breast, and felt panic rising in its stead. Somehow he had to turn them all from this plan of Bryagh's. For a moment he toyed with the wild idea of snatching up Angie, cage and all, and making a run for it. Even as he thought this, it came to him that it was not such a wild idea after all. Until he was able to see Angie close to Bryagh – and Bryagh was about his own size – he had not realized how big he was. Even squatting on his haunches, as he was now, his head was in the neighborhood of nine feet off the floor of the cave. Standing upright on all four feet, he would probably measure six feet or better at a front shoulder, with as much as half that length again of powerful, limber tail. If he could catch the other dragons all looking the other way for a moment ...

But then it sank in on him that he did not know the way out of this underground place. He had to assume that a further opening dimly seen at the cave's far end led to a passage which would take him to the surface. Some faint, Gorbash-memory seemed to assure him this was so. But he could not count on the subconscious memories of this body he was inhabiting. If he should lose his way – be trapped with his back against some wall, or in some blind passage – the other dragons might well tear him apart; and Angie, even if she survived that battle, would lose her only possible rescuer. There had to be another way.

'Wait a minute,' he called out. 'Hold on!'

'Shut up, Gorbash!' thundered Bryagh.

'Shut up, yourself!' Jim bellowed back. 'I told you my brains were busy. They just came up with the best idea yet.'

Out of the corner of his eyes he saw Angie sitting up in her cage with a dazed expression, and felt relief. The sight gave him courage and he doubled the volume of his voice.

'This is a female george you've got here. Maybe that didn't strike any of you as something important; but I've been aboveground often enough to learn a thing or two. Sometimes female georges are especially valuable—'

At Jim's shoulder, Smrgol cleared his throat with a sound like an air-hammer biting into particularly stubborn concrete.

'Absolutely correct!' he boomed. 'It might even be a princess we've got. Looks to me something like a princess. Now, a lot of you nowadays don't know what princesses are; but in the old days many a dragon found a whole pack of georges after him because the george he picked up turned out to be a princess. When I fought the ogre of Gormely Keep, he had a princess locked up along with his pack of other female georges. And you ought to have seen the georges when they got that princess back. Now, if we stake this one out, they might send a regular army against us to try and get it back ... No, staking it out's too risky. Might as well just cut our losses and eat—'

'On the other hand,' shouted Jim, quickly, 'if we treat her well and hold her – 'it,' I mean – for a hostage, then we can make the georges do anything we want—'

'*No!*' roared Bryagh. 'It's my george. I won't stand for—'

'*By my tail and wings!*' The tremendous lung power of Smrgol cut the other dragon off. 'Are we a community, or a tribe of mere-dragons? If this george is actually a princess and can be used to stop these shelled georges from hunting us all over the landscape, then it's a community property. Oh yes, I see some of you with the gold-lust still in your eyes; but just stop and think that the life-lust is maybe something just a little bit more important. How many of you here would like to face just a single george in his shell, with his horn aimed at you? Eh? We've had enough of this nonsense. The boy here's got a real idea – surprised I didn't think of it myself. But then my nose wasn't itching; his was. I vote we hold the george here hostage until young Gorbash can go find out what it's worth to the other ones. How about it?'

Slowly at first, and then with mounting enthusiasms, the dragon community voted to do as Smrgol had suggested. Bryagh completely lost his temper, swore for forty straight seconds at near full dragon-volume, and stamped out of the meeting. Seeing the excitement was over, other members of the community began to drift off.

'Come, my boy,' Smrgol puffed, leading the way to the cage, and covering it once more with the tapestry. 'Pick up the whole thing, there. Careful! Not too quickly. You don't want to shake the george around too much. Now, follow me. We'll take it up to one of the topside caves opening on the cliff face. Georges can't fly, so it'll be safe enough there. We can even let it out of the cage and it'll get some light and air. Georges need that.'

Jim, carrying the cage, followed the older dragon up a number of winding passages until they came out into a small cave with a narrow – by dragon standards – opening on thin air. Jim set the cage down, Smrgol rolled a boulder into place to block the entrance by which they had come, and Jim stepped to the edge of the outer opening to look around at the countryside. He caught his breath at the, sight: one-hundred-plus feet of sheer cliffside drop to the jagged rocks below.

'Well, Gorbash,' said Smrgol, coming up beside him and draping a friendly tail over the younger dragon's armor-plated shoulders. 'You've talked yourself into a job. Now, my boy, I don't want you to be offended at what I'm going to say.'

He cleared his throat.

'The truth is,' he went on, 'just between the two of us, you really aren't too bright, you know. All that running around on the surface you used to do and consorting with that fox, wolf, or whatever-it-was friend of yours was not the right sort of education at all for a growing dragon. Probably I should have put my foot down; but you're the last of our family, and I… well, I thought there wouldn't be any harm in letting you have a little fun and freedom when you were young. I've always backed you up before the other dragons, of course, because blood's thicker than water, and all that. But brains really aren't your strength—'

'I may be brighter than you think,' Jim said, grimly.

'Now, now, don't be touchy. This is just between you and me, in private. It's no disgrace for a dragon to be thick-headed. It *is* a disadvantage in this modern world, though, now that georges have learned how to grow shells and long, sharp horns and stings. But the point I want to impress on you is something I wouldn't admit to any other dragon. If we're to survive, sooner or later we're going to have to come to some kind of terms with these georges. This constant warfare doesn't seem to be cutting down *their* numbers much, but it's decimating *our* ranks. Oh, you don't know what that word means—'

'Of course I do.'

'You surprise me, my boy.' Smrgol looked at him, startled. 'What's it mean, then? Tell me!'

'"The destruction of a considerable part of – that's what it means."'

'By the primal egg! Maybe there's hope for you after all. Well, well. What I wanted to do was impress you with the importance of your mission, and also with its dangers. Don't take chances, Grand-nephew. You're my only surviving relative; and, in all kindness I say it – in spite of all that muscle of yours – any shelled george with a bit of experience would chop you up in an hour or so.'

'You think so? Maybe I'd better make it a point to keep well out of sight—'

'Tut-tut! No need to get touchy. Now, what I want to do is try and find out from this george here where it came from. I'll leave, myself, so as not to frighten it unduly. If it won't talk, leave it here where it's safe and fly up to that magician who lives by the Tinkling Water. You know where that is, of course. Due northwest of here. Start negotiations through him. Just tell him we've got this george, what it looks like, and that we want to discuss terms for a truce with the georges. Leave it up to him to make arrangements. And whatever you do' – Smrgol paused to look Jim sternly in the eyes – 'don't come back downcave to me for more advice before you leave. Just go. I'm having trouble enough holding control here with what prestige I have. I want to give the impression you're capable of handling this all by yourself. Understand?'

'I understand,' said Jim.

'Good.' Smrgol waddled to the open-air entrance of the cave. 'Good luck, boy!' he said, and dived off.

Jim heard the beating of his great, leathery wings descending and dying out in the distance. Then he turned back to the cage, pulled the tapestry off it once more, and discovered Angie huddled in the back of it, as far away from him as she could get.

'It's all right,' he told her, hastily. 'It's just me, Jim ...'

He was hunting about for some part of the cage that would open up. After a second, he found a door with a heavy padlock on it, but there was no key. Experimentally, he took hold of the door with one large, clawed paw, grasped a cage bar with another, and pulled. The padlock twanged and disintegrated, the cage bar broke into pieces, the door flew open. Angie screamed.

'It's just me, I tell you, Angie!' he said, annoyed. 'Come out, now.'

Angie did not come out. She scooped up one of the broken pieces of bar and held it like a dagger, underhanded, with its sharply splintered end toward him.

'Stay away from me, dragon!' she said. 'I'll blind you if you come close!'

'Are you crazy, Angie?' cried Jim. 'I tell you it's *me*! Do I look like a dragon to you?'

'You certainly do,' said Angie, fiercely.

'I do? But Grottwold said—'

At that moment the ceiling seemed to come down and hit him on the head.

... He swam back to consciousness to find Angie's concerned face hovering over him.

'What happened?' he said, shakily.

'I don't know,' she said. 'You just suddenly collapsed. Jim – it really is you, Jim?'

'Yes,' he said, stupidly.

'...' said Angie.

He did not catch exactly what she said. Something peculiar was going on in his head, like a mental equivalent of the sort of double vision that sometimes follows a concussion. He seemed to be thinking with two minds at once. He made an effort to settle down with one set of thoughts; and succeeded in focusing in, mind-wise, after a fashion. Apparently with an effort he could keep his mind undivided.

'I feel like somebody hit me over the head with a club,' he said.

'You do? But, really, nothing happened!' Angie was sounding distressed. 'You just went down as if you'd fainted, or something like that. How are you feeling now?'

'Sort of mixed up in the head,' Jim answered.

He had pretty well conquered the impulse to think on two tracks at once; but he was still aware of something like a separate part of his mind sitting, contained but apart, in the back of his consciousness. He made an effort to forget it. Maybe, if he ignored it, the feeling would go away. He concentrated on Angie.

'Why is it you believe it's me, now, and you didn't before?' he demanded, sitting up on his dragon-haunches.

'I was too upset to notice you were calling me by my name,' she said. 'But when you kept using yours, and then when you mentioned Grottwold, I suddenly realized it could be you, after all, and he'd thought of sending you to rescue me.'

'Thought! Hah! I told him to get you back or else! But he told me I was only supposed to project, and other people probably wouldn't even see me. Only you would.'

'What I see is one of the dragons they have here. You've projected, all right. But you've projected your identity into a dragon-body.'

'But I still don't see – Wait a minute,' said Jim. 'I thought earlier I must be speaking dragon. But if I'm speaking dragon, how come you can understand me? You ought to still be speaking English.'

'I don't know,' said Angie. 'But I could understand the other dragons, too. Maybe they all speak English.'

'They don't – I don't. Listen to what I'm saying. For that matter, listen to the sounds *you're* making.'

'But I'm speaking ordinary, colloquial—' Angie broke off, with an odd look on her face. 'No, you're right. I'm not. I'm making the same sort of sounds you're making, I think. Say "I think."'

'I think.'

'Yes,' Angie said, thoughtfully, 'it's the same sounds; only your voice is about four octaves or so deeper than mine. We must both be speaking whatever language they have here. And it's the same language for people and dragons. That's wild!'

'"Wild" is the word for it,' said Jim. 'It can't be! How would we learn a complete new language, just like that?'

'Oh, I don't know,' said Angie. 'It *could* be, in the case of a subjective transfer, such as we both had in order to get here. Maybe the universal laws are different here and there's only one language possible, so that when you talk in this world, or wherever this is, your thoughts automatically come out *in* this one language.'

Jim frowned.

'I don't understand that,' he said.

'I guess I don't either. Anyway, it doesn't matter. The main thing is, we can understand each other. What did he call you – that other dragon?'

'"Gorbash." It seems that's the name of his grand-nephew, the one whose body I'm in. *His* name's Smrgol. Evidently he's almost two hundred years old and he's got a lot of authority with the other dragons. But never mind that. I've got to send you back; and that means I've got to hypnotize you first.'

'You made me promise never to let anyone hypnotize me.'

'That was different. This is an emergency. Now, where's something to rest your arm on? There, that rock will do. Step over here.'

He pointed to a loose boulder, one of several in the cave. This particular one was about waist high on Angie. She went over to it.

'Now,' said Jim. 'Lay your forearm down on top of it as if it was a table. That's right. Now concentrate on being back in Grottwold's lab. Your forearm is getting lighter. It's rising, rising—'

'Why hypnotize me?'

'Angie, please concentrate. Your forearm is getting lighter. It's rising. It's lighter, it's rising, rising. It's getting lighter. It's rising—'

'No,' said Angie, decisively, taking her arm off the boulder. 'It's not! And I'm not about to be hypnotized until I know what's going on. What happens if you hypnotize me?'

'You become able to concentrate completely on being back in Grottwold's lab and so you reappear there.'

'And what happens to you?'

'Oh, my body's there, so any time I don't want to be someplace else, like here, I return to it automatically.'

'But that's supposing you're just a disembodied spirit. Are you sure you can go back that easily if you're in another body, like this dragon one?'

'Well …' Jim hesitated. 'Of course I am.'

'Of course you're not!' said Angie. She looked upset. 'This is all my fault.'

'Your fault? This? Of course not. It's Grottwold's—'

'No,' said Angie, 'it's mine.'

'It isn't, I tell you! Maybe it isn't even Grottwold's fault. His equipment could have just had some kind of a breakdown that sent you out, body and all, and made me end up in this Gorbash-body instead of completely apporting.'

'His equipment didn't break down,' Angie insisted. 'He just went ahead the way he always does and experimented without knowing what he was doing. That's why it's all my fault. I knew he was like that, but I didn't tell you because we needed the extra income; and you know how you are.'

'How I am? No,' said Jim, grimly. 'How am I?'

'You'd have fussed at me; and worried about something happening – and you'd have been right. Grottwold's just like a baby with a shiny toy, playing with that equipment of his, in spite of the degrees he has. Anyway, it's settled.'

'Good,' said Jim, relieved. 'Now, just put your arm back on the top of that rock and relax—'

'I didn't mean that!' said Angie. 'I mean there's no way I'm going to go back without you.'

'But I can go back just by not wanting to be someplace else!'

'Try it.'

Jim tried it. He closed his eyes and told himself that he no longer wanted to be anyplace else but back in his own body. He opened his eyes again, and Angie was standing watching him with the walls of the cave all around them.

'You see?' said Angie.

'How can I want to be someplace else while you're still here?' Jim demanded. 'You've got to go back safely to our own world, before I can want to be back there, too.'

'And leave you here alone, not knowing whether you'll ever make it or not, and Grottwold without the slightest idea of how he sent me here in the first place, so he'd never be able to send me back again? Oh, no!'

'All right! *You* tell me, then. What else is there to do?'

'I've been thinking,' said Angie, thoughtfully.

'About what?'

'That magician the other dragon was talking to you about. The magician you were going to open negotiations with, on me.'

'Oh, him,' Jim said.

'That's right. Now, you know that these georges – these people they apparently have around here – are never going to have heard of me. The first thing they'll do when the magician carries word to them about me is look around to see who they know who's missing; and they're going to find no one is. Then, if I'm not one of their own people, why should they get into any negotiations to get me back from the dragons – let alone give the kind of concessions your grand-uncle seems to want—'

'Angie,' Jim explained, 'he's not my grand-uncle. He's the grand-uncle of this body I'm in.'

'Whatever. The point is, once the georges figure out I don't belong to them, they won't have any interest in saving me. So, when you go to the magician—'

'Wait a minute! Who said I was leaving you, to go anywhere?'

'You know as well as I do that that's what you have to do,' Angie answered. 'You know we don't have a chance any other way. But it might be, it just barely might be, that this magician can help us both get back. If nothing else, you could teach him to hypnotize both of us at once, so that we'd go back together, or something – Oh, I don't know! It's the only chance we've got, and you know it as well as I do. We've got to take it!'

Jim opened his mouth to contest this point and then closed it again. As usual, she had exercised that verbal judo of hers to leave them both on her side of the argument.

'But what if the magician doesn't want to help?' he protested feebly. 'After all, why should he help us, anyway?'

'I don't know; but maybe we can find some reason,' said Angie. 'We have to.'

Jim opened his mouth and once more closed it again.

'So off you go and find him. And when you do, be honest with him. Simply tell him about our situation with Grottwold. Ask him if there's any way he can help us get back, and any way we can make it worth his while. We've got nothing to lose by being open and straightforward with him.'

To Jim's mind this did not ring like the foregone conclusion it apparently was to Angie. But she was winning.

'And leave you here, meanwhile?' was all he could manage to say.

'And leave me here. I'll be just fine,' Angie answered. 'I heard what you said at the end, down in the big cave. I'm a hostage. I'm too valuable to hurt. Besides, the way that old dragon was talking to you, the Tinkling Water must be close. You can probably go there, talk to that magician and get back in an hour or two. It's just about the middle of the day here – hadn't you noticed? You can learn what to do and get back here safely before night.'

'No.' Jim shook his head. 'If I hypnotize you, at least you'll get home. We start playing games like this magician business and maybe neither one of us will. I won't do it.'

'Well, I won't let you hypnotize me,' said Angie. 'I'm not going to leave you here with maybe no way to get back, or something worse, even. So what are you going to do?'

She had, Jim thought, a neat way of sealing up all the exits except the one she wanted him to use.

'All right,' he said finally and unhappily.

He walked to the edge of the sheer drop, then caught himself and teetered there.

'What's wrong?' demanded Angie.

'I just thought,' Jim said, a little thickly. 'Gorbash obviously knew how to fly. But do I?'

'You could try it,' she suggested. 'It'll probably just come to you. I'd think it would, instinctively, once you were in the air.'

Jim looked down at the jagged rocks far below.

'I don't think so,' he said. 'I really don't think so. I think I'd better move the boulder there and go back down the inside route.'

'Didn't the old dragon – What's his name...?'

'Smrgol.'

'Didn't old Smrgol warn you not to come downcave again? What if you meet him on the way and he says you're not to go, after all? Besides, the Tinkling Water may be far enough away so you'll *need* to fly to get there.'

'True,' said Jim, hollowly. He thought it over. There seemed to be no alternative. He shuddered and closed his eyes. 'Well ... here goes nothing.'

He jumped outward and began to flail his wings wildly. The air whistled about him as it might if he was either flying or falling like a stone. He was sure he was falling. There was something like a sudden soundless explosion in the back of his head, and his wings stretched, slowed and began to encounter resistance. He could feel air against their undersurfaces in the same way the back pressure of the water on an oar can be felt by somebody rowing.

Hope flickered faintly alight in him. If he were going to smash on the ground, he certainly should have done it by this time? On the other hand, maybe he was just managing to delay his descent, sliding down at a steep angle toward a collision with the rocks some distance from the base of the cliff?

He could stand the suspense no longer. He opened his eyes and looked.

4

Once more, as when he cried out on seeing Angie, he had underestimated dragon capabilities. The ground was not rushing up to meet him. To the contrary, it was far, far, below him, odd little patches of wood alternating with open country. He was at least a couple of thousand feet up and climbing rapidly.

He paused for a moment and his wings stiffened out automatically in glide position. Still, he did not descend. He woke abruptly to the fact that he was soaring – instinctively riding a thermal, an uprising current of warm air, after the fashion of balloonists, sailplaners and the large birds of his own remembered world. Of course! He kicked himself mentally for not thinking of it before. The larger birds were mainly soaring birds because of the effort required for them to fly. He remembered now hearing that most of the heavier hawks and eagles would refuse to fly on days that were completely windless.

The same thing had to be true – or more so – for dragons, with their enormous weight. Evidently, like the lion, who could make a very fast charge but maintain it for only a small distance, a dragon's great muscle power could lift him quickly to soaring heights. But from then on it must be a matter of his riding the available winds and thermals.

Apparently, such riding was instinctive stuff to his Gorbash-body. Without conscious thought he found he had lined himself up with the sun above his right shoulder and was sailing northwestwardly away from the cliff face where he had taken off. In fact, the cliff itself was now dwindling into inconspicuousness behind and below him. Far away on the rim of the horizon before him was the dark-green belt of a wide-stretching forest. It moved steadily toward him, and he toward it without effort; and almost without his being aware of it, he began to enjoy himself.

It was hardly the time for such self-indulgence, particularly with Angie held prisoner behind him in a cave; but Jim found it so difficult not to feel good that he finally relaxed and allowed himself to do so. For one thing, it was just past noon of a thoroughly superb day sometime in late spring or early autumn. The sky was a lucent blue, touched here and there by just that small number of little, fleecy clouds that would serve as grace notes to set off the beauty of the day as a whole. Even from a couple of thousand feet up (dragons apparently shared the telescopic vision of the large birds of prey as well as their soaring inclinations) the gorse-fuzzed open moors, the pines and oak tree clumps he saw below him had a sort of dewy freshness about their appearance. With Gorbash's acute sense of smell, Jim could even catch the faint medley of green odors rising from the countryside; and the scent slightly intoxicated him.

He felt powerful, capable and a little reckless. In fact, for two cents he would go back and face down the whole rest of the dragon community, if necessary, to free Angie. The double-thinking back part of his mind even seemed strangely sure none of the others could match him at flying. He puzzled over that impression, then remembered that Smrgol and even Bryagh had referred to Gorbash spending more of his time aboveground than was usual for dragons. Perhaps because he had been out of the caves more and had had to fly more frequently, Gorbash was in better training than the others?

An unanswerable question. But it reminded him of all the other questions that his incredible adventure raised. This world had more unreal elements in it than a sane mind could imagine. Dragons – let alone dragons that talked – were incredible. Somehow this world must have a set of physical and biological laws that made this possible; and someone with a doctorate in history, with a fair number of science courses along the way, ought to be able to figure those laws out – and, having figured them out, make use of them to his and Angie's advantage.

He would have thought that language would be the main problem in this other world. Only, it wasn't. The more he thought of it the surer Jim was that he, in this Gorbash-body, was not talking modern English – or any other form of English. Apparently he was talking dragon with no trouble at all; although the mental channels that seemed to translate this into modern English – colloquial modern English at that – in his head, were puzzling, to say the least. As a medievalist, Jim could both speak and read Middle and Old English, and with a doctorate he could also read and make himself understood in modern French and German. In addition to these languages, he had a smattering of modern Spanish, a few words of modern Italian, and a good knowledge of all the Romance languages in their medieval forms. Finally, he could read both classical and church Latin with facility, and work his way through classical Greek with the help of a dictionary in that language.

All in all, a pretty fair set of qualifications for anyone adventuring into any period of the European Middle Ages. Only, it seemed, none of these were useful. It was not his major areas of interest that he would find useful here but his minor ones. Still, there had to be a system of logic behind any operating environment; and if he kept his eyes open and put two and two together ...

He soared on steadily through the air, thinking intensely. But his thoughts eventually went in a circle and ended up getting nowhere. He simply did not have enough data yet to come to conclusions. He gave up and looked around below him once more.

The wood had evidently not been as close as he had first thought. Although he was making very good time indeed – Jim estimated his air speed as somewhere in the area of fifty to seventy miles an hour – the green band of trees was still the same small distance off. On the other hand, he did not seem to be tiring at all. In fact, he felt as if he could soar like this indefinitely.

He did feel the first, slight tickling of an appetite, however. He wondered what, as a dragon, he ate. Not – he winced away from a thought – no, definitely not human beings. If that was ordinary dragon fare, he'd just have to go hungry. Perhaps the magician could help him out in the food department as well as with the means of getting Angie and himself home again.

He was finally beginning to get close to the wood now. He could make out separate trees. They were all pine, spruce and balsam, growing close together. For the first time a doubt crossed his mind. If he had to search through that forest on foot ... But then he reassured himself. He could not have been expected to know exactly where this Tinkling Water place was, or Smrgol would not have reminded him that it lay to the northwest. On the other hand, if it had been a hard place to find, the older dragon, with the low opinion he had of Gorbash's mentality, would have given more explicit directions and double-checked to make sure his grand-nephew had them straight.

Possibly there would be something he could see from the air, Jim thought, as he began to swoop down on a long arc that would bring him in close above the treetops.

Suddenly, he saw it: a tiny clearing among the trees with a stream running through it and cascading over a small waterfall at its upper end. Beside the stream was a pool with a fountain, and a small, oddly

THE DRAGON AND THE GEORGE

narrow, peaked-roof house surrounded by grass and flower beds, except where a gravel path led from the edge of the dense woods up to the house's front door. A signpost of some sort stood to one side of the path just before the door.

Jim set down on the path with a thump.

In the silence that followed his rather heavy landing, he distinctly heard the sound of the water of the fountain falling and splashing in the pool. It did, indeed, tinkle – not like the sound of small bells, but with the very distant, fragile notes of glass wind chimes, clashing in the light breeze. The sound was somehow inexpressibly lulling to the nerves, and the rich and mingled odors rising from the blossoming flowers in the flower beds reinforced the effect; so that all at once Jim felt as if he had been plunged into a dream place where nothing was quite real and certainly nothing was overly important.

He moved slowly up the path and paused to read the signpost before the house. The sign itself was a plain, white-painted board with black lettering on it. The post on which it was set rose from among a riot of asters, tulips, zinnias, roses and lilies-of-the-valley, all blooming in complete disregard for their normal seasons. Printed on the board in black, angular letters was the name S. Carolinus. Jim went on up to the front door, which was green and sat above a single red-painted stone step.

He knocked.

There was no answer.

In spite of the soothing effect of the fountain and the flowers, Jim felt a sinking sensation inside him. It would be just his luck and Angie's to arrive at the residence of S. Carolinus when S. Carolinus was not within it.

He knocked again – harder, *this* time.

The sound came of a hasty step inside the house. The door was snatched inward and a thin-faced old man with a red robe, black skull-cap and a thin, rather dingy-looking white beard stuck his head out to glare at Jim.

'Sorry, not my day for dragons!' he snapped. 'Come back next Tuesday.'

He pulled his head back in and slammed the door.

For a moment Jim merely stared. Then comprehension leaked through to him.

'Hey!' he shouted; and pounded on the door with some of his dragon-muscle.

It was snatched open furiously once more.

'Dragon!' said the magician, ominously. 'How would you like to be a beetle?'

'You've got to listen to me,' said Jim.

'I told you,' Carolinus explained, 'this is not my day for dragons. Besides, I've got a stomach ache. Do you understand? This-is-not-my-day-for-dragons!'

'But I'm not a dragon.'

Carolinus stared at Jim for a long moment, then threw up his beard with both hands in a gesture of despair, caught some of it in his teeth as it fell down again, and began to chew on it fiercely.

'Now where,' he demanded, 'did a dragon acquire the brains to develop the imagination to entertain the illusion that he is *not* a dragon? Answer me, O Ye Powers!'

'The information is psychically, though not physiologically, correct,' replied a deep bass voice out of thin air beside them and about five feet off the ground – causing Jim, who had regarded the question as rhetorical, to start.

'Is that a fact?' said Carolinus, peering at Jim with new interest. He spat out the hair or two still remaining in his mouth and stepped back, opening the door. 'Come in, Anomaly – or do you have a better name for yourself?'

Jim squeezed through the door and found himself in a single cluttered room which evidently took up the full first floor of the house. It contained pieces of furniture and odd bits of alchemical equipment indiscriminately arranged about it. S. Carolinus closed the door behind him and walked around to face Jim again. Jim sat down on his haunches, ducking his head to avoid hitting the ceiling.

'Well, my real name is James – Jim Eckert,' he said. 'But I seem to be in the body of a dragon named Gorbash.'

'And this,' said S. Carolinus, wincing and massaging his stomach, 'disturbs you, I gather.' He closed his eyes and added faintly, 'Do you know anything that's good for an unending stomach ache? Of course not. Go on.'

'I'm afraid not. Well, the thing is – Wait a minute. Are you talking dragon, or am I talking whatever language you're talking?'

'If there's a language called "dragon,"' said S. Carolinus, grumpily, 'naturally, you're talking it. If you were talking it, I'd *be* talking it with you – naturally. Actually we're simply talking. Will you stick to the point? Go on about yourself.'

'But, I mean, do dragons and humans here – I mean georges – speak the same language? I mean, I seem to be speaking your language, not mine—'

'Why not?' Carolinus said, closing his eyes. 'In the domain of the Powers there is only one language possible – by definition. And if you're not talking to the point in five seconds, you're a beetle, on general principles.'

'Oh. All right. Well,' Jim explained, 'the thing is, *I'm* not so interested in getting out of this dragon-body as I am in getting back to where I came from. My – uh – Angie, the girl I'm going to marry—'

'Yes, yes, on October thirteenth,' said Carolinus impatiently. 'Get on with it.'

'October thirteenth? This October? You mean in just three weeks?'

'You heard me.'

'But, I mean – so soon? We didn't hope—'

Carolinus opened his eyes. He did not mention beetles, but Jim understood immediately.

'Angie—' he began hurriedly.

'Who is where?' Carolinus interrupted. 'You're here. Where's this Angie?'

'At the dragon cave.'

'She's a dragon, too, then?'

'No, she's human.'

'I see the difficulty.'

'Well, yes – No,' said Jim. 'I don't think you do. The difficulty is, I can send her back, but possibly I can't get back myself; and she won't go without me. Look, maybe I better tell you the whole story from the beginning.'

'Brilliant suggestion,' said Carolinus, wincing and closing his eyes again.

'You see,' said Jim, 'I'm a teaching assistant at a place called Riveroak College. Actually, I ought to be an instructor in the English Department …' He ran rapidly over the whole situation.

'I see,' Carolinus replied, opening his eyes finally. 'You're sure about all this, now? You wouldn't prefer to change your story to something simpler and more reasonable – like being a prince ensorceled into a dragon by a rival with access to one of those Inner Kingdom charla-tans? No?' He sighed heavily and winced again. 'What do you want me to do about it?'

'We thought you might be able to send both Angie and myself back where we belong.'

'Possible. Difficult, of course. But I suppose I could manage, given time and a proper balance between Chance and History. All right. That'll be five hundred pounds of gold or five pounds of rubies, payable in advance.'

'What?'

'Why not?' Carolinus inquired, frostily. 'It's a fair fee.'

'But—' Jim almost stammered. 'I don't have any gold – or rubies.'

'Let's not waste time!' snapped Carolinus. 'Of course you have. What kind of a dragon would you be without a hoard?'

'But I don't!' Jim protested. 'Maybe this Gorbash has a hoard some-place. But if so, I don't know where it is.'

'Nonsense. I'm willing to be reasonable, though. Four hundred and sixty pounds of gold.'

'I tell you I don't have a hoard!'

'All right. Four twenty-five. But I warn you, that's my rock-bottom price. I can't work for less than that and still keep house and goods together.'

'I don't have a hoard!'

'Four hundred, then, and may a magician's curse – Just a second. You mean you really don't know where this Gorbash-hoard is?'

'That's what I've been trying to tell you.'

'*Another* charity patient!' exploded Carolinus, flinging skinny fists in the air, furiously. 'What's wrong with the Auditing Department? Answer me!'

'Sorry,' came the invisible bass voice.

'Well,' said Carolinus, calming, 'see that it doesn't happen again – for another ten days at least.' He turned once more to Jim. 'Haven't you any means of payment at all?'

'Well,' Jim said, cautiously, 'about this stomach ache of yours. I've just been thinking ... Does it go away after you eat something?'

'Yes,' said Carolinus, 'as a matter of fact it does, temporarily.'

'I was just thinking you might have what people where I come from call a stomach ulcer. People who live and work under a good deal of nervous pressure often get them.'

'People?' Carolinus looked at him suspiciously. 'Or dragons?'

'There aren't any dragons where I come from.'

'All right, all right,' said Carolinus, testily. 'You don't have to stretch the truth like that. I believe you about this stomach devil. I was just making sure you knew what you were talking about. Nervous pressure – exactly! These ulcers, how, do you exorcise them?'

'Milk,' said Jim. 'A glass of cow's milk six or eight times a day until the symptoms disappear.'

'Ha!'

Carolinus turned about, darted over to a shelf on the wall and took down a tall black bottle. Uncorking it, he poured what looked like red wine into a dusty glass goblet from one of the nearby tables, and held the goblet up to the light.

'Milk,' he said.

The red liquid turned white. He drank it off.

'Hmm!' he said, with his head on side, waiting. 'Hmm.'

Slowly a smile parted his beard.

'Why, I do believe,' he said, almost gently, 'it's helping. Yes, by the Powers! It is!'

He turned to Jim, beaming.

'Excellent! The bovine nature of the milk has a remarkably placating effect on the anger of the ulcer, which must, by-the-bye, be a member of the family of Fire Demons, now I come to think of it. Congratulations Gorbash, or Jim, or whatever your name is. I'll be frank with you. When you mentioned earlier you'd been a teaching assistant at a college I didn't believe you. But I do now. As fine a small bit of sympathetic magic as I've seen for weeks. Well, now' – he rubbed bony hands together – 'to work on your problem.'

'Possibly ...' said Jim, 'if you could get us together and start out by hypnotizing us both at once—'

Carolinus' white eyebrows shot up on his forehead like startled rabbits.

'Teach your grandmother to suck eggs!' he snapped. 'By the Powers! That's what's wrong with the world today! Ignorance and anarchy!'

He shook a long and not-too-clean forefinger under Jim's muzzle.

'Dragons galumphing hither and yon – knights galumphing yon and hither – naturals, giants, ogres, sandmirks and other sports and freaks each doing their billy-be-exorcised best to terrorize his own little part of the landscape. Every jackanapes and teaching assistant in his blindness setting himself up to be the equal of a Master of the Arts. It's not endurable!'

His eyes lit up exactly like live coals and glowed fiercely at Jim.

'I say it's not! And I don't intend to endure it, either! We'll have order and peace and Art and Science, if I have to turn the moon inside out!'

'But you said for five hundred – I mean, four hundred pounds of gold—'

'That was business. This is ethics!' Carolinus snatched up some more of his beard and gnawed on it for a moment before spitting it out again. 'I thought we'd chaffer a bit about price and see what you were worth.

But now that you've paid me with this ulcer spell ...' His tone became thoughtful suddenly; his eyes dimmed, unfocused, and seemed to look elsewhere. 'Yes. Yes, indeed ... very interesting ...'

'I just thought,' Jim said, humbly, 'that hypnotism might work, because—'

'Work!' cried Carolinus, returning abruptly to the here and now. 'Of course it'd *work*. Fire will work to cure a bad case of the dropsy. But a dead-and-cindered patient's no success! No, no, Gorbash (I can't remember that other name of yours), recall the First Law of Magic!'

'The what?'

'The First Law – the *First Law!* Didn't they teach you anything at that college?'

'Well, actually, my field was—'

'Forgotten it already, I see,' sneered Carolinus. 'Oh, this younger generation! The Law of Payment, you idiot! For every use of Art of Science, there is a required or corresponding price. Why do you think I live by my fees instead of running through the aleph tables? Just because a number is transfinite doesn't mean you can use it to get something for nothing! Why use hawks and owls and cats and mice and familiars instead of a viewing crystal? Why does a magic potion have a bad taste? Everything must be paid for, in *proportion!* Why, I wouldn't have done what this wooden-headed Grottwold amateur of yours did without having built up ten years' credit with the Auditing Department first; and I'm a Master of the Arts. He's pushed his debit right to the breaking point – it can't go any further.'

'How do you know?' asked Jim.

'Why, my good teaching assistant,' said Carolinus, 'isn't it obvious? He was able to send this maiden of yours – I assume she is a maiden?'

'Well—'

'Well, well, call her a maiden for form's sake. Academic question, anyway,' Carolinus snapped. 'The point I'm making is that he was able to send her back completely, body and all; but he only had enough credit with the Auditing Department after that to transport your spirit, leaving your body behind. Result, you're an Imbalance in the here and now – and the Dark Powers love something like that. Result, we have a nice, touchy situation – now that I look a little deeper into it – ready to turn things here very much for the worst. Hah! If you'd only been a little more clever and learned, you'd have realized you could have had my help without paying for it with that ulcer exorcism. I'd have helped you anyway, just in order to help myself and all of us here.'

Jim stared at him.

'I don't understand,' he said, finally.

'Naturally not – a mere teaching assistant like yourself. All right, I'll spell it out. The fact of your appearance here – yours and this Angie's – has upset the balance between Chance and History. Upset it badly. Imagine a teeter-totter, Chance sitting on one end, History on the other, swinging back and forth – Chance up one moment, then Chance down and History up. The Dark Powers love that. They throw their weight at the right moment on a side that's already headed down, and either Chance or History ends permanently up. One way we get Chaos. The other we get Predictability and an end to Romance, Art, Magic and everything else interesting.'

'But ...' Jim found himself drowning in a sea of words, 'if that's the case, what can we do about it?'

'Do? Push up when the Dark Powers push down. Push down when the Dark Powers push up! Force a temporary balance and then hit them head on – our strength against their strength. Then, if we win that final battle, we can set your situation to rights and be back on permanent balance again. But there'll be trouble, first.'

'Look here, though—' Jim was beginning.

He was about to protest that Carolinus seemed to be making the situation out to be far more complicated than was necessary. But he had no chance to finish his sentence. Just then a loud thud outside the house shook it to its foundations; and a dragon voice thundered.

'*Gorbash.*'

'*I* knew it,' said Carolinus. 'It's already started.'

5

He led the way to the door, threw it open and strode out. Jim followed. Sitting on the path about a dozen feet from the door was Smrgol.

'Greetings, Mage!' boomed the old dragon, dipping his head briefly. 'You may not remember me. Name's Smrgol. You remember that business about the ogre of Gormely Keep? I see my grand-nephew got to you, all right.'

'Ah, Smrgol. I remember,' said Carolinus. 'That was a good job you did.'

'He had a habit of dropping his clubhead after a swing,' Smrgol explained. 'I noticed it along about the fourth hour of the battle. Left himself wide open for just a second. The next time he tried it, I went in over his guard and tore up the biceps of his right arm. After that it was just a matter of finishing.'

'I remember. Eighty-three years ago. So this is your grand-nephew?'

'I know,' said Smrgol. 'A little thick-headed and all that – but my own flesh and blood, you know. How've you been getting along with him, Mage?'

'Well enough,' said Carolinus, dryly. 'In fact, I'll venture to promise this grand-nephew of yours will never be the same again.'

'I hope so,' Smrgol said, brightening. 'Any change is a change for the better. But I've bad news, Mage.'

'Don't tell me!'

'Don't ... ?' Smrgol stared.

'I was being sarcastic. Go on, go on,' said Carolinus. 'What's happened now?'

'Why, just that that young inchworm of a Bryagh's run off with our george.'

'WHAT?' cried Jim.

The flowers and grass lay down as if in a hurricane. Carolinus tottered, and Smrgol winced.

'My boy,' he said, reproachfully. 'How many times must I tell you not to shout? I said Bryagh's taken the george.'

'WHERE?' Jim yelped.

'Gorbash!' said Smrgol severely. 'If you can't talk about this in a polite tone, we won't include you in the discussions after this. I don't know why you get so excited whenever we mention this george.'

'Listen—' said Jim. 'It's time you found out something about me. This george, as you call her, is the woman I—'

His vocal cords seemed to become paralyzed suddenly. He was unable to say another word.

'—and to be sure,' Carolinus interrupted quickly, shoving into the gap caused by Jim's sudden and unexpected silence, 'this is a matter of concern to all of us. As I was telling Gorbash, the situation is bad enough already without our making it worse. Eh, Gorbash?'

He bent a penetrating eye on Jim.

'We want to be careful and not make it any worse than it is already, don't we? We don't want to disturb the already disturbed fabric of things any more than it already is. Otherwise, I might not be able to be of any help.'

Jim found his vocal cords suddenly free to operate again.

'Oh? Oh ... yes,' he said, a trifle hoarsely.

'And to be sure,' repeated Carolinus, smoothly, 'Gorbash has asked the right question. Where has Bryagh taken this so-called george?'

'Nobody knows,' Smrgol answered. 'I thought maybe you could find out for us, Mage.'

'Certainly. Fifteen pounds of gold, please.'

'Fifteen pounds?' The old dragon visibly staggered. 'But, Mage, I thought you'd want to help us. I thought you'd – I don't have fifteen pounds of gold. I lived up my hoard a long time ago.'

Shakily, he turned to Jim.

'Come, Gorbash, it's no use. We'll have to give up our hope of finding the george—'

'No!' cried Jim. 'Listen, Carolinus! *I'll* pay you. I'll get the fifteen pounds somewhere—!'

'Boy, are you sick or what?' Smrgol was aghast. 'That's only his asking price. Don't be in such a sulphurous hurry!'

He turned back to the magician.

'I might be able to scrape together a couple of pounds, maybe, Mage,' he said.

They dickered like fishwives for several minutes while Jim sat quivering with impatience; and finally closed on a price of four pounds of gold, one pound of silver and a large flawed emerald.

'Done!' said Carolinus.

He produced a small vial from his robes and walked across to the pool at the base of the fountain, where he filled the vial about half full. Then he came back and searched among the soft grass around the edge of one flower bed until he found a small, sandy, open spot between the soft green blades. He bent over and the two dragons craned their necks down on either side of him to watch.

'Quiet now,' Carolinus warned. 'I'm going to try a watchbeetle – and they're easily alarmed. Don't breathe.'

Jim held his breath. Carolinus tilted the vial in his hand and a drop fell on the little sandy open spot with a single glass-chime musical note. *Tink!* Jim could see the bright sand darken as the moisture sank into it.

For a second nothing happened; then the wet sand cracked, opened, and a fine spray of lighter-colored, drier sand from underneath spouted into the air. A small amount of this under sand grew about a depression that sank and became a widening hole, like the entrance to an anthill. An occasional flicker of small black insect limbs could be seen, rapidly at work. After a second the work ceased, there was a moment of silence, and then an odd-looking black beetle popped halfway out of the hole and paused, facing up to them. Its forelimbs waved in the air and a little, squeaky voice like a cracked phonograph record repeating itself far off over a bad telephone connection came to Jim's ears.

'Gone to the Loathly Tower. Gone to the Loathly Tower. Gone to the Loathly Tower.'

The watchbeetle stopped abruptly, popped back out of sight and began churning away inside the hole, filling it in.

'Not so fast!' Carolinus snapped. 'Did I give you leave to go? There're other things than being a watchbeetle, you know. There're blindworms. Come back at once, sir!'

The sand spouted into the air once more. The watchbeetle reappeared, its front limbs waving agitatedly.

'Well, well – speak up!' said Carolinus. 'What about our young friend here?'

'Companions!' creaked the watchbeetle. *'Companions! Companions!'*

It ducked out of sight again. The sand began to work itself smooth once more; and in a couple of seconds the ground looked as if it had never been disturbed.

'Hmm,' Carolinus murmured thoughtfully. 'It's the Loathly Tower then, that this Bryagh of yours has taken the maiden to.'

Smrgol cleared his throat noisily.

'That's that ruined tower to the west, in the fens, isn't it, Mage?' he asked. 'Why, that's the place the mother of my Gormely Keep ogre came from, as the stories go. The same place that loosed the blight on the mere-dragons nearly five hundred years ago.'

Carolinus nodded, his eyes hooded under his thick white brows.

'It's a place of old magic,' he answered. 'Dark magic. These places are like ancient sores on the land, scabbed over for a while but always breaking out with new evil whenever the balance of Chance and History becomes upset.'

He went on musingly, speaking almost more to himself than to Jim and the older dragon.

'Just as I feared,' he said, 'the Dark Powers haven't been slow to move. Your Bryagh belongs to them, now – even if he didn't, before. It'll be they who caused him to take the maiden there, to become a hostage and weapon against Gorbash here. It's a good thing I took a stern line with that watchbeetle just now and got the full message.'

'Full message?' Jim echoed, puzzled.

'That's right – the full message.' Carolinus turned commandingly upon him. 'Now that you know your lady's been taken there, no doubt you're all ready to go to her rescue, aren't you?'

'Of course,' said Jim.

'Of course *not!*' snapped Carolinus. 'Didn't you hear the second part of the watchbeetle's message? "Companions!" You'll have to have companions before you dare venture close to the tower. Otherwise your Angela and you are both doomed.'

'Who is this Angela?' Smrgol asked, puzzled.

'The Lady Angela, dragon,' said Carolinus. 'The female george Bryagh took to the tower.'

'Ah,' said Smrgol, a little sadly. 'Not a princess then, after all. Well, you can't have everything. But why does Gorbash here want to rescue her? Let the other georges do whatever rescuing there has to be—'

'I love her,' said Jim, fiercely.

'Love her? My boy,' Smrgol scowled, aghast, 'I've put up with a good deal of your strange associates in the past – that wolf and so forth. But falling in love with a george! There's a limit to what any decent dragon—'

'Come, come, Smrgol,' said Carolinus, impatiently. 'There are wheels within wheels in this matter.'

'Wheels ...? I don't understand, Mage.'

'It's a complex situation, derivative from a great many factors, unobvious as well as obvious. Just as in any concatenation of events, no matter how immediate, the apparent is not always the real. In short, your grand-nephew Gorbash is also, in another sense, a gentleman named Sir James of Riveroak, obligated to rescue his lady from the Dark Powers now controlling Bryagh, the Loathly Tower, and the Powers-know-what-else. In words of one syllable, therefore, he whom you know as Gorbash must now embark on a quest to restore the balance between Chance and History; and it is not for you to criticize or object.'

'Or understand either, I suppose,' Smrgol said, humbly.

'One might say that,' barked Carolinus. 'In fact, I do!' His voice softened somewhat. 'We're all caught up in a new battle for freedom from domination by the Dark Powers, Smrgol. And it's going to be a battle that makes your set-to with the ogre of Gormely Keep seem unimportant. You can stand aside if you want, but you can do nothing to change what's coming.'

'Stand aside? Me?' Smrgol huffed. 'What kind of dragon do you take me for? I'm with Gorbash – and with you too, Mage, if you're on the same side he is. Just tell me what to do!'

'I am,' said Carolinus, dryly. 'Very well, Smrgol. In that case, you'd better get back to the other dragons and start making them understand what's at stake here and just where Bryagh, you, and Gorbash stand on matters. As for you—' he turned on Jim.

'I'm headed for that tower, like it or not,' said Jim.

'Do, and you'll never see your lady again!' Carolinus' voice cracked like a gunshot. His eyes were burning once more. 'Do it, and I wash my hands of you; and if I wash my hands of you, you've no hope! Now – will you listen?'

Jim swallowed his immediate impulse to take off then and there. There might be something in what Carolinus was about to say. In any case, he and Angie would still need the magician's help to get home again, even after Angie was rescued. It would hardly be wise to make an opponent of Carolinus now.

'I'll listen,' he answered.

'Very well, then. The Dark Powers have taken your lady to their tower for the very reason that they hope to draw you into their territory before you've gathered the strength to oppose them. They want you to come immediately to the rescue of the Lady Angela; because if you do, you'll be easy to defeat. But if you hold off until you've gathered the companions the watchbeetle indicated, it's they who can be defeated. Therefore, you're foolish if you go now.'

'But what'll they do to Angela – I mean, Angie—' said Jim, 'when they see I'm not coming right after her? They'll figure she's no good as a means to stop me, and do something terrible to her—'

'They cannot?' Carolinus snapped. 'By taking the lady they've over-extended themselves, made themselves vulnerable. If they treat her any way but well, all who might oppose them – man, dragon and beast – will form a solid front against them. There're rules at work here; and just as if you go now to her rescue you will certainly lose, so if they harm their hostage *they* will certainly lose!'

Jim found himself wavering in his firm intention to go after Angie at once. He remembered his earlier determination to figure out the system by which this world operated. If Carolinus was correct ... and the magician was a very convincing arguer ...

'But you're sure she'll be all right if I don't get to that tower right away?' Jim asked.

'She'll only be other than all right if you do go now.'

Jim gave in with a deep sigh.

'All right,' he said. 'What do I do, then? Where should I go?'

'Away!' said Carolinus. 'That is, in exactly the opposite direction which you would use in returning to the dragon cave from which you came.'

'But, Mage,' put in Smrgol, puzzled, 'away from the cave is exactly toward the fens and the Loathly Tower. And you just finished saying he shouldn't go to the tower—'

'Dragon,' cried Carolinus, wheeling on Smrgol. 'Have I got to argue with *you*, now? I said "away!" I didn't say "to the tower." The Powers give me patience! Have I got to explain the intricacies of Advanced Magics to every dumbwit and numbskull who flies in here, or don't I? I ask you?'

'No!' said the deep bass voice out of thin air.

'There,' Carolinus said in a relieved tone, mopping his brow. 'You heard the Auditing Department. Now, no more talk. I've got my hands too full as it is. Off with you to the dragon cave, Smrgol. And away with you, Gorbash, in the opposite direction!'

He turned around and stamped into his house, slamming the door shut behind him.

'Come, Gorbash,' boomed Smrgol. 'The Mage's right. Let me get you started in the right direction, then I'll leave you on your own. My, my, who'd have thought we'd run into such interesting times in my old age?'

Wagging his head thoughtfully, the elderly dragon sprang into the air, leathery wings opening out with a thunderous clap, and mounted skyward.

After a second's hesitation, Jim followed him.

6

'You can just see the beginning of the fens, there – that misty, bluish line beyond that bit of forest coming in from the north and stretching out like a finger across your way.'

Smrgol, soaring alongside Jim, broke off as they left the thermal they had been rising upon and had to use their wings to get to another. The prevailing breezes seemed to be blowing against them.

Jim noticed that the older dragon had a tendency to fall silent when he had to exert himself flying. It gave the information Smrgol seemed determined to impart something of a fragmentary feeling.

'Nothing important comes out on the fens nowadays to concern our people, of course. Except, that is,' Smrgol went on abruptly as they caught another thermal and started on a long, buoyant glide toward the dimly seen fens, 'for the mere-dragons. Relatives of ours, as you know, Gorbash. Distant, naturally. You'll have some fifteenth or sixteenth cousins among them without a doubt, though probably they won't remember the connection. Never were a very solid branch of the family to start with; and then when this blight hit them – well, they generally fell apart.'

Smrgol paused to clear his throat.

'Took to living separately, even from each other. There are no good caves out there among all that bog and water, of course. They must be feeding themselves mostly on fish from the sea, nowadays, I don't wonder. Only an occasional sandmirk, sea lizard or stray chicken is to be found in that sort of territory. Oh, there are a few smallholdings and impoverished farms on the borders of the fens, and occasionally they can be raided. But even those'll have suffered from the blight; and everything they own'll be stunted or hardly worth the eating to a healthy dragon like you or me, boy. Why, I've even heard some of our mere-dragon relatives have fallen so low as to try and exist on garden truck. Heard of one even eating cabbages. Cabbages! Unbelievable ...'

Once more they had to use their wings to reach another thermal;

and by the time they got to it and Smrgol took up talking again, it was obvious to Jim's ears that the older dragon was definitely winded.

'Well, there you have it … Gorbash …' he said. 'I guess that covers it, pretty well. Keep … your head, my boy. Don't let your natural … dragon fury run away with you; and you can't help … But do well. Well, I guess I'd better be turning back.'

'Yes,' said Jim. 'Maybe you'd better. Thanks for the advice.'

'Don't thank me … boy. Least I can do. for you. Well … good-bye, then …'

'Good-bye.'

Jim watched Smrgol fall off in a sloping dive, turning a hundred and eighty degrees as he swung to catch a lower thermal and the wind from the seacoast, which was now behind him. Smrgol dwindled quickly and Jim turned his attention back to what lay ahead of him, personally.

Below him at the moment, the forest and open ground over which Jim had approached the woods holding Carolinus' house had given way to a wide landscape of desolate moors, interrupted by strands of just a few trees, and some poverty-stricken huts made of what looked like fallen branches tied together in bundles, the roofs thatched with hay or grass. The inhabitants of these, when surprised outside their dwelling, invariably scurried for shelter at the sight of Jim winging overhead. They were dressed in furs rather than in more conventional clothes and did not appear to be a very attractive people.

However, as Jim continued on his flight, these habitations became more and more occasional and finally disappeared altogether. The moors were ending now and the forest Smrgol had pointed out was close. Unlike the coniferous woods around the Tinkling Water, this other growth was apparently of deciduous trees such as oaks and willows. They all seemed curiously leafless for this time of year and their branches, seen from above, had a gnarled and tangled look that gave the forest a particularly forbidding look; as if it was the kind of place that would not easily let out again anyone who wandered into it on foot. Jim felt a twinge of smugness at being able to soar safely above it.

In fact, once again the intoxication of being airborne was making him feel better than conditions justified. He had no real idea of what he was headed into; but that did not seem to disturb his cheerful feeling. He had wanted to go to the Loathly Tower and Carolinus had argued against it. But here he was, at Carolinus' direction, going toward it anyway. Whatever the reason was for his being headed in this direction, what he was doing at the moment felt to him particularly *right* …

Now, the far edge of the forest was almost underneath him. Beyond, there was nothing but the green fenland, stretching to a misty deeper-blue line which must be the open sea. The fens was a good-sized area, he saw, a greenly lush, low-lying wilderness of land and water. It filled the landscape before him to the skyline in all directions except straight ahead, where the sea blue showed.

He searched about it with the telescopic vision of his dragon-eyes for some sight of a structure which could be the Loathly Tower, but he could pick out nothing. The breeze that had been blowing against him dropped abruptly, and a new, light wind began to push from behind him. He stretched his wings to it, and let it carry him, gliding at a small angle down the invisible air surface as if it was some miles-long, magic slide. The fenland rose to meet him: spongy, grass-thick earth, broken into causeways and islands by the blue water, thick-choked itself in the shallower bays and inlets with tall seagrass and club rushes.

Flocks of water fowl rose here and there like eddying smoke from one mere, drifted over and settled on the surface of another, a few hundred yards away. Their cries, thinned by the distance, came faintly to Jim's hypersensitive ears.

Ahead, heavy clouds were piling up above the coastline to the west.

Jim soared on, above the still water and the soft grass, smelling the distant saltwater. He looked worriedly at the declining sun which was just now beginning to slip down behind the thick cloudbank he had just noticed. It would be nightfall before long. He was hungry and he had absolutely no notion of what he should do once it was dark. Certainly, he could not continue in the air. It would not be pleasant to fly full-tilt into the ground because he could not see where he was going. It would not be pleasant, in fact, to fly full-tilt into one of the bays or meres. He could land and travel onward on foot – but there would probably be bogs.

The sensible thing once the sun set, he thought, would be to spend the night on one of the small land patches below him. Not that such a prospect sounded very comfortable. Also, *he* would be completely exposed down there if anything decided to creep up on him.

Jim was brought up short in his thoughts at this point by the sudden remembrance of what he was. He had, he realized, been thinking like a human, not like a dragon. What, in its right mind, would want to creep up on a dragon? Outside of a knight in armor. And what would a knight in armor be doing prowling around in the dark? Or another dragon, for that matter? The only other dragon he had any reason to fear around here, if Smrgol's report on the mere-dragons had been correct, was Bryagh; and Bryagh would be making a mistake if he came anywhere near, in the mood possessing Jim right now.

In fact, thought Jim, he would like nothing better than to get his jaws and claws on Bryagh right now. He felt a grim and sullen anger begin to kindle in him like a hot coal fanned to life just beneath his breast-bone. The feeling was rather enjoyable. He let it kindle and grow until it suddenly occurred to him that it was a dragonly, rather than a human, anger he was feeling. Perhaps this was what Smrgol had been talking about when he had advised Gorbash not to let his dragon-fury run away with him.

Jim made a determined effort to put the emotion aside, but the inward fire he had kindled did not seem disposed to go out that easily. He struggled with it, alarmed now, and – as luck would have it – just at that moment he caught sight of another dragon shape, down on one of the spits of land directly in front of him.

The other dragon was concerned with something lying in the grass. What it was, Jim could not make out from this height and angle; but in any case, its identity was academic. The sight of the other dragon had been all that was needed to bring to full flame the fury now within him.

'Bryagh!' The word snarled, unbidden in his throat.

Reflexively, he nosed over and went into a dive like a fighter plane, his sights locked on the target below.

It was a dive sudden enough to take the dragon underneath utterly by surprise. Unfortunately, it had one natural drawback. Even a small flivver airplane with its motor cut off makes a noticeable amount of noise descending in a steep dive; and a large dragon such as Gorbash had no less air resistance than the average two-seater light airplane. Moreover, the dragon below had evidently had some experience with such a noise; for without looking upward he made one frantic leap and went tumbling head over tail out of the way as Jim slammed down onto the ground at the spot where a second before the other had been.

The attacked dragon came to the end of his tumbling, sat up, took a look at Jim and began to wail.

'It's not fair! It's not fair!' he cried in a – for a dragon – remarkably high-pitched voice. 'Just because you're bigger than I am! And I had to fight two hours for it. It almost got away half a dozen times. Besides, it's the first good-sized one to wander out onto the fens in months, and now you're going to take it away from me. And you don't need it, not at all. You're big and fat, and I'm weak and hungry ...'

Jim blinked and stared. He glanced from the dragon down to the thing in the grass before him and saw that it was the carcass of a rather old and stringy-looking cow, badly bitten up and with a broken neck.

Looking back at the other dragon again, he realized for the first time that the other was little better than half his own size, and so emaciated that he appeared on the verge of collapse from starvation.

'... Just my luck!' the other dragon was whimpering. 'Every time I get something good, someone comes along and takes it away from me. All I ever get is fish—'

'Hold on!' said Jim.

'—Fish, fish, fish! Cold fish, without any warm blood in them to put strength in my bones—'

'Hold on, I say! SHUT UP!' Jim bellowed, in Gorbash's best voice.

The other dragon stopped his complaining as abruptly as if he was a record player whose plug had been pulled.

'Yes, sir,' he said, timidly.

'What're you talking about?' demanded Jim. 'I'm not going to take your cow away from you.'

'Oh no, sir,' said the other dragon; and tittered as if to show that nobody could accuse him of not knowing a good joke when he heard it.

'I'm not.'

'He-he-he!' chuckled the smaller dragon. 'You certainly are a card, your honor.'

'Dammit, I'm serious!' snapped Jim, backing away from the carcass. 'Go ahead, eat! I just thought you were someone else.'

'Oh, I don't want it. Really, I don't! I was just joking about being starved. Really, I was!'

'Look,' said Jim, taking a tight rein on his dragon-temper, which was beginning to rekindle, 'what's your name?'

'Oh, well,' said the other. 'Oh, well – you know—'

'WHAT'S YOUR NAME?'

'Secoh, your worship!' yelped the dragon, fearfully. 'Just Secoh, that's all. I'm nobody important, your highness. Just a little, unimportant mere-dragon.'

'You don't have to swear it to me,' said Jim. 'I believe you. All right, Secoh' – he waved at the dead cow – 'dig in. I don't want any myself, but maybe you can give me some directions and information about this territory and what lives here.'

'Well ...' Secoh hedged. He had been sidling forward in fawning fashion while the conversation was going on, until he was once more almost next to the cow. 'If you'll excuse my table manners, sir. I'm just a mere-dragon—' And he tore into the meat before him in sudden, ravenous fashion.

Jim watched. His first impulse was the compassionate one of letting the other get some food inside him before making him talk. But, as he sat and observed, Jim began to feel the stirrings of a not inconsiderable hunger himself. His belly rumbled, suddenly and audibly. He stared at the torn carcass of the cow and tried to tell himself it was not the sort of thing any civilized person would want to eat. Raw meat – off a dead animal – flesh, bones, hide and all ...

'Say,' said Jim, drawing closer to Secoh and the cow, and clearing his throat, 'that does look rather good, after all.'

His stomach rumbled again. Apparently his dragon-body had none of his human scruples about the eat-ability of what he was looking at.

'Secoh?'

Secoh reluctantly lifted his head from the cow and rolled his eyes warily to Jim, although he continued to chew and gulp frantically.

'Er, Secoh – I'm a stranger around these parts,' said Jim. 'I suppose you know your way around pretty well. I – Say, how does that cow taste?'

'Oh, terrible – Mumpf—' said Secoh with his mouth full. 'Stringy, old – awful, really. Good enough for a mere-dragon like me, but not for—'

'Well, about those directions I wanted ...'

'Yes, your worship?'

'I think – Oh, well, it's your cow.'

'That's what your honor promised,' replied Secoh, cautiously.

'But you know, I wonder,' Jim grinned confidingly at him, 'I just wonder how a cow like that would taste. You know I've never tasted anything quite like that before?'

'No, sir.' A large tear welled up in Secoh's near eye and splashed down upon the grass.

'I actually haven't. I wonder – it's up to you, now – would you mind if I just tasted it?'

Another large tear rolled down Secoh's cheek.

'If – if your honor wishes,' he choked. 'Won't you – won't you help yourself, please?'

'Well, thanks,' said Jim.

He walked up and sank his teeth experimentally into a shoulder of the carcass. The rich juices of the warm meat trickled over his tongue. He tore the shoulder loose ...

Some little time later, he and Secoh sat back, polishing bones with the rough upper surfaces of their forked tongues, which were abrasive as the coarsest sandpaper.

'Did you get enough to eat, Secoh?' Jim asked.

'More than enough, sir,' replied the mere-dragon, staring at the denuded skeleton with a wild and famished eye. 'Although if you don't mind, your honor, I've got a weakness for marrow—'

He picked up a thighbone and began to crunch it like a stick of candy.

'Tomorrow we'll hunt up another cow and I'll kill it for you,' said Jim. 'You can have it all to yourself.'

'Oh, thank you, your honor,' said Secoh, with polite lack of conviction.

'I mean it – now, about this Loathly Tower, where is it?'

'The wh-what?' stammered Secoh.

'The Loathly Tower. The Loathly Tower! You know where it is, don't you?'

'Oh yes, sir. But your honor wouldn't want to go there, would your worship? Not that I'm presuming to give your lordship advice—' Secoh cried suddenly, in a high and terrified voice.

'No, no. Go on,' said Jim.

'—but of course I'm only a little, timid mere-dragon, your honor. Not like you. But the Loathly Tower, it's a terrible place, your highness.'

'How terrible?'

'Well ... it just is.' Secoh cast an unhappy look about him. 'It's what spoiled all of us, you know, five hundred years ago. We used to be just like you other dragons – Oh, not so big and fierce as you, of course, sir. But then, after that, they say the Dark Powers got pushed back again and sealed up, and the tower itself broken and ruined – not that it helped us mere-dragons any. Everybody else just went home and left us the way we'd become. So, it's supposed to be all right, now. But all the same I wouldn't go near there if I was your worthiness, I really wouldn't.'

'But what's there that's so bad?' demanded Jim. 'What sort of thing, specifically, is it?'

'Well, I wouldn't say there was any *thing* there,' replied Secoh, cautiously. 'It's nothing your worship could exactly put a claw on. It's just that whatever or whoever goes near it – without belonging to it, I mean – it does something to them, sir. Of course, it's the evil sorts that head for it in the first place. But sometimes things just as strange seem to come from it, and lately—'

Secoh caught himself and became very busy searching among the bones of the cow.

'Lately, what?'

'Nothing – really, nothing, your excellency!' cried Secoh, a little shrilly, starting up. 'Your illustriousness shouldn't catch a worthless little mere-dragon up like that. We're not too bright, you know. I only meant ... lately the tower's been a more fearful place than ever. No one knows why. And we all keep well away from it!'

'Probably just your imagination,' said Jim, shortly.

He had always been a skeptic by nature; and although this strange world was clearly full of all sorts of variances with the normal pattern of things as he knew them, his mind instinctively revolted against too much credit in the supernatural – particularly, he thought, the old B-movie horror, type of supernatural.

'We know what we know,' said the mere-dragon with unusual stubbornness. He stretched out a scrawny and withered forelimb. 'Is *that* imagination?'

Jim grunted. The meal he had just gulped down had made him drowsy. The gray last light of day was leaden in its effect upon his nerves. He felt torpid and dull.

'I think I'll grab some sleep,' he said. 'Anyway, how do I find the Loathly Tower from here?'

'Just go due west. You won't be able to miss it.'

A shiver was to be heard in the last words of the mere-dragon, but Jim was becoming too sleepy to care. Dimly, he heard the rest of what Secoh was telling him.

'It's out along the Great Causeway. That's a wide lane of solid land running due east and west through the fens for about five miles, right to the sea. You just follow it until you come to the tower. It stands on a rise of rock overlooking the edge of the ocean.'

'Five miles ...' Jim muttered.

He would have to wait until morning, which was not an unpleasant prospect. His armored body seemed undisturbed by the evening temperature, whatever it was, and the grassy ground beneath him was soft.

'Yes, I think I'll get some sleep,' he murmured. He settled down on the grass and yielded to an impulse of his dragon-body to curl his long neck back and tuck his head bird-fashion under one wing. 'See you in the morning, Secoh.'

'Whatever your excellency desires,' replied the mere-dragon in his timid voice. 'You just settle down over here, and if your worship wants me, your worship has only to call and I'll be right here ...'

The words faded out on Jim's ear as he dropped into sleep like an overladen ship foundering in deep saltwater.

7

When he opened his eyes, the sun was well above the horizon. The bright, transparent, cool light of early morning lit up the clear blue arch of sky overhead. The seagrass and the club rushes swayed slightly in the early breeze that was sending a series of light ripples over the stretch of shallow lake near where Jim lay. He sat up, yawned expansively and blinked.

Secoh was gone. So were the leftover bones.

For a second Jim felt a twinge of annoyance. He had been unconsciously counting on tapping the mere-dragon for more information about the fens. But then the annoyance faded into amusement. The picture of Secoh stealthily collecting the denuded bones in careful silence and sneaking away before daybreak tickled Jim's sense of humor.

He walked down to the edge of the lake and drank, lapping like some enormous cat and flipping several pints of water into his throat with each flick of his long tongue. Satisfied at last, he looked westward toward the misty line of the ocean and spread his wings –

'Ouch!' he said.

Hastily he folded the wings again, cursing himself mentally. He should, of course, have expected this from the way Smrgol had run out of breath while flying yesterday. The first attempt to stretch Gorbash's wings had sent what felt like several keen-edged knives stabbing into muscles he had seldom used before. Like anyone else who has suddenly overexercised a body out of shape for such activity, he was stiff as a board in that portion of his body he had most need of at the moment.

The irony of it did not escape him. For twenty-six years he had gotten along quite nicely without wings. Now, after one day's use of them, he was decidedly miffed to have to proceed on foot. His amusement gone, he turned his head toward the ocean and set about following a land route.

Unfortunately, it could not be a direct route. Instinctively, he tried to travel on land as much as possible, but often he had to jump small ditches – which caused his wings to spread instinctively and sent fresh stabs of pain into his stiff flying muscles – and once or twice he had to actually swim a ditch or small lake too wide to jump. This taught him why dragons preferred to walk or fly. Unlike humans, they apparently had a slightly higher specific gravity than water. In other words, unless he swam furiously, he had a tendency to sink. And his dragon-body, Jim found, had a near-hysterical fear of getting any water up its nose.

However, proceeding by these methods, he finally gained a rather wide tongue of land which he assumed to be the Great Causeway that Secoh had spoken about. He had seen nothing else to compare with it in the fens and, if further proof were needed, it seemed to run westward as far as he could see, as straight as a Roman road. It could almost, in fact, have been built there: it was several feet higher than most of the surrounding bits of land, covered with bushes and even an occasional tree.

Jim rolled on the grass – he had just finished swimming one of the stretches of water too wide to jump – and flopped, belly-down, in the sun. A tree nearby kept the sun out of his eyes, the heat of the daystar's rays were soothing to his stiff muscles and the grass was soft. He had walked and swum away most of the morning and the midday hush was relaxing. He felt comfortable. Dropping his head on his foreclaws, he dozed a bit . . .

He was awakened by the sound of someone singing. Lifting his head, he looked about. Someone was coming out along the causeway. Jim could now hear the dry clopping of a horse's hooves on the firm earth, the jingle of metal, the creak of leather, and over all this a fine, baritone voice carolling cheerfully to itself. Whatever the earlier verses of the song had been, Jim had no idea. But the chorus he heard now came clearly to his ear.

'... *A right good spear, a constant mind –*
A trusty sword and true!
The dragons of the mere shall find
What Neville-Smythe can do!'

The tune was one of the sort that Jim may have heard somewhere before. He was still trying to decide if he really knew it or not, when there was a crackling of branches. A screen of bushes some twenty feet away parted to disgorge a man in full plate armor, with his visor up and a single strip of scarlet pennon afloat just below the head of his upright lance; he was seated on a large, somewhat clumsy-looking white horse.

Jim, interested, sat up for a better look.

It was, as things turned out, not the best possible move. Immediately, the man on horseback saw him and the visor came down with a clang, the long lance seemed to leap into one steel-gauntleted hand, there came a flash of golden spurs, and the white horse broke into a heavy-hooved gallop, directly for Jim.

'A Neville-Smythe! A Neville-Smythe!' roared the man, muffledly, within his helmet.

Jim's reflexes took over. He went straight up into the air, stiff wing muscles forgotten, and was just about to hurl himself forward and down on the approaching figure when a cold finger of sanity touched his mind for a fraction of a second and he flung himself instead into the upper branches of the tree that had shaded his eyes.

The knight – as Jim took him to be – pulled his horse to a skidding stop on its haunches directly under the tree; and looked up through the branches at Jim. Jim looked back down. The tree had seemed fairly good-sized when he was under it. Now that he was up in it, with all his dragon-weight, its branches creaked alarmingly under him and he was not as far above his attacker's head as he would have preferred to be.

The knight tilted back his visor and canted his head back in order to see upward. In the shadow of the helm Jim made out a square-boned, rather lean face with burning blue eyes over a large, hooked nose. The chin was jutting and generous.

'Come down,' said the knight.

'No thanks,' replied Jim, holding firmly to the tree trunk with tail and claws.

A slight pause followed in the conversation as they both digested the situation.

'Damned caitiff mere-dragon!' said the knight, finally.

'I'm not a mere-dragon.'

'Don't talk bloody nonsense!'

'I'm not.'

'Course you are.'

'I tell you, I'm not!' said Jim, feeling a preliminary stirring of his dragonly temper. He got it back under control, and spoke reasonably. 'In fact, I'll bet you can't guess who I really am.'

The knight did not seem interested in guessing who Jim really was. He stood upright in his stirrups and probed upward with his lance through the branches, but the point came a good four feet short of Jim.

'Damn!' said the knight, disappointedly. He lowered the lance and appeared to think for a moment. 'If I take off my armor,' he said, apparently to himself, 'I can climb that goddam tree. But then what if he flies down and I have to fight him on the bloody turf, after all?'

'Look,' called Jim, 'I'm willing to come down' – the knight looked up eagerly – 'provided you're willing to listen with an open mind to what I have to say, first.'

The knight thought it over.

'All right,' he said, at last. He shook the lance at Jim, warningly. 'No pleas for mercy, though!'

'Of course not.'

'Because I shan't grant them, dammit! It's not in my vows. Widows and orphans, men and women of the Church and honorable enemies surrendering on the field of combat. But not dragons!'

'No,' said Jim, 'nothing like that. I just want to convince you of who I really am.'

'I don't care who you really are.'

'You will,' Jim said. 'Because I'm not really a dragon at all. I've been put under an ... ensorcelment to make me look like a dragon.'

'A likely story.'

'Really!' Jim was digging his claws into the tree trunk, but the bark was flaking away under his grasp. 'I'm as human as you are. Do you know S. Carolinus, the magician?'

'I've heard of him,' grunted the knight. 'Who hasn't? I suppose you'll claim he's the one who ensorceled you?'

'Not at all. He's the one who's going to change me back as soon as I can find the lady I – to whom I'm affianced. A real dragon ran off with her. That's what I'm doing so far from home. Look at me. Do I look like one of your ordinary mere-dragons?'

The knight considered him.

'Hmm,' he said, rubbing his hooked nose thoughtfully. 'Come to think of it, you are a size and half on what I usually run into.'

'Carolinus found my lady had been taken to the Loathly Tower. He sent me out to find some Companions, so I could go and rescue her.'

The knight stared.

'The Loathly Tower?' he echoed.

'That's right.'

'Never heard of a dragon – or anyone else in his right mind, for that matter – wanting to go to the Loathly Tower. Shouldn't care to go there myself. By heaven, if you *are* a dragon, you've got nerve!'

'But I'm not,' said Jim. 'That's why I've got – er – nerve. I'm a gentleman like yourself, bent on the rescue of the lady I love.'

'Love?' The knight reached into a saddlebag, produced a piece of white cloth and blew his nose. 'I say, that's touching. You love this demoiselle of yours?'

'Doesn't every knight love his lady?'

'Well ...' The other put his handkerchief away again. 'Some do, some don't, politics being what it is these days. But it *is* a coincidence. You see, I love my lady also.'

'Well, then,' said Jim, 'that's all the more reason you shouldn't interfere with me in my efforts to rescue mine.'

The knight went into one of his moments of obvious thought.

'How do I know you're telling the truth?' he said, at last. 'Bloody dragons could say anything!'

Jim had a sudden inspiration.

'I'll tell you what,' he said. 'Hold your sword up, point down. I'll swear on the cross of the hilt that what I say is true.'

'But if you're a dragon what good will that do? Dragons don't have souls, dammit!'

'Of course not,' retorted Jim. 'But a Christian gentleman does; and as a Christian gentleman, I wouldn't dare forswear myself, now would I?'

Jim could see the knight visibly struggling with the inverted logic of this for several moments. Finally he gave up.

'Oh, well,' he said, held up his sword by the blade and let Jim swear on it.

He put the sword back in its sheath. Jim let go the trees and half jumped, half flapped down to ground.

'It might be...' said the knight, moodily, staring at Jim as Jim stood up on his hind legs to dust the bark and twigs from his foreclaws. 'There was a palmer in gray friar's-cloth came to the castle last Michaelmas and spoke a rhyme to me before he left:
'"Betyde thee weale yn any fyght
When'ere thou kens: thy cause ys right."'
But I don't see how it applies.'

'Don't you?' said Jim, thinking rapidly. 'I'd say it was obvious. Because I'm bent on rescuing my lady, if you tried to kill me, your cause would be wrong. Therefore weale wouldn't have betyded you.'

'By St. John!' said the knight, admiringly. 'Of course! And here I thought I was just out after some mere mere-dragon today! What luck! You're sure this cause of yours is right? No doubt about that, I suppose?'

'Of course not,' said Jim, frostily.

'Well, then, I *am* in luck. Naturally, I'll have to demand permission of my lady, since there's another demoiselle involved. But I can't see her objecting to an opportunity like this. I suppose we'd better introduce ourselves, since there's no one around to do it for us. I take it you know my arms?'

He swung his shield around for Jim's inspection. It showed, on a red background, a wide X of silver, like a cross lying over sideways, above a rather fanciful-looking animal in black, which Jim made out to be lying down in the triangular space under the lower legs of the X.

'The gules, a saltire silver, of course,' went on the knight, 'are the Neville of Raby arms. My great-grandfather, as a cadet of the house, differenced with a hart lodged sable – and, of course, I'm in the direct line of descent.'

'Neville-Smythe,' said Jim, remembering the name in the song he had just heard and any memories he could dig up on the subject of heraldry. 'I bear – in my proper body, that is—'

'Assuredly, sir,' Neville-Smythe agreed.

'An – gules, typewriter silver on a desk sable. Sir James Eckert, Knight Bachelor.' Jim suddenly remembered something Carolinus had mentioned in explaining him to Smrgol and took a chance on gaining a little authority. 'Baron of Riveroak. Honored to make your acquaintance, Sir Brian.'

Neville-Smythe lifted off his helm, hung it on the pommel of his saddle and scratched his head puzzledly. He had light brown hair, rather compressed by the helm; and now that his face was out in the sunlight, it could be seen that he was no older than Jim. What had given the impression of a greater maturity in the shadow of the visor was a very deep tan and little sun wrinkles around the outer corners of Neville-Smythe's blue eyes. Also, a white scar seamed his lower right cheek down to the jawline, adding a veteran-like touch to his appearance.

'Typewriter ...' Sir Brian was muttering to himself. 'Typewriter ...'

'A – local beast, rather like a griffin,' said Jim, hurriedly. 'We have a lot of them in Riveroak – That's in America, a land over the sea to the west. You may not have heard of it.'

'Damme if I have,' replied Sir Brian, candidly. 'Was it there that you were ensorceled?'

'Well, yes and no,' said Jim, cautiously. 'I was transported to this land of yours by magic, as was the lady – Angela. Then when I woke, I found myself bedragoned.'

'Were you, now?' Sir Brian had bright-blue eyes, amazingly innocent-looking in comparison to his tanned and scarred face. 'Angela, eh? Fair name, that.'

'As she herself is fair,' answered Jim, gravely.

'You don't say, Sir James! Perhaps we ought to have a bit of a go on behalf of our respective ladies while we've got the chance, before we get to know each other too well for it.'

Jim swallowed.

'On the other hand,' he said, quickly, 'you were telling me about your lady. What was her name?'

'The Lady Geronde.' Sir Brian began to fumble about his saddlebags. 'I've got her favor here, someplace. Wear it on my arm when I expect to run into someone, of course, but when one's out hunting dragons – Half a moment. It must be right here under my hand . . .'

'Why don't you just tell me what it's like?' Jim suggested.

'Oh, well.' Sir Brian gave up his search. 'It's a kerchief, you know. Monogrammed "G.d'C." The Lady Geronde Isabel de Chaney, presently chatelaine of the Castle Malvern. Her father, Sir Orrin, went off to the wars against the Eastern heathen three years ago Whitsuntide, less five days; and there's been no word of him since. If it weren't for that and the fact that I have to do all this scurrying around the countryside, winning worship and so forth, we'd have been married by this time.'

'Why do you do it, then? Go riding around the countryside, I mean?' Jim asked, curiously.

'Good Lord, Geronde insists on it! Once we're married, she wants me to come home safe, you know.'

Jim did not follow this argumental development in the conversation. He said so.

'Why, how do you people manage things, overseas?' demanded Sir Brian. 'Once I'm married, with my own lands, I've got to produce my own levy of men if my lord or the King calls on me for service in war. If I don't have a name, I'll be forced to march out with a raggedy-breeched bunch of bumpkins and clodpoles out of my own fields, who'll like as not take to their heels at the first sight of trained men-at-arms, and probably leave me no choice but to die on the spot for honor's sake, if not for other reasons. On the other hand, if I'm known about as a warrior of some worth, I'll have good, experienced men coming and wanting to serve under my banner, because they know, do you see, that I'll take good care of them. And, by the same token, they'll take good care of me.'

'Oh,' said Jim.

'And besides,' went on Sir Brian, ruminatively, 'this chasing about does keep one in shape. Though I must say the mere-dragons we have around here don't give you much of a workout. That's why I had high hopes of you there for a moment. Doesn't do to practice with the neighbors, you know. Too much chance of a lost temper and a feud resulting.'

'I see,' said Jim.

'However,' said Sir Brian, brightening, 'all's well that ends well. And this quest of yours to rescue your lady can certainly be worth a dozen mere-dragons to my reputation. Though, as I say, I'll have to get permission from Geronde, first. Happily, Castle Malvern's only a day and a half's ride from here. *Long* days, though; so hadn't we better be moving?'

'Moving?'

'Traveling. Covering distance, Sir James!' Brian squinted up at the sun. 'We've only about a half-day's light left to us now, and that means noon or better of the second day before we can see the gates of Castle Malvern. So, shall we?'

'Hold on a minute,' said Jim. 'You're talking about both of us going to this Castle Malvern. Why?'

'My good sir, I explained why,' said Sir Brian with a touch of impatience, reining his horse about so that it faced to the east. 'The Lady Geronde must give her permission, first. After all, my first duty's to her.'

Jim stared.

'I still don't follow you,' he said, at last. 'Permission for what?'

But Brian was already walking his horse away from the ocean. Jim hurried to catch up with him.

'Permission for what?' he repeated.

'Sir James,' said Brian, severely, turning his head to look Jim squarely in the eyes – on horseback, his head was just about level with Jim's as Jim walked on all fours. 'If this continued questioning is a jest of some sort, it is in sorry taste. What else could I seek my lady's permission for, than to accompany you on your quest and make one of the Companions you told me you were seeking?'

8

They went along silently, side by side. Brian stared straight ahead as he rode, looking somewhat stiff-faced and offended. Jim was busy adjusting to the idea of the knight as a Companion.

He had not really paid that much attention when Carolinus had echoed the watchbeetle in saying that Jim would gather Companions to aid him in rescuing Angie and facing up to the Dark Powers. But as far as he had thought about it, he had assumed he would be selecting those who would join him. He had not really envisioned them thrusting themselves upon him.

Obviously, Brian was not likely to be a liability as a Companion. Plainly, he had no lack of courage and his appearance testified to some experience in combat. But beyond these things, what did Jim really know about the man? Nothing, in fact, except for the meager facts of his name, arms, and the identity of his lady.

On the other hand, was it wise to look a gift horse in the mouth? Carolinus had spoken of forces at work and given the impression that inhabitants of this world were about to be divided by them into two camps – that of the Dark Powers and that of those who, like Jim, were in opposition to them. If that was the case, then it ought to be possible to identify the camp to which any particular individual belonged by watching to see who and what he lined up with.

Brian had lined up with Jim. Therefore, he ought to be in the camp of those opposing the Dark Powers, by definition ...

Jim came up out of his thoughts to realize that the knight was still riding alongside him stiffly, with a very obvious, if invisible, chip on his shoulder. A small apology might be in order.

'Sir Brian,' said Jim, a little awkwardly. 'Excuse me for not understanding that you were offering yourself as a Companion. The truth of the matter is, things are different where I come from.'

'Doubtless,' said Brian, unsmilingly.

'Believe me,' said Jim, 'there was no jest of any kind involved. It was just my own lack of – er – wit, that kept me from understanding what you were talking about.'

'Ah,' said Brian.

'Naturally, I couldn't ask for a better Companion than a gentleman like yourself.'

'Quite.'

'And I'm overjoyed to have you with me.'

'Indeed.'

Jim felt like someone knocking on the door of a house in which the owner was home but obstinately refusing to answer. A touch of annoyance tweaked at him; and on the heels of this came an idea at which he nearly smiled visibly. Ignorance of other people's customs could work both ways.

'Of course, if only I'd known your Social Security number right from the start,' he said. 'It would have been different.'

Brian's eyes flickered. They continued to travel on side by side in silence for perhaps another full minute before the knight spoke again.

'Number, Sir James?'

'Why, yes,' said Jim, raising his eyebrows. 'Your Social Security number.'

'What bloody number is that supposed to be?'

'Don't tell me,' said Jim, 'you don't have Social Security numbers here?'

'Blind me if I ever heard of any such thing!'

Jim clicked his tongue sympathetically.

'No wonder you thought it odd of me, not understanding the offer of your Companionship,' he said. 'Why, where I come from nothing can happen unless a gentleman's Social Security number is known. Naturally, I thought you were withholding yours for good reasons of your own. That's why it didn't dawn on me that you were offering me Companionship.'

'But I haven't got one to withhold, dammit!' protested Sir Brian.

'Haven't got one?'

'By St. Giles, no!'

Jim clicked his tongue again.

'That's the trouble with living out in the provinces, here,' Sir Brian said in an aggrieved tone. 'They've probably been using these what-do-you-call-it numbers for a twelvemonth now at Court; and none of us out here have ever heard of them.'

They went on a little farther in silence.

'*You've* got one, I suppose?' Brian said.

'Why – yes,' Jim answered. Hastily, he delved into his memory. '469-69-9921.'

'Damned fine figure.'

'Well…' Jim decided he might as well pick up some credit while the opportunity existed. 'I am Baron of Riveroak, after all.'

'Oh, of course.'

They rode on a little farther.

'I say,' said Brian.

'Yes, Sir Brian?'

Brian cleared his throat.

'If I was to have a something-number of my own, what would you venture to say it might be?'

'Well, I don't know …'

'Well, well, I shouldn't ask it, I suppose. Puts me at a disadvantage, though.' Brian turned a troubled face to Jim. 'Here you tell me your number and I can't reciprocate.'

'Think nothing of it,' said Jim.

'I *do* think something of it, though.'

'You shouldn't,' Jim insisted. He was beginning to feel a little guilty in spite of himself. 'I'm sure your number, if you had one, would be a very good one.'

'No, no. Probably quite an ordinary figure. After all, what am I? Just an outlying knight bachelor, no chansons about me for the minstrels to sing, or anything like that.'

'You underestimate yourself,' said Jim, uneasily. The ploy was getting out of hand. 'Of course, I wouldn't know what the official number would be; but in my country I'd guess you'd be at least a' – he had to think rapidly to count the digits in his own Social Security number – '387-22-777.'

The eyes Sir Brian turned on him were as round as dinner plates.

'Really? You think so, do you? All that?'

'At least that.'

'Well, well. What was it again?'

Jim slowly repeated the number he had given Brian several times over until the knight had it by heart; and they went on cheerfully together, chatting like old friends. Like Companions, in fact, thought Jim.

Brian, having gotten over his stiffness of manner, turned out to be eager to talk. Specifically, his topic of conversation was the Lady Geronde, who was apparently not only the most beautiful of women, but a collection of all the other talents and virtues as well. Over and above Geronde, however, the knight was a repository of local gossip, both bloody and salacious. Jim had never considered himself to be someone easily shocked, but what he was now hearing was startling.

He was, in fact, learning fast. His mind had been translating the language and actions of Sir Brian into the fuzzy, quasi-Victorian image of a stage Englishman that most Americans carried around in that part of their mind reserved for stock characters. Now, a closer acquaintance with the knight was destroying that particular image rather thoroughly.

To begin with, Brian was entirely physical, pragmatic and human. 'Earthy' might have been a better word. The taboo areas in his cosmos were restricted to those of religion and a handful of ideals and principles. Curiously, he seemed perfectly capable of highly idealizing something as an abstract idea, and at the same time ruthlessly being honest about it as a specific reality – all without seeing any particular conflict between these attitudes. For example, Jim learned, to Brian his King was at once a majestic figure anointed by God, a ruler by divine right for whom Brian would die without question if the need arose, and at the same time a half-senile old man who was drunk half the time and could not be trusted with the more important decisions of his kingdom. The lady Geronde was somehow both a goddess on a pedestal, above and beyond the touch of gross males, and a thoroughly physical human female with whom Brian's hands were quite familiar.

Jim was still trying to fit this double view of the knight into a pattern with the other things, like intelligent dragons, talking watchbeetles and the existence of Dark Powers, which he had so far discovered in this world, when the daylight began to wane and Brian suggested they look about for a place to camp overnight.

They had left the fens well behind by this time, and had spent several hours striking at an angle northeast through the rather unpleasant wood Jim had flown over the day before and congratulated himself on not having to traverse at ground level. Happily, now, they had left it behind for a much less forbidding forest, still mainly populated by oaks and elms, but in the shape of larger specimens of these, which had killed off the more tangled undergrowth underneath them, so that the going was easier. They came at last to a small clearing by a brook, which in the last rays of the afternoon sun, filtering through the high branches of the trees, looked almost as inviting as Carolinus' property by the Tinkling Water.

'Should do us quite well, I'd think,' Brian observed, cheerfully.

He dismounted, unsaddled his horse, rubbed it down with some handfuls of grass he pulled up, and left it tied on a long tether to crop its dinner from the clearing. For himself, Brian produced from his saddlebags something dark which was evidently smoked meat. For Jim, there was nothing; and, although his stomach twinged reproachfully at him, Jim could not really blame the knight for not offering to share the food. What had made a rather adequate meal for the man would have made a single, unsatisfyingly small gulp for the dragon. Tomorrow, Jim promised himself, he would find some excuse to leave Brian for a while and find a cow ... or something.

He became aware that Brian was lighting a fire, something he viewed with only academic interest at first, out of his own newly discovered indifference to external temperatures. But, as the sun went lower behind the trees, its light reddened to the color of bright blood and deep shadows started forming between the surrounding tree trunks; and the fire, now blazing away heartily on the dry, fallen branches that Brian had accumulated, began to take on the appearance of the only mark of cheerfulness in the growing darkness.

'Getting chilly,' observed Brian, hunching his shoulders and standing close above the fire.

He had divested himself of helmet, gloves and the plate armor from his legs, leaving only his upper body metal-covered. His hair, recovered from the pressure of tilt helmet, had expanded to show itself as quite a mane. It gleamed with ruddy highlights from the fire, as he stood facing the flames.

Jim drew close on the fire's other side. It would not have occurred to him to think of the night as growing chilly, but he was conscious of a sort of depression of the spirit which had come on him with the disappearance of the sun. The forest about them, which had seemed so friendly in the daylight, now began to acquire an ominous and threatening appearance as night closed in. Looking around, Jim could almost swear that the surrounding darkness was a physical entity trying to push inward upon them, only held back by the dancing light of the fire.

'Where are we?' he asked Brian.

'Lynham Woods,' said Brian. He, too, looked about at the wall of night surrounding the circle of firelight. 'Not such a bad place, ordinarily. But there's a difference about this night, wouldn't you say, Sir James? One gets the feeling there's something afoot out there in the dark, somewhere.'

'Yes,' Jim agreed, feeling a small, involuntary shudder inside him.

To his dragon-senses Brian's description was unpleasantly accurate – it did indeed feel exactly as if something was prowling out there in the woods, somewhere beyond the firelight, circling their camp and waiting for an opportunity to pounce.

'Stars,' Brian commented, pointing upward.

Jim looked up between the treetops. Now that the sun was completely down, some stars were visible. No moon, but some stars. However, even as he watched, they began to disappear one by one, as if an invisible curtain was being drawn across the sky.

'Clouds,' said Brian. 'Well, there's one comfort. With a cloudy sky, it shouldn't get as cold here before morning as it might if the sky were clear. A clear sky and I'd have ventured to guess at a touch of frost before dawn. It's cool for this time of year.'

The clouds to which Brian had referred had by this time covered all portions of the sky visible beyond the treetops. The clearing now seemed englobed in unrelenting lightlessness.

Slowly, the knight sat down by the fire and began to replace the cuisses and greaves he had earlier removed from his legs.

'What is it?' asked Jim. 'What're you doing that for?'

'I don't like it,' Brian said shortly. 'There's something amiss this night. Whatever it is, it'll find me armed and ready for it.'

He finished getting his body armor back on and went to get his helmet and lance from where he had placed them with his saddle and other gear. He drove the butt of the lance into the ground beside the fire, so that it stood point upward by his right hand, and put the helmet on, leaving the visor up.

'Let us keep facing each other with the fire between us, Sir James,' he said. 'That way we can watch all about us, as far as the firelight shows.'

'Right,' Jim replied.

They stood facing each other. After a little while a sound began, very faint and faraway at first.

'A wind,' Brian remarked.

It was indeed the sound of a wind. They could hear it far off, almost as if it was hunting among the bushes and the limbs of the trees. The sound of it rose, fell, and moved from quarter to quarter, but always off in the distance. Then, gradually, it began to come closer, as if it had been quartering the forest for them and was now closing in.

Still, in the clearing, not a breath of air stirred, except that drawn in by the updraft from the dancing flames of the fire. Brian threw more of the dried branches upon the blaze.

'My special thanks to St. Giles, whose day this is,' muttered the knight, 'and who moved me to gather wood enough to last until dawn.'

The wind drew closer. They could hear the sound of its passage, now loud in the near-distance. It breathed closer and closer to them, leaving a sighing and groaning of branches where it passed. It was loud now, loud enough so that they had to raise their voices above its sound to speak to one another. Then, suddenly, it was on them.

It blew directly into the clearing with an abrupt force that threatened for a second to push them off their feet. The fire shot up a long trail of sparks into the darkness and its flames guttered nearly to extinction, so that the gloom all around suddenly flooded in on them, and they were peppered in the face by a shower of dried twigs and dead leaves.

Then, as quickly as it had come, the wind was gone. The fire flamed up again and the darkness was pushed back once more. Without warning, there was silence.

The wind had gone.

Brian sighed softly within the open visor of his helmet.

'Stand to watch, Sir James,' he said softly. 'Now, it comes.'

Jim stared at the knight.

'It comes—' he started to echo.

And then he heard it.

It was so small and distant at first, he thought it was only a singing in his eardrums. Then it grew ever so slightly in volume and he identified it for what it actually was: a continuous, high-pitched chittering – like the wind, now off at a distance, but gradually growing closer. He sensed something mindless about that chittering, something that made the skin crawl on the back of his dragon-neck, instinctively.

This body reaction stirred Jim almost more than the sound itself had done. What could there be out in woods like this, at night, of which even a dragon would be afraid? He opened his mouth to ask Brian what was making the noise; and found the question stuck in his throat. An almost superstitious fear checked him. If he asked Brian, and Brian told him, then whatever was moving in on them would become undeniably real. As long as he still did not know, it could be that it could all turn out to be an illusion, a bad dream from which he would awaken to a sunlit morning.

But as they stood, the chittering grew slowly louder and closer – and there was no awakening from a nightmare.

'Sir Brian,' he said, at last. 'What is it?'

The knight's eyes, within the firelit gloom of his visor, burned strangely on Jim.

'You don't know? Sandmirks, Sir James.'

The moment Brian spoke the identifying word, something in the very blood and bones of Gorbash passed knowledge on to the mind of Jim – and he knew without further asking what they looked like, those hunters out in the night, circling ever closer and closer to this campfire and the two of them who waited here.

In his mind's eye Jim saw them, something of a cross between a rat and a ferret in shape and the size of small dogs. Their eyes would shine red, reflecting the light of the flames when they came close enough, but their black, coarse-haired bodies would remain invisible in the darkness as they passed around and around the clearing, just beyond the reach of the firelight. And from their mouths would continue to come this same mindless chittering that was like the claws of spiders running up and down Jim's spine and into his brain.

'What they do here,' said Brian, 'this far from the sea, only the devil that helped them knows. Their proper runs are the cold salt beaches. Little shore animals and the poor castaways who have the ill luck to wash ashore at night are their proper prey. Here is an enemy against which my sword and your claws, Sir James, will be small help.'

'If they come close enough—'

'They will not, while the minds are in our bodies. These are craven creatures, whose weapon is madness.'

'Madness?' Jim echoed. The word had slid along all his nerves like an icy knife.

'What else did you think their noise meant?' Brian said. 'The story is that they're possessed of the souls of other animals who have died insane, or in great torment, and so they are full of the stuff of madness, which they pour out on the night air to infect the minds of such as you and I. I know not how it is with you, Sir James, but Saint Giles has always been a good friend to me and he did not advise me to gather this huge pile of firewood for nothing. It's my counsel that we turn to that good saint, and to God with all his angels, for none else can aid us, here.'

The knight drew his sword, rested it point down on the earth before him, and taking the hilt of it in both his hands, bowed his head above it in prayer. Jim stood still, watching the armored man, the fire and the surrounding darkness, hearing the steadily growing sound of the chittering.

He was not at all religious himself; and somehow, in this particular moment, something in him rebelled at the thought of turning, or even pretending to turn, to religion for help. On the other hand, he could not help envying Brian for being able to find such a backup available and waiting.

For, whatever the truth was about the souls of animals who had died insane or in torment, there was no denying the fact that some quality in the chittering went clear through the conscious, logical, upper part of Jim's mind into the old, primitive levels behind it, and plucked the chords of atavistic fears he had not known he possessed. Deep within him, from the very first moment in which he recognized the chittering as something more than a singing in his ears, was the impulse to turn and run from it. To run and run, until either he could hear it no more, or his heart would burst from the effort of running.

In the end, that must be what all victims of the sandmirks did – run until they could run no more. And then, at last, with their prey exhausted and helpless, the black, fiery-eyed, humping shapes would close in, chittering, to kill and feed. While his conscious mind still worked, Jim recognized the fact that if he ran, he was lost. Like Brian he must stand here and fight back against the noise that was gnawing away at his sanity.

He could not bring himself to follow Brian's example; but there had to be other things he could do to set up a defense against the calling of the sandmirks. The multiplication tables?

He tried them. For a while, he was able to concentrate on them; and he congratulated himself on finding a weapon. But after he had run through all those that he knew readily and had started again on them, he found that the second time through they did not shut out the chittering as well as they had the first time. The third time he went through them, they were hardly any help at all, not much more than meaningless sounds muttered under the breath.

He searched his mind as best he could under the effect of the sandmirk voices – which were now clearly circling the camp at a distance of no more than fifty yards away or so – for something stronger than the multiplication tables with which to oppose them. In desperation, he began to recite the argument of his doctorate thesis on the changes in social custom deriving from the rise of the cities in France during the Hundred Years' War. Night after weary night, after all other work had been done, he had sat in the single light of his desk lamp, hammering out that thesis. If there was protective magic in anything he knew, it would be in that.

'... *Examination of the direct effects of the English military incursion into western France in the two decades immediately following the thirteen-fifties,*' he muttered, '*show a remarkable process of change at work unrecognized by the very people caught up in it. Particularly the port of Bordeaux ...*'

Suddenly, to his joy, he realized it was working. All those midnight hours of effort he had put into the thesis had created a piece of mental machinery with a momentum that was too powerful for the chittering of the sandmirks to clog and stop. As long as he could keep the words of it running through his head, he could hold them off. It was as if the chittering was blocked now by a barrier that allowed only the harmless noise of it wash over the barrier's top. The thesis had been two hundred and twenty double-spaced pages of typescript when finished. He would not reach the end of his material too soon, as he had with the multiplication tables. He glanced across the fire at Brian, and found the other still praying. Neither one of them dared take time off to speak with each other, but Jim tried to signal with his eyes that he was holding his own and he thought that Brian understood and returned a like message.

The sandmirks were close now – just outside the circle of firelight; and the sound of their voices was so shrill and encompassing that Jim could hardly hear the sound of his own voice in his ears. Nonetheless, he and Brian were holding their own and the predators in the darkness would not dare attack while their prey still had the will and the strength to defend themselves. As Jim watched, Brian reached down to throw a couple more of the dead branches on the fire.

Flames spurted up on the new fuel; and for a second, straining his eyes, Jim thought he had a glimpse of shadowy shapes slipping back out of sight into the further darkness. He and Brian continued their watch, and their own private litanies.

The night wore on.

The fire blazed. The sandmirks continued to circle, never stopping for one moment their invitation to terror. Croaking, with voices gone hoarse from steady, long use, Jim and the knight faced each other above the fire. Sir Brian swayed a little with weariness; and Jim felt himself also growing light-headed with exhaustion. The dark continued unbroken around them. The raw, damp scent of dawn was in the air, but daybreak was yet some time off.

And now, for the first time since he had begun to recite his thesis, Jim felt the pressure of the sandmirk voices beginning to crumble away the barrier he had erected against them. His exhausted memory fumbled, lost its place on the remembered page it was quoting, and found it again. But in that second of weakness the effect of the chittering had gained ground. It pierced through the words Jim painfully uttered; and its power was growing steadily.

Jim became conscious that Brian had stopped speaking. Jim also stopped and they stared at each other across the fire while the sound of the chittering soared in volume all around them, lifting triumphantly into the night.

The knight reversed his sword, picking it up to hold blade upward in both hands.

'In God's name,' said Brian, in such a torn and ragged voice that Jim could hardly understand him, 'let's go to them, while we still have the strength to do so.'

Jim nodded. In the final accounting, to charge death was preferable to fleeing from it in sick fear. He stepped around the fire to stand, beside Brian.

'Now!' said the knight in his husk of a voice, raising his sword overhead –

But before they could charge the almost invisible foe that encircled them, a scream almost worse than the chittering split the darkness to their right. At once, the sound that had driven them to the edge of madness ceased utterly, to be followed by the noise of many small bodies crashing away in flight through the woods.

Another scream sounded, this time straight ahead and farther out. A moment of waiting followed, during which the sounds of flight had all but died in the distance; and then came a third scream, farther off yet.

'By Saint Giles!' whispered the knight in the stillness. 'Something's killing them ...'

He had hardly finished before a fourth scream came, this time a long distance off. After that, utter silence.

Numbly, Brian moved to build up the fire. It crackled, blazed afresh and the shadows drew back a long distance. Jim glanced upward.

'Look,' he said. 'I think...'

Brian looked. An edge of cloud was pulling back from a few stars that were still visible; and the sky behind the stars was paling.

'Yes. Dawn,' said Brian.

They stood watching as the sky turned toward light and the remaining stars faded to invisibility.

'But what was it that came to our rescue?' the knight asked.

Jim shook his head.

'I don't know,' he said, hoarsely. 'I can't guess what—'

He broke off.

Something had moved – a blacker black within the darkness of the still-deep shadows beyond the firelight. It moved again and came forward slowly, stepping into the light. A four-legged shape as large as a small pony, green-eyed, with long narrow muzzle, half-parted to show white, gleaming teeth and a tongue as red as the fire flames.

It was a wolf. A wolf double the size of the largest wolf Jim had ever seen in a zoo or on film. The green eyes went past the knight and the fire to burn savagely upon Jim.

'So it's you,' a deep, harsh voice from the scimitar-armed jaws said. 'Not that it makes all that difference. But I thought as much.'

9

The mind can take only so much before reaction sets in. With all Jim had been through since he had ended up in this world, and particularly after the ordeal he had just gone through as the prey of the sandmirks, he should not have been struck numb by the fact that now it was a wolf who could talk like a man. But he was.

He sat down on his haunches with a thump. If he had been in his regular human body, he probably would have collapsed on the ground. But the effect was the same. He struggled to find his voice while the monster wolf walked forward to the fire.

'Who – who're you?' he managed at last.

'What's the matter, Gorbash?' snarled the wolf. 'Sandmirks got your memory? I've only known you for twenty years! Besides, there's few living who'd mistake Aragh for any other English wolf!'

'You're who – Aragh?' croaked Brian.

The wolf glanced at him.

'I am. And who are you, man?'

'Sir Brian Neville-Smythe.'

'Never heard of you,' growled the wolf.

'My house,' said Sir Brian stiffly, 'is a cadet branch of the Nevilles. Our land runs beyond Wyvenstock to the Lea River on the north.'

'None of my people up there,' grated Aragh. 'What're you doing down here in my forest?'

'Passing through on our way to Malvern, Sir wolf.'

'Call me Aragh when you talk to me, man.'

'Then address me as Sir Brian, Sir wolf!'

Aragh's upper lip began to curl back from his gleaming teeth.

'Wait—' said Jim, hastily.

Aragh turned to him, lip uncurling slightly.

'This Sir Brian is with you, is he, Gorbash?'

'We're Companions. And actually I'm not really Gorbash. You see …' Jim tried hastily, with his weary throat, to explain the situation that had ended up bringing Brian and him to this place.

'Hmpf!' Aragh growled, when Jim had finished. 'Pure nonsense, all of it. You always did get yourself mixed up seven different ways every time you tried something. However, if this Sir Brian's committed himself to fight alongside you, I suppose I can put up with him.'

He turned to Brian.

'And you,' he said. 'I'll hold you responsible for taking good care of Gorbash. Soft-headed he is, but he's been a friend of mine for years—'

A light went on in the back of Jim's mind. This Aragh must be the wolf friend of Gorbash's which Smrgol had talked disapprovingly about, the one Gorbash had associated with while he was growing up.

'—and I don't want him chewed up by sandmirks, or anything else. D'you hear me?'

'I assure you—' Brian was beginning stiffly.

'Don't assure me. Just do it!' snapped Aragh.

'About those sandmirks,' Jim put in hastily, once more in an effort to turn the Brian-Aragh conversation from possible disagreement, 'they almost had us. Didn't that sound of theirs bother you?'

'Why should it?' said Aragh. 'I'm an English wolf. You don't catch me thinking of two things at once. Sandmirks belong on the seashore. They'll know next time what'll happen if I catch them here in my woods.'

He snarled softly, as if to himself.

'You mean to say' – Brian took off his helmet and stared at the wolf in a sort of wonder – 'you could hear that chittering and not be troubled by it?'

'How many times do I have to say it?' growled Aragh. 'I'm an English wolf. I suppose if I sat around like some people and just listened, I might have noticed the noise they were making. But the second I heard them, I said to myself, "That lot's got to go!" And that's all I had on my mind until they went.'

He licked his lips with his long tongue.

'All except for four of them,' he said. 'They're no good for eating, of course. But they do scream well when you break their necks. I heard *those* noises they made, never fear!'

He sat down on his haunches in turn and sniffed at the fire.

'World's going to pot,' he muttered. 'Few of us left with any sense at all. Magicians, Dark Powers, all that nonsense. Break a few necks, tear a few throats out in the good old-fashioned way, and see how long these sandmirks and their sort'll go on acting up! See how much trouble the

Dark Powers would be able to stir up after a few doses like that to their creatures!'

'Actually, how long *have* you known Sir James?' inquired Brian.

'Sir James? Sir James? He's Gorbash, far as I'm concerned,' Aragh growled. 'Gorbash he's always been. Gorbash he'll always be, in spite of any spell-and-body nonsense. I don't believe in people being one person one day, then somebody else the next. You do what you want. As far as I'm concerned, he's Gorbash. Twenty years, to answer you. And didn't I say twenty years? Why?'

'Because, my good fellow—'

'I'm not your good fellow. I'm nobody's good fellow. I'm an English wolf; and you'll be wise not to forget it.'

'Very well. Sir wolf—'

'That's a bit better.'

'Since you've very little sympathy with the quest that Sir James and I are on, and since I see dawn is now breaking, it only remains to thank you for your assistance against the sandmirks—'

'Assistance!'

'Call it what you will. As I was saying' – Brian put his helmet back on, picked up his saddle and went to his horse – 'it only remains to thank you, say adieu and resume our travel to Castle Malvern. Come, Sir James—'

'Wait a minute!' snarled Aragh. 'Gorbash, what do you think you can do against those Dark Powers, anyway?'

'Well ... whatever I have to,' Jim answered.

'To be sure,' growled the wolf. 'And what if they send sandmirks against you again?'

'Well ...'

'I thought so,' said Aragh with bitter satisfaction. 'Up to me, as usual. Give it up, Gorbash. Stop this madness of thinking you've a human mind in you and go back to being a plain, straightforward dragon again.'

'I can't do that,' said Jim. 'I've got to rescue Angie—'

'Who?'

'His lady,' put in Brian, stiffly. 'He's explained how that other dragon, Bryagh, stole her off to the Loathly Tower.'

'His lady? His LADY? What's the times coming to, a dragon mooning about over some female human and calling her his "lady"? Gorbash, give up this nonsense and go home!'

'Sorry,' said Jim through his teeth. 'No.'

Aragh snarled.

'Damned idiot!' He got to all four feet. 'All right, I'll come along and make sure the sandmirks don't get you. But – only sandmirks, mind! I'm not going to be a party to the rest of this ridiculousness of yours!'

'Damme if I remember your being invited,' said Brian.

'Don't need to be invited.' Aragh's upper lip began to curl again as his head turned toward the knight. 'I go where I wish, Sir knight, and I'd like to see any try to stop me. I'm an English—'

'Of course you are!' Jim broke in, 'and there's no one we'd rather have with us than an English wolf. Is there, Brian?'

'Speak for yourself, Sir James.'

'Well, there's no one I'd rather have with me, besides Sir Brian here,' said Jim. 'Sir Brian, you have to admit those sandmirks were more than we could handle ourselves.'

'Hmph!' Brian looked as if he was being asked to agree to having a tooth pulled without without as much as a drink by way of anesthetic. 'Suppose so.'

He suddenly swayed where he stood and the saddle dropped out of his hands to thump on the ground. He walked heavy-footedly over to the nearest tree and sat down with a clatter of metal, his back to the trunk.

'Sir James,' he said hoarsely, 'I must rest.'

He leaned his head back against the tree trunk and closed his eyes. In a moment he was breathing heavily, with deep inhalations of air, just on the edge of snoring.

'Yes,' said Jim, looking at him. 'We both had a night with no rest. Maybe I should catch some sleep, too.'

'Don't let me stop you,' said Aragh. 'I'm not the sort to need a nap every time I turn around; but come to think of it, I might just trail those sandmirks and make sure they kept going once they left here.'

He glanced at the rising sun.

'I'll be back about midday.'

He turned about and effectively disappeared. Jim had a glimpse of him slipping between two tree trunks and suddenly there was no sound or sign that the wolf had ever been there. Jim lay down on the grass himself, tucked his head under a wing, and closed his eyes ...

But, unlike Brian, he did not find himself falling asleep.

He persisted in keeping his eyes closed and his head wing-tucked for perhaps twenty minutes before he gave up and sat up once more to look around him. Much to his own surprise, he was feeling quite well indeed.

He remembered now that the hoarseness of his own voice had

disappeared while he was standing around engaged in the three-cornered conversation with Aragh and Brian. Evidently his fatigue had vanished at the same time. These things were remarkable; but apparently dragons simply had better recuperative powers than humans. He looked at Brian, who was now frankly snoring the snores of utter exhaustion and had slid down the tree trunk until he was very near to lying flat on the grass. The knight ought to be out of things at least until noon. Which left Jim with that much time to kill. He thought once more about something to eat.

He got to his feet. Now might be the very time to look around and see if anything was available. About to wander off, he checked himself. What if he lost his way in the wood and could not find the route back here? Perhaps he should mark the trees as he went –

He broke off his thoughts, mentally kicking himself for an idiot. Of course, on foot he could easily get lost. But who said he had to go on foot? Experimentally, he stretched his wings and found that all the stiffness and soreness was gone out of them. With an explosion of air, he leaped from the clearing and headed skyward. Behind him, Brian slid all the way down on to the grass and snored ever more loudly.

But within seconds the knight was forgotten below him. It was a sheer pleasure to be on the wing again. A few vigorous flaps took him above treetop level. He banked in a circle to take a look back down at the clearing and set up a memory of its appearance from the air, then mounted higher to relate it to its immediate surroundings. High up, he was happy to see that both it and the stream running through it were quite distinguishable from a distance.

Leaving Brian and the clearing to take care of themselves, he banked again and began to quarter above the wood, examining it.

From the air it looked more parklike than it had on the ground. The large trees were spaced evenly enough so that he could get a fair to good view of the earth between them: Unfortunately for his stomach, nothing was in sight that looked like food. He looked about for Aragh, but found no sight of the wolf, either.

There seemed to be little point to his soaring above the forest, except for the pleasure of doing so and the fact that he had time to spend. A finger of guilt touched his mind. He had hardly thought of Angie since he had met the knight. Was she really all right? Perhaps he should make some effort to go and find out for himself?

With these thoughts, he let himself go with the thermals, an uneasiness in him like the memory of the chittering the sandmirks had made that could make the skin on the back of his neck crawl in recollection.

The only way to settle this uneasiness, he told himself now, was to go and make sure that Angie was all right. Carolinus' directions to stay away from the Loathly Tower until he had gathered the Companions who would aid him to overthrow the Dark Powers really did not make sense. He should decide, for himself, what to do—

He woke suddenly to the discovery that he was already at an altitude of at least several thousand feet and just rising into a tailwind blowing directly for the fens and the seashore – back the way he and Brian had come. Already, in fact, he was riding that air current in a long, soaring glide which would bring him eventually to ground at the point where the Great Causeway met the ocean. As he realized this, he heard echoing in his mind the memory of the chittering sandmirks. Overriding this was a knife-thin whisper calling him to the Loathly Tower.

'Now ...' the whisper was saying. 'Go now ... don't delay ... go alone, now ...'

He checked himself with a chill of horror, and fell off sharply in a long, turning bank that would bring him down and back toward the woods where he had left Brian sleeping. Almost as soon as he had turned, the echoing memory and the whisper were gone, like Aragh a short while back, as if they had never been.

Had he actually heard them? Or had he merely imagined them?

He shook the questions from him with an effort of will. He had certainly not imagined that he had unconsciously lifted to an altitude and a wind that would have carried him directly to the Loathly Tower. It gave him an uneasy feeling to find himself so vulnerable to a call from that direction. He had not been so, yesterday, even when he was headed on foot toward the tower. Somehow, the sandmirks' chittering had opened up a channel through which the Dark Powers could call him to them. And if this were so, even though the ugly, small creatures had been driven off, the Dark Powers had won something by their attack.

Or – was it that simple? Aragh had certainly put in an appearance in the nick of time. Wasn't the coincidence of the sandmirks' arrival just a little too good to be true? What if the Dark Powers had never intended that the sandmirks should destroy him? What if, for their own purposes, what they wanted was not the death of Jim Eckert, but his coming to their tower?

That was another chill thought.

Jim found himself wishing he had Carolinus nearby to question. But something told Jim that if he should turn and fly to the Tinkling Water now – even assuming he could get there, find Carolinus in and manage to return to Brian by noon – the magician would not be pleased to see him. Carolinus had made quite a point of Jim's following the path that would lead to his gaining of Companions, before he did anything else.

Well, Jim thought, soaring low once more over the Lynham Woods back toward the clearing where Brian was sleeping, he had acquired two of the Companions so far, at least. Brian and Aragh. Now that he was turned resolutely away from the Loathly Tower once more, he found his momentary suspicion of Aragh had evaporated. Hadn't Aragh been a close friend of Gorbash for years? Not that the wolf wasn't a grim enough character in his own right; but there was nothing secret, dark or hidden about that grimness. What he was, was all on the surface for anyone to see.

Jim checked himself as he soared over a small, dark object on the ground below. Turning back, he swept in and came down to land heavily beside it.

It was a dead sandmirk. Clearly one of the four Aragh had killed the night before.

Jim examined it. Here, after a fashion, was food; but he found that Gorbash's stomach recoiled from the thought. Why was not clear; but the reaction was undeniable. A tentative parting of Jim's jaws above the corpse brought a definite wave of nausea to the dragon-stomach. Apparently, Aragh had known what he was talking about earlier when he mentioned that sandmirks were no good for eating.

Jim left the carcass to some beetles and a few flies which were beginning to circle it, took to the air again and began his search for the clearing. It did not take him long to find, but the interval was enough for him to come to some conclusions about fueling this oversize body of his.

The touch of nausea had effectively cured his earlier appetite. Which made it pretty clear that it was only appetite, and not hunger, that he had been feeling. He and Secoh had divided the cow between them – in hindsight, Jim admitted that he had taken the lion's share of the meat – and even that large meal had not exactly filled up the stomach of Gorbash. In spite of this, he had really not been suffering for food, since. To be sure, he was ready to eat again at first opportunity, but he felt none of the interior hollowness and discomfort of real hunger. Apparently dragons were able to go for some time between meals, really stocking up only when fuel was available. The pattern of dragon feeding was obviously something like an enormous meal once a week or thereabouts. If so, he could probably go at least a few more days before really needing to eat. However, when he did, he had better do a good job of it . . .

By this time he had relocated the clearing and was gliding in to a landing on its grass. Brian, he saw, was still there, and still snoring.

A glance at the sun told Jim there were still at least three hours to go until noon, if not more than that. He walked to the stream, drank deeply, and flopped down on the grass. His outing had relaxed him. He felt limp and at peace with the world. He tucked his head under his wing once more without hardly thinking about it, and fell instantly asleep.

He woke to the voice of Brian, once more heartily rendering his musical promise of what the mere-dragons might expect from a Neville-Smythe.

Sitting up, Jim saw the knight sitting naked in the stream, happily splashing himself with what must be some fairly cold water and singing. His armor was laid about on the grass and his clothing was spread out and draped on sticks rammed into the turf, so that the various garments were spread to the sunlight. Jim got to his feet and walked over to examine the clothing. He assumed that Brian had washed it and that it was spread out like this to dry. But he found it already dry.

'Fleas, Sir James,' called Brian cheerfully. 'Fleas! Damme if they don't seem to love a gambeson under armor for breeding in more than any other cloth a gentleman might wear. Nothing like a good hot sun, or a good hot fire, to drive them out of the seams, eh?'

'What ... ? Oh, yes. You're right,' said Jim. 'Nothing like it, as you say.'

It had not occurred to Jim that body vermin might be as universal a problem on this medieval world as it had been in medieval times back on his own world. He took a second to be grateful for the fact that, evidently, his dragon hide was far too thick and tough to be bothered by the pesky creatures; then he glanced at the sun and saw that it was standing directly overhead.

'Aragh back yet?' he asked.

'He's not here,' said Brian.

'Not here?' growled the voice of Aragh. He slid into sight from behind a tree that should have been too small to hide him. 'I got back some time ago. Who says I'm not here?'

'No one, Sir wolf,' Brian said, cheerfully, rising from the stream. Stripping the water off his body and limbs with his hands, he walked over to his clothes and began putting them on, without bothering with further self-drying. 'We'll be ready to travel in a wink!'

It was slightly more than single wink's worth of time, but not too much more, before Brian had himself dressed and armored and his horse saddled. He swung himself up into the saddle.

'Shall we go?' he asked.

'Fine,' said Jim.

Aragh melted into the woods and disappeared. Jim and Brian, side by side, followed after the wolf.

They found him sitting down, waiting for them two clearings farther on.

'I see,' he growled. 'One of these poke-along, take-forever-to-get-there trips. Is that what it's going to be? All right. I can dawdle along at a walk as well as the rest of you.'

He fell in level with them and they paced forward together.

'I don't intend to trot my horse in the heat of the day, just to please you,' said Brian.

'Why not? Trot's the only pace to move at,' muttered Aragh. 'All right. Suit yourself. Oh, not that way, Sir knight. This way.'

'I know the route to Malvern Castle,' Brian said, stiffly.

'You know a route,' said Aragh. 'I know the shortest one. You'll be a day and a half, heading in that direction. I can bring you there before sunset. Follow me – or not. Makes no difference to me.'

He headed off to their right, tail swinging low behind him. Jim and Brian halted, looking at each other.

'But that way leads to the *lower* reaches of the Lyn River,' Brian protested. 'The closest ford's fifteen miles upstream.'

'It's his woods, though,' said Jim. 'Maybe we ought to trust him.'

'Sir James—' Brian began. 'Oh, very well!'

He turned his horse's head in the direction Aragh had taken and together they moved after the wolf, catching up with him a little farther on.

They rode through the warm hours of the afternoon. The forest opened out even more, but never quite ceased being a forest. To begin with they did very little talking, Aragh and Brian growling 'Sir knight' and 'Sir wolf' at each other whenever Jim tried to draw them into any kind of conversation. But gradually the atmosphere thawed on the pleasant discovery by the two that they had at least one thing in common: a detestation of someone named Sir Hugh de Bois de Malencontri.

'... sent his beaters through my woods!' snapped Aragh. 'My woods! As if it was his private preserve. I broke up his hunting for him. Hamstrung half a dozen horses and—'

'I say, not the horses!'

'Why not?' Aragh said. 'You humans in armor make yourselves safe by riding on somebody else's four legs. Catch an English *wolf* letting anybody laze about on his back!'

'A gentleman has a use for a good steed. Not necessary for game, though. Always dismount, myself, to go after a boar with a boarspear.'

'Ah? Twenty or thirty of you at once, no doubt!'

'No such thing. I've gone into a thicket by myself, alone, several times!'

'Well, that's something,' said Aragh, grudgingly. 'No boar's a picnic. No brains, but no picnic either. Will charge anything. The only way to handle one is step aside and cut him up. Break a leg or two for him, if you can.'

'Thanks, I prefer the boarspear. I take his charge. Crosspiece keeps him from getting at you. Then it's hang on until you can let go for a moment to get a falchion into his throat.'

'Suit yourself,' Aragh growled. 'Anyway, de Bois' fine gentlemen didn't like being on their feet. I killed two, crippled eight, before the main party came up with crossbowmen.'

'Well done!'

'Eh? All in the day's work. I missed de Bois himself, though. He knocked somebody else out of the saddle, took his horse and ran before I could follow. No matter,' Aragh snarled lightly to himself. 'I'll catch him one of these days.'

'Unless I get to him first,' said Brian. 'By St. Giles! He had the affrontery to pay his court to the Demoiselle Geronde. Hah!'

'The de Chaney ... ?'

'Exactly! My lady. I drew him aside at my lord the Duke's Christmas feast, nine months since. "Lord Baron," I said, "a word in your ear. Keep your bastard's breath out of my lady's face or I may be forced to hang you by your own guts."'

'He said?' growled Aragh.

'Oh, some nonsense about having his verderers skin me alive if he ever caught me near his lands. I laughed.'

'And then?' put in Jim, fascinated.

'Oh, he laughed, too. It was my lord Duke's Christmas feast – peace on Earth, good will and all that – neither one of us wanted to make a public fuss. And that was how matters stood when we parted. I've been too busy with mere-dragons and now this quest of yours, Sir James, to get around to keeping my promise to him. But I really must, one of these days.'

And so on ... in the same vein.

About midafternoon, they came out abruptly through a screen of trees and bushes onto the banks of the River Lyn. Without pausing, Aragh stepped off into the water and proceeded to head across the stream, immersed almost to his backbone. Jim and Brian stopped.

'But there's no ford here, dammit!' said Brian.

'With weather the way it's been for the past month and this time of year,' said Aragh over his shoulder, 'there is – for this week and the next. But suit yourself.'

In fact, the wolf was nearly to midstream now and his neck and head were still well above the surface of the water. Brian grunted and urged his horse down the bank. He began to ride across.

'I think I'll fly,' Jim announced, looking at the river with disfavor.

He had not forgotten his swimming sessions in the fens. He leaped into the air, and with a few wingbeats passed over the heads of the others to land on the far bank and watch Aragh climb dripping back onto dry land. They waited together for Brian.

'Must say you knew what you were talking about,' said the knight, grudgingly, to Aragh as he came ashore. 'If this is Malvern Wood on this side, which it should be—'

'It is,' said Aragh as they moved off together into the forest.

'—we should indeed see the walls of the castle there before nightfall,' concluded Brian. 'I must say, being on my lady's land is almost like a homecoming to me. If you'll notice, Sir James, how peaceful and pleasant things are here—'

A *thwack* resounded, and a three-foot arrow stood suddenly in the ground a few paces in front of them.

'Hold!' cried a high-pitched voice, the voice either of a woman or a young boy.

'What the hell?' demanded Brian, reining up and turning in the direction from which, judging by its angle in the turf, the arrow had come. 'I'm going to crop myself some archer's ears—'

Thwack! sounded another arrow, materializing in the trunk of a tree a foot behind and an inch or two to the right of Brian's helmet.

'I'll take care of this,' Aragh grunted, on a low note, and vanished.

'Hold where you are, Sir knight!' cried the voice again. 'Unless you want me to put an arrow through that open visor of yours – or into one of your eyes, dragon! Don't move a muscle until I come to you.'

Jim froze where he was. Brian, also, he saw, was prudently not moving.

They waited.

10

It was a golden afternoon. In the Malvern Wood birds sang and a little breeze blew past Jim and Brian. Time went by and nothing else happened.

A deer walked across the open space between two trees about twenty yards from them, paused to look interestedly at the two unmoving figures and continued on, out of sight. A badger galumphed past, ignoring them completely in the tough, deliberate manner of its species.

Jim's feet were beginning to go to sleep, when he heard a droning sound in the air. A bumblebee buzzed into their vicinity, circled twice and then flew into the opening in the knight's visor. Jim waited interestedly, sleeping feet forgotten, for the explosion he was sure would come; but he had underestimated the self-control of Sir Brian. Neither sound nor movement emanated from the knight; although with his acute dragon hearing, Jim could now hear the bee buzzing hollowly around in the helmet and falling silent intermittently, which meant it must be landing on lip, nose or ear momentarily to assess the situation.

Eventually the bee flew out again.

'Sir Brian?' said Jim, questioningly, for he had actually begun to wonder if the knight was still conscious within his armor.

'Yes, Sir James?'

'Something's wrong. Whoever shot at us must have run off, right afterwards. Or something. We've been standing here twenty minutes. Why don't we go look?'

'Perhaps you're right.'

The knight reached up, snapped his visor down and reined his horse behind the tree the arrow was stuck in. No further shots came in their direction. Jim followed him; and keeping some trees always as a screen between themselves and the point from which the arrow had probably been launched, they circled around to investigate.

The woods appeared as quiet and untenanted as they had been all day, for perhaps a hundred yards' distance. Slightly beyond, however, the two came upon a slim figure in brown hose and doublet, with a peaked hat over shoulder-length red hair, kneeling on the grass with a longbow and quiver of arrows laid to one side, massaging the furry neck of a large black shape.

The large black shape was Aragh's. He was lying on his stomach in the grass, his long muzzle stretched out on his forepaws and his eyes half-closed, growling softly to himself as the slim hands worked on his neck and scratched under his ears.

'What devil's spell is this?' roared Brian, pulling his horse to a halt as he and Jim came up.

'You,' said the figure kneeling on the grass, glancing up at him, 'guard your tongue, Sir knight! Do I look like the devil?'

Clearly she – for obviously the figure in the doublet and hose was no boy – did not look like any devil. The word 'angel' might have fitted better, if it had not been for her rather steely gray eyes and the deep, practical tan of the skin on her face and uncovered hands and forearms. Aside from those two ordinary aspects, however, she appeared almost too good to have been cast from the ordinary human mold.

Even kneeling in the grass as she was, she was obviously almost as tall as Jim or Brian. Her legs were long, her waist tiny, her shoulders delicate but wide, and the curves of her body such as an artist of Jim's world might come up with for the illustration of some advertiser's commercial daydream. Her hair, a few shades darker than Brian's in the sunlight, was touched with highlights of honey-colored gold. She had a delicate curving jawline, a perfect mouth, a perfect nose and those same eyes which – except for the steeliness Jim had already remarked – had also to be considered perfect.

'No,' admitted Brian. 'But what're you doing to the wolf to make him growl like that?'

'He's not growling,' she said fondly, stroking his neck. 'He's purring.'

Aragh opened his left eye and rolled it up to look at Brian and Jim.

'Mind your own business, Sir knight,' he grated. 'Up under the ears there, again, Danielle ... Ah!'

He went back to his growling.

'I thought you were going to take care of things, Sir wolf!' said Brian, gruffly. 'Do you know we stood there for—'

'The knight's a Neville-Smythe,' snarled Aragh to the girl, lifting his head from his paws. 'The dragon's an old friend of mine named Gorbash – thinks he's a knight, too, right at the moment. Sir James of something. Can't remember the Christian name of the Neville-Smythe.'

'Sir Brian,' said Brian, taking off his helm. 'And the good knight with me, who's been ensorceled into a dragon's body, is Sir James, Baron of Riveroak, from a land across the sea.'

The girl's face lit up with interest. She scrambled to her feet.

'Enchanted?' she asked, approaching Jim and looking closely into his muzzle. 'Are you sure? I don't see human eyes within the beast eyes, as they say you should. Can you tell people what you were, Sir James? What was it like being enchanted? Did it hurt?'

'No,' said Jim. 'Just, all of a sudden, I was a dragon.'

'And before that you were a baron?'

'Well ...' Jim hesitated.

'I thought so!' she said, triumphantly. 'Part of the spell keeps you from telling who you really were. I mean, undoubtedly you were the Baron of Riveroak, but you were probably a lot more than that. A hero of some kind, probably.'

'Well, no,' said Jim.

'How would you know? This is exciting. Oh, my name's Danielle. I'm the daughter of Giles o' the Wold; except that I'm on my own, now.'

'Giles o' the Wold?' Brian echoed. 'He's that outlaw, isn't he?'

'He is now!' she flashed, turning on him. 'He was a gentleman of rank once, though his true name I will tell to none.'

Aragh growled.

'No offense,' said Brian with surprising mildness. 'I thought Giles o' the Wold, though, was of the King's Forest, up beyond Brantley Moor?'

'So he is,' she said. 'And there he and his men are, still. But, as I say, I now live apart from him.'

'Ah,' said Brian.

'Ah, yourself!' she said. 'Why should I spend my days with a bunch of men either old enough to be my father, and women just as old, or clodpated young bumpkins who turn red and stammer when they speak to me? My father's daughter deserves better than that!'

'Well, well,' said Brian.

'And again, well!' She looked from Brian to Jim and her voice softened. 'I feel no need to crave pardon, Sir James, but it's only fair to say I'd not have shot at you if I'd known you and this knight to be friends of Aragh.'

'That's all right,' said Jim.

'Quite all right,' echoed Brian. 'However, if you're through tickling the wolf, my lady o' the Wold, perhaps we three should be moving on. We want to get to Malvern Castle before the gate's locked for the night.'

He reined his horse about in the direction they had all been heading originally and began to ride off. Jim, after a moment's hesitation, moved after him. A second later they were joined not only by Aragh, but by Danielle, her bow and quiver slung upon her shoulder.

'You're going to Malvern Castle?' she asked. 'Why?'

'I must ask permission of my lady Geronde de Chaney to companion Sir James here in the rescue of his lady.'

'His lady?' She turned on Jim. 'You've got a lady? Who is she?'

'Angela, uh ... de Farrel, of Trailercourt.'

'Odd names you have overseas,' commented Brian.

'What does she look like?' demanded Danielle.

Jim hesitated.

'She is fair,' Brian put in, 'according to Sir James.'

'I'm fair,' said Danielle. 'Is she as fair as I am?'

'Well ...' Jim stumbled. 'Yes and no. I mean, you're different types ...'

'Different types? What does that mean?'

'It's a little hard to explain,' said Jim. 'Let me think about it. I'll think of a better way to explain it after I've had a chance to mull it over.'

'All right. You mull,' said Danielle. 'But I want to know. Meanwhile, I think I'll come along with the rest of you to Malvern Castle.'

Brian opened his mouth. For a second he looked as if he would say something. But then he closed his mouth again.

They moved along together, Danielle refusing an offer from Brian to mount her behind him on his horse. She could, she stated, outrun the heavy white charger any day in the week. Certainly she could out-walk him.

Jim was more than a little baffled by Danielle. He had been prepared to take on in the way of Companions any who could be useful to him. When Brian had cropped up, he had wrestled a bit with the idea of the knight simply declaring himself in. Once he had accepted that idea, however, Aragh's joining them had seemed almost natural. But this girl – to be one of his Companions, to face the Loathly Tower and the Dark Powers and rescue Angie? In no way could he envision her being useful. Granted, she was good with a bow and arrow ...

He lost himself in the mental puzzle of trying to reconcile all the unbelievable elements of this place he and Angie had fallen into. The dragons, the magician, the sandmirks (if he had seen them on film in a late, late movie he would have sneered at them), Aragh, and now this russet-haired goddess with a bow and arrow who talked like – he did not know what she talked like. Except that he was becoming more and more wary of finding himself in a conversation with her. She had a directness which literally scared him silly. What gave her the idea that she could ask any question she felt like?

Of course, he did not have to answer. But not answering simply made him look as if he were dodging something. The nub of the problem was that Jim had been very strictly trained not to ask embarrassing questions; and apparently Danielle had no inhibitions at all in that area.

The next time she asks me something I don't want to answer, he told himself, I'll simply tell her it's none of her business—

'Ridiculous!' he heard Brian saying to Aragh, 'I tell you. From this angle we have to come in behind the castle, at the Little Lyn Stream, where the curtain wall is up on a rock and there's no way in, even if someone on the wall recognizes me.'

'We come in facing the gate, I tell you!' snarled Aragh.

'Back!'

'Gate—'

'Look,' said Jim hastily, waking once more to his role as peacemaker between these two. 'Let me ask somebody local. All right?'

Peace at any price.

He turned aside from their line of march through the apparently unending wood, and searched about for a source of directions. It certainly could not be too hard to find someone. Granted, there seemed to be no other humans about. But in this world, everything seemed capable of speech – dragons, watchbeetles, wolves ... An exception might be the flora. So far he had seen no evidence that trees, flowers or bushes could speak. But if he could only find an animal or insect ...

However, annoyingly, just at the moment, there was nothing in sight. He wandered on, looking for anyone at all: a mouse, a bird... Suddenly he almost tripped over a badger, in appearance a twin to the one he had seen galumphing by while he and Brian were holding their positions at the command of Danielle.

'Hey, wait!' he cried.

It did not seem disposed to wait. Jim flipped himself into the air on his wings and thumped again to earth, this time facing the badger.

He had it backed up against a bush. It bared its teeth in true badger fashion. Badgers, Jim remembered a zoologist saying once at a rather drunken faculty party, would tangle with anybody. This one was obviously not about to spoil the general reputation of its kind, in spite of the fact that Jim-Gorbash outweighed it something like a hundred to one.

'Take it easy,' said Jim. 'I just want some information. We're headed toward Castle Malvern. Will this way bring us up behind it, or to its front?'

The badger hunched its shoulders and hissed at him.

'No, really,' Jim persisted. 'I'm just asking.'

The badger snarled and made a lunge for Jim's left forefoot.

When he snatched the foot back, the badger turned with a speed that was surprising in a creature of its apparent clumsiness, slipped around the bush and disappeared. Jim was left staring at nothing.

He turned away to find Brian, Danielle and Aragh behind him, all in a row, staring at him.

'I just wanted to get some directions from someone who knew ...' he began; but his voice died in his throat at the sight of their stares. They were looking at him as if he had taken leave of his senses.

'Gorbash,' said Aragh, at last, 'were you trying to talk to that badger?'

'Why, yes,' said Jim: 'I just wanted to ask someone who knew the local area whether we would come out behind Castle Malvern, or in front of it.'

'But you were talking to a *badger!*' said Danielle.

Brian cleared his throat.

'Sir James,' he said, 'did you think you recognized this particular badger as someone you knew who had also been ensorceled? Or is it that in your country badgers can talk?'

'Well, no – I mean, I didn't recognize this badger; and no, in my country badgers can't talk,' said Jim. 'But I thought ...'

His voice failed. He had been about to cite as evidence his experience that dragons, watchbeetles and wolves could talk; but faced with those stares, he got the abrupt but certain feeling he had just managed to make a fool of himself.

'Mixed up in the head, that's what he is!' Aragh said, gruffly. 'Not his fault!'

'Well,' said Jim, defensively. 'I talk, and I'm a dragon.'

'Don't dragons talk where you come from, Sir James?' asked Danielle.

'We don't have dragons where I come from.'

'Then what gave you the idea they didn't talk?' demanded Aragh. 'Been overworking your brains, Gorbash, that's the trouble. Try not to think for a while.'

'We have wolves where I come from' – Jim turned on him – 'and they don't talk.'

'Wolves don't talk? Gorbash, you're addled. How many wolves do you know?'

'I don't exactly know any. But I've seen them in ... I mean, on ...'

Jim realized immediately that the words 'zoos' and 'films' would mean as little to the three in front of him as 'Social Security number' had meant to the knight, earlier. In whatever language he was speaking now, they would be nothing but meaningless noises.

'How about watchbeetles?' he demanded desperately. 'When I talked to Carolinus, he poured some water on the ground and a watchbeetle came to the surface and spoke.'

'Come, come, Sir James,' said Brian. 'Magic, of course. It had to be magic. Watchbeetles can't talk, any more than badgers can.'

'Oh, well,' said Jim feebly. He gave up. 'Never mind. As Aragh says, maybe I've been thinking too much. Let's forget it and get going again.'

They took up their route once more, and a sudden shower caught them unexpectedly. For a moment, as the raindrops pelted down hard about them, Jim looked around for shelter – then recognized that the three with him were completely ignoring the wetting. Hard on this came his own recognition that his own armored hide was scarcely conscious of the moisture; and he decided to ignore it also. After a bit, the rain ceased and the sun tried to come out.

It was now in a quarter of the western sky which caused Jim to guess at a time of about 5 p.m. – an hour Brian and Danielle would probably refer to as midway between none and compline, from the canonical hours commonly in use in the Catholic Middle Ages. Momentarily, Jim ran back over his memory to fix those hours in his mind. The earliest was 'matins,' at midnight. Then came 'lauds,' at first daylight – call it plus or minus 5 A.M., depending on the season of the year. Then 'prime,' at sunrise – call that 6 A.M. Then 'terce,' midmorning – say, 9 A.M. 'Sext,' at noon. 'None' at midafternoon – 3 P.M. 'Vespers' at sunset – 5 P.M. or later ... Finally, 'compline,' before retiring; which would probably be no later than an hour or so after sunset, particularly if you were a monk and had to look forward to getting up at midnight.

He had reached this point in delving his memory, when Aragh abruptly put his nose up into the air.

'I smell smoke,' he said.

Jim sniffed the breeze which was blowing from them, not toward them. His dragon's sense of smell was not so much inferior to the wolf's but that he could smell smoke himself, now that his attention had been called to it. If they could smell it when the wind was carrying the odor away from them, then whatever was burning must be merely a short distance in front of them.

Aragh broke into a trot, and Brian spurred his horse to keep up. Jim increased his pace and Danielle ran easily alongside him. They went a short distance, emerged from among the trees and stopped, to find themselves in a clearing, at one end of a double row of huts made of mud and wattle, with straw-thatched roofs. Several of these were still smoking. The short rain had fallen here, too, and the bare earth between and around the huts was darkened and, in trampled spots, muddied by the water. The trees and the thatches still dripped moisture and the air was soft and damp. On it, here, the smell of smoke was strong. It hung still, for the breeze had now stopped.

The village – if that was what it was – was silent, with no one to be seen moving about it. Except for the few huts that had caught fire – only to have their flames apparently put out by the shower – there was nothing at all happening. The only people were four or five who had evidently fallen asleep about the street or in the doorway of some hut or other. About a dozen feet in front of Jim, as he pushed past Brian and Aragh for a better look, was a half-grown girl in a robe of coarse brown cloth, lying on her side with her back to them and her black hair spread on the mud.

Jim stared. Had the people here been having some sort of celebration, at which they became so intoxicated that they did not stir to put out the fires which drunken accident had started on their meager dwellings? He took one step more toward the girl to wake her up and ask her – and at that moment some twelve or fifteen men on horseback, with steel caps, half-armor and drawn swords, rode out from between the last huts at the far end of the village and turned to face Jim and the others.

The scene before Jim seemed to jump abruptly, like a faulty movie film, from one frame to the next. All at once, he saw the village with a difference: the people lying about were not merely sleeping, they were dead – killed – and their slayers were at the other end of the village street. He took a third step forward, looked at the dead girl before him, and from this fresh angle saw her arms stretched out before her without hands. They had been cut off at the wrist.

The smell of smoke now seemed to fill his brain. He launched himself into the air, swooping forward and down upon the mounted men. He saw their swords up, catching the watery sunlight as he drove into them, but he felt no blows. Three of the horses went down under the impact of his body and he tossed two of their falling riders aside with his clawed forepaws, cutting the third man – the one most directly in front of him – almost in half with one snap of his jaws. On the ground now, Jim reared up, striking out with claws, teeth and wings at once.

The action around him was a blur. He saw an arrow sprout suddenly, half out of the metal breastplate of a rider; and some gleaming metal drove into the fray on his right. The point of Brian's lance carried one rider clear off his horse and into another rider, who also flew from his saddle. Then the lance was dropped, and Brian's sword was cutting right and left; while under him the clumsy white charger – abruptly transformed – reared, screaming, lashing with its front hooves and savaging with its teeth, to beat to the ground the lighter horses about it.

At Jim's left a rider suddenly vanished from his saddle; and for one insane moment it was Aragh riding the mount instead, his jaws grinning as he launched himself from the leather under him into another of the opposing riders—

All at once, it was over. Two or three of the mounted men-at-arms, and as many riderless horses, were dashing off. Aragh, on the ground now, was tearing out the throats of any who still lived. Jim checked himself, snorting heavily through his nostrils, and looked around.

Neither Aragh nor Brian seemed to have been touched. Danielle, Jim was glad to see, was still several houses down the street, approaching them at a walk, bow still in hand and an arrow ready but not strung. She had stood back, it seemed, sensibly, and used her weapon as it ought to be used – from a distance.

Jim looked down at his own forearms and body. He was covered with blood, some of which was probably his own; but he felt nothing. Within, he was conscious of two conflicting emotions struggling for ascendancy. The dragon in him was savagely disappointed that there were no more enemies to kill; the man felt as if he badly wanted to be sick.

11

'Hold still!' said Danielle. 'How can I wash you off if you keep moving?'

He wanted to tell her that it was the dragon-adrenaline in him that was still making him twitchy. But he did not know how to explain this in terms she would understand. What had triggered him off had been a purely human horror at seeing the dead girl without hands, but after that he had been pure dragon. Or had he? An impulse made him stop and question this. Perhaps not. Maybe he was in some ways as savage as Aragh, or Brian or those men he had killed.

'That's all right,' said Danielle, having gotten him cleaned up. She was a competent, but not necessarily sympathetic, nurse. 'You're cut up more than a little; but nothing important. Three or four of the cuts could use some oil and bandages. But if you keep them clean, they should all heal well, despite the lack. Don't roll in the dirt, Sir James.'

'Roll? Why would I want to roll—' Jim was beginning, when Brian, who had been busy taking off his helm and gauntlets after retrieving his lance and checking it for damage, interrupted.

'It's plain to see,' he said, 'there's been no less than an attack on Malvern Castle. That lot of swine would not be foraying in such a manner unless the Malvern force at least were shut within walls and unable to sally. We'd best go carefully to get a look at the castle before we let the countryside know of our numbers and whereabouts.'

'Catch me approaching any castle any other way.' Aragh was standing nearby. Though his words were in character for the wolf, the tone was unusually mild. 'And what if the castle is no longer in the hands of your lady? Shall we turn back?'

'Not far,' Brian answered, tightly. His jaw muscles were lumped and the bones of his face seemed to stand out sharply under the skin. 'If the castle is taken, I have a lady either to rescue or avenge – and that takes precedence over my desire to help Sir James. If unfriends indeed hold the castle, we must find another place for ourselves this night. There's an inn not too far off. But first, let's go see how matters stand with the castle.'

'I can go and get back with no one seeing me,' said the wolf. 'Better the rest of you wait here.'

'Those who got away might come back with help, if we stay here,' put in Jim.

'Not with night coming on,' said Brian. 'Still, it won't be long until dark for us, as well. Perhaps it's best if you do scout the castle alone, Sir wolf. I and the others will head for the inn, to see if that's open to our using, or has been misused like this village. But wait – you don't know where the inn is.'

'Tell me,' said Aragh. 'Though, given a little time, I could find it easily enough myself.'

'Due west of the castle is a small hill with a crown of beech trees against the sky. If you look south from that hill's top, you'll see a place where the trees darken in a hollow, about two arrow-flights distant. You won't be able to see the inn, itself; but under those trees you'll find both it and the stream that runs by it.'

'Soon,' said Aragh, and was gone.

Jim, Danielle and Brian headed off through the wood, Brian leading.

'All this is familiar land to me,' he explained. 'As a boy I was a page here for three years, to learn my manners from Sir Orrin. My lady and I have walked or ridden over every foot of this ground, since.'

The sun was setting now, and long shadows stretched out from the trees across the grass. They were not forbidding shadows, however, as they had been in Lynham forest, the night before. The evening hush lay on everything and, with half the sky overhead painted pink, for a moment the world about them seemed a different one from that holding the village they had just left.

But the moment passed. The light continued to fade and they came at last to a spot where Brian stopped abruptly, holding up his right hand to halt Jim and Danielle.

'The inn's just beyond these trees,' he told them. 'But walk and talk softly. Sound carries in this place, particularly when there's no wind.'

They moved forward quietly together and gazed out from the shadows of the trees which the knight had indicated. They saw an open glade perhaps four hundred yards across at its narrowest. The stream Brian had spoken of to Aragh was ditched to flow completely around a long, stout building of logs, built in the center of the glade on a grassy mound of earth. that seemed artificially raised within the circle of land. At the far end of the building – actually an extension of it – stood a sort of half-open shed in which two horses could be seen tethered, their heads in some sort of wall trough, feeding.

'The inn door's open, and the shutters are folded back from the windows,' muttered Brian. 'So they're not in a state of siege. On the other hand, it can hardly be a trap with men waiting for us inside, seeing there are only those two horses in the stable. Nor would these two feed so quietly if other horses had been taken off into the woods nearby to trick us. Those in the stable would be eager to get loose and join their stablemates. Nonetheless, we'd best wait for Aragh. Indeed I believed that, swiftly as he travels, he'd be here before us.'

They waited. After only a few minutes, there was a movement behind, and Aragh was once more with them.

'Your fear's justified, Sir knight,' he said. 'The castle is barred and guarded. Also, I smelled blood spilled on the ground before the main gate, and the armed men on the walls talk of their lord, Sir Hugh.'

'*De Bois!*' The name seemed to stick deep in Brian's throat.

'What other Sir Hugh could it be?' Aragh's red jaws laughed in the last of the light. 'Rejoice, Sir knight! We'll both have our chance at him, shortly.'

'Rejoice? With my lady no doubt in his hands, as well as her castle?'

'Perhaps she escaped,' put in Jim.

'She's a de Chaney, and holds the castle for her father, who *may* be dead in heathen lands. She'd defend the castle to the death or her own capture.' Brian's teeth clicked together. 'And I won't believe in her death until I've had certain proof of it. Therefore, she's captured.'

'Have it your way, Sir knight,' said Aragh.

'I most surely shall, Sir wolf. And now, we need to scout this inn more closely to make sure it holds no trap for us.'

Aragh's jaws laughed again.

'Did you think I'd come to meet you here without first taking a look at that box down there? I came up close behind it, before coming to you here, and listened. There's an innkeeper, his family and two men servants. Also one guest. And that's all!'

'Ah,' said Brian. 'Then we go in.'

He started off and the rest of them caught up with him, walking openly across the glade in the last of the light; but a slight frown grew on the knight's face as they got closer to the ditch that separated them from the open front door.

'It's not like Master Dick Innkeeper not to be out of doors by this time to see who we are and what intentions we have,' he said.

Nonetheless, he kept walking forward. His armored feet rang

hollowly on the rough-hewn planks of the bridge crossing the ditch before the inn's door. He stepped onto the artificial island on which the inn was built, mounted its slight slope and walked into the gloom within, where what looked like a single torch had been lighted against the darkness. The others followed him in and found him stopped dead still, a pace inside the building.

He was staring at a lanky figure seated in a rough chair with his hose-clad legs propped up on the table before him. In one hand, the seated figure held the longest bow Jim had ever seen; and the other held an arrow loosely fitted to the string.

'And perhaps you'd better tell me who you are, now,' the figure said in a soft tenor voice with an odd, musical lilt to it. 'I can put an arrow through each of you before one of you could take a step, you should all know. But you do be seeming a strange pack of travelers to be together on the road, and if you have something I should be hearing, I'm prepared to listen, look you.'

12

'I'm Sir Brian Neville-Smythe!' said Brian, harshly. 'And you might think twice about whether you could put arrows through us all before one of us could reach you. I think I might just reach you, myself!'

'Ah no, Sir knight,' said the man with the bow. 'Do not be thinking of that armor of yours as something to make you different from the rest. At this distance the lady's doublet and your steel coat are the same as nothing to my arrows. The dragon a blind man could not miss, look you; and as for the wolf—'

He broke off suddenly, and laughed noiselessly for a second.

'It is a wise wolf, then,' he said, 'and a sly one as well. I did not even see him go.'

'Master bowman,' said Aragh's voice from out of sight beyond the open doorway. 'You'll have to leave that inn, someday, and travel in the woods. When that day comes you'll be breathing without a throat before you can close your fingers on a bowstring, some moment when you least expect it, if either Gorbash or Danielle o' the Wold is harmed.'

'Danielle o' the Wold?' The bowman peered at Danielle. 'That would be this lady, now, whose face I cannot see any more than I can see the faces of you others, for the glare of the sunset light behind you. Would you be of some relation to a Giles o' the Wold, lady?'

'My father,' said Danielle.

'Indeed! He is a man, then, and an archer – if report be true – whom I am most wishing to meet.' The bowman raised his voice. 'Rest you easy, Sir wolf. The lady will not be harmed by me, now; neither at this moment nor any other.'

'Why do you want to meet my father?' Danielle asked, sharply.

'Why, to be talking to him about bowmanship,' said the man at the table. 'I am Dafydd ap Hywel, look you, a man of the longbow, the same which was first made and used in Wales, and which has since falsely come to be called an English weapon. So I am traveling about to teach these English archers that it is none of them can come near to matching

694

a Welshman like myself, whether at mark or at rover, or at length of flight, or anything at all they wish to try with bow, string and shaft – and this because I am blood of the true bowmen, which they are not.'

'Giles o' the Wold can outshoot you twice over, any day!' said Danielle, fiercely.

'I do not think he will, indeed,' Dafydd said, gently, peering at her. 'But I do have a great wish to see your face, lady—' He lifted his voice. 'Innkeeper!' he called. 'More torches, here! And you have more guests also, look you!'

A faint sound came of voices and footfalls farther back in the building; and then light spilled through the doorway in the shape of a square-bodied, middling-tall man of about forty, holding a burning torch in one hand and carrying three unlit in his other fist.

'Sir knight – lady – dragon …' he said, a bit breathlessly, and began to stick the unlit torches in wall sockets around the room and light them.

As the new flames flared up, Jim could see that Brian's face was hard.

'How is this, Dick Innkeeper?' he said. 'Do you treat all old friends this way – hiding in the back of your inn until some other guest summons you forth?'

'Sir Brian, I – Forgive me—' Dick Innkeeper was obviously not used to apologizing; and the words came with difficulty. 'But my roof is over my head and my family alive only because of this guest. You may not know it, messire, but Malvern Castle has been taken by Sir Hugh de Bois de Malencontri—'

'I know it,' Brian interrupted. 'But you seem to have been spared.'

'Spared, we *have* been,' said the innkeeper, turning from setting the torch from which he had been lighting the others into the last wall socket. The red light showed all their faces clearly now. 'But only because of this bowman. It was two days since that he stopped here for the night; and early yesterday we heard horses outside and both went to the door to see fifteen or twenty men-at-arms riding out of the wood to my door.

'"I don't like this," I said to him, as we stood in the doorway together.

'"Do you not, my host?" he answered; and, without saying anything further to me, stepped out of doors and called to them to come no nearer.'

'It was no great thing,' said Dafydd, from the table, on which his feet were still cocked, although he had now laid aside his bow and arrow. 'They were a quarter of the way clear of the wood, and not an archer or crossbowman among them.'

'Even so,' said Brian, staring interestedly at him. 'Dick spoke of fifteen or twenty, and all mounted. Not likely they'd stop at your word.'

'Never they did,' the innkeeper explained. 'Whereupon he slew five of them in the time it takes me to draw a single breath. The others fled. When I went out to gather the bodies afterwards, every arrow was through the same place on each dead man's chest armor.'

Brian whistled.

'My lady Danielle,' he said, 'it strikes me your father may have something to do in outshooting this man of the Welsh bow, after all. I take it, Dick, those fellows of Sir Hugh's haven't been back?'

'They may come if they wish,' said Dafydd, mildly. 'I am not a man of great dispute, but I have said they shall not come in here, and they shall not.'

'Not likely,' said Brian. 'Sir Hugh's not fool enough to waste any more men than he has already, even to take an inn as valuable as this one.'

It was unfortunate – also involuntary – but at the word 'valuable' Jim felt again that sensation that had kindled in him back at the dragon cave, when the word 'gold' had been mentioned. Unfortunately, avarice seemed to be a built-in dragonly vice. He forced the reaction out of his mind. The innkeeper was still talking.

'... But what would you wish in food and drink, Sir Brian?' he was saying. 'I've meats both fresh and salted, bread and fruits of the season ... ale, beer and even French wines...'

Jim felt a new sensation kindle in him.

'And what can I give the dragon?' The innkeeper had turned to Jim. 'I've no cattle, swine, or even goats. Perhaps, if the good beast—'

'Dick,' said Brian, severely, 'this gentleman is Sir James Eckert, Baron of Riveroak in a land beyond the seas. He's been ensorceled into this dragon shape you now see him in.'

'Oh! Forgive me, Sir James!' Dick Innkeeper wrung his hands. Jim stared at him, fascinated, having never seen it done before. 'How can I make amends for my stupidity? Twenty-three years keeper of this inn, and never before have I failed to know a gentleman when he stepped through my door. I—'

'That's all right,' Jim said, awkwardly. 'It's a natural mistake.'

'No, no, Sir James!' said Dick, shaking his head. 'You're kind; but one who keeps an inn doesn't make mistakes, natural or otherwise, or he doesn't stay long in business. But what, then, can I bring you to eat, Sir James? Will you dine on what I can supply the others? I know not what food is preferred in lands beyond the seas. True, my cellar is stocked with great variety—'

'Why don't I just take a look down there,' said Jim. 'You did mention
... wine?'

'Indeed. Wine of Bordeaux, of Auvergne, of—'

'I think I'd like a little wine.'

It was a massive understatement. The moment the innkeeper had
mentioned the word 'wine,' Jim had experienced a glow inside him that
very nearly equaled the feeling he had had at the mention of gold. In
addition to their taste for treasure, it appeared, dragons had a fondness
for wine.

'And I'll find something down in your cellar to eat,' he said. 'Don't
bother about me.'

'Then perhaps you'd come with me, Sir James,' Dick offered, turning
toward an interior doorway. 'I think you can get through here all right?
As for the entrance to the cellar, since we need to pass casks through it,
it should be wide enough and the staircase stout enough to bear you ...'

Talking, he led Jim through the doorway, down a passage that was
narrow but adequate for Jim to pass, and into a large room that was
obviously a kitchen. In the kitchen wall to their right a wide door stood
open, with steps leading downward beyond it. Jim followed the innkeeper into the cellar.

The cellar, in fact, turned out to be worthy of the innkeeper's evident
pride in it. Apparently it ran a full length of the inn building and was
a storehouse of everything from what might be found in a medieval
attic to what might be found in a medieval castle store-house. Clothing,
furniture, sacks of grain, bottles full and empty, casks of drinkables ...

'Ah,' said Jim.

... And toward the far end a forest of hooks in the heavy wood beams
overhead supported heavy planks of smoked meats, including a small
wilderness of good-sized hams.

'Yes,' said Jim, stopping by the hams, 'this should do me nicely.
Where was that wine you were talking about?'

'All along the far wall, Sir James,' said Dick, bustling about. 'In the
bottles – but perhaps you'd want to taste the wine I've got in casks, of
which there's a greater assortment ...'

He was rummaging on a dark shelf – the cellar was unlit except for
the single torch he had carried down. Now, he came up with a large
container of darkened leather, with a wooden handle fixed to it by
metal straps. It looked as if it might hold perhaps three-quarters of a
modern American gallon. He handed this to Jim.

'Why don't you try the various wines – the wines are at this end of
the row, beer and ale at the other – while I take some meat and drink

up to Sir Brian and the others? I'll be back shortly, to carry up what you choose.'

'Don't bother,' said Jim, craftily. 'Actually, the furniture up there doesn't suit this dragon-body of mine too well. It's embarrassing trying to eat with other humans in their natural bodies. Why don't I just eat and drink down here?'

'Whatever you wish, Sir James.'

Dick went off, considerately leaving the torch he had brought down in a holder near the wine casks.

Jim rubbed his forepaws together, looking around him ...

13

Jim woke, under the vague impression that a conversation was going on somewhere in his vicinity. A pair of voices, both male, seemed to be talking in attempted hushed tones; but which, under the stress of emotion on the part of one voice or another, broke out occasionally to sound louder than its owner intended. Waking up a little more, but without opening his eyes, Jim identified one voice as Brian's, the other as that of the innkeeper.

Jim listened idly, only half paying attention to what he heard. He felt far too comfortable to concern himself about anything. For the first time since he had found himself in this body, his stomach was comfortably upholstered. He felt no further inclination to add to its contents, no matter what might be available within arm's reach. And the wine had been all that a dragon could have expected. Nor were there any noticeable aftereffects. Perhaps dragons did not get hangovers ... ?

He was gradually drifting back to full consciousness as he lay there. His eyelids were bright with what must be additional torchlight – he remembered that the torch Dick had originally left had guttered out sometime before he was through eating and drinking; but his dragon-body was quite at home in the dark, and also by that time he knew the location of everything in the cellar which interested him. The two voices were now completely understandable, so that he found himself following the conversation in spite of himself, and despite the fact that the two were obviously trying not to disturb him.

'... But Sir Brian,' the innkeeper was saying, forlornly, 'hospitality is one thing; but—'

'The bowman may have saved you from that small pack of rascals,' Brian answered, sternly, 'but if Sir Hugh's to be driven off and you and your family live once more in full safety, it'll be Sir James here, as well as myself, who'll provide you with that peace. How will you answer my lady, once she's been put back in possession of her castle, when she hears that you begrudged one of her rescuers a little food and drink?'

'A little!' Jim could imagine Dick wringing his hands again. 'Forty-six of the choicest hams! A quarter of a tun of Bordeaux and perhaps two dozen bottles of other wines! Three such meals by Sir James, Sir Brian, and you'll see me a ruined man!'

'Lower your voice!' Brian snapped. 'Want to wake the good knight with your complaining and crying? For shame, Master innkeeper! I've been with Sir James since two days ago and he's not eaten until now. It may well be he won't need to eat again until the castle's recovered. But, in any case, I've told you I'd see you paid for any costs he puts you to.'

'I know, Sir Brian. But an innkeeper can't merely put your pledge instead of food before hungry guests, with the explanation that his cellar's empty. It takes time to gather such a store of foodstuffs as I have – had – downstairs here. As it is, ham alone is going to be a rare dish under my roof until Eastermass of next year—'

'Hush, I say! Come away!' hissed the knight sternly.

The torchlight and the sound of footsteps withdrew together.

Jim opened his eyes in utter darkness. The strong jaws of his conscience began to nibble at him. This strange world with its talking creatures, its magic and its Dark Powers, had somehow put that part of him to sleep. Now it awoke, a giant with its strength re-doubled. However fairy-tale his existence appeared to be here, this was in fact a world where people were born in the ordinary fashion, suffered and died – were killed, too, like that poor child in the village with her hands cut off. He remembered how, back in his own world, he had wished to change modern times for a medieval period when problems were more solid and real. Now, here he was, surrounded with solid and real problems even if the rules were a little different – and far from appreciating that solidity and reality, he was acting as if it were some kind of dream in which he had no responsibility.

The innkeeper had a point. He had more than a point – he had a serious problem that was the result of Jim's simply helping himself to whatever and how much of the man's stock-in-trade had tickled Jim's appetite. The ripoff was no less than it would have been if Jim had walked into a supermarket back in his own world and made off with a hundred and twenty-six full-sized hams and twenty cases of wine.

And the fact that Brian had made himself responsible for the cost of the gargantuan meal made it no better. To begin with, Jim had no idea that he and the knight had become close enough friends so that one might be expected to undertake such an obligation for the other. Guiltily, Jim had to admit that if the situation were reversed, he, with his own world's twentieth-century attitudes toward someone he had only known for a couple of days, would have felt that the other had gotten himself into the situation and that it was up to the fellow to get out of it on his own ...

An inspiration broke suddenly upon Jim like the light of a torch abruptly kindled in a pitch-black cellar. Some of Gorbash's memories seemed still to linger in this body Jim was using. Perhaps the memory of where Gorbash kept his hoard was still there also, if only he could evoke it. If he could discover where the hoard was, he could pay back Dick Innkeeper himself, and rid his conscience of its uneasy sense of obligation to the knight.

Feeling much better, now that he had thought of this, Jim roused himself and, with a dragon's sureness in the dark, strode back along through the cellar and up its stairs into the kitchen. No one was there but a stout woman of about the innkeeper's age, who bobbed him a curtsey when he appeared.

'Uh, hello,' said Jim.

'Good morning, Sir James,' replied the woman.

Jim went down the passageway and into the tavern room. He felt shamefaced about the idea of encountering the innkeeper or Sir Brian, but the room when he stepped into it was empty. Once more the front door was open – a natural response to the need for some circulation of air, Jim realized, since the windows of the inn, even unshuttered, were mere slits – designed more for defense than for light and ventilation. He stepped outside and heard the voices of Brian and the innkeeper again, but from a distance. They were down at the stable end of the building, concerned with Brian's white warhorse, which had also been slightly cut up in the fight at the village.

Talk of the horse's cuts reminded Jim of his own. He had hardly been conscious of them yesterday. Today, however, he felt them – not seriously, but in the same way half a dozen small razor cuts might feel on his face after he had done a clumsy job of shaving. His Gorbash-body felt a sudden impulse to lick them; and he discovered that his supple neck and long tongue had no trouble reaching any of the wounds.

With the cuts all cleaned by his tongue, the discomfort from the wounds fell to a point where he could ignore them. He sat up and looked around, to discover Aragh sitting on his haunches not ten feet from him, watching.

'Good morning,' said Jim.

'It's good enough,' said Aragh. 'Spent the whole night inside that place, did you?'

'Well, yes,' answered Jim.

'Suit yourself,' Aragh said, grimly. 'You'll never catch me going into one of those boxes.'

'You didn't come in at all?'

'Of course not,' growled the wolf. 'That sort of thing's for humans. Something soft about all humans, Gorbash, even if they can hold their own like that knight and the bowman. I don't mean just soft in the body, I mean soft in the mind. Takes ten years for one of them to be able to take care of itself, and they never get over that. They remember being petted and fed and looked after; and later on, when they get the chance, they try to set up things so they get petted and cared for some more. When they get old and feeble, that's all they're good for – more petting and caring. Not for me, Gorbash! The first warning I'll get that I'm growing feeble is going to be when somebody who oughtn't to be able to, tears my throat out!'

Jim winced slightly. This assessment of human nature, coming on top of his guilt about last night's indulgence, struck a more tender spot than it might have done otherwise. Then he thought of something.

'You liked having Danielle scratch under your ears, yesterday,' he said.

'*She* did it. I didn't *ask* her to,' Aragh replied, gruffly. 'Wait'll she catches up with you!'

'Catches up with me?'

Aragh's jaws parted in one of his noiseless wolf-laughs.

'I know her. You and your nonsense about having a human lady, Gorbash! Now, you've got two!'

'Two?' said Jim. 'I think you're imagining things.'

'I am? Go see for yourself. She's just off there in the trees with that bowman.'

Jim looked away in the direction Aragh's muzzle was pointing.

'Maybe I will,' he said.

'Good luck!' Aragh yawned and lay down in the sun, jaws on fore-paws, eyes closed.

Jim went off toward the area Aragh had indicated in the surrounding woods. Stepping into the shade of the first big trees, he saw no one. Then his dragon-ears caught a murmur of voices that would have been inaudible to his human ones, coming froth a short distance farther off. Feeling like an eavesdropper, he moved quietly toward them, and halted when the speakers came into view.

They were standing in a small opening among the trees. The grass under their feet, the sunlight upon them and the tall elms all around them framed a picture that was almost too perfect to believe. Danielle, in her hose and doublet, looked as if she had just stepped out of a book of legends; and Dafydd, who stood with her, was hardly less imposing.

The bowman wore his bow and quiverful of long arrows – Jim got the idea that these two items were never more than an arm's length from him, even while he slept. Danielle, however, had left her own bow and arrows someplace else. She wore no weapon except the knife at her belt; although this, with its six-inch sheath outlining a near-equal length of blade, was certainly nothing to ignore.

'… After all,' she was saying, 'you're just a common bowman.'

'Not common, lady,' Dafydd replied softly. 'Even *you* ought to recognize that, look you.'

He stood over her. Danielle was tall, but Dafydd was a good deal taller. Jim had not really appreciated the Welshman's height, on seeing him seated in the inn. Grottwold might have been as tall; but beyond the overall inches, any similarity between the two men ended. Dafydd was as straight and supple as his own bow and his shoulders were as wide as the inn's front door. His face was of the sort usually described as 'chiseled' – straight nose, square jaw, level eyes, but all without the heavy boning of someone like Brian. His voice was soft and musical; and he had been entirely right about himself as a bowman – or anything else. He was not at all common.

Jim, watching, found himself completely caught up in wonder at Danielle's attitude. How, he wondered, could she prefer someone like himself – that is, if Aragh was telling the truth – to this medieval superman? For the moment, he had forgotten entirely that he was in a dragon's body, not in his ordinary human form.

'You know what I mean!' said Danielle. 'Anyway, I've had enough of bowmen to last me for a lifetime. Besides, why should I care about you, bowman or not?'

'Because I find you beautiful, lady,' Dafydd answered, 'and I remember nothing in all my life that I found beautiful that I did not want it; and, wanting, never ceased from striving for, until I gained it.'

'Is that so? I'm not some bauble to hang on your baldrick, Sir bowman! As it happens, I'll say who gains me!'

'Indeed, you shall. But shall no one else while I live – as you may now know from my telling you of it.'

'Hmph!' Danielle did not exactly toss her head, but Jim got the strong impression that for two cents, or its medieval equivalent, she would have. 'I'm going to marry a prince, when I marry. What can you do against a prince?'

'Against prince, king, emperor, God or Devil – the same thing I would do against any man or beast who came between me and the lady I wanted. One or the other of us would go down; and that is not likely to be myself.'

'Oh, of course not!' sneered Danielle.

She turned and marched away from Dafydd. Jim woke suddenly to the fact that she was coming straight for him and that in a moment he would be discovered. There was hardly anything to do but pretend he had just arrived. He stepped forward, out of the trees.

'There you are, Sir James!' Danielle called, happily. 'Did you have a good night's sleep? How are your wounds?'

'Wounds?' echoed Jim. She had certainly not dignified his cuts with the name of 'wounds' when she had cleaned him up yesterday. 'Oh, fine! Yes, I slept like a log!'

'Dear Sir James,' she said, reaching him. 'I've been waiting for you to wake up so that we can talk some more. There were things I wanted to know, you remember. Shall we take a walk, just the two of us?'

'Well ... sure,' said Jim. He had come into these woods with the firm intention of settling any foolish notions Danielle might have about him. Face to face with her, he felt his confidence evaporating. 'Oh, good morning, Dafydd.'

'Good morning, Sir James,' said the bowman, pleasantly.

Danielle already held Jim by the forearm and was leading him off into the wood at an angle to the route he had taken on coming here.

'I'll talk to you later in the day,' Jim called over his shoulder to Dafydd.

'Indeed now, we shall, Sir James.'

In a moment the small clearing was out of sight. Danielle led the way through the trees for some distance, but soon slowed her pace.

'Have you remembered anything?' she asked.

'Remembered?' Jim echoed.

'Of who you were, besides being Baron of Riveroak.'

'Well ... who could I be?' Jim said. 'I mean, just being Baron alone—'

'Come, Sir James,' said Danielle, impatiently. 'A gentleman isn't just his rank. For that matter, he can have many ranks. Isn't our Lord Duke also Count of Piers, Steward of the East Marches and lots of other things? And as for our King in England, isn't he also King of Aquitaine, Duke of Brittany, Duke of Caraballa, Prince of Tours, a Prince of the Church, a Prince of the Two Sicilies, Count this, Count that ... and so on, for half an hour? Baron of Riveroak is probably the *least* of your titles.'

'What makes you think so?' asked Jim, feebly.

'Why, because *you've* been enchanted!' Danielle snapped. 'Who'd bother enchanting a mere baron?'

Her manner softened. She reached up to pat him gently on the end of his muzzle. To Jim's surprise, the touch of her hand was a very pleasant thing. He wished she would do it again – and a small twinge of jealousy toward Aragh stirred within him.

'There! Never mind,' she said. 'It's the enchantment that keeps you from remembering. Are you sure it didn't hurt?'

'Not at all,' said Jim.

She looked dubious.

'We used to do a lot of talking about magic in my father's band, in the wintertime. There wasn't much else to do from December until March, once we got snowed in, but sit around the fire and talk. Of course nobody knew – but everybody seemed to think there'd have to be this one, sudden, terrible flash of pain when you changed forms. You know, the same way it would be if you were getting your head cut off, just before your head rolled on the ground and you were really dead.'

'It didn't happen that way with me,' said Jim.

'You've probably forgotten it – just like you've forgotten being a prince.'

'Being a prince?'

'Probably,' Danielle answered thoughtfully. 'Of course, you could have been a king or emperor; but somehow that doesn't seem to fit you like being a prince. What did you look like?'

'Well …' Jim coughed self-consciously. 'I was about as tall as Brian, say, and about the same weight. My hair was black and my eyes were green. I'm twenty-six—'

'Yes,' said Danielle, decisively, 'that's the right age for a prince. I was right.'

'Danielle …' said Jim. He was beginning to get a little desperate. 'I wasn't a prince. I happen to know I wasn't a prince. I can't tell you just how I know; but believe me. Take my word for it – I *know* I wasn't a prince!'

'There, there,' said Danielle, 'don't worry about it. It's undoubtedly just part of your ensorcelment.'

'What is?'

'Thinking you know you weren't a prince. Undoubtedly, whoever ensorceled you didn't want you realizing who you really are. Let's not talk about it any more now, if it upsets you. Do you happen to know how you can end the enchantment?'

'You bet,' said Jim, fervently. 'If I can get Angela – my lady – back, I'll get out of this dragon-body in a hurry.'

'Well, that's not hard, then. All you have to do is get your Companions together, go to the Loathly Tower, get this Lady Angela and send her back wherever she came from.'

'How do you—?'

'I've been talking to Sir Brian,' said Danielle. 'How many more Companions do you have to get?'

'I don't know,' Jim answered. 'But you realize, once I get Angela free I'll be going back with her.'

'Going back with her … ?'

'I love her.'

'No, no,' said Danielle. 'You'll see, that's just another part of the enchantment. Once you're disenchanted, you'll see her as she really is; and realize you're not in love with her at all.'

'As she really is?' Jim echoed, bewildered. 'Now look, Danielle, I *know* how she really is. She … I … we've known each other very well for a year and a half, now.'

'That's what the enchantment makes you think. It came to me suddenly, last night. The reason you couldn't answer the question I asked you about whether she was as fair as I am was because, although you knew better, the enchantment was making you think she *was*. Nobody,' Danielle insisted, 'is as fair as I am. But I don't blame you for not being able to see that, while you're ensorceled this way.'

'But—'

'Come, Sir James. You're going to have to face facts, eventually. Look me right in the eyes and tell me you really believe this Angela is as fair as I am.'

Jim stopped, to keep from running into her. She had stepped around in front of him and was gazing directly into his eyes from less than a foot away.

He gulped. The absolute hell of it was, she was right. Much as he loved Angie, this suntanned figure of perfection would win any beauty contest between them in the moment of its announcement. But that was beside the point. It was Angie he wanted, not five feet eleven inches of—

'That's beside the point, Danielle,' he made himself say. 'It's the Lady Angela I'm concerned with; and I'm the one she's concerned with. Even if you could convince me things were different, I don't think you could convince her.'

'Oh? Hmm,' Danielle said, her fingers playing with the hilt of her knife. 'Well, well. She and I can settle that little matter by ourselves when the *time* comes. But, Sir James, hadn't we better be heading back to the inn? The others will be wondering that you should keep me apart alone with you all this time.'

'You're right,' said Jim, and headed back with her.

It was not until he was a half-dozen steps along the way that he realized she had conned him again. Who was likely to wonder about his spending time with Danielle as long as he was still in the body of a dragon?

When they did arrive back at the inn, they found a table with benches – something like a picnic table – set up outside the front door. Brian and Dafydd were seated at it with leather drinking mugs and a bottle of wine before them. Aragh sat on his haunches at the foot of the table, his head well above the boards.

'Sir James!' Brian called, as Jim and Danielle emerged from the wood. 'Come join us! We have plans to make for the retaking of my lady's castle.'

Jim felt the pit of his stomach drop slightly. He had gathered earlier that Brian had definite intentions of evicting Sir Hugh de Bois de Malencontri and freeing his Geronde, but he had not bothered to think seriously about what the knight might do. Now, however, that they were down to the point of action, he recalled that the situation was somewhat unbalanced between their own numbers and those of the castle's probable occupiers. This discrepancy would not have bothered him so much if he had not gathered that Brian was the sort of individual who, having made up his mind to do something, was certain to do it.

He lumbered up and sat himself down at the open end of the table, opposite Aragh.

'Sir James,' said Brian. 'Oh, by-the-bye – would you like some wine?'

'Ye – No,' said Jim, remembering his existing debt to the innkeeper.

'Very well. Sir James, I have some sorry news for us,' Brian went on. 'The good bowman here tells me that he sees no reason to join forces with us against Sir Hugh, his principles being—'

'"Let be who will leave me be,"' put in Dafydd. 'Not that I do not wish you well, whatever. But it is not a quarrel of mine.'

'Likewise,' went on Brian, 'Sir wolf here considers the matter of my lady and myself to be no quarrel of his; and he has reminded me that his promise to join us extended only insofar as we have to deal with sandmirks.'

'Oh.'

'Therefore,' said Brian, cheerfully. 'Clearly, it is to be you and I alone against Sir Hugh and his men. For that reason, let us put our heads together, for we will have need of what cleverness we can muster.'

'Well, there you have it, Gorbash,' said Aragh, with grim relish. 'That's what you get for thinking you're human. Only humans would consider taking a castle full of enemies, when there were only two of them and the castle is built to keep out an army.'

'It's certainly not sensible, Sir Brian!' put in Danielle, who was standing by Aragh, petting him behind the ears. 'You have to admit that!'

'Sensible or not,' Brian resumed, his jaw muscles bunching, 'my lady is held and I will loose her. By myself, if need be. But I believe I can count on Sir James.'

'It's not Sir James' duty to free your lady!' said Danielle. 'His duty's to free himself from his enchantment by getting the Lady Angela out of the Loathly Tower. In fact, it's his duty *not* to risk his life – and that rescue – by trying anything as foolish as taking Malvern Castle, two-handed!'

'I constrain none,' said Brian. His burning-blue gaze swung around to lock with Jim's. 'Sir James, how say you? Are you with me in this matter, or do I proceed alone?'

Jim opened his mouth to make his apologetic excuses. Attacking the castle with Aragh and Dafydd help to put matters, perhaps, faintly within the realm of success. Without them, such an attack would be nothing less than suicidal. Better to make the situation plain to Brian right now, than to have to back out later.

But, oddly, the words seemed to stick in his throat and would not come out. Jim was under no circumstances the bravest man around – and he was no better a dragon than he was a man, as far as courage went. On the other hand, there was Angie ... for whose rescue Carolinus assured him he would need Companions – and if he let Brian down now, it was not to be expected that Brian would still come along to the Loathly Tower to help him. Also, there was something about the knight's determination ... and something, as well, about this crazy world he was now in: unbelievable as it seemed, there was something in him – in the human, not dragon, part of him – that wanted to try taking Malvern Castle, even if he and Brian must make that attempt alone.

'Well, Sir James ... ?' said Brian.

'Count on me,' Jim heard himself saying.

Brian nodded. Dafydd refilled his jack with wine, held it up to Jim and drank it off in silent toast.

'Oh, yes!' Danielle flashed, turning on the bowman. 'And you were the one who would put yourself up against prince, or king or emperor, and were so sure it wouldn't be *you* who would go down!'

He looked at her in surprise.

'This is none of my concern, as I said,' he answered. 'How is it you're making a comparison between this and what I would do for you, in your own case?'

'Sir Brian needs help! Does Sir James hang back and say it's none of his concern? He does not! I wondered about your courage with all those fine speeches you've been making. I see I was right to wonder!'

Dafydd frowned.

'Ah,' he said, 'you mustn't go making talk like that. My courage is as good as any man's – and, in fact, I think better.'

'Oh?'

He stared at her with a sort of slow wonder.

'You will be pushing me into this, now?' he said. 'Indeed, I see you will.'

He turned to Brian.

'What I said was no less than the truth,' he told the knight. 'It is nothing to me, one way or the other, about this Sir Hugh of yours. Nor am I some knight errant, look you, to go rescuing maidens. That is for those of you who are liking such things. But for this particular maiden with us now, and no other, you may count on me, too, for what I can do to aid.'

'Good man – !' Brian was beginning, when Aragh interrupted.

'You've got visitors, Sir knight. Turn and look.'

Brian turned. They all turned.

Emerging from the trees opposite the inn were the first of a number of men, all in steel caps, brown, green or russet hose, and leather jackets with metal plates fastened thickly upon them, wearing swords at their belts and with longbows and quivers of arrows slung from their shoulders.

'It's all right, Sir Brian,' said Danielle. 'It's just Giles o' the Wold, my father.'

'Your father?' Brian turned back swiftly to dart a suspicious glance at her.

'Certainly!' Danielle explained. 'I knew you'd need help, so I asked one of Dick Innkeeper's sons to ride secretly last night on one of his father's horses to summon him. I said to tell him you'd be glad to split whatever wealth was to be gained from Sir Hugh de Bois and his men in retaking the castle.'

14

Brian stared at her for a second longer, then turned back to look at the newcomers, who were already halfway across the open ground to the inn. Slowly he got to his feet. Dafydd rose also, casually, his hand on his quiver. Jim found himself getting to his feet as well, and Dick Innkeeper materialized in the inn door, stepping out to join them. Only Aragh stayed seated, his jaws laughing.

The man in the lead was a lean individual who looked to be in his fifties. The ends of hair seen escaping from under his steel cap were iron gray, and his short, curly, jutting beard was pepper-and-salt in color. Beyond his air of authority, he seemed little different from the men behind him, except that the weapon at his belt was not the short sword the others wore, but rather a longer, two-handed weapon like Sir Brian's.

He came up to the ditch girdling the inn, crossed its bridge and stopped before the knight.

'I'm Giles o' the Wold,' he said. 'And these are my free brothers and companions of the forest. I take it you're Sir Brian Neville-Smythe?'

'I am,' Brian answered, stiffly. 'Master outlaw, I wasn't the one who invited you here.'

'I'm aware of that,' said Giles. Above his beard, his face was tanned to almost the color of old leather and the skin had gone into small, shrewd wrinkles. 'My daughter sent for me—'

He glanced past Brian for a moment.

'I'll talk to you later, girl,' he said. 'Now, Sir knight, what matters who sent for me? If you need assistance, here am I and my men, and the price of our aid's not so high as to be beyond reason. Shall we sit like reasonable men and discuss it, or should my lads and I turn around again and go?'

Brian hesitated a second – but only a second.

'Dick,' he said, turning to the innkeeper. 'Bring another jack for Giles o' the Wold; and see what his companions will have.'

'Ale,' answered Dick, in a somewhat grim voice, 'is all I have in such quantity.'

'Ale, then,' said Brian, impatiently. 'Bring it!'

He sat back down at the table. Giles took the other end of the bench that Dafydd had been sitting on.

Giles looked curiously at Aragh, and then at Jim.

'The wolf I know – by reputation, if nothing else,' he said. 'The dragon – My daughter's message said you were a knight under enchantment?'

'This is the good Sir James,' Brian explained. 'The bowman next to you is Dafydd op – What's that family name of yours, Master archer?'

'Hywel,' said Dafydd, pronouncing it with a lilt that Jim knew his own tongue certainly could not have managed. 'I am in England to teach the English that the longbow, as well as the true blood of they that best use it, are from Wales alone; and it is also that I am going to marry your daughter, Master Giles.'

'He is not!' cried Danielle.

Giles' bearded face parted in a smile.

'If you ever get her permission,' he said to Dafydd, 'come talk to me about it. You might have to concern yourself not only with my feelings in the matter, but the intentions of some score or so younger members of my band.'

'You've a clerkly way of talking, Master outlaw,' said Brian as Dick came out with bottles and another jack for Giles, followed by his two men servants rolling a cask through the door into the yard.

'Use your caps,' they could hear him directing the outlaws who came clustering around. 'I've no store of jacks for such a number as this.'

'I've been that, too,' Giles answered Brian, carelessly. He took off his own steel cap and tossed it on the table, filled his jack from one of the bottles and drank deeply. His sparse hair stirred a bit in the light breeze that was blowing. 'Now, Sir knights, Friend Welshman and Master wolf, I've heard some little about you all—'

His glance touched for a second on the unusual length of the longbow leaning against the table at Dafydd's side.

'—But to save time, perhaps it's best you tell me from the beginning all that bears on the matter here, including that about each of you.'

They told him – Jim starting off, Brian taking up the story after he had met Jim, Aragh carrying the tale on from the defeat of the sand-mirks, and Danielle, Dafydd and the innkeeper putting in their own reports. Giles drank and listened.

'Well, gentles and others,' he said, when they were done. 'Maybe I've brought my lads here on a fool's errand after all. My daughter's message gave me to believe you'd a chance to take this castle that only needed a few more stout fighters to secure. But a mixed bag you are – I mean no offense by that – and I know Malvern Castle, which is not a cattle shed to be taken by a rush and a few blows. My lads are fine bowmen, and swordsmen if need be, but no men-at-arms. My pardon to all, but how in hell did you think you might take half an acre of stone walls from perhaps fifty men in no less than half-armor and used to such defense?'

Brian scowled.

'I know Malvern Castle inside out,' he said. 'Fifty men scattered about it won't be more than two at a time in any one place. Here are three of us, at least – four if the wolf had joined us – who are each more than a match for any two of them in any place, at any time.'

'I'll not deny that,' said Giles. 'But you'd need to be in the castle itself to match them. So, to take first things first, what magic had you planned to use to get into the castle?'

'Malvern will have food stored for siege,' said Brian. 'But that has to be dull stuff. There's better provender here. Sir Hugh tried to take this inn and failed – I don't doubt he knew there were choice wine and meats here. It was my thought that I could disguise myself as Dick Innkeeper, driving a wagonload of choice food as a peace offering to the new commander of Malvern. The wolf would ride along in the wagon as a dog of the inn, to snarl at any of the common sort that might be tempted to filch the dainties it carried before they reached Sir Hugh. Then, once within, and hopefully in the presence of Sir Hugh himself, he and I would kill the baron, and strive to reach my lady's quarters, where she will be held prisoner—'

'Why?' asked Giles.

'Why what, Master outlaw?'

'Why do you think the Lady Geronde will be locked in her own quarters?'

'Because,' said Brian, with obviously hard-held patience, 'Sir Hugh would waste no time in taking over the lord's chambers; and there'd be no place else but my lady's room below the solar, to keep anyone like her prisoner in good health and safety. Strong men have been known to last little more than a few days in dungeons, of which Malvern has two, and none of the nicest. Anyplace else in the castle my lady could not be guarded from her own people, who might help her to escape, or to attempt such an escape that death would put her beyond her captors' power. Nor could she be safely guarded elsewhere from Sir Hugh's own men, some of whom at least – as you'd know, Master outlaw, having lived long enough to have a knowledge of men-at-arms – will be no more able than brute beasts to think of the consequences for what they do, when drink is in them.'

'Granted,' Giles acknowledged. 'Go on, Sir Brian. You've slain Sir Hugh and guards and broken into the lady's room. Now what?'

'Now, the good Sir James, who has been on wing and waiting, sees our signal from the balcony of my lady's chamber. He swoops down and carries her away to safety and to rouse a force from the country-side, to retake the castle. Nothing is left but for the wolf and me to escape, ourselves – if God wills it.'

'God?' snarled Aragh, abruptly. 'Your god, knight, not mine! If anyone saves Aragh, it'll be me. When I was half grown and a full-grown sow bear broke my right foreleg, so that in no way could I run, was it the god of humans who saved me? No, it was I – Aragh! I stood, and fought and got my teeth through the fur and loose skin to the great vein in her throat, so that she died and I lived. That's the way it's always been for an English wolf – the way it will always be. Keep your god if you wish, Sir knight, but keep him to yourself!'

He paused, licked his jaws with one flick of his red tongue and yawned elaborately.

'But I forget,' he said. 'I'd already told you this business of your lady and the castle has nothing to do with me.'

'So. Then what of your plan, Sir Brian?' said Giles.

Brian scowled.

'Master outlaw, I'll remind you once more – it wasn't I who invited you here. Here, we're trying to decide what force is needed for a rescue, but how to do it with what we've got. If we lack the wolf, we lack him, that's all.'

'How ... ?' Giles began. 'No, with all respect, Sir Brian, I think this trip of mine has been—'

'Wait a moment, Father!' said Danielle. 'I was the one sent for you.'

She turned and looked directly at Aragh. Aragh opened his jaws in silent laughter.

'This is Aragh!' he growled. 'Did you think I was another lovesick bowman?'

'No ...' Danielle replied, 'I thought you were Aragh, my wolf-friend, who'd never betray me, any more than I'd betray Aragh. When I sent for my father and his men, it never crossed my mind that Aragh would abandon his friends, such as Sir James and myself. But, since he has—'

She turned back to the table.

'I may not be a match for any two men-at-arms, except with bow and from a safe distance,' she said. 'But I can be even more useful than a wolf for attracting attention away from Sir Brian, and with the help of surprise I could even aid in killing Sir Hugh and freeing Geronde. Once that's done, of course, I may not be so likely to fight my way to freedom, but I have an advantage over Aragh – like Sir Brian, I can leave my rescue to God.'

'Girl—'

'Hush, Father! I'm my own mistress, now. So. Sir James – Sir Brian – count me with you in your attempt on the castle.'

She looked back at Aragh.

'And you may sleep in the sun!' she snapped.

Aragh opened his jaws, licked them again and closed them. Then he did a thing that astonished Jim: he whined.

'No, you don't!' Danielle said, fiercely. 'You had your chance. Now I'm going into that castle, and you're not going to have anything to do with it!'

Aragh's head dropped. It lowered and lowered until his nose almost touched the ground. He all but crept toward Danielle and pushed his head against her knees.

For a moment she merely glared at him. Then she sat down with a thump and put her arms around his furry neck and hugged his head to her.

'It's all right ... it's all right,' she said.

'I wouldn't have let Gorbash get hurt, either,' growled Aragh, in muffled tones into the padding of her doublet. 'I was just going to wait until time to go. What good am I if I can't kill for my friends?'

'Never mind.' She rubbed behind his ears. 'It's all set straight, now.'

'I'll even get this knight out safely, afterwards.'

'I know you will,' said Danielle. 'But maybe you won't have to.'

She looked up from where she sat to her father.

'Now that Giles o' the Wold knows he'll have three strong allies inside the castle, maybe he can consider making use of himself and his men after all to take the castle?'

'Daughter,' said Giles, 'you stay clear of the whole affair.'

'That's right,' Aragh insisted, pulling his head out of her embrace. 'I go. You don't, Danielle!'

'All right,' she replied. 'I won't go into the castle. Anything I can do outside, I'll do. Father ... ?'

Giles refilled his jack and drank thoughtfully.

'My lads and I are no good unless we can get inside, too,' he said. 'If there was some way you could open the gate for us ...'

'If it's to be a taking of the castle,' said Brian, 'I can then barricade my lady and myself in her quarters. Sir James, instead of carrying her off, can land somewhere within the walls and attract attention, during which the wolf can slip down, slay the guards and open the gate—'

He turned to Aragh.

'There's a rope hoist to the right side of the gate, within,' he said, 'by which one man may lift the bar. With your teeth in that rope, it should lift easily. Then throw your weight on the right-hand gate door – note, Master wolf, the *right-hand* door, not the left – and you should be able to swing it out enough for the archers to get in.'

'Good enough, as far as it goes,' said Giles. 'But the gate won't stand unbarred for more than a moment, I think, even if it takes a dozen men together to cut down the wolf. And it'll take more than a moment or two for all of us, even at a dead run, to cross the open ground that I remember lies about Malvern Castle. Because it's from the nearest cover we must come, certainly. They'll have lookouts on the battlements against anyone creeping close, unseen.'

'Shoot the lookouts first,' Dafydd suggested.

The Welshman had been so silent that Jim had almost forgotten he was there. Now, they all looked at him.

'How, Master Dafydd?' Giles asked, ironically. 'With head and shoulders only for target above the walls, and at a distance of close on half a mile? Clearly you've not seen Malvern Castle and the land it stands on.'

'I can do it,' said Dafydd.

Giles stared at the younger man for a long moment. Gradually he leaned forward, peering closely into Dafydd's calm face.

'By the Apostles,' he said, softly. 'I do think you mean that!'

'I know what it is that I can do,' Dafydd said. 'I would not say it, else.'

'You do ...' said Giles, and paused. 'You do ... and you'll never have to prove to me anything more about the bow and men of Wales. I know of no man living, or of any bowman in memory, able to make such a shoot and kill the men on watch. There'll be at least three, maybe four, of them on that front wall, or this Sir Hugh is no soldier; and you'll have to kill them all at near the same time, or the last one to fall will raise the alarm.'

'I have said what I can do, look you,' said Dafydd. 'Let us pass on to other things.'

Giles nodded.

'The thing at least seems possible,' he agreed. He turned to Brian. 'There'll be smaller details to keep us busy the rest of today and the evening. Twilight or dawn were the best times to surprise them; and dawn preferable, since it gives us as many hours of light after as we wish. So, we can take our time with the details. Meanwhile, let's agree on the pay for my lads and me. Sir Hugh's men will have some gear of weapons and armor which should come to us. In addition, it's only just that Malvern Castle should ransom itself – say, for a hundred marks of silver.'

'If my lady chooses to reward you after she and hers are free,' said Brian, 'that's up to her. I've no authority or right to spend what belongs to the de Chaneys.'

'There won't be any de Chaneys if Sir Orrin's indeed dead among the heathen, and the Lady Geronde isn't rescued – and you need us for that!'

'Sorry,' said Brian.

'All right, then...' The sun wrinkles around the corners of Giles' eyes grew deeper. 'Let us have Sir Hugh to ransom. He'll have family or friends who'll pay for his safe return.'

'No,' said Brian. 'I've said he's to die. And he is. Not only I, but the wolf's vowed it. And Aragh's a part of this, as much as you and your men.'

'Don't think to take his throat from my teeth, Master outlaw!' Aragh snarled.

'For my lads to risk their lives to gain only some metal and war tools is not enough,' said Giles. 'We're a band of free men, and they won't follow me at that price, even if I ask it.'

He and Brian argued for some little time, without getting to a solution.

'See here, Master Giles,' said Brian, at last. 'I've no hundred silver marks of my own to give you; but you'll have heard of me as one who pays his due. I'll give you my knight's word to speak of you and your men to my lady; and she's not the sort to let service go unrewarded. If, however, for some reason payment can't come from her, I'll myself undertake to pay you as I manage to gather that sum, or any part of it, until it's all accounted for. Damme, now, more than that I can't say!'

Giles shrugged.

'I'll talk to my lads.'

He got up from the table and went to gather his men into a huddle at a distance large enough to give their discussion privacy.

'Don't worry, Sir Brian,' said Danielle, quietly, to the knight, 'they'll agree.'

In fact, in about fifteen minutes Giles came back and announced agreement. Behind his back, Danielle smiled at the others sitting around the table.

'Let's get on to the details, then,' Giles went on, sitting once more. 'Sir Brian, you can hardly wear sword and armor when you drive the provision cart into the castle. On the other hand, you're not likely to be able to do much against men-at-arms, to say nothing of Sir Hugh himself, if you're naked. How to get your weapons and armor into the castle? Perhaps Sir James could carry them in a bundle and drop them to you – but then, there would be the time necessary for you to don them, and once Sir Hugh's men had seen a dragon deliver them to you—'

'Once inside the keep, with only one or two armed men for escort to Sir Hugh,' said Brian, 'the wolf and I can kill them quietly and make a few minutes in which I can dress and arm myself. As for my weapons and armor, these will be with me in the cart. They'll be hidden under the provisions, and the wolf may lie on top of all.'

'And no one,' snarled Aragh, 'will rummage beneath me to find them – I promise you.'

Giles nodded, slowly.

'Still ...' he said to Brian, 'even if you appear the perfect innkeeper, or innkeeper's assistant, Sir Hugh and his men are bound to be wary, suspecting some attempt at rescue of your lady—'

'Ha!' said Dick, who had been standing in the doorway of his inn.

He turned about and vanished into the dark interior.

'What ails him?' said Giles, looking at the now-empty entrance to the building.

'As it happens,' Brian said, 'I'd thought myself about Sir Hugh suspecting me. I've got an answer to that worked out. To start with, I'll go to the castle this afternoon. Ride as close to the walls as I can safely, in armor, considering he'll have crossbows from the walls of Malvern Castle even if he failed to bring some with him; and challenge him to come out and settle the matter by single combat—'

'What silly sort of knight's trick is that?' broke in Giles. 'By the scar on your face, you ought to know better than that, Sir Brian. Why should Sir Hugh come out to fight you, when he can simply stay safely in the castle and keep all he's got?'

'Exactly!' said Brian. 'I count on him doing just that.'

'But all you'll accomplish is letting him know you're outside Malvern Castle.'

'Exactly. Then, when he sees the provision cart I'm driving closely pursued by a knight in armor on a white horse, he'll be all the more ready to swing wide the gates, let the cart in and believe the man driving it.'

'And how's that to be arranged, unless you've two suits of armor and a twin to wear one of them? To say nothing of the fact—' Giles broke off, abruptly. 'By the way, Sir Brian, does this Sir Hugh know you by sight?'

'He does,' said Brian, grimly.

'Then what if he's on the wall when you drive up? Do you think rough clothes'll keep him from recognizing you?'

'Dick Innkeeper has a false beard among some stuff left here by several strolling players who could not pay their shot,' said Brian. 'With that to cover most of my face, I stand a chance; and beyond that – well, I have to take some risks.'

'A beard?' Giles hesitated. 'That's a thing I hadn't thought of. This innkeeper's a man of possessions. It might work.'

'A man with a large cellar,' said Brian. He paused and listened, cocking his head toward the doorway behind him. 'And here, I think, comes the answer to your objection of a moment since ...'

A thumping sound came from inside the inn. All turned to see a shape materialize in the doorway, filling it. It was a shining figure in full plate armor, with beaked helm and closed visor; and in one mailed fist it carried a mace.

15

'By God!' Giles exclaimed, sitting back down on the bench, picking up his jack and drinking deeply from it. Like all the rest, except Brian, he had half risen to his feet at the sight of the figure in the doorway. 'You don't want to startle an old bowman so, Master Innkeeper – if it is indeed you, in that suit. You might have had an arrow through you before you were recognized!'

'That was my own thought, also,' said Dafydd.

'Your pardon, Sir James, lady, and my masters,' boomed Dick's voice hollowly inside the helm. 'As Sir Brian has just said, my cellar is large. And an inn acquires many things from its various guests over a pair of lifetimes – for my father kept it here, before me. But can I not pass for a knight, think you? Particularly on horseback and from a distance?'

'Hmm,' said Giles, getting up again to examine the innkeeper more closely. 'I'd counsel you not to wear that assortment of metal in actual battle, Master Innkeeper. Now that I look close, you've got parts of four different suits upon you, none of which fits as armor ought. Can you raise your right arm above your head?'

Dick tried. The arm creaked halfway to shoulder height and stopped with a clank.

'Yes,' said Giles, 'I thought so. Your couter on that arm is overlarge, and your pauldron too small for a man of your shoulder. But from a distance ... from a distance, and sitting on a horse, you might pass.'

'Good,' Brian said, briskly. 'Something to eat then, Dick, and I'll ride to the castle to present Sir Hugh with my challenge.'

'I'll go along with you,' Jim offered. 'I'd like you to point out where you want me to land inside the walls.'

'I'll go, too,' said Giles, 'along with six of my lads, who'll each lead five to eight other bows against some particular part of the castle, once we're inside. We all need to look Malvern over and make our plans.'

'And I,' said Dafydd, 'will have a glance at those walls where the lookouts may be standing.'

'We might as well make it a bloody picnic,' grunted Brian. 'Anybody else want to come along, eh? How about you, Sir wolf?'

'What for?' Aragh replied. 'I'll go in with you and Gorbash; and stay with you, killing all I find, until it's over and I go out again. That takes no study or planning.'

The meal was served, as Brian requested; and a little more than an hour later all those who had spoken about going stood in the cover of a thick clump of beech trees, looking out at the broad stretch of cleared ground around Malvern Castle. Brian, armored and with spear upright in hand, rode his white warhorse forward at a walk to within perhaps sixty or eighty yards of the castle gate. There he stopped, and shouted to the heads whom those in the woods could see showing above the merlons and crenels of the battlements.

'He makes a brave show,' said one of the outlaws.

'It's a custom of knights to do so, Jack,' replied Giles, dryly.

'You were not wrong indeed, Master Giles,' said Dafydd. The Welsh bowman was shading his eyes with one hand, peering at the heads on the walls. 'It is, in fact, close to half of one of your English miles. But at dawn the wind should fall, and with no strong cross-breeze I see no trouble with up to six of them. I will mark the nearest crenel to each steel cap I see, then first shoot one watchman and wait for the others to look out, which they will surely all do when they see their comrade struck dead, and no one in view in the open ground. I will have five other arrows stuck in the ground before me, and I will put those in the air so close together that the five looking out will die almost at once – Hold, the knight speaks!'

In fact, Brian had begun to issue his challenge. A headgear brighter than the others had appeared on the battlements and the individual wearing it had called out something. Brian was responding. The fact that he was facing away from those in the forest edge caused a good share of what he said to be lost, even to Jim's sharp dragon-ears. Those words that Jim heard, however, were nearly all obscenities. He had not realized Brian had such a command of colorful language.

'Now, Sir Hugh answers,' said Giles, for Brian had fallen silent and the voice that had shouted earlier was making itself heard again – though none of its words were understandable to those at the forest's edge. 'It'll be Sir Hugh, beyond a doubt, because of the high crest and visor of the helm that takes the light so. That's a headpiece for horseback.'

'Master Giles,' asked Dafydd, looking sideways at the outlaw, 'is it that you ever wore such a helm and armor yourself, now?'

Giles glanced back for a second.

'If you ever do become one of the family,' he said, 'you can ask me that again. Otherwise, I don't hear such questions.'

'Now come the bolts,' commented the outlaw whom Giles had addressed as Jack. 'Best he turn and ride now. There – he does so!'

Brian had turned his charger and was galloping away from the castle.

'Can the crossbows get through his armor with their bolts at that distance?' asked Jim, fascinated.

'No,' said Giles. 'But they can cripple his horse – and that's a beast worth twenty farms, if it's worth one. Ah, they've missed ...'

A swarm of what looked like little black match-sticks against the blue of the sky was descending around Brian and his galloping steed. Jim was puzzled about how Giles could be sure the quarrels from the crossbows had all missed, when most of them seemed still to be in the air. A matter of the trained eye, he supposed. In fact, by the time he finished his thought the missiles had fallen either behind or to one side or the other of the running horse.

'And that's that!' said Jack, spitting on the ground. 'Sir knight'll be in the woods with us here before they can rewind those engines for a second shot. Give me two of our better men and the horse would have been down within ten strides – and the knight, too, with any luck.'

Dafydd, leaning on his great bow, looked aside and down at Jack. For a second it looked as if he would say something, but then he turned his attention back to the approaching Sir Brian.

'Good, Master Welshman,' said Giles, softly. He had been watching the tall young man. 'A slow tongue indicates a wise head.'

Dafydd said nothing.

In the next moment Brian came riding into the shadows of the forest and pulled his snorting charger to a stop. He wheeled the animal around, pushing up his visor.

'Half thought they might make a sally after me,' he said. 'But I see not.'

He swung down from the saddle with surprising lightness, considering the weight of metal he was carrying.

'You tempted those crossbows closer than I should have,' said Giles.

'Blanchard of Tours, here,' Giles answered, slapping the white horse affectionately on one sweaty shoulder, 'is faster than most would guess.'

He looked around at them.

'What do you think of what you saw?' he asked.

'Judging by the heads on that front wall,' said Giles, 'your Sir Hugh has at least the fifty men with him. But he's got no archers, or he would have used them against you right now; and his men with the crossbows were nothing admirable. Draw me a plan of the castle, now, while we have it out there in front of us; so I can gain some idea of where my lads should go, once they're inside.'

Brian drew the dagger from his belt, bent stiffly at the waist and began to scratch on the ground.

'As you see,' he said, 'Malvern's more wide than deep. The top of the keep you can barely see from here. It's in the left corner of the rear wall, its upper part rising above the towers in the other three corners – which are watchtowers and granaries, only. The Lord of Malvern's chambers are just under what was the original top floor of the keep, back when the keep was the same height as the watchtowers. My lady's grandfather added two more floors and a new battlement floor above the keep, so as to give Sir Orrin and his new bride separate bed space, with a solar above them for good measure, and the new battlement floor above the solar, with supplies of heavy stones there to cast down and kettles for the heating of oil to pour on any who might try to scale the keep's outer walls.'

His dagger scratched in the dirt.

'Below and before the keep, in Sir Orrin's time,' he explained, 'was added a great hall, mainly of wood – the original walls and towers of the castle are stone, as you see. This filled up much of the old court-yard. It is joined to the keep as high as the first floor and has served both as dining hall and as barracks for the large number of men Sir Orrin would gather about him from time to time when he went off to war. Stables of wood and outbuildings were also added inside the outer walls, so that there's much that can burn – but look that Sir Hugh's men don't try to set fires to cover their escape, once we're inside and they find themselves losing the fight. Of your men, Master outlaw, there should be a party to secure every tower, another party to hold the courtyard, and yet another strong party to invade the keep by way of the great hall. I, and possibly Sir James, will already be in the upper levels of the keep when you and your men come through the gate – if so we be still alive. Now, give me your questions ...'

Giles, Dafydd, and even some of the other outlaws Giles had brought along proceeded to do so. Their queries had mainly to do with dis-tances and angles within the castle.

Jim found his attention wandering. What he himself wanted, he thought, was to get a direct look at the inside of those walls – and there was no reason he should not be able to do so. Flying high enough, and in a direct line, on a pass that took him by but not directly over the castle, he should be able to use his telescopic vision to get a pretty fair view of everything inside. At a sufficient distance, he might not even be noticed by Sir Hugh's men; or, if he was, they might merely take him for a large bird.

Even if they identified him as a dragon, a dragon who was simply passing by and apparently paying no attention to them should hardly be cause for alarm or speculation. At the same time, it probably would not hurt to make his overflight just at twilight, when at the end of the day and their evening meal, the watchers on the castle walls would be least likely to be alarmed by something passing high overhead.

Accordingly, he waited until the questions of the others had been answered to Brian's best ability and they had all returned to the inn. Once there, however, he took Brian aside and explained what he planned to do.

'What I mainly want to be sure of,' Jim said, 'is where I ought to land, when I come in.'

'My lady's main chamber has a balcony – but a small one,' Brian pointed out. 'The solar above has no balcony, but very large windows through which you might fly directly.'

Jim felt doubt stir in him.

'I don't know that,' he said. 'I haven't had all that experience in flying.'

'Then,' said Brian, 'there's only the battlement floor – the open top level of the keep. In fact, it might be the best place for you to land, since there'll be at least one guard on duty there, and possibly someone else belonging to Sir Hugh in the solar. So that if you can slay those and fight your way down to Geronde's floor, you'll have made all safe to the top of the keep; and in case of anything going amiss, you can carry her off from there by air, to safety.'

Secretly Jim had a few doubts about his ability to carry the weight of an adult human, and still fly. True, his wings were capable of exerting tremendous lift for a short time. But he was fairly sure that he would not be able to soar with the added burden of a grown woman; and if he could not soar, how far could he fly by wing power alone? For safety, it should be at least to the edge of the surrounding wood, which Giles had pointed out was half a mile away. But there was no point in loading these doubts on Brian. The knight had enough uncertainties already to trouble him, although Jim had to admit that Brian showed little sign of being overwhelmed by them.

'I'll let you know what I see,' Jim said.

But he did not. Half an hour later, he cruised past the castle at about twelve hundred feet altitude and his telescopic vision failed to catch one of the guards so much as looking up, let alone watching in his direction. Nor did he discover anything about the castle that was different from what Brian had said. He checked out the battlemented roof of the keep and saw only one man on guard there, as Brian had guessed. Things were working out almost too predictably to be interesting.

He circled back at a distance and landed at the inn just as darkness was closing in. To his surprise, most of the outlaws – except Giles and a few of his subsidiary leaders – were already asleep, the ale apparently having assisted them to slumber. Brian, with no more than a normal amount of wine in him, was also slumbering. So was Danielle. Aragh had gone off into the night woods and would probably not return until morning. Even Dick Innkeeper, with most of his family and employees, was asleep – except for one older woman who was supplying wine to Giles and ale to his outlaw lieutenants.

Disgruntled, Jim settled down in the main room of the inn, tucked his head under his wing, and prepared himself to spend a sleepless night ...

It seemed he had only blinked and then again lifted his head from under his wing, however, to find activity all around him.

Dick, his family and the servants were bustling about. Danielle was bandaging Aragh's neck – the wolf had somehow managed to get himself hurt or wounded during the night. Giles was seated at a table, drawing plans of the castle on thin leather sheets, in quintuplicate for his lieutenants; and Dafydd, working in a concentration that hinted he would not welcome interruption, had set up a small pair of pan balances and was weighing half a dozen of his arrows, one at a time, then slightly but meticulously trimming their shafts and feathers. Brian, seated at a table a few feet away, was eating an enormous breakfast of bacon, bread and cold beef, with several more bottles of wine.

Outside, it was still dark. Far from being daybreak, it was not even first light. Jim guessed the hour to be about 4 A.M.

He looked enviously at Brian. Anybody who could have that kind of appetite before the sun was up, on a day when he might well expect to be killed—

'Ah, there, Sir James,' said Brian, waving his jack. 'Have some wine?'

Jim decided he deserved a drink, in spite of his debt to Dick Innkeeper. 'Yes,' he said.

Brian uncorked a fresh bottle and passed it over. Jim took it in one claw grasp and put it to his jaws, swallowing its contents in a gulp.

'Thanks,' he said.

'Dick!' roared Brian. 'Wine for Sir James!'

Dick Innkeeper came up, wringing his hands.

'Sir knight, please,' he said, 'not another quarter tun of Bordeaux—'

'Nonsense!' said Brian. 'Of course not! Just a few dozen bottles, or their equivalent. Just enough to wet the good knight's throat.'

'Oh, in that case ... of course, of course ...'

Dick hurried out of the room. Jim heard him shouting for one of the manservants.

What appeared a few minutes later was not a few dozen bottles of the innkeeper's best, but a small cask holding no more than ten gallons or so of good, if second-rate, wine. But the cask was full and Jim, with a momentary wistful thought for the vintages he had sampled in the cellar, settled down to its contents philosophically. After all, not even a dragon could have the best of everything all the time.

He sat drinking with Brian and gradually absorbing the bustle going on around him. Everybody was very busy and very businesslike. He heard a great deal of sharpening of weapons, making of last-minute repairs in equipment, checking of maps, and directions and orders. Correspondingly, he noted almost a complete lack of the cheerful jokes and insults that had been a noticeable part of the give-and-take between the outlaws, in particular, the day before. Now, everybody was serious. Torches smoked and glared everywhere. People went back and forth at high speed, each one engaged in some task that did not brook interruption. Giles was neck-deep in lieutenants, and unapproachable. Aragh, bandaged, soon went out; and Danielle was now nowhere to be seen. Dick and his staff were like the captain and crew of a ship fighting a hurricane. Finally, even Brian gave up the wine bottles and suggested in a friendly voice that Jim get the hell out, take a walk or something, because it was time he was seeing to Blanchard and his weapons.

Jim took the advice and left the inn for the deep, chilly, pre-dawn darkness outside. He was feeling a distinct loneliness and awkwardness, like a stranger at a large family gathering; and this feeling was reinforced by a sort of gentle melancholy induced by the wine he had just drunk. He was not really lonely for his own world – strangely enough, with all its hard, medieval realities, he was discovering he liked it here – but for somebody to whom he could anchor. Preferably Angie; but, failing that, anyone who could give him a feeling of belonging, instead of one of being a sort of wandering soul adrift between worlds.

He looked around again for Aragh and remembered he had seen the wolf leave the inn immediately after Danielle had bandaged him. But neither his dragon-nose or ears gave him any evidence that the wolf was anywhere in the vicinity; and Jim had seen enough of Aragh to know that unless the other was plainly in evidence, his chances of finding him were close to non-existent.

Jim gave up and sat down by himself in the darkness. Behind him were the noise, the odors, and the light of the inn. Before him were the solid blackness of the trees and overhead a thickly overcast sky, through which the faint gleam of an obscured moon came milkily now and then, low in the western quarter of the heavens. The moon would be down, soon, and there would be no light at all.

He might well be dead at the end of this day that would soon be dawning. The thought brought with it no particular fear but an increase in the feeling of melancholy. If he could be cut, as he had been in the brawl at the village, he could be seriously wounded or killed. In which case he would die here, at some impossible remove from everything he had ever identified with. Nobody would even know of his death. Even Angie, assuming she survived the Loathly Tower and the Dark Powers which Carolinus had talked about, would probably never know what had happened to him. He might not even be missed ...

He was sinking steadily deeper into a sort of luxurious self-pity, when he realized that he was no longer sitting on the ground. He was, instead, lying down on it, about to turn over on his back, spread his wings and roll back and forth on the rough, sandy soil. Echoing in his mind, just in time to stop him, came the remembered words of Danielle: 'Don't roll in the dirt, Sir James!'

He had wondered at the time why she should think he would ever want to roll in the dirt. Now he understood. Thinking about his cuts had reminded his subconscious of them. The day after he had gotten them, they had smarted like small shaving cuts; but he had come to ignore them and they had passed out of mind. Now, however, he realized that they were healing; and, in the process of doing so, they had developed a new sensation: they itched.

A good scrub against the hard earth would be a satisfying way of scratching those itches. Of course, it would also not only reopen the cuts, but get dirt and infectious materials ground into them.

He sat up again. Of course, Danielle was right. The worst of it was, though, that now that he had recognized the itch feelings, they redoubled, as if fiendishly and consciously determined to drive him crazy. He forced his body onto all four of its legs. If Brian could remain motionless with a hornet buzzing around the inside of his helmet, he ought to be able to ignore a little itching.

On his feet again, he could now smell the coming day – not an odor he could identify precisely, but a generally damp, fresh variation in the night breeze that was blowing in his direction. His ears caught the faint sound of paws on ground, and suddenly Aragh was before him.

'They all awake in there?' growled the wolf, softly. 'Time they were moving!'

'I'll tell them.'

Jim turned toward the inn door; but just at that moment it opened, and Giles stuck his head out.

'Sir James?' he asked, quietly. 'Have you seen the wolf?'

'He has,' snapped Aragh. 'I'm here. What are you whispering for, Sir outlaw?'

Giles pulled his head back in and shut the door without answering. He had not, in fact, been whispering. His voice had only been lowered – as had Aragh's a second before. Almost immediately, the door opened again and Giles with his lieutenants came out, followed by Danielle.

'Dick Innkeeper's gone to put his armor on, and harness the horses,' she told her father. 'His men have the cart already loaded. Sir Brian's still with him, over at the stables.'

'All right. Jack, will you tell the knight that we're ready to move?' Giles asked. 'The rest of you go assemble your lads.'

Jack went down along the building toward the stables; the other lieutenants moved out into the darkness, to where the rank and file of the outlaws had set up camp.

Fifteen minutes later, they were on the march. Brian on Blanchard, Giles on one of the inn horses that gleamed a strange, pale grayish-white in the murkiness, and Jim on foot, led the march. Behind them came Dafydd and Danielle, followed by the wagon driven by Dick, then the general body of the outlaws. Aragh had disappeared into the darkness of the forest at their first movement, growling that he would meet them at the edge of the forest facing the castle.

The promise of daylight began to deliver itself as they moved. It was a good hour yet till sunrise when they left the inn; but as they wound their way among the trees, the taller trunks began to emerge from the darkness as the sky overhead lightened. As these two things happened, the light wind dropped, just as Dafydd had predicted, and the mist filling the lower levels of the forest gradually became visible; it was a landscape of white, black, and gray they moved through – a land fit for spirits and night demons. In the semi-gloom of the emerging day, the earth underfoot was a dark platform and the mist a ghostly blanket reaching twice a man's height up into the trees, so that to the right, left, and all about, things were hidden. Even the gradually brightening sky was swag-bellied with thick, cold clouds.

They moved with little talk, the mist, clouds and darkness acting like a smothering blanket upon any enthusiasm. The wagon, weapons and armor jingled. The hooves of the horses thudded on the earth. Their breath – and Jim's – smoked as white as the mist in the damp, cold air. Gradually the light became true daylight and the mist began to thin; and almost before Jim was ready for it, they reached the edge of the wood looking out on the plain where Malvern Castle stood. The last mist still trailed in streamers across the open ground, and the tops of the stone walls and towers rose from it like the upper parts of some castle half drowned by the sea. Suddenly, even as they halted and looked, the first rays of the rising sun slid through the treetops to the east and struck at a long slant into the mist, thinning it further.

Slowly, the plain began to become fully visible, everything on it sharply seen, down to the very stones at the base of the battlements.

Jim glanced up once more at the sky. The heavy cloud cover was beginning to be torn open in places by the upper winds, although the air was still calm at ground level. Enough of the clouds remained, and hung low, however, so that for the first time it occurred to him that he would not be able to fly high in approaching the castle. If he was to come in by air to the top of the keep during the next half-hour or so, he would have to fly at little more than a few hundred feet; and there would be no disguising to those on watch about the castle walls and towers that a dragon was coming – nor the destination to which that dragon was heading.

16

'Right!' said Brian, loudly and cheerfully. 'Everybody present? How about Sir wolf?'-

'Worry about yourself, Sir knight,' answered the voice of Aragh. 'I've been here long enough to kill twenty sheep.'

'All right,' said Brian. 'Make ready, then. Master Giles, you know your men and your bow work. I know my part. Do you take charge of your archers, including the Welshman. Sir James, Dick, wolf – to me here.'

The expedition split into two groups.

Dafydd, a few yards off by himself, was carefully unwrapping one by one the cloths in which he had individually cased the arrows on which Jim had seen him working at the inn. He handled the shafts delicately, planting six of them before him point-down in the earth and sliding the other two into his quiver. Dick descended from the horse he had ridden here; and now that Jim saw it clearly in the daylight, he noticed that the light-brown animal had been liberally powdered with flour or some other white substance to lighten it to something like Blanchard's color. Brian swung down from Blanchard now and began transferring to the smaller, whitened horse the breastplate and body armor his charger customarily wore.

'Like rider, like steed,' he said. 'You and your mare here will be a pair for unfit armor, Dick. The chaufrain's too wide for her head, the crinet too long for her neck. But she can carry them a short while without too much trouble. The petrel's also too wide for her chest, but that can hang loose. On the other hand, I can buckle the flanchards tight around forearms and shoulder and they'll carry almost as well as they do on Blanchard.'

'It's still not going to hang well,' said Danielle. 'And that horse's coloring is poor. I don't see why you don't just let the innkeeper ride *your* horse.'

Brian frowned.

'Wish me no bad luck, mistress,' said Dick, cheerfully, out of the depths of his helmet. 'I've stabled such horses before. I can ride most beasts; but I'd not throw leg over one like Blanchard for a hundred pounds of silver. Not only would he not endure for a moment anyone but his master on his back, but having thrown me, he'd hardly be content to stand. He'd turn on me with hooves and teeth, as he's been trained, until either he had me killed, or I managed to escape.'

'Quite right,' said Giles, turning from his own men. 'The knight knows what he's about, Danielle. Try not to command everyone, for once. Horses such as Blanchard wouldn't be worth the duke's ransom they are, if they were the sort that could be found on any farm. I'd wager Sir Brian paid a heavy penny for this one.'

'My full inheritance,' grunted Brian, hard at work fastening the second horse's straps. 'The armor's my father's; but all else that came to me went to buy Blanchard. Never made a sounder move. He'll face lance, battle-axe, mace or sword, and defend me if I'm down against any man or beast that lives. I can ride him with knees alone and both hands busy with shield and weapon. And damned few other warhorses can match him for weight or strength.'

He glanced at the innkeeper.

'No offense to you, friend Dick,' he said. 'But even if Blanchard'd carry you, I'd not let him. He's my horse alone.'

'No fear, Sir Brian. I'm happier on Bess here, in any case.' Dick hesitated. 'But will you not at least wear a chain shirt under your cloth one?'

'Chain shirt alone won't do, anyway, if I run into Sir Hugh in full armor,' said Brian. 'He's a whoreson, but he knows how to fight. And if one of his men should think to search me early and find the mail, the alarm'll be sounded ahead of time. No, best to take the chance and dress later.'

'You don't make the most likely innkeeper, either,' Danielle remarked.

That much, Jim thought, was true. Sir James was clad in tight leather breeches with belt and sheath knife that had originally belonged to Dick's son, a loose gray shirt and a clumsy, thick, dark cloak. As clothes, nothing was wrong with them. They would have looked all right on someone like Dick, himself – assuming that the breeches could have been gotten to fasten around the innkeeper's relatively thick waist. But the trouble with them on Brian was the way he wore them. Jim's earliest impression of the knight had been of piercing blue eyes, the erect carriage that comes from living in the saddle and bearing armor, and an aggressively jutting chin. All these were still very visible, in spite of the humbleness of the garments that now clothed him.

'I've the beard, here,' said Dick, producing it from among the load in the wagon. 'It's not an exact match for your hair, Sir Brian; but then it's not unknown for a man with brown hair your color to have a beard touching on the red. These threads go over your head under your own hair to fasten in on … and if you then comb your own hair forward to mingle with it in front, as the player showed me … Let me assist you, Sir Brian …'

Together, they got the beard on. It did, indeed, go a long way to disguise the knight, giving him an unkempt, raffish look above which the blue eyes looked merely villainous.

'You might try slouching a bit,' said Danielle.

'Like this?' asked Brian.

He tried, without any great success.

'I'm not a damned jack-o-motley, you know!' he fumed at them all, finally. 'Leave be! I'll either coney-catch Sir Hugh and his men, or not, as God wills!'

He got up on the seat of the wagon, and picked up the reins of the two horses harnessed to it.

'Ready?' he demanded.

'Ready, Sir Brian,' said Dick, who was already mounted on the whitened and armored Bess.

'Give me a good lead, now, so that they don't see you having to hold Bess back from catching me.'

'Yes, Sir Brian.'

'And you, Giles, don't forget to leave a party on the gate. If Sir Hugh's first warning is to look out his chamber window and see fighting within the walls, he'll stop to arm and armor himself before all else. Once he shows up, full-accoutered, make sure those in the gate party stand back and try only to keep him from a horse, until I myself—'

'Or I,' interrupted Aragh.

Brian glanced at him, impatiently.

'Sir wolf,' he said, 'what might you do with a man in full armor?'

Aragh snarled softly, leaping up to settle himself in the wagon.

'Sir knight,' he said, 'someday you may see.'

'At any rate,' Brian went on, turning back to Giles, 'hold the gate and keep Sir Hugh from horse!'

'Fear not, Sir Brian,' said Giles. 'I've some little knowledge of such things.'

'Doubtless. But saying it makes all certain.' Brian flipped the reins he held, starting his wagon horses forward. 'Now – for God and my lady!'

He drove out of the woods.

Out on the small plain surrounding the castle, the last of the mist had now disappeared and the gray stone walls were warmed by the clear yellow light of early day. Brian whipped the wagon horses into a trot, and then into a clumsy gallop along the tracks leading toward the castle gate.

'Not yet, Master Innkeeper! Not yet ... *Now!*' snapped Giles; and Dick kicked Bess into movement, clanking out from the screen of trees at what was already a gallop.

Giles glanced at Jim.

'Yes,' said Jim, 'I'd better get started.'

He badly wanted to stay and see whether the gate would be opened for Brian and Aragh, and whether Dick would be able to turn and get back safely. But he must take off in the opposite direction to approach the castle from an angle and altitude where he would not immediately be spotted.

He turned, accordingly, and ran back some distance in the wood before leaping into the air and mounting to just above treetop level. Looking back over his shoulder, he saw he was now far enough from the castle so that the trees hid him from the viewers on the battlements, and commenced to fly in a wide circle toward the back of Malvern.

Shortly, he caught his first thermal. Circling up on this, he found himself just under the cloudbank, which was unbroken here but showed openings toward the north and west. On impulse, he decided to fly up through the clouds and see if it was possible to get above them.

It turned out to be so; although he had to climb nearly twelve hundred feet to achieve it. Once above the clouds, he headed directly toward the castle, looking for a gap in the white masses below him through which he could orient himself. Locating one, he soared toward it and looked through at an angle that gave him a view of both the plain and Malvern. No wagon or armored figure on horseback was in sight, but there was a patch of sunlight on the ground to the west of the castle, indicating another rift in the clouds somewhere above it.

He lifted his head, searched for this other rift from above and found it, not far off. He soared to it, saw the castle at a sharper angle below and identified the roof of the keep. He was about three-quarters of a mile from it and about a thousand feet above. He went into a dive, not through the rift, but through the clouds just beyond it, directly above the castle.

For a long moment he was wrapped about and blinded by cloud mist. Then suddenly he was back in open air again and the castle was right under him. Half folding his wings, he dropped like a stone from a catapult, arcing to its target. At the last moment he pulled up and, with a thunderclap of cupped air, slammed down on the top of the keep.

Only one guard met him. The man gaped, turned and disappeared down the stone stairway leading to the floor of the solar, below. Jim plunged after him, gained the solar and ducked in time to avoid a spear flung through the air. Instinctively, he struck out with a wing, and that powerful member literally picked up the man-at-arms and slammed him against a wall, to drop and lie still.

The dragon-blood of Jim – or Gorbash; under these conditions it was impossible to identify whose blood it was – was up and boiling!

He heard the sound of steel clashing on steel below him and plunged down the next flight of stairs to catch a momentary glimpse of a tall, slim girl in white holding a short pike and facing out an open doorway. He brushed past her as she cried something he could not understand and tried to stick him with the pike. But by that time, he was through the door and into a short corridor where Brian, wearing only a helmet and with the rest of his armor in a pile at his feet, was holding off three men-at-arms with his sword.

Jim slammed into the three and they went down.

'Thanks!' gasped Brian. 'Hold the lower stairs, will you, Sir James? And aid the wolf, if need be. He's either opened the gate by this time, or they have him dead. Bring word as to which – if you can.'

Snorting, long red tongue flickering out between parted jaws, and wings half raised, Jim hurled himself down the last flights of steps. At the bottom he discovered a large, dim hall to his right, somewhat divided by curtains, beyond which came the sounds of fighting and the shouts of men. To his left was a doorway to open sunlight. He went through.

To his right now, around a curving wall of weathered logs, he saw the space of an interior courtyard and the castle gates, one of which was swung partway inward and open. Two fights were going on in the courtyard. One was over by some open sheds containing horses, where five of Giles' men were engaged with swords against about the same number of Sir Hugh's men-at-arms. Just inside the gate, a shouting semi-circle of nearly a dozen more men-at-arms had Aragh against the battlement, none of them apparently too eager to be the first to close with him, but all trying by sword feints and gestures to hold his attention long enough for someone else to get in a blow.

'ARAGH!' thundered Jim, using his full dragon-voice.

He plunged at the semi-circle, which disintegrated as he hit it.

Immediately, he was fighting four men, Aragh was killing three others, and the rest were fleeing.

'Where's Giles?' Jim shouted at the wolf as he finished off three of his own four opponents and saw the other turn and run.

'Inside the hall,' Aragh panted, 'when last I saw him.'

'Sir Hugh?'

'No sign of him.'

'He's not in the keep!' Jim said. 'I just came from there. Brian's getting into his armor. I'll check the rest of the castle.'

He leaped into the air and with one pump of his wings put himself atop the wall. To right and left he saw the bodies of several men-at-arms down and motionless, a single arrow through the chest of each. The battlements were abandoned except by the dead.

Jim wondered where Dafydd was. Still back in the forest? Or had he come in and joined Giles' men, who were fighting in the hall or otherwise?

At that moment, an entrance on the far side of the keep suddenly disgorged men-at-arms carrying the same sort of short pikes that the girl had brandished. They bore down on the fairly even battle that was going on near the stables between some of their comrades and the outlaws.

The dragon-fury was now completely in possession of Jim. He leaped from the wall at this new body of the enemy. None of them had been looking up and he cannoned into them without warning. Suddenly he was in the midst of battle, hissing, roaring, fighting with teeth, claws and wings all at once, balanced on his hind legs like some gigantic bird of prey.

They melted about him. It was like battling straw men armed with candy-cane weapons. The pikes broke at his touch; he flung the men who carried them about like dolls. A savage feeling of power flamed up in him. Out of the corner of one eye he saw Aragh again surrounded by a fresh group of Sir Hugh's retainers and thought of going to the wolf's aid as soon as he had finished matters where he was. What was it Aragh had said about seeing that Gorbash got back safely? But Jim needed nobody's help. Who could stand against a dragon? No one. He was invincible, and when this was over he would remind them all of that – wolf, outlaws; knight ... Then, abruptly, the men-at-arms who had been attacking him began to shout and yell triumphantly.

'Gorbash!' howled Aragh. *'Gorbash!'*

Was the wolf calling for help? Jim looked and saw Aragh hard-pressed, but in no way badly wounded or in trouble.

'The hall, Gorbash!' cried Aragh.

Jim looked, between the pikeheads that came flashing at him suddenly with renewed vigor. The main doors of the hall were opening; and slowly, as he watched, a ponderous figure all in mirror-bright armor, already mounted with long lance in one gauntleted hand, rode out through the opening.

The armored figure did not appear to be in a hurry. It rode out into the center of the courtyard, turned its head in the direction of the wolf, looked toward Jim, then put its horse into a leisurely trot and rode – not at either one, but out of the castle gate.

Howls of reproach and anger replaced the shouts of triumph of the men-at-arms. They retreated from Jim and Aragh. Some dropped weapons and tried to run. Aragh was immediately upon those who ran from him, bringing them down from behind; but Jim ignored the men-at-arms falling away from him.

'You clean up here, Aragh!' he roared at the wolf. The feeling of unmatchable power was blazing in him now, and he could not wait to close with the mounted figure he had just seen. 'I'll go get him!'

'No! Stay! Hold, Sir James – !'

It was another fully armored figure, shouting, bursting out of the same exit from the keep that Jim had used. Brian, fully dressed and weaponed at last, ran heavily toward the stables, where horses still neighed and pulled at their tethers, upset by the excitement around them.

'*Too late!*' Jim thundered, joyously. 'I spoke for him first!'

He took to his wings, lifting up and over the wall. Outside, the armored figure on the horse was already three-quarters of the way to the forest edge.

'Surrender, Sir Hugh!' shouted Jim at full volume. 'I'll get you, anyway!'

He had expected the escaping knight, particularly after showing he was the kind to leave his men to die while he saved himself, to do nothing but put his heavy roan into a panic-stricken gallop at the sound of a dragon-voice and the sight of dragon-wings swooping after him. To Jim's surprise, however, Sir Hugh pulled his steed to a stop, turned and lowered his lance to attack position. Then he broke the horse into a run, charging directly for Jim.

Jim almost laughed. The man had lost his head. Either that, or else he had faced the fact that defeat and death were inescapable and had decided to go down fighting. At the same time, it was odd; and Jim had a sudden, reasonless memory flash of Smrgol, demanding of the other dragons in the cave: 'How many of you here would like to face just a single george in his shell, with his horn aimed at you?'

Then he and Sir Hugh came together with a crash, an unbelievable impact that in one blinding, pain-shot moment blotted out sight, thought, memory and all else ...

17

'My boy ...' said Smrgol's voice, brokenly, 'my boy ...'

It had seemed a very long time now that Jim had been conscious of shapes moving around him, of alternate periods of light and darkness, of voices that came and went ... voices familiar and voices strange. But he had paid little attention to them, lost as he was on a sea of pain which sucked him down, now and again, into dark waters of unconsciousness, then let him return partway to reality. The pain had become the whole world to him lately. It filled his mind completely. It dissolved his body in sensation. No one part of him suffered; it was his total being. And this situation had continued and continued ...

But now, with his identification of Smrgol's voice, the waters of the pain-ocean receded a little. The reduction in discomfort made him feel almost comfortable – almost luxurious. What pain remained was like an old disability, grown into a companion over the years, something that would be missed if it were suddenly to disappear altogether. He tried to focus his eyes on the large, shadowy shape near him.

'Smrgol?' he asked.

The voice that came from his throat was a ghost-voice, a wraith of that dragon-resonance with which he had become familiar since he had first awakened on this different world in Gorbash's body.

'He spoke to me!' It was Smrgol. 'Praise to the Fires! He'll live! Wolf, call the others! Tell them he's going to live, after all. Tell them to come, quickly!'

'I'll go,' snarled the voice of Aragh. 'But I said he would. Didn't I say he would?'

'Yes, yes...' Smrgol's voice was throaty. 'But I'm an old dragon; and I've seen so many go down before those horns of the georges ... Gorbash, how do you feel? Can you talk ... ?'

'A little ...' Jim whispered. 'What happened?'

'You were an idiot, boy, that's what happened!' Smrgol was trying to sound stern and was not succeeding very well. 'What gave you the wild idea you could take on a shelled george – one on a horse at that – single-handed?'

'I mean,' husked Jim, 'what happened to me?'

'You got a horn – a lance, they call it – through you, that's what happened. Anyone but a dragon would've been dead by the time he hit the ground. Anyone but one of our branch of the family would've died within the hour. As it is, it's been eight days now with you teetering on the edge; but now that you're back enough to answer me, it'll be all right. You'll live. A dragon that's not killed outright survives – that's the way we are, boy!'

'Survives ...' echoed Jim. The word had a strange sound in his ears.

'Of course! As I say, that's the way we are. Three more days and you'll be on your feet. A couple of days after that and you'll be the same as ever!'

'No,' said Jim, 'not the same ...'

'What're you talking about? Nonsense! I say you'll be as good as ever, and you will! Don't argue with me, now. I say you will!'

The old dragon went on talking, but Jim found his mind slipping back into dark waters once more. He would not argue with Smrgol. There was no point to it. But that did not mean he was allowing the old dragon to convince him. There was a change in him now; and he would never be the same again.

That recognition of a change stayed with him in the days that followed. As Smrgol predicted, he mended rapidly; and as he mended he began to respond to the visitors coming to see him. From them he slowly pieced together what had happened to him since that second in which he and Sir Hugh had crashed together outside the castle walls.

He understood now why the dragons, magnificent animals as they were, were still correct in fearing an armored knight, particularly one on horseback and armed with a lance. Over a ton of horse, man and metal – moving at speed of better than ten miles an hour with all that mass concentrated on the sharp point of a sixteen-foot shaft – gave awesome penetrating power. In Jim's case the lance had missed his heart and both lungs, or even Gorbash's constitution could not have saved him. The point of the weapon had entered high on his chest where the massive pectoral muscle of the left wing was not thick, and gone clear through him to emerge beside the left scapular with about eight inches of point and shaft. In addition, the back twelve feet of the lance had broken off, leaving a short stub of thicker shaft protruding from the entry point in his chest.

At first, the others had thought him dead. Certainly Hugh de Bois had thought so; for, without waiting to make sure, he had climbed back on his horse – which had gone down in the collision – and ridden off before he could be chased and caught by Brian on one of the castle horses.

The others had gathered around Jim on the plain, where he lay unmoving; and it had been Aragh who had first established that he still breathed, if only barely. They had not dared move him, as he was clearly on the very precipice edge of extinction. So they had built a makeshift hut of poles and branches over him where he lay, covered him with cloths and built a fire within the shelter to keep him warm while the wolf went for S. Carolinus.

Carolinus had come, accompanied by Smrgol, to whom he had somehow gotten word. At the magician's direction, the old dragon had used his strength to do what the others had seen no way of doing, even if they had been willing to risk it. Smrgol had carefully drawn out the broken shaft.

With the wound cleared, Jim had bled heavily for a while, but eventually the bleeding had stopped; and Carolinus had announced that since Jim had survived so far, nothing more was to be done for him. The magician had made ready to leave.

'But there must be something we can do!' Danielle insisted.

'Wait,' snapped Carolinus, 'and hope.'

He left.

They built the hut into a more permanent structure. Smrgol and Aragh took turns sitting with him, occasionally with Danielle, Brian, or one of the other humans for company; and they waited. Finally the day had now come on which he answered Smrgol.

Now, all were coming around to talk to him and convey their satisfaction that he had survived. Each of them had an individual way of doing this: Smrgol lectured him. Aragh growled sourly at him. Danielle insisted that he had been stupid, but thought at the same time that it was rather princely of him to hurl himself to almost-certain death; she was briskly unsympathetic, but very gentle in changing his bandages, which she would not allow anyone else to touch. Giles was curious as to the style of fighting Sir James had known in his proper body, and came close to hinting that Jim must have had some secret ploy up his sleeve or he would not have risked making a frontal attack on Sir Hugh in the first place. Dafydd came and sat and worked at his fletcher's craft of arrow-making, and said nothing.

Geronde de Chaney (who had been the girl in white, with the pike, in the keep) came by and promised him revenge. She wore a bandage herself on her right cheek.

It appeared that Sir Hugh had originally ridden up with a half-dozen followers and obtained entrance to the castle by saying he had word of her father's death. Once inside, the men with him had overpowered the gate guards and let in the rest of his retainers. With the castle in his hands, he had admitted he knew nothing about her father; but since he intended to have Malvern, he told her he expected her to marry him immediately. When she refused, he had threatened to disfigure her in stages by slashing first her right cheek, then three days later her left, then three days after that by cutting off her nose, then by putting out her eyes one at a time until she gave in. She had defied him and now would carry the scar on her cheek for the rest of her life. She was a frail, rather ethereal-looking maiden with ash-blond hair and detailed plans for cooking Sir Hugh over a slow fire as soon as she could make him her prisoner.

Brian brought wine and sat and drank with Jim, telling his bad jokes and endless stories, some of which were apparently true – according to Aragh or Smrgol – but all of which were incredible.

Dick Innkeeper sent the last of his hams to tickle Jim's appetite.

Actually, Jim found that for the first time in his dragon-body appetite was missing. The wine was pleasant on his throat; but even that did not tempt him except in what, for a dragon, were very small quantities.

Nevertheless, he mended. He took to sitting outside in the sun, and the clear, bright light of early autumn warmed his body even if it did not touch the inner coldness that had come to swell in him. The truth was that Death, in the shape of Sir Hugh's lance, had come too close. The broken spear was out of his body now and most of the pain was gone, but there was still a low-level general interior ache that stayed with him and nourished a bleakness of spirit. The color had gone out of things, the uniqueness and value out of the people about him. Even the thought of Angie dwindled in importance. His mind held only one overriding thought: he would never attack an armored knight head-on again. He would, in fact, never attack anything again but in the easiest and surest way. Only survival was important; and it did not matter how survival was accomplished, just so that it was ...

Perhaps, the thought came to him much later, the others might have noticed this change in him and would have worked to reverse it, if it had not happened that, just at that time, as soon as he was well enough to participate, he was drawn into their discussion about what should be done next.

'... The decision,' said Brian firmly at length, 'must rest with you, Sir James. Geronde, he lent us his aid to get you free from Sir Hugh, and I'm in his debt for that. If he wishes to go first to the rescue of his lady – and Lord how can I object to that, seeing he's helped me to recover mine – I must go. You know that, milady.'

'Of course I do,' Geronde said, quickly.

They were all – except Smrgol, who had flown back on business of his own to the dragon cave – sitting at the high table of the castle hall after dinner and Jim was slaking an appetite for wine that had greatly recovered. Geronde was seated on the other side of Brian from Jim, and she leaned around the knight now to look directly into the dragon's eyes.

'I'm as much in debt to Sir James as you are, Brian,' she said, 'and bound like you to honor his decision. But, Sir James, I only want you to consider the advantages of moving against Hugh de Bois at just this time.'

'Advantages for you, perhaps,' Aragh growled at her. The wolf was always uncomfortable inside any building, and this made him even more bad-tempered than he was ordinarily. 'I've no use for a castle. Nor should you, Gorbash!'

'But you wish an end to Sir Hugh as much as we,' Geronde said to him. 'You should want to go after him now, just as we do.'

'I'll kill him when I find him; I won't hunt him. I hunt for food – not, like you humans, for anything cold or warm, wet or dry, that takes your fancy,' snarled Aragh. 'And Gorbash is like me, not like you.'

'Gorbash may well be like you,' Geronde retorted. 'Sir James is not. And Sir James will be back in his own proper body one of these days. When that day comes, he may have need for a castle. Under law, I cannot acquire Sir Hugh's land and castle as long as there's doubt whether my father lives or not; and Malvern Castle and lands will go to Sir Brian as my husband, on our marriage, in any case. Meanwhile, once Sir Hugh is taken care of, we'll need a reliable neighbor; and the Bois de Malencontri is not an ill estate, even for a' – she glanced briefly down the length of the high table at Danielle – 'person who may be of considerable degree.'

'I say again, castles and lands are nothing to me,' snarled Aragh. 'What good are cold stone and dry earth? And I also say again they should be nothing to you, Gorbash. If Smrgol were here, he'd tell you that, too. In any case, I've been with you to guard your back and stand with you against the Dark Powers, not to help you gain human toys. You start lusting after things like that, Gorbash, and we go different ways!'

He rose to all four feet, turned and trotted from the hall, the castle people moving out of his way as he came close to them.

'Indeed,' Dafydd agreed, when the wolf was gone, 'and he could be right at that. Defending yourself is one thing, going to seek the killing is quite another, no matter how good the reason, look you.'

'Don't listen to them, Sir James,' said Danielle. 'You don't need them, anyway. If you don't take that castle, somebody else will. Isn't that right, Father?'

'Since there's pay in it, count on me and my lads,' Giles said to Lady Geronde. He turned to Danielle. 'But it's business – business only – that takes us there. Beyond that, leave me out of this.'

'I've promised you and your band half of the wealth Castle Malencontri contains,' Geronde assured him. 'You know it should be worth your while. Sir Hugh has been robbing his lesser neighbors for years.'

'And I've agreed,' said Giles. 'It's not me you need consent from. It's Sir James.'

Jim started to shrug before he remembered his dragon-body was not equipped to do so. Carolinus had told him that Angie would not be in discomfort while she was waiting for him to rescue her. A few more days, he thought now, out of his new inner bleakness – even an added week or two – should make little difference. Besides, just in case Carolinus couldn't get the two of them sent back to where they belonged, a castle and lands would not be a bad thing for them to own. The need for food and shelter – good food and comfortable shelter – was as much a reality here in this world as pain itself. And realities were not to be ignored.

'Why not?' he said. 'All right, I'm in favor of moving on Hugh de Bois de Malencontri and his property now.'

The moment he said it, a strange sort of ripple seemed to run through the air in the hall, something like the momentary shimmer of a heat wave, and the bleak feeling inside him expanded into a sensation of hollowness as if he and Gorbash's body together were only a shell enclosing nothing at all. Jim blinked, half inclined to think his eyes were playing tricks on him because of the wine or the smoky atmosphere of the candle-lit room. But the impression was gone in the same instant it had seemed to exist; so that he found himself unsure he had really felt anything in the first place.

He looked around at the others, but they seemed to have noticed nothing, except for Dafydd, who was looking at him penetratingly.

'Good,' said Geronde. 'It's settled, then.'

'I do not think it is good,' Dafydd put in. 'In my family, from father to son and mother to daughter for many generations now, there have been eyes to see warnings. And a moment past the candle flames here all bent, though there was no wind in the hall. I do not think this going after Sir Hugh now is good at all.'

'Aragh frightened you, that's all,' said Danielle.

'I am not frightened. But, no more than the wolf, am I a knight to be holding or taking of castles.'

'I'll make you a knight,' Danielle told him. 'If I make you a knight, will that do away with your doubts?'

'For shame, Danielle!' said Giles. His face had darkened. 'Knighthood is no jest.'

Dafydd got to his feet.

'You are making sport of me,' he said. 'But since you will do this thing, I'll do it also, because I love you. For now, I will go out into the clean air and the clean woods by myself.'

He, too, left the hall.

'Here, here!' said Brian, cheerfully. 'Let's have an end to doom-saying for a bit. Fill your cups! We've agreed now. To the soon taking of Sir Hugh and his castle!'

'And Sir Hugh himself, one day closer to the fire,' added Geronde.

They drank.

Early the next day they set off, without Aragh but with Giles' outlaws reinforced by some forty men drawn from Malvern Castle and the other de Chaney estates. Geronde herself had been fiercely eager to come with them; but her sense of duty to the castle and lands of her father was capable of overriding even her thirst for vengeance. So, she had agreed to stay behind. They saw her standing on the castle wall, looking after them, until the trees of the forest blocked her from view.

The morning was overcast as it had been on that day when they had retaken Malvern Castle from Sir Hugh. This day, however, the clouds did not clear. Instead they thickened, and soon a light, steady drizzle began.

Their way led at first through alternate woods and open spaces, but as the morning wore on the tree cover became general, the ground low-lying and wet. They were moving into an area of small lakes and bogs, and the wagon track they were following soon became miry and slippery. Their party straggled, and separated into groups spread out over half a mile.

But more than their pattern of travel seemed affected by the grayness of the day: the damp dullness of the atmosphere seemed to produce a sullenness of temper. Those on foot, like the outlaws and the forty men from the Castle Malvern lands, trudged along head-down against the falling water, their bowstrings cased, their weapons hooded. The outlaws' previous custom of rough jokes and friendly insults had vanished. When they spoke it was sourly, expressing their dissatisfaction with the weather, the route, and the probable cost – in deaths and wounds – of reducing the castle they were going to assault. Old arguments were dredged up between individuals and tempers grew short.

Even the leaders of the expedition seemed affected by the general change in attitude. Giles was grim, Danielle sharp-tongued and Dafydd completely uncommunicative. It was as if the whole party was reacting to a feeling that something was wrong.

Jim took refuge, at last, at the head of the column with the single exception to this general malaise: Brian on Blanchard was his invariable self. There was something cheerfully spartan and unyielding about the knight. His personal world appeared to have had all its essential questions and uncertainties settled long ago. The sun might shine, snow might fall, wine might flow or blood be spilled – but all these were surface variations, to be ignored ordinarily as beneath notice. Brian gave the impression that he would joke with his torturers as they were stretching him on the rack.

Jim told him about the way the others were acting, particularly the leaders.

'Shouldn't worry about it,' said Brian.

'But it's important to keep everybody working together, isn't it? For example, what if Giles suddenly decided to pull out with all his band? We'd be left with the forty men from Malvern, half of whom don't look as if they know anything about fighting.'

'I don't think Giles would do that,' said the knight. 'He knows there's wealth to be got for him and his lads in Sir Hugh's stronghold. Also, he's agreed to go – and was a gentleman once, pretty clearly, though he won't admit it now.'

'Well, even if Giles personally can be counted on,' Jim added, 'there could be trouble with Danielle and Dafydd that might end up involving her father. Dafydd's been saying less with every mile, and Danielle won't let up on him. Actually, she shouldn't be along on this, anyway, except that nobody seems to have had the guts to tell her she couldn't come.'

'Master Welshman wouldn't have come without her.'

'True,' Jim admitted. 'But you have to concede she's no warrior—'

'Are you sure about that?' asked Brian. 'Ever seen her shoot?'

'Just that time her arrows came at us. And in the looted village. All right, she can handle a bow—'

'Not just a bow,' the knight said. 'She draws a longbow with a hundred-pound pull, like half the archers in her father's band.'

Jim blinked. Years ago in college, he had taken a passing interest in bow-hunting. Practicing at targets, he had begun with a forty-pound bow and graduated to a sixty-pound one. Sixty pounds had felt, to him, like the practical limit – and he did not consider himself weak.

'How do you know?' he asked.

'Saw her shooting after you were lanced, at the taking of Malvern Castle while some fighting was still going on.'

'She was at the castle?' Jim asked, startled. 'I thought she stayed in the woods. But how could you tell, just seeing her shoot?'

Brian looked sideways at him with curiosity as they moved forward together.

'It's a strange land you must come from overseas, James,' he said. 'By watching the arrow as it leaves her bow, of course.'

'Watching her arrow?'

'See how much it lifts as it leaves the string,' Brian explained. 'When I saw her, she was still aiming under her mark at ten rods' distance. Pull no more than an eighty-pound bow myself. Of course, I'm no archer. But Mistress Danielle is no weakling.'

Jim trudged on alongside Blanchard and the mounted knight for a long moment of silence, absorbing this.

'If she pulls a hundred-pound bow, what does Dafydd pull?'

'Lord, who knows? A hundred-and-fifty? Two-hundred? Even more than that? The Welshman doesn't fit any ordinary suit of clothes. You've seen he's his own bowyer and fletcher – and a rare craftsman at both. I wager there's not an archer in Giles' band – assuming he could draw it when he got it – who'd not give ten years' earnings for that bow of Master Dafydd's. With the longbow, the secret's all in the taper towards the ends of the bowstave, you know. Even allowing for the man's strength, it's not just a case of cutting himself a heavier, longer bow that lets him shoot the flights he does, and that accurately. There's a cunning and an art built into his weapon that goes beyond the skill of the ordinary bowyer. You heard Giles when Master Dafydd first undertook to slay the guards on the castle walls from the edge of the woods. And, of course, the same holds true for the arrows the Welshman makes. Any of these outlaw lads'd no doubt trade half the teeth in his head for a quiverful of those.'

'I see,' said Jim.

The information sank into the back of his mind and lay there leadenly. Once upon a time, he realized, before his encounter with Sir Hugh, he would have found this kind of information fascinating. Now, it only left him vaguely resentful – against Dafydd for possessing such knowledge and skill, and toward Brian for the condescension he thought he heard in the knight's voice when explaining it to him.

He said nothing more; and Brian, after making a few further remarks aimed at continuing the conversation, gave up and turned Blanchard about to trot back down the track and check on the rest of the expedition. Left alone, Jim plodded on, scarcely noticing where he was going. He realized he was traveling by himself now, but that suited his present mood. He had no wish for company – particularly for the company of these medieval characters, both beast and human.

In fact, now that he glanced about, himself, he could see neither people nor horses, nor anything of the wagon track they had been following. Undoubtedly the track had taken one of its reasonless curves – like a footpath, it had evidently developed along the route of easiest travel. There was no construction to it as a road at all, with the result that it often went widely out of its way to avoid a patch of bushes which a man with an ax could have cleared in an hour or two of work. It had probably detoured; and he, tied up in his thoughts, had unconsciously taken the direct route, straight ahead – in which case, he would be running into it again shortly, when it curved back to its base line of direction.

Meanwhile, as Jim was telling himself, the isolation was not unwelcome. He had had it with strange worlds, talking creatures, blood, battle, superhumans and supernatural forces – all of these in the context of a primitive technology and elemental society.

When you got down to it, he thought, there was a limit to how much living you could do with animals. Smrgol and Aragh, as well as the other dragons, were animals in spite of the fact that they could talk. For that matter, the humans he had met were no better – human animals, operating by custom, instinct or emotion, but never by civilized thought. For all her beauty, Danielle was hardly more than a fur-clad female out of the Stone Age. Similarly, for all his craft and skill, Dafydd could have stepped right out of a Cro-Magnon hunting party. Giles was a clever old criminal, no more; and Brian was a pain-indifferent killing machine who thought with his muscles. As for Geronde – she was a pure savage in her happy anticipation of the torture she would inflict on her enemy once she had captured him.

What had made him think – back in the cleanliness and comfort of the twentieth-century world he belonged to – that *he* would ever find it attractive, let alone pleasant, to live with people like these? Their redeeming qualities were nil. Any obligation or affection he might think he was developing toward them was nothing but the product of a false romanticism.

He broke off at this point in his thoughts to realize that he had been traveling for some time and had not yet come upon the wagon track or seen any sign of the rest of the party. Possibly the wagon track had run out. Possibly they had turned off on some other route. Possibly, even, they had decided to halt for the day – because the rain was now coming down quite heavily. Well, in any case, they could take care of themselves; and he could rejoin them tomorrow. He felt no need of their company; and with his dragon's insensitiveness to temperature and weather, it made little difference to him that the day had grown wet and chilly.

In fact, now that he thought of it, it suited his own mood to have the day drawing to a prematurely gray close and the skies pouring down upon the dripping trees and sodden earth that surrounded him.

Nevertheless, he looked about, picked out a grove of trees and walked over to it. It was a simple matter to pull up some of the larger saplings by the roots and lean their tops together, teepee-fashion, to produce a makeshift shelter. The interlaced tops, still thick with leaves, did provide him some protection against the falling rain.

Jim curled up inside the shelter with a good deal of satisfaction. The day was gathering into gloom, now. He had no idea where the others were, he could not find them if he wanted to, and that was as it should be. They could not find him either – and *that* was as it should be ...

He was preparing to tuck his head under a wing, when a sound registered on him that he had been hearing faintly but which had been growing slowly in volume for some time. For a second his mind refused to identify it; and then recognition came, clear and unmistakable.

Sandmirks – approaching.

18

Jim was out of the shelter before he realized he had moved – and was ready to run. What checked him was the same instinct he felt at the time he had encountered sandmirks before: the wordless understanding that to try to run from them was the beginning of the end. It was a knowledge that came from the deepest levels of Gorbash's brain.

He stood where he was, in the increasing darkness, his jaws parted, his tongue flickering in and out between them. His breath was snarled in his throat. If he had any idea in which direction Brian and the others could be found, there might be some sense in running. If he could reach them, there was perhaps safety in numbers. Just why there should be, he was not quite sure; but the impression persisted, instinctively. Furthermore, he knew that sandmirks vastly preferred to attack a helpless and outnumbered victim. Maybe a large group of humans or animals together could resist the fear the sandmirks tried to breed in the minds of those they wanted to destroy and devour. If the victims could resist, then they might be able to attack the sandmirks in turn. The sandmirks, as he had seen, were not likely to stand against those who had no fear of them – witness, the speed with which they had fled when Aragh had driven them off.

But which way should he go to find the expedition against Sir Hugh? As he had considered earlier, they might have diverged from the path or halted for the night, some time since. They might even have turned back. If he began to run and it turned out he was headed in the wrong direction, he would be running into the sandmirks' jaws.

One thing was certain: he had no Aragh to come to his rescue here. Even if the wolf had hung around Malvern long enough to see whether Jim would, indeed, go along on the expedition, he would have had his worst fears confirmed long since; and he would have taken off in a direction back to his own woods. He would be miles beyond hearing the voices that were closing in on Jim now.

Fear and rage, combined, flared like living flames inside Jim. The breath snarled once more in his throat. His head darted left and right, reflexively, like the head of a driven animal hearing the sounds of the beaters closing in on it from all sides. There had to be some way out. Some way ...

But there was none.

The frantic, instinctive darting of his head slowed and then stopped. The rage in him died. Now he was only afraid, and the fear filled him completely. At last, he faced the fact that he was right to be afraid: there was something wrong with him if he was not. It was death he heard coming – his death.

He stood in the rainy darkness, hearing the chittering of the sand-mirks growing closer. They were only minutes away from surrounding him now. He had no place to flee to; and it would be too late to flee once they had arrived. His mind reached the furthest possible limit of despair and went beyond, into a kind of limitless, colorless clarity.

He saw himself clearly now. He had wandered off, rehearsing in his mind all the things he could find wrong with Brian and the others. But the arguments against them that he had summoned up were only a smoke screen for what was wrong with himself. It was not Brian, Smrgol, Aragh and the others who were so much less than he, but he who was so much less than they. If it had not been for the accident that had landed him in the powerful flesh he now wore, he would be nothing. In his own body he would not have been able to qualify as the least member of Giles' band. Could he pull a hundred-pound longbow, let alone hit anything with an arrow from it? Could he, clad in the best armor in the world and mounted on the best warhorse, delude himself that he could last as an opponent of Brian's or Sir Hugh's for two minutes?

He knew better now. It was very ego-pampering to cannon into men-at-arms whom he outweighed five to one and send them flying. It was very comfortable to tell people living in a rigidly stratified society that he had been a baron, and let them surmise that he had perhaps been a prince. But what had happened when a real lance actually went through him? All at once the fun had gone out of the game. He was ready to pick up his marbles and go home.

Now, alone, with the sandmirks closing in on him, and facing himself at last, he saw that this was no soft world he and Angie had landed in. It was a hard one; and all those he had met here – Smrgol, Brian, Aragh, Giles, Dafydd, Danielle, even Secoh and Dick Innkeeper – were battle-scarred survivors of it. They were survivors because they had the courage required to survive. That courage he had resented in them when he had flown onto the lance point of Hugh de Bois and discovered that he could be killed, just like anyone else. The discovery had woken him to a realization of how little of their sort of courage he had ever been called on – in his own world – to show.

Now it no longer mattered whether he could be courageous or not, because he was going to die, anyway. The sandmirks were just beyond the trees that ringed him; and the panic born of their chittering was beginning to eat at his brain. They would be certain of him this time. He had not even a campfire to keep them at a distance. Cleverly, once again, they had come on a rainy, cloud-thick night when a dragon could not take to the air for fear of flying blindly into a tree or cliff; and when he, like any ordinary earth-bound animal, could only attempt to escape on foot. The only difference now from the time before was that he had at last come to terms with himself – a single, small triumph, the one thing that made him different from a simple dragon-victim.

The breath checked in his lungs. For a moment even the sandmirk voices were forgotten. He had, at least, a final choice. He would die either way, but he could still choose how. What was it he had said to Carolinus, back when they first met? '... But I'm not a dragon'?

Nor was he. Gorbash might have no choice in this situation, but he was Jim Eckert, who had. He could go down, he could die, still trying to reach the Loathly Tower and rescue Angie – by himself, if necessary – not as a helpless meal for sandmirks.

It might be death to fly, but he preferred that death to staying here. He gaped his jaws and roared at the sandmirks. He crouched and sprang upward into the rain and the darkness; and the sound of the chittering faded quickly to silence and was lost, far below and behind.

Pumping his wings, he reached for altitude. It was a forlorn hope to think that the cloud cover would be low enough for him to mount above it. And, even if it was, and he did, above those clouds and rain on a night like this one where would he find thermals to soar on? A good wind could save him – but weather like this did not go with strong, steady winds above a layer of rainclouds. If he could not soar, sooner or later he would become wing-weary and start to lose altitude. After that the crash to earth would be inevitable.

But for now, his strength was still with him. He beat upward through the downpour. Darkness surrounded him – before, behind, above, below. He felt as if he were hanging still in a wet and lightless void, exerting all his strength but going nowhere. No pause came in the rain, no rift in the darkness overhead to show a patch of starlit sky.

Judging by the altitude he had gained previously in a first few minutes of upward flying, he thought he should easily be above five thousand feet by this time. He tried to remember what he knew about rain-clouds. Most precipitation, he vaguely remembered learning once, fell from nimbostratus; altostratus or cumulonimbus clouds. Cumulonimbus were low-lying, but the other two were in a middle range – up to twenty thousand feet or so. Clearly, he could not fly above twenty thousand feet. His lungs were the lungs of any animal adapted to a planetary surface. He would run out of oxygen at that altitude – even if the cold of the higher air did not freeze him.

A faint but steady wind pushed the rain along at his present altitude; and instinctively he had been heading into it to gain lift. He took a chance now and stiffened out his wings in soaring position while he caught his breath. He had no visible evidence that he was losing altitude, but he could feel the pressure of the air on the underside of his wings; and this sensation sent clear signals to his dragon-brain that he was now on a shallow glide back toward the ground. He dared not prolong the glide. He might be losing altitude faster than he thought.

He began to use his wings again, and his pressure points signaled that he was once more gaining altitude, though at a slow rate. His mind, working at a steady white heat from the moment he had decided to leave the sandmirks on the ground behind, now tossed something at him out of the very back of his reading experience: a passage from a very old book dealing with somebody lost underwater who no longer knew even which way was up to the surface. He had thought, when he had read that passage, that what was needed in such a situation was some sort of diver's personal sonar. That memory triggered off in his mind the recollection that not only was his dragon-voice of unusual proportions but his eyesight and hearing were unhumanly sensitive. Bats could fly blind at night, or even – as experimenters had discovered – when the animals had been physically blinded, because of their echo-sounding – their sonar. What if he could do something like that?

Jim opened his mouth, gathered the full force of his lungs, and sent a wordless cry booming out into the falling rain and darkness around him.

He listened ...

He was not sure whether he had heard anything echoing back at him. He boomed again. And listened ... and listened ... straining his ears. This time, he thought he heard an echo of some sort.

Once more he boomed, and once more he listened. This time, clearly, an echo returned. Something was below him and off to his right.

Lowering his head toward the ground below, he boomed again.

His dragon-hearing was evidently quick to learn. This time he was able to make out, not only a general echo, but some differences in the areas from which the echoes came. Far to his right, the response was soft, close to his right it was sharp, and far to his left it became soft again. If these were any indication, they should signal a hard surface almost directly underneath him.

He checked on that thought. It was not so likely that the echoes indicated hard surface, as that they did a reflective one. This could mean that right under him was an area of open land, while to right and left were areas where tree growth interfered with echo response.

He stopped experimenting and resumed flying, while he thought this out. The real problem, he told himself, was to discover if he could determine the distances between himself and the source of the echoes. A sort of glee ran through him. It was not that, even now, he had any real belief in his ability to save himself – win an overall victory against the sandmirks. He was merely doing something about his situation.

He flew for a while, again deliberately trying to gain altitude – enough so that he would be able to tell by what he heard whether there was any real difference between the echoes he had caught at a lower altitude. He once again stiffened his wings into soaring position and sent his pulse of sound winging into the rain-drenched darkness.

The echoes came back – and for the first time hope leaped up within Jim. For what he was hearing was essentially the same distribution of strong echoes and weak – indications of high reflective surfaces adjoining softly reflective ones – in the same directions in which he had found them before, but with a very clear weakening of the echoes – an obvious indication that the echoes' strength might be usable as indexes to his height.

He was now caught up in what he was doing. A fever of optimism burned inside him. The odds were still large against his being able to learn anything in time to let him land safely; but the odds had been astronomical against him before.

He continued alternately to fly, soar, experiment with changes in altitude. His life-and-death situation helped him learn: his ability to interpret what he was hearing was growing by leaps and bounds. Not merely was his hearing becoming more sensitive, but also more selective; so that he was able to distinguish not merely two types of surfaces below him, but perhaps half a dozen – including a thin streak of sharp, almost metallic echo which might indicate a stream or river.

Also, little by little, his skill in using the information from the echoes was increasing. Gradually building in his mind, like the negative of a photograph, was an image of the area below. He could now ignore two sounds which – had he considered them earlier – might have kept him from trying the experiment: the noise of the falling rain, hissing around him, and the steady sound of it beating on the earth below. His dragon-hearing apparently was capable of control by conscious intent.

For a moment it crossed Jim's mind that dragons might have more in common with bats than was generally thought. Certainly their wings were like enormous bat wings. If he was able to do what he was now doing, possibly any dragon could; and it was surprising that most dragons believed nighttime to be a time when they could not fly unless by a bright moon.

Of course, he remembered, dragons obviously had a different orientation to darkness than humans did. He remembered how he had felt in the dragon caves – he had not had so much as a touch of claustrophobia. As a dragon, he did not mind being underground, or enclosed in darkness. Similarly, in the cellar of Dick Innkeeper, the fact that the torch had gone out while he was eating had left him completely undisturbed. Darkness as such, and the inability to see, held no terrors for him. It struck him now that the real reason for other dragons' fear of flying at night, when they could not see, was that for them aboveground was considered a strange and possibly dangerous place; and the lack of light to fly by was a good excuse not to go there. Gorbash, Jim remembered, was thought of as an almost unnatural dragon for spending so much time aboveground. Now, Gorbash's abnormal attitude, complemented by Jim's normal human attitude that the surface was a good place on which to be, opened up a whole new dimension in dragon night travel.

Meanwhile, although he was gaining more and more control over his situation, Jim had no way of judging his altitude. It did no good to know that he was getting closer and closer to the ground, if he had no way of guessing when getting close changed abruptly to being there!

It occurred to him that he had only one solution: he could fly down toward the stronger echoes, coming as close to their source as he dared, and hope that when he got very near there would be enough light – even on this dark night – for him to pull up at the last moment. The attempt would be a bit like playing Russian roulette; but what other choice had he?

Putting himself into the shallowest of glide paths, he began to descend. As he did, inspiration came to him for a second time. He remembered the streak of particularly sharp echoes and his own guess that it might represent a river or creek, with a highly sound-reflective surface. He altered his path slightly toward that particular echo. If he was fated to crash-land, he would have more hope if he came down on water than on earth or into a grove of sharp-branched trees.

He continued his descent, sending out pulses of sound as he went. The echoes came back, more and more sharply, more and more swiftly. Straining his eyes, he peered ahead; but all he could see was blackness. Closer he came, and closer – and still he could see absolutely nothing.

Abruptly, he pulled up; and as he did so his tail, hanging down behind him, splashed through water. A split second later he was climbing again, and cursing his own stupidity.

Of course, dammit! Voice, ears – he had completely forgotten nose. Suddenly he had *smelled* water! His dragon-olfactory sense might be no match for Aragh's superb physical instrument, but it was a great deal more sensitive than a human's. He checked his climbing instinctively and went again into a shallow glide, once more aimed toward the water echo below. But this time he paid attention to the odors reaching his nose.

Conscious awareness, he found himself thinking, was a wonderful thing. What he now identified through his nostrils should have been apparent to him on the way down before, but because he had not been expecting to use his sense of smell to orient himself, he had paid no attention. Now, deliberately sniffing, he smelled not only water, but grass, pine needles, leaves and the damp earth itself.

Coming down over what he now knew was water, he smelled soil to right and left of it. He had been right: it was a small river, perhaps fifty yards wide. He descended until his tail touched water, and then rose a little and drifted toward the smell of earth on the right. He glided at an angle toward it, and –

Oops! He pulled up just in time as he smelled a stand of elm trees rising thirty feet into the air above the right bank, directly in his path. Beyond them was a scent of grass and earth. He glided down again above the bank's edge beyond the trees, veered just off it over the water, once more –

And pancaked into the liquid below.

Jim made a tremendous splash. But the water by the bank turned out to be only shoulder-deep on him – perhaps the height of a man. He stood in the stream for a moment, the cool liquid streaming slowly around him, savoring the simple feeling of being safely on the surface of the earth again.

After a few moments, the rapid beating of his heart slowed and he turned and climbed out of the water onto the bank, his head dizzy with success.

It occurred to him, tantalizingly, that he might even have succeeded in coming down safely on the bank itself. Then he rejected the thought. Landing on something solid was more than a bit risky. It would be wiser to wait until he had practiced these new nighttime skills some more.

His headiness began to fade. It was a great thing to be alive and to have escaped the sandmirks, but he was still without Companions or a plan of action.

He was no strong staff for Angie to lean her hopes of rescue on, he thought now, in guilty reaction; but he was all she had. Briefly, he thought of waiting until morning and then taking wing to see if he could find Brian and the rest. Then he remembered how he had already promised to help them take Hugh de Bois' castle first. His change of heart would probably be excuse enough for the troupe to consider itself free of any obligation to help him with Angie. Even if they didn't, he now realized how far he was from understanding his strange new friends. All of them, even the humans, thought and acted according to standards entirely different from his. It was a sobering example of how one could speak the same language as someone else without being on the same mental wavelength at all.

He needed to get straightened out on the way his medieval friends thought and felt, before he made any more mistakes about them and this world; and the obvious person to help him was Carolinus.

He lifted his head. It had almost stopped raining while he was coming in for a landing and during these heavy thoughts. In fact, the clouds seemed to be thinning a trifle. He thought he saw a milky gleam behind one patch of them that could be the moonlight struggling to get through.

If the moon came out – or even if it didn't, he thought, now – he ought to be able, once airborne, to locate the Tinkling Water again. His wing muscles, which had been tiring while he tried to interpret the echoes he heard from the ground, now felt rested once more – another instance of the amazing dragon-strength and endurance. It was too bad dragons could not be studied by competent physiologists, zoologists and doctors of veterinary medicine to find out how they managed to have such physical gifts.

Jim took off with a bound into the now-rainless air – and a little afterward, as he soared in a direction he could only hope was toward Carolinus' cottage, the moon came out to reveal the silver-black landscape about nine hundred feet below him. Five minutes later the sky was all but clear and he was in a long glide toward the woods holding the Tinkling Water, which he could see now, less than two miles ahead of him. He had only been off in his heading by about five compass points.

19

Among patches of white moonlight and India-ink shadows, Jim landed with a thump on the gravel path leading to Carolinus' front door. Far off in the woods some sleepy bird clucked loudly enough to be overheard by Jim's dragon-ears. Otherwise, there was complete silence.

Jim hesitated. No light at all showed from the windows of the house; and now that he was here, he was feeling a reluctance to awaken the magician.

As he stood indecisively, a conviction began to creep over him that the building was not merely shut up for the night, but was deserted. In the little clearing, an air of abandonment and emptiness hung on the air itself.

'So, there he is!' growled a voice.

Jim spun around.

'Aragh!' he shouted.

The wolf was approaching from the shadows at the edge of the clearing. Jim was so glad to see him, he could have hugged him. Behind the lean, gleaming-eyed shape strode a larger, familiar dragon-figure.

'Smrgol!' said Jim.

He had not realized until this moment how he had come to feel for these two, and for Brian and the others. It became clear to him that the space between contrasting life forms in this world was not so great as in the world he had left. Life and death were next-door neighbors; similarly, love and hate were as close as two doorways at the end of a corridor, and if you did not learn to hate someone within a short space of time, you learned to love.

'What are you two doing here?' he asked.

'Waiting for you,' Aragh snarled.

'Waiting for me? But how did you know I was coming here?'

'The Mage did,' said Smrgol. 'He called me here yesterday by a cliff sparrow who brought me his message. *"Dragon,"* he said, when I got here, *'James Eckert, whom you know as Gorbash, and I each have long*

757

*journeys to make – alone. If I make mine, I'll find you all together, later
on. If lames James makes his, he'll come looking for me, here. Wait for
him, and tell him what I just told you. Also, tell him that the hour is close
and the battle is greater than I thought. More than one plane is involved
– can you say that word, dragon?"*

"'Plane,'" I said. And then: "'What does it mean, Mager?'"

"'Very good,'" he said. "'And never mind what it means. James will
understand. More than one plane is involved, and if we can fight together
to save the sickness here from spreading out over all, so much the better
our chances. But if we can't fight together, still it behooves each of us to
fight on as he can, alone; for if our opposition succeeds, there'll be nothing left for any of us... Have you got all that, dragon?'"

"'I can recite all the legends from the First Dragon on—'" I was starting
to tell him, but he cut me short.

"'And never mind legends either right now, if you please, Smrgol,'" he
said. "'Also tell that wolf—'"

"'Aragh?'" I asked. "'Is he coming here, too?'"

"'Naturally. He'll be wanting to know what's got into James. Now stop
interrupting!'" he said. "'Tell the wolf to go find the knight, the bowman,
the outlaw and his daughter, and tell them all that they're needed for
the last battle. Also, there's no use in their going on to Malencontri. Sir
Hugh and his men have already turned aside to answer the call of the
Dark Powers in the Loathly Tower, whose minions they now are. Even
if Sir Brian and the others should take Castle Malencontri now, it'd be
worthless to them. For if the Dark Powers win, Sir Hugh will gain it back
with one stroke of his sword on its gate and a single crossbow bolt over its
walls. Tell them that they'll see me before the Loathly Tower, if I return
from my journey. Likewise, they'll see James there if he returns safely
from his. And so farewell.'"*

'And so farewell'?' Jim echoed. 'Was that part of the message?'

'I don't know. But they were his last words,' said Smrgol. 'Then he
disappeared – you know, the way magicians do.'

'What was your journey, Gorbash?' asked Aragh.

Jim opened his mouth and closed it again. It would not be easy – or
comfortable – to explain to these two about his recent inner pilgrim-
age into self-examination and self-discovery, which Carolinus by some
magical means seemed to have anticipated.

'Someday, maybe,' he said, 'I might be able to tell you. But not right
now.'

'Oh, one of those journeys,' Aragh growled, leaving Jim uncomfortably uncertain as to how much the wolf actually knew or understood.

'All right, you're here. Let's get to this Loathly Tower, then, and settle matters!' His teeth clashed together on the last word.

'Gorbash and I will go,' said Smrgol. 'You forget, wolf, you've a message to the knight and his company. In fact, you were probably supposed to go right away, when I told you.'

'I'm at nobody's orders,' said Aragh. 'I wanted to stay to see Gorbash safely back from this journey of his, and I did.'

'You'd better go now,' Smrgol insisted.

'Ha!' snapped Aragh. 'I will, then. But, save a couple of those Dark Powers for me, Gorbash. I'll catch up with you.'

The shadows seemed to close about him; and he was gone.

'Not a bad sort – for a wolf,' said Smrgol, glancing back into the darkness, for a second. 'Touchy, though. But then, they all are. Now, Gorbash, as soon as it's dawn, we'd better be pressing on to the Tower. So what you'd better do is get some rest after your long journey the Mage talked about—'

'Rest?' said Jim. 'I don't need rest!'

And in fact, even as the words popped out of his jaws, he realized that they were correct. He felt fine.

'Perhaps you don't think you need rest, my boy,' Smrgol was saying severely. 'But a dragon of any experience knows that to be in good fighting trim he needs sleep and food—'

'Food?' Jim asked, suddenly alerted. 'Have you got something to eat?'

'No,' Smrgol replied. 'And all the more reason you should plan on getting five or six solid hours of slumber—'

'I couldn't sleep.'

'Couldn't sleep … ? A dragon who can't sleep? Enough of these wild stories, Gorbash. Any dragon, and particularly one of our family – can always eat, drink or sleep—'

'Why not take off right away?' Jim asked.

'Fly at night?'

'There's a bright moon,' Jim said. 'You just saw me fly in here.'

'And very reckless it was. Youngsters like you always like to take chances. They get away with something nine hundred and ninety-nine times out of a thousand. Then, one day, their luck turns sour and they wish they'd listened. But by then it's too late. What if while you were in the air the sky'd clouded up before you realized it, and suddenly you found you couldn't see the ground?'

Jim opened his jaws to tell the older dragon what he had discovered about flying in utter darkness and rain, then decided to leave well enough alone.

'Come come,' said Smrgol, gruffly. 'No more of this nonsense. We both need sleep.'

Something about Smrgol's insistence touched the new sensitivity of Jim's emotional perceptions. He looked at Smrgol as closely as he could without seeming to openly study the older dragon. There was something different about the large body he saw, something hard to pin down but undeniably different from the last time he had seen Gorbash's grand-uncle. Suddenly it struck him what it was.

Smrgol's left eyelid was half closed. It drooped down over the long, narrow eye. Smrgol's left wing also drooped, slightly but visibly; and as he stood on all fours the older dragon seemed to be resting most of his weight on his right two legs. Jim had seen physical signs like these before – if not in dragons. His grandfather had shown similar marks of physical distortion on one side of his body following his first stroke, three years ago.

But dragons didn't get – Jim checked the thought. Apparently they did, if they were old enough or otherwise vulnerable. In any case, whether they did or not was unimportant here. What mattered was that Smrgol was now crippled; and whether he understood the exact nature of what had happened to him or not, he was in no condition to fly right now.

'All right,' said Jim. 'I guess I can wait until morning.'

Smrgol would be no better in the morning, but a few hours would give Jim some time to puzzle out a way of handling the situation. He tucked his head under one wing and pretended to go to sleep. His ears caught what he thought might be a faint sigh of relief, and when he peered out from under his appendage a few minutes later, Smrgol also had his head tucked in and was beginning to snore lightly.

Jim fell asleep while he was still pondering what should be done, but woke with the answer already formed in his mind.

'Smrgol,' he said, once they were both awake in the dawn of a new day, 'I've been thinking—'

'Good boy!'

'Er – yes,' Jim said. 'And what came to mind was this. I should probably fly to the Loathly Tower as quickly as I can. If Carolinus is right about Sir Hugh and his men being headed there, then the Dark Powers are probably gathering all their forces. Who knows what they're likely to come up with? Thousands of sandmirks – or anything! Meanwhile, why don't *you* go secretly on foot back to the dragon caves, so that no one will know you're planning to gather the other dragons, get them together—'

Smrgol coughed self-consciously.

'My boy,' he said. 'I meant to say something to you about that. As a matter of fact ... well, the others aren't coming.'

'Not coming?'

'They voted against it. I did what I could, but ...'

Smrgol let his voice trail off.

Jim did not press him. He could imagine why the other dragons had voted against it, if Smrgol had already had his stroke when he tried to talk them into coming. An overage and crippled leader was not one to inspire followers with a thirst for combat. Besides, Jim had acquired enough knowledge of dragons by now, both through his Gorbash-body-and-brain and from association with Smrgol and the others, to know that they were basically conservative. *Let's sit tight, and maybe it'll all blow over*, would be basic dragon philosophy.

'Well, that's even better!' said Jim, quickly. 'That means you'll be free to walk towards the fens while I fly there, and act as liaison with any of our side that you run into on the ground.'

'"Liaison"?' Smrgol said, suspiciously. 'Is that a word you got from Carolinus or that knight?'

'No ... Well, maybe. At any rate, it means—'

'I know what it means,' said Smrgol, sadly. 'It's just that it's such a george type of word for you to be using, my boy. Well, well, you really need me to go towards the fens on foot?'

'I think it'd be wise,' Jim answered. 'That lets me head right for the tower, and leaves you to take care of ... well, everything else.'

'That's true.' Smrgol's glance darted for a second to his left side. 'Perhaps I ought to do just that ...'

'Good!' said Jim. 'All right then, I'll be taking off right away.'

'Good luck, Gorbash!'

'Good luck to you, too, Grand-uncle!'

Smrgol's eyes lit up happily at the last word.

'Well, well, Nephew – don't just stand there. You said you were leaving. Get on with it!'

'Right!' answered Jim; and leaped into the air.

The new morning was as free of rain and clouds as the previous day had been full of them. A stiff wind was blowing toward the fens. At about six hundred feet, Jim spread his wings into soaring position and rode the airstream like an eagle. He had hardly been in the air five minutes, however, before the wind inexplicably changed direction a full hundred and eighty degrees and began to blow inland from the fens, against him.

He tried shifting to various altitudes in an effort to find at least one where this contrary wind did not blow; but it seemed to be everywhere. Battling it for some time, he made very slow process. If this kept up, he might as well have joined Smrgol at making his way to the fens on the ground. In fact, if things didn't improve—

The wind quit abruptly. Suddenly, there was no breeze at all. Caught unprepared, Jim lost nearly five hundred feet of altitude before he could adjust himself to the new conditions and start hunting for thermals.

'What next?' he asked himself.

But there was no next. The air stayed dead calm, and he continued, working his way from thermal to thermal, mounting on one and gliding forward to catch another and climb again. It was faster than walking, but still not the swiftest way of traveling.

By the time he reached the fens, it was midmorning. He made out the line of the Great Causeway and began to work his way out above it at a height of merely a couple of hundred feet.

The land end of the Great Causeway was thickly enough covered with trees and bushes to look similar to the forest land behind the moors and above the fens. The vegetation stood with leaves and branches motionless under the clear autumn sun, as Jim alternately soared and flew above it. Nothing could be seen on the ground, under or between the trees, that Jim could make out. No human or animal figure – not even a bird or cloud of insects – showed itself below. The emptiness of the scene was at once both forbidding and reassuring. Jim found himself being lulled into nearly forgetting why he had come here. Reasonlessly, there came into his head a fragment of a poem he had tried to write in his undergraduate days, before he had sensibly decided to be a teacher:

An hour, an hour ... another hour ...
Without a difference I can see,
Like faceless children on a wall
That stretches to eternity ...

'Jim Eckert! Jim Eckert!'

A tiny voice, calling from far off, roused him from his thoughts. He looked around but could see nothing.

'Jim Eckert! Jim Eckert!'

A shiver went down his back and spread out to chill his whole body as it came again, more loudly; and now he pinpointed its location as somewhere on the causeway up ahead.

'Jim Eckert! Jim Eckert!'

It was full-strength now, a dragon's voice, but not the voice of a dragon with the volume of a Smrgol or Bryagh.

Jim stared ahead, raking the causeway with his sharp vision. Finally he caught sight of something gray that moved slightly, far up in a patch of tall grass surrounded by trees and bushes. He swooped toward it.

As he approached, he saw what he had already almost guessed to be the source of the calling. It was Secoh, down on the ground, his wings spread out over the grass on either side of him, like some captured bird cruelly stretched on display. The mere-dragon was lifting his head, almost hopelessly, from time to time to call.

Jim was almost above the mere-dragon now. Secoh had plainly not yet seen him approaching – not surprising, considering that Secoh was facing in the wrong direction. Jim thought swiftly. The calling of his real name was eerie; and there was something more than that – something unnatural about the odd position in which Secoh was extended – that made even the thought of answering the mere-dragon an uneasy one.

Jim hesitated; and as he hesitated, the momentum of his glide carried him beyond Secoh and the mere-dragon caught sight of him.

'Jim Eckert! Jim Eckert!' Secoh cried. 'Don't go! Come back and listen to me, first! I've got something to tell you. Please come back! Oh, help me! Help, your worship! I'm just a mere-dragon ...'

Jim glided on, closing his ears to the cries fading behind him; but there was a war going on within him. Somehow Secoh had learned to call him by his right name. That meant the mere-dragon had either really discovered something, or else the Dark Powers were using him as an intermediary. Could the Dark Powers be ready to negotiate Angie's release?

He kept a firm grip on the hope that sprung up in him at that last thought. Negotiation was a possibility ... and if, on the other hand, Secoh had only discovered something useful, Jim would be foolish not to take advantage of it. Also, although Jim sternly throttled down the idea that emotion had any strong influence over whatever decision he might make, he was touched by the note of despair in Secoh's voice and the mere-dragon's desperate appeal for help.

Grimly, Jim banked into a turn, beat his wings for more altitude and started to glide back.

Secoh was in the same spot, his position unchanged. He set up a chorus of glad cries as he saw Jim once more coming toward him.

'Oh, thank you, your highness! Thank you, thank you ...' he babbled as Jim slid in to land on the grass beside him.

'Never mind all the thanking!' snapped Jim. 'What's this you've got to tell me—?'

He broke off, for he had just noticed the reason for Secoh's unnatural, spread-eagled position. Cleverly hidden in the grass were pegs driven into the earth, to which Secoh's wingtops and toes had been cinched tight by leather cords.

'Hold, dragon!' cried a voice.

Jim looked up. A figure in bright armor, which he had last seen coming at him on horseback, lance in hand, stepped out from the cover of trees on his right; and all around Jim, shoulder to shoulder, a solid ring of crossbowmen had appeared, their weapons aimed and cocked, the quarrels pointed at Jim's chest.

Secoh wailed.

'Forgive me, your greatness!' he cried. 'Forgive me! I couldn't help it. I'm just a mere-dragon and they caught me. The Dark Ones told them that if they made me call you by that name, you'd come and they could catch you. They promised to let me go if I could get you to come. I'm just a mere-dragon and nobody cares about me. I had to look after myself. I had to, don't you see? I *had to* ... *!*'

20

The figure in armor walked intrepidly forward until he stood less than three feet from Jim's jaws. He put his visor up and Jim saw a square, cheerfully brutal countenance with a large nose and pale, cold, gray eyes.

'I'm Sir Hugh de Bois de Malencontri, dragon,' he said.

'I know you,' Jim answered.

'Damme if I see why you're any different than any other dragon,' said Sir Hugh. 'Still, who's to argue if it makes Them happy. Tie him up, lads. He's too heavy for the horses, but we'll make a sledge and drag him on it to the tower.'

'Please, Sir knight, your lordship, will you untie me now?' Secoh called. 'You've got him. Will you just cut these tight thongs and let me go—'

Sir Hugh looked over to Secoh and laughed. Then he turned back, considering Jim.

'Sir knight! Sir knight!' Secoh quivered all through his body. 'You promised! You promised you'd let me go if I got him to come. You wouldn't go back on your knightly words, would you, your Royalty?'

Sir Hugh looked at the mere-dragon again and burst into a roar of bass-throated laughter.

'Hark at him! Hark to the dragon! Knightly honor, he says! Knightly honor to a *dragon?*'

His laughter cut off abruptly.

'Why, dragon,' he said to Secoh, 'I want your head for my wall! What sort of jack-fool would I be to turn you loose?'

He turned away; and as he did so a deadly shower came down from the clear sky – a rain of clothyard shafts whistling upon them. Half a dozen of the crossbowmen fell. The rest, some with arrows in them, broke for the cover of the trees. Four shafts fell around Sir Hugh, and one long arrow drove through the top edge of his left pauldon to ring

765

loudly on the breastplate below, but without penetrating the second thickness of armor.

Sir Hugh swore, snapped down his visor and also ran heavily for the trees. A second flight of arrows descended in a large circle among those same trees, but it was impossible for Jim to tell what damage they had done. He heard the sounds of feet running away, of a man in armor mounting and galloping off. Then silence. He and Secoh were unhurt, but alone except for the dead and dying crossbowmen on the ground about them.

A whimper from Secoh brought Jim's attention back to the mere-dragon. He stepped over and drove the claws of one forepaw into each of the pegs holding Secoh down, in turn, and pulled them out. They came up easily to his muscles. Secoh immediately sat up and began biting through the leather thongs that had held the pegs to his toes.

'Why didn't you pull the pegs out yourself?' Jim asked Secoh. 'It's not easy, stretched out like that, I know, but any dragon—'

'They had all those bows and swords and things,' said Secoh. 'I'm not as brave as you are, your magnanimity. I couldn't help being afraid; and I thought maybe if I did what they wanted, they'd let me go.'

He stopped biting through the thongs and cowered.

'Of course, I understand how your worship would feel. I shouldn't have called you down to land here—'

'Forget it,' said Jim gruffly.

Secoh took him at his word and went back to biting through leather.

Jim made a small tour around the fallen crossbowmen. But there was nothing to be done for any of them. Those who were down were either already dead or within minutes of dying; none of them yet retained enough consciousness to realize that someone was standing over them. Jim turned away just in time to see Secoh preparing to take off.

'Wait a minute!' he snapped.

'Wait? Oh, of course – wait. I understand, your highness!' Secoh yelped. 'You thought I was about to fly away. But I was just stretching the cramp out of my wings—'

'You aren't going anywhere,' Jim said, 'so settle down and answer a few questions. Who told you to call me Jim Eckert?'

'I already said!' protested Secoh. 'The george – the knight – told me; and the Dark Ones told him.'

'Hmm. And how did they catch you in the first place?'

Secoh looked unhappy.

'They – they put out a fine piece of meat,' he said. 'Half a large boar … lovely, fat meat, too.'

A tear trickled down from the eye on the side of his head nearest Jim.

'Such lovely, fat meat!' Secoh repeated. 'And then they didn't even let me have a bit of it. Not a bite! They just aimed their crossbows at me and tied me up.'

'Did they say why?' Jim asked. 'Did they give any reason for guessing I'd be along, so you could call me down in the first place?'

'Oh, yes, your worship. They talked about it a lot. The knight said you'd come at just this time, and after they caught you the six men he named must take you without delay to the tower; and he with the rest would catch up with them on the way.'

'Catch up?' Jim frowned.

'Yes, your importance.' Secoh's eyes looked suddenly a good deal shrewder than Jim had ever seen them before. 'This knight was going to stay behind to lay a trap for the other george – your friend. And that was something he wasn't supposed to do: the Dark Ones had sent him out just to get you, and come right back. But he really has a terrible anger against your friend, you know, the one who goes around chasing us mere-dragons all the time. So this knight was going to catch your friend in spite of what the Dark Ones wanted—'

Secoh stopped to shiver.

'That's what's so terrible about them, these georges,' he went on. 'Nobody can make them do what they're told, not even the Dark Ones. They don't care for anything, just as long as they can go riding around in their hard shells and sticking their sharp horns into poor mere-dragons like me, or anyone they want to. Imagine somebody else going ahead and doing just what he wanted after the Dark Ones had given him orders!'

'I wonder where they all went when they ran off from here though?' Jim wondered.

'The knight that was here and those crossbowmen?' Secoh nodded his head back toward the mainland end of the Great Causeway. 'There's a swamp off to the left there where you'd drown in a minute if you couldn't fly, your highness. But the Dark Ones showed that knight a way through it. He and his men have gone out there, and they'll be circling around to get back on the causeway behind your friends who shot all the arrows in here, just now. I know, because that's the way this knight told his men they'd surprise and take your friends after you'd been dragged off to the tower.'

'That means they've cut us off from the mainland—' Jim was beginning, when he became aware that he had been listening to the sound of approaching horses' hooves for some seconds; and a moment later Brian rode into the clearing.

'James!' cried the knight, joyously. 'There you are! I've been feeling seven sorts of rascal for trying to talk you into that assault on Malencontri. After you disappeared yesterday, I got to pondering and it struck me that we'd probably been counseling you against your duty; and you'd determined to go it alone, after all. Said as much to Giles, Dafydd, and Danielle; and blind me if they hadn't all been thinking along the same lines themselves. First the wolf, then you, gone. Bad omens, those, for a group of Companions, eh? So we'd already turned toward the fens here, when the wolf caught up with us last night – Hullo! Is that one of our local dragons you've got here?'

'Secoh, your mightiness!' yelped the mere-dragon, hastily. 'Just Secoh, that's all. I know you well, your georgeship, and admired you from afar, many times. Such speed, such dash—'

'Really?'

'Such kindness, such gentleness, such—'

'Oh, not all that, actually—'

'I said to myself, a knight like that'd never hurt a poor mere-dragon like me.'

'Well, of course,' said Brian, 'I would have, you know. Chopped your head off if I could have caught you, just as I would any other dragon. But I take it you're on our side now, from seeing you here with James.'

'Your ... ? Oh, yes sir, yes. I'm on *your* side.'

'Thought so. Struck me you had the look of a fighter about you the moment I noticed you there. Lean, hard-muscled, deadly – not like most of the other local dragons I've seen.'

'Oh yes, your knighthood. Lean—'

Secoh, who had half spread his wings as if he was about to try leaving once more, broke off, checking himself in midmotion to stare at the knight. Brian, however, had turned back to speak to Jim.

'Others'll be here in a minute—' he had begun.

'Wrong,' said a sour voice. 'I've been here since before you rode in. But I was busy tracking our enemies. They went off into a swamp by the causeway. I could have tracked them there, too, but decided to come back and see how Gorbash was. Are you all right, Gorbash?'

'Fine, Aragh,' said Jim, for the wolf had stepped into the clearing as he was talking.

Aragh looked at Secoh and grinned evilly.

'"Hard-muscled" and "deadly"?' he said.

'Never mind all that now, Sir wolf,' said Brian. 'Important thing is we're all together again, and the next step calls for a bit of planning. As soon as – Ah, here they are, now.'

Dafydd, Giles and Danielle, together with the rest of the outlaws, had in fact been coming into the clearing from the moment Aragh had appeared. The outlaws were already moving around the fallen forms of the crossbowmen, retrieving their arrows. Dafydd paused in the center of the clearing and looked about.

'Carried my shaft off, he must have,' the bowman said to Jim. 'Was he wounded, then?'

'That was your arrow that hit Hugh de Bois? I should have known it,' said Jim. 'It went through part of his armor but not through the rest.'

'It was a blind loose,' said Dafydd, 'with a dropping shaft because of the trees between us. Yet I am not happy hearing that I put point in him but did him no harm.'

'Peace!' Danielle said to him. 'With the intercession of Saint Sebastian, you couldn't have done more from that distance on such a shot. Why do you keep pretending you can do the impossible?'

'I am not pretending, whatever. As for "impossible," there is no such a thing as an impossible, but only a thing the doing of which has not yet been learned.'

'Never mind that now, I say,' Brian interrupted. 'We're back together with Sir James and there's a decision to be made. Sir Hugh and his crossbowmen, having escaped us here, have taken refuge in a swamp. Should we follow them, post a force to hold them from returning, or press on to the tower, leaving them behind us? For myself, I would not willingly leave enemies free to follow upon my rear guard.'

'And they aren't just in the swamp,' said Secoh loudly and unexpectedly. 'By this time they're back on the causeway.'

Everyone turned to look at the mere-dragon; who wavered and seemed on the verge of cringing under so much attention, but ended by straightening his spine and staring back at them.

'What's this?' said Giles.

'Hugh de Bois and his men are fighting under the orders of the Dark Powers in the tower,' said Jim. 'Secoh here tells me the Dark Ones told Hugh how to get through the swamp safely and back on the causeway. That means they're on firm ground somewhere between us and the mainland.'

'No argument, then,' said Brian. 'The Tower before and those crossbowmen behind are no situation to wish for. Let's turn and go back to meet them.'

'I don't know …' said Jim. There was an uneasiness in the pit of his stomach. 'The rest of you go meet them, if you think that's best. I've got to get on to the Loathly Tower. Somehow, I've got the feeling time's running out.'

'Ha?' said Brian, and became suddenly thoughtful. 'That was the feeling that came on me when I found you gone yesterday. In some sort, I've got it with me even now. Perhaps best you and I together go on toward the tower, James, and to whatever awaits us there. The rest can hold here and deal with Sir Hugh and his men if they try to pass.'

'I'm going with Gorbash,' said Aragh.

'And I, too,' said Dafydd, unexpectedly. He met the eyes of Danielle. 'Do not look at me so. I said the taking of castles was not my work – nor was it, at all. But when, in Castle Malvern, the flames all bent and there was no wind, a coldness came into me. That coldness is still there, and my mind is that it will never leave me until I seek out and help to slay its source.'

'Why, you *are* a knight,' said Danielle.

'Mock me not,' said the Welshman.

'Mock? I'm not mocking you. In fact, I'm going with you.'

'No!' Dafydd looked over her head at Giles. 'Make her stay.'

Giles grunted.

'You make her stay,' said the older man.

Danielle put her hand on the knife at her belt.

'No one makes me stay – or go – or anything else,' she said. 'In this hap, I'm going.'

'Giles,' Brian put in, ignoring her, 'can you hold Sir Hugh and his men, alone?'

'I'm not quite alone . . .' Giles said, dryly. 'I have my lads here. And the Malvern Castle stalwarts! Sir Hugh and his troop will pass into Heaven before they pass us by.'

'Then let's go on, in God's name!'

Brian remounted his horse and started down The the causeway. Jim fell in beside the large white charger.

'. . . Any more objections?' Danielle was challenging Dafydd.

'No,' the bowman answered, sadly. 'Indeed, a part of the cold feeling was that you would be with me when the final time came. As the shadows point, the day will wend. Let us go, then.'

The two of them fell in behind Jim and Brian, and their voices dropped to confidential tones, not so low but that Jim could not have used his dragon-ears to overhear what they were telling each other, but low enough so that he could give them the privacy of ignoring them. Aragh came trotting up on the other side of him from Blanchard.

'Why so glum, Sir knight, and Gorbash?' he said. 'It's a fine day for slaying.'

'In the matter of this tower and those within it,' said Brian, shortly, 'we go against something that touches our souls.'

'The more fool you, for having such useless, clogging things,' Aragh growled.

'Sir wolf,' said Brian, grimly, 'you understand nothing of this, and I'm in no mind to instruct you.'

They continued to travel in silence. The air stayed windless and the day seemed hardly to alter with the ordinary movement of time. Gradually the horizon, where land met sea, began to be visible as a gray-blue line ahead of them, still some miles distant. Jim looked up at the sky, puzzled.

'What time is it, do you think?' he asked the knight.

'Shortly before prime, I should say,' responded Brian. 'Why?'

'Prime ... ?' Jim had to pause to remember that prime was noon. 'Look how dark it's getting!'

Brian glanced around and also raised his gaze skyward before looking back down to Jim. To the west, above them, although the sun still floated in an apparently cloudless sky, a sort of darkness of the air itself seemed to dull the colors of heavens and landscape. Brian looked sharply to his front.

'Hullo!' he said. 'See ahead, there!'

He pointed. Jim looked. Before them the causeway now held only an occasional tree or clump of bushes intermixed with the tall fenland grass. Somewhere up there – it was impossible for the eye to measure exactly how distant – the grass was being pressed down along what seemed to be a sharp line extending across the causeway and out into the fen on either side. Beyond that line everything looked coldly gray, as if seen under a chill and winter sky.

'It's moving this way,' said Aragh.

It was.

It took a moment or two of watching for Jim to make it out, but by watching the grass bend and rise again it was possible to discover that the line, whatever it might be, was creeping slowly forward. It was as if some heavy, invisible fluid slowly and heavily flooded outward along the causeway, overwhelming the meres and islands of the fens. Jim felt a slow chill mounting his spine as he watched.

Instinctively, Jim and the knight came to a halt as they watched; and Aragh, seeing them stop, also halted. He sat down now and grinned at them.

'Look up, and west,' he said.

They looked. For a second Jim's hopes bounded upward at seeing what he thought was a dragon shape about four hundred feet above the causeway, soaring in their direction. But then a difference gradually registered upon him. This was no dragon, or anything near the size of a dragon, although it was too large to be any soaring bird. It looked to be half again the wing-spread of an eagle, but it had an odd, heavy-headed silhouette that gave it a vulturous look. Jim squinted hard into the sky, but the strange darkness of the air baffled him in his efforts to make out the flying shape's detail.

It was coming straight for them, gliding. All at once, as the flying shape grew closer, Jim began to resolve the features of that odd, bulky head. He soon saw it clearly – and his vision blurred, refusing to accept what his mind recorded. It was a huge, dun bird – all but the head. Its head was the head of a woman, her pale face staring forward and down at Brian and himself, her lips parted, showing pointed white teeth.

'Harpy!' said Brian beside him, on a slow intake of breath.

It came on.

Surely, thought Jim, it would veer aside at the last moment; but it continued to swoop directly toward the two. Now he saw why his eyes had refused to focus on that white face. It was not merely that it was human and female. More terrible than that, it was completely mad. The frozen features of insanity rode above the pinions of the huge, winged creature swooping toward them –

Abruptly it was on them, driving at Jim's throat; and everything seemed to happen in a single moment.

A dark shape shot into the air toward the harpy just before it reached him. Long jaws clicked on emptiness where a fraction of a second before the white face had been, and the harpy screamed hideously, jerking aside into Brian, half tumbling the knight from Blanchard's back before its long wings caught on the air and beat upward once more to safety.

On the ground, Aragh was snarling softly to himself. Brian pulled his body upright again in the saddle. The harpy, its strike missed, was now winging away from them through the air, back toward the tower.

'It's well for you the wolf turned it away,' said Brian, somberly. 'Its bite is poison. I own that hell-face had me spellbound and frozen.'

'Let it try again,' said Aragh, viciously. 'I don't miss twice.'

A voice broke in on them, wailing from out over the still fenwater to their left.

'No! No! Turn back, your worships! Turn back! It's no use. It's death for you all, up there!'

They turned their heads.

'Why, dammit!' Brian exclaimed. 'It's that mere-dragon of yours.'

'No,' said Aragh, testing the air with his nose. 'Another. Different scent.'

A mere-dragon, looking enough like Secoh to be a twin, was perched precariously on a small tussock of half-drowned soil and marsh grass about forty feet out from the causeway.

'Oh, please!' it cried, stretching out its wings and fanning them to maintain its balance on the tussock. 'You won't be able to do any good; and we'll all suffer for it. They're woken up now in the tower, and you'll just make Them angry if you go there!'

'Them?' called Jim. 'You mean the Dark Powers?'

'Them – Them!' wailed the mere-dragon, despairingly. 'Them that built and live in the Loathly Tower, that sent the blight on us five hundred years ago. Can't you feel Them, waiting for you there? Can't you smell Them? They that never die, they who hate us all. They who draw to Them all terrible, evil things ...'

'Come here,' said Jim. 'Come onto the causeway here. I want to talk to you.'

'No ... no!' whined the mere-dragon. He threw a terrified glance at the line approaching over the grass and water. 'I have to fly – get away!' He flapped his wings, rising slowly into the air. 'They've broken loose again and now we're all lost – lost—'

A breeze out of the chill wintriness beyond the moving line seemed to catch the mere-dragon and whirl him away into the sky. He went, flying heavily, back toward the mainland, crying in a thin, despairing voice.

'*Lost ... lost ... lost!*'

'There, now,' said Brian. 'What was I telling you about mere-dragons? How can a gentleman gain honor or worship by slaying a beast like that—'

In midsentence, the words died on his tongue. While they had been talking to the mere-dragon, the line had come upon them; and as Brian spoke, it passed beneath them. The cold winter colors beyond it enclosed them, and the knight and Jim looked at each other with faces gone ash-colored and pinched.

'*In mantis tuas, Domine,*' said the knight, softly, and crossed himself.

All about and around them, the serest gray of winter light lay on all things. The waters of the fens stretched thick, oily and still between the patches of dull-green grass. A small, cold breeze wandered through the tops of the bullrushes, making them rattle together with dry and distant sounds, like old bones cast out into some forgotten churchyard. The trees stood helpless and quiet, their leaves now dried and faded like people aged before their time; while all about, a heaviness – as of hope gone dead – pressed down on all living things.

'Sir James,' said the knight in an odd, formal tone and with words Jim had never before heard him use, 'wit thee well that we have in this hour set our hands to no small task. Wherefore, I pray thee that, should it be thou alone who return and I am slain, thou shalt not leave my lady nor those who are of my kindred live on in ignorance of mine end.'

'I – I'll be most honored to inform them—' Jim answered, awkwardly, from a dry throat.

'I thank thee for thy most gentle courtesy,' said Brian, 'and will do in like event for thee, so soon as I may find ship to take me beyond the western seas.'

'Just – tell Angie. My lady, Angela, I mean,' said Jim. 'You needn't worry about anybody else.'

He had a sudden mental picture of the strange, brave, honest character beside him actually leaving home and family to head out over nearly three thousand miles of unknown ocean in obedience to a promise given a near-stranger. The image made him wince inside, in its comparison to the picture he had of himself.

'I shall do so,' said Brian – and at once reverted to his ordinary self, swinging down out of his saddle onto the ground. 'Blanchard won't go another inch, damn him! I'll have to lead him—'

He broke off, looking back past Jim.

'Where'd the bowman and Mistress Danielle go?' he asked.

Jim turned. Brian was correct. As far as the eye could see, there was no sign of the two who, they had assumed, were following them.

'Aragh?' Jim asked. 'Where did they go?'

'They fell behind, sometime since,' said the wolf. 'Perhaps they changed their minds about coming with us. They're back there somewhere. If it weren't for the trees and bushes, you might still see them.'

A moment's silence followed.

'Then, let's on without them,' said Brian.

He tugged at the bridle of Blanchard. The white horse reluctantly took one step, then another. They moved off. Jim and Aragh fell into step alongside.

✳

As they traveled onward, the dreariness all around and pressing down upon them had the effect of stifling conversation. Even existing seemed to be an effort under its influence, and each movement of their bodies required a conscious exertion of will; their arms and legs were like lead weights swung heavily and reluctantly into each slow, necessary step. But the effect of their silence was worse, for it left them isolated, each set off alone in the dark pool of his own thoughts. They moved as if in some pale dream, speaking now and then for a moment, then falling silent.

As they progressed, the causeway narrowed. From forty yards across, it dwindled until it became as many feet. The trees, too, shortened and became more stunted – more twisted and gnarled – and under their feet the thinning grass revealed a different soil, an earth lacking in the rich blackness of the fenland toward the main shore. Here it was sandy, with a sterile, flinty hardness. It crunched under their weight and under the hooves of Blanchard, and was at once unyielding and treacherous.

The white warhorse checked himself suddenly. He tossed his head and tried to back up instead of going forward.

'What the hell!' exploded Brian, tugging on the reins. 'What devil's into him now—'

'Listen,' said Jim, who had also stopped.

For a moment, Jim could almost make himself believe he had imagined what he had just heard. But then it sounded again and began to grow in volume. It was just ahead of them and getting closer: It was the chittering of sandmirks.

The volume soared upward. Clearly, the sandmirks were not just in front of them, but all around. The dark predators had simply not all given voice, to start with; but now they were in full chorus. Jim felt the sound they made reaching through, once more, to the old primitive areas of his midbrain. He looked at Brian and saw the knight's face beneath the open visor of his helmet; it looked drained of blood, its skin fallen in to the bones like the face of a man ten days dead. The chittering was rising to a crescendo and Jim felt the ability to think slipping from him.

Beside him, Aragh laughed his silent laugh.

The wolf threw back his head, opened his long jaws, and howled – a long howl that cut like a razor slash across the sound of the sandmirks. It was not merely lupine night music from some moonlit hilltop that Aragh uttered, but a call that began on a low note and climbed in tone and volume to a pitch greater than all the chittering; then it fell again, dropping ... dropping into nothingness. It was a hunting howl.

When it ceased, there was silence. Only silence. Aragh laughed again. 'Shall we go on?' he said.

Brian stirred like someone coming out of a dream, and tugged on the reins. Blanchard stepped forward. Jim, too, moved; and they once more took up their journey.

The sandmirks did not begin their chittering again. But as the knight, the dragon and the wolf moved on, Jim could hear innumerable small ripplings in the water and rustlings behind the trees, bushes and bull-rushes that surrounded them – a noise that paralleled their path and kept up with them, as if a small army of heavy-bodied rats was providing them with escort. He did his best to put that sound from his mind. An instinctive terror was inspired by the noise of those feet and bodies alone; and he had other terrors to watch for.

But the watching was becoming more difficult.

'Getting darker, isn't it?' Jim said, finally. 'And misty.'

They had gone perhaps a mile and a half since they had crossed the line. And the sky had, indeed, been blackening. It was not a natural darkness, but a sort of thickening of the air, a premature night that seemed to be coming over them. With it came low clouds above their heads, and banks of mist, moving at water level off to either side of the causeway.

Abruptly, Blanchard balked again. They stopped. But around them the noise of the sandmirks began to mount toward a frenzy of invisible movement. There was something triumphant about their mad activity. Unexpectedly, ahead and off the causeway to the right, rang out a single, heavy splash, like the sound of something large heaving itself out of water onto land. Aragh's nose lifted abruptly, and he growled, deep in his throat.

'Now,' he said.

'Now what? What comes?' Brian demanded.

'My meat,' snarled Aragh. 'Stand clear!'

Stiff-legged, he walked a few paces forward from them and stood, tail hanging in a low arc, head a little down, jaws slightly open, waiting. His eyes burned red in the dimness.

Now Jim's nose caught the scent of whatever it was Aragh had smelled. The odor was oddly familiar – and then he realized it was the same scent he had been picking up from the sandmirks, who had kept company with them. Only, this was stronger and far more rank. Now, too, his ears picked up the sound of something heavy-bodied approaching them from down the causeway – the sort of creature that would go through bushes rather than around them.

Brian drew his sword. Aragh did not turn his head, but his ears flicked at the sound of metal sliding against metal.

'*My meat*, I said,' he repeated. 'Stand back! Go when I say.'

Jim found his every muscle tensed, his eyes almost aching with the effort to see through the gloom to what was coming. Then, all at once it was visible, moving toward them: a great, black, four-legged shape, its close body hair still gleaming slickly from the waters it had just left. It made no effort to hide, but came on until it was less than three times its own body length from Aragh. Then it reared up and from its throat came a sick-sounding chuckle that was a deep-toned version of the same chittering the three intruders here had heard earlier.

'Apostles guard us!' Brian muttered. 'Is *that* a sandmirk ... ?'

A sandmirk it was, but many times the size of the smaller creatures that had now three times awakened an ancient fear in Jim. This individual was at least as large as an adult grizzly bear; in fact, very nearly the size of one of the great Kodiak Island brown bears. Aragh, standing forward to challenge it, seemed in comparison to have shrunken from pony-size to the dimensions of a small dog.

But the wolf showed no signs of backing off. From his throat came the steady, slow rumble of a growl, unvarying and continuing. For a long moment the monster sandmirk stood swaying a little on its hind legs, chuckling its bass chitter. Then it moved forward, yet upright – and suddenly the fight had begun.

It was a flurry of action, too fast for human or dragon eye to follow in detail. For all its size, the great sandmirk could move its body and legs with vision-blurring speed. Only, Aragh was faster. He was in, out, around, up and down on the towering black figure, so swiftly and continuously that Jim's eyes gave up trying to follow his actions.

As suddenly as they had come together, the two parted. Aragh stood back, head low, sounding his steady growl while the huge sandmirk panted, swaying on its heavy hind legs, its black coat marked here and there with lines of red.

Aragh's growling now broke off, though his tense watching of his opponent did not relax an inch.

'Go!' he said, without turning his head. 'The others won't follow you as long as I hold their mother in play. And they won't mob me to help her, because they know that the first five to reach me will die; and none of them want to be among those.'

Jim hesitated. Brian spoke for both of them.

'Sir wolf,' he said, 'we can't leave you to face these odds alone—'

But before the last words were out of his mouth, battle had been joined again. Once more, the movement was too fast to follow; but this time it lasted longer – until a sudden, ugly, breaking sound rang out and Aragh leaped back to stand on three legs, his left foreleg dangling.

'Go!' he snarled, furiously. 'I told you – go!'

'But your leg—' Jim began.

'Did I ask your help?' Aragh's voice was thick with rage. 'Did I ever ask help? When the she-bear caught me when I was a cub, alone and with three legs I killed her. I'll kill this Mother of sandmirks, again with three legs and alone! *Go!*'

The monster now wore a bright pattern of red, bleeding slashes all over her body. But though she panted hoarsely, she did not seem weakened, or slowed. Nevertheless, Aragh's decision to fight alone was plainly not to be altered; and to throw away the wolf's deliberate sacrifice of himself was unthinkable. Certainly, if he was killed, it would only be a matter of time before the sandmirks would finish the other two.

Brian looked at Jim.

'Let's go,' said Jim.

The knight nodded. He tugged on the reins of Blanchard and led the horse forward. They moved off, as the wolf and the giant sandmirk matriarch closed in combat again behind them.

The sounds of fighting behind them soon died in the distance. The darkness and the mist enclosed them. But Aragh had been right about one thing: none of the smaller sandmirks followed them. They plodded on; and for a long time neither of them spoke. Then Brian turned his head to Jim.

'A very worthy wolf,' he said, slowly.

'If that big sandmirk kills him—' Jim began, and heard the sentence die in his mouth.

He had been about to promise revenge upon the killer, and then it had come to him that he could do nothing. If the huge black creature should kill Aragh, there was no way he could find her again; and if he found her, there was no way he could destroy her before she and her legion of children killed him. He was not an English wolf, to ignore the effect of the chittering voices.

It was bitter for Jim to face the fact that he was helpless to strike back against a cruel wrong. Intolerable. He had reached his present age never having cause to doubt that injustice must eventually be brought to book, and that any unfairness of life must, in the end, be balanced. Now he had to accept the debt of Aragh's possible self-sacrifice, know-ing it might be something he could never pay back. Marching slowly along under the eerie and unnatural darkness that held the fenlands, he forgot for the moment where he was, and what might become of him, in the internal struggle of finding some way to live with that debt.

It was hard to let go of cherished illusions; but he had no choice. Gradually, as he faced that fact, his convulsive grip on the belief that life *must* be fair, or else it could not be endured, relaxed; and he saw one more shackle upon the strength of his individual spirit fall away and sink into the waters of oblivion.

'Getting darker, isn't it?' Brian's voice roused him from his thoughts.

Jim looked around. They had gone perhaps a mile and a half since leaving Aragh and the sandmirks behind; and indeed the air had further thickened, even as the mists were closing in solidly on either sides of the causeway.

'Much more of this,' Jim said, 'and we won't be able to go on.'

It was by now all but impossible to see any distance farther than the water's edge on either hand or for more than a dozen yards in front of them. They drew the cold viscousness of the air into their lungs, and it seemed to settle and pool there, stifling them. Walking had become even more of a labor as their wills sagged under the sense of depression which pressed without letup upon them. Nor was this all; for with the additional darkening had come a blanketing of sound. The noise of their footsteps and hoof-treads on the sandy soil was all but lost to their ears; and even their voices seemed to sound distant, thin and faraway.

'Brian?' called Jim, groping through the gloom.

'Here, James ...' The dim outline of the armored knight moved toward Jim and blundered against him, as they both came to a halt.

'I can't see to go any farther,' Jim said.

'Nor I,' Brian admitted. 'We shall have to stay where we are, I suppose.'

'Yes ...'

They stood facing each other, but no longer able to make out the features of each other's faces; they were lost in an impenetrable darkness. And this darkness became even blacker, until any last intimation of light was gone and the obscurity was total. Jim felt chill, hard, iron fingers grip his left shoulder.

'Let us hold together,' said Brian. 'Then, whatever comes on us, must come on us at the same time.'

'Yes,' Jim agreed.

They stood in silence and in lightlessness, waiting for they did not know what; and soon the blackness about them pressed further in on them, now that it had isolated them, and was nibbling at the very edges of their minds. Out of the nothingness came no material thing;

but from within Jim crept up, one by one, like blind white slugs from some bottomless pit, all his inner fears and weaknesses, all the things of which he had ever been ashamed and striven to forget, all the maggots of his soul ...

He opened his mouth to speak to Brian – to say something, anything, to break the black spell upon him. But he found that already a poison had been at work within him. He no longer trusted the knight: for he knew that evil must be in Brian because of the evil he had rediscovered in himself. Slowly, stealthily, he began to withdraw from under the other's touch.

'Look!' Brian's voice came suddenly to him, distant and strange, sounding like the voice of someone who has gone a long way off. 'Look back the way we came!'

Jim turned. How he knew the proper direction to look, in that nothingness, he was never able to tell. But he turned; and he saw, faraway – so very far away that it was like the glimmer of a star seen across uncounted light-years of space – a tiny, distant point of light.

'What is it?' he gasped.

'Don't know,' replied the distorted, toy-like voice of the knight. 'But it's coming this way. Look at it grow!'

Slowly, very very slowly, the far-off light waxed and advanced. It was like a keyhole into daylight, enlarging as it came closer. The minutes ticked off, measured second by second in the beating of Jim's heart. Finally, the light stretched tall, lengthening as it came on like a knife slit cut through a cloth of darkness.

'What is it?' cried Jim, again.

'I don't know ...' the knight repeated.

But both of them felt the goodness of it, as it came. It was life and courage again; it was a power against the power of dark helplessness that had threatened to overwhelm them. They felt their strength returning as it came on, brightening; and Blanchard stirred beside them, stamping his hooves on the hard sand and whinnying.

'This way!' called Jim.

'This way!' shouted Brian.

The light shot up suddenly in height, reaching for the heavens, as if activated by the sound of their voices. Like a great rod it advanced, upright, toward them, now broadening as it approached. The darkness was rolling back and lifting. The black was graying once more into a thick twilight, then the twilight thinning and dispersing. The scuffing sound of feet nearing them came to their ears, they heard a sound of slow breathing, and all at once –

It was daylight again.

And Carolinus stood before them dressed in his robes, a high-pointed hat on his head, holding erect before him – as if it was blade and buckler, spear and armor, all in one – a tall, carven staff of wood.

'By the Powers!' he said, gazing at them. 'I got to you in time!'

Jim and the knight looked at each other like men snatched back from the brink of a cliff. Blanchard tossed his bridled head and stamped his feet again, as if to reassure himself that he was once more upon the solid earth of a world he knew.

'Mage,' said Brian, 'my thanks!'

'The fabric of Chance and History was stretched this time in your favor,' said Carolinus. 'Otherwise, I could never have reached you in time. Look!'

He lifted the staff and drove it point-down into the sand at his feet. It went in, and stood upright like the denuded trunk of a tree. He gestured at the horizon and they looked around.

The darkness was gone. The fens lay revealed, far and wide, stretching back the way they had come and, up ahead, going perhaps another half-mile to where they met the thin dark line of the sea. The causeway had also risen in altitude; until now, where they stood, they were perhaps twenty feet above the level of the surrounding landscape. Far ahead to the west, the sky was on fire with sunset. It lighted all the fens, the meres and the causeway with a red glow which lay bloodily on earth and grass and stunted trees; and it pooled just ahead, around a low hill, at a rise of a hundred feet or more above the seashore where, touched but uncolored by that same dying light there loomed over all, amongst great, tumbled boulders, the ruined, dark and shattered shell of a tower as black as jet.

21

This much and little more they saw in the brief minute or so that the light lasted, for the sun was on the very lip of the sea horizon and went down as they watched. Night – true night, this time – came in front the east in one swift stride.

Carolinus had been bending over something on the ground beside his staff. A little flame now leaped up beneath his hands; and going a little off to one side, he brought back some dry branches fallen from one of the causeway's dwarfed trees. He threw these on the flame, and a fire blazed up, lighting and warming them.

'We're still within the circle of strength of the Loathly Tower,' said the magician. 'Stay within ten paces of the wand if you care to be sure of your own safety!'

Tucking up his robe, he sat down cross-legged before the fire.

'Lie down, Sir knight,' he said, 'and you, too, my enchanted friend. When that sun comes up again, you'll find you'll need all the rest you've been able to get.'

Brian obeyed willingly enough, but Jim sank reluctantly to the ground by the fire.

'What about Angie?' he asked. 'We haven't seen any sign of Bryagh. Do you suppose—?'

'Your damsel's in the tower,' Carolinus interrupted him.

'In there?' Jim started up. 'I've got to—'

'Sit down! She's perfectly safe and comfortable, I promise you,' said Carolinus, testily. 'The forces in strife here don't center around her – not for the present, at least.'

He winced, and reached into his robes to produce a flask and a small cup made of cloudy glass. He poured white liquid from the flask into the cup and sipped it.

'What the devil?' said Brian, staring.

'How do you know?' Jim demanded of the magician. 'How can you tell—?'

'By the Powers!' snapped Carolinus. 'I'm a Master of the Arts. How do I know? Forsooth!'

'Pardon me,' said Brian, his blue eyes staring. 'Is that *milk* you're drinking, Mage?'

'A bit of a sympathetic magic, Sir knight, for an ulcer-demon that's been plaguing me lately.'

'Tell me how!' Jim asked again.

'I should think there'd be danger of it giving you a flux,' said Brian, frowning. 'Children, now ...'

'I will not tell you!' exploded Carolinus. 'Did I spend sixty years to get my degree, only to be demanded an account of my methods at every turn? If I say Saturn is in the ascendant, Saturn *is* in the ascendant. And if I say the maiden is perfectly safe and comfortable, then the maiden is perfectly safe and comfortable. By the Powers!'

He snorted indignantly to himself.

'Listen to me, my young friend,' he went on to Jim, draining his cup and tucking it with the flask back out of sight in his robes, 'you may have a little kitchen knowledge of Art and Science, but don't let that give you delusions of understanding. You're here for a purpose, which comes into operation after sunrise tomorrow – just like this knight.'

'I, too, Mage?' inquired Brian.

'Do you think you just happened to run into our mutual friend, here?' Carolinus asked. 'You laymen always think of Chance as a random operative factor. Nonsense! The operations of Chance follow the most rigid rules in the universe. Chance is invariably determined by the point of greatest stress between the other Prime Operators, such as History and Nature – particularly History and Nature, I might say, since as any fool knows, their particular strife makes changes in the pattern almost hourly. Otherwise, the universe would become so orderly we'd all die of sheer boredom. Listen to me, then—'

He pointed a long, bony forefinger at Jim.

'Nature is always at work to establish a balance of factors, which the operation of History is as unfailingly and continuously at work to disturb. The rub to all this lies in the fact that the new balance may always be established at more than one point, and it is in the determination of exactly which point that Chance – as a compensating element – enters the equation. This truth is the basis on which all magic, as a product of Art and Science, is constructed. *Now* do you understand the situation we have here?'

'No,' said Jim.

'Oh, go to sleep!' cried Carolinus, throwing up his arms in exasperation.

Jim blinked.

… And it was morning.

He sat up in amazement and found himself yawning. On the other side of the staff – or wand, as Carolinus had called it – Brian was also sitting up with a look of surprise. Carolinus was already on his feet.

'What happened?' asked Jim.

'I sent you to sleep. What d'you think happened?' retorted Carolinus. He produced his flask and cup, poured himself some milk and drank it down, making a face. 'I'm beginning to hate this stuff,' he grumbled, putting the utensils back out of sight again: 'Still, there's no doubt it's working. Come now!'

He turned snappishly on Jim and Brian.

'On your feet! The sun's been up for an hour and a half and our forces are strongest when the sun is in the ascendant – which means, we have our best chance of conquering before midday.'

'Why didn't you wake us up earlier, then?' asked Jim, getting to his feet as Brian also rose.

'Because we had to wait for them to catch up with us?'

'Them? What them?' asked Jim. 'Who's going to catch up with us?'

'If I *knew* who, exactly,' said Carolinus, gnawing on his beard, 'I'd have *said* who. All I know is that the situation this morning implies that four more will join our party – Oh, so they're the ones!'

He was staring over Jim's shoulder. Jim turned and saw the approaching forms of Dafydd and Danielle, followed by two dragon shapes a little farther down the causeway.

'Well, well – Master Bowman!' said Brian, heartily as Dafydd came up. 'And Mistress Danielle! Good morning!'

'A morrow it is, but whether good or not, I'd not wish to guess,' said Dafydd. He looked around. 'Where is the wolf, Sir knight?'

A cloud crossed Brian's face.

'You haven't seen him?' Jim asked. 'You must have passed him. Some ordinary-sized sandmirks and one particularly large one caught us, and he stayed behind to fight the large one. You must have passed the place where we left them fighting.'

'Left them?' cried Danielle.

'It was the wolf demanded it,' said Brian, grimly. 'We wouldn't have left, otherwise – as I think you might know, mistress!'

'We saw neither him, nor any sign of sandmirks or battle,' said Dafydd.

Jim stood silent. It was like absorbing a hard blow to the stomach to hear this, for all that he thought he had faced the fact the day before that he might never see Aragh alive again.

'Just because he asked you,' Danielle said, fiercely, 'you didn't have to leave him alone to face—'

'Danielle,' Carolinus interrupted. She turned to face him.

'Mage!' she said. 'You here? But you were a hundred years old even when I was little. You shouldn't be here!'

'I am where I must be,' said Carolinus. 'As was your wolf; as are Sir James and Sir Brian. Accuse them not. It was the task of Aragh to stay and fight alone, so that these two could come to this place at this time. That's all, and there's no more to be said!'

His old eyes were steady on her. Her own became unhappy, and she turned away from him.

'I'll go look for him ...' said Jim, half to himself. 'As soon as this is all over, I'll go and find him.'

'Perhaps,' said Carolinus, dryly. He looked past Jim once more. 'Good morrow, dragons!'

'Secoh!' Brian exclaimed. 'And – who's this?'

'Smrgol, george!' huffed the older dragon. He was approaching with a pronounced limp and with his left wing draped on the back of the mere-dragon. His left eyelid was now drooped almost shut. 'Give me a minute to catch my wind! Not as young as I used to be; but I'll be all right in a moment. Look here who I've brought with me!'

'I – I wasn't too keen on coming,' stammered Secoh to Jim. 'But as your wor – I mean, as you know, your grand-uncle can be pretty persuasive.'

'That's right,' boomed Smrgol, evidently having recovered the larger share of his breath in the moment of pause while the mere-dragon spoke. 'Don't you go calling anybody "your worship." Never heard of such stuff!'

Then he turned to Jim, himself.

'And letting a george go in where he didn't dare go, himself! "Boy," I said to him, "don't give me this nonsense about being only a mere-dragon! Mere's got nothing to do with what kind of dragon you are. What kind of world would it be if we all went around talking like that?"'

Smrgol tried to mimic someone talking in a high voice, but succeeded in lifting his tones only into the middle-bass level.

"'Oh, I'm just a plowland-and-pasture dragon. You'll have to excuse me. I'm just a halfway-up-the-hill dragon ...'" "BOY!" I said to him, "you're a DRAGON! Get that straight, once and for all time! And a dragon ACTS like a dragon, or he doesn't act at all!'"

'Hear, hear!' said Brian.

'Did you hear that, boy?' Smrgol demanded of the smaller dragon. 'Even the george understands *that* fact of life!'

He turned to Brian.

'Don't believe I've met you, george.'

'Brian Neville-Smythe,' said Brian, 'knight bachelor.'

'Smrgol Dragon,' said Gorbash's grand-uncle. He ran an approving eye over Neville-Smythe's armor and weapons. 'Good harness! Wager you carry your shield somewhat high when fighting on foot.'

'Matter of fact, I do. But how did you know?'

'Shiny place there on your rerebrace where the elbow cop's been rubbing back against it. Good shield tactics against another george, but I wouldn't advise you to try it on me. I'd have my tail between your legs and you off your feet in a second.'

'Is that a fact?' said Brian, plainly impressed. 'Remarkably sporting of you to tell me so! I'll remember that. But aren't you making it rather hard on the next dragon I fight, if it isn't you?'

'Well, I'll tell you,' rumbled Smrgol, clearing his throat. 'Pardon me – I've been thinking, for some time, that maybe you georges and us dragons could stop fighting and get together. We're really a lot alike in many ways—'

'If you don't mind, Smrgol,' cut in Carolinus sourly. 'We're not exactly oversupplied with time to chat. It'll be noon in—'

He was interrupted, in his turn, by a cry from Danielle. The rest turned to see her running down the causeway. Limping slowly toward them on three legs was the figure of Aragh.

Danielle reached him and dropped on her knees beside the wolf, hugging him. Sticking out a long tongue, he tried to lick her left ear, which was the closest part of her he could reach, held as he was. After a moment, however, he pulled from her grasp and walked on up to the rest of them, in spite of her efforts to make him lie down and let her examine the broken leg. Only when he had joined the group did he lie down and give in to her.

'... You ought to know better than to walk on this!' she was saying.

'I didn't walk on it,' said Aragh. His jaws grinned evilly at them all. 'I walked off it.'

'You know what I'm saying!' Danielle flashed. 'You know better than to travel on it.'

'What else could I do?' he snarled. 'I killed the Mother, but the kits are all around us. They want your meat after those in the tower get through with you. They want lots of meat to start feeding up a new mother. None of you can handle them but me. With me beside you here, they'll stay their distance.'

'We thought you dead,' said Brian, somberly.

'Dead, Sir knight?' Aragh glared at him. 'Never count an English wolf dead until you see his bones well bleached by the sun.'

'Enough chitchat!' Carolinus snapped. 'Time moves, and both Chance and History change. As I was saying, it'll be noon in – When will it be noon, you?'

'Four hours, thirty-seven minutes, twelve seconds, at the second gong,' replied the invisible voice Jim had heard before. There was a momentary pause; and then a mellow, chimed note sounded on the air. 'Chime, I mean,' the voice corrected itself.

Carolinus muttered something under his breath. Then he addressed them all.

'Come on, now,' he ordered. 'Stay together. And stay behind me!'

He pulled the staff from the ground; and they all moved off in the direction of the tower, Brian now back in Blanchard's saddle since the horse seemed to have ceased his objections to going forward.

With their first steps, however, the day which had dawned as bright, clear and ordinary as any day anywhere, began to cloud and darken and its air to thicken as it had the day before. Swiftly, this time, the mist closed in on the sea side and on the waters to either side of the causeway. The clouds became a solid bank, lowering until they touched the top of the tower, to hang literally no more than a hundred feet over the challengers' heads. The dreary, drab chillness of the day before settled down on the group and added. its weight once more to Jim's spirits.

He looked around him.

Surprisingly, none of this strangely assorted bag of individuals who were his Companions appeared to show any sign of being affected by the fresh demonstration of the power of whatever lived in the Loathly Tower. Aragh was limping along on three legs, grumpily assuring Danielle he would lie down, and stay lying down, in a moment so that she could set and splint the broken leg. Carolinus, leading them all, looked as if he was merely out for a brisk walk and his wand was no more than a staff to help him along. Dafydd was carefully untying the cords binding what looked like a plastic tube that had encased the string of his bow against the overnight dampness. After a second's puzzling, Jim suddenly realized that it must be a length of animal gut – probably pig or sheep – which had been carefully cleaned, dried and put to that purpose.

Smrgol marched along quite stoutly, his bad wing and some of his weight bearing on the mere-dragon beside him. On the other side of the old dragon rode Brian, and the two of them were now in earnest conversation.

'… About this business of people and dragons getting together,' said Brian. 'It sounds interesting – must say that. But hardly practical, d'you think? We'd be bound to run into a lot of rock-hard prejudice against, on both sides.'

'Got to make a start sometime, george,' said Smrgol. 'There's times when it'd pay to work together – like now, for instance. Not that you're not right, of course. For example, you'll notice I couldn't get any more of the dragons from our cave to join me here.'

'Ah, yes,' said Brian, nodding.

'Not that they're fearful, you understand, george. I don't think that for a minute. But when you live for a couple of hundred years – with luck, that is – you hardly feel like risking everything on the first chance that comes along. I'm not excusing it, you understand; it's just the way we are. Knight-erranting may make sense for you georges. Dragon-erranting would make no sense, at all, to us.'

'Well, then, where's the hope?'

'The hope's in us – you and me, george – and of course Gorbash here, the Mage, young Secoh alongside me here, that bowman and the female george with him, the wolf, mage and all. If we can pull this off – defeat the Dark Powers, that is, and win a victory – it'll be a tale to tell for five hundred years. Now, I don't know about you georges, but we dragons love tales. That's what we do in the caves, you know, for months on end, lie around telling each other tales.'

'Months? Really?' said Brian. 'I'd hardly think – months?'

'Months, george! Give a dragon a few pieces of gold and jewels to play with, a good cask of wine to drink and a good story to listen to – and he's happy. Why, if I could count the times I told the story of how I slew the ogre of Gormely Keep, all those years ago – Oh, of course the younger dragons all groan and moan when I mention it; but they curl up, fill their flagons and listen all the same, for all they've heard it time and again.'

'Hmm,' murmured Brian. 'Now that I think of it, we humans do a bit of sitting around and listening to old stories ourselves. Particularly in winter, you know, when it's hard to get about and there's not much to do if you could. By St. Denis, I cut my teeth on some of those old tales – they were one of the things that made me want to be a knight.'

'Exactly!' said Smrgol. 'Exactly the same with us dragons! Every dragon hearing the tale of how we defeat the Dark Powers here at the tower will want to go out himself and team up with some georges and maybe a wolf or some such, and have a like adventure of his own. From that, it's only a step to working together …'

'Tell me something,' Jim said to Carolinus, abandoning the knight–dragon conversation to catch up with the magician and walk a half-pace behind him, 'what's the price that has to be paid for the magic you used to drive away the darkness yesterday?'

'It's already paid,' replied Carolinus. 'The first to invoke magic incurs the debit. Counter-magic only balances the ledger. Not so with this—'

He lifted the staff and shook it slightly in the air before Jim's eyes.

'I had to go a long way to get this,' he explained. 'And I had to mortgage a lifetime of credit with the Auditing Department to make the journey. If we should lose here, I'm destroyed as a mage. But then, if we lose, we're all destroyed, anyway.'

'I see,' said Jim, soberly. He thought for a minute. 'What is it, exactly, that lives in the Loathly Tower?'

'What *lives* there just now, I don't know yet – any more than you do. What *is* there – neither alive nor dead, but just in presence on that spot – is the manifestation of Evil, itself. There's nothing we or anyone else can do to get rid of that. You can't destroy Evil, any more than the creatures of Evil can destroy Good. All you can do is contain one or the other, if you're strong enough, and render it momentarily ineffective in your own situation.'

'Then how can we do anything about the Dark Powers … ?'

'We can't – as I just said. But we can destroy the creatures, the tools by which Evil is currently working its will. Just as its creatures, for its purpose, will be trying to destroy us.'

Jim felt a cold lump in his throat. He swallowed.

'You must have some idea,' he said, 'of what kind of creatures they'll be, the ones who'll be trying to destroy us.'

'We already know who some of them are,' Carolinus answered. 'Sir Hugh and his men, for example. Also, the sandmirks. In addition—'

He stopped speaking and walking as abruptly as if he were an automaton that had been turned off. Jim checked himself, too, staring at the tower. From the windows just below its ruined battlements, figures had come boiling out – several dozen at least of great-winged, heavy-headed shapes that dipped and swung in the air about the top of the tower, screaming.

For a second they swarmed there, like a cloud of giant gnats. Then one of them swooped down toward the Companions—

And plummeted from the air like a body flung from the top of a cliff, a slim shaft impaling its body. It struck heavily, dead upon the causeway at Jim's feet, its woman's face frozen in a silent, maniacal scream.

Jim turned to see Dafydd standing with a fresh arrow already drawn to his bow. The screaming had cut off, completely and suddenly. Jim looked up and saw that the tower had no longer any swarm about it.

'Indeed, it will be no trouble if they are all of that size and swiftness,' said Dafydd, coming forward to reclaim his arrow from the slain harpy. 'A child could not miss at such a distance!'

'Don't mislead yourself, Master Bowman,' said Carolinus over his shoulder as he began to walk forward once more. 'It won't be anything like that easy with the others—'

He had turned his head west again as he spoke, and once more he broke off, stopping sharply. He stared down at a patch of grass in which, apparently, something lay hidden. Above the long beard his old face grew bony and grim. Jim stepped forward to see what had caused the magician's reaction.

With a shuddering wave of nausea, he twisted his head away again, just as the others came up to look. Lying in the grass before them was what had once been a man in armor.

Jim heard Brian's deep intake of breath as he sat on Blanchard.

'A most foul death,' said the knight, softly, 'most foul ... most foul ...'

Getting down from Blanchard, the knight went down on his armored knees beside the dead body in the grass, joining his steel gauntlets in prayer. The dragons were silent. Dafydd and Danielle stood with Aragh, none of them saying anything.

Only Carolinus, among the humans, bent his fierce old eyes on the scene before them with something besides horror. The magician poked with his staff at a wide trail of slime that led around and over the body and back in the direction of the tower. It was the sort of trail a garden slug leaves; only, to leave such a trail the slug would have had to be two feet wide where it touched the ground.

'A worm ...' said Carolinus to himself. 'But it was no worm that killed this man so. Worms are mindless. Something with great strength and patience plucked and crushed, in that slow fashion—'

He stared at Smrgol suddenly; and Smrgol bobbed his massive head in an oddly embarrassed gesture.

'I didn't say it, Mage,' the old dragon protested.

'It'll be best none of us says it until we're sure,' retorted the magician. 'Come along!'

Brian rose from beside the corpse; made a small, helpless gesture over it, as if he wished to straighten out the limbs but saw the utter futility of bringing anything like decent order to what remained; and climbed back on Blanchard. The group went on up the causeway to perhaps a hundred yards from the tower; and here Carolinus stopped, driving his wand once more into the earth so that it stood upright.

Aragh dropped, panting, into a lying position and Danielle, getting to her knees beside him, began to set and splint his leg, using some dry, fallen limbs from a stunted tree nearby and a sleeve of her doublet cut into strips.

'Now,' said Carolinus; and the word tolled on Jim's ear like the sound of a bell.

The mist had closed in on them. Whiteness was on all sides and close overhead. Only the tiny plain where they stood below the tumbled boulders of the tower hill, the boulders themselves and the tower were clear of it. Or was it quite clear? Tendrils of mist drifted above it below the clouds, and something about the air and the light filtering through the clouds themselves baffled the eyes and made it hard to focus on any one thing.

'As long as my wand and I stand,' said Carolinus, 'no power of theirs can completely take from us light, breath or strength of will. But stay within the space the wand keeps clear, or it and I may not be able to protect you. Let our enemies come to us here.'

'Where are they?' asked Jim, glancing around.

'Patience,' said Carolinus, sardonically, 'they'll come soon enough; and not in such form as you may expect.'

Jim looked around himself at the causeway's end: the boulders and the tower. No breeze stirred from out of the mist. The air was heavy and still. No, it was not exactly still; it seemed to shiver faintly, with a quivering unnaturalness, like that of an atmosphere dancing to heat waves. Only, here it was all dim, wintry and chill. As Jim noted this trembling of the air, there came to his ears – from where, he did not know – a high-pitched, dizzy singing like that which sometimes accompanies delirium or high fever.

When he looked again at the tower, it seemed to him that the appearance of the structure itself was distorted by these happenings. Although it had seemed only an ancient, ruined shell of a building, between one heartbeat and the next it had appeared to change. Almost, but not quite, he thought he caught glimpses of it unbroken and alive, thronged about with half-seen figures. His heart thudded more strongly; and the causeway and the tower upon it seemed to shake with every contraction of his chest, seemed to go in and out of focus, in and out, in and out ...

Then he saw Angie.

He knew he was too far from the tower to see her as clearly as he now saw her. At this distance, in this light, her face should have been hard to make out. But he saw her both from a distance and as if from close up, with a sharp and perfect clarity. She stood in the slight shadow of a ruined doorway opening on a balcony halfway up the side of the tower. Her blouse stirred to the slow movement of her breath. Her calm blue eyes stared closely into him. Her lips were half parted.

'Angie!' he cried.

He had not realized how much he had missed her. He had not understood how much he had wanted her. He took a step forward and found his way blocked by something as unyielding as an iron bar set in posts of concrete. He looked down. It was only the length of the wand, held in the old arm of Carolinas, but it was a barrier beyond his strength to pass.

'Where?' Carolinas demanded.

'There! On the balcony of the tower, there! See?' Jim pointed; and the others lifted their heads to peer where he indicated. 'In the doorway! Can't you see? Up on the side of the tower, in the doorway!'

'Not a thing!' said Brian, gruffly, dropping the hand with which he had been shading his eyes.

'Maybe,' said the mere-dragon, doubtfully. 'Maybe . . . back in the shadows, there. I'm not sure, really.'

'Jim,' said Angie.

'There!' cried Jim. 'You hear her?'

He pushed the restraining staff once again. But it was no use.

'I can hear you, Angie!' he shouted.

'You don't have to raise your voice,' she answered, softly. 'I can hear you, too. Jim, it's all right. It's just all those others that don't belong here. If you come up by yourself and get me, I can leave, and we can go home and everything will be fine.'

'I can't!' cried Jim, almost sobbing, for Carolinus' staff would still not let him pass. 'They won't let me go!'

'They've got no right to keep you, Jim. Ask the Mage what right he has to keep you, and he'll have to let you go. Ask him, and then come up here by yourself to get me.'

Jim turned, raging, on Carolinus.

'What right—?' he began.

'STOP!' Carolinus' voice went off like a cannon exploding in Jim's ears.

It dizzied, deafened and half blinded him, so that vision and hearing were blocked as if by thick, soft barriers. His unnaturally keen vision and hearing of Angie were gone, but he could still make himself think he saw her – as a shadow-in-shadow in the doorway behind a balcony on the tower.

'Why?' Jim turned on Carolinus in fury.

The magician did not back off an inch. His dark eyes glittered above his white beard.

'By the Powers!' he shouted, and his words came very clearly to Jim's ears. 'Will you walk blindly into the very first trap They set for you?'

'What trap?' Jim demanded. 'I was just talking to Angie—!'

The sentence broke off on his lips as Carolinus swung his staff to point. About the tease of the tower, between it and the boulders on the slope, had just arisen the wicked head of a dragon as large as Jim himself.

Smrgol's thunderous bellow split the strangely singing air.

'Bryagh! Traitor! Thief – inchworm! Come down here!'

The distant dragon opened his mouth. His booming answer rolled down to them.

'Tell us about Gormely Keep, old bag of bones!' he thundered. 'Ancient mud puppy, fat lizard, scare us with words!'

'Why, you—' Smrgol lurched forward.

'Hold!' shouted Carolinus; and Smrgol reared high, checking himself, his heavy foreclaws digging deep into the sandy soil as his body came down.

'True ...' he rumbled, his eyes hot.

'Old iguana! Go sleep in the sun!' Bryagh taunted.

But the older dragon now turned away, without answering, to the magician.

'What's hidden, Mage?' he asked.

'We'll see.'

Carolinus' voice was tight. He raised his staff and brought it down endwise, three times, on the earth. With each impact the whole causeway seemed to shake.

Up among the rocks, one particularly large boulder tottered and rolled out of the way. Jim's breath shuddered in his throat and he heard Brian, behind him, grunt hoarsely. Secoh cried out on a thin, sharp note.

In the space that the dislodged boulder had revealed, a huge, slug-like head lifted from the ground. It raised up even higher as they watched, yellow-brown in the harsh sunlight, its two sets of horns searching as its upper body waved from side to side, revealing a light external shell, a platelet with the merest hint of a spine. Its horns twitched and the eyes on the end of the primary pair aimed themselves at the group below. Slowly, it began to creep down the slope toward them, leaving a glistening trail on boulders and sand behind it.

'The Worm,' said Carolinus, softly.

'... that can *be* killed,' growled Smrgol, thoughtfully. 'Though not easily. Blast it, I wish it were Bryagh alone!'

'Nor is it those two alone.' Carolinus struck at the ground three times again.

'Come forth!' he cried, his old voice piping high on the quivering air. 'By the Powers! Come forth!'

And then they saw it.

From behind the great barricade of enormous rocks near the top of the tower hill, there slowly raised a bald and glistening dome of hairless gray skin. Gradually, this revealed two perfectly round blue eyes, below which was exposed no proper nose but, instead, two air slits side by side, as if the whole of the bare, enormous skull was covered with a simple sheet of thick skin. As it rose still farther, this unnatural head – as big around as a beach ball – showed its wide and idiotically grinning mouth, entirely lipless and with two jagged but matching rows of pointed teeth.

With a clumsy, studied motion, the whole creature rose to its feet and stood among the boulders. It was man-like in shape, but was clearly nothing ever spawned by the human race. A good twelve feet in height it stood, a rough patchwork of untanned hides studded with bones, bits of metal and clusters of tiny color points that could have been gems and made a kilt around its thick waist.

But this was not the extent of its difference from the race of man. It had, to begin with, no neck at all. Its unnatural hairless, near-featureless head was balanced like an apple atop perfectly square shoulders of gray, coarse-looking skin. Its torso was one straight trunk, from which arms and legs sprouted with disproportionate thickness and roundness, like sections of pipe. Its knees were hidden by its kilt and its lower legs by the rocks; but the elbows of its oversize arms had unnatural hinges to them, while the lower arms were almost as large as the upper and near-wristless, and the hands themselves awkward, thick-fingered parodies of the human extremities, with only three digits, one of which was a single-jointed, opposed thumb.

The right hand held a club, bound with rusty metal, that surely not even such a monster should have been able to lift. Yet one thick, crook-fingered hand hefted it lightly, as deftly as Carolinus had carried his staff.

The monster opened its mouth.

'*He!*' it went. '*He! He!*'

The sound was chilling. It was an incredibly bass titter, if such a thing can be imagined. And though the tone was about that of the low note of a three-valve tuba, it clearly came from the creature's upper throat and head. Nor was there any real humor in it. Having sounded its voice, the monster fell silent, watching the advance of the great slug with its round, light blue eyes.

Jim found his dragon jaws open, panting like a dog after a long run. Beside him, Smrgol stirred slowly.

'Yes,' he rumbled sadly, almost as if to himself, 'what I was afraid of. An ogre.'

In the silence that followed, Sir Brian got down from Blanchard and began to tighten the girths of his saddle.

'So, so, Blanchard,' he crooned, softly. But the large white horse was trembling so violently it could not stand still. Brian shook his head, and his hands fell from the girths. 'I must fight on foot, it seems,' he said.

The rest were watching Carolinus. The magician leaned on his staff, looking very old indeed, the lines looking even deeper in the ancient skin of his face. He had been watching the ogre, but now he turned back to Jim and the other two dragons.

'I'd hoped all along,' he said, 'that it needn't come to this. However' – he waved his hand at the approaching worm, the now-silent Bryagh and the watching ogre – 'as you see, the world goes never the way we want it, but must be haltered and led.'

He winced, produced his flask and cup, and took a drink of milk. Putting the utensils back again, he turned to Dafydd.

'Master Bowman,' he said, almost formally. 'The harpies are again in the tower, but when the others attack they'll be out again. See how the clouds overhead now sag down from the tower's height.'

He pointed upward. It was true: the cloud cover now bellied down like the worn-out ceiling of some ancient room. The thick, eye-baffling vapor hung less than thirty feet above their heads.

'The harpies will come diving swiftly out of that cover,' said the magician, 'giving you all but no time whatsoever to shoot before they're on you. Do you think you can hit them with those arrows of yours under such conditions?'

Dafydd cocked an eye upward.

'If the clouds come no lower—' he began.

'They cannot,' said Carolinus. 'The power of my staff holds them at no closer than this.'

'Then,' Dafydd replied, 'provided they come no faster than the one I shot a short while ago, I have a fair chance, look you. I do not say that one may not get through, for I am but a man, after all – though there have seen those who thought I was something more, with bow and arrow. But it is a fair chance I can put a shaft through each of them before it can do us harm.'

'Good!' said Carolinus. 'More than a fair chance, none of us can ask for. Don't forget that their bite is poisonous, however, even when the harpy itself is dead.'

He turned back to Brian.

'I'd suggest, Sir Brian,' he said, 'particularly since you're to be on foot, that you take the worm. You'll be most useful that way. I know you'd prefer that renegade dragon, but the worm is the greater danger to the others who have no armor.'

'Difficult to slay, I imagine?' queried the knight, stopping from adjusting the armstrap on the inner face of his shield to squint up the slope at the approaching slug shape.

'Its vital organs are hidden deep inside it,' Carolinus explained, 'and, being mindless, it will fight on long after being mortally wounded. Cut off those eye stalks and blind it first if you can.'

'What—' Jim began, then found his voice hampered by the dry throat. He had to swallow before he could continue. 'What am I supposed to do?'

'Why, fight the ogre, boy! Fight the ogre!' roared Smrgol; and the inhuman giant up on the slope, hearing him, shifted his round-eyed gaze from the worm to fasten it on the old dragon. 'And I'll take on that louse of a Bryagh. The george here'll chop up the worm, the Bowman'll deal with the harpies, the Mage'll hold back the evil influences, the wolf keep off the sandmirks – and that'll be that!'

Jim opened his mouth to cure Gorbash's grand-uncle of what seemed a bad case of false optimism – then suddenly realized that it was nothing of the kind. Smrgol was deliberately trying to pass the matter off lightly in order to put heart in Jim. This, when the old dragon was himself half dead and certainly no match for the powerful young Bryagh.

Suddenly Jim felt as if his heart had turned over in his chest. He looked around him at the others. If the old and crippled Smrgol was no match for Bryagh, was Brian any more a match for that obscene worm now only about thirty yards off? Was it a fair match, Aragh on three legs, for all the wolf's indifference to their chittering, against the horde of small sandmirks that remained alive? And Dafydd, miracle archer that he was, how could he hope to shoot down without error harpies that could appear practically on top of him without warning? Finally, was it fair to expect the old magician by himself to hold down all the impalpable evil in this place while the battles were going on?

Jim himself had a good reason for being here: Angie. But the others were here primarily because of him, involved by him in a fight where the odds would all be against them. Guilt moved deep inside Jim and weakened his legs. He turned to the knight.

'Brian,' he said. 'You and the others don't need to do this—'

'Lord, yes!' replied the knight, busy with his equipment. 'Worms, ogres – one fights them when one runs into them, you know.'

He considered his spear and put it aside.

'No, not as long as I'm to be on foot,' he murmured to himself.

'Smrgol,' Jim said, turning to the dragon, 'don't you see? Bryagh's a lot younger than you. And you're not well—'

'Er ...' Secoh muttered, hastily, and broke down in what seemed to be embarrassment and confusion.

'Speak up, boy!' rumbled Smrgol.

'Well ...' stammered the mere-dragon, 'it's just – wh-what I mean is, I couldn't bring myself to fight that worm or that ogre. I really couldn't. I just sort of go to pieces when I think of one of them getting close to me. But I could, well, fight another dragon. It wouldn't be quite so bad – not so frightening, I mean – if that dragon up there were to break my neck ...'

He broke down and stammered incoherently.

'I know I'm sounding silly ...'

'Nonsense! Good lad!' bellowed Smrgol. 'Glad to have you! I can't quite get into the air myself at the moment – still a bit stiff. But if you could fly over and work that sea lizard down this way, where I can get a grip on him, we'll stretch him out for the buzzards.'

He dealt the mere-dragon a tremendous thwack with his tail by way of congratulations, almost knocking the other off his feet.

Jim turned back to Carolinus.

'There's no retreat,' said the magician, before Jim could speak. 'This is a game of chess where, if one piece withdraws, all on his side fall. Hold back the creatures, all of you, and I'll hold back the forces; for the creatures will finish me if you go down and the forces finish you if they get me.'

'Now, look here, Gorbash!' Smrgol shouted in Jim's ear. 'That worm's almost down here. Let me tell you something about how to fight ogres, based on experience. You listening, boy?'

'Yes,' said Jim, numbly.

'I know you've heard the other dragons calling me an old windbag when I wasn't around. But I *have* conquered an ogre – the only one of our race to do it in the last eight hundred years. They haven't. So pay attention, if you want to win your own fight.'

Jim nodded.

'All right,' he said.

'Now, the first thing to know' – Smrgol glanced at the oncoming worm and lowered his voice confidentially – 'is about the bones in an ogre.'

'Never mind the details,' said Jim. 'What do I *do?*'

'In a minute, in a minute ...' Smrgol answered. 'Don't get excited, boy. An excited dragon is a losing dragon. Now, about the bones in an ogre. The thing to remember is that they're big – matter of fact, in the arms and legs they're mainly bone. So there's no use trying to bite clear through. What you want to do is get the muscle – that's tough enough, as it is – and hamstring. That's point one.'

He paused to look significantly at Jim. Jim managed with an effort to keep his mouth shut and be patient.

'Now, point two,' Smrgol went on. 'Also connected with bones. Notice the elbows on that ogre. They aren't like a george's elbows. They're what you might call double-jointed. Why? Simply because, with the big bones they've got to have and the muscle on them, they'd never be able to bend a bone more than halfway up before the bottom part'd bump the top, if they had a george-type joint. Now, the point of all this is that when that ogre swings his club, he can only swing it in one way with that elbow. That's up and down. If he wants to swing it side to side, he's got to use his shoulder. Consequently, if you can catch him with his club down and to one side of his body, you've got an advantage; it takes him two moves to get it back up and in line again – instead of one, like a george does.'

'Yes, yes ...' said Jim, watching the advance of the worm.

'Don't get impatient, boy! Keep cool! Now, his knees don't have that double joint, so if you can knock him off his feet you've got a real advantage. But don't try that unless you're sure you can do it; because once he gets his arms around you, you're a goner. The only way to fight him is in and out – fast. Wait for his swing, dodge it, dive in while his arm is down, tear him up, get back out again. Got it?'

'Got it,' said Jim, numbly.

'Good! Whatever you do, remember, don't let him get his grip on you. And don't pay any attention to what's happening to the rest of us, no matter what you think you hear or see out of the corner of your eyes. It's everyone for himself, once things start. Concentrate on your own foe. And, boy ...'

'Yes?' Jim answered.

'Keep your head!' The old dragon's voice was almost pleading. 'Whatever you do, don't let your dragon-instinct get in there and run away with you. That's why the georges have been winning against us all these years, the way they have. Just remember you're faster than that ogre and that your brain'll win for you if you stay clear, keep your head and don't rush. I tell you, boy—'

He was interrupted by a sudden cry of joy from Brian, who had been rummaging around in the panniers behind Blanchard's saddle.

'I say,' shouted Brian, running up to Jim with surprising lightness and agility, considering the weight of his armor. 'The most marvelous stroke of luck! Look what I just found!'

He waved a wispy length of white cloth at Jim.

'What?' Jim demanded, his heart leaping.

'Geronde's favor! And just in time, too. Be a good fellow, will you,' Brian went on, turning to Carolinus, 'and tie it about my vambrace, here on the shield arm ... Thank you, Mage.'

Carolinus looked grim, but nonetheless tucked his wand into the crook of one arm and with his freed hands fastened the cloth around the armor of Brian's left forearm. Brian turned about, drove his spear into the ground and tethered Blanchard's bridle to it. Then, catching up his shield position, he turned back and drew his sword with his other hand. The bright blade gleamed even in the dull light. He leaned forward to throw the weight of his armor before him; and ran at the worm, which was now hardly more than a dozen feet away.

'A Neville-Smythe! A Neville-Smythe! Geronde!' he shouted as they came together.

Jim heard but did not witness the impact of their collison. For just then everything began to happen at once. Up on the hill, Bryagh screamed suddenly in fury and launched himself down the slope and into the air, wings spread like some great bomber gliding in for a crash landing. Behind Jim was the frenzied flapping of leathery wings as Secoh took to the air to meet him – but this was drowned by a sudden, short, deep-chested and grunting cry, like a wordless shout. Lifting his club, the ogre had stepped clear of the boulders, coming straight down the hill with heavy, ground-covering strides.

'Good luck, boy!' said Smrgol in Jim's ear. 'And Gorbash—'

Something in the other's voice made Jim turn his head to look at him. The ferocious mouth-pit and enormous fangs were close to him, but behind them Jim read an unusual expression of affection and concern in the dark dragon-eyes.

'Remember,' Smrgol said, almost softly, 'that you are a descendant of Ortosh and Agtval, and of Gleingul who slew the sea serpent on the tide banks of the Gray Sands. And be, therefore, valiant. But remember, too, you are my only living kin and the last of our line – and be careful!'

The old dragon's voice stumbled and choked. It seemed to struggle for a fraction of a second before it went on.

'And – er – good luck to you, too – er – James!'

Then Smrgol's head was jerked away as he swung about to face Secoh and Bryagh, who came crashing to earth entangled together, almost on top of him. Jim, turning back toward the tower, had only time to take to the air himself before the rushing ogre was upon him.

He had lifted on his wings without thinking, out of his dragon-instinct when attacked. He was aware of the ogre before him, halting now, its enormous gray feet digging deep into the ground. The rusty-banded club flashed before Jim's eyes and he felt a heavy blow high on his chest that swept him backward through the air.

He flailed with his wings to regain balance. The oversize idiot face was grinning only a couple of yards from him. The club swept up for another blow. Panicked, Jim scrambled aside in midair, retreating, and saw the ogre sway forward a step. Again the club lashed out – quick! How could something so big and clumsy looking be so quick with its hands? Jim felt himself smashed out of the air down to the ground, and a lance of bright pain shot through his right shoulder. For a second a thick-skinned forearm loomed over him and his teeth met in it without thought.

He was shaken like a rat by a terrier, and flung clear. His wings beat for the safety of altitude and he found himself about sixteen feet off the ground, staring down at the ogre, who grunted and shifted the club to strike upward. Jim cupped air with his wings, flung himself backward and avoided the blow. The club whistled through the unfeeling air; and, sweeping forward, Jim ripped with his teeth at one great shoulder before beating clear. The ogre turned to face him, still grinning. But now blood welled and trickled down where Jim's teeth had torn, high on the shoulder.

Abruptly, Jim realized something.

His panic was gone. He was no longer afraid. He hung in the air, just out of the ogre's reach, poised to take advantage of any opening; and a heat of energy, a sharpness of perception was coursing all through him. He was discovering that, with fights – as with a great many similar things – it was only the beforehand part that was bad. Once battle was joined, several million years of instinct took over and there was no time or thought for anything but confronting the enemy.

So it was, now.

The ogre moved in on him again and that was his last intellectualization of the fight; for everything else was lost in the moment-to-moment efforts to avoid being killed and, if possible, to kill, himself.

It was a long, blurred time – about which, later, he had no clear memory. The sun marched up the long arc of the heavens and crossed the midday point and headed down again. On the torn, sandy soil of the causeway he and the ogre turned and feinted, smashed and struck at each other. Sometimes he was in the air, sometimes on the ground. Once he had the monster down on one knee, but could not press his advantage. At another time they had fought halfway up the slope to the tower and the ogre had pinned him in a cleft between two huge boulders. The club was hefted for the final blow that would smash Jim's skull. Then he had somehow wriggled free, between the very legs of his opponent; and the battle was on again.

Now and then, throughout the fight, he would catch brief kaleidoscopic glimpses of the combats being waged about him: Brian, wrapped about by the blind body of the worm, its eye stalks now hacked away, and the knight striving in silence to draw free his sword and sword arm, which were pinned to his body by the worm's encircling form. Or there would roll briefly into Jim's vision a tangled, roaring tumble of flailing, leathery wings and serpentine bodies that was Smrgol, Bryagh, and the mere-dragon. Once or twice he had a momentary view of Carolinus, still standing erect, his staff upright in his hand, his long white beard flowing forward over his gown, like some old seer in the hour of Armageddon. Then the gross body of the ogre would blot out his vision and he would forget all but what was before him.

The day faded. A mist pressed inward from the sea and fled in little wisps and tatters across the battlefield. Jim's body ached and his wings felt leaden. But the ever-grinning ogre and his sweeping club seemed neither to weaken nor to slow. Jim drew back in the air for a moment, to catch his breath; and in that second he heard a voice cry out.

'Time is short!' it called, in cracked tones. 'We are running out of time! The day is nearly gone!'

It was the voice of Carolinus.

Jim had never heard it raised before with such a desperate accent. Even as he identified it, he realized that it had sounded clearly to his ears – and that for some time now, upon the causeway, except for the ogre and himself there was silence.

He had been driven back down from the slope to the area from which he had started. To one side of him, the snapped ends of Blanchard's bridle dangled limply from the earth-thrust spear to which Brian had tethered the horse before advancing against the worm. A little off from the spearshaft – from which the terrified horse had evidently broken free – stood Carolinus, leaning heavily on his staff, his old face shrunken, almost mummified in appearance, as if life had been all but drained from it.

Jim turned back to see the ogre nearly upon him once more. The heavy club swung high, dark and enormous in the dying day. Jim felt in his limbs and wings a weakness that would not let him dodge in time; and with all his strength, he gathered himself and sprang instead up under the sweep of the monster's weapon and inside the grasp of those cannon-barrel-thick arms.

The club glanced off Jim's spine and he felt the ogre's arms go around him, the double triad of bone-thick fingers searching for his neck. He was caught, but his rush had knocked the ogre off its feet. Together they rolled over and over, on the sandy earth, the ogre gnawing with his jagged teeth at Jim's chest and striving to break the spine or twist the neck, while Jim's tail lashed futilely about.

As they rolled against the standing spear and snapped it in half, the ogre found his neck hold and commenced to twist Jim's neck as if it was a chicken's being wrung in slow motion.

A wild despair flooded through Jim. He had been cautioned by Smrgol never to let the ogre get his arms around him. He had disregarded that advice and now was lost, the battle was lost. Stay away, Smrgol had warned, use your brains.

But the wild hope of a long chance sprang suddenly to life in him. His head was twisted back over his shoulder and he could see only the darkening mist above him; but he stopped fighting the ogre and groped about with both forepaws. For a moment of eternity, he located nothing – and then something hard nudged his right foreclaw, a glint of bright metal flashed before his eyes. He gripped what he had touched, clamping down on it as firmly as his clumsy claws would allow –

And, with every ounce of strength that was left to him, he drove the broken half of the snapped spear deep into the middle of the ogre, who now sprawled above him.

The great body bucked and shuddered. A wild scream burst from the idiot mouth beside Jim's ear. The ogre let go, staggered back and up, and tottered to its feet, towering above Jim as the stone edifice itself towered above them both.

Again, the ogre screamed, stumbling about like a drunken man, fumbling at the broken end of the spear that was sticking out of him. Jerking at the shaft, he screamed again; and lowering his unnatural head, bit at it like a wounded animal. It splintered in his teeth. He then screamed a final time and fell to his knees. Slowly, like a bad actor in an old-fashioned movie, he rolled over on his side and drew up his legs like someone with a cramp. An ultimate scream was drowned in the bubbling in his throat; black blood trickled from his mouth. He lay still.

Unsteadily, Jim crawled to his feet and looked about him.

The mists were, oddly, drawing back from the causeway and the thin light of late afternoon stretched long across the bouldered slope, the tower above it and the small plain below. In the rusty light, Jim saw that the worm was dead, literally hacked in two. Aragh lay, grinning, a splint on his broken leg. Brian, in bloody, dented armor, leaned wearily on a twisted sword not more than a few feet from Carolinus. Dafydd was down, his shirt half torn off, the shape of a harpy sprawled motionless across his chest. Danielle stood above him, an arrow still notched to her own bow. As Jim watched her, she slowly lowered her weapon, cast it aside and dropped down beside the Welshman.

A little further off, Secoh raised a bloody neck and head above the motionless, locked-together bodies of Smrgol and Bryagh. The mere-dragon stared dazedly at Jim. Jim moved painfully, over to him.

Looking down at the two immense dragons, he saw that Smrgol lay with his jaws locked in Bryagh's throat. The neck of the younger dragon was broken.

'Smrgol.' Jim croaked.

'No ...' gasped Secoh. 'No good! He's gone ... I led the other one to him. He got his grip – and then he never let go ...' The mere-dragon burst into sobs and lowered his head.

'They all fought well,' creaked a strange, harsh voice.

Jim turned and saw the knight standing at his shoulder. Brian's face was as white as sea foam below the now-helmetless tousled brown hair. The flesh of his features seemed fallen in to the bones, like the face of an old man. He swayed as he stood.

'We have won,' said Carolinus. 'At a price!'

He turned to Danielle. Jim and the knight turned with him. She was still beside Dafydd; but she had pulled the harpy from Dafydd's upper body, and the shreds of his shirt. Brian's helm, now filled with water from beside the causeway, was with her and she was gently sponging a red tear that ran from near the joining of Dafydd's neck and left shoulder to his middle ribs.

Jim, the magician and the knight walked together to stand over the two of them. With his shirt off, Dafydd's upper body looked twice as large as it had, clothed. It was a sculptor's find of a chest: the shoulders lay back, square and incredibly, broad of bone, and powerful muscle lay in cables across the bowman's lean torso from the pectorals to the abdominals, as if molded by an anatomist building a display model. But the body was limp now, and still.

'Indeed,' said Dafydd to Danielle, so faintly that, had it not been for the utter stillness now all about them, the three watchers would not have understood him, 'you are wishing the impossible. As the Mage, said, their bite is death, and I feel that death now in me.'

'No,' said Danielle, sponging away at the ragged slash the harpy's teeth had made in him.

'But it is so,' Dafydd insisted, 'though I wish it were not so, for that I love you. But to every bowman comes death, in time. I have always known this, and am content.'

'You are no longer merely a bowman.' Danielle's voice was steady and composed. 'I made you a knight and you are a knight; and as a knight, it's ungentlemanly of you to take leave without my permission. And I do not wish you to go. I will not let you go!'

With a strength that startled Jim, for all that Brian had told him about how she pulled a hundred-pound warbow, Danielle lifted his upper body easily in her arms, laid his head against her shoulder and held him to her.

'I have you,' she said; and though her eyes were perfectly dry and her voice quite calm, almost businesslike, the sound of it wrung Jim's very guts, 'and I'll never give you to anything else – even to death – unless you want to leave me. You have to tell me you want to leave me, or else you can't die.'

Dafydd smiled faintly.

'Indeed ...' he said; and in that moment after, in which he said nothing, Jim was ready to believe that the single, faintly breathed word had been his last.

But the bowman spoke again.

'Then it's true, that you really wish me to live. If so then death must come, get me against my will, which I do not think it or any other thing can do, since never have I been forced against my will nor shall be now, look you.'

He closed his eyes, turned his head a little to rest against her breast and said nothing more. But his chest continued slowly to rise and fall steadily.

'He'll live,' Carolinus said to Danielle. 'He asked no price for coming here, and not even the Auditing Department can ask a price of him, now that he's helped win this day.'

The girl did not answer the magician, but bowed her head above Dafydd's slowly moving chest and sat holding him as if she would sit there forever, if necessary. Jim, Brian and the magician turned back to Aragh, and to Secoh, who had conquered the explosion of his grief and now sat quietly above the body of Smrgol.

'We have won,' said Carolinus. 'Not again in our lifetimes will this place gather strength enough to break out against the world.'

He turned to Jim.

'And now, James,' he said. 'You wanted to go home. The way is open.'

'Good,' said Jim.

'Home?' asked Brian. 'Now?'

'Now,' said Carolinus. 'He has wished from the beginning to return to his own place, Sir knight. Fear not, the dragon who's the original owner of this body James has been wearing will remember all that's happened here and be your friend.'

'Fear?' Brian somehow managed to dig up a spark of energy to spend on hauteur. 'I fear no dragon, dammit! It's just that … I shall miss you, James!'

Staring at Brian, Jim saw the knight's eyes unexpectedly brimming with tears. He had forgotten learning, in his studies of the European Middle Ages, that people cried then as naturally as they laughed; his own self-conscious twentieth-century self felt acute embarrassment at the sight.

'Well, you know …' he muttered.

'Well, well, James,' said Brian, wiping his eyes on a trilling end of Geronde de Chaney's favor. 'What must, must! In any case, in respect to the old boy here' – he nodded at the dead Smrgol – 'I'm going to see what can be done about this dragon-human alliance business, so I'll be seeing a fair amount of whoever owns this body you've been in, and it'll be somewhat like having you around, in any case.'

'He was great!' burst out Secoh, staring at the body of the old dragon at his feet. 'He made me strong – for the first time in my life. Anything he wanted, I'd do it!'

'You come along with me, then, to vouch for the dragon end of things,' said Brian. 'Well, James. I suppose it's good-bye, then—'

'Angie!' cried Jim, suddenly remembering. 'Oh – excuse me, Brian. But I just remembered. I've got to go get her out of the tower.'

He spun around.

'Wait!' said Carolinus.

The magician turned to face the edifice itself; and raised his wand.

'Deliver!' he cried. 'You are vanquished. Deliver!'

They waited.

Nothing happened.

22

Carolinus struck his wand once more, endwise, upon the hard sand.

'*Deliver!*' he cried.

Once more they waited. The slow seconds stretched out into minutes.

'By the Powers!' Suddenly, strength seemed to have flowed back into S. Carolinus. His voice was once more full and he looked to have grown six inches. 'Are we to be flouted? *Auditing Department!*'

Something happened then that Jim was never to forget. The memorability of it lay not in what happened, but in the quality of the event. Without warning, the whole earth spoke – the sea spoke – the sky spoke! And they all spoke with the same, single, bass voice that had responded from thin air to Carolinus before, when Jim was present. This time, however, nothing was apologetic or humorous about the voice.

'DELIVER!' it said.

Almost in the same second, something dark came swiftly out of the blackness of the arched, ground-level entrance to the tower. Drifting down the slope toward them, it seemed to float; but it arrived more quickly than its leisurely velocity indicated. It was a mattress of intertwined fir boughs, the needles still fresh and green upon them; and on that mattress Angie lay, her eyes closed.

The mattress reached them and settled to the ground at Jim's feet.

'Angie!' he exclaimed, bending over her.

For a moment a deep fear had stirred in him; but then he saw that she was breathing steadily and calmly, as if only sleeping. In fact, as he watched, she opened her eyes and looked up at him.

'Jim!' she said.

Scrambling to her feet, she threw her arms around his scaly neck and hung on to him. Jim's heart did a flip-flop in his chest. His conscience ripped him like a bandsaw for not having thought of her more during the past days, for not having managed to come for her sooner.

'Angie ...' he murmured tenderly – and then something struck him. 'Angie, how did you know it was me, and not some other dragon?'

She let go and looked up at him, laughing.

'Know it was you!' she exclaimed. 'How could I miss, after all this time in your head—'

She broke off suddenly and stared down at herself.

'Oh, I'm back in my own body, again! That's better. That's much better!'

'Head? Body?' Jim's mind wobbled between two incredible questions; and finally chose the one that sounded the more ominous. 'Angie, whose body were you in?'

'Yours, of course,' she said. 'That is, I was in your mind, which was in your body – or Gorbash's body, to be exact. At least, I was – unless I'm dreaming now. No, there they all are, just the way they should be: Brian, Dafydd, Danielle and the rest.'

'But how could you be in my mind?' demanded Jim.

'The Dark Powers, or whatever they call themselves, put me there,' said Angie. 'I didn't catch on, at first. Right after Bryagh brought me here, I got sleepy and lay down on those fir branches. The next thing I knew, I was in your head – seeing everything that was going on. I could tell what you were thinking, and I could almost talk to you. At first I thought some accident had happened; or maybe Grottwold had been trying to bring us back and got us mixed up together this time. Then I caught on.'

'Caught on?'

'The Dark Powers had put me there.'

'The Dark Powers?' Jim asked.

'Of course,' said Angie, calmly. 'They were hoping I'd want to be rescued so badly that I'd keep trying to push you to come to the Loathly Tower here, alone. When I was about half asleep, I thought I heard some voice or other talking to Bryagh about ways of getting you to come after me without Companions to help you.'

'How did they know?' Jim frowned.

'I don't know, but they did,' said Angie. 'So, when I remembered that, it wasn't hard to guess who'd put me in your mind, and why. As I say, I couldn't really *talk* to you, but I could make you feel the way I was feeling, if I sort of pushed hard enough, mentally. Remember when Brian told you he had to get Geronde's permission to be a Companion of yours and you would both have to go to Castle Malvern, first? You remember how you suddenly felt guilty about turning your back on the tower, with me there? Well, that was me in your mind. I'd just woken up there, and didn't realize why. Then it hit me that you might be in pretty terrible danger going on to the tower alone, if Carolinus had insisted you get some Companions before trying it; and I remembered what I'd heard when I was falling asleep. I put two and two together, and stopped wishing you'd come to rescue me. The moment I did that, I could tell that you began to feel better about going with Brian to Castle Malvern.'

She ceased talking. Jim stared at her, too full of questions to sort out what he wanted to ask first. Now that he had a moment to notice, he realized that apparently Angie had grown in translating to this other world. He had thought of Danielle as tall, but now he saw that Angie was equally so. Not that she looked any the worse for the increase in size. To the contrary –

Carolinus clicked his tongue.

'Two minds in one body!' he said, shaking his head. 'Highly irregular! Highly! Even for the Dark Powers, that's taking a chance. Could be done, of course; but—'

'But wait!' Jim had found his voice. 'Angie, you said Gorbash was in my mind, too? How could he be?'

'I don't know how, but he was,' Angie said. 'He was there already when I got there. I couldn't communicate with him, though. You had him sort of locked up.'

Jim winced internally. Now that Angie had identified Gorbash as the other mind in the back of Jim's, he could feel the original owner of the dragon body strongly. Gorbash had evidently returned to his own head back during that moment in the dragon caves, when Jim – alone with Angie – had been as good as knocked out by some invisible force. Now Jim could feel Gorbash clearly – wanting control of his own body again.

'*Three!*' Carolinus was saying, staring at Jim.

'What do you mean, "locked up"?' Jim asked Angie, feeling a twinge of conscience toward the dragon.

'I don't know how else to describe it,' said Angie. 'You've been sort of holding his mind down with yours – that's the best explanation I can give you. I didn't *see* any of this, you understand, I could just feel what was going on. He couldn't do a thing unless you got emotionally wound up about something and forgot him for a moment.'

'Three!' Carolinus repeated. 'Three minds in one skull! Now that really is going over the line, Dark Powers or not! Auditing Department, are you copying all this—'

'Not their fault,' said the voice out of thin air.

'Not ...'

'Not the fault of the Dark Powers that Gorbash was there,' explained the Auditing Department. 'They did put the Angie-mind in with the

James-mind, but the responsibility for the presence of the Gorbash-mind lies outside our departmental area.'

'Ah. Complicated matter?' asked Carolinus.

'Decidedly. Wheels within wheels. So if you'll start to straighten things out as soon as possible—'

'Count on me,' said the magician. He turned back to Jim and Angie. 'All right, now. What do you want? Am I to send you both back?'

'That's right,' said Jim. 'Let's go.'

'Very well,' said Carolinus. He looked at Angie. 'And *you* wish to return?'

She looked at Jim for a moment before answering.

'I want whatever Jim wants . . .' she said.

Jim stared at her, bewildered.

'What sort of an answer is that?' he asked. 'What do you mean?'

'I mean what I say,' Angie said, with a hint of stubbornness in her voice. 'I want what you want – that's all.'

'Well, I want to go back, of course. I just said so.'

She looked away from him.

'Very well,' Carolinus agreed. 'If you'll both move over here by me—'

'Wait!' said Jim. 'Wait just a minute!'

He turned to face Angie.

'What's all this?' he demanded. 'Of course we're going to go back – just as quick as we can. What else can we do? There's no choice about this!'

'Of course there's a choice,' said Carolinus, irritably.

Jim looked at the magician. The old man appeared tired and cross.

'I say, of course there's a choice!' repeated Carolinus. 'You've now got sufficient credit with the Auditing Department for a return. You can spend it all going back; or stay and keep some of it to help build your life here. It's up to you. Make up your mind, that's all!'

'Stay, James,' said Brian, quickly. 'Malencontri can be yours – yours and the Lady Angela's, just as we promised earlier. Together, our two estates and families will be too strong for any enemies.'

Aragh growled, a wordless sound. When Jim looked over at him, the wolf glanced away.

Jim turned back at Angie. He was feeling completely mixed up.

'Come on,' said Angie, putting her hand on his massive dragon-shoulder. 'Let's go and talk for a second.'

She led him toward the side of the causeway. By the edge of the water, they stopped and Jim heard the lapping of tiny waves against the edge. He looked down into her face.

'Did you really know everything I did?' he asked.

She nodded.

'Everything you did and thought!'

'Hmm.' Jim remembered a stray thought or two he had had about Danielle.

'That's why I believe you ought to think about this.'

'But what do *you* think?' he insisted.

'I said what I think. I want whatever you want. But what do *you* want?'

'Well, of course I want to get back to civilization. I'd think we'd both want that.'

Again she said nothing. It was very irritating. It was as if she forced his words to hang in the air in front of his nose, staring back at him.

'Hmm!' he growled to himself.

It was ridiculous, he thought, to suppose that he could want anything other than to go back. His job was waiting for him at Riveroak, and sooner or later they would be finding someplace to live – admittedly, nothing palatial – but it would be at least a one-room and kitchenette. And later on, when they both had teaching positions, they could move up to something better. Meanwhile, back there they had all the blessings of civilization – doctors, dentists, accountants to figure out their bills, time off every summer to do what they liked ...

Moreover, all their friends were back there: Danny Cerdak; and, well, Grottwold ... Here, there were only a bunch of strange characters they had met only the week before last: Brian, and Aragh, Carolinus, Danielle, Dafydd and the dragons and so forth ...

'To hell with it!' said Jim.

He turned around to take his decision back to Carolinus, with Angie trotting along beside him. No one was looking at them now, however. All were facing the approaching figures of Giles o' the Wold and the men with him. The little army was a sorry looking lot, and many bore evidence of wounds, but they were smiling through their weariness as they began to report the final rout of Sir Hugh's men, now fleeing back in the direction of Castle Malencontri.

'And Sir Hugh?' Brian asked.

'Alive, worse the luck,' Giles told him. 'Though he was reeling a bit in the saddle, the last I saw of him. One of my men got a shaft through his armor, and he'd be losing blood. Less than half his men go back with him.'

'Then we can take Malencontri before he can recoup his losses,' Brian exclaimed. Then he frowned uncertainly and turned his face toward Jim. 'That is, we could, if we had reason ...'

'I'm staying here,' Jim told the knight gruffly.

'Hurrah!' shouted Brian, throwing his helmet into the air and catching it, as if he was twelve years old.

'Very well!' Carolinus said, testily. 'If that's your decision. You realize that if you spend your credit with the Accounting Department to get your own body back here, you won't have enough left over to change your mind and return whence you came? You'll have enough to get you started here, but not enough to get moved back, after all.'

'I understand. Of course, I understand that.'

'All right, then. Stand back, all the rest of you! We're going to be having two bodies where one is now. All right, then' – Carolinus lifted his staff and thumped its end down on the earth – 'there you are!'

And there he was.

Jim blinked. He found himself looking directly into the dangerously toothed jaws of a dragon-muzzle less than six inches from his nose; and clutching a pillow to his body, which was now dressed only in what seemed to be a white hospital gown.

'Just who do you think you are?' demanded the dragon-jaws.

Jim took a couple of steps backward, partially to keep himself from being deafened and partially to get a better look at what was confronting him.

'Gorbash?' he said.

'Don't try pretending you don't know me!' said the dragon, which Jim was now seeing entire.

It – Gorbash – was a very large and fierce-looking animal. Larger and fiercer than Jim had realized, from his experience inside the body.

'Of – of course I know you,' Jim gasped.

'You certainly do! And I know *you*. I ought to. Who do you think you are, taking over somebody else's body, doing what you want with it and treating the dragon who really owns it as if he just appeared in it yesterday? All the time using it the way you choose to. Mishandling it, taking risks with it! Would anybody believe what this george did with my body in just the first few days after he had it?'

Gorbash turned appealingly to the others standing around.

'Shut me up completely. Wouldn't let me twitch a muscle – in my own body, mind you! Then, before I could think, he went headfirst off a cliff and started flailing around with my wings so much that I could barely get them beating properly in time to keep us from smashing on the rocks. Then, he nearly got the Mage here to turn us into a beetle.

Next, he overflew and got my muscles stiff. Then, instead of resting up, he swims – mind you, swims – across all sorts of water in the fens. Never a thought about our toes and vicious sea turtles or giant sea lampreys come into the tidewater. And that's only the beginning. Then—'

'I – I didn't end up in your body on purpose,' protested Jim.

'But you certainly acted like you owned it from the minute you got there! And don't interrupt!' Gorbash roared, resuming his appeal to the audience. 'And that was just the beginning. He nearly got us eaten by sandmirks, *did* get us nearly killed by the horn of that other george, and never a bite to eat or a drop to drink ... er, except for that time at the inn. But that hardly counts!'

'Oh, it doesn't, doesn't it!' cried Secoh. 'I heard about that feast of yours at the inn. All the lovely meat without hardly any bones you could stuff into you! All the rich, rich wine! It wouldn't be James who wanted to drink that cellar dry, and you know it as well as I do—'

'WHAT? *Shut up, mere-dragon!*' boomed Gorbash.

Secoh gave a sudden bounce that landed him nose to nose with Gorbash, who reared back instinctively.

'*I will not shut up!*' roared Secoh. 'I don't have to shut up! I'm as good as any other dragon, mere-born or not.'

'Mere-dragon, I'm warning you...' Gorbash began ominously, beginning to hunch his shoulders and gape his jaws.

'You don't scare me!' cried Secoh. 'Not anymore, you don't. It was your own grand-uncle taught me I didn't have to bow down to anyone. Death before dishonor! I've just fought a dragon as big as you were – to the death! Well, anyway, I helped your uncle fight him. *He* didn't scare me and *you* don't scare me. *You* haven't done anything – all you did was get carried along by what James wanted to do with your body. But you'll go around preening yourself for the next hundred years, talking about how you were in a fight with an ogre! All right, you go ahead, but don't try to push me around. I'll tear your wings off!'

And Secoh snarled into the very teeth of the bigger dragon.

Gorbash bobbed his head and looked uncertain.

'Yes, and another thing!' said Secoh. 'You ought to be ashamed of yourself! If your grand-uncle was alive, *he'd* certainly tell you so. He was a real dragon! You're just one of those fat cave lizards. Here, James made you famous and all you can do is complain ...'

'Ha!' said Gorbash – but he said it without quite the force he had in his words a moment before. He looked away from Secoh toward the others. 'I don't have to worry about what some mere-dragon thinks.

The rest of you were around and saw how it was with this george taking over my body—'

'And a good thing he did!' Danielle interrupted, sharply. 'You don't sound like anyone I'd trust to face an ogre.'

'I—'

'Gorbash,' said Aragh, grimly, 'you never had much in the way of brains ...'

'But I—'

'Nor will I stand by and hear Sir James maligned,' Brian announced. The knight's face was set and dark. 'Another word from you, dragon, about this good knight and gallant gentleman and I'll find yet one more use for my sword this day, bent as it is from the worm.'

'I'll help!' said Secoh.

'Enough!' snapped Carolinus. 'Dragons, knights – you'd think there was nothing in the world but fighting, ready as you all are to do it at the drop of a leaf. Enough of this now! Gorbash, another word from you and you can be a beetle, after all!'

Gorbash collapsed abruptly. He thumped down on his haunches and began making choking noises.

'You don't have to cry!' said Danielle, slightly less sharply. 'Just don't go around making foolish statements like that.'

'But you don't know!' mourned Gorbash, in his sub-bass voice. 'None of you know! None of you understand what it's been like. One minute, I'm counting my diam – cleaning my scales. And the next, I'm in some tiny magician's room aboveground, and this george – I don't know if he was the Mage there or not – bending over me. Naturally, I get up and start to tear him apart, but all I have is a sort of george-body, no claws at all, no teeth to speak of... And a lot of other georges come in and they try to hold me, but I get away and run out of this large castle I'm in and some georges dressed all in blue, with clubs, corner me; and one hits me over the head with his little club. That george's head I've got can't even stand a little hit like that; and the next thing I know I'm back in my own body, but this george called James is already there, and he keeps me crowded back into a corner so that I can't do a thing unless he's so busy he almost forgets about me. I can't even do anything when he's asleep, because when he goes to sleep the body goes to sleep and I have to go to sleep, too. That time in the inn when we drank a little wine is the only time I got loose at all, and if I hadn't been so hungry and thirsty—'

'Gorbash,' said Carolinus. 'Enough.'

'Enough? Oh, all right.' Gorbash gulped and fell silent.

'Speaking of wine, Mage,' said Brian, a little hoarsely, into the still-ness. 'Can you do something? It's been a day and a night since any of us ate. A day since we drank – and nothing but the water of the few fresh ponds of the meres for drinking, even now.'

'Also, if nothing else,' put in the clear voice of Danielle from where she still sat on the ground beside the bowman, 'Dafydd needs shelter and warmth for the night; and he's in no condition to travel. Can't your Auditing Department do something for him, after all he did for it?'

'His credit lies in another area,' Carolinus explained.

'Look,' said Jim, 'you said I'd have some credit left over with the Auditing Department even after getting my body back, if I decided to stay here. Let's use some of that to get food, drink and shelter for everyone.'

'Well, perhaps . . .' Carolinus answered, gnawing his beard. 'However, the Auditing Department doesn't keep a kitchen and a cellar stocked for entertainment. But I *can* use some of your credit, James, to move everyone to where food and drink are available.'

'Go ahead,' Jim suggested.

'All right, then' – Carolinus raised his staff and struck its end against the ground once more – 'done!'

Jim stared around him. They were no longer on the fenland causeway by the Loathly Tower. They were back once more before the establish-ment of Dick Innkeeper. The sunset was rosy behind the treetops to their west and a gentle twilight held everything. A mouth-watering smell of roasting beef came from the open doorway of the inn.

'Welcome, welcome, travelers!' called Dick, himself, bustling out of the open door. 'Welcome to my inn, whoever ye may—'

He broke off, his jaws dropping.

'Heaven help me!' he cried, turning to Brian. 'Sir knight, Sir knight, not again! I can't afford it. I simply can't afford it, no matter how many times you're affianced to milady in the castle. I'm only a poor inn-keeper, and my cellar holds only so much. Here you are now with not one dragon but two, and at least one other – uh—' He stared doubtfully at Angie, and at Jim, still dressed in his hospital gown. 'Gentleman and lady?' he wound up a questioning note; and added hastily, 'Plus the Mage, of course. And all the rest . . .'

'Know you, Dick,' said Brian, sternly, 'that this other gentleman is Baron James Eckert of Riveroak, just lately freed from his ensorcelment

into the body of the dragon, after slaying an ogre at the Loathly Tower
and defeating the Dark Powers who threatened us all. This is his lady,
the Lady Angela. Over there you see the dragon – Gorbash, by name
– in which the ensorcelment took place. You can even see the scar of
Sir Hugh's lance upon him. Beside him is a dragon of the meres and
fens – Secoh, by name – who despite his smaller size has fought most
valiantly this day—'

'No doubt, no doubt!' Dick was wringing his hands. 'A worthy company, indeed. But Sir knight, *someone* must pay me this time. I ... I
must insist.'

'Unfortunately, Dick,' said Brian, 'sensible as I am of your situation
and the strain our party threatens to put upon it, I am not wealthy
myself, as you know. Nonetheless, as I did previously, I will pledge—'

'But pledges do me no good, Sir knight – with all respect!' cried Dick.
'Can I feed other travelers with the pledges, which is all I will have left
after you and your friends have been accommodated? And if I cannot
feed travelers, what will become of me and mine?'

'Carolinus,' Jim offered, 'I've still got some credit left, haven't I? Why
don't we use that to pay Dick?'

'It's not that kind of credit,' said Carolinus, grumpily. 'For an instructor in the arts, your ignorance is appalling sometimes, James.'

'Dick Innkeeper,' said Danielle, and her voice had an edge to it that
made all look at her, 'whether or not you feed and house me, or these
others – all but one – means nothing to me. But Dafydd needs warmth
and sustenance; and I give you fair warning, if it becomes necessary
for—'

'Not necessary,' growled Aragh. 'Though if it comes to that, there is
an English wolf at your side. But we've no problem here. Gorbash can
afford to pay for the best for all – and will!'

'I ... ?' Gorbash grunted like a dragon just hit in the solar plexus by
a particularly powerful ogre. 'I? I've practically nothing, no hoard at all
to speak of—'

'You lie!' cried Secoh. 'You were next of kin to that great dragon, your
grand-uncle. As next of kin, you've been told where his hoard lies; and
since he was very old he was very rich from years of hoarding. You have
two hoards, let alone one; and you're a wealthy dragon!'

'But I—' Gorbash began.

'Gorbash,' said Aragh, 'I've been a friend when you had none other,
except your grand-uncle. This day you've lost him. You owe a debt to
James and these others who've made life safe for you and touched you
with the mantle of their courage. The least – I say, the least – you can

do to discharge a part of that debt is to cease whining about what little you'll pay here. If you can't do that, you're no friend of mine and I leave you alone in the world.'

'Aragh—' began Gorbash, but the wolf turned his back. 'Wait, Aragh! Of course I didn't mean ... Of course, I'm happy to make a, well, a celebratory feast in honor of my grand-uncle who slew the ogre of Gormely Keep and today in his old age ... Well, what more do I need to say? Innkeeper, your best for these people, and you shall be paid in gold before we leave.'

In a daze, Jim found himself ushered into the inn just behind Danielle and Dafydd, who was carried gently to the best bed and tucked in to recover under Danielle's care. In another room, Jim struggled into a number of clothes brought up from the store in the inn's basement; and eventually emerged, richly clad, with Angie, onto the grounds outside, to find that tables and benches laden with the materials for a feast had been already set up.

While they had been inside, the sunset had died completely and now night was come. Great torches on tall standards blazed all about them and made a warm cave in the new night. Their fires crackled and sparked around the long table with benches on either side. The surface of the table was hidden under roasts and joints, fruits and cheese and other food of all kinds; while at the far end stood a massive hogshead of wine, already tapped, and before that, a row of drinking vessels both human- and dragon-sized.

'Well done!' said the hearty voice of Brian behind them, and Jim and Angie turned to see the knight emerge from the inn, his eyes fixed on the table. 'Dick Innkeeper has sent to tell Geronde we're here. She'll be joining us in a bit. Dick's really done us up well, eh, James?'

Brian had also dressed. He was out of his armor and wearing a scarlet robe Jim had never seen before. Jim suspected the knight of also benefiting from the inn's store of clothing. In the robe, belted around his narrow waist by a broad tapestry-like gold cloth holding a dagger in a gold sheath skeined with ivory threads, Sir Brian Neville-Smythe was a noble figure. The sight of him reminded Jim of his own inadequacies.

'Brian ...' he began, awkwardly, 'I should tell you something. You see, I really don't know a great deal about using a sword and shield, or a lance, or a great many things like that. I'm not sure how much use I'll be as a friend – now that I'm staying. I'm not even in training for the sort of thing you take for granted. It's not as if I still had Gorbash's dragon body, with all its muscles ...'

Brian smiled.

'Well now, James,' he said, 'indeed, it will be a pleasure for me to train you myself in the noble use of arms and all else that becomes a gentleman of your rank. As for muscle, it would be strange if one of your size and thews could not make a good man of deeds.'

'Size ... ?' Even as Jim echoed the words, he realized he had been aware of what Brian was talking about for some time; in fact, ever since his mind had returned to his own body.

He had not paid real attention to it until this moment. He had seen how Angie had grown in translating to this world. But as he compared himself now to Brian, he faced the fact that beside him the knight looked no larger than a half-grown youth.

Understanding woke inside him.

He had forgotten one thing – or, in fact, a number of things: the suits of medieval armor he had seen in museums, the plans for medieval boats, buildings and furniture ... In the European Middle Ages the average size of men and women was much smaller than it had become by the twentieth century, his own time. Jim had been merely middling tall in his own time and place. Here, he was a giant.

He opened his mouth to explain this, but before he could speak he felt Angie squeeze his arm. Behind Brian, others were coming out of the inn. Danielle, and Giles o' the Wold, closely followed by Carolinus, and two sons of Dick Innkeeper, who carried wooden platters and goblets. The heavy shapes of Gorbash and Secoh had also loomed up in the torchlight out of the darkness beyond the open terrace and now Aragh slipped up, too, to join them. There was a clean, fresh splint on the wolf's broken leg.

'The innkeeper says all is ready,' he growled.

'God be thanked!' commented Giles. The leathery face of the outlaw leader was bent into new creases by a rare smile. 'For, I vow, we were all close to failing there for lack of proper meat and drink.'

'Amen!' said Brian, limping a little as he led the way toward the benches and the tables. 'Take seats, friends, and let us all be joyous, for we're given pains enough in life so that we should not lack will to make good use of pleasure such as this, when it is truly earned.'

If you've enjoyed these books and would
like to read more, you'll find literally thousands
of classic Science Fiction & Fantasy titles
through the **SF Gateway**

✳

For the new home of
Science Fiction & Fantasy . . .

✳

For the most comprehensive collection
of classic SF on the internet . . .

✳

Visit the SF Gateway

www.sfgateway.com

Gordon R. Dickson (1923 – 2001)

Gordon Rupert Dickson was born in Alberta, Canada, in 1923 but resided in the United States from the age of thirteen. Along with Robert A. Heinlein, he is regarded as one of the fathers of military space opera, his *Dorsai!* sequence being an early exemplar of both military SF and Future History. Dickson was one of the rare breed of authors as well known for his fantasy as his SF – *The Dragon and the George*, the first novel in his Dragon Knight sequence, was shortlisted for the World Fantasy Award and won the British Fantasy Award. Dickson's work also won him three Hugos and Nebula. He died in 2001.